JEANNE WHITMEE OMNIBUS

Oranges & Lemons

This Year, Next Year

Also by Jeanne Whitmee

ORANGES AND LEMONS
THIS YEAR, NEXT YEAR
THE LOST DAUGHTERS
THURSDAY'S CHILD
EVE'S DAUGHTER

JEANNE WHITMEE OMNIBUS

Oranges & Lemons
This Year, Next Year

JEANNE WHITMEE

A *Time Warner* Paperback

This omnibus edition first published in Great Britain by
Time Warner Paperbacks in 2002
Jeanne Whitmee Omnibus Copyright © Jeanne Whitmee 2002

Previously published separately:
Oranges & Lemons first published in Great Britain in 1993 by Judy Piatkus
Published by Warner Books in 1994
Reprinted 1999
Copyright © Jeanne Whitmee 1993

This Year, Next Year first published in Great Britain in 1995 by Judy Piatkus
Published by Warner Books in 1995
Reprinted 1999
Copyright © Jeanne Whitmee 1994

The moral right of the author has been asserted.

A CIP catalogue record for this book is available from the British Library.

ISBN 0 7515 3297 5

Printed and bound in Great Britain by Clays Ltd, St Ives plc

Time Warner Paperbacks
An imprint of
Time Warner Books UK
Brettenham House
Lancaster Place
London WC2E 7EN

www.TimeWarnerBooks.co.uk

Oranges & Lemons

Chapter One

Shirley was tired, hungry and, although it was only hours since she had left London, she was homesick already.

Standing there along with all the other children in the crowded reception centre, she felt oddly isolated. Many of them were crying for a variety of reasons – insecurity, hunger, fear. But although there was a huge lump in Shirley's throat and a queer sinking feeling in her tummy, she refused to give in to her own despair. Instead her small dimpled chin jutted out defiantly and her mouth set in an almost belligerent pout, determined not to make what her grandmother called an 'exhibition of herself'.

Hitching the string of the cardboard box containing the hated gas mask a little higher on her shoulder, she brushed fussily at the creases in the skirt of her best pink coat. The train had been crowded and hot and she'd been obliged to share a seat with some of the kids from the 'Buildings' – the very children her grandmother always warned her to avoid. 'Play with them and you'll come home with ringworm – nits too, more than likely,' she would warn, adding darkly: 'All them curls'll have to come orf if you do, my gel. Shaved to the bone your 'ead'll be if you bring them filthy things 'ome 'ere.' Itching at the very thought, Shirley scratched surreptitiously at her auburn curls and hopped from one foot to the other. She'd been wanting to go to the lav for hours, but she'd made herself wait. Not like Tilly Marks, who had already wet herself twice and stank to high heaven.

1

In the little corrugated-iron village hall at Houlton, the villagers came and went throughout the long hot afternoon, patriotically doing as the posters and leaflets had urged them, offering to share their homes with those less fortunate than themselves as part of the war effort. Outwardly, they were motivated by sacrifice and patriotism, but many had other motives of their own; like the childless Tom and Jenny Baker, who willingly took two children, seeking to fill their empty hearts as well as their home. They chose the ones who looked most in need of the abundance of love they had to give, bearing the two little girls off, all smiles, to the high tea Jenny had been preparing all morning. Farmers Bill and Ted Bates, on the other hand, chose four of the biggest and strongest-looking lads. With the village boys being called up almost straight out of school, they would need all the help they could get to provide the extra crops the government would soon be urging them to produce. If they played their cards right this war could be the making of them, provided they could get enough help. There were those who took the children out of what they saw as their Christian duty, like the two Miss's Pimm from Ivy Cottage. Whoever shared their spartan home would need to get used to kneeling for prayers twice a day in the sanctified front parlour, not to mention attending chapel three times every Sunday. So, as the late summer afternoon gently dissolved into evening the villagers came and went; making their choices, pledging their sacrifices, happily bearing home their prizes, or simply making the best of a bad job.

Finally only Shirley Rayner and Tilly Marks were left. Miss Grace, the vicar's sister, appointed as billeting officer, glanced anxiously down the hall at the two little girls and then at her Women's Voluntary Service helper in the sturdy shape of Edith Phipps, the postmaster's wife.

'Oh, dear. It looks as though we're left with those two on our hands,' she said. 'I confess I can understand why no one wanted to take the one in the mackintosh.' She wrinkled her nose. 'She really does smell quite dreadfully.

But the other one – she looks different, quite a cut above the others.'

Edith Phipps folded her fleshy mouth into a disapproving line. 'Different all right. Looks a proper little madam to me; a handful if ever I saw one.' Folding her arms over her vast bosom, she glanced patronisingly at Ellen Grace's stringy, unfulfilled body. 'If you'll pardon me saying so, Miss Grace, those of us who've had children of our own will have seen it in her right away. That's why she's been passed over.'

Ellen glanced at the children again. Shirley's pink coat with its velvet collar and her red-gold curls topped by a large pink butterfly bow were in sharp contrast to the waiflike Tilly's blatant poverty. Wearing an overlong, shabby brown mackintosh passed down by an elder brother, grubby plimsolls and no socks, Tilly Marks looked the very picture of dejection. Her mousy hair hung like chewed string around her pinched little face and the traces of something hurriedly eaten still ringed her mouth stickily. Edith Phipps followed Ellen's gaze.

'That little thing now – a hot bath and a good meal and she'll be good as new,' she said. '*Better*, in fact.' She looked at the child speculatively, her head on one side. 'Head lice, I shouldn't wonder, but some green soft soap and a sharp haircut'll make short work of them. I'll take her if you like,' she offered decisively. 'Just for a few days, mind, till we find a permanent home for her. I've still got some of my Sylvia's little frocks packed away upstairs. I'll soon fix her up respectable.'

Ellen cheered up. 'Oh, would you? That *is* kind. But what am I to do about the other one?'

'Holly Jarvis'll just have to take her,' Edith said, her lips tightening.

'Oh, do you think so?' Ellen looked doubtful. 'We can't force people, you know. I did ask, of course, but with her only being caretaker at Longueville Hall it was hardly up to her.'

Edith sucked in her cheeks again. She deeply resented the Jarvises, envious of their cushy job up there at the

3

Hall, living on the fat of the land with their employers hardly ever there. 'Well, just as you see fit, of course, Miss Grace,' she said, making it clear that she felt the Jarvises were getting off scot-free. 'But we are going to be at war after all, and even people like the Darrents will have to make sacrifices. There must be at least eight bedrooms in that rambling great place, and them Darrents and their stage friends are only there once in a blue moon. They could very easily take six kiddies, let alone one.' She fixed Ellen with her beady brown eyes. 'If you want my opinion, I think it's a crying shame for folk like them to have two homes when there are some poor souls with no roof over their heads.'

'Well, of course I do take your point,' Ellen said guardedly. 'But the Darrents are rather special and they have been *very* generous. You know they've done a tremendous lot for this village.'

Edith said nothing, indicating her disapproval by drawing her breath in sharply and folding her arms. It was easy enough to curry favour by chucking money about when you had more than enough of it. 'I believe the Jarvises are caring for the Darrents' child for the duration,' Ellen went on hopefully. 'She's at a boarding school on the east coast, but it's closing down in case of an invasion.'

Edith sniffed. 'All the more reason for them to take another, then. One child will rattle around that great house like a pea in a bottle.'

'Well, I suppose I've no choice but to ask,' Ellen said. 'Even if they take her on a temporary basis it would help. I'd willingly take her back to the Rectory, only now that the new curate has the spare room there's no room.'

''Course there isn't. Besides, you've done your share.' Edith looked pityingly at Ellen. The poor thing wasn't used to work, apart from parish visiting. And try as she would she couldn't imagine her coping with any child, let alone *that* one. 'Just you take her to the Hall,' she advised. 'We're all putting ourselves out, so why not them Jarvises?'

Ellen walked down the length of the hall to where the children waited, stretching her austere features into her version of a kindly smile. To the children who watched her bearing down on them she looked like a tall skinny angel of doom with her long teeth bared and her colourless hair escaping from its bun in cobweblike wisps. Ellen addressed Tilly first, holding a lace-edged hanky to her nose and trying hard to summon up Christian compassion for the odoriferous child.

'Mrs Phipps is going to take you home with her, er . . .' She peered at the label tied to the child's collar, while still keeping her distance. 'Tilly, is it?'

'Yes, miss.' Tilly wiped her nose on the sleeve of her raincoat.

'Oh, dear. Haven't you got a handkerchief, child?' Ellen asked.

Tilly shook her head. 'No, miss.'

'Oh, well, it can't be helped then, I suppose. Run along then.'

Tilly picked up the brown-paper carrier bag that contained her few pathetic possessions and made her way resignedly towards the waiting Mrs Phipps.

Watching Tilly go, Shirley felt her throat constrict. Was she going to be left here alone all night? Fighting down panic, she bit down hard on her lower lip to stop it from quivering. Ellen turned to her.

'You come along with me, dear. We're going for a little walk. I'm sure we'll find a nice new home for you.'

Shirley watched as the fat lady with the WVS armband round the sleeve of her cardigan propelled Tilly Marks through the door, pushing her ahead of her with the tip of her umbrella. Shirley's fermenting resentment exploded into anger. Tilly might niff a bit but the old cow needn't treat her like something the cat had sicked up. It wasn't fair.

'I wanna go 'ome,' she said in a loud clear voice.

Ellen looked startled. 'I'm afraid that's out of the question, dear,' she said, 'Now, if you'll just come along with me.'

'I ain't goin' nowhere wiv no one.' Shirley's rosebud lips set in a determined pout and the cornflower-blue eyes flashed. 'I ain't gonna to be pushed about like *that*.' She pointed at Mrs Phipps's retreating broad back. 'I wanna go 'ome.'

Ellen sighed. It seemed that Mrs Phipps had been right and the child's angelic appearance was deceptive. 'Come now, dear,' she said soothingly 'We must all exercise self-denial. Our country is about to be at war and we're all going to have to do things we don't wish to do. Once Mrs Phipps has given – er – Tilly a bath and a change of clothes she'll be kindness itself to her, I promise you. Now, the place I have in mind for you is very nice indeed. I'm quite sure you're going to like it. And there'll be another little girl there who is just about your age.'

Shirley could see that she was fighting a losing battle. She'd have to give in – at least for the time being. After a long thoughtful pause, she picked the shiny red cardboard suitcase that Gloria had bought from Woolworth's for her just yesterday. If she didn't do as the woman said, she might get left behind. But if she didn't like the place they found for her she'd soon let them know.

The round blue eyes that looked up at Ellen glittered determinedly. 'All right then – but if I don't like it I'll bleedin' run away.'

Trying hard not to show how profoundly shocked she was, Ellen led the way. Her brother Bertram had worked in an East End parish in his younger days. He had warned her that these children would probably be coarsely spoken. It was difficult to know how to deal with it. If she admonished the child there might be more trouble. On the other hand, putting a child who used language like that into the home of people like the Darrents seemed, well, almost sacrilegious, especially when their own only daughter was to be there for the duration. The Darrents had made a more than generous donation to the organ fund only last month – *and* given the use of their garden for the church fête. If this girl proved to be a bad influence on little Imogen it would look so appallingly *ungrateful*.

As they set off down the lane towards Longueville Hall she glanced down anxiously at the small neat figure trotting beside her. She was clean enough, allowing for the rigours of the train journey; a sweetly pretty child – until she opened her mouth. But there was something about the way she was dressed – flashy was the word that sprang to mind. Indeed, if it wasn't for her charitable upbringing Ellen might almost have called the pink coat and patent-leather sandals *common*. She sighed. When she had taken on the job of billeting officer for the village she hadn't foreseen so many difficulties. 'Oh, dear, I do hope I'm doing the right thing,' she muttered anxiously under her breath.

To Shirley the walk seemed endless. In fact it was a little under half a mile. At the end of a lane they came to a pair of tall wrought-iron gates set in stout brick pillars, each topped by a stone eagle. Shirley perked up. It was just like something out of the film Gloria had taken her to see the previous week, *Wuthering Heights*. That posh family called Linton had lived in a place like this. Her interest aroused, she quickened her pace to keep up with Ellen's long strides and together they walked up a tree-lined drive. Eventually it opened onto a circular carriage sweep with a majestic copper beech in the centre. And Shirley stopped in her tracks to gasp. The house was magnificent. It was built of mellow red brick, square, with two rows of long, white-painted windows, topped by a roof that swept down over them and had little dormer windows jutting out from it. The front entrance had shallow steps leading up to it, flanked by white pillars, topped by a little pointed roof. She had seen nothing like it outside of the cinema.

'Ooo-er . . .' She looked up at Ellen. ''Ere – this ain't *it*, is it?'

'It certainly is,' Ellen assured her. 'The house is called Longueville Hall and it belongs to two very famous people.'

'Cor, go on – *who*?' Shirley's blue eyes were round with interest.

'Their name is Darrent. Mr Tony Darrent, who is an actor, and his wife, Leonie Swann, who sings on the stage in, er, musical comedies.' Would the child know what she was talking about? It seemed she did.

'Get *orf*! You're 'avin' me on,' she said disbelievingly. 'You don't mean the Tony Darrent what's on the pictures? I seen 'im in *The Prince of Hearts*.'

'I believe he has made some moving pictures, yes,' Ellen said disapprovingly. Did Londoners really take children as young as this to the cinema?

Suitably impressed, Shirley fell silent. Just wait till she told Gloria about this. Tony Darrent was Gloria's favourite star. She had photos of him, cut out of film magazines, pinned up on the walls of the bedroom they shared.

Walking up the wide steps, Ellen pulled the shiny brass bell beside the front door. It echoed through the house grandly. Shirley glanced up at Ellen.

'P'raps they're out,' she said hopefully, suddenly over-awed by the dignified splendour of Longueville Hall. But almost immediately the door was opened by a man wearing a green baize apron, his shirt sleeves rolled up above his elbows.

Ellen treated him to a smile that reminded Shirley of the coalman's horse when you gave it a carrot. 'Oh, good evening, Mr Jarvis. I'm so sorry to trouble you, but, er, is your wife in?'

The man held the door open for them. 'Come in, Miss Grace. Molly's in the kitchen.'

They followed him through a hall with a black-and-white marble floor and Shirley gazed in amazement at the beautiful pictures on the walls and the wonderful staircase that curved up from it in a rising sweep. At the top a tall window cast shafts of golden evening sunshine down into the hall, turning the gilded wrought-iron baluster to gleaming gold. Jim Jarvis talked as he led the way.

'We were expecting the Darrents for the weekend and Molly has been getting ready for them all day but Mr Darrent has just telephoned to say they might not be able to get down with things being all at sixes and sevens. There's some talk of all the theatres being closed down.'

He shrugged resignedly. 'Can't be helped. I suppose our problems are nothing when you think of what those poor souls in Warsaw are going through. The war coming is bound to upset everything. I dare say they'll be making us dig up the tennis court to grow potatoes before long.' He opened a door and stood aside for them to pass, shaking his head at Ellen. 'It'll be a sight worse than the last lot, Miss Grace, you mark my words. We're all in for it this time and no mistake; at home as well as at the front.'

Ellen nodded her agreement. 'They do say we'll be safe here in Northamptonshire, though,' she said, 'with our only industry being footwear.'

Jim shook his head. 'No knowing what they'll have to turn their hands to, though,' he said darkly. 'Once they've made enough army boots they'll likely have to go over to munitions, I shouldn't wonder. And once the Hun gets wind of that . . .'

Ellen looked round for Shirley, who was still standing at the foot of the staircase, staring goggle-eyed around her.

'Come *along*, child,' she said sharply. 'Don't dawdle when Mr Jarvis is waiting for you.' She didn't want the Jarvises to think she was soft – or that she was personally responsible for bringing them this particular child.

Shirley followed the two adults through a short corridor to another hallway, much smaller and less opulent than the main hall. It had linoleum and a red carpet runner on the floor. Through an open door Shirley saw a small room equipped with a sink and shelves. In the centre was a table on which stood more silverware than she had ever seen before. As well as cutlery there were candelabra, fancy dishes, tea and coffee pots. Her eyes as round as saucers, she asked:

'Ooo-er. Are all those things made of real silver, mister?'

Jim looked down at her, seeming to notice the child for the first time. A smile tugged at the corners of his mouth. 'They certainly are, missie. Take a lot of looking after, too, I can tell you.' He smiled at Ellen, who returned his smile nervously. 'Come on in, Miss Grace. Molly'll be pleased to see you. You look fagged out. I dare say you could do with a cup of tea.'

'C'n I 'ave one too, mister?' Shirley piped up. Then, to Ellen's chagrin: 'Me stummick finks me froat's cut.'

The kitchen was huge, nothing like Ma's kitchen behind the little greengrocer's shop in Angel Row, which was a tight squeeze when the four of them sat down to eat in it. Shirley's eyes were round as she looked around her. A massive dresser filled one wall. On its shelves were an impressive array of blue and white dishes, everything from the tiniest cream jug to an enormous meat dish that would hold a whole suckling pig. The floor was made of polished red tiles and in the centre stood a large scrubbed-top table, covered now by a red chenille cloth edged with a bobble fringe. But best of all was the smell. The mingled aromas of apple pie and steak-and-kidney, fruitcake and scones filled the air. It made Shirley's mouth water and her tummy rumbled audibly.

Molly Jarvis stood by the big black cooking range that was set in a deep recess lined with tiles. She wore a bright print overall and her round pink face shone with good humour and the exertion of her afternoon's cooking.

'Well, what a nice surprise! Come in, Miss Grace. I've got the kettle on.' She wiped her plump freckled hands on a snowy tea towel and pulled out a chair. 'Sit down and – oh . . .' She caught sight of Shirley. 'Now then, who might this little lady be?'

'This is Shirley Rayner. I do hope you won't mind.' Ellen smiled apologetically. 'I've really come to ask a favour. All the other evacuee children have been placed. There's just this one left and I wondered – I know it's an imposition – if you, er . . .' She trailed off at the look on Molly Jarvis's face. She was looking down at Shirley, shaking her head and tutting under her breath. Ellen winced. She might have known it was out of the question to bring the child here.

'Poor little scrap, did no one want you then, lovie?' Molly sank to her knees, undoing the buttons of Shirley's pink coat. 'Don't you worry. Nanny Jarvis'll find you a comfy bed. Now – when did you last eat, my pretty?'

The lump came back to Shirley's throat and her eyes began to sting. It had been all right till now. Back at the reception centre she could have taken on the lot of them and given as good as she got. But this woman's kind voice and gentle brown eyes completely disarmed her. Suddenly her lower lip began to tremble and she felt very small and very sad. 'B-breakfast-time,' she mumbled.

'*Breakfast?*' Molly Jarvis looked up accusingly at Ellen. 'You mean these little mites haven't had a bite since they left London?'

Ellen's sallow cheeks flushed a deep brick red. 'I was given to understand that the WVS gave them all tea and buns at the railway station,' she mumbled guiltily.

'*I* never got none,' Shirley complained. 'The big boys pushed us little 'uns out and got back in the line. There weren't none left when it was my turn.'

'Weren't *any* left,' Ellen corrected under her breath, wincing at the appalling grammar and horrible cockney accent. If only the child would keep *quiet*. 'You're, er, sure the Darrents won't mind?' she ventured, looking hopefully at Molly. 'I mean, I know it isn't quite what one would wish, but under the circumstances . . .' She lowered her voice. 'At least this one is *clean*. Some of them were quite revoltingly dirty.'

'Mind? Of course they won't.' Molly stood up, folding Shirley's coat over her arm. 'I told Madam on the telephone that you'd been round enquiring and she said she would leave it to my discretion. She'll be company for Imogen. The child would have been lonely, leaving all her school friends behind.' She smiled down at Shirley. 'There'll be someone for you to play with after tomorrow, lovie. And I've cooked enough for an army so we'll get you fed directly.' She smiled reassuringly at Ellen. 'Now, don't you fret, Miss Grace. I'll take good care of her.'

Jim watched his wife affectionately. She'd be in her element with children to care for again. She had missed young Imogen sadly when the child had been sent away to school. Hardly surprising since she had cared for her since the day she was born.

Taking in an evacuee was the least of their worries. They'd been anxious for a while in case the Hall might be requisitioned for a hospital or taken over by the military. If that happened they'd lose their position as caretakers. On the other hand, if the war went on long enough even old stagers like Jim would be called up and Molly would never manage this place on her own. But so far he had kept these worries to himself. Molly was worried enough as it was about the uncertainty of the future. Looking across at her as she fussed with the child he felt his heart lift. There was happy anticipation written in every line of her face. It was an ill wind, he told himself. At least having children to care for again would taken her mind off the war.

In the flat over the Rayners' greengrocer's shop in Angel Row, Gloria was getting ready to go to work. They were showing *Stage Door* at the Adelphi this week. It was all about a group of girls starting out in show business and Gloria loved it. Standing each night in her place behind the back row of the circle, she identified with the budding young actresses in the story, sharing their hopes and aspirations. And she never tired of the beautiful tragic bit where Andrea Leeds climbed to the top floor to throw herself to her death. It was so sad and so lovely. It had made her cry at every performance. As she slipped into the plum-coloured uniform with its gilt frogging, she glanced round the little bedroom. It seemed so quiet and empty without Shirley. Gloria swallowed the lump in her throat. Where was she now, she wondered? Would somebody kind take her in? Would Shirley be missing her too? How long before she could go and see her? She hated to think what was going to happen to them all once this war got under way. It was almost too frightening to think of. She'd been a small child when the last war ended so she couldn't remember what it had been like, but everyone said it was terrible, and that this one would be worse.

There was talk of all theatres and cinemas closing. If that happened she would lose the job she loved so much. Thank God there was always the shop to fall back on. Ma and Pa were always glad of extra help. The little shop which sold fruit and flowers as well as vegetables had always done well. 'Slap bang between the 'orspital and the cemetery. If we don't catch 'em goin' one way, we gets 'em going the other.' It was Pa's favourite joke. He said that folks would be turning vegetarian if the war went on long enough, and they'd make their fortunes. 'Just s' long as we don't all get gassed or blown to kingdom come first, that is,' he'd chuckle. It was just Pa's lugubrious sense of humour, his way of keeping himself cheerful. 'Whistling in the dark,' Ma called it. She would give him a shove and tell him not to be barmy, but it scared Gloria half to death.

It was only a matter of hours since Shirley left but already she was missing her unbearably. Ever since her daughter had been born nine years ago the little girl had been her whole life. She had named her after the multi-talented child star Shirley Temple, confident that she'd grow up to be just as engaging and cute; pinning all her own relinquished dreams and ambitions on her. Every week as soon as she was paid she'd go down to the market and buy remnants of pretty material to make little dresses just like the ones Shirley Temple wore in her films; glad of the apprenticeship she had served with a court dressmaker in the West End, which had furnished her with the know-how and skill.

Gloria had always been mad about films, which was why she hadn't minded too much when she was not allowed to resume her dressmaking apprenticeship after Shirley had been born. She had already seen the advertisement for usherettes needed at the nearby Adelphi cinema and, although Ma said it was a waste of her training, she applied.

She took Shirley along to the pictures as soon as she was old enough to sit still, and enrolled her little daughter on her fifth birthday for the sixpenny Saturday-morning dancing classes in the Mile End Road, where she soon learned to tap, pirouette and pose as engagingly as her famous namesake.

Gloria had been barely seventeen when Shirley was born. Ma and Pa had been shocked and horrified when they first learned that their only daughter was 'in trouble'. But once the initial shock had subsided they made the courageous decision to live down the shame and the gossip and to stand by her. Although they had asked Gloria repeatedly to tell them who the father was, she steadfastly refused to reveal his identity. There was little point in telling them anyway. When she broke the news to him that she was expecting he had dropped a bombshell of his own, admitting that he was already married. He had made it clear that she was on her own and that he wanted nothing more to do with her. He had even tried to argue that the child could not be his. Deeply hurt and disillusioned, Gloria hadn't set eyes on him since, and after the initial pain of his betrayal she told herself she was better off without him. She had steered clear of men since Shirley was born, too. Her only heroes were the ones she admired from afar on the silver screen; Clark Gable and Robert Taylor were her favourites. Recently a British actor had appeared who promised to be just as famous, Tony Darrent, who looked like a blond version of the handsome Errol Flynn. At least it was safe to love them, she told herself. They wouldn't let her down.

Shirley grew up calling her grandparents Ma and Pa just as Gloria did. It had come naturally and somehow none of them had ever got round to telling the child that Sid and Ada Rayner were really her grandparents. It wasn't until the rumours of war began to look like a frightening reality that Gloria decided that the time had come to make the truth about their relationship known to her. If they were going to be parted she wanted to have things straight. Besides, it was surely only a matter of time before some busybody outside told her, and she didn't want it to come as a shock. Sitting in front of the dressing table now, Gloria remembered the day just two weeks ago when she had told her.

It was Sunday and she had taken Shirley Up West to Hyde Park for the afternoon. It had been a lovely warm day and Ma had packed sandwiches and a flask of tea for them. Sitting on the grass by the Serpentine, eating their picnic, Gloria had said suddenly:

14

'What would you say if I told you Ma wasn't your real mum, Shirl?'

The child looked round, only half listening as she threw a handful of crumbs to the waiting sparrows. 'Dunno – why?'

'Because she *isn't*, Shirley.' Gloria caught at the child's arm and looked into her eyes, demanding her attention. 'I mean it, Shirl. Ma *isn't* your real mum.'

Sobered by Gloria's serious expression, Shirley asked suspiciously: 'Who *is* my mum then?'

'Me. I am, love.'

For a second the child stared at her, open-mouthed, then she laughed and said: 'Oh, that's all right then.' Taking another sandwich from the basket, she began to munch happily. 'I thought you were gonna tell me I was an awful, like in *Heidi*.'

Gloria had laughed, weak with relief. Grasping the child, she hugged her till she had begged for mercy. 'Well, you're not an *awful*. You're my little girl and I love you very much.' Tears in her eyes, she looked down at Shirley. 'Do you love me too?'

Embarrassed by Gloria's display of emotion, the child had struggled out of her arms, pushing her away, embarrassed. 'Get orf, Glor, don't be soppy.'

But later that night, when they were both in bed and Gloria thought she was asleep, Shirley's plump little arms crept round her neck.

'Is it true, what you said this afternoon?' she whispered in her ear. 'Are you really my mum?'

Gloria hugged her close. 'Yes, it's true all right.'

'Why didn't you never tell me before?'

'I don't know really,' Gloria said truthfully, tucking the covers around them both. 'I just didn't, that's all.'

'I'm glad you're my mum, Glor.' Shirley snuggled close. 'An' I do love you.' She stopped, frowning as a thought occurred to her. ''Ere – do I have to call you Ma now?'

Gloria smiled and buried her face in the soft red curls. 'Don't you dare,' she said. 'Just as long as we both know, it don't matter, does it?'

'No.' Shirley frowned into the darkness with the effort of working it all out. 'But – if you're my mum, who's my dad then?'

Gloria bit her lip. 'You ain't got one, love.'

'Why not? Everyone else has. I thought you had to have a dad.'

'Well, you *don't*,' Gloria said firmly. 'There's some as do have one, and some as don't. And don't you let no one tell you no different. You an' me, we've both got Pa. We'll share him, eh?'

The explanation seemed to satisfy Shirley as she slipped a thumb into her mouth and cuddled closer.

Gloria held her little daughter. Lying awake long after the child slept, she reflected that there might not be many more chances to share moments of closeness like this. When they first started talking about war and the possibility of evacuating the children, she had been adamant that she wouldn't let Shirley go, but Pa had talked her round, making her see the sense of it. Pa was too old to join up, but he had volunteered for the Air Raid Precautions. He had fought in France in the last war and he knew a thing or two about what might happen. He warned that they'd probably close all the schools in the East End anyway and that clinched it as far as Gloria was concerned. She wanted Shirley to have a better education that she'd had herself. She wanted her daughter to be someone when she grew up. Not for her the wasted life, watching the world go by on celluloid from behind the back row of the Adelphi. Since making up her mind, she had tried not to think about it too much. Maybe it wouldn't happen after all. Maybe there wouldn't be a war. Old Mr Chamberlain was doing his best, wasn't he? He'd talk that Herr Hitler round, no danger. But after Hitler's troops goose-stepped into Poland things began to look black. It seemed to Gloria that all her worst fears were being realised. There was little doubt that she and Shirley were going to be parted.

After she and the other mothers had seen the children off on a packed train bound for an undisclosed destination that morning, Gloria had come home and sobbed inconsolably, sitting at the kitchen table behind the shop. Ma, with characteristic blunt stoicism, told her to pull herself together and dry her tears.

'You think your Pa and I wanted to see 'er go?' she asked. 'That little kid's all the world to us, but it's for the best, gel. Think yourself lucky that you've no man to lose, too,' she added. 'A lot of them women'll be sayin' goodbye to their 'usbands any day now. An' a lot of 'em won't be comin' back. Our Shirl'll land on her feet, you just see if she don't. Born lucky, she was.'

Gloria ran a comb through her hair and stood up. Better get off to work while there was still work to go to. She sighed and pushed the little pillbox hat that completed her uniform into her bag. It was such a lovely evening; hard to imagine the horrors that were taking place across the sea in Europe. It was a shame to be shut in when the sun was still shining. She'd walk to the Adelphi and make the most of it.

As she walked down Angel Row she looked at the newly erected blast walls that shielded each house, and the hastily constructed air-raid shelters that had been built in the street months ago. Fire buckets and sandbags stood in readiness beside street doors in case of incendiary bombs, and in every outhouse a stirrup pump and long-handled shovel stood in readiness. What unimagined evils were in store for them all? she asked herself despairingly. What with bombs, poisoned gas and everything else they were threatened with, they'd be lucky to be here this time next year. Pa had been right. Shirley was better out of it.

In the little room under the eaves, Shirley lay in the spotless white bed, bathed, fed and comforted by the woman who insisted on being called 'Nanny Jarvis'. It was a nice room, all painted white with a funny sloping ceiling and a little window that looked out over the treetops. It had white curtains with a pattern of pink roses and a frilled bedspread to match. There was a soft rug on the floor and a washstand with a big bowl and jug. They were

17

patterned with roses too, to match the big chamber pot under the bed.

'This will be your room while you're here,' Nanny Jarvis had told her.

'Won't I have to share it with no one?' Shirley asked, her heart sinking a little. Ever since she could remember she had shared a bed with Gloria. She had never in her whole life slept alone and the bed felt so big and empty.

As though reading her thoughts, Nanny Jarvis said: 'Don't worry. Tomorrow you won't be lonely any more. Imogen will be home in the afternoon.'

'Who's Imo-gen?' Shirley found the name difficult to say. She'd never heard the name before and privately she thought it rather ugly.

'Imogen is Mr and Mrs Darrent's daughter. She's just your age,' Nanny said. 'You and she will get along like a house on fire. Such fun you'll have. Won't that be nice?'

Tucking in the blankets, she kissed Shirley's forehead and said good night, leaving her alone to think over all the bewildering events of the day. She had never been in a house as big as this. You could get lost among all the passages. She couldn't imagine ever knowing her way around it. There were even two lots of stairs and she'd had a bath in a real bathroom with black and white tiles and soft white fluffy towels. It had two big mirrors you could see yourself all over in and you didn't have to go outside to the lav. At home they washed in the kitchen and had a bath once a week in the big tin tub that hung on a nail in the yard next to the outdoor 'khazi' as Pa called it.

Now that it was almost dark outside she could hear all the strange sounds of the country. An owl hooted eerily and she discovered that the strange rustling sound she could hear, like hundreds of people whispering, was the wind shaking the leaves on the trees. She missed the sound of the traffic rumbling by in the Whitechapel Road, the rumble of cartwheels and the heavy clop-clop of the drayman's big grey horses. At home in Angel Row the Prince of Wales would be chucking out about now. If she was at home she'd hear Joey Harris, the cobbler from up the street, making his unsteady way home. 'Red Sails in the Sunset', he always sang, or sometimes, if he was feeling sad, 'The Miner's Dream of Home'. She liked to hear him: it made her feel safe. Tears stung her eyes. Soon it would be time for Gloria to come home from the Adelphi. Sometimes she brought her sweets on a Saturday night, or maybe a bag of crisps. And if she was still awake she'd let her sit up in bed and eat them – because it was Saturday and no school tomorrow.

This final thought was too much and Shirley stuffed one small fist into her mouth, tears squeezing out from under her tightly closed eyelids. All her toughness and determination to stand firm dissolved like the candyfloss she had eaten on Hampstead Heath on Bank Holiday Monday. She felt bleak and lost and alone.

'I – I want – Glor,' she hiccupped. 'I want M-ma – and Pa and *Glor*.'

At breakfast next morning she sat silently at the kitchen table, eating little. Molly thought she looked peaky and said as much to Jim when he came into the scullery to change his boots. He smiled and shook his head.

'She's bound to be feeling strange, love, and a bit homesick,' he said. 'Tell you what, I'll take her to the village with me to pick up your groceries, then she can help me finish cleaning the silver. She seemed really taken with it yesterday. We'll need to find out what's going to happen about schooling for the kiddies, too. I don't know how the village school is going to fit them all in.'

Fortified by the cornflakes and boiled egg that Nanny Jarvis insisted on feeding her, standing over her while she ate, Shirley seemed to cheer up and went off happily enough with Jim Jarvis, sitting proudly beside him in the elderly Austin Seven. She was wearing her favourite yellow-and-brown dress with a jaunty bow to match in her red-gold curls.

'I ain't never been in a motorcar before, mister,' she said as they drove out through the gates and set off along the road into the village, ''Ere, 'as Tony got one like this 'n' all?'

19

Jim chuckled. 'Mr Darrent has a car but not like this. His is a Rolls-Royce. And by the way, young lady, better not let him catch you calling him Tony. It's Mr Darrent to the likes of us.'

Shirley coloured. She was so used to Gloria referring to her idol by his Christian name that it came naturally to her. 'What's a Rolls-Royce?' she asked.

'You'll see,' Jim told her. 'You'll see, missie. All in good time.'

As they drove, Shirley noticed things that had escaped her yesterday. She pointed to a herd of black and white cows grazing peacefully in a field.

'What are them things, mister?'

Jim smiled. 'Those are cows. That's where our milk comes from.'

Shirley stared at them in surprise. 'Go on. You're pullin' me leg,' she said, searching his face. 'Milk comes from the milkman.'

Shirley waited outside the village store while Jim went in with the order Molly had made out for him. Across the road was the post office – not at all like the one back home in Whitechapel. This one had a thatched roof and a garden in front with brightly coloured flowers growing in it. A huge tabby cat sat in the window, sunning himself among the dummy packets of Nestlé's chocolate and adverts for Mazawatte tea and Reckitt's Blue. Shirley walked across to press her nose against the window, making faces at the cat, who stared unblinkingly back at her with an expression of disdain. After a moment or two a girl came out of the shop. Shirley looked at her – then looked again, staring in amazement. It was Tilly, but a very different Tilly from the one she had seen on the end of Mrs Phipps's umbrella yesterday afternoon. This Tilly wore a clean blue cotton-print dress. Her hair had been cut very short, which seemed to alter the shape of her face, and her skin shone with cleanliness.

'Wotcher, Tilly,' she said amiably.

Tilly looked back at her. 'Wotcher. I gotta new frock.'

'Yeah. Looks nice. What's your lady like?' Shirley asked.

'Orl right.' Tilly sniffed. 'She cut me hair and made me 'ave a barf, but she give me a lotta new clo's. 'S all right 'ere,' she concluded. 'Grub's a bit funny, though. There ain't even a fish 'n' chip shop.'

'I had a ride in a motor car,' Shirley boasted. 'I'm livin' in a house just like on the pictures. It's got *'undreds* of rooms.'

Tilly wrinkled her nose disbelievingly. 'You ain't. You tells lies, Shirley Rayner. My mum says you and your Gloria's always been too big for yer boots.'

'It's *true*, I tell you.' Shirley pointed. 'That's the car over there, see? An' this house where I'm stoppin' belongs to two film stars.'

'Dirty *liar*.' Tilly stuck her tongue out as far as it would go. 'You'll be struck dumb if you're not careful, tellin' whoppers like that. Always thinks yerself better than the rest of us, don't you – you 'n' your poncy dancin' an' yer Shirley Temple frocks.'

'At least they're *my* frocks – not someone else's,' Shirley jibed.

The dart found its mark. Tilly's pasty cheeks reddened. 'My mum says you're a bastard, so *there*.'

Shirley's jaw dropped. She'd heard the word before, but she didn't know what it meant, only that it had to be something really bad by the venomous way people always said it. Her quick redhead's temper roused, she took a step towards the other child, her blue eyes blazing and her hand raised. But she stopped in her tracks as burly Mrs Phipps came out of the shop.

'Now then. What's going on here?' she challenged.

'She was gonna clout me,' Tilly wailed, pointing accusingly at Shirley. 'She's been tellin' 'orrible lies and now she's tryin' to 'it me.'

Shirley burned with the injustice of it. 'She called me a bastard,' she protested.

Mrs Phipps gasped and flushed a deep crimson. 'Wash your mouth out with soap, you wicked girl,' she said, outraged. She put a protective arm round Tilly and drew her into the shop doorway. 'Go away, you dreadful child.

I know your sort, you little demon. Don't you dare come here making trouble, or I'll be onto Miss Grace about you.' She flapped at Shirley with both hands. 'Go on – shoo. Get off with you now.'

When Jim Jarvis came out of the village store ten minutes later, he found Shirley waiting for him in the car. She looked subdued and thoughtful. 'All right, love?' he asked.

She nodded uncertainly. 'Mr Jarvis . . .' She looked up at him with large round cornflower-blue eyes. 'Mr Jarvis, what's a bastard?'

Chapter Two

Leonie sat in her dressing room and stared moodily at her reflection in the mirror.

'It's so bloody unfair,' she wailed as Tony poured them another whisky each. 'What's the point anyway?'

'With the bombardment they're expecting, it would be mad to encourage people to assemble in large numbers,' Tony explained patiently. 'Think of the casualties.'

His wife shrugged her beautiful shoulders, totally unable to visualise this bombardment everyone was talking about. Things like that only happened in other, uncivilised countries. They didn't happen in England, surely? 'But what's going to become of *us*?' she wailed. 'Is this to be the end of my career? Just when I was getting such divine notices, too. I suppose the new show will have to be shelved now and as for the film Peter was talking about . . .'

Peter Jason was the couple's agent and he'd had them both in the office only a week ago with an exciting proposition: a new high-budget musical film with Leonie and Tony starring.

Unlike Leonie, Tony was guiltily grateful for this respite. He had yet to tell her that he didn't want to do it. Sitting down beside her, he took both her hands in his. 'Darling, listen. This shut-down thing is only temporary. It has to be. One of the most vital things in wartime is to keep morale high. And how can they do that without entertainment? They'll have to find some way to start up again, you'll see.'

'People won't want to go out to the theatre if they insist on keeping up this ridiculous blackout idea,' Leonie said pouting. 'Especially when they still have the wireless to listen to in their own homes.'

Tony laughed. 'They'll soon get tired of that, darling. You have to admit it's pretty dreary stuff.' He patted her shoulder. 'Cheer up. You'll see, everything will sort itself out. Maybe we'll join Basil Dean's ENSA and entertain the troops.'

Leonie threw back her head and snorted derisively. '*ENSA*? By all accounts they're taking anyone – raw amateurs. You know the joke they're already making about it: Every Night Something Awful. Being involved with that is hardly likely to enhance my career, is it?'

Tony looked at Leonie's lovely reflection in the dressing room mirror with iits border of light bulbs. She really was incredibly self-centred, but even when she was being shrewish and petulant she was still devastatingly beautifull.

They'd been married now for almost eleven years. Tony had been playing juvenile leads with Birmingham rep when they first met. The year was 1928 and he was twenty-seven, and just recovering from the break-up of his disastrous early marriage to Gillian Fane, who had since made her name in Hollywood. Leonie had been plain little Eileen Smith then, the pretty, stage-struck daughter of a local butcher. She never missed a performance and every night there she'd be, waiting for him outside the stage door, just to smile shyly and exchange a few words. He'd been flattered by her open admiration. In spite of his talent and good looks, the break-up of his marriage and the loss of his baby son had dealt him a devastating blow, undermining his confidence badly.

When the theatre had run a talent competition, Eileen had entered. He'd been amused to see her name on the list, thinking it was just another ploy to attract his attention, but it turned out that she really did have talent. When her turn came to perform, she stood in the middle of the stage, looking tiny and fragile in a scarlet dress, and sang 'After the Ball', incorporating a floaty little dance she had choreographed herself. Her voice was surprisingly strong and melodious for someone so young and she moved with a natural grace and charm. Watching her that evening he suddenly saw, too, that she was more than just the pretty teenage girl he had taken her for. Her dark hair was cut in a fashionable bob, and her deep violet eyes were large and lustrous, fringed with silky black lashes. Tony was utterly captivated.

She had won the competition, of course. Tony and two other members of the company had made up the panel of judges. He had talked them into it, but they hadn't taken much persuasion. The Darrent family had been well known and respected in the theatre for five generations. Tony instinctively knew star quality when he saw it, however raw and unpolished it might be. He was easily able to convince his fellow judges that little Eileen Smith had been blessed with a very special gift. With his contacts he could help her build a remarkable career if she would let him, and when over dinner later that evening he outlined his plans to Eileen, her eyes had sparkled up at him with undisguised delight.

In spite of Eileen's parents' horror and disapproval at the idea of her throwing in her lot with a 'strolling player', she had left home and joined Tony in London and with his help and enthusiasm she had climbed effortlessly from one success to another. Tony worked hard with her to iron out the flat Midlands vowels and improve her diction. He took her to dancing classes and persuaded his agent to take her on. Together he and Peter had dreamed up a new and more glamorous name for her – Leonie Swann, soon to be displayed in lights outside one of London's leading theatres. Since then they had starred together in three long-running West End musicals and their highly successful film, *The Prince of Hearts*. Two years ago Leonie had signed a recording contract with Parlophone, making records of all the hit songs from her shows.

On the first night of their current West End hit, *Sunshine Sally*, she had received the accolade all young actresses dreamed of. After the show she had had an unexpected visit in her dressing room from none other than the master himself, Noël Coward. He had pushed in among all the other well-wishers, a bottle of champagne in his hand with which to toast her, hinting that he intended to write a musical play especially for her. In view of all this it was hardly surprising that Leonie had become obsessed with her career, Tony reminded himself. Or that she resented the approaching war, which to her was simply a tiresome obstacle to her ascendant star.

Tony knew of old that Leonie could be formidable when thwarted. He recalled the last time her career had been temporarily halted – when she had discovered that she was pregnant a year after their marriage. For himself, Tony had been overjoyed at the prospect of a child. He had never quite recovered from the loss of contact with his small son, Marcus, now living with his mother in far-off America. But Leonie did not share his enthusiasm. In fact, she made herself quite ill with dismay.

Her pregnancy had been difficult and fraught with sickness, which hadn't helped. She was moody: tearful and petulant by turns, fretting constantly about the frustrating interruption of her career, the ugly thickening of her petite figure and what she saw as her ruined looks.

When she went into labour and suffered three long days of excruciating agony, Tony had begun to fear for her sanity. When the newborn baby girl was finally put into her arms, she had screamed at the nurses hysterically to take it away and turned her face to the wall.

But the moment when Tony first took his little daughter in his arms and looked down at her was a memorable one. He would name her Imogen after his mother, he decided. He hoped fervently that Leonie would come to love the child in time, but if she could not, then it would be up to him to be mother and father to her.

Once the hell of childbirth was over, Leonie had recovered remarkably quickly from her ordeal. When her looks and figure returned without any effort and she found that her voice, far from being ruined, had gained a new mature depth and richness, she put the past months behind her. But she made no real attempt to be a mother to the child. The couple bought their first permanent home, Longueville Hall, a beautiful Georgian manor house deep in the leafy countryside of Northamptonshire, and engaged the homely Jarvises: Molly as housekeeper and nanny to Imogen, and her husband, Jim, as gardener and handyman.

It was only when Tony tried to resume the passionate relationship they had enjoyed before Leonie's pregnancy that he began to realise that things between them would never be the same again. Imogen was three months old and they were spending their first weekend at their new country home. Leonie had slept alone since the birth, protesting that she was not yet fit to allow his lovemaking. But Tony himself had spoken to the doctor, who had seemed surprised, assuring him that there was no reason for them not to resume a normal married life together. So when Leonie had fought him off and dissolved in floods of tears, making him feel a brute, Tony had been upset and perplexed. Over the following weeks and months he had been patient, but the situation had not improved. Finally Leonie had told him that she could not risk another pregnancy and for that reason she refused to allow him back into her bed except on very rare occasions. Even then she was tense and rigid with apprehension, despite all his loving reassurances.

His first affair had been little more than a desperate attempt to bring her to her senses. He made sure that she found out and when she did she was furious. But his triumph was short-lived when he realised that it was bruised pride and not a broken heart that angered her. She told him coolly that if he must have affairs he must insist on his discretion. She would not tolerate being made to look a fool. She would also prefer to remain in ignorance about his extramarital activities. Finally Tony was forced to acknowledge that Leonie's beautiful head housed a hard and calculating brain, and her exquisite body, a heart as cold as ice. At times he even questioned whether she had married him simply to fulfil her ambitions as an actress.

As the years passed they learned to come to terms with the sad charade that was their marriage. In public they were the well-known romantic theatrical couple beloved of the popular press. Their successful marriage was a show-business legend. In private, although they continued to support each other professionally, Leonie reserved all her emotion for her career, while Tony went from mistress to mistress, searching in vain for the loving closeness so sadly lacking in his marriage. He was a handsome man with a passionate nature, a popular romantic actor whom women fantasised over and queued to see. In the course of his work he came into close contact with many beautiful actresses. There was never any shortage of women both in and out of the business who were eager to minister to his physical needs; indeed, an affair with Tony Darrent was something of an achievement to many of the young aspiring starlets who vied for his attention at first-night parties.

If Leonie resented his brief and frequent flings, she gave no hint of it, choosing to turn a blind eye as long as she was left alone. As for Tony, none of his affairs meant more to him than mere physical gratification – until the day almost a year ago when he had walked into his agent's office and met Claire DeLisle, Peter Jason's new secretary. From that moment his whole life had changed.

'Have another drink. It'll make you feel better.' Tony refilled his wife's glass. 'Tell you what, we'll drive up to Houlton tomorrow afternoon. Imogen will have arrived by then and we can all be together for a few days.'

Leonie pulled a face. 'Do you think it's wise to leave London? Suppose Peter wants to get in touch – or Noël?'

'I doubt if either of them will be making firm plans over the next few weeks,' he said. 'But if they do, they both know how to use a telephone.' Standing behind her, he laid a hand on her shoulder, looking at her reflection in the mirror. 'Chamberlain is making a broadcast to the nation on Sunday morning. I'd like us all to be together when we hear what he has to say.'

As Leonie looked up and met the gravity of his expression, her mouth began to tremble with apprehension. 'Tony, you don't think that ghastly little man Hitler will *really* drop bombs on us, do you?' Her lovely eyes widened with sudden panic. 'Tell me the truth: are we all going to be killed?'

'Of course we're not,' Tony said, squeezing her shoulder reassuringly. 'I'm sure it's just the frenzied raving of a madman. All the same, there's no sense in taking chances. The government has been far too complacent as it is. I think that the countryside will be safer for the time being. Maybe you should stay there with Imogen for a while. At least until we see the way the land lies.' He stood up and moved towards the door. 'I'll ring Nanny and Jim now, shall I? Say we're joining them tomorrow.'

Leonie sighed, her shoulders slumping disconsolately. 'Oh, if you must. What an absolutely *bloody* choice – buried dead in London or buried alive in the country?'

'While I'm gone perhaps you could start packing up here,' he suggested, looking round at the litter of clothes strewn around the dressing room. Leonie was notoriously and incurably untidy. 'Then we can make an early start tomorrow morning.'

But when he returned ten minutes later, Leonie still sat where he had left her, staring gloomily into the mirror, her eyes blank.

'Nanny tells me she's taken an evacuee,' he told her. 'A little girl of Imogen's age.'

'Really?' Leonie said abstractedly, leaning forward to pluck out a stray eyebrow hair.

He looked round with irritation. 'Leonie, you haven't even started to get your things together. We may not be coming back here, you know. It's possible the run may have to be suspended indefinitely.'

She shrugged. 'Letty can do it. What else is a dresser for?'

He sighed. 'Darling, I've *told* you. Letty has joined up.'

She turned to stare at him. 'What on earth do you mean, joined up?'

'She's going into the ATS. She rang to say so this morning. We're on our own now.'

'Oh, really! It's *too* tiresome. Everyone seems to have gone quite mad.' She stood up and switched off the dressing-table lights. 'Be an angel and pack for me, will you, darling? Shove as much as you can into a bag and leave the rest where it is. It's all too boring for words, this absurd war thing.' She swung her silver fox furs around her shoulders, picked up her gloves and bag and walked to the door. 'I've got the most fearful headache coming on. I'm going home to lie down.' She blew him a kiss. 'See you later.'

Tony waited until her footsteps had died away, then went into the corridor and lifted the receiver of the pay-telephone. He slipped two pennies into the slot, dialled the number and waited, breathing in the dusty stuffiness that all backstage corridors have and listening to the unnatural silence all around him. Normally at this time of day the theatre was a hive of activity, ringing with the sound of excited voices, alive with the buzz of anticipation and the tension generated in the hour before curtain-up. Now the dressing rooms were dark and empty, and no good-natured banter came from the stage hands in the prop room as the stage manager coaxed and chivvied them. Listening to the telephone ringing, he visualised the great stage on the floor above: the red plush curtain raised on the sightless, gloom-filled cavern of the auditorium; the ropes and pulleys hanging from the flies above, swaying slightly in the draught – like a forest of hangman's nooses. Tony shuddered. Empty theatres always gave him the creeps. So full of ghosts, so redolent of heightened emotions and shattered dreams. Suddenly he felt desperately lonely, as though he were the only person left alive in a doomed world.

At the other end of the line there was a click as the receiver was lifted and he heard Claire's cool tones say: 'Good afternoon. Peter Jason Theatrical Agency.'

The utter normality of her voice was as comforting as a light switched on in a dark room. Tony hastily pushed button A. 'Darling, it's me. I was praying you wouldn't have gone home yet.'

'*Tony* . . .' Her voice was breathless with relief. 'Thank God! I was terribly worried. I rang the theatre earlier but there was no reply. No one seems to know what's going on except that all places of entertainment are closing down indefinitely.' There was a pause, then she said: 'I suppose there's absolutely no chance of the weekend we were planning?'

'I'm sorry, darling. It's out of the question now, I'm afraid. I can't tell you how disappointed I am.'

'Me too.' There was a pause, then she said quietly: 'This wretched war scare is messing up everything, isn't it?'

'I'm afraid it's more than just a scare now, darling. It looks pretty certain that we're in for it. But I had to ring you. Nothing will change between us, Claire. I want you to know that whatever happens I love you. I always will.'

'I love you too. Oh, darling, what are we going to do?'

'I'm driving up to Houlton first thing in the morning. Imogen's arriving there today. Her school has closed. I'm trying to persuade Leonie to stay there with her for a while. After that, God only knows what will happen.'

'And you? I've been wondering all day. Will you be called up?'

He sighed. 'It'll be a while before they get round to calling up my age group, but with my flying experience I really feel I should volunteer.' He heard her stifled gasp at the other end of the line and said quickly: 'Darling, can we meet now – before I leave? Even if it's just for an hour?'

'I wish we could. I can't bear the thought of you going away without seeing me. We might . . . we could all be dead this time next week.'

'Don't say things like that.' There was a pause, then he said: 'Look, I'm at the theatre. There's no one else here. I'm packing up Leonie's things. Can you come round here now?'

'Of course I can.' He heard her catch her breath in what sounded almost like a sob. 'If I can get a taxi I'll be there in ten minutes.'

' "I love my ceiling more
Since it was a dancin' floor for-*or* my love." '

Wearing her best pink dress with the frilly skirt and lace collar, Shirley pirouetted daintily for Molly and took a bow. Molly clapped enthusiastically.

'Bravo! Every bit as good as the real Shirley.'

'Aren't you a clever little girl then? Where did you learn to sing and dance like that?'

'At the dancing classes down the Mile End Road,' Shirley told her proudly. 'I've been going every Sat'day morning since I was five.'

'And who made you this pretty dress?' Molly fingered the rose-pink crêpe de Chine, examining the hand-finished seams and hems with approval.

'Gloria. She makes all my things for me.'

'Is Gloria your big sister?'

'No. She's my mum.' Shirley wriggled into the chair more comfortably and took a deep swig of the glass of home-made lemonade Molly had poured her. After lunch Jim had driven into Northampton in the Austin to meet Imogen's train at the Castle Station. Knowing that train timetables were erratic owing to the evacuation programme, he had started out early, right after lunch, leaving his wife and her new small charge to get to know one another better. Nanny Jarvis had taken Shirley on a tour of the grounds. Wide-eyed she had viewed the kitchen garden, immaculately kept by Jim, and the steamy hothouse with its pungent mingled odours of tomatoes and exotic fruits. Discreetly hidden behind a mellowed red-brick wall, against which espaliered pear and nectarine trees grew, was the swimming pool the Darrents had had installed the previous year, its turquoise water sparkling in the sunshine. Last of all Shirley had been introduced to Toffee, Imogen's piebald pony, who grazed happily in a paddock all his own that was at least ten times bigger than the Rayners' back yard.

After gazing in awe at these hitherto undreamed-of delights, Shirley said half to herself: 'I wish Tilly Marks could see all this.'

Misunderstanding, Nanny Jarvis said: 'Then you must ask your little friend Tilly along to tea one day soon.'

In return for the guided tour, Shirley had changed into the pink flounced dress and entertained Nanny with a song and dance from her extensive repertoire. Now they were having a companionable break together, with lemonade and home-made biscuits.

'Y'see,' Shirley went on conversationally as she bit into a biscuit, 'Ma and Pa are Glor's mum and dad really. I ain't got a dad of me own. But it don't matter. Glor *said* so.'

'I see.' Molly was silent, her head bent over her knitting. Jim had told her about the embarrassing question Shirley had asked him on the way back from the village this morning. Obviously Gloria Rayner was an unmarried mother. But it was clear that Shirley was a very much loved and wanted child for all that.

'Why's Imo-gen gone back to school?' Shirley asked suddenly. 'The 'olidays ain't over yet.'

'She went back two weeks ago,' Molly explained. 'St Margaret's broke up at the end of June this year because a lot of the parents had booked holidays abroad. They were afraid that if they didn't go in early summer the war might prevent them going at all.'

'I ain't never been on 'oliday,' Shirley said thoughtfully. 'Only to Southend on August Monday – oh, an' once Glor an' me went to Kent for the 'op pickin'.' She smiled reminiscently. 'That was *lovely*.' She looked at Molly, her head on one side. 'Where's abroad?'

'Abroad? Oh, France and so on. Across the water.'

'Cor – would they go in a boat? Pa went in a boat when he was a soldier in the Great War. He told me about it.'

'They must all be missing you very much,' Molly said. 'Tell you what, shall we send them a postcard to let them know you're safe and happy?'

Shirley gasped and clapped a hand over her mouth. Gloria had given her a stamped addressed postcard, tucking it into her luggage when she packed. She should really have posted it that morning but she had forgotten. There had been so many new things to see and do. She told Molly about the card and ran off to her room to get it. Together they composed a message for it and Nanny wrote it out for her, then Shirley sat at the kitchen table and copied it onto the postcard in her best writing, the tip of her tongue protruding from the corner of her mouth. At last it was done and she handed it to Molly for her approval.

'You've done that very nicely,' Molly said smiling. 'Now, shall we walk down the lane to the postbox with it?'

As they walked, Molly looked down at the little girl trotting beside her. Shirley was a lovely child: bright, clever and pretty. Very different from her poor, plain, inhibited Imogen. It would do Imogen good to have a companion as outgoing as Shirley – provided they got along together. For all her privileged background, Imogen had never known the security of a loving family as this child had. Sadly, Leonie had never taken to her for some reason and the fact that the child had grown up to be plain and gauche hadn't helped the situation.

Imogen was painfully thin. No amount of feeding ever seemed to fill out the child's spare frame. Her mousy hair was straight and lifeless and she had worn spectacles from the age of four to correct a pronounced squint. Although Molly loved the child dearly she sometimes despaired of her. How could the offspring of such glamorous and attractive parents turn out so plain? She seemed to have inherited all the wrong attributes of each. Her father's strong nose sat incongruously on her mother's delicate facial bone structure; her father's long arms and legs looked somehow all wrong on the fragile body she had inherited from her mother. When her permanent teeth appeared they were large and strong, like Tony's, not small and pearly like Leonie's. They threatened to overcrowd her mouth and were already being corrected by the use of an ugly brace, adding to the catalogue of disadvantages cruel fate had already dealt her.

34

As they were walking back from the pillar box Jim passed them in the car and waved cheerily. Shirley peered into the car's rear window as it passed, curious to catch a glimpse of her new playmate. The face that looked back at her from under the straw school hat was not encouraging. Sharp grey eyes stared coldly at her through a pair of ugly steel-rimmed spectacles. Shirley lifted her hand in a tentative greeting, but Imogen turned her head away, pretending not to notice. Shirley looked up at Molly.

'She's a bit stuck-up, ain't she?'

Molly smiled. 'She'll be all right once you get to know her, my duckie, never you fear.'

When they reached the house, Imogen was standing in the drive, surrounded by her school trunk and all her other belongings, waiting for Jim to put the car away. Shirley looked with interest at the tennis racquet and the hockey stick leaning against the expensive suitcases. She saw now that the other girl wore a long school-uniform dress made of green-and-white checked gingham, topped by a green blazer, its pocket embroidered with a badge worked in gold thread. On her head was the regulation summer boater, sitting straight on the lank hair and secured by elastic under the chin. On the girl's feet was the ugliest pair of shoes that Shirley had ever seen; black and heavy, with laced-up fronts. Shirley was infinitely grateful that she didn't have to wear such monstrosities. But the critical way Imogen's eyes took in her own pink flounced dress and patent dancing pumps made Shirley blush indignantly. The unspoken criticism in the candid grey eyes was plain to see.

Molly ran forward to embrace the child warmly. 'There you are, then, my duckie. Was the train journey horrid and tiring? Are you hungry?' She turned to Shirley, standing apart, her eyes wary. 'Look, this is your new little playmate, Shirley Rayner. Shirley is from London. She's an evacuee and she's going to stay with us. Say how-do-you-do nicely, pet.'

Imogen, who had returned Molly's hug warmly, turned cold, resentful eyes on Shirley. Reluctantly she extended

35

her hand. 'How do you do,' she said in what to Shirley was an excessively posh voice. Her eyes did not meet Shirley's and her long pointed nose averted itself as though to avoid an unpleasant smell.

'Please ter meecher,' Shirley returned carefully in the proper polite way that Gloria had taught her. She reached out to shake Imogen's hand but the other girl's arm was hastily snatched back before their fingers could meet. As Imogen turned and walked ahead of her with Molly, Shirley quite plainly heard her say:

'How long will *she* be staying here, Nanny? She's *frightfully* common, isn't she?'

Shirley stared at the tall, straight back of the girl in front. Disappointment engulfed her. She had never met anyone quite like Imogen Darrent before and she was filled with dismay at the odd feeling the other girl gave her. 'She ain't a bit pretty. She looks just like Key'old Kate in the *Beano*,' she whispered to herself. 'And she don't like me.'

Shirley was used to the petty spite and occasional jealousy of her schoolmates in the East End. But they spoke their minds. They voiced their grievances to her face in no uncertain terms, and that she understood and could cope with. Shirley was well able to stand up for herself and could give as good as she got, both verbally and physically. But Imogen didn't challenge, she merely condemned without words, dismissing with a single scathing glance. Her cold, silent disdain precluded all retaliation, and her attitude of superiority stirred up a bewildering mixture of unfamiliar emotions inside Shirley which made her feel very uneasy indeed.

Claire had obviously been lucky enough to find a taxi at once since it was less than ten minutes later that Tony heard her footsteps descending the stairs and echoing down the empty corridor outside the dressing room. He opened the door and looked out eagerly, his heart quickening as it always did at the sight of her.

Claire was the opposite to Leonie in every way including her looks. She was tall, almost as tall as Tony. She wore very little make-up and with her taste for plain, classic styles some people might almost have called her ordinary – until they looked more closely. Then they saw that with her naturally blonde hair and straight, slender figure she was attractive in a quiet, subtle way that was all her own. For Tony her eyes were her best feature. They were a deep turquoise blue, the colour of the sea on a summer's day, and they shone with a transparent honesty and candour, rare in the other women he had known. Her taste in clothes was conservative; not for her the furs and luxurious fabrics that Leonie loved. Her style, like her personality, was quieter, but no less attractive. This afternoon she wore a grey suit and a white silk blouse – the ordinary clothes worn by a thousand secretaries every day in London. Yet Claire wore them with a flair and an easy elegance that was all her own. Tony felt his heart contract with love as he held out his arms to her. She quickened her pace, running into them, and for a moment they clung to each other wordlessly.

'Thank you for coming, darling,' he said at last, drawing her into the dressing room and closing the door. 'Damn this war! All our plans . . .'

She took his hand urgently. 'Listen. I can't stay long. I told Peter I was slipping out to the post office. I've got to clear my desk before I can leave. Peter's closing the office tonight for a couple of weeks, so I've got some time off.' She looked into his eyes. 'How long do you intend to stay at Houlton?'

His heart quickening, he said: 'I haven't thought. A couple of days perhaps. Why?'

'Friends of my family have a little holiday cottage on the east coast. I've got a key. I can always go there if they aren't using it. I thought I might go for a few days. You could join me.' The blue-green eyes gazed into his, pleading silently, and he felt his heart melt with longing for her. She wound her arms around his neck. 'A few days to ourselves – just the two of us. It may be the last chance we get to be together. Please say yes, darling.' Her body pressed close to his was irresistible and he crushed her to him, kissing her deeply.

'When will you be going?' he asked, his lips against hers.

'First thing tomorrow morning. I'm taking the car. I expect I'll have to sell it when I get back. There won't be any petrol for private motorists, so they say. We must make the very best of the next couple of weeks. It might be the only chance we'll ever get.'

He released her and took out his diary. 'Give me the address. I'll join you the moment I can.' He scribbled down the address, then drew her down onto the couch. 'Don't let's talk any more. Just hold me for a few minutes, then I'll put you into a taxi and send you back to the office.' He kissed her. 'I promise I'll be there, darling. I'll manage it somehow, come hell or high water.'

The four of them sat at high tea in the kitchen. Molly had prepared all Imogen's favourites: home-cooked ham with a crisp salad from the garden, strawberry blancmange and cream and a big chocolate cake with a rich fudge frosting. But the atmosphere was, as Jim said later to his wife, 'that thick you could have cut it with a knife'.

'I had a phone call from your daddy while I was getting tea,' Molly said. 'He and Madam are coming up tomorrow. Won't that be nice?'

Imogen nodded. 'It seems ages since they were here last.' All through the meal she had ignored Shirley, pointedly talking to Jim and Molly about subjects in which she was unable to join. She spoke of her school friends and her teachers, her achievements on the sports field, and how lovely it would be to be home with the Jarvises indefinitely.

'I went along to see Mr Hawkins at the village school this morning,' Jim told her. 'The children are to have an extra week's holiday while he and his staff sort out how all the newcomers are to be fitted in.' He smiled. 'That'll give you two girls a chance to get to know one another, won't it?'

Molly picked up his lead, trying to draw Shirley into the conversation. 'Shirley thinks Toffee is lovely, don't you duckie? And I'm sure she'd like you to teach her to ride, Imogen – and to swim in the pool. Looks like the weather's really settled. You two are going to have a grand old time together, I know.'

Shirley, who had been feeling sad and left out, looked hopefully at Imogen, but the other girl just shrugged her shoulders noncommittally and changed the subject. Later, Molly pressed them into taking a walk together. Walking along the lane in the evening sunshine, Shirley looked at Imogen and said:

'Will you really teach me to ride and swim? If you do, I'll teach you to tap-dance if you like.'

Imogen turned and looked her in the eyes for the first time. Her grey-eyed gaze was icy cold. '*Tap-dance*? Why on earth would I want to do that? And you might as well know now that no one is allowed to ride Toffee but me. You'd probably ruin his mouth.' She pulled at a blade of grass and walked on ahead of Shirley, easily outstripping her on her long legs.

Burning with indignation, Shirley hurriedly caught up with her, 'I wouldn't *touch* his mouth,' she protested. 'I like 'orses. I give the milkman's 'orse a carrot every mornin' and it ain't ruined '*is* mouth yet. An' plenty of people wants to tap-dance. I go to the classes down the Mile End Road. The teacher says I'm a dead ringer for Shirley Temple.'

Imogen stopped walking to stare at Shirley. 'I'm sorry, but I don't understand a *word* you're saying,' she said.

Shirley stopped in her tracks as the other girl walked on. She was cut to the quick. There it was again: no argument, nothing she could come back at; just that dismissive put-down – as effective as a smack in the mouth. Shirley ran after the other girl and trotted beside her lanky form.

'Don't s'pose you could do it anyway on them skinny legs,' she said breathlessly, trying hard to goad Imogen into retaliation. When there was still no response she added: 'You're a stuck-up cat, Imo-gen Darrent. I don't like you an' I don't like your name – so there.'

Imogen turned abruptly, almost causing Shirley to bump into her. 'Go *away*,' she hissed. 'When my mother and father come tomorrow I'm going to ask them to send you away. We don't want nasty little London children who can't speak properly here.' She took a step forward, towering over Shirley. 'And another thing. Don't you dare call Mrs Jarvis Nanny. She's not your nanny and never will be.' And without another word she walked back to the house, leaving Shirley gazing open-mouthed after her.

Once again that night Shirley cried herself to sleep. If only Gloria were here! She wrapped her arms around herself, pretending it was Gloria cuddling her, but it wasn't the same. She thought of them all, Ma, Pa and Gloria, sitting round the kitchen table having their dinner without her. When would she see them all again? Maybe *never*. The thought made her panic badly. She'd write tomorrow and ask to be taken home again. It was horrible here now that snotty Imo-gen had arrived. She spoiled everything. What did *she* have to complain about? Her mum and dad were coming tomorrow, then Shirley would really feel out of it and alone. She snuffled unhappily into her pillow, trying to gain solace from the forbidden thumb in her mouth, till at last a restless, dream-filled sleep claimed her.

After breakfast next morning Imogen went off, wearing jodhpurs and a yellow polo-necked sweater, to see her pony. Shirley stayed behind in the kitchen, hanging around and begging to be given a job with which to fill her time. Molly glanced at Jim anxiously.

'Didn't you want to go with Imogen to see Toffee?' she asked.

The one thing Shirley had never done was tell tales. Among her contemporaries in the East End it was an unwritten law that you didn't tell of people, however rotten they were to you. 'No,' she said. 'Didn't feel like it this mornin'. I'd rather help you wash up, Nan – er, Mrs Jarvis.'

When the washing-up was done, Jim provided her with a soft duster and set her on the task of polishing the brass door plates in the hall. Alone with Molly in the kitchen he said:

'Those two don't seem to be hitting it off, do they? I suppose it's only to be expected. Chalk and cheese they are if ever I saw it. Chalk and cheese.'

'They'll shake down,' Molly said hopefully. 'They'll find something in common eventually. The trouble with Imogen is that she's never been asked to share. She asked me this morning if we couldn't send Shirley away. I was quite shocked.'

'The poor kid may have a lot to share materially,' Jim said perceptively. 'But I don't think it's that that worries her. She's afraid of sharing you, my love.'

'*Me?*' Molly turned to look at him.

Jim nodded. 'You're the most important person in that child's life. You're her rock – her security; the one person she can rely on to be always there and always loving. And she could see you were taken with pretty little Shirley. She feels threatened.'

Molly frowned. 'Oh, dear. I never thought. I was just trying to get them to be friends. What can we do about it?'

'Nothing, love,' Jim said resignedly. 'This war is going to change a lot of things. A lot of people are going to have to learn to compromise. And if you ask me, most of them'll be a lot better for it.'

When the silver-grey Rolls drew up outside the front door of Longueville Hall that afternoon, there was great excitement. Tony and Leonie had been too busy working to see anything of their daughter during the holidays, so this visit was a bonus. Imogen had been waiting ever since lunch, not moving from her place at the landing window from where she would get the first glimpse of the car as it drove in through the gates. The moment she saw it she gave a shout and ran down into the hall.

'Nanny, Jim, they're here!' Pulling open the heavy oak door she ran down the steps into the drive and hurled herself into her father's arms, almost knocking him off his feet as he got out of the car. Shirley watched in silence from inside the door where she stood concealed in the shadows.

'For heaven's sake, Imogen,' Leonie said irritatedly as she watched the display of excited emotion. 'Give your father time to draw his breath.'

Tony hugged his daughter and whispered in her ear: 'Go and give Mummy a kiss.'

Imogen obediently walked round to the other side of the car and held out her arms to her mother. Leonie bent and offered her cheek for the child to kiss, delicately fending off her hands for fear of sticky marks on her eau-de-Nil linen suit.

Shirley watched with eyes like saucers. She had never seen two such glamorous people before. She could hardly believe that she was about to meet the stars she had seen on film at the Adelphi; Leonie Swann herself, and the man whose handsome face had looked down at her from the bedroom walls for the past year. Seeing him in the flesh gave her a funny feeling. She was astonished to see that apart from his expensive clothes and posh car, he looked just like anyone else as he laughed and hugged his daughter. Leonie, on the other hand, was quite different. Standing in the drive, tapping her foot impatiently, she was the very picture of glamour and sophistication – everyone's idea of a film star, in fact. In her pale-green suit and white shoes, she looked very elegant; her face was like some exquisite flower and her mass of dark hair was piled on top of her head in a glorious profusion of curls.

Jim, who had followed Imogen down the front steps, began to unload suitcases from the car's boot.

'Come along now, duckie,' Nanny Jarvis laid a gentle hand on Shirley's shoulder. 'Come and be introduced. No one's going to bite you.' She noted with approval that the child had changed – without being told to – into a pretty pink-and-white-checked gingham dress with a white collar and tiny puffed sleeves. Shirley looked up at her and took the hand that was offered, allowing herself to be led down the front steps. For all the world – as Molly said later – like a lamb to the slaughter.

'Good afternoon, Mr Darrent – Madam,' Molly said respectfully. 'I hope you had a good journey. This is little Shirley Rayner, the evacuee I told you about.' She gave Shirley a little push towards Tony. 'Say how-do-you-do,' she prompted under her breath.

Shirley held out her hand. 'Please ter meetcher,' she said with a shy smile.

Tony shook her hand solemnly. 'Hello, Shirley. I'm pleased to meet you too. I hope you'll be happy here at Longueville Hall.'

Leonie brushed past Imogen and walked round the car. 'My God, I expected some little ragamuffin. What a beautiful child!' she said loudly. 'Where on earth did you find her, Nanny?'

Molly tried not to wince as she registered the crestfallen expression on Imogen's face. 'The, er, billeting officer, Madam. I didn't go down to the hall. Miss Grace brought her up here herself.' She turned towards the house. 'If you'd like to come in, I've laid tea in the drawing room. I'm sure you must be dying for a cup of tea.' But to her dismay Leonie remained where she was, her eyes fixed on Shirley.

'What did you say your name was, darling?'

'Shirley, Mrs – er, miss. Shirley Rayner.' Shirley blushed to the roots of her auburn hair and Leonie's silvery laugh rang out delightedly.

'Tony, listen to the way she speaks. She's the perfect cockney answer to Shirley Temple. Isn't she pure heaven?'

Tony slipped an arm round Imogen and walked up the steps with her. He sensed the child's humiliation, felt the tension in her shoulders and silently cursed Leonie's brash insensitivity. Couldn't she see what she was doing to the girl? Why couldn't she at least pretend to be interested in her own daughter for once?

In the drawing room Leonie inisisted that both children should be allowed to have tea with them. Tony could hardly argue. It would look bad to leave the evacuee child out, yet he knew perfectly well that Leonie was only amusing herself. All through the meal she asked questions, gaining the child's confidence and flattering her outrageously. With careful coaxing she got her to reveal that her clothes had been made by her mother and copied from her namesake's film costumes, that she attended dancing classes every Saturday morning and that her mother was a cinema usherette. Even more embarrassing, she also persuaded the child to part with the information that her mother was unmarried and that they lived with the grandparents above their greengrocer's shop in Whitechapel. At last, unable to stand any more, Tony turned to Imogen who sat silent and white-faced on the settee beside him.

'And how is Toffee?' he asked. 'Have you ridden him yet? And tell us about your swimming and tennis. Did you do well this summer?'

Imogen's face brightened. 'I was chosen to play in the school tournament,' she said. 'I was the youngest ever to be chosen.'

'And did you win?' Leonie asked coolly, one eyebrow arched enquiringly.

Imogen coloured. 'No,' she admitted. 'But I almost won the junior swimming cup.'

'Almost isn't winning, is it, darling?' Leonie said, helping herself to another scone. 'Still, I'm sure you'll try harder next year.'

'Let's all go and see Toffee,' Tony said brightly. 'We'll go and see if Nanny can let us have some carrots and sugar lumps, shall we?'

That night Shirley went to bed happy. Mrs Darrent, or Leonie, as she insisted on being called, really liked her. She had said she wanted to see her dance. That'd shown that snotty, stuck-up Imo-gen where she got off. She closed her eyes and popped her thumb into her mouth. If only Gloria could see her! If she could only tell her that she was going to dance in front of Tony Darrent tomorrow. Maybe it wouldn't be too bad here after all.

* * *

In their bedroom on the first floor overlooking the garden, Leonie faced her husband angrily.

'You're only staying till tomorrow afternoon? But why? You never told me before. What's going on, Tony?'

'Nothing's *going on* as you put it.' Tony sighed and began to pull off his tie. 'If you want me to see Peter for you, if you don't want everything to grind to a halt, then I've got to go back to town and keep a finger on the pulse.'

Leonie gave a derisive snort. '*Finger on the pulse?* Don't make me laugh. Who is she this time?' Her eyes glittered challengingly.

'What do you care?' Tony picked up his dressing case and moved towards the door. 'I'll sleep in the dressing room. I'm sure you'll be happier alone.'

'For Christ's sake, Tony. What will the Jarvises think? It was your idea to share a room when we're here, so as to keep up appearances.'

'Don't worry. I'll remove all traces in the morning,' he said over his shoulder. 'And I'll be gone tomorrow night.'

'If you think I'm going to be buried alive by myself here while you go off whoring yourself stupid . . .' Her voice trailed off as the door closed firmly behind him. She swore loudly and hurled her hairbrush at the wall. This time it was serious. All her feminine intuition told her so. This time he was actually in love. And she wasn't bloody well having it.

'. . . I have to tell you now that no such undertaking has been received and that therefore this country is at war with Germany.'

Tony and Leonie, the Jarvises and both children sat silently in the library listening to Mr Chamberlain's announcement on the wireless. When it was over they stared at each other in stunned silence for a moment, then Tony stood up and switched off the set.

'Well, that's it, I'm afraid. Official confirmation of what we all knew anyway.'

For a moment they looked at each other, then Jim asked: 'Will you be joining up, sir?'

Tony shrugged. 'I don't know. Perhaps the RAF could use me. We'll all have to wait and see what happens.'

At that moment the air-raid siren began to wail its mournful warning and Leonie jumped to her feet, clapping her hand to her mouth. 'Oh, dear God, they're here already!'

The threats and fears of the past months were at last reality. The war had begun in earnest.

Chapter Three

It was late when Tony arrived at the cottage. He'd got hopelessly lost in the winding Suffolk lanes and eventually stopped at a pub to ask the way. The locals sitting outside in the evening sunshine with their mugs of ale had stared in amazement at both him and the car and he had begun to wish he'd left the Rolls behind and borrowed Jim Jarvis's baby Austin. But that would have aroused Leonie's suspicions even more. He couldn't understand why she was so angry about his leaving. She certainly didn't want his company. He had felt mean leaving Imogen so soon, but he'd promised to make it up to her later. He might even have time on his hands if the shut-down lasted long.

Holly Cottage was at the end of a lane that was little more than a cart track. It was thatched, with whitewashed walls and a garden that was a profusion of late-summer colour. Through the car's open window he caught the scent of roses and saw that they were climbing over the tiny front porch, fat and pink and evocatively fragrant. Hearing the car bumping along the track, Claire came out to meet him. She wore a blue cotton dress and sandals, her legs were bare and brown and her fair hair was streaked with sunlight. He felt the familiar rush of love for her.

They went inside with arms round each other and he found himself in a room with a beamed ceiling, so low that it only just cleared his head. Claire had drawn a low table up in front of the stone fireplace between twin settees. It was laid for two with a single lighted candle in a brass candlestick in the centre. He smiled at her.

'You've been busy.'

'Busy counting the hours,' she said. 'So – it's happened. We're at war.'

'We are indeed.'

She went to him and wound her arms around his neck in the way that he loved. 'Do you think it's possible to pretend it isn't happening – just for a while?'

He kissed her. 'We can try.'

She had cooked chicken and fresh green vegetables and potatoes, all of which she'd bought from the farmer at the top of the lane. Tony had brought a couple of bottles of his best Chablis, smuggled out of the cellar at Longueville Hall. He chilled them in a bucket of ice-cold water from the wall in the back garden. Finally, replete and relaxed, they sat together close to each other, finishing the last of the wine and gazing dreamily into the dying embers of the apple-wood fire.

Tony sighed deeply. 'This is wonderful – idyllic.'

'You don't regret coming then?'

He frowned as he looked down at her. 'Regret it? Of course not. Why do you say that?'

She shook her head. 'After I'd asked you I felt guilty. This is a time when families should be together. I was only thinking of myself.'

He drew her head down onto his shoulder. 'What Leonie and I share could hardly be called family life. You know that as well as I do.'

'But there's Imogen.'

Tony sighed. 'Yes, there's Imogen. But I'll make it up to her. Now that she's going to be at Houlton for the duration there'll be plenty of opportunities. This time is just for us, my darling. For a little while we'll be thoroughly selfish. We won't think of the past of the future or of anyone but ourselves. Will you promise me that now?'

He didn't say 'It may be our last chance', but she read it in his eyes as she took his face between her hands and kissed him. 'I promise. Whatever else happens, this time – these few days – belongs only to us . . . for ever.'

On the floor above, reached by a tiny twisting staircase, was one large bedroom. Tiny dormer windows peered out from under the thick thatch both front and back. The room was cool, dim and cosy. Under the sloping ceiling the large double bed with its brass bedstead was covered by a patchwork quilt. Claire had made it up with lavender-scented sheets from the airing cupboard in the tiny bathroom next door. On the dressing table was a small glass vase with three pink cabbage roses she had picked from the garden; their scent filled the room. For the rest of his life Tony was never able to smell roses without thinking of Claire, that room and those few precious stolen days. Slightly tipsy with wine and the scent of roses, they undressed slowly, pausing to kiss and caress, and finally they tumbled into the big feather bed together to make love in an atmosphere of peace and tranquillity they had never known before.

Long after Claire slept in the crook of his arm, Tony lay awake. He was reluctant to waste this precious time in sleep, wanting to store every moment of it, filing it away in his memory to feed on in the dark days to come. God only knew when they would find another opportunity to be alone together like this – if ever. If only he and Claire could have met years ago! His life would have taken a totally different direction; he would doubtless have developed into another kind of person; even his career would have expanded and grown. All his acting life so far had been spent playing lightweight parts. He had drifted from juvenile leads into light romantic heroes and now that he was approaching his middle years he could see the dreaded path that lay before all so-called matinee idols looming ahead, unless he could make the necessary departure soon. He had seen it so many times in the past: the toupee to cover the thinning hair, the specially made corset to whittle the bulging waistline, the carefully applied make-up and lighting on stage and the dark glasses worn in public to conceal the puffy eye-bags and incipient wrinkles. Finally, the ultimate humiliation; the incognito trip to a Swiss clinic for plastic surgery in a last desperate attempt to maintain the illusion of youth. It was all so sad and pathetic and Tony was determined not to let it happen to him.

The worst of it was that he had never intended his career to take that direction. It had always been his ambition to be a classical actor in his family's tradition. Shakespeare had provided wonderful parts for great actors of all ages, beginning with Romeo and ending with Lear. His father, the respected and well-loved Richard Darrent, had played them all to great acclaim. Tony longed to play them too. But somehow Leonie's career had come between him and his aspirations. Starring with her, the first of her successful plays had labelled him as a romantic lead and the outstanding success of their film, *The Prince of Hearts*, seemed to have set the seal, typecasting him for ever.

It had been ten months ago, on his thirty-eighth birthday, that he had made the momentous decision to change course. He'd gone to his agent's office that morning determined to achieve his aim, even if he and Peter Jason, who had been his agent for the past twelve years, had to part company.

Walking up the stairs in a positive mood, he had thrown open the door, determined that this time he would have his way. At the desk in the outer office sat a girl, her fair head bent over her work. Tony paused. Miss Harrison, the elderly secretary who had worked for Peter as long as Tony could remember, was nowhere to be seen. When the girl looked up at him he saw that her eyes were startlingly blue. He was reminded of the Mediterranean and for a moment his reason for coming was completely forgotten.

'Yes – can I help you?' She smiled disarmingly, obviously completely unaware of who he was.

'I'd like to see Peter, please. I have an appointment.'

The girl drew the appointment book towards her. 'What name?'

Tony was faintly amused. He was used to being recognised everywhere he went and had certainly always received VIP treatment in this office. Little Miss Harrison would have been on her feet by now, fussily offering him a chair, a cup of coffee and one of the home-made fairy cakes she always brought for her elevenses. He cleared his throat.

'Tony Darrent.' He was slightly abashed to hear himself using his 'actor's voice'.

The girl simply nodded and stood up. 'Oh yes, that's right. I'll just slip in and see if Mr Jason is ready for you.'

When she got up and moved out from behind the desk Tony saw that she was tall and slim with an extremely good figure, accentuated by the plain skirt and blouse she wore. She had classic looks; a flawless complexion, straight nose and wide mouth. When she spoke he saw that her teeth were white and even; but it was her eyes that mesmerised him. Their astonishing blue gaze quite took his breath away with their candid directness and her smile lit them brilliantly. It was as though the sun suddenly shone, warming him through and through with its glow.

When she came out of the office a few moments later she was smiling apologetically. 'You can go in now, Mr Darrent,' she said. Then, a little shyly: 'I think I owe you an apology. I should have recognised you – at least known your name. It was unforgivable to keep you waiting. I come from the Channel Islands, you see, and we haven't had any of your films over there.'

'Please don't apologise.' Tony held out his hand. 'How do you do, Miss – er?'

'DeLisle.' She put her cool hand into his. 'Claire DeLisle.'

Sitting opposite Peter in the office, Tony asked: 'Where's Miss Harrison?'

'Retired last week. She was long past the age. We all miss the old dear. She'd been with us for years.'

'And the new girl?'

'Daughter of a distant cousin of mine. She was born and bred in Jersey – wanted to come over and sample life in the great metropolis. She just happened to write to me at the right time.' He nodded and offered Tony his silver cigarette box. 'Very efficient. I couldn't have chosen better if I'd advertised the job.' He raised an eyebrow at Tony as he lit his cigarette. 'What can I do for you?'

Tony leaned back in his chair and blew out a cloud of smoke. 'I know I've mentioned this before, Peter, but I want to go legit.'

Peter sighed. 'Oh, dear. I thought you'd forgotten all that nonsense.'

'Well, I haven't. I want you to let it be known that I'm available for classical roles.'

Peter rubbed his chin. 'Aren't you forgetting something? You've got a contract to finish. Three more films to make, including this extravaganza with Leonie.'

'I'll buy out of it – anything.' Tony leaned forward and stubbed out his barely smoked cigarette. 'If I don't do it now, Peter, I'll never do it at all.'

'Christ, you're really serious, aren't you?' Peter Jason got up and went to a filing cabinet in the corner. From the top drawer he took out a bottle of whisky and two glasses. Pouring two generous measures, he passed one to Tony. 'Come on,' he said. 'Whatever it is, you'd better get it off your chest.'

Tony took a deep draught of his whisky and looked at his agent over the rim of the glass. 'It's nothing new. You know that I've always wanted to be a classical actor. After all, it's what I was brought up on. I just drifted into popular light stuff along with Leonie. I'll be forty before you know it and if I don't do something about it now it'll be too damned late.'

'Have you talked this over with Leonie?'

Tony shook his head impatiently and reached for another cigarette. 'What kind of question is that? You know we never talk. I'm in deadly earnest about this, Peter. I'm sick of dancing to Leonie's tune, playing the adoring husband *and* leading man. Any ham with good teeth and a modicum of talent could do what I do. Look, I made Leonie what she is, but somehow along the way I messed up my own career doing it.'

Peter shook his head. 'You could lose a hell of a lot of money, you know.'

Tony glared at him. '*You* could, you mean.'

Carefully containing his patience, Peter ignored the barbed remark. 'Look, supposing – just *supposing* I could get you a season at Stratford, there's no guarantee you'd be right for it. It could be a disaster. You could make a laughing stock of yourself.'

'Thanks for the vote of confidence,' Tony said wryly.

'I'm just being realistic. I've every confidence in you, Tony, but you're the matinee-idol type. And the British public – and that includes critics – tends to like actors doing what they've seen them do successfully time and again.'

'Bugger the British public,' Tony said explosively. 'And *that* includes critics.'

'They put you where you are, Tony, and don't you forget it,' Peter admonished with a frown. 'Look, you're going through a bit of a midlife crisis. Don't tear up your contract. I'll see if I can wangle you a guest appearance at Stratford next season. You can work it in between shooting. How's that?'

'Hold a bloody spear, you mean. Don't patronise me, Peter. This isn't the old cliché of the clown who wants to play Hamlet. I'm deadly serious. I won't consider anything less than a lead.'

A spark of annoyance flickered in Peter's eyes as his patience began to wear thin. 'Look, Tony, to be frank, companies like Stratford expect classical training, RADA at the very least. I'm not at all sure that I could convince them that –'

'RADA?' Tony sprang to his feet and glowered angrily down at his agent. 'My family have been in the theatre for the past five generations. My grandfather played Horatio to Irving's Hamlet. My grandmother understudied Ellen Terry. And everyone remembers my father, Richard Darrent. His name is a bloody *legend*, for Christ's sake. Don't you talk to me about RADA! I learned my craft where it should be learned, in the theatre – from real pros. And I started learning it the minute I was born.' He walked towards the door. 'If you don't believe in me, Peter, then you only have to say so and I'll find an agent who does.'

When he'd gone, slamming the door behind him, Peter Jason threw up his hands in exasperation. '*Actors!*' he muttered, flapping his hands towards the door. 'Egotistical bloody hotheads, the lot of them. Sometimes I wonder what I'm doing in this business.'

As Tony stormed through the outer office, he was halted by a cool voice.

'Is anything wrong, Mr Darrent? You look upset.'

He turned to see Claire looking at him, her blue eyes genuinely concerned. Suddenly his temper evaporated and he smiled shamefacedly. 'Oh, not really. I got a little overheated in there. Look – tell Peter I said I'm sorry, will you?'

'Of course I will. Do you want to go back and tell him yourself?'

Tony shook his head. 'No. Just tell him for me.'

'Is there anything I can do? I mean – I don't want to intrude, but if you want to talk about it? Sometimes it helps.'

'You're right.' He smiled at her. 'Let me buy you lunch.'

Claire blushed. 'Oh, I didn't mean . . . I wasn't . . .'

'I know you weren't. But you're right, I do need to talk to someone impartial. Please have lunch with me.' He looked at his watch. 'I'll pick you up at one. Do you like the Savoy Grill?'

'I'd prefer somewhere less – er . . . There's a little restaurant round the corner from here. They do a very good plaice and chips.'

He laughed and was about to ask if she was shy about being seen with him in public, then he remembered that she really had no idea just how well known he was. Unlike most of the women he met, she was genuinely friendly and utterly guileless. It was as soothing and refreshing as summer rain. 'All right,' he said. 'I'll pick you up at one and you can take me there. I'll look forward to it.'

Peter hadn't managed to get him a leading part with a Shakespearean company, but Tony hadn't minded too much. After that first lunch with Claire his obsession had lessened. She was so sweet and sincere. She understood how he felt, almost without his telling her. It was uncanny.

He popped into the office several times a week after that first meeting, but Peter was relieved to find that his failure to get his best client the part he wanted was received with a surprising tolerance. Tony's visits were merely an excuse for seeing Claire. Eventually he gave up pretending and began to invite her out regularly. Her quiet calm was becoming addictive to him. Being with her was becoming a necessity. They kept to quiet places, mainly because Claire preferred them. Sometimes she would cook him a meal in her tiny flat in Earls Court, where he found the kind of relaxation he had almost forgotten existed.

He hadn't bargained for falling in love. When he first realised what was happening to him he was alarmed and dismayed. It was a complication he hadn't encountered before. Their relations had so far remained chaste. Claire was reluctant to sully their relationship by making it physical too soon, but Tony had to face that what he felt for her was deeper than anything he had ever known before – even for Leonie in their early days together. He tried not seeing Claire, but it hadn't worked. When they were apart he couldn't concentrate, couldn't work, couldn't think of anything but her, and when he had turned up at her flat two weeks later he found her in tears because she felt the same. They had fallen into bed together there and then. After that he knew there would never be anyone else for him but Claire. As soon as he could he would tell Leonie and ask her for a divorce. Then came the serious possibility of war with all its attendant complications and insecurities. They had decided to wait and see. Perhaps – vain hope – it wouldn't happen after all. But now it had.

He wakened to the scent of fresh coffee and someone shaking his shoulder. Opening his eyes he stared disbelievingly up at her, his eyes slightly unfocused. She laughed down at him.

'Wake up, dozy. Drink this coffee and get dressed. We're going for a walk.'

He sat up, brushing his dishevelled hair out of his eyes. 'What time is it?'

She held the bedside clock up for him to see and he stared at it. '*Half-past seven?* There's no such time. Come back to bed.' He reached out for her but she jumped back out of his reach.

'Not on your life. The sky's blue and the sun is shining. The sea is just across that field. I want to walk beside it with you; making footprints on the sand; breathing the air before anyone else has. Just the two of us with no one else about.' She pulled the bedclothes off him and threw him a sweater and slacks from the bag he had brought. 'Here, put these on.'

The air was salty and fresh with the tang of early autumn. They walked with their arms around each other's waists across the field to the dunes and down onto the hard sand at the water's edge, then suddenly Claire was pulling her sweater over her head, stepping out of her cotton skirt and kicking off her sandals.

'Come on, let's go for a swim.'

'In *there*? Now? It must be freezing.' But she was gone, running into the surf to plunge under the first wave that rolled in. Tony hopped on one foot, taking off his shoes, undoing his slacks. A moment later he joined her, gasping as the icy water splashed remorselessly over his warm skin. Claire laughed, bobbing on the water like a seal yards away from him. Droplets of sea water sparkled on her eyelashes and flew around her in a glittering shower as she shook her head. She dived and came up in front of him. Grasping his shoulders she pushed him under.

'There. Now you're in. Race you to the breakwater.'

Gasping and laughing he struck out and followed her powerful crawl, but he couldn't catch her up.

Later, as they lay drying in the shelter of a deep sandy dune on Claire's outspread skirt, he asked her where she had learned to swim like that.

'When you grow up surrounded by sea you have to learn to swim well,' she told him.

She talked affectionately about her home in Grève de Lecq, in Jersey, and the loving family she had left there running their boatbuilding and chandlery business. In return he told her about his early childhood, touring theatres and living in digs with his mother and father; the heartbreaking parting when he was sent away to boarding school and, later, his first small parts in rep where he began his career as student assistant stage manager. Claire knew about his consuming ambition to be a classical actor. Her quiet confidence and steadfast faith in him buoyed him up as nothing else could.

'It was a happy childhood,' he told her, gazing up into the dissolving morning haze. 'But I missed having a stable family home. Till I met you I didn't know what a real home was – or how wonderful and special it felt to have the love of a real woman.'

He dried her with his sweater, brushing the fine sand from her smooth skin, following his caressing fingers with his lips until he had kissed every inch of her. Finally they made love there on the sand and vowed their love for each other for the thousandth time. As they lay watching the sun slowly climbing the sky, Claire said suddenly:

'Tony, I've been thinking. Now that we're actually at war, maybe I should join up – the ATS or the WAAF.'

He raised himself on one elbow to look down at her. 'But if you do that I'll hardly ever see you.'

She reached up to pull him down to her, holding him close, her lips against his cheek so that he wouldn't see the pain in her eyes. 'Let's face it, darling. It could be almost impossible to us to meet again once things begin to hot up. Anyway, I dare say you'll do the same yourself. With your flying experience you'd be of immense value to the RAF.'

'I know,' Tony said thoughtfully. Flying had been his hobby and relaxation for years. When they bought Longueville Hall he had joined the flying club at nearby Sywell aerodrome, from where he flew regularly. For the past two years he had been a voluntary instructor, working with beginners as often as his professional commitments allowed. The thought of Claire joining up and putting herself in danger turned his blood to ice. 'What about your folks, though?' he asked. 'Shouldn't you just go home? If I can't see you I'd like to think of you safe among your family.' The sunlit morning seemed suddenly dark with storm clouds, but he pushed the shadows from his mind determined not to be depressed. Getting to his feet, he took her hands and pulled her up with him.

'What did we promise? No war, no problems, just here and now and *us*.'

She smiled into his eyes. 'You're right. I'm sorry, darling.'

They walked back across the field in their crumpled clothes to eat an enormous breakfast outside in the tangled garden and plan what they would do with the rest of the day.

Leonie was bored. She was also furious with Tony. How could he just go off like that and leave her here alone with Imogen? Especially after it had been announced that they were actually at war. They'd even had their first air raid, too – almost as soon as the announcement was made. Well, if not an actual raid, a *warning* of one. It had been dreadful. That ghastly Mrs Phipps from the post office had come trundling up the drive on her bicycle wearing a World War I tin helmet to ask if they'd filled the bath and every other receptacle with water. Being in the WVS seemed to have gone to the woman's head. Leonie had sent her off with a flea in her ear. Bossy old bag! And now Jim Jarvis had started talking about digging up the tennis court to grow potatoes. She had told him what she thought of that idea, too.

'If there has to be a war, Jim, there also has to be some place where we can get away from it,' she told him firmly. 'And as far as I'm concerned, it's here at Longueville Hall.'

There was only one thing to break the terrible monotony and that was the evacuee child, Shirley. She was absolutely fascinating. The way she spoke and some of the expressions she used were straight out of Dickens, yet she looked like an angel with her red-gold curls and cornflower-blue eyes. Why couldn't she – Leonie – have managed to produce a child who looked like that instead of Imogen? Really, the girl seemed to grow plainer and duller by the minute.

On Monday morning she had telephoned Peter Jason at his office in Charing Cross Road. When there was no reply she rang his home number.

'I've closed the office for a couple of weeks, Leonie,' he told her. 'Till we see how the land lies.'

'But Tony said he was going back up to town especially to see you,' Leonie said plaintively. 'Here I am at Houlton, all alone, waiting for him to bring me some news. Our whole *future* is at stake, Peter. I think it's rather selfish of you to take a holiday at a time like this.'

Peter swallowed his irritation and thought quickly. He had guessed months ago that there was something going on between Tony Darrent and Claire. Privately he thought Tony must be mad to play around so close to home, but it wasn't his place to tell him what to do with his life. Claire had told him she was going to Suffolk and hearing about Tony's disappearance he didn't have to be a genius to guess that he was probably with her.

'I'm not on holiday, Leonie,' he said. 'I've only closed the office. I'm available here at home to all my special clients and Tony knows that.'

'So you'll be seeing him there at Richmond?'

'Undoubtedly,' Peter said warily.

'So – have you any news? What about the new film, Peter? And has Noël been in touch?' Leonie bit her lip in anguish. 'God! I don't think I can *bear* much more of this uncertainty. What a time for a war to start!'

'Don't worry, darling,' Peter said soothingly. 'It's my guess that things will soon be back to normal. Entertainment will be the order of the day. It's just a question of when and where to put it on.'

'Oh, well, I suppose I'll have to leave it all in your capable hands,' she said resignedly.

'That's right. Just you enjoy relaxing with little Imogen,' Peter advised. 'Let Tony and me do the worrying for you.'

She replaced the receiver with a trembling hand. Her arrogance and impatience were a protective shell that was becoming more fragile with each passing day. It concealed her innermost secret feelings of fear and insecurity. Fear of his new situation – the war and its unknown evils – and insecurity about her crumbling marriage.

Tony had had plenty of affairs. She was so used to them now that she could read the signs as easily as ABC. She always knew when they were about to begin and she could follow their progress through from climax to conclusion by Tony's moods. She even welcomed them. When there was a new woman in his life he was always in a good mood, at his most handsome and charming. With the adrenaline flowing copiously he did his best work and when he was engaged in chasing some dumb blonde or dizzy brunette he was a tolerant working partner and amusing companion, seeming to see the world through rose-coloured glasses. But this time it was different. He was never in the same mood twice; preoccupied and pensive one minute, elated the next. And she was sure he hardly heard a word she or anyone else said to him.

It had all begun with his obsession to play a classical role. That frightened her more than anything. She would never have admitted to anyone, not even Tony himself – least of all to Tony – but she was terrified of being left to carry a show alone. His abandonment of their marriage, she could stand. In truth there had been no marriage for years, and she was willing to admit that it was largely her fault. But if Tony stopped acting with her, if their celebrated partnership on stage were to end, she was terribly afraid that it could be the end of her career.

But what to do about it? Who *was* she, this very special woman who had finally won Tony away from her in mind as well as body? Not knowing tore her nerves to shreds. It was like fighting an enemy blindfold with one hand tied behind her back. It was Leonie's guess that she was a classical actress – well known, beautiful, young? *Younger than she?* Leonie would be thirty next birthday and she was having trouble coming to terms with the fact.

60

Sitting there, staring unseeingly out of the window, she visualised them playing opposite each other at Stratford or in London – Hamlet and Ophelia; Romeo and Juliet even. Tony was still youthful and athletic enough to get away with Romeo. Consumed with jealousy, she got up and paced the room, racking her brain for something to do to take her mind off the demons that gnawed mercilessly at her.

In the paddock Imogen, dressed in jodhpurs and a white shirt, was putting Toffee through his paces; trotting him round and putting him over the small jumps placed at intervals around the field. Shirley watched enviously from the fence. Imogen had hardly spoken to her since their first meeting. She behaved as though Shirley didn't exist, doing all the things she always did when she was at home and making no attempt to share anything with her unwelcome 'playmate'.

The weather was fine – what Jim Jarvis called an Indian summer – and Shirley had worn her selection of cotton dresses in rotation. Today, in a desperate attempt to attract someone's attention, she had chosen the buttercup yellow with panels piped in white. She wore her white ankle socks and sandals with it and got Nanny Jarvis to tie a big white bow in her hair. Even Imo-gen's *unschool* clothes were dowdy to Shirley's eyes, but she had the uncomfortable feeling that they had what Gloria would have called 'class' and she found this slightly intimidating.

Apart from Imo-gen's obvious dislike of her, Shirley liked it here. It was very different from the little shop in Angel Row. Never in her life had she had so much open space in which to play, so much green grass to run on or such fresh air to breathe. Instead of the weekly bath in the tin tub in the kitchen, in water shared with Gloria, she had one all to herself every night before bed in the big white bath that was almost big enough to swim in. And she had never tasted such delicious food. Home-made bread, fresh farm butter and eggs, and milk that came up every morning from the farm in a gleaming churn, still warm from the cow. At first she had been sceptical about drinking it. It didn't seem right somehow – having milk that came out of an animal instead of a bottle. But once she had tasted its delicious creaminess she soon changed her mind. Porridge and cornflakes would never be the same again.

In spite of Imo-gen's mum's interest in her, Shirley hadn't been asked to dance for the Darrents and now Mr Darrent had left for London again. Everyone seemed so preoccupied now. The only exciting thing that had happened was when the siren had sounded soon after the old man on the wireless had said there was a war on. That horrible fat lady from the post office had come up to the house that morning in a funny tin hat slipping over her eyes. She'd tried to boss everyone about, telling them what to do. Mrs Darrent had told *her* where to get off and no mistake. She'd called her a rude word that Shirley wasn't allowed to say. She had enjoyed that.

'Go on – give us a go,' she called out as Imogen trotted past on the pony. Imogen ignored her as usual, but just at that moment Nanny Jarvis appeared with two glasses of milk and a plate of biscuits on a tray.

'I thought you girls would like your elevenses out here as it's such a lovely morning,' she said. Putting the tray down on a bench, she called to Imogen, 'Come and have your milk and then you can let Shirley have a ride.'

'She can't ride,' Imogen returned with a toss of her head.

'Never mind. You had to learn once too, didn't you? You can hold the reins and lead her round the paddock.' She smiled down at Shirley. 'You'd like a ride on the pony, wouldn't you, duckie?'

'Yes please.' Shirley took her glass of milk and drank thirstily, looking at Imogen over the rim of her glass and trying to assess her reaction. The other girl took her own glass and drank with dainty sips.

'You've got milk all round your mouth,' she told Shirley scathingly. 'It looks disgusting.'

'That's all right.' Nanny handed Shirley a handkerchief. 'You were thirsty, weren't you?'

62

Shirley wiped her mouth and handed back the hanky, staring back at Imogen. 'Can I get on now then?' she asked with a sidelong look at Nanny Jarvis.

Looking furious, Imogen walked silently with her to the waiting pony and stood holding the reins, resentment in every gesture. 'Well, what are you waiting for? Aren't you going to get on?' she asked coldly.

Nanny stepped forward and lifted Shirley into the saddle. 'You're supposed to show her how to mount and give her a leg up,' she admonished Imogen. 'You're not a very good teacher, are you?'

Shirley smiled. 'Thank you, Nanny,' she said.

When Nanny was out of earshot Imogen mimicked Shirley's cockney accent: '*Fank you, Nanny,*' she jibed. 'Little angel, aren't you? Little goody-goody. I thought I told you not to call her Nanny.'

'Shall if I want,' Shirley said defiantly. 'Anyway, she told me to.'

'I see. You always do what people tell you, do you? Well, so does this pony.' She threw the reins across Toffee's neck and gave his rump a sudden slap. The startled pony began to canter round the field, taking the small jumps with glee, delighted at his sudden freedom. Shirley held onto his mane determinedly, trying not to let Imogen see how scared she was. When they came round to where Imogen stood the girl gave the pony another slap, harder this time, making him increase his pace and set off on a second circuit.

'P-please – m-make 'im s-stop!' Shirley could feel herself gradually slipping sideways out of the saddle and her heart was bumping with fear, but Imogen only laughed mercilessly.

Suddenly there was a shout. 'Imogen! Catch those reins at once. Stop that pony this minute before there's an accident.'

Shirley saw Imogen's gaze freeze with dismay as she saw her mother running across the grass. Leonie climbed the paddock fence quickly and ran forward to catch the pony's bridle, bringing him to a halt. 'Are you all right?'

she asked a quivering Shirley who hung half in and half out of the saddle. Lifting her gently to the ground, she turned to a sheepish-looking Imogen. 'Here, take him back to his stable and give him a rubdown,' she said sternly. 'And don't you *ever* let me catch you doing anything so spiteful again, you horrid child.' As her daughter walked away, leading the pony, Leonie looked down at Shirley.

'Are you hurt, darling?'

The kind words brought a lump to Shirley's throat. 'N-no,' she said. *She* wasn't hurt, but her pride and her feelings were. It wasn't fair. She'd done nothing to Imogen. Why should she want to hurt her?

Leonie seemed to understand. Bending to wipe a smudge from the child's face with her own handkerchief, she said: 'Poor sweetie, you're trembling. Tell you what, you shall have lunch with me today. And we'll make horrid Imogen have hers in her room. How's that?'

Shirley shook her head vigorously. 'I'm not very 'ungry.'

'But you will be by then. I'm having fresh salmon. You can have some too if you like. And afterwards I'll play the piano and you can dance for me as you promised. How's that?'

It sounded lovely and Shirley longed to agree, but how could she make Mrs Darrent see that if she did, it would only make matters worse between herself and Imogen. 'Can – Imo-gen come too?' she asked. 'She never meant to make the 'orse go too fast. She was just tryin' to learn me to ride.'

Leonie looked taken aback for a moment, then she laughed. 'Well, well. What a generous little girl you are! Very well, if that's what you want. I've got some news for you both anyway.'

Shirley changed out of the dirtied buttercup-yellow dress into her pink and white polka-dot. Imogen, however, appeared in the dining room still wearing her jodhpurs and shirt. Leonie looked at her disapprovingly.

'I hope you've at least washed your hands. You look a perfect disgrace, child.'

Molly, who heard the remark as she came in with the first course, said: 'I tried to get her to put on something more suitable when you said the children were to lunch with you, Madam, but she insisted on staying in those things.'

'It's quite all right, Nanny. I'm sure it's not your fault. We both know that Imogen is incurably stubborn, don't we? She gets more like a donkey every day.' Leonie smiled at Shirley. 'You look perfectly *sweet*, darling.' She winced slightly as Shirley began to slurp her soup. 'But, er, when you eat soup you hold your spoon *so* – do you see?'

Imogen picked up her own spoon and bent her head over her plate. Under her breath, and just loud enough for Shirley to hear, she said: 'Common little pig.'

Shirley turned to look at her. She took in the lank mousy hair, the large front teeth with their ugly brace, and the resentment that gleamed at her from behind the steel-rimmed spectacles. And for the first time in her short life she knew the meaning of the word hate.

Imogen blushed bright red. 'Don't you know that it's rude to stare?' she demanded.

'Children, *please*.' Leonie glared at them both. 'Any more and you'll have to finish your lunch in the kitchen.' She helped herself to salad and passed the bowl across the table. 'Now listen. I've had a telephone call this morning from Mr Hawkins, the headmaster of the village school. He's beginning the new term next week. Just to begin with and because there are so many evacuees, it is to be divided into two groups. Half will go in the mornings and half in the afternoons. The under tens – that's you – are to go in the mornings and as you're the same age you'll be in the same class. Won't that be nice?'

Imogen put down her knife and fork and looked at her mother. 'Why do I have to go to the village school?' she asked. 'I don't like the village children. They're dirty.'

'Don't be difficult, Imogen,' Leonie said coldly. 'There's a war on. You're lucky to be getting into a school at all. And you'll be able to sit next to Shirley here. She certainly isn't dirty. Which is more than I can say for you at this moment.'

Crushed and crimson-faced, Imogen lowered her eyes and the rest of the meal was eaten in silence. When the time came for Leonie to invite Shirley to dance, Imogen asked to be excused, but Leonie shook her head.

'No, Imogen. You are to come to the drawing room with Shirley and me.' She led the two girls across the hall into the drawing room and sat down at the piano.

'Shirley is going to entertain us,' she told a reluctant Imogen. 'It will do you good to see what some little girls can do when they try to please their parents.'

To the strains of 'Animal Crackers' Shirley did her favourite song-and-dance routine as taught by Miss Kent at the Saturday morning dancing classes, her feet in their white sandals tapping away on the parquet floor of the drawing room. When it came to an end, Leonie clapped delightedly.

'That was *sweet*, darling. You must dance and sing for us again soon. What a clever little girl you are.'

Stony-faced, Imogen asked: 'May I go now, please? It's time to feed Toffee.'

'Oh, go along then if you must,' Leonie said. 'But first say thank you to Shirley for entertaining us so nicely.'

Blushing furiously Imogen muttered a grudging 'thank you', but when Leonie turned her back she surreptitiously wrinkled her nose and thrust out the tip of her tongue. Shirley returned the gesture, withdrawing her tongue and adjusting her sunny smile quickly as Leonie turned back again.

Later that night, when she passed Imogen's bedroom door, she heard her crying and felt a stab of guilt. Was it because she'd got told off for making the pony run fast? No. It'd be because she didn't want to go to a school that wasn't posh. That was the sort of thing Imo-gen would cry about. Why should she feel sorry for her?

Tony and Claire crossed the field hand in hand. Every morning since they'd arrived the sun had wakened them.

Although it was September there was only the faintest nip of autumn in the air and the breeze from the sea was fresh and invigorating. Tony, who had spent most of his life in cities, inside theatres, knew he could soon get to like the open-air life, especially if it were shared with Claire. Each morning they had swum in the sea, then returned to the cottage to laze. In the afternoons they worked in the cottage garden. Claire said it was the least they could do for their hosts in return for their rent-free stay. After an early supper they climbed the stairs and lay together in the big brass bed, talking, making love and talking again, until sleep overtook them.

This morning, as they reached the far side of the field and climbed the stile that gave onto the dunes, Claire said: 'Isn't it funny, you can't even see the sea from here. Until you climb to the top of that ridge of sand you wouldn't know it was there.'

'You would. You can hear it,' Tony said. 'Stop and listen.'

They stood quite still together hand in hand, listening to the sounds of the morning. High above, almost hidden by the haze, a skylark sang, its pure, silvery notes mingling with the roar of the waves as they washed the pebbly shore. Then Claire's hand tensed in his as another, more intrusive sound cut rudely into the peace of the morning. She looked apprehensively at Tony, who frowned.

'What? What is it?'

But Claire didn't have to look. She already knew. It was the sound of a tractor. And as they climbed the soft, slippery sand of the dunes the mechanical rumble was joined by the clang of metal and the voices of men, talking and laughing together as they worked. Standing at the top of the ridge they watched them filling sandbags and throwing them onto a trailer. Further along the beach another team was hammering steel posts into the sand and nearby they saw huge coils of barbed wire. Without voicing their thoughts, both knew that this was the end of their stolen time together. The end of love and happiness, the end of peace. A cloud momentarily crossed the sun and Claire shivered.

'It's going to rain,' she said, turning away. 'Let's go back.' In her heart she knew that the time had come to pack and leave.

On the day that term began at St Luke's village school, Shirley was up early. She was looking forward to it. She was lonely for the company of other children and she hadn't seen any of her old schoolmates since she arrived at Houlton – apart from Tilly Marks, and you couldn't count her. Tilly was a year younger and in a different class anyway.

Shirley and Imogen ate breakfast together in the kitchen and while they ate Nanny Jarvis packed each of them some biscuits for their mid-morning 'lunch'. Imogen was pale and silent. She wore her school skirt and a dark-green jumper with a white blouse underneath. Shirley privately thought it was a bit silly to wear thick clothes when it was still quite warm. She had chosen her blue and white gingham for her first day at the new school and she knew she looked nice in it. Gloria always liked her in that. On the other hand Imo-gen did look quite smart, she told herself, giving the other girl a sidelong look.

Nanny kissed them both goodbye and wished them a happy day and Jim walked down to the lane with them. He showed them the armband he would soon be wearing.

Shirley examined it carefully. 'What's LDV stand for?' she asked.

'Local Defence Volunteers,' Jim told her proudly. 'All the men who haven't joined up are getting together to protect our own village from danger, like a little army. We'll have proper uniforms when they're ready but till then we're wearing these armbands.'

When they got to the ornate gates that had so impressed Shirley on the day she arrived, he told them that all the iron railings and gates throughout the country would soon be taken down and collected for something called salvage. 'To help make aeroplanes,' he explained.

Shirley said she thought that was a shame and that an aeroplane with wrought-iron gates would surely be too draughty, which made Jim laugh.

Imogen did not join in their good-humoured chatter. Walking on Jim's other side, she was silent and tense.

He left them at the top of the lane and as soon as he was out of sight, Shirley said: 'Come on, Imo-gen, let's be friends.' She reached out and tried to take the other girl's hand, but Imogen rejected it with a shrug of her shoulder, quickening her pace to walk on ahead.

'I don't make friends with girls who show off,' she said. 'You think you're really clever, don't you? Sucking up to Nanny and Jim and my mother and getting them all to make a fuss of you. Well, I *hate* you and I always will, so there. I'm going to get my daddy to send you away when he comes home again.'

'You can't. You've gotta do everythin' you can to help the war,' Shirley said, her chin thrust out and her lower lip trembling. 'There's gonna be bombs in London. That's why all the kids've gotta come 'ere. You don't know nuthin', Imogen Darrent.'

'I know you're a nasty little show-off. You're common and you've got no manners. You're a – a *slum* child.'

Shirley's throat ached with the pain of the other girl's insults but she refused to give Imogen the satisfaction of seeing her cry. Blinking hard at the threatening tears, she burst out: 'How'd you like ter leave yer 'ome and yer mum and dad and go where people don't want you? You're ugly and mean an' 'orrible, Imo-gen Darrent, an' I don't *want* to be friends with you now. Not *ever*.'

She ran on ahead, her gas mask in its cardboard box bumping uncomfortably against her back. In the High Street she was comforted by the sight of a group of children from Whitechapel. Running up with a shout of greeting, she joined them as they converged on the school building next to the church. She'd find her own way and make her own friends just like she always had. Under her breath she said one of the forbidden words with immense satisfaction.

'*Bugger* you, Imogen Darrent. *Be* rotten then. See if I care.'

Chapter Four

Anticlimax was the word everyone was using. Weeks had gone by now since war was declared and so far nothing had happened. When the first siren had sounded that Sunday morning they had all feared the worst. Everyone in Angel Row was convinced that the bombs and poison gas were about to be showered on them, but so far there had been nothing.

In spite of the unexpected lull, Pa had made the most of his newfound authority as an ARP warden, making himself thoroughly unpopular with all the neighbours with his shout of 'Put that light out!', and Ma had set to work clearing out the large cupboard under the stairs and making it comfy, because right from the start she had announced her veto against the street shelters.

'The kids've already started peein' in 'em,' she said, wrinkling her nose. 'What with them an' the courtin' couples they ain't fit for decent folk to sleep in. If I'm gonna be buried alive I'll be buried in me own 'ome in comfort and that's flat.' And both Gloria and Pa knew by the set of her mouth that nothing on this earth – Hitler's Luftwaffe included – would shift her.

To Gloria's delight the Adelphi had opened its doors again within the first fortnight, as did most of the other cinemas and theatres. Working hours were not quite the same as before, though. Because of the blackout the theatres put on only one performance each night instead of two, with two matinees a week. And the cinemas opened at two and closed at ten.

As the nights began to draw in, the blackout made things difficult. There were no street lights. Shop as well as house windows were dark. Even the cars and buses had their headlights muffled, which made crossing the road after dark hazardous. But people were gradually getting used to finding their way around with the help of dimmed torchlight and the difficulties were met, for the most part, good-humouredly. Every day there were hilarious new stories of adventures – and misadventures the previous night on the way home.

Gloria still missed Shirley sorely. There were letters, of course. They wrote to each other every week without fail, but the laboriously penned letters in Shirley's rounded handwriting told Gloria very little about the things she really wanted to know. When her first postcard had arrived Gloria hadn't known whether to believe what the child had written or not. She knew her daughter was no liar, but, an avid cinema-goer from an early age, Shirley was given to daydreams and romancing. Perhaps, in her own way, she was just making the most of the traumatic break. But on making some enquiries about the address Gloria soon discovered that her daughter really *was* living in the country home of Tony Darrent and his wife Leonie Swann. Shirley had written that Mrs Darrent – or Miss Swann – had even asked her to dance for her and told her she was clever. Gloria was ecstatic with pride. She told all her friends at work about it, though most of them received the story with scepticism, exchanging disbelieving looks when her back was turned. They all knew of Gloria's high-flown ambitions for her daughter.

In the bedroom they had shared, the magazine pictures of Tony Darrent still adorned the walls and sometimes when she lay looking up at them, Gloria tried to imagine what it would be like actually sharing a home with her idol. Not that he was there much. According to Shirley's letters he had left his wife and daughter in the country and gone back to London the moment war was declared and he hadn't been back since. Gloria wondered if he and the glamorous Leonie were as happy together as the magazines would have their readers believe.

In the corner by the wardrobe the wind-up gramophone stood on its table, the pile of well-played records they both loved standing idle beside it. Listening to them without Shirl made Gloria cry so she didn't put them on very often now. There were all the songs from the Shirley Temple films, 'The Good Ship Lollipop', 'Animal Crackers' and the others, bought for Shirley to practise her dancing to. Then there were Gloria's favourites, 'Dancing in the Dark', 'The Way You Look Tonight', 'They Can't Take That Away From Me' and all the other lovely romantic numbers from Fred and Ginger's films. The hit from last year that Shirley and she had played till it almost wore out was the jolly 'Beer Barrel Polka', but Gloria's latest favourite was the hit from the new film *The Wizard of Oz*, 'Somewhere Over the Rainbow'. She had bought that one just last week after hearing it on the wireless. Listening to its wistful lyrics, she knew Shirl would love it and she longed to be able to play it to her.

Already she was saving up to make the trip up to Northamptonshire to see her. That would be a real treat. As well as looking forward to seeing Shirley she was dying to get a glimpse of her favourite stars – or at least to see the place where they lived. She'd begun to hope that maybe if things stayed as they were, she could even bring Shirley home again, though when she had suggested it to Pa he had shaken his head pessimistically.

'I don't trust this quiet,' he told her, sucking his breath in noisily and gazing up suspiciously at the sky. 'Them Gerries know 'ow to lull you into a false sense of security. Look at what they done already, over there in Poland and Czechoslovakia. Mark my words, one o' these nights they'll be over here – *then* we'll cop it. You leave the kiddie where she's safe, gel.'

His words struck a deathly chill through Gloria's bones and she prayed he was wrong. But all the same – better to be on the safe side.

Among the girls she worked with there were often tears these days. Ma had been right; the husbands and 'young men' of most of Gloria's workmates were being called up or volunteering for service. In one way Gloria was glad she didn't have to go through the heartbreak, though in another she longed to be part of it all. Since Shirley's birth she had kept out of the way of fellers. The decent ones steered clear of her once they knew she had a kiddie anyway, and the ones who were interested were mainly after one thing. And anyway, most of the blokes her own age or older were either married or spoken for – not that *that* stopped some of them. A long time ago Gloria had made up her mind that, sadly, marriage wasn't for her. Not now. And after what had happened to her she wasn't prepared to risk her trust again. But the atmosphere of war, of sacrifice and emotional partings, of the longed-for letters and the prospect of ecstatic reunions stirred her to a new restlessness, making her wonder wistfully at times what her life might have been like, if things had been different.

The shortages that everyone had warned about hadn't occurred yet, though there was talk of rationing and price controls to come into effect soon. It was rumoured that ration books had already been printed and lay in big stacks somewhere up at Whitehall, waiting to be distributed. Here again, Pa was sceptical.

'It'll be a case of business as usual for them as can afford it, you see if I'm not right,' he predicted. 'Black market, just like it was in the last lot. Folks like us, tryin' to earn a decent livin' 'll be expected to keep prices low and to 'and most of our profits over to the bloody government. The workin' classes don't never win.'

When Shirley came out into the playground with her small group of friends, she saw that they were at it again. Over in the corner behind the lavs, well out of view of the school windows, a group of six or seven girls – some evacuees and the rest village kids – were gathered round a lonely figure in a green jumper. It had been going on ever since the first day of term. Even where Shirley stood on the steps she could hear their taunts floating across the playground:

73

'Polly Longfrock. She talks with a plum in her gob. Too posh for the likes of us. Go on, let's hear you speak then. Stuck-up cat. Teacher's pet. Rotten little snob.'

Shirley could see Imogen from where she stood. She was taller than the other kids. Her face white, she stood with her back pressed against the wall, red-eyed from crying. At first they hadn't been able to get to her. She'd remained aloof, ignoring them just as she had Shirley. But the constant jeers and taunts had chipped away her natural reserve until at last her persecutors found to their delight that they could make her cry whenever they wanted to. To begin with Shirley thought she would probably tell the teacher, or her mum, who would come down to the school and have it stopped. But to her surprise Imogen said nothing. Although each day must have been sheer misery, she never breathed a word about it to anyone, not even Shirley, who was obviously aware of her predicament.

'Come on, Shirl. Come and play skipping with us.' One of the group tugged at her arm. But Shirley shook her head.

'In a minute.'

Imogen had been nasty to her and when the teasing first began Shirley had felt triumphant. That'd show her what it felt like to be on the outside – disliked and unwanted. But as it went on getting worse day by day, it began to make her feel uncomfortable, then guilty and finally angry. It was unfair, so many against one – and for so long. She admired Imogen for not splitting, too. If she wanted to she could have had them all caned for what they were doing.

Making up her mind suddenly, Shirley strode determinedly across the playground and shoved her way through to the front of the gang of jeering kids.

'Wanna play skippin' with us, Imo-gen?'

The gang stopped their jeering and stared at her in surprise. Imogen stopped weeping and looked up. The ringleader, an older girl with sharp, spiteful features, was the first to break the shocked silence.

74

'Whatcher wanna play with a four-eyed snob like 'er for? She's ugly. Look at 'er teeth, they got iron bands on 'em.'

Shirley turned to face the girl, looking her up and down critically. 'Look oo's talkin'. *You* ain't got much room to shout, 'ave yer?' she said. 'Yer frock's all mucky and yer nose needs wipin'. Ain't you got an' 'anky? Uses yer sleeve, do yer?'

The rest of the gang began to snigger and their leader turned away, unwilling to provoke any more of Shirley's blunt criticisms.

'Aw, come on,' she said. 'Let's leave 'em to it. They ain't worth botherin' with.' From a safe distance she called: 'You wait, Shirley Rayner. I'll get you for this.'

'Smack yer silly face for you if you try,' Shirley returned shrilly.

The hubbub of playtime, momentarily stilled by the heated exchange, soon resumed and Shirley turned to Imogen. 'You all right?'

'Yes.' Imogen nodded, dabbing her eyes and putting her spectacles back on again. She sniffed and looked at Shirley. 'Thank you for making them stop.'

Shirley shrugged. ''S orl right. 'T ain't fair, six onto one. Do you wanna play skippin' then?'

Imogen smiled gratefully. 'Can I really? Yes please.'

Shirley's group, who had watched the whole encounter with fascination, accepted Imogen without questions. Seeing Shirley in action, they knew better than to object. For the rest of playtime they took turns at the rope and Imogen proved herself adept at the skill, executing 'bumps' and even 'double bumps' with an expertise that earned her the respect of every one of the group.

As Shirley was walking out through the school gates at lunchtime, Imogen caught up with her. 'Shall we walk home together?' she asked.

Shirley looked round. ''S orl right. Them kids won't touch you again.'

'I know,' Imogen said. 'I'd like to walk with you anyway.' She gave Shirley a sidelong glance. 'May I?'

'If you want.' Suddenly Shirley smiled at her. 'Come on. I've got a penny in me knickers pocket. We'll get some gobstoppers at the shop. Race you – last one there's a soppy 'aporth.'

'Why didn't you never split on 'em?' Shirley asked with her mouth half full of bread and jam.

The girls were sitting under the hedge in the field next to Toffee's paddock. Nanny Jarvis had packed up raspberry jam sandwiches and a bottle of lemonade so that they could have a picnic. She'd been relieved and delighted to see the two of them getting along at last.

Imogen pulled at the long grasses. 'I didn't think anyone would be on my side,' she said.

'The teacher would've,' Shirley said. 'She'd've given 'em the cane.'

Imogen lifted her shoulders helplessly. 'They'd have been worse than ever to me if I'd sneaked, though, wouldn't they?'

Shirley had to agree that they probably would. 'What about your mum then? She'd've gone down there and given 'em what for, wouldn't she?'

'I don't think so.' Imogen sighed. 'Mummy doesn't like me, you see. She'd probably have been pleased.'

Shirley was shocked. 'She must *like* you. You're 'er little girl.'

Imogen shrugged. 'I heard her telling Nanny once that she never wanted a baby at all. She thinks I'm ugly just as those girls at school do. She wishes I'd never been born.'

Shirley stared at her incredulously. At home in London she knew a few mums who didn't seem to care all that much. She knew some kids who didn't have proper clothes or even enough to eat. But if anything went wrong, or someone did something to hurt their kids, they sprang fiercely to their defence like enraged tigresses defending their cubs. The attitude Imogen described was totally alien to her. She had always thought that posh kids had more of everything – including love.

'I thought ladies always wanted babies,' she said thoughtfully. 'If they don't, why do they keep 'avin 'em?

P'raps it's 'cause she don't see you much. What with you bein' away at boardin' school an' everythin'. Glor and me ain't never been away from each other. We even sleep together at 'ome.'

'Who's Glor?'

'Gloria. She's my mum. I ain't got no dad so me an' Glor, we share everythin'.'

Imogen looked at her with envy. 'I bet you wish she was here.'

Shirley nodded. 'Yes. But she's savin' up to come an' see me. That's if your mum'll let 'er.'

'Of course she will. Mummy'd do anything for you. I expect it's because you're pretty.'

'Is that why you hated me?' Shirley asked. 'Were you jealous?'

'*No*.' Imogen looked away. 'Well – a bit.' She selected a juicy grass and began to chew it. 'I can't help being ugly. It's not my fault.'

'You're not *really* ugly,' Shirley said, studying Imogen closely. 'If you didn't wear them specs, an' that – that wotsname thing on your teeth . . .'

'I won't always have to wear them,' Imogen told her quickly. 'The dentist says that by the time I'm twelve or thirteen I'll be able to do without the brace. And if I keep wearing my glasses my squint will come right too – eventually.' She looked at Shirley's hair with envy. 'I wish my hair curled like yours, though.'

'You could do it up in rags,' Shirley said helpfully. 'I'll 'elp you if you like. Ain't you got any nice frocks?'

Imogen shook her head. 'Mummy says there isn't any point. Apart from school I only come here to Houlton and most of the time I just play in the garden or ride Toffee.'

Shirley was silent, assessing her new friend. 'I bet Glor'd make you some frocks,' she said. 'She gets lovely stuff down the Brick Lane market. It's ever so cheap. When she comes we'll ask her, shall we?'

Imogen smiled. 'Do you really think she would?' She paused, licking her lips nervously. 'Shirley, I've been thinking. There's something I want to ask you.'

'Yeah? Go on,' Shirley encouraged.

'Well, you said once that you'd teach me to tap-dance.'

Shirley grinned delightedly. 'I will if you want.'

Imogen blushed. 'I thought if I could do something like that Mummy might like me better.' She bit her lip anxiously. 'I'm terribly clumsy, though, I'll probably be no good at it.'

''Course you will,' Shirley said cheerfully. 'You should'a seen some o' them in our class. Like cart 'orses they was when they first come. Now they can dance as good as Ginger Rogers.' She stopped, her face suddenly serious. 'Tell yer what, Imo-gen. If I learn you to dance, will you learn me to talk proper?'

Imogen looked surprised. 'Do you *want* to? I thought everyone hated the way I speak.'

'Nah – they're all jealous really. That's why they tease you. Didn't you know that? They used to do it to me – cause of me frocks an' that. That's how I know.' She paused to frown thoughtfully. 'I wouldn't talk like it at school – not at first. But I'd like to know how to so's you 'n' me could talk the same – when we're here at 'ome.'

'At *h*ome,' Imogen corrected with a smile.

'At *h*-ome. That be''er?'

Imogen shook her head. 'Be*tt*er, you mean.'

'Right, be*tt*er.' Shirley's face broke into a delighted grin. 'See? I'm learnin' real quick.'

'You can ride Toffee whenever you want,' Imogen offered. 'I'll show you how to ride him properly. Maybe Daddy will even get you a pony of your own.'

'Cor!' Shirley's hand flew to her mouth as she gasped with delight. The two girls laughed delightedly. Suddenly the future looked much brighter – for both of them.

Claire had decided to go home. She would remain in London for a while, however. There seemed to be no immediate danger. Her family in Jersey didn't seem unduly troubled about the war in Europe. Surely it wouldn't affect them? The War Office had said that the Channel Islands would be of no strategic value to either side. The tourist office was still advertising holidays as usual and there really seemed no cause for concern. They urged their daughter to return home again as soon as possible. She would surely be safer there than in London and, like Tony, they were horrified at her notion of joining one of the women's services. So Claire had decided she would stay with Peter Jason till he had managed to find a suitable replacement and then leave for Jersey. The longer she remained, the harder the parting with Tony would be for her.

When they left Suffolk they had returned to London separately; she to her flat in Earls Court; he to the Mayfair apartment he and Leonie occupied when they were working in town. Apart from the taped windows and heaps of unsightly sandbags, precautions they were already used to, London looked the same. So normal that it was hard to believe that the country was at war. There had been no onslaught of menacing bombers as prophesied and people were beginning to tell each other that all Hitler's dark threats were just so much sabre-rattling. Places of entertainment reopened and the city's night life slowly began to return to normal. In spite of the blackout it was a case of business as usual, and the public let out its collective long-held breath.

One of Tony's first priorities was a visit to Peter Jason's home in Richmond. He found him and his wife, Eve, having tea in the pleasant garden that ran down to the river. They looked happy and relaxed, sitting on the lawn in the autumn sunshine. Eve welcomed Tony warmly and went off into the house to get another cup.

'I've been hoping you'd come. I've got good news, old boy,' Peter said brightly. 'Theatres are to open again the week after next; at least, that's the latest tip that going round.'

'I was hoping you'd have something a bit more positive to tell me,' Tony said tetchily. The sight of Peter sitting there dressed in flannels and an open-necked shirt, puffing away on his pipe as though all was right with the world, caught him on the raw. 'Have you been lazing about here like this ever since I last saw you? Haven't you done anything at *all* on our behalf?'

Peter frowned. 'As it happens, I reopened the office unofficially last Monday,' he said. 'I've been going up to town every morning – and working my backside off at home the rest of the day, if you really want to know. What's the matter with you? It's the same for all of us, you know. I stand to lose by the war, too. I'm losing my secretary for a start.'

'I know.' Tony sank into a deckchair and pushed his fingers through his hair. 'I'm sorry, Peter. It's just the uncertainty. Good news about the theatres, of course. Am I to take it that *Sunshine Sally* is to open again, then?'

Peter shook his head, puffing thoughtfully at his pipe. 'Well, no. There was a meeting of management and backers yesterday. As you know, the run was to have ended at the beginning of December anyway and the bookings were all cancelled with the shutdown. At the meeting the general consensus was that *Sunshine Sally* was too frivolous a subject for the present climate, so it was decided unanimously to call it a day as from now.'

'What about the new film?'

Peter shrugged. 'As that's a light-hearted subject, the same probably goes for that too. For the time being, anyway.'

'I see.' Tony could hardly conceal his relief. 'Were you there – at the meeting, I mean?' he asked.

'Yes – on your behalf. I tried to get hold of you as soon as I heard about the meeting, but I couldn't locate you anywhere. By the way, Leonie has been onto me several times. I let her think we'd been in touch.'

Tony gave him a sheepish sidelong glance. 'I see. Thanks, Peter. So – not such good news after all. Seems we're in for a long rest.'

A smile twitched at the corners of Peter's mouth and he paused to refill his pipe. 'As a matter of fact, no. At least, not in your case. The backers were talking about putting on something patriotic to stir up the right spirit and lift morale. It seemed likely that they were prepared to put their money where their mouths were, so I suggested Shakespeare – *Henry V*.'

Tony sat upright in his chair, his attention suddenly riveted. 'Go on. Did they buy it?'

'They were very enthusiastic and so was the management. Striking while the iron was hot, I went on to suggest you for the name part.'

Tony held his breath. 'And . . .?'

'They weren't too sure at first, then I reminded them about your long family tradition of classical acting.'

What Peter had actually said was that people who wouldn't normally touch anything by William Shakespeare with a barge pole would flock to see it if Tony Darrent were starring.

'I see. That did the trick, did it?'

Peter smiled. 'Certainly did. They want to see you as soon as possible. Graeme Hamilton will be directing. I know you and he get along well together. And I insisted that you're to have your choice of supporting cast. If you're agreeable I'll start drawing up the contract at once, then you and Graeme can get together and talk about auditioning.'

Tony was elated. All he could think about was getting to a telephone to tell Claire. Then a sobering thought struck him. 'What about Leonie? Have you told her about *Sunshine Sally* closing and the film being postponed?'

Peter took his pipe out of his mouth and studied the bowl. 'No, old son, I rather thought that was your province.'

Tony sighed. 'She's not going to like it one little bit. And you *are* her agent.' He brightened. 'Tell you what. Why don't you and Eve come up to Houlton for the weekend?'

'Sorry, can't be done. Too much on at the moment.'

'You mean you don't want to face up to your responsibilities.'

'Not mine – yours. You could always find her a part in *Henry*, I suppose.'

81

Tony shook his head. 'Come off it, Peter. Leonie's a musical-comedy actress. She couldn't handle a Shakespeare role and you know it. It might be different if it were some other play, but *Henry V*? Not a chance. The only female part is Princess Katherine and she doesn't speak French for a start. Apart from that there's only the serving girl, and I can't see her taking kindly to that.'

'Mmm.' Peter thought for a moment. 'ENSA would be ideal for her, of course. They'll be looking for glamorous singers to entertain the troops.'

Tony winced. 'I wouldn't suggest it if I were you. Not if you want to walk away with your teeth intact.'

They both laughed, then Peter said casually: 'Everything all right between you two, is it?'

Tony looked up. 'Of course. Why do you ask?'

Peter leaned out of his chair to tap out his pipe against the table leg. 'I've noticed that your latest, er, *diversion* seems to be touching you a little more deeply than usual, if you don't mind my saying so, old boy. I just wondered if Leonie might have noticed too. Women have an uncanny instinct for that kind of thing.'

'None of your business, actually, Peter,' Tony said bluntly. 'But as it happens it's over anyway.'

'Really? Maybe that's just as well – for all concerned.'

Pretending he hadn't heard, Tony got to his feet. 'I'd better be off,' he said. 'I've one or two other calls to make. Tell Eve I'm sorry to rush off, will you. And if you change your mind about that weekend at Houlton . . .'

Peter returned his wave and watched him stride away across the lawn towards the house. 'Handsome sod,' he muttered to himself. How many hearts had he carelessly and unfeelingly broken over the years? Claire had told him of her intention of returning home as soon as she returned from Suffolk and he'd guessed that her decision had more than a little to do with Tony. Would she be going home to Grève de Lecq as heartwhole as she had left it? Shrugging, he told himself that Tony was right. It was none of his business and anyway, there was nothing he could do about it. Perhaps now that Tony was getting the role he wanted, he would settle down and stop womanising. This time it had done neither his work nor his temper any damned good at all.

Leonie had agreed enthusiastically to Shirley's request to have her mother at Houlton for the weekend. Anything to lift the sheer boredom of being buried alive in this hole while Tony had the satisfaction of getting a new show off the ground. At the time she agreed to Gloria's visit she hadn't known that Tony would also be home that weekend.

He arrived quite unexpectedly on the Friday evening and after dinner he told her about his visit with Peter down at Richmond. He had already told her over the telephone a week ago that the show would not reopen but after dinner that evening he broke the news to her that there was no part for her in the new production that was to take its place. Leonie was incredulous. She had been prepared for *Sunshine Sally* to close. The run had been almost at an end anyway. But she'd thought then that she had the new film to look forward to, not to mention Noël's half-promised play. Now it looked horribly likely that she was doomed to stick out the duration of the war on her own at Longueville Hall while Tony cavorted around the West End stage brandishing a sword and making a complete twerp of himself in hose and doublet. If she wasn't so angry she could have laughed.

'How convenient! Just what you wanted. Congratulations, darling.' Her eyes flashed dangerously. 'It won't run, of course. Who do you think will want to come and see you in that dreary old drivel? And may one ask why isn't there a part for me in it?'

'There's only one female part of any importance,' he explained. 'That of Princess Katherine. And most of her lines are delivered in French.'

'I could learn.'

Tony shook his head irritably. 'You're not right for it, Leonie. Katherine is shy – timid almost.'

'I *am* an actress, just in case you've forgotten.'

'A musical actress. It's just not *you*, Leonie.'

'Oh, come on, Tony.' She tossed back her hair. 'Surely we could get someone to write in some numbers for me.'

He snorted irritably. 'Don't talk such utter rubbish.'

'Why is it rubbish? They do it all the time in Shakespeare plays. What about *Midsummer-Night's Dream* and *Twelfth Night*?'

'They are musical plays. This is a drama.' Tony strode across the room to take a cigarette from the box on the coffee table and light it. 'Anyway, it's already cast.'

There was a long silence as Leonie watched him walk to the window and blow out a cloud of smoke. 'I see,' she said. 'So there's really no more to be said, is there?'

'Not really, no.'

Leonie took a cigarette herself and lit it with deliberate calm. 'May one ask who she is – this Sarah Bernhardt you've chosen to play opposite you?'

'Her name is Juliet Fabergé. She's a relative newcomer.'

Leonie laughed. 'The stage name is a little pretentious, don't you feel?'

'As it happens it's her own. She's half French.'

'How convenient. Aren't you lucky?' Leonie drew hard on her cigarette and narrowed her eyes at him through the smoke. 'She's young, of course. Attractive?'

'Naturally. You don't imagine I'd pick an ugly old crone to play the part of a beautiful young French princess, do you?'

Leonie stubbed out her half-smoked cigarette viciously. 'No, darling. That wouldn't be your style at all. Clever of you to pick an unknown, too. She won't take any of the limelight from you, will she? You'll be able to bag top billing – *and* get the best of the notices.' She threw him a challenging look. 'What did she have to do to get the part? Or shouldn't I ask?'

'Don't be so bloody childish.' Tony turned angrily and took a step towards her, then checked himself and took a deep breath. 'Look, Leonie, I'm really sorry there isn't anything on offer for you at the moment, but there will be.

Peter's working hard on it. I'm pretty sure he'll be able to get you some radio work and maybe some concerts too – personal appearances. There's some talk of entertainment for the factory workers.'

'Factory workers, eh?' Leonie laughed. 'What *fun*! It's a wonder to me that you haven't suggested sending *me* into a factory – or down a coal mine, perhaps. I'm sure you'd love to see me packed off to help the war effort.'

When Molly Jarvis returned to the kitchen with the coffee tray, she shook her head. 'Going at it hammer and tongs up there, they are,' she told Jim. 'Seems Mr Tony is going to do a Shakespeare play in London and there isn't a part for Madam in it.'

Jim grinned wryly. 'Oh dear, oh dear. That'll have set the cat among the pigeons and no mistake. Is she mad with him?'

'Mad isn't the word,' Molly told him, unloading the tray and beginning to wash up. 'She's in one of those sharp-as-a-dagger moods of hers. Claws out, ready to fly. I wouldn't be in his shoes.'

Tony and Leonie passed the evening in tense silence, speaking to each other only when they were obliged to. In their room later Tony collected up his things. 'I'll sleep in the dressing room.'

'No!' Leonie turned to him suddenly. 'Darling, don't go. I'm sorry if I was bitchy. It's just so dreary here all by myself with nothing to do and nothing to look forward to. I was disappointed, that's all.'

Tony sighed. 'Of course. I understand.'

She held out her arms to him. 'Stay with me tonight, darling. I've missed you.'

She wore a peach chiffon negligee trimmed with cream lace, and with her dark hair tumbling over her shoulders she looked quite breathtakingly beautiful. At one time Tony would have been delighted at her gesture, but now he had to force himself to put his arms around her and hold her close. He felt sorry for her. She was having a

85

rough time and she was desperately worried about her future career. He knew and understood that. In the past, if she had looked at him like this, clearly inviting him to make love to her, he'd have taken up the offer gladly, whether or not there was someone else in the offing. But ever since the arrival of Claire in his life he had found himself wanting to be completely faithful to her.

Leonie looked up at him, her lips soft and inviting. 'We are friends again, aren't we, darling?'

'Of course.'

'Then . . . shall we go to bed?' There was a flicker of uncertainty in the eyes that held his. She was losing him; she could feel it – sense it in every nerve. And she knew that if she lost him, she would lose everything. She would never act again without his guidance and support. Her first reaction had been to make him suffer for indulging his own ambitions without a thought for hers. But common sense stepped in, telling her that if she were to win him back she must play the right cards. Tony was a sensual man, and he had loved her devotedly and passionately – before Imogen. However much she feared another pregnancy, she must allow him back into her bed. Not only that, but she must prove to him that she could give him more than any of the other women in his life; that she was the only woman who could truly satisfy him.

Slipping her arms out of the peignoir she let it slip to the floor with a soft whisper. Tony stared at her, transfixed. It was so long since he had seen her naked that he had forgotten the exquisite beauty of her body, her perfect proportions, the high, firm breasts and smooth creamy skin. Her eyes were dark and luminous as she stood motionless, barely breathing as she looked up at him. Her lips, devoid of make-up, were petal-soft and full. He felt his heart beginning to quicken and took an involuntary step backwards, physically resisting the magnetic pull of her.

'What is it, darling?' She took a step towards him. 'You're not still cross with me?' She loosened his robe and slipped her arms around his waist, running her fingers lightly up and down the bare skin of his back. 'Please, darling – please love me. It's been so long.'

Almost without being aware that he did it, his arms pulled her against him. 'I – thought you didn't . . . that you were afraid that . . .'

'You'll be careful.' Her lips were warm against the corner of his mouth. 'You know how to be careful. It'll be all right, won't it, darling? I do love you so. I always have – always will. I need you – now.'

His control snapped. After all, she was his wife, he told himself as he bent to scoop her up into his arms. If he wanted to make love to his wife, surely to God there was nothing wrong in that? Putting her down on the bed, he threw off his robe and joined her there. Leonie enfolded him in her arms and gave herself with all the passion she possessed, carefully closing her mind to the risk she was taking – the possibility that so repelled her. Closing her eyes, she concentrated on the art of lovemaking, employing all the little tricks she had learned to please him in the old days; teasing, holding back a little and then throwing aside all inhibitions to let the searing fire of her unleashed passion devour them both.

Driven by the powerful urge she created in him, Tony was momentarily oblivious. He was aware of nothing but two bodies sharing one all-consuming sensation. Time hung suspended. No one and nothing else existed for him. But at the moment of climax it was Claire's face he saw and not Leonie's. Throwing back his head, he cried out her name.

As he collapsed on top of her, his body trembling convulsively, Leonie felt numb with shock and fear. *Claire*, so that was her name? Who was she? Leonie knew no one of that name, but there was no denying that Tony had thought only of her while they made love. She turned her face into the pillow. In that moment she knew the bitterness of defeat.

Gloria felt as though she'd been travelling for weeks. The train from Euston had been late and from the start the platform had been full of impatient, bad-tempered passengers, nerves frayed by the delay. Gloria climbed aboard, fending off the thrusting elbows of her fellow travellers with her suitcase. She found a seat, only to give it up fifteen minutes out of London to a frail old gentleman who looked perilously close to collapse.

The journey to Northampton had taken more than twice as long as it should, and then she had discovered that Houlton was a six-mile bus ride out of town – and that the railway and bus stations were inconveniently situated on either side of the town. Finally she had alighted from the green single-decker bus outside Houlton post office, lugging her heavy suitcase wearily after her. It wasn't that she had brought that many clothes, but at the last minute she had decided to bring the gramophone and records. Shirley might as well have the benefit of them. Gloria never got time to play her records nowadays anyway, what with her civil-defence classes and fire-watching duty at the Adelphi.

'Can you tell me the way to Longueville Hall?' she asked a man coming out of the Post Office.

'Yes. Walk up to the crossroads.' He pointed. 'Then take the left fork. There's a lane about half a mile along. Turn down there and you'll come to it. Big gates with the name carved in the pillars.'

It sounded quite a walk. Gloria picked up her case resignedly, fervently wishing she'd left the gramophone at home. 'How far down the lane is it?' she asked.

'Oh, not far,' the man said cheerfully. 'About three-quarters of a mile, I'd say.'

She felt as though she'd been walking for hours when a car drew up beside her and a voice said: 'Hello there. You wouldn't be Mrs Rayner, would you – Shirley's mother?'

Gloria blushed bright red as she turned and found herself looking straight into the eyes of the man she had adored from afar. 'Oh – er, yes. I am.'

He smiled the famous smile and reached across to open the passenger door for her. 'Wonderful. Jump in. Just throw your suitcase into the back.'

Gloria sank gratefully into the leather upholstery of the Rolls and breathed in the perfume of wealth and success. If only all the others at the Adelphi could see her now! If only she had a camera with her.

'Jim, our handyman, has been up to the village to meet the last two buses,' Tony Darrent was saying to her. 'He brought the children with him. They were so disappointed when you weren't on either bus.'

Gloria wanted to tell him she was sorry she was late but that she was glad it was in his car she would arrive. But when she opened her mouth to speak, something seemed to have happened to her throat and no sound came out. She thought of all the cool, smart, sophisticated things she would have said if she was like Joan Crawford or Bette Davis. Instead she sat with her eyes on the road and her cheeks pink, mumbling her thanks and making a stumbling apologetic remark about the trains and the weather. She was glad she'd worn the blue coat she had made herself, though, and the little frothy black hat perched on top of her blonde Veronica Lake hairstyle. Everyone had said she looked nice when she was ready to leave this morning.

They drove in through the gateway. Tony explained to her that the gates had been taken for salvage and that new wooden ones were being made. When she saw the house she caught her breath in wonderment. Fancy her Shirl living in a place like this! It was just like something off the pictures. Tony pulled up outside the front door. It opened and out tumbled Shirley with another, taller child. Shirley hurled herself down the steps and into Gloria's arms. Laughing and crying both at the same time, they clung to each other, hugging and kissing, while Imogen stood to one side, looking awkward.

'Glor, this is my friend Imogen.' Shirley pulled Gloria across to where the other girl stood.

'Hello, Imogen.' Gloria held out her hand. 'Pleased to meet you. Shirl has told me such a lot about you in her letters.'

The girl shook hands solemnly. 'Good afternoon, Mrs Rayner. We've been looking forward to your visit.'

'Gloria, please. Everyone calls me that.'

'Nanny Jarvis has had tea ready for ages,' Shirley said, pulling her mother up the steps. 'Come in and meet everyone else.'

But a smiling Molly Jarvis, who was waiting in the doorway, insisted that Gloria be allowed to go to her room to freshen up after her journey. Tea could wait another few minutes, she told the excited girls.

Gloria was totally stunned by everything she saw. She had expected to be sharing Shirley's room and when Mrs Jarvis had shown her to a room of her own on the first floor she had been slightly disappointed at first, but when she saw inside she changed her mind. The room was enormous and airy. You could have dropped the whole of the flat in Angel Row into it and still had room to spare. The furnishings were luxurious and it had the most breathtaking view of the garden. Standing at the window looking out she saw acres of green lawns and flowerbeds. She was surprised to see that there were still flowers blooming, too, even though it was well into autumn. She could see the sparkle of glass in the distant kitchen garden, and she even fancied she could glimpse the blue water of the swimming pool Shirl had written about. The whole house was like something out of a fairy tale.

But the thing that had shaken her even more than the house was Shirl. She had grown so much, for a start. Her skin and eyes glowed with health and the sun had sprinkled freckles across her nose and cheeks. Her limbs had rounded out, too. Now she looked more like the real Shirley than ever before. But it was the way she *spoke* that really shook Gloria. The natural cockney tones had faded almost to nothing. She spoke with what Pa would have called a 'plum in her mouth'. Gloria couldn't make up her mind whether she liked it or not. It was a little worrying – almost as though Shirley were growing away from her and turning into someone entirely different. On the other hand, this might just be the chance to get one foot on the ladder to success that Gloria had always dreamed of for her.

Unaware of the ordeal she was putting her guest through, Leonie had insisted that they all took tea together in the drawing room. Gloria changed into her best black skirt and new little blouse-jacket she had made out of a remnant of scarlet crêpe-de-Chine. Leonie admired it at once.

'I saw one just like it in *Vogue* last week,' she observed. 'By Molyneux.'

Gloria, who was trying hard to drink her tea with one finger daintily crooked, said: 'That's right, Molyneux. I got the idea from *Vogue*. Ma's friend at the newsagent's lets me have it if she's got a copy left over. I copy the fashions out of it.'

'How *clever*! It must save you an absolute fortune in dressmaker's fees.'

Gloria laughed. 'It's a case of 'avin' to. If I didn't make my own things I'd have to buy cheap 'n' cheerful.' She glanced across at Shirley sitting there so politely, eating her little cucumber sandwiches as to the manner born. 'I brought the old grammy, Shirl,' she said. 'And all the records you like. You'll be able to practise your dancin' now.'

'Oh, how *kind*,' Leonie said. 'They must have been so heavy for you to carry. But there was no need. I've been playing the piano for Shirley to dance to.'

Gloria felt slightly crestfallen. 'Oh, I see. That's very good of you.'

'Not at all. I've nothing else to do at the moment and Shirley is so talented. It's a joy to watch her.'

Gloria looked across the room at her daughter and wondered if it was her imagination that the child avoided her eyes. She cleared her throat and turned her attention to Imogen, who seemed almost as ill at ease as she was. 'Do you dance, lovie?' she asked.

Imogen looked at Shirley, who nudged her and whispered, 'Go on. Tell them.'

'Shirley's been teaching me, actually.'

'And she's doing ever so well,' Shirley put in. 'Soon as we've got a routine worked out for her she's going to do it for you, Mrs Darrent.'

91

Leonie's delicately arched eyebrows rose slightly. 'Well, *well*.' She smiled at Gloria. 'These two are terribly good for each other, you know. They surprise me more each day. At first I thought they'd never hit it off, but now they're just like sisters.'

The door opened to admit Tony. Oblivious to the impact this entrance had on Gloria, he glanced round the room, slightly surprised to find a tea party taking place. 'Ah, there you are, then. Any tea?'

'Of course, darling. I was beginning to wonder where you'd got to.' Leonie said, reaching for the teapot. 'Our guest must think you dreadfully rude, coming in so late.' She treated Gloria to one of her blinding smiles. 'I think you'd better ask Gloria to forgive you, don't you?'

Gloria blushed as Tony turned his attention upon her. Sitting beside him in the car she had hardly dared to look at him. Now that they were face to face she saw that he was far better-looking than any of his pictures.

'Please, Gloria, forgive me,' he said theatrically, bending towards her. He added in an undertone: 'If you don't, my wife will never speak to me again.'

Gloria giggled, acutely embarrassed. Did people like them always talk like this – in riddles and put-on voices so that you'd no idea what they meant and what they didn't? Tony had seemed so ordinary and friendly in the car earlier. Now it was almost as though he and his wife were acting in a play. She wished she could escape and be alone with Shirl.

Leonie, the smile still firmly glued to her face, was shrewdly studying the pretty cockney girl who was Shirley's mother. She was younger than she'd imagined, and attractive in an obvious sort of way. Out of the corner of her eye she observed that Tony thought so too. But then Tony had always had an eye for this kind of girl – at least, he had before this present infatuation had taken hold of him. The girl was quite besotted with him, of course; speechless and practically paralysed with adoration. Leonie took in the flushed cheeks and shining eyes. It was quite pathetic really.

It was then that the idea hit her – hit her with such a force that she almost dropped her cup. It was so simple, and – she hoped – so effective. Very carefully, so as not to let her excitement show, she put down her cup and said evenly:

'When the girls have gone to bed, you *will* dine with us, won't you Gloria?'

Gloria bit her lip uncertainly. She'd never actually *dined* before. Suppose she disgraced herself – used the wrong knife and fork or something? 'Oh, well . . .' she began.

'There'll only be us,' Leonie went on hurriedly. 'We don't stand on ceremony. And we'd *love* to have your company, wouldn't we, Tony?'

'Sorry – what?' Tony, who hadn't been listening, looked at the expectant, upturned faces and realised that his agreement on something or other was required. 'Oh, *yes*,' he said enthusiastically. 'Of course.'

Leonie smiled. It would work, this plan of hers. It would be an absolute piece of cake.

'I'm planning a Christmas charity concert,' Leonie announced, smiling at Gloria across the lighted candles. 'I haven't found a suitable venue yet but I'm confident that I soon shall.' She helped herself to more cheese and biscuits. 'I'd like to have your permission for darling little Shirley to perform,' she went on, smiling at Gloria. 'I was going to ask you that anyway, but now that I've met you I've had the most *marvellous* brain wave.' Enjoying the suspense she was creating, she bit into a cracker and chewed thoughtfully. 'You're so clever with your needle, Gloria. What would you say to designing and making the costumes? We'd put your name on the programme, of course. Can't you just see it? *Costumes by Gloria Rayner*. It's such a pretty name.'

Gloria's mouth dropped open in surprise. '*Me*? Oh, but surely I live too far away to be of any help to you?'

Leonie smiled. 'Ah, yes, but you see I've thought of that.' She looked at Tony. 'My husband is to open soon a new play in the West End, but he'll be joining us here every weekend, won't you, darling? In fact, he'll be helping me with the production. He could pick you up at some given point and drive you up.'

Gloria looked doubtfully across at Tony. 'I have to work till half-ten on Saturdays.'

'And so will I once we open,' Tony put in. It was the first he'd heard of this concert idea and he was wondering just what Leonie was up to.

'Well, of course. I've thought of that,' Leonie said. 'Tony, you could collect Gloria from her cinema and drive her up here on Saturday nights after the show. We'd have all day Sunday and then you could drive back to town on Monday mornings.' She turned to Gloria. 'I don't suppose you have to go in till the afternoons, do you?'

'Well, no, but . . .'

'It would mean you'd see Shirley every weekend, too, of course,' she went on, playing her trump card. 'It would mean *so* much to her, I know.'

Gloria felt a tingle of excitement. The dining room with its gleaming table, flowers and candles had impressed her enough. But now this . . . 'Well, if you really think I could do it. It sounds ever so exciting.' Turning to Tony, she asked shyly: 'What do you think, Mr Darrent?'

He gave Gloria the smile his fans described as 'bone-melting'. 'I think it's a splendid idea, Gloria. I'm sure we'll all have the most tremendous fun. And please – you will call me Tony, won't you? After all, if we're all going to be working together we might as well be chums.'

Chapter Five

Leonie's Christmas charity concert promised to be an enormous success. The snap decision to organise it had surprised even her, but once it was made she had thrown herself into the project with the energy and enthusiasm usually reserved for her stage performances. She became so engrossed that she almost forgot her original reason for initiating it. Almost – but not quite. Tony certainly seemed more relaxed since he'd been seeing Gloria regularly. So far she had no evidence that his interest in the girl was more than friendly, but from the adoring, goggle-eyed way that Gloria looked at him she felt sure it was only a matter of time before an affair started. Tony never could resist flattery. Maybe she would help him forget the woman who had bewitched him and they could all get back to normal.

The venue she finally found was a disused cinema in Northampton. Just before the outbreak of war it had been scheduled for demolition, but the town council, who had purchased it in order to carry out a redevelopment scheme, now indefinitely postponed, had succumbed to Leonie's charm and lent it willingly and free of charge when told that the proceeds of the concert were to go to the war effort.

To Leonie's delight, she found that the interior was still intact, complete with seating and even a workable front drop. She set an army of voluntary helpers to work cleaning, repairing faulty equipment and making good where necessary.

Leonie occupied herself with compiling a variety programme of sketches and musical numbers taken from West End shows. She wheedled and cajoled permission from her various friends in the business, getting them to waive royalty fees by various means – some more devious than others. She decided to do a couple of numbers herself – songs that she would dedicate emotionally to all the wives and girlfriends left behind – and she had also persuaded one or two actor friends who were, like her, temporarily 'resting' to come and take part as celebrity guest artists. The supporting company she made up from members of local amateur dramatic and operatic societies, each one carefully auditioned and hand-picked.

At home Shirley rehearsed Imogen mercilessly. Using Gloria's wind-up gramophone, they rehearsed in secret in the swimming-pool changing room, well out of sight and sound of the house. Shirley was determined that the routine she had worked so hard to create must be perfect before Leonie was allowed to see them perform. She had chosen the music from Gloria's collection of records. It came from an Astaire–Rogers film and the song was 'Isn't This a Lovely Day?' Imogen, being taller, was to take the part of Fred and Shirley was Ginger. Gloria had been let in on the secret. She was to make white trousers and a striped blazer for Imogen and a long dress with romantically swirling skirt and puffed sleeves for Shirley. Jim Jarvis, who was building most of the scenery, had been persuaded to paint a bandstand backcloth to represent the one in the film.

When they performed their dance for Leonie she was almost speechless with amazement. She could hardly believe her gangling, awkward daughter could move so gracefully. In the sleek trousers and blazer Gloria had made her, she danced her part in the duo to perfection. There and then, to their delight, she allotted the girls the closing spot in the first half of the show.

Unaware of Leonie's plan for her, Gloria was enjoying her part in the preparation for the concert too. All her spare moments were taken working away on the sewing machine in the parlour in Angel Row. Leonie had provided most of the material, bought or begged from her various contacts in the theatrical-costumier trade. One hire firm had given her some costumes intended for disposal and Gloria had worked hard replacing beads and tarnished sequins, washing and starching collars and cuffs and generally transforming them until they looked as good as new.

But what she loved best was her weekends at Houlton. Every Saturday night after the last showing at the Adelphi she could change quickly and hurry to the corner of the street where Tony would pick her up in his car. Those drives through the frosty winter nights in Tony's Rolls were the highlight of her week, the most romantic thing that had ever happened to her.

At first Tony had chatted amiably to her during the drive about everyday things like her job and the films they had both enjoyed. Soon she forgot her awed shyness and learned to relax in his company. Then one night he suddenly said: 'Tell me about yourself, Gloria. You talk about Shirley and your job, but never about yourself.'

She felt herself blushing. 'There's nothing much to tell,' she told him. 'I was born and grew up in Whitechapel. I went to the council school till I was fourteen, then left to be apprenticed to Maison Juliette, a court dressmaker in the West End.'

'So that's where you learned to be such a wizard with the needle?'

'That's right.'

He glanced at her. 'Why did you give it up?'

Gloria shrugged. 'My Shirley came along. I thought her dad was going to marry me, but I was wrong. Turned out he already had a wife. Ma and Pa were good, letting me stay on and keep her. Well, when I was ready to work again they wouldn't have me back at Juliette's so I took the job at the Adelphi.'

'And you like it?'

'It's all right. The hours are a bit funny, but I love seeing all the films. I'd have liked to be an actress myself,' she

97

admitted shyly, looking down at her hands. 'I don't suppose I'd ever have been clever enough, though, but maybe Shirl will some day.'

'And Shirley's father?' Tony glanced at her again and she felt herself going hot. Her kind of people didn't talk much about love and anyway most folk steered well clear of any mention of Shirley's dad.

'Oh, him. He hopped it,' she said. 'Scared stiff I'd make trouble for him, I expect. Never saw him again after I told him about the baby.'

'What rotten luck for you. Did you love him?' When she paused he added: 'I'm sorry, Gloria. I shouldn't have asked. Does it still hurt?'

'No,' she said truthfully. 'I was very young, not much more than a kid. Silly, too, I dare say. It seemed like the end of the world at the time, but now – well, I've got Shirl now, haven't I? She makes up for everything.'

'So there's never been anyone else?'

'No. Well, there wouldn't be, would there? No decent feller wants to take on some other bloke's kid.'

'That's rather a cynical way of looking at it.'

Gloria shrugged. 'Dunno about cynical. It's how it is. I don't mind. I've got used to it now.'

Tony was silent, his eyes on the dark road in front of him. Everyone had their problems. Not everyone could walk away from them. But Gloria's resigned acceptance was touching.

After that the horizons of their conversations during the drives widened and their acquaintance began to develop into a sincere friendship. Tony found her down-to-earth logic and candour refreshing. He felt she understood the human condition in a way that was unusual in women. Unlike most of the women he knew, she accepted people as they were and wasn't continually trying to change them to suit her. Perhaps best of all, they moved in entirely different circles and he knew that anything he said to her was unlikely to reach the ears of any of his own acquaintances.

When he asked her if she liked Shakespeare and she admitted that she didn't know, he brought her a ticket for the play. She went Up West on her evening off and sat enthralled in her front stall at the New Theatre, watching a new swashbuckling Tony Darrent playing Henry V with a vitality and panache that held her spellbound. Sitting there among the smart people in the posh seats, she was glad she had decided to wear the little black silk evening jacket she'd copied from a Hartnell design. Watching her painstakingly embroidering the shoulders with beads and sequins, Ma had admonished her for the waste of time and money. 'You'll never wear it. You know you won't,' she'd said. 'Where do you ever go to wear a thing like that?' But Gloria had hoped that some day an opportunity would come along.

Tony had invited her to come backstage afterwards and tell him what she thought of the show. She had never been backstage in a real theatre before and she wondered if she really dared go. At last her curiosity and the desire to see Tony and congratulate him got the better of her shyness. The stage doorkeeper had been told to expect her. He took her along to Tony's dressing room, where she found him sitting in front of the mirror, wearing a dressing gown and taking off his wig and make-up.

'Gloria!' He turned to beam at her, his eyes still smudged with black liner. 'How pretty you look! I was afraid you might not come. Just give me a minute and we'll go upstairs for a drink.' He turned back to the mirror and lavishly applied more cold cream. 'I want to hear your opinion of the play. Your honest opinion, mind – warts and all.'

She was so flattered that he actually wanted to know what she thought. *Her* – Gloria Doris Rayner from Angel Row who'd hardly known that William Shakespeare existed till tonight.

Seated in the cosy little bar that Tony called the green room, Gloria sipped her port and lemon, glancing hesitantly at him.

'I liked the play ever so much,' she said slowly. 'I'll be honest with you; I thought I wouldn't be able to understand it – written all them years ago – but I did. Well, most of it, anyway. It was a lovely story, specially the bit where he falls in love with the French princess.' She smiled at him shyly. 'I thought you were ever so romantic in that bit.'

'You haven't told me what you thought of the rest of my performance, though,' Tony said earnestly. 'Any fool can be romantic looking at a pretty girl like Juliet.'

'You're teasing me now,' Gloria said. 'You don't need people like *me* to tell you how good you are.'

'Ah, but that's where you're wrong. I do.' He put down his glass and leaned towards her. 'You see, I'll let you into a little secret. I've never actually played Shakespeare before. And this production was put on especially for people like you, Gloria. People who aren't familiar with Shakespeare, I mean. It's meant to bring him to the people – show that his plays are not just for the wealthy and privileged but for everyone to enjoy.'

Gloria looked at him with rounded eyes. 'No kiddin'? Are they really?'

'Of course. He wrote them for ordinary people back in the sixteenth century. They were performed right here in London, down by the Thames in open-air theatres. People would come in and walk about, eat, meet their friends. Theatregoing was a glorious, informal occasion in those days.'

'Didn't the actors mind? I mean – all that noise when they were trying to act.'

Tony laughed. 'I suppose they were used to it.' He covered her hand with his and looked into her eyes. 'So you enjoyed it? You're not just trying to please me?'

'Oh, no. I mean *yes*. It was lovely.'

'Marvellous.' He gave her hand a squeeze. 'I'd better get you home now or your mother will be worrying.' He tossed back the last of his drink and stood up, holding out his hand to her.

Long into the night Gloria lay thinking; about the brave, romantic King Henry; about Tony and the way he had held her hand. He was so wonderful, and she was so lucky to know him. Oddly enough she hadn't told her friends at work about the Saturday-night drives and their long talks. They wouldn't have believed her. And anyway, it was much too special to share.

Sundays were hard work in many ways: going to the theatre and fitting costumes; improvising; solving problems when someone dropped out of the cast and a person of an entirely different size and shape took over. Most weekends she came home with piles of more work to do – repairs, alterations – but she didn't mind. Watching the rehearsals and seeing the show slowly taking shape was so exciting. And being with Shirley, seeing how happy she was, was more than adequate reward.

Early on Sunday mornings Shirley, who was fast asleep when Gloria arrived late on Saturday night, would creep into her bedroom and wake her by snuggling up beside her. They would cuddle up together and tell each other all their news. It was most special hour in the week for both of them. One Monday morning at the beginning of December, as Shirley and Gloria were saying their goodbyes, Gloria whispered:

'Ma wanted me to tell you you're to come home for Christmas. And if things stay quiet like they are now you might be able to stay for good soon, Shirl. Won't that be lovely?' She was dismayed to see the child's face drop momentarily. *She'd rather stay here*, she told herself. This is getting to be more her home now than Angel Row is. The sad, unhappy feeling clouded her mind for the rest of the day.

At last the week of the concert arrived. By the time Tony and Gloria left London on the Saturday night, the first performance was already over. As she climbed into the passenger seat Gloria remarked wistfully that she wished they could have been there.

Tony shrugged. 'We saw the dress rehearsal last Sunday.'

'Yes, but with an audience it's so much more exciting. I'd love to have seen how the girls went down in their number.'

101

'The audience will have loved them,' Tony said with a smile. 'Imogen has surprised us all and it's all down to Shirley, you know.' He smiled at her. 'You have a very talented daughter.' After a pause he added: 'The only thing that worries me is what Leonie will do with herself once it's all over.'

'Won't she be in another play? I mean, doesn't she want to act any more?' Gloria asked.

'At the moment there isn't much call for her kind of work. There will be soon, of course. But try telling her that.'

Gloria was silent. Over the past weeks she had sensed the tension between them and guessed that their marriage wasn't as happy as the press and magazines would have the fans believe.

He turned to look at her as though he had read her thoughts. 'You must have noticed these past weeks that our marriage isn't all it should be.'

Gloria shifted uncomfortably in her seat. 'It's none of my business,' she muttered.

He went on as though he hadn't heard: 'Leonie and I haven't been . . . what you'd call close since Imogen was born.' He looked at her. 'In a way I'm rather like you, Gloria. I have a daughter whom I love, but because of her I have to face life without the kind of love all human beings have a right to.'

'I'm sorry.' It sounded so inadequate, but she didn't really understand what he meant and she couldn't think of what else to say.

He smiled at her. 'You don't make judgements, do you? You're a good friend, Gloria. May I tell you something? Completely in confidence, of course.'

'Well . . . yes, of course – if you want to.'

'I know I can trust you, you see. There aren't many people I can say that to, believe me.' He slowed down and pulled the car over to the side of the road, switching off the engine. Taking out his cigarette case he offered her one, then took one himself and lit them both. In the brief flare of the match she saw the pain in his eyes and wondered what she was about to hear.

'There's someone else in my life, Gloria.' He inhaled deeply and blew out the smoke. 'Not just an affair, but someone very special, whom I love very deeply. She and I were going away together. I was about to ask Leonie for a divorce. Then came this damned war.'

'Oh.' She swallowed the shock that quickened her heart and made herself look at him. He had wound down the window and was leaning his elbow on the frame. In the darkness his eyes shone luminously as though there were tears in them. 'Do you . . . do you still see each other?' she asked, sensing his need to talk about it.

'No.' He looked at her. 'Her home is in the Channel Islands. She came to London to work. She's gone back there to be with her family. It was I who urged her to go, because she'll be safe there. But, *Christ*, Gloria, I miss her.'

'I see.' She bit her lip, wishing she could think of something more intelligent to say. She was beginning to sound like a parrot, What did he really expect of her? Suddenly he threw away his cigarette and wound up the window.

'I'm sorry, Gloria. I'm embarrassing you with my confidences. I've no right to burden you with it. It's just that sometimes I feel I'll go stark, staring, bloody mad if I can't talk to someone about her. And you – well, you're always so sympathetic, because you've been through it too.'

Immediately she understood. He saw her as a friend, impartial and outside his class; someone he could trust and confide in. It was a tremendous compliment, yet here she was offering him no help or comfort at all. Reaching out she touched his hand.

'Tony, I'm really glad you feel you can talk to me. Of course I understand and if ever I can do anything to help, anything at all, I'll be glad to. I . . . I want you to know that.'

His fingers curled round hers warmly and he looked at her for a moment, a smile on his lips. Then he leaned forward, cupped her chin and kissed her very gently on the lips.

'Bless you, Gloria. You'll never know how much that means to me.' A moment later he had switched on the ignition bringing the car instantly to life. They were on their way once more to Houlton, just as though nothing had happened. But for Gloria, staring dazedly into the darkness, life would never be quite the same again.

When they arrived at Longueville Hall the atmosphere was electric.

'A man came from the paper and took photos of us all,' Shirley said, jumping up and down with excitement. 'He took *ever* so many of Imogen and me. They're going to be in the paper on Monday. Not just the little paper we get here, but the big London ones too. Imogen was nearly sick before we went on.' She giggled, grasping her friend's hand. 'But once we started off she never got one step wrong and we got *ever* such a lot of clapping when we was – *were* finished. The curtain had to go up again *twice* so's we could take another bow. It was *lovely*. Ooh, I nearly forgot.' She pulled a carefully folded programme out of her pockct. 'Look – here's your name. It says, Costumes by Gloria Rayner.'

Gloria looked proudly at her name printed in bold type on the programme. So Leonie had been true to her word. Gloria thought briefly of the secret Tony had told her and felt slightly guilty about knowing it. She turned to Imogen. 'Did you enjoy being in the concert then, lovie – once your nerves settled down?'

The girl nodded, smiling happily. 'Oh yes, thank you. It was marvellous.'

Gloria couldn't help noticing the child's glow of pride when her mother said:

'They both did very well indeed. I was proud of them.' Leonie clapped her hands. 'Now let Nanny take you off to bed. If you don't get your sleep you'll get no applause on Monday night at all.' She looked at Tony. 'And if I don't get a large gin and tonic soon I shall expire. Fix some drinks, darling, will you?'

Christmas at Angel Row was not the success Gloria had hoped for. Jim Jarvis put Shirley on the train at Northampton two days before Christmas Eve, and Pa was there waiting to meet her at Euston. All the way to Whitechapel on the Underground the child chattered away about the concert, her friend Imogen and her famous parents, and Jim and Molly Jarvis, none of whom Pa knew from Adam, as he pointed out later to his wife in the privacy of the kitchen.

'She's come 'ome a little stranger,' he complained.

'She's grown a lot,' Ma observed with a sniff. 'Grown *up* too. A damn sight too fast if you asks me. All this actin' on the stage an' livin' with them bohemian theatricals 'as gone to 'er 'ead.'

Although Shirley had looked forward to being at home and seeing her grandparents again, she found it oddly disappointing. The shop and the flat in Angel Row seemed to have shrunk. She was sure everything wasn't this small when she was last here. The bedroom she shared with Gloria seemed so cramped and she missed having a bathroom and an indoor lav – or loo, as the Darrents called it. Going out into the yard on cold dark evenings was an inconvenience she had happily forgotten all about, and reacquainting herself with it was irksome, to say the least.

Ma had done her best with the Christmas dinner, but food shortages were already beginning to bite and the turkey they normally had was replaced this year by a rabbit; stuffed and roasted, but sadly lacking in festive appeal. Gloria had made Shirley a new party dress, of white organdie, spotted with blue. She had made one for Imogen too, at Shirley's request, making a note of the measurements used for her concert costume and choosing some taffeta in a deep gold shade that she found in the market. Ma and Pa's present to Shirley was a little gold bracelet with her name engraved on a heart-shaped locket.

After the crackers had been pulled, the mottoes read and the hats tried on, there was nothing to do except play Ludo with Gloria or listen to the wireless, and Shirley found it hard to conceal her boredom. What made things worse was that Gloria had to work on every day except Christmas and Pa was on duty at the ARP post most evenings. Once the holiday was over things were slightly better. Shirley helped Ma in the shop, putting potatoes and vegetables into bags for the customers, but, although she didn't say so, she found it poor substitute for her daily rides on Toffee or the country walks she and Imogen enjoyed, making up stories for each other as they walked and daydreaming about the exciting things they would like to see happen in their grown-up future lives.

The day after Boxing Day Gloria had the afternoon off and she took Shirley Up West to see *Gone With the Wind*. Gloria enjoyed it enormously, weeping copiously into her handkerchief in all the sad bits. But the three and a half hours running time proved too much for Shirley, who shifted uncomfortably in her seat for much of the last hour. At home over tea, when Ma asked her if she had enjoyed the film Shirley shook her head.

'It was boring,' she announced.

Gloria looked stunned. 'How can you say that, Shirl? Vivien Leigh was lovely in it. It got an Academy Award nomination too.'

'I don't care. It was boring.' Shirley began to get down from the table, but Ma frowned at her and tapped the table sharply with her knife.

'Just a minute, milady. What d'you say 'fore you get down?'

Shirley pulled down the corners of her mouth. 'Nanny Jarvis doesn't make us say it,' she mumbled sulkily.

'Well, more's the pity,' Ma retorted. 'When you're in this 'ouse, my gel, you does as *I* says, never mind this Nanny Jarvis o' yours we keep hearin' so much about.'

'Thank-you-for-my-tea-may-I-get-down?' Shirley chanted.

Ma folded her arms and nodded. 'You may.' When Shirley had gone upstairs she turned to Gloria. 'That child is gettin' too big for 'er boots if you asks me,' she said. 'If you're not careful you'll 'ave trouble with 'er.'

'It's the war,' Gloria said unhappily. 'She don't know where she belongs any more. She'll be gone the day after tomorrow. Don't let's make her miserable, Ma.'

Tight-lipped, Ma began to clear the table. She said nothing but the look on her face and the clatter of the dishes said it all for her. It wasn't only Shirley who was changing. There had been a change in Gloria too since she'd been making those weekend visits to the country. Ma had watched it taking place as the weeks went by. Ideas above her station were what she'd be getting next.

The new year came in quietly enough, but soon changes began to creep into the everyday lives of people in city and countryside alike. The ration books everyone had been talking about were issued early in the New Year, much to Nanny Jarvis's dismay.

'How shall we ever manage on *this* much food a week?' she wailed, staring at the books. 'We'll all starve.'

But Jim protested that they certainly would not starve – not while he could still hold a spade. In spite of Leonie's objections he had finally managed to get her to agree to his 'digging for victory', as all the posters urged. He had already begun to plant potatoes on what was once the tennis court and now he was wondering how hard he'd have to fight for permission to keep some chickens and maybe even a pig. With his Home Guard duties, he was busy almost round the clock, and if it hadn't been for worrying about Hitler's invasion he would have been enjoying every minute.

In the next village an aircraft factory had been built. It had been assembled hurriedly, appearing to sprout from the ground almost overnight like a gigantic mushroom to turn out the urgently needed planes. Engineers and fitters were already being recruited and there was even talk of women being employed there.

Leonie was working again at last and only came up to Houlton at weekends. This week after the charity concert Peter Jason had telephoned to say that, following the publicity the show had attracted, he'd had several offers for her. The best of these was to make a series of radio shows for the BBC's Forces Programme. She was to sing special songs dedicated to the wives and families of servicemen in a programme which would be called *With Love from Leonie*.

'It seems you put such feeling into the songs you sang at that concert of yours that they can't wait to sign you up,' he told her.

It hadn't taken her long to decide to accept. She longed to get back her status as a popular artist once again and she was confident that she could manage a radio show without Tony's support – though she let Peter believe she had accepted the offer out of patriotism. She insisted that she must be allowed to choose her own music and write her own material, presenting it in her own style, and left Peter to negotiate the contract for her.

Tony was still playing to packed houses in *Henry V* at the New Theatre. His notices had been encouraging and he was happy to have achieved his ambition to play a classical role successfully. Claire wrote regularly and lovingly from her home in Jersey. When the run of *Henry* came to an end he planned to go over and visit her before joining the RAF. It would be so wonderful to see her and share a summer break. During the week he and Leonie occupied the Mayfair flat together fairly amicably, mainly because their paths rarely crossed; she was working in the daytime, he in the evenings.

Shirley and Imogen found school easier as the spring term progressed. Many of the first evacuees had gone home again, leaving more space in the overcrowded classrooms and playground. Shirley enjoyed her first game of snowballs and built her first snowman that winter. She and Imogen tried sliding on the village pond and got a good scolding from Nanny Jarvis when they fell in and came home shivering and covered in green slime.

With the spring came more changes. In May the prime minister, Mr Chamberlain, died and the flag on the school was lowered in respect. Some weeks later the girls came home from school one afternoon to find Nanny and Jim huddled over the wireless in the kitchen, shushing them as they tumbled noisily through the door.

'My God, we're done,' Jim muttered, his face ashen. 'The lads have been beaten back into the sea. We're done for. Gerry'll be coming now and no mistake.'

Nanny burst into frightened tears and Imogen ran to her and began to cry in sympathy.

'What's happened, Jim?' Shirley whispered, frightened by his solemn face. 'Is Hitler coming?'

'The soldiers we sent over to fight are coming home, lass,' he said. 'But England's tougher than to let one setback make her roll over and die. We'll see them off, don't you fret.'

After that everyone was talking about the little boats that went to Dunkirk in France to help bring the soldiers back. There were stories of trains full of them seen in the town, dirty and battered, their uniforms in rags. The news bulletins were full of what was called the Battle of Britain. No one was allowed to speak while the wireless was on in case some vital scrap of information was missed. When they weren't listening to the news they were listening to *With Love from Leonie*, which was on every week and proving to be one of the most popular programmes on the Forces Programme. It was earning Leonie Swann more fans than she had yet had in all her career. Shirley and Imogen didn't know what to make of it, but they were encouraged by Jim's assurance that the new prime minister, Mr Churchill would certainly win the war for them and make everything come right. Jim always knew best. After all, he was in the Home Guard. He had a proper soldier's uniform and a real gun now, so he must know what he was talking about.

As the year progressed, Gloria's visits to Houlton grew fewer. Ma hadn't been well, and with Pa down at the ARP post so much she had to help in the shop and flat when she wasn't at work; besides, she really couldn't afford the train fare very often. One evening in July she finished her shift in a light-hearted mood. It was warm and still quite light as she came out of the staff entrance of the cinema and waved a cheery goodbye to her friends. Life wasn't so bad. They were all getting used to the changes, and she was lucky. Apart from parting her from Shirley, the war didn't seem to have made all that much difference to her life. Pa was always shaking his head and foretelling gloom and doom. He'd come home from the ARP post with stories about things being worse than they were led to believe and news of German planes seen flying over the southeast coast. He used words like 'reconnaissance' and spoke of German spies parachuted in secretly to infiltrate and undermine them all. She and Ma took these rumours with a pinch of salt. She was smiling to herself about his bizarre stories as she reached the corner of the street – then suddenly she stopped in her tracks, her heart leaping into her throat, as a man stepped out of the shadows in front of her.

'Gloria – don't be frightened. It's only me.' He reached out a hand to steady her.

She let out her breath in a sigh of relief. '*Tony*! You did give me a turn.' She looked up at him. He wore a raincoat and a trilby hat pulled down well over his face. Under it his face looked pale and haggard. 'Is anything wrong?' she asked, concerned. 'Shirley . . . ?

He took her arm. 'No, Shirley's fine. Look, I've got to talk to you, Gloria. The car's along here – please . . .' Without waiting for her answer, he hurried her along the street.

As they got in, he didn't start to speak but drove, his eyes concentrating on the road and his lips set in a grim line. Gloria became anxious when ten minutes later he was still driving.

'Tony – look, Ma will be expecting me. She'll wonder where I am. Where are we going?'

'Maple Court – to the flat,' Tony said. 'Leonie's gone home for the weekend and I . . .' His voice faltered and he said no more. Gloria looked at him, concerned for him now. Her own problems were forgotten. There was obviously something seriously wrong. He needed a friend – needed *her*. This was no time to be thinking of herself.

110

The flat took her breath away. Unlike Longueville Hall it was ultramodern and more glamorous than anything she had ever seen. If it hadn't been for Tony's obvious desperation she would have liked to look round. In the hall he pulled off his coat and hat and threw them both carelessly into a cupboard. Gloria looked at him helplessly.

'What's wrong? Please tell me.'

He took a crumpled letter out of his pocket and thrust it into her hand, then walked through into the kitchen to stand with his back towards her, staring out of the window. Slowly and uncertainly she smoothed out the single sheet of notepaper and began to read.

Dear Tony Darrent,

I am Claire's elder brother. I know about your secret relationship as she and I have always been very close and she confided in me. I knew she would want me to write to you at this time. One week ago, on 28 June, the Germans bombed our island. Here at Grève de Lecq we were safe, but my sister was shopping that day in St Helier. Tragically she was in a building which caught a direct hit and was killed along with many others. The funeral was yesterday. I am so sorry to bring you this news.

Yours in deep sorrow,
Gerald DeLisle.

Gloria caught her breath. 'Oh, God, Poor Tony!' She ran to him and took his shoulders, turning him towards her. Tears were streaming down his cheeks and he shook his head at her wordlessly. Throwing her arms around him, she held him close, drawing his head down onto her shoulder and rocking him as she would have rocked Shirley. 'Don't cry,' she whispered into his hair. 'She can't have suffered, poor girl. Oh, Tony, *please* don't cry like that.'

His harsh sobs tore at her heart. She felt so helpless. Keeping one arm round him, she helped him into the hall and pushed open a door that turned out to be a bedroom. Pushing him down onto the bed, she pulled off his shoes and drew the counterpane up over him. Back in the living room she opened the cocktail cabinet and searched through the bottles till she found some brandy. Splashing a generous amount into a tumbler, she went back to the bedroom with it and sat on the side of the bed.

'Here, drink this. It'll help.' She slipped an arm round his shoulders and held the glass to his lips. As the warming liquid slipped down his throat, he gradually calmed.

'I loved her,' he whispered. 'She was the only woman I've ever truly loved. I was going over to see her next month – and now . . . I can't believe it. Oh, God, I can't believe it.' He looked at her. 'I keep thinking I'm dreaming and I must wake up in a minute.'

Her throat tight with tears, she stroked his face. 'I know, I know. It's terrible.'

'How will I bear it, Gloria? How will I go on – acting, both on stage and off? I can't even let Leonie know. It goes too deep for me to risk the look of triumph I know I'd see in her eyes. She knew there was someone special, you see. How will I . . . ?'

'You still have Imogen,' Gloria reassured him. 'You still have a daughter, Tony, and she needs you. She always will. That's what I told myself when Jack took off and left me to face it alone.' She pulled him close. 'At least you know she died loving you. You didn't get dumped like I did. You'll have that love to cherish for the rest of your life now. It can never die now and no one can take it away from you.'

He dropped his head onto her shoulder and his arms around her tightened. 'Thank you, Gloria. What would I have done without you?'

After a moment or two she gently freed herself from his clinging arms. 'Look, why don't you get undressed and into bed properly?' she said. 'I'll make you a hot drink. Have you had anything to eat?' He shook his head. 'Right. I'll make you some scrambled eggs. I know it won't make the hurt go away, but you'll feel better able to face it with some food inside you and a night's sleep.'

She got up and opened the glass door to the adjoining bathroom. It was cool, green and sweet-smelling. 'I'll run you a bath,' she said over her shoulder. 'You can have it while I do the eggs.' She turned to look at him lying there on the bed, staring numbly at the ceiling. 'Come on, love. Please try – for me.'

Sitting opposite him at the kitchen table half an hour later, she coaxed him mouthful by mouthful through the plate of eggs and toast, just as she had done with Shirley when she had the measles the year before. Gradually he began to look a little better. The colour came back into his ashen cheeks and the haunted look began to clear from his eyes. When he had finished, Gloria said: 'Go to bed now and try to get some rest. I'll wash up these dishes, then I'll be off home.'

He reached out a hand to grasp hers as she began to rise from the table. 'Please don't go.'

She stared at him. 'I *must*, Tony.'

'No. Please. I need you. I don't want to be alone tonight.'

She carried the dishes to the sink, her mind racing. What would she tell Ma? What would people say if they found out she'd stayed here all night? She turned to say something, but the look of mute appeal overrode her anxieties. 'All right,' she said. 'If you really want me to, I'll stay.'

She insisted that she would make herself comfortable on the settee in the living room where she could hear him if he called. She dozed a little on and off, her ears alert for the smallest sound. Eventually she must have fallen asleep and she had no idea how long she slept or what the time was when she was wakened by a hand on her shoulder. She sat up with a start. '*What* – who . . . ?'

'It's all right, it's only me.' Tony lowered himself onto the settee beside her. 'I can't sleep, Gloria. It's useless. I keep seeing her face . . . hearing the crash . . . the screams. Every time I close my eyes I can see her lovely body all broken and bloody. I keep wondering if she knew – if she thought of me. Christ, I can't bear it, Gloria.'

'Shh.' She sat up and slipped an arm around his shoulders as he sat there with his head in his hands. 'I think you should see a doctor tomorrow,' she told him, stroking the dishevelled hair back from his brow. 'You'll make yourself ill if you go on like this. Go back to bed, Tony, I'll get you some aspirin.'

But he held tightly on to her hand. 'Come with me – please.'

She couldn't bring herself to refuse, but went with him willingly. In the bedroom she slid fully dressed into the rumpled bed beside him and held him close in her arms. 'I'm here,' she whispered. 'Go to sleep. I'll still be here when you wake. I promise.'

He clung to her like a frightened child, his face buried in her neck. 'I insisted on her going home, Gloria,' he said. 'It was I who sent her to her death.'

'No, no. You mustn't think of it like that. You thought you were doing the right thing.' She held him till he calmed, then lay very still, hardly daring to breathe. Gradually she heard the pattern of his breathing change until, after a few minutes, she knew he had fallen at last into an exhausted sleep.

As the dawn crept in, reaching fingers of thin light into the corners of the unfamiliar room, she marvelled at the strangeness of life. Who would have ever thought that she would be here, in bed with the man whose unattainable image she had loved for so long – bringing him comfort of the most innocent kind? If it hadn't been for the war . . . life was full of surprises . . . Her eyelids drooped, heavy as lead. They closed and finally she slept too.

'Where the bloody 'ell have you been?' As Gloria crept in through the back door, Ma faced her with arms folded challengingly over her heaving bosom. 'Pa an' me've been up half the night, worried out of our wits about you. Sat 'ere till nearly two o'clock this mornin', we did.'

'I went home with a friend,' Gloria muttered, avoiding her mother's steely eyes.

'You lyin' little bitch. Now tell me the truth or I'll take me 'and to you. You're not too old for it, y'know.'

114

'Oh, don't go on so Ma.' Gloria sank wearily into a chair. 'Is there any tea going?'

'Tea?' Ma had worked herself up into a state and she wasn't going to be cheated out of a showdown by Gloria's apathy. 'You stop out all night. like some alley cat, then you come waltzin' in 'ere calmly askin' for *tea*?' She stood demandingly over Gloria. 'Come on then, let's 'ave it. What friend is this? One of the girls at the Adelphi treated 'erself to a posh car now, 'as she?'

'I don't know what you mean.'

'Oh, no? Well, I'll tell you, shall I? Your father was on his way 'ome last night when he sees you gettin' into this big car. So whose car was it? That's what I want to know. And what were you up to? As if I didn't know.'

'I *was* with a friend,' Gloria said. 'A friend who's just lost someone very close. I offered to stay the night. That's all there is to it.'

'So why couldn't you come and let us know first? And why didn't you tell me that in the first place?'

'Because you kept *on*.' Gloria's voice trembled, close to tears. Lack of sleep and the emotionally fraught hours behind her had left her completely drained. 'For heaven's sake, Ma, where did you think I was? I'm not a giddy schoolgirl. I never go out with men. I haven't since before Shirley. You ought to know that by now.'

'And you better not, my girl.' Ma took a step towards her. 'It's *'im*, isn't it? That Tony Darrent? You're soft on 'im. I've seen it comin'.' She shook her head exasperatedly. 'Wake up, gel. He'll 'ave 'is fun and then drop you just like the other one did. A gel like you don't stand a chance with 'is sort. Wake up and use yer loaf 'fore it's too late.'

Gloria didn't wait to hear any more. Getting up, she flung out of the kitchen and up the stairs to the privacy of her own room. There she threw herself down on the bed and buried her face in the pillow. How could she have fooled herself into thinking just a few hours ago that her life could be untouched by the war? It would lay its evil hands on them all before it was over. No one would escape. All the pent-up emotion she had generated last night erupted. The tears flowed and she sobbed till her whole body ached; for Tony; for poor dead Claire, whom she had never met; and for Shirley, who was slowly slipping away from her. But most of all for the love that had been steadily growing in her heart since last Christmas. The love that she knew could never be returned.

For Shirley and Imogen the long hot summer holiday was a delight. Tony did not buy Shirley the pony Imogen had promised, but he did buy the girls a bicycle each and they rode out on most days with packed lunches or teas to explore the countryside.

Gloria managed to get up for the occasional weekend visit, but Shirley hardly seemed to notice whether she was there or not. She never saw Tony again once all that summer. Molly Jarvis told her that as soon as the run of his play finished in September he was going to join up. Gloria reluctantly accepted that Ma's remarks had been unacceptably close to the truth. He had needed her that night when he was so upset, but she meant no more to him than a shoulder to cry on. Maybe the memory of it even embarrassed him. Sadly, she took his pictures down from her bedroom walls. He was still the most beautiful man and the best actor she had ever seen, but somehow she no longer saw him in quite the same way. He was a *man* to her now with all a man's faults and frailties; a man – not a star. She went to work, helped Ma in the shop in her spare time and looked forward to the time when the war would be over and she could have Shirley back. Surely once it was over she would want to come back and carry on just as they used to – wouldn't she?

At Longueville Hall Imogen taught Shirley to swim and in return Shirley taught Imogen how to sing 'Over the Rainbow' like Judy Garland and how to curl her hair. Both girls helped Jim Jarvis with his digging for victory. But their favourite pastime was playing at 'shows'. Shirley would choose the music and teach Imogen the words.

Together they would choreograph dance routines and stage their performances in the garden with all Imogen's dolls and teddies for an audience. While the Battle of Britain raged, while the Germans invaded the Channel Islands and England tensely defended its shores and awaited the same fate, the children played, made up stories and confidently planned a golden future.

On Saturday 2nd September Sid Rayner left Ma and Gloria to the Saturday afternoon shoppers' rush and, with his ARP satchel and steel helmet slung over his shoulder, set off to put in his shift at the ARP post. At the top of Angel Row he stopped to wait for the traffic to thin before crossing the road.

'Lovely afternoon, Sid,' called a fellow shopkeeper. 'Just the weather for goin' down to Southend for the day, eh?'

'Chance'd be a fine thing,' Sid pointed to his satchel and steel helmet. 'On duty, me.'

'Best o'luck then, mate.'

On the next corner Pa looked up, his attention suddenly caught by a low rumbling sound. The next moment he stood riveted to the spot, staring dumbly into the clear blue summer sky, High above him rode a great V-shaped flotilla of black planes – hundreds of them, the sound of their engines gathering to a roaring crescendo. As he stood staring up at them, Pa could see smaller fighter planes sparkling in the sunlight as they darted in and out, like pilot fish among a herd of whales. Along with others he stood on the pavement and watched, almost mesmerised by the sight. Then, in the distance, he heard a long whining scream followed by an explosion that shook the ground. Immediately there were cries of alarm as people began to scatter, running for the shelters. Quickly donning his helmet, Pa ran the rest of the way to the post. As he ran along the street, head lowered as though running into a storm, he thought of Ma and Gloria and hoped they were taking cover, but once he arrived there was little time for worrying. The bombs were falling thick

117

and fast all around by now. Word came in that the target was the docks. One bomb hit an electricity main and all the lights went out. Pa set about putting the emergency supply – candles in jam jars – into operation.

Long after the sun had done down that night, the eastern sky was brighter than day. Great plumes of smoke, blood-red flames and showers of dancing sparks provided a macabre firework display as building after building succumbed to the onslaught. To those who gazed helplessly up at the sky that night it was as though the city had become a living hell. The long-threatened, long-dreaded Blitz had begun.

Chapter Six

The success of the radio programme *With Love from Leonie* was greater than anyone could possibly have foreseen. Articles about Leonie and her life and career appeared in the *Radio Times* and several of the popular women's magazines. But when Leonie agreed to give an interview to a journalist from *Home and Beauty*, she found the woman inquisitive to the point of impertinence.

'Our readers are always fascinated by a star's education and family life,' she gushed, pencil poised over her notebook. 'We all know, of course, that you are married to Tony Darrent and have a little daughter, but could you tell me something about your own childhood, Miss Swann?'

Somewhat dismayed, Leonie cleared her throat. 'Oh, it was really very ordinary,' she said, playing for time. 'I'm sure your readers would be dreadfully bored.'

'Not at all. We find that our readers like to identify with their favourite stars,' the woman said. 'And if your background is as mundane as theirs it makes them feel closer to you.'

As mundane as theirs. What a cheek! As if she was going to admit to a mundane background. Clearly she was going to have to invent something. Leonie shuddered inwardly as she recalled the poky little flat above the little butcher's shop in Snow Hill, Birmingham, where the pungent odour of raw meat seemed to permeate everything and where the sawdust from her father's boots crept into every corner. She pictured her mother standing over

119

the copper in the washhouse at the rear of the shop, boiling her father's bloodstained overalls. She had hated it all then and she hated it now. 'I grew up in the country,' she heard herself saying in a clear, positive tone, 'I was always surrounded by animals.' Well, at least that was true, even though she didn't add that they were dead ones, dissected ready for the table. 'We had a beautiful old house,' she went on. 'Standing in its own parkland, looking back I suppose it was quite a privileged child-hood, really.'

The woman looked suitably impressed. 'You were an only child?'

'Oh, yes,' Leonie said firmly. She had always *felt* like an only child. Her brother, Norman, was six when she was born. He had resented her as a baby and they had never got along. He had left school at fourteen, a gangling, pimply youth, to help their father in the shop. Her only vivid memory of him was when she was in her early teens and he'd begun to hang around her bedroom door, a lecherous leer on his face, trying to catch a glimpse of her undressing. She had caught him once looking through her bedroom keyhole and threatened to tell Dad. They hadn't spoken to each other much after that.

'I see.' The woman was scribbling rapidly. 'And you said your background was ordinary. You're too modest.' She looked up. 'So you grew up in the country? That must be why you choose to live there yourself.'

'Yes, Longueville Hall is very similar to my own child-hood home, which is what attracted me from the moment I first saw it.'

'Your father – was he in, er, farming?' The journalist looked up enquiringly.

'In a way.' Leonie searched her mind for a suitable title. 'I suppose you could call him an, er, a landowner.'

'You're being modest again, aren't you, Miss Swann?' The woman wagged her finger and smiled archly. 'What you really mean is that he was the local squire; lord of the manor. How fascinating! So with that kind of family background I suppose you must have been presented at court?'

God! Had she gone too far? To hide the flush that was slowly creeping up her neck, Leonie got up and crossed the room to take a cigarette from the box on the mantelpiece. 'Actually no,' she said, making a flamboyant show of lighting it and blowing smoke at the ceiling. 'Mummy wanted me to have a coming-out ball like all my debutante friends, of course, but I wasn't in the least interested in that kind of thing. A career in music and singing was my ambition. I wasn't interested in snaring a rich husband.'

'I see. So you intended to go into the theatre from quite an early age?'

'Oh, yes.'

'Did you meet opposition from your parents?'

'Not really. Thcy were always very keen on the theatre themselves,' Leonie said. 'There were always lots of house parties at home. The house was always full of famous people. It was the most tremendous fun.'

'How exciting! Tell me about your first job. I did hear that it was your husband who discovered you.'

Leonie smiled. 'That's right. As I was saying, our house was always full of theatrical celebrities. I was singing at one of our weekend house parties. Tony was there and he confessed to me later that he was quite captivated. Afterwards he begged me to go to London and meet his agent.'

'And he fell in love with you too. How romantic!' The interviewer looked around her. 'This is a beautiful flat, Miss Swann. You and Mr Darrent live here when you are working in London, I suppose?'

'That's right.'

'So brave of you to stay in London. You're not worried about the bombing at all?'

'So far we've been lucky; only the odd broken window, though the raids have been a strain, of course. But I'm leaving London shortly on a tour of army camps. I'm not allowed to tell you where – it's all terribly hush-hush.'

'I do hope that doesn't mean that *With Love from Leonie* is to come to an end. It's compulsive listening for so many people.'

'Oh no. We shall be broadcasting some more programmes later.'

'All your fans will be reassured to know that. And what about your husband?'

'Now that the run of his play has ended, his plans are quite fluid,' Leonie said cagily.

'There has been a whisper that he may go into the RAF.'

Leonie smiled. 'We'll have to wait and see. He's very keen to do his bit for the war in whatever way he can.'

In fact, Tony had already spoken to his old friend Johnny Langdon from the flying club. Johnny was now a wing commander in the RAF and over lunch at the Garrick Club the previous week Tony had asked about his chances of getting a commission. Johnny had pursed his lips doubtfully.

'I'm afraid your age is pretty much against you, old chap. The job is pretty arduous, you know.'

'I think I'm fairly fit, and at thirty-nine I'm hardly over the hill,' Tony protested.

But Johnny drew in his breath and shook his head. 'Most of the fighter pilots are pretty well just out of the sixth form and even some of them crack up under the strain. Of course, with your flying experience there must be some way you could be useful. Look, why don't you go along and offer your services – see what happens? I'm sure they'll be able to find you something.'

Tony was disappointed and more than a little put out. He had expected to be snapped up and given a commission right away. He wanted to fly a Spitfire, not a desk, but, all the same, he went along a couple of days later and volunteered his services.

After a rigorous medical, he was told that he was unfit for flying duty and advised off-the-record by a kindly and well-meaning medical officer who was secretly a fan of his that he could most certainly serve his country better by remaining in his own profession and entertaining the troops. Tony was shattered. His medical report, which he insisted on seeing, showed that he had raised blood pressure, poor muscle tone and – most depressing of all – fallen arches. He resolved to do something about all three as soon as possible.

The only person to whom he confided his ignominious rejection was Peter Jason. The block in Charing Cross Road where Peter previously had his office suite had been badly bomb-damaged in October and Peter had now set up a temporary office in his own house in Richmond. When Tony told him that his plans for joining the RAF had been shattered, Peter heaved a sigh of relief.

'Well, at least you've got it out of your system,' he said. 'As a matter of fact, something has just come up which I think might interest you. I'd made a note to ring you about it in the morning, so I'm particularly pleased you've dropped in today.' He looked up at Tony. 'Heard of the Crown Film Unit?'

Tony nodded. 'Aren't they the people who are doing the war documentaries?'

'That's right. Well, now another group is getting started. They're calling themselves Combat Films. A team of documentary filmmakers have got together to make some realistic, dramatised war documentaries. Churchill is behind it all the way. Apparently he's very keen. So as to get the realism they want, they'll be filming during actual battles wherever possible. And of course people with your kind of experience will be invaluable.'

Tony looked doubtful. 'But surely if the accent is to be on realism they won't want well-known actors taking part?'

'It wasn't just acting that I had in mind. Some of these chaps are from the world of commerce. The stuff they've been turning out – training films and such – is very different from what's planned, so they're going to need help with the direction. Then if – as they hope – they cast actual servicemen with no previous acting experience they'll need someone to coach them. Last but not least there's your flying experience, of course. There's no end to the ways you could help. It could be a rewarding and fascinating job and one that will last for the whole duration of the war if you want it to.' He pushed his cigarette box across the desk. 'So what do you say? I can tell you now that they'd jump at the chance to have you on the team.'

Tony took a cigarette and lit it thoughtfully. 'Well, it sounds interesting, I grant you, but won't it be at the expense of my acting career? It could be hard to pick up the threads again when the war is over.'

'I've already thought of that,' Peter told him. 'You can always fit in the odd play or film. Leave it to me. I won't let your name fade out.'

Tony brightened. 'All right then. If they'll have me I'll give it a try.'

'*Have* you? They'll consider themselves bloody lucky to get you, believe me.' Peter pressed the button to the intercom and asked his new secretary to bring in some coffee. It was late November now, and he'd been concerned about Tony since the summer. He looked gaunt and ill. Peter wasn't surprised he had failed the RAF medical. He seemed to have lost all his enthusiasm and even some of his confidence, too. Shrewdly, he guessed that Claire's death had a lot to do with it.

After the girl had brought the coffee and withdrawn, he decided to bring the subject into the open. Maybe it would help Tony to talk about it. 'Are you feeling better now?' he asked. 'You've been pretty depressed over the past few months, haven't you?'

Tony picked up his cup, carefully avoiding Peter's eyes. 'I suppose I have. The war – one thing and another – you know . . .' He trailed off, knowing that he had no hope of fooling Peter. He had the sharp-eyed, shrewd perception that all good agents have, and a sixth sense where a client's state of mind was concerned.

'It was Claire's death, I dare say,' Peter went on softly. 'It hit me hard too. She was an exceptionally lovely girl. It was a terrible tragedy. The family is still badly shaken. The occupation of the Channel Islands is a stinking business, too. It must be hell for them, having to put up with all that the occupation entails after losing their only daughter because of the bastards. But life has to go on, old chap. A lot more have lost loved ones since this damnable bombing started. We aren't the only ones. Before we're finished the cost in human lives will be enormous.'

Tony gulped at the scalding coffee. 'We were in love, Peter,' he said bleakly. 'Really in love, I mean. It wasn't just some cheap affair.'

'I'd guessed as much.'

'The awful thing is that it was I who urged her to go home. I can't shake off the feeling that it's some hellish kind of retribution.'

'None of us could possibly have foreseen what would happen. Who could possibly have predicted the German occupation of the Channel Islands?' Peter reached across to touch Tony's sleeve. 'You and Leonie – is there any comfort to be had in that quarter?'

Tony shook his head. 'She didn't know – and she never must now. What Claire and I had was too precious to risk cheapening it – especially now that the memory of her is all I have left.'

Peter sighed. It was much worse than he had thought. 'Look, old boy, you've grieved enough,' he said at last. 'It's not good to bottle things up like this. Put some of that emotional energy into this job. You can make a huge success of it, I know you can. Go home and make plans; offer them your ideas and innovations.'

Tony looked at him. 'All right, I will. I suppose you're right, Peter. Tell them I'm on. I'm already beginning to look forward to it.'

The article about Leonie in *Home and Beauty* was published two weeks later. The magazine had given it a centre-page spread with glamorous colour photographs of both the Mayfair flat and Longueville Hall. Leonie sat in satin lounging pyjamas, draped decoratively over a Regency chaise longue; Leonie wearing jodhpurs and feeding sugar lumps to Toffee, with on either side of her, her daughter and the evacuee she had generously taken to her heart. The caption under the photograph made it appear that Shirley was her daughter and Imogen the evacuee. When Tony pointed this out, Leonie shrugged it off as immaterial. Reading on through the article, he laughed derisively.

'Where the hell did they get all this stuff about your family being the local gentry?'

Leonie blushed. 'You know what these people are,' she said defensively. 'They don't want the truth, they obviously wanted something glamorous. So I gave them the kind of thing I thought they'd enjoy.'

Tony put down the magazine and looked at her. 'Do you ever think about your parents, Leonie?'

She shrugged. 'Not often, why?'

'How do you think they'll feel when they read this?'

'How should I know? It's more than likely they won't even see it. The *Daily Herald* is more their style than *Home and Beauty*.'

'Have you listened to the news or read the papers lately?'

'Not specially – why?'

'Don't you know that Birmingham is being razed to the ground in much the same way that Coventry was? Doesn't it ever occur to you to wonder if they're all right?'

Leonie got up and walked to the fireplace, turning her back on him. 'Have *they* ever wondered if *I'm* all right? They could have got in touch at any time over the years. They haven't. They don't even know they have a granddaughter.'

'Maybe the time has come to put that right. That brother of yours is probably in the forces by now. Things might be hard for them.'

His soft tone angered her and she rounded on him. 'You've become boringly sanctimonious lately, Tony. Since when have you been worried about other people's feelings, especially my parents'? As for Norman, a dose of strong discipline is just what he needs. Why should I worry about him?'

He shrugged. 'War makes one think. It brings out latent qualities in all of us; the best in some, the worst in others.'

'I suppose you think this job you're taking qualifies you as some sort of hero,' she snapped. 'I'm off to entertain the troops, remember. All over Christmas I'm going to have to pig it in a series of dreadful barracks. I'm doing my bit, too.'

The words were hardly out of her mouth when the siren began its doleful wail. She broke off. '*Hell*, they're early tonight.'

Tony stood up and held out his hand to her. 'Shall we go to the shelter?'

She grasped his hand and stood looking up at him. 'I'd rather stay here. Tony, why are you so distant? You've been so far away these past months, there's just no reaching you. Is something worrying you? It's not the medical you had – you're not seriously ill, are you?'

Softening a little, he pressed her hand. 'No, of course I'm not – unless you count fallen arches as serious.'

They laughed together and the tension eased. Suddenly she looked up at him beseechingly. 'Tony, let's go to bed. It's been so long. You haven't made love to me since that night at Houlton . . .'

The first bomb of the raid fell somewhere down by the river, rattling the windows, and Tony's arm went round her in an instinctively protective gesture. 'We really should go to the shelter.'

She began to unbutton his shirt. 'But we won't – will we? Please, darling. I hate the shelter. Let's stay here.'

With the blackout curtains in Leonie's bedroom drawn back they could see the winter night sky lit up by searchlights and barrage. With each succeeding explosion Leonie's need seemed to grow. It was as though her urgent desire to survive manifested itself in frenetic lovemaking, and her passion built to a crescendo that was heightened by an explosion so near at hand that the whole building shook and trembled around them. Leonie clutched feverishly at Tony, her long fingernails painfully tearing at the skin on his back as she strained her body upwards beneath him. In a frenzy of elation her mouth sought his voraciously and he was suddenly struck by the

127

unpleasant notion that she was trying to devour him, to join his body permanently to hers so that he would never again be free of her.

'Now – *now*,' she hissed into his ear. 'Make it happen. Oh, God, I want – I want . . .' Suddenly her body arched and convulsed, then she slowly relaxed, letting out her breath in a long low howl of animal pleasure.

Unfulfilled, Tony rolled away from her. He felt utterly repulsed. In that moment he loathed himself and knew that he never wanted to touch her again, but before he could escape she fastened her fingers round his arm, holding him captive.

'Darling, don't go. Don't leave me – not yet,' she said breathlessly. 'God, it was marvellous – wasn't it? I'll tell you a secret. I adore making love during an air raid. It's even more exciting than a thunderstorm – wild and primeval.' She leaned over to growl softly into his ear. 'It brings out the animal in me.' She pressed her lips to the pulse in his neck and ran her hand down the length of his thigh.

He lay quite still, wanting nothing more than to get away from her. He could never live through a raid without thinking of Claire; dying her death with her; feeling her pain; suffering again the devastating loss. The thought of the same situation causing Leonie's sexual excitement sickened him. He lay quite still, listening as her breathing steadied; praying that she wouldn't expect him to begin the whole nauseating charade again. Suddenly to his horror, she looked into his eyes and said softly: 'It's over, isn't it – between you and Claire?'

He froze. It was as though someone had kicked him hard in the solar plexus, taking his breath away. Sitting up, he stared down at her, his heart thudding raggedly. 'What – what do you know about Claire?'

She smiled languorously up at him. 'Nothing really. You called out her name once when we were making love. I knew then that it must be serious. It hurt, Tony. It made me realise how much I love you. But it's over now, isn't it? I always know when your affairs are over. I'm going to be the important one in your life from now on. I can make you happy again just like before. Haven't I just proved it?'

Nausea almost overwhelmed him as he shook off her hand and got out of bed. 'The raid – it's getting too hot for comfort.' He was pulling on a sweater and slacks. 'Get up, Leonie. We're going to the shelter.' He was already moving towards the door.

She slipped her long legs over the edge of the bed and stood up. Making no attempt to cover her nakedness, she stood between him and the door. Winding her arms around his neck, she pressed herself against him seductively.

He put her firmly from him. 'Get dressed, Leonie.' Reaching for her dressing gown, he draped it around her shoulders. 'We owe it to Imogen not to take stupid risks like this. She's the one we have to think of.'

'*Imogen*?' Her eyes glittered angrily. 'Is she all you can think of?' She shrugged the gown to the floor and he looked at her standing before him, nude and with that blatant, predatory gleam in her eyes. She laughed suddenly and held out her arms. 'Stop being so stuffy, Tony. Come back to bed. You know you want to. Let's make a night of it like we used to in the old days.'

To his horror he felt himself becoming aroused and his stomach lurched sickeningly. He thought of Claire and what he saw as his disloyalty to her memory. 'Put some clothes on, for Christ's sake,' he snarled, turning away in disgust.

She remained where she stood, her eyes glistening with angry tears. 'You go to the shelter if you're so bloody scared,' she snapped. '*I'm* not going.'

'Then stay here,' Tony threw over his shoulder as he flung out of the room.

The tears welled up and began to slip down her cheeks. 'That's right, *coward* – scuttle off to save your worthless bloody skin,' she shouted at his retreating back. 'I'm staying here and I don't care if I do get killed. *You* obviously don't give a damn.' But Tony was already out of hearing as he made his way to the shelter shared by the other residents of the flats.

Leonie was turning back towards the bed when there was a massive explosion as a bomb fell in nearby Green Park. It threw her so violently back against the wall that all the breath was dashed from her body and her teeth seemed to rattle in her head. Plaster showered down from the ceiling, coating her hair with white powder and clinging to her eyelashes. On the other side of the room splinters of glass from the bedroom window showered the carpet and dressing table. Still winded by the blast, Leonie slid down the wall to land in a crumpled heap on the floor. She watched numbly as ornaments toppled and smashed. The shredded brocade curtains fluttered like ribbons and the aroma of Joy mingled with the stench of destruction as the contents of a smashed perfume bottle made a widening stain on the carpet.

As the floor beneath her feet began to shudder and tremble, Leonie leaped to her feet and let out a terrified shriek. Sobbing with fear, she snatched up a dressing gown, pulled it round her, thrust her feet into slippers and wrenched open the door. As she made a frantic dash for the staircase she knew with fearful certainty that she wanted nothing more than to stay alive.

The train journey back to London from Northampton that Sunday evening took more than twice as long as it should. Perched uncomfortably on her case in the crowded corridor, Gloria was tired and dispirited. She should have been fire-watching at the Adelphi last night but she had changed with Freda Harris so that she could go and spend a weekend with Shirley, yet the child had barely seemed to notice that she was there half the time. There was a party on in the village hall the next week and she and Imogen were providing the entertainment. They were doing the Fred-and-Ginger routine they'd done last Christmas for the concert and they were much too busy rehearsing to be bothered with her. She had spent most of the weekend helping Molly Jarvis in the kitchen.

'You mustn't mind them,' Molly had told her good-naturedly, sensing her disappointment. 'Just be glad Shirley is so happy here and away from all that dreadful bombing.'

But Gloria wasn't happy. Each time she saw Shirley the child seemed more distant than the last. There was no hope of her coming home this Christmas and Gloria had a horrid suspicion that she wouldn't want to anyway.

'I wonder you don't move up here yourself,' Molly said one evening as they sat over bedtime cocoa. 'Several of the London mothers have, you know. With their husbands away at the war, there's no reason for them to stay in London any more. And this is a better place for the boys to come on leave to than poor Blitz-torn London.'

Gloria shook her head. 'My job is in London,' she said. 'Ma and Pa too. They're Londoners through and through. They'd never dream of leaving and I don't think they'd expect me to.'

Jim looked up from his Sunday paper. 'But if you were to be – if the worst happened, what would become of Shirley?' he asked. 'Have you ever thought about that?'

Molly shot him a warning frown, but he ignored it. 'These things have to be considered,' he said insistently. 'There are cinemas here, you know, Gloria. I dare say you'd get another job easy enough.'

Gloria shook her head doubtfully, but Jim's words gave her food for thought. He was right, of course. If anything happened to her, Shirley would have no one. The child was still only ten. It would be a terrible thing to be left at that age. There would still be Ma and Pa, but whole families were often wiped out in one raid. It happened all the time. Of course they were careful. They always went to the shelter when the siren went – even Ma, in spite of her misgivings. They spent most of the air raids down the Underground nowadays. Sometimes it could be quite good fun even if there wasn't much sleep to be had. There was a great feeling of comradeship and sometimes there was entertainment too. They sang to drown out the sound of the bombs and keep their spirits up.

Later, when she was in bed, she thought again about Jim Jarvis's remarks. Twice the shop in Angel Row had suffered bomb damage, though so far they hadn't actually been bombed out. On each occasion they'd had to manage without water and electricity for several days and the rear wall was still shored up and likely to stay that way now for the duration. The whole street was a far cry from what it had been. But they put up with it and managed the best they could. Ma and Pa prided themselves that they had carried on business without a break and they promised their customers that as long as they were still there and could get up to Covent Garden of a morning they would trade as usual. But Gloria could see the strain on her mother's face as night after night of bombing took its toll of her health, and Pa came back from the ARP post after his spells of duty looking gaunt and exhausted. Neither of them was getting any younger. Maybe if she could find a place to rent in Houlton she could persuade Ma to come too. Pa would never leave his beloved ARP but he could always come up for the occasional rest. Best of all, they could be with Shirley. They could be a family again. That was the important thing.

Over the breakfast washing-up next morning, she asked Molly about the Darrents. She hadn't seen either of them for months. She knew Leonie was busy with her broadcasts, but it was Tony she really wanted to hear news of.

'Madam is off to entertain the troops over Christmas,' Molly told her. 'And Mr Tony has joined this film unit. They're making war documentaries.' She shook her head ruefully. 'Between you and me, it sounds just as dangerous as going to war.'

'He didn't join the air force then?'

'Bless you, no. Unfit,' Molly said.

Gloria's heart plummeted. 'You mean he's ill? Something wrong with him?'

Molly shook her head, 'Just his age, I think. They only want the really young boys for the flying, apparently. It's full of strain, all that night flying and getting shot at. I don't mind telling you, Jim and I were relieved when he didn't go. But this documentary thing sounds almost as bad. They're going to film in the battle zones, so I hear.'

'So he'll be flying anyway?' Gloria asked fearfully.

'I don't really know all the ins and outs of it, but it seems he's there to teach the young servicemen how to act,' Molly explained. 'And to direct too – something like that. All I do know is that we hardly see either of them these days.' She shook her head. 'That poor child won't see her parents at all this Christmas. I'm really glad she's got Shirley. Those two kiddies are real pals now, you know. Inseparable, as they say.' Her face suddenly brightened. 'Tell you what – why don't you come here for Christmas? Bring your mother and dad too if they'll come. I'm sure the Darrents wouldn't mind.' She raised her eyes to the ceiling. 'All those rooms up there empty. It seems a shame not to give a London family a rest from the bombing.'

On the interminable journey home Gloria thought about Molly's offer. She doubted whether she could persuade Ma and Pa to go to the country, even for the weekend, but she might go herself if the holiday was long enough to make it worth while. She'd get Shirley the best present she could find and make her some new dresses. She could hardly believe the rate at which the child was growing. Somehow or other she had to win her back again, she told herself desperately as she rocked backwards and forwards in the gloomy corridor as the train crawled onwards.

If she were truthful with herself she'd have to admit that she had hoped to see Tony this weekend. She hadn't seen him since that night last July when they spent the night together. She wondered if he was over the loss of his Claire yet. Time and again she relived that night, remembering his anguish and her own bewilderment. What would have happened, she wondered, if he had wanted to make love to her? What would her response have been? Deep down she knew that at the time she would have refused. But now, in retrospect, her view was very different. Perhaps she should have offered him the comfort of her body. It would have been an adult, womanly gesture, something she could have done for the man she loved and admired so much, to help him to bear his suffering. And now she had lost her chance to give the only thing she had to give; and perhaps to mean more to him than a mere passing confidante. She would never know now what the outcome might have been. And the worst of it was that Ma still didn't believe her when she insisted that nothing had happened.

As the train pulled in to Euston Station the siren was wailing. Wearily Gloria followed the crowd down onto the Underground platform and there she stayed till first light when the 'all clear' sounded, getting what rest she could, her head pillowed on her small weekend case.

As she walked out of the station at Whitechapel, devastation faced her. She picked her way through streets piled with the rubble and debris of last night's raid. The acrid stink of burning filled the air and water from the fire hoses glistened on the road and formed sooty puddles everywhere. The whole landscape had changed. Bombed houses stood with rooms exposed to view, torn wallpaper hanging in shreds. In one a picture still hung pathetically askew from its nail. Broken and charred timbers and joists hung precariously overhead, some with scraps of blackened linoleum still attached to them. And in the midst of all this hellish devastation, exhausted, dispirited people scrabbled among debris looking for any small possessions that might have survived intact.

Anxious about Angel Row, Gloria quickened her steps. But as she turned the corner into Grainger Street she stood still and gasped with shock. There was nothing. The whole street had gone; houses, shops and, most shocking of all, the Adelphi. Where the cinema had stood there was nothing but a heap of smoking rubble. Her hand to her mouth, Gloria began to run. On the corner a group of grey-faced men were standing. She recognised one of them as an ARP warden from Pa's post.

'Were there any casualties?' she asked breathlessly.

The man looked at her wryly. 'What do you think, luv? They all copped it.'

'*All?*'

'We dug two out of the rubble still breathing but I'd be surprised if they lived long enough to get to the hospital,' he said bluntly.

'There was a girl fire-watching at the cinema,' Gloria said, her heart in her mouth. 'Freda – Freda Harris. Please, can you . . .?' The man was shaking his head.

'Cinema copped it first. Direct hit.' The man looked at Gloria's white face. 'Friend o' yours, was she?' Gloria nodded numbly. 'Well, she couldn't've known anything, luv. Must've been instantaneous. Lucky it was a Sunday and no performance,' he added. 'Could've been much worse.'

Could have been much worse. The words echoed in Gloria's head all the way back to Angel Row. If she hadn't gone to Houlton for the weekend, if she hadn't got Freda to change places with her, she – or what was left of her – would be lying in the mortuary now. Instead she would have Freda's death on her conscience for the rest of her life. By the time she reached Angel Row, which, to her enormous relief, was mercifully still more or less intact, she had made up her mind what she must do.

When Gloria had first tentatively voiced her intention of going to Houlton for the duration, Ma had been tight-lipped.

'You must do as you think fit, o'course,' she said noncommittally.

But Pa had taken a more practical view. 'The girl's right, Ma,' he said. 'She's got young Shirl to think of. We wouldn't want the kiddie to be left motherless, now would we?'

'Don't you see, Ma?' Gloria urged her mother. 'If I hadn't gone to Houlton last weekend I'd have been dead now. Poor Freda got killed instead of me. I'll never forgive myself for that. But it made me see what might still happen if I stay here. I'm not just thinking of myself.' She paused to lick her lips, assessing her mother's reaction. 'In fact, you could come too if you'd a mind to.'

135

Ma's eyebrows shot up. '*Me*? Leave London? And who do you think'd look after your pa and run the shop if I upped and slung me 'ook?'

'I'd be all right –' Pa ventured bravely, but the look on Ma's face silenced him in mid-sentence.

'*No*,' she said, leaning back in her chair and folding her arms. 'I ain't movin' from my 'ome an' my shop. Not while it's still standin'. If that 'itler wants to make me give in 'e's gonna 'ave to kill me first.'

Gloria sighed. 'Mrs Jarvis asked me to invite you both for Christmas,' she said. 'Why don't you come? We could all be together again, even if it was only for a few days.'

At last Ma gave in and the three of them travelled to Houlton for the Christmas holiday. Ma was grudgingly impressed by the size of Molly Jarvis's kitchen, the big, shiny refrigerator and the massive range. And though she made no comment, her eyes widened at the freshness of the home-grown vegetables and farm produce that they took for granted in the country. But when Gloria asked if she had changed her mind about going to live there, she shook her head stubbornly.

'I was born and bred in the dear old Smoke and that's where I'll stop till me time's up,' she said with a sniff. 'You can 'ave too much fresh air, you know,' she added darkly. 'Catches me at the back o' the throat somethin' chronic sometimes, it does.' She wrinkled her nose. 'All them farmyard pongs can't be 'ealthy either if you asks me.'

Ma and Pa hadn't seen Shirley for almost a year and they were both astonished by the way she had grown. On Christmas night they all gathered in the drawing room to watch the girls dance for them and, though Ma pulled down the corners of her mouth in mock disapproval, she couldn't disguise her pride in her talented granddaughter. However, she couldn't resist warning Gloria later.

'Mark my words. All this performin' will go to the child's 'ead. 'Fore you know it she'll be wantin' to go on the stage proper.' She sucked in her breath and shook her head. 'An' we all know where *that* leads.'

Gloria stayed on for a week after the holiday and tried to get a job, but it wasn't as easy as Jim seemed to think.

None of the Northampton cinemas had any vacancies. Without work she couldn't even begin to make plans to settle and at last she was obliged to return to London with a promise from Jim and Molly that they would keep their eyes and ears open and get in touch the moment they heard of anything going.

It was several weeks later that the letter arrived from Jim. When Gloria opened it, a small newspaper cutting fluttered to the floor. Picking it up, she saw that it was an advertisement from a local paper. Women were needed to work in the new aircraft factory. Sitting back in her chair at the breakfast table, she read it thoughtfully, then passed it across to Pa, who studied it carefully, his lips moving as he read.

'Well, it's a job,' he said, looking up at her at last. 'And I heard tell that women are going to get called up if things go on the way they are. I dare say if you was in war work that wouldn't 'appen. It says 'ere they pay you while you train, too. It's worth thinkin' about.'

Gloria sighed. 'Factory work, though, Pa. That's something I never thought I'd come to.'

Pa looked again at the cutting. 'Where is this Boothley Bottom place anyway? Funny name.'

'It's about three miles from Houlton. The next village.'

'So you'd be close to Shirl.' He handed back the scrap of paper with a shrug. 'Well, it's up to you, gel. Make up your own mind. Don't ask your ma, though. You know what she'll say.'

Gloria took his advice. For the next few days she did a lot of thinking, not mentioning the letter to her mother at all. Ma was still waging her fierce, unbending one-to-one war with Hitler and she saw Gloria's plans to move away from London as 'giving in'. Then suddenly it seemed that everywhere Gloria looked there were articles about women going into war work. It stood to reason that there weren't going to be enough men to staff the factories with them all being called up, but so far there had been resistance to the idea of women taking over. Now, though, the newspapers and magazines were full of it.

Posters began to appear everywhere; an emotive image of a willowy feminine figure, arms outstretched in glorious triumph as a factory spewed out shoals of aeroplanes in the background. Mr Bevin appealed to the patriotism of all women to step into the breach to save their country. Gloria decided to apply.

On the day she received the letter, telling her she had been selected for an interview, she broke the news to her mother.

'The shop can't support all of us anyway, Ma,' she said. 'You know how hard up we've been since my money stopped coming in. I'd have had to get another job soon, and what is there here for me? There's hardly a cinema round here left standing.'

'Why beat about the bush? You've made up your mind anyway, ain't you?' Ma said, tight-lipped. 'I don't know why you're makin' out you're asking for *my* advice. You've known all along you were goin'. Admit it.'

'I've *got* to go, Ma. Can't you see, I miss Shirl and I want to be with her?' Gloria pleaded. 'She's growing up without me. Sometimes I feel as if she's not mine any more.' She reached across to take her mother's hand. 'If I can find a little place to rent, you and Pa could come too. Please, Ma.'

Ma snatched her hand away abruptly. 'Go on then, you go if you must. I ain't stoppin' you. But don't expect me to up and run.'

Resigned to her mother's stubbornness, Gloria stood up. 'All right, Ma. I really *would* like us all to be together somewhere safe for the rest of the war. But if you won't come, you won't. I've got to think of Shirl first. You've forced me to make the choice.'

Unblinking, Ma watched her walk out through the door. She made no attempt to stop her or to protest any further. But as the door closed behind her only daughter her hands clenched into fists at her sides and her eyes filled with rare tears.

'*Bugger* that there 'itler,' she muttered thickly, thumping one fist down on the table. ''E's gorn and done it now all right. If I could only get me 'ands on 'im I'd squeeze the life out of the little bleeder.'

The interview at the aircraft factory at Boothley Bottom went well, but Gloria could see right from the start that the work was very different from anything she had ever done before. And it was obvious that the hours were such that it would be impossible for her to have Shirley to live with her. It was made clear to her that, unfettered, she would be free to work the maximum hours, and the wages offered for shift work took her breath away. Never in her wildest dreams had she envisaged earning so much. There was a hostel for unmarried female workers too, which meant cheap living, and a hot meal could be had in the works canteen at the end of every shift. Gloria worked out that on that kind of money she might actually be able to buy a home of her own in a few years' time; if she saved up really hard and provided the war lasted that long. A little cottage perhaps, somewhere pretty and peaceful where she and Shirley could settle down together after the war. Maybe she could even find enough to pay for Shirley to go to a private school where she could learn the things Gloria yearned to know more about – how to speak French and appreciate great writers like Shakespeare. Talking to Tony and seeing him act in the theatre had made her regret all the gaping holes in her own education and wish for better for her daughter. A whole exciting new future seemed to open tantalisingly before her as she sat there waiting to hear if the job was hers.

All the way back to Longueville Hall on the bus Gloria kept thinking of the new job she'd been offered and wondering if she could really take it. It would all depend on Molly Jarvis – or rather the Darrents. She kept her fingers crossed, hoping her bright new dream wasn't about to crumble.

The moment Molly looked at her she knew. 'You've got it. I can tell by that sparkle in your eyes,' she said with a smile.

Gloria slipped off her coat and sat down at the kitchen table. 'There were ten of us interviewed. Eight of us were offered jobs,' she said. 'The two who didn't get chosen had young kids. It's too bad, you know. The pamphlets all said there'd be crèche facilities for women with kiddies, but there's no such thing at that factory.'

Molly nodded sympathetically as she poured boiling water into the teapot. 'Typical. They want the women to work but they don't make the proper provisions. If you ask me, it's a woman they want, organising things up there at Whitehall.'

Gloria cleared her throat. 'The thing is, Molly, I'd have to work shifts – all night sometimes – and live in the hostel, which means . . .'

'That you'd like Shirley to stay on here with us.' Molly finished the sentence with a smile. 'It's all right, I'd foreseen that. Don't worry, dear.'

But Gloria shook her head. 'It's good of you and I'm grateful, but it isn't really what I wanted. I was looking forward to Shirl and me being together again. The thing is, the money's so good I couldn't afford to turn it down. I'll pay you extra, of course.'

'For what that little one eats? I should think not. Anyway we all love having her here. You know that.'

When she came home from school, Shirley too was happy with the news. A little *too* happy for Gloria's peace of mind. The two little girls hugged each other and danced ecstatically round the kitchen at the news that Shirley would not be leaving Longueville Hall. Later, when they were alone, Gloria asked Shirley how she felt about having her close at hand.

Shirley looked at her mother's wistful face and knew she needed reassurance. 'It'll be lovely,' she said. 'I'll be able to see you much more often and you'll be able to come to all our concerts and everything – yet I'll still be able to stay here with Imogen and Nanny and Jim.'

'Don't you miss London at all?' Gloria asked.

Shirley bit her lip, trying to assess the reaction her mother wanted from her. 'Well, I do a bit,' she said. 'I miss Ma and Pa and you, of course. But everyone says it's horrible in London now. Miss Frost, our teacher, says it'll never be the same again.'

'I don't suppose it will,' Gloria said sadly. 'That's why I thought maybe we might stay here after the war, buy a little place, just me and you. And perhaps when Pa and Ma retire they'll come too. Would you like that?'

'Ye-es.' But for Shirley 'after the war' was another world. It was impossible to foresee the kind of life she might have after the war. She'd be grown-up then; a new, different, exciting person to whom anything might happen.

'Come and give us a cuddle,' Gloria invited, holding out her arms. Shirley came to her willingly enough, but in her arms the child already felt different. She was losing the comforting chubbiness of childhood and the old intimacy they had shared was fading. Her body was already beginning to develop adult characteristics, growing slender and firm. She was supple and strong from regular exercise and her dancing. So much about her was different; her speech, her manners . . . With a sudden stab of regret Gloria realised that she even smelled different. Shirley was almost eleven, she reminded herself. Before she knew it she'd be a young woman.

Chapter Seven

At first Gloria found the work at Boothley aircraft factory hard going. It was repetitive and boring, and during the training period and the few months following she often thought despairingly that she would never stick it. But whenever she was tempted to quit she made herself think of the money she could save. Closing her eyes she would visualise the pretty little cottage with roses and geraniums in the front garden and the idyllic life she and Shirley would live there. It never failed to spur her onwards.

The hostel was spartan, but the food in the canteen wasn't bad and the friendship of her workmates more than made up for the home comforts she missed. They were a mixed bunch of women of all ages and from varying backgrounds. On her bench there was a doctor's daughter who hadn't fancied the services but wanted to do her bit, a middle-aged woman who had worked all her life as a hotel manageress, a housewife who had never been out to work in her life before and an ex-parlourmaid who insisted that she had once worked for six months at Windsor Castle.

As the weeks became months Gloria gradually settled into the routine. The work became easier as she grew more adept and the off-duty hours were enhanced by the company of the other women. It wasn't long before they discovered her dressmaking skill, and she found that she could make herself some extra money doing alterations and adding innovative touches to tired, much worn dresses. Disappointingly, she didn't see Shirley nearly as often as she had hoped to because of the odd hours she worked, but in the school holidays she spent as much time as she could over at Houlton.

On Saturday evenings dances were run in Boothley Bottom village hall. Gloria had never been much for dancing. Her unsocial hours as a cinema usherette had precluded it and in the first few weeks at the factory she was so exhausted that all she wanted to do on her Saturday evening off was fall into bed and sleep. But her roommate, Jane, finally persuaded her to go with a crowd of the other young women and she found that after her first stumbling efforts she soon picked up the steps and began to enjoy herself. It was nice to have a reason to get dressed up again, to do her hair and put on make-up, and to talk to men other than the bossy middle-aged foremen at the factory. Soldiers from a nearby army camp often attended the dances. Most of them were awaiting embarkation orders so the faces were always changing. It wasn't possible to form any lasting friendships, but nevertheless the dances made a pleasant diversion to the week's hard work.

Monthly lunchtime concerts were something the workers looked forward to at the factory, and great excitement was generated when the news went round that Leonie Swann was to be the next star turn. There was standing room only that day, and Gloria's workmates were impressed when she told them that she actually knew the star and that her daughter had been evacuated to her country home. Some of them looked sceptical, so to prove that she wasn't shooting a line she volunteered to go up and speak to Leonie when she toured the factory after the concert. To her dismay and humiliation, the star received her friendly overture with a look of shocked surprise, staring through her as though she had never seen her before. As the little party moved on, the accompanying foreman turned to mouth a silent admonishment at Gloria, shaking his head at her behind Leonie's back. As she returned, red-faced, to her bench, the other girls lowered their eyes. Her friend Jane leaned close and said above the din of the machinery:

'Take no notice, love. Wouldn't have hurt the stuck-up cow to give you the time of day.' She nudged Gloria good-naturedly. 'Cheer up. It's nearly three. *Music While You Work*'ll be on in a minute and we can have a good old sing.'

1941 was a busy year for everybody. In September Tony's first film, *Blitz*, was released. It had been shot during some of the worst of London's air raids and highlighted the courage of the civil-defence workers, the ARP and the Auxiliary Fire Service in particular. *On Target* came out soon after. It was a half-hour documentary about a bombing raid, filmed during an actual raid over Germany with members of the RAF taking part. Both films were hailed as successful morale boosters and Tony's skills as a director were highly praised.

Leonie's career was climbing from strength to strength. Her tour of army camps had been so successful that another, more extensive tour was planned. Her records were selling as fast as they came out and her face was on the cover of one magazine or another almost every week.

At Longueville Hall Shirley and Imogen were busy with school work. Soon they would sit for the scholarship, hoping for a place at the high school. Imogen had the advantage, the curriculum at her private school having been much more extensive than anything the village school could offer. Shirley feared privately that her friend would sail through the exam, leaving her behind, so she resolved to work really hard in order to keep up. She couldn't bear the idea of Imogen moving on without her. The alternative, from what she could gather, was to remain at the village school till she was fourteen and then go into a job in a shop or one of the many shoe factories. She knew instinctively that if she were to let that happen, life and all its delights would travel on without her.

In the evenings, after the girls were in bed, Molly and Jim would sit in the kitchen with their cocoa, listening to the radio. As the months went by Jim's face grew grimmer each night as he listened to the nine-o'clock news.

Nothing seemed to be going right for poor old England. They had held Hitler at bay so far and the bombing raids didn't seem as bad as they had been, but overseas the news was critical. Jim reckoned that winter must surely be the worst England had ever known. In December came the shocking news that Pearl Harbour had been bombed, knocking out many American ships and taking a heavy toll of lives. On Christmas Day, as the Jarvises once again shared their festivities with Gloria and the other Rayners, Hong Kong fell. February saw the surrender of Singapore, quickly followed by Rangoon and Burma. Things looked very black indeed and Jim began to fear that the worst might happen, they could be losing the war.

He didn't communicate his fears to Molly. She had enough to cope with, running the house and making the rations go round. The one bright spot, as Jim saw it, was that America had joined the fight at last. It must be a sad day for many American homes, but it was a huge relief that Great Britain no longer stood alone.

In the early spring of 1942 Imogen and Shirley sat the scholarship examination. Rigid with nerves they sat in the big room that was the top class of the village school. The headmaster, Mr Hawkins, invigilated, looking up ferociously over the tops of his spectacles whenever anyone fidgeted or coughed. Halfway through, they were allowed out into the playground for a break. Shirley found Imogen and grasped her hand excitedly.

'How did you get on?'

Imogen pulled a face. 'Not bad. You?'

'Easy. The sums were cushy and the English comp was *fun*.' She jumped up and down gleefully. 'I bet we both pass. Just think – we'll be High School girls, Imo. Won't it be smashing?'

Imogen was more blasé about the prospect. 'It's got to be better than this hole anyway,' she said as they filed back into the building for the second half of the exam.

It was June when four of the pupils were called to Mr Hawkins's office and told that they had achieved a place at the high and grammar schools. The one boy was a local child. Two of the three girls were Shirley and Imogen, and the fourth, surprisingly, was Tilly Marks, now unrecognisable as the grubby waif taken in by Mrs Phipps at the post office. That evening Jim put through a telephone call to the hostel at Boothley Bottom to give Gloria the news. She walked back into the communal rest room with shining eyes.

'You'll never guess what. My Shirl's gone and got herself a place at the high school,' she said triumphantly. 'My kid's gonna *make* something of herself.'

Jane and the others crowded round her with congratulations, hugging her and patting her back. 'That's lovely, Glor. Wonderful news.'

The letter had travelled all round England by the time Leonie received it. She was up in Orkney, performing for the officers and men of HMS *Erebos*. From the envelope she saw that it had been sent first to the BBC, then on to the London flat; from there to Longueville Hall, where Jim had forwarded it to her in Orkney. She turned the tattered envelope over in her hand. In one corner the sender had printed in large black capitals: PRIVATE AND CONFIDENTIAL, which explained the forwarding. The BBC usually kept her fan mail until she was in London. She did not recognise the handwriting and the envelope was of a cheap quality, as was the flimsy sheet of notepaper it contained. It was headed with the name and address of a bank and read:

Dear Eileen,

I read the piece about you in an old copy of *Home and Beauty* in the doctor's last week and felt I had to write to you. It's funny but I don't remember our house in the country or all them stars we used to entertain at weekends. You must have a different sort of memory to me, our Eileen.

Mum and Dad have had a very hard time of it, what with the bombing and everything. Dad can't work no more. He relies on me to keep him and Mum. I didn't

146

get taken in the army because of an injury to my leg five years ago when a car knocked me off the delivery bike. It left me with a bad limp and it's a job for me to get about sometimes. All we've got is the shop and I have to manage it on my own now. It's a hard life, our Eileen. Not like yours.

We've been bombed twice. Last time Mum was in hospital for three weeks with shrapnel in her back.

We could do with a bit of that money you're earning, our Eileen, and I'm sure you'll want to send us some now that you know how bad things are. But don't let Mum and Dad know. They're too proud to ask for anything, as you know.

Maybe that magazine would like to know about your *real* family and upbringing. But I'm sure it won't come to that, will it, Eileen, you being so loyal and all?

Hoping this finds you as it leaves me, I remain, your affectionate brother,

Norman.

Speechless with fury, Leonie crushed the note in her hand and hurled it across the room. Of all the slimy little toads! How dare he imagine he could blackmail her? And in such crude, blatant terms too. *Our Eileen*, indeed. But after a moment's thought she got up and retrieved the letter, smoothing it out again and rereading it thoughtfully. He'd do it. There was no doubt about that. It was just the kind of thing he'd enjoy. He had always been jealous of her. Mum and Dad had been getting on when she was born. They had always wanted a girl and Norman's nose had been put well and truly out of joint by her arrival. Oh yes, he'd take great delight in seeing her exposed as a liar and a poseur, especially now that she had made a success of her life. She bit her lip hard. If *only* she hadn't made up that ridiculous story. But as she thought about it she could see that she could turn the situation to her advantage. She remembered the conversation she'd had with Tony and his remark about the war bringing out the best in some, the worst in others. It might be nice to be able to write and tell him she had re-established contact with her family and was sending money to help them. Maybe it would help to improve their relationship. No need to mention Norman's letter, of course.

She and Tony saw each other rarely nowadays and when they did he was decidedly cool towards her. He'd shown absolutely no inclination to sleep with her since that night when the flat had been bombed. She had wondered lately if he'd found a new girl in that film company of his; or even if the mysterious Claire could have returned to claim his affections. How much would Norman settle for? she wondered. She pulled her chequebook out of her handbag and unscrewed her fountain pen. He might have the cheek of the devil and a certain ratlike cunning, but Norman had never been all that bright. She'd try him with fifty. That should keep him quiet.

Shirley and Imogen had just broken up for the summer holidays when Tony took his much needed break. He'd been working flat out for a year now and he had just come back from Tobruk in Libya, getting the film crew out just in time before the disastrous fall. He had found the work exciting and exhilarating at first, but lately the tension had begun to chip away at his nerves. He found himself running out of ideas, too. What he really needed, he told himself, was to get away from it all and recharge his batteries. He decided to take a couple of weeks off while the editing and cutting of the latest film was taking place. He'd go down to spend it with Imogen at Houlton. He had written to Leonie to tell her, asking if there was any chance of her joining him there. He pointed out how long it was since they spent any time with the child. But she'd replied rather tetchily that it was out of the question and that she'd have thought that if he had leave he might have made the effort to spend it with her up in Scapa Flow, where she was dying of boredom. To her annoyance Tony replied that he felt Imogen deserved a treat after passing her scholarship exam.

As it happened, his visit coincided with Gloria's holiday. As soon as she learned the dates, she made arrangements with Molly to stay at Longueville Hall so that she could be with Shirley. But when she heard that Tony was to be there too, she was filled with apprehension. He might think it a cheek for her to invite herself there for her holiday. He might not want to have her around; he might feel awkward about the night they had spent together at the Mayfair flat. It seemed so long ago now, but she hadn't forgotten it and she doubted very much that he had either.

She need not have worried. When she got off the bus at Houlton post office, Tony and the two girls were there to meet her. Tony was at the wheel of the camouflaged car provided by the film company. As she stepped down from the bus, he got out of the car to take her suitcase from her, a smile of welcome on his face.

'Gloria! How nice to see you. It's been simply *ages*.'

He looked thinner, but fit and handsome, tanned from his recent visit to the Libyan desert. Gloria was glad she had let Jane do her hair in the new upswept style that was becoming so popular, and that she had stayed up to finish the blue dress that she'd copied from the one Ingrid Bergman had worn in *Casablanca*. All the girls swore that she looked the image of Ingrid in it and that the blue was the very same colour as her eyes. She smiled shyly back at Tony.

'It's ever so good of you to come and meet me,' she said politely.

'Not a bit.' He hoisted her case into the boot and slammed it shut. 'These two would never have forgiven me if I hadn't.'

By now Shirley was out of the car too, hugging her mother and chattering excitedly. 'I've got to have a uniform,' she announced. 'For the high school. It's brown with a yellow hat band and a badge. It's hard to get some of the things but when the older girls grow out of theirs or leave, they sell their uniforms. There's a special sale on at the school tomorrow and Imo and I are going with Nanny to see if there's anything that will fit us.'

Gloria hugged her daughter. 'What a good idea! I'll come too and make sure you've got everything you need. Can't let my clever little girl go to her posh new school without the proper uniform, can I?'

Shirley glanced at Imogen and lowered her voice. '*Glor* – don't call me that,' she whispered.

The girls sat in the back of the car and Gloria sat in the front with Tony. All the way back to the Hall he kept the conversation flowing; asking about her job at the factory; talking about the girls, their success at winning scholarships and the way they had both grown since he last saw them. Gloria felt shy and awkward with him, and deflated at Shirley's obvious embarrassment. Tony was making polite small talk as though she were some casual acquaintance to whom he was trying extra hard to be nice – someone he had only just met. Clearly he wanted to pretend that his confidence and the intimate moments they had shared that night at the flat had never happened.

At Longueville Hall he took her case from the boot and carried it into the house for her. Molly stood in the hall, waiting to welcome her, her round face beaming with pleasure.

'Welcome home, my dear. We've all been looking forward to seeing you so much.' She took both Gloria's hands and looked her up and down, shaking her head and exclaiming at her thinness. 'My, but you've lost weight. You mustn't overdo it, you know.'

'Fat chance of doing anything else,' Gloria said with a laugh. 'I was quite glad to lose a few pounds. It doesn't bother me. Munitions work is the best slimming treatment I know.'

But Molly shook her head. 'I read where a lot of girls have gone down with TB from overdoing it in factories. These long shifts ruin your health. It's not natural, working all the hours God sends like that.' She smiled. 'Anyway, I'm going to make sure you get a good rest and plenty of wholesome food while you're here. At least I can send you back in good shape.'

Upstairs Gloria found Tony putting her case at the foot of the bed in the room she always occupied. The window was open and the curtains fluttered in the breeze. The room was filled with the scent of summer: newly mown grass, roses and lavender. Gloria went to the window and leaned out, breathing deeply. 'Mmm. It's lovely to think I've got seven whole days to enjoy this,' she said.

Tony crossed the room to stand behind her, looking over her shoulder. 'Gloria,' he said softly. His tone made her turn to look at him and she saw that his eyes were serious. 'I want you to know that I haven't forgotten what you did for me that night. I'll appreciate it for the rest of my life.'

She shook her head, suddenly lost for words. 'It was nothing.'

He reached out and grasped her shoulders, turning her so that she was obliged to look at him. 'Oh, but it was. It meant a very great deal to me. I've realised since that it must have been difficult, explaining your absence that night, and yet you didn't even hesitate when I asked you to stay.'

'I told my parents I'd been with a friend. It was all right.'

'You're sure?'

'Of course.' She smiled wryly. 'Anyway, there's been more to worry them since then.'

'They're all right?'

'As well as can be expected, what with the bombs and everything.'

He smiled. 'That's good. Well, anyway, I wanted you to know that I'm grateful. And it's good to see you again, Gloria.'

'It's good to see you too, Mr Darrent.'

His eyebrows rose. 'Oh *dear*. I thought we'd agreed on Tony.'

She blushed and looked away. 'It was a long time ago. I didn't know if . . .'

He squeezed her shoulders, then let his hands drop to his sides. 'And if I can make your holiday happy and relaxed, please let me. I'm at your service, madame.' He laughed and tipped up her chin. 'Come on, relax and smile for me. We can be friends, can't we, just as we were before?'

'Of course. Thank you – Tony.'

'That's good. Now you'd better unpack and get downstairs. Nanny's got the biggest tea you've seen since before the war waiting in the kitchen and I don't know about you, but I'm ready to do it full justice.'

Gloria had looked forward to going with Molly and the girls to buy the school uniforms next morning, but at breakfast Molly insisted that there was no need.

'I know what they need, my dear. You just stay here and put your feet up.'

'Oh, but I'd like to come,' Gloria assured her. 'It's a special occasion, isn't it – buying her school uniform?'

Molly looked uncomfortable but Shirley was more direct. 'It's all right, Glor,' she said. 'See, if there's just the three of us we can get a lift there and back in Mr Morris's grocery van. He goes into Northampton on Mondays to pick up the magazines from the wholesaler's. We often go. Nanny sits in front with him and Imo and me squeeze in the back. He doesn't mind if there's only the two of us and we sit still.'

'Oh, I see,' Gloria said.

Molly's face was flushed with embarrassment. 'He helps us out because Jim lets him have our surplus vegetables,' she said. 'We all have to do what we can for each other with the shortages and everything. It's not that we don't want your company, dear, but queuing for the bus can take so long now that they've cut down the service.'

'Oh, that's all right,' Gloria said with a smile. 'I shall look forward to a mannequin parade when you get home.' She opened her handbag. 'Here, let me give you some money.'

But Molly waved a hand. 'Pay me when I get back,' she said. 'I've got no idea what we'll be able to get secondhand at the school, but at least we won't have to part with our precious coupons. We'll go to the Co-Op for the rest, if that's all right with you.' She bustled round, pulling on her coat and reaching for her handbag. 'Now, come along, you girls. No dawdling. We don't want to keep Mr Morris waiting. He said he'd be at the end of the lane at half nine.'

Trying hard to fight down the feeling of disappointment, Gloria wandered out into the garden. Of course Molly was right, it would have been tiring, waiting around for buses. Much better to accept a lift when it was offered. It was Shirley's dismissal that hurt. She was so proud that her daughter was going to get a real education, but wounded that she wasn't allowed to share in her achievement. 'It's only natural,' she told herself, trying to justify the child's attitude. 'Molly has done everything for her for almost three years now. And after all, it's only a few school clothes. Shirl still likes the dresses I make for her specially.'

'You're looking very pensive.' Tony had come round the end of a tall yew hedge and was facing her before she noticed him. 'What is it – lost something?'

'I'm beginning to wonder,' Gloria said, half to herself. 'Molly has taken the girls into town to buy the new school uniforms.'

'And left you behind?'

Gloria shrugged dismissively. 'Not on purpose. They had the chance of a lift in someone's van and there was only room for three.'

Tony frowned. 'But I would have driven you all in.'

'Molly wouldn't ask. I expect she thinks you need a rest – and to save your petrol allowance, too.'

'All the same . . .' He grinned at her ruefully. 'I do know what you mean. It's the girls, isn't it? Do you get the feeling sometimes that you're surplus to requirements?'

She sighed. 'I do.'

'Me too, but it's hardly surprising, is it?' he said. 'We've been off doing our bit for the war, you and me, but life has to go on. Let's just be grateful for the Mollies and Jims of this world.'

'Oh, I *am*,' Gloria said quickly. 'When I think of some of the people Shirley might have been billeted on. I wouldn't want you to think . . .'

'I *don't*.' He slipped an arm around her shoulders. 'It's just that sometimes we look at the children and wonder what we're missing, but sadly there's nothing we can do about it.' He smiled. 'I'll tell you what. Why don't we slip off for the day ourselves? We could have lunch at a little place I know where you can still get a good steak. When they come back they can just miss *us* for a change. What do you say?'

She bit her lip. 'Oh, I don't know – do you think we should?'

'Yes, I most definitely do.'

They looked into each other's eyes and laughed. Gloria felt herself beginning to relax as Tony took her hand and drew her along with him towards the garage. As they passed the hedge that separated the lawn from the kitchen garden, Jim could be seen hoeing between the rows of lettuces. Tony put a finger to his lips and they both ducked down, chuckling like a couple of children playing truant.

The car wasn't as comfortable as the Rolls, but to Gloria it was a treat to ride in any car. Tony explained that he'd had to lay the Rolls up for the duration.

'I used to get her out now and again, but now that the private petrol ration has been withdrawn I can't run her,' he explained. 'I'm lucky to have the use of this old bus, even though she is a bit of a rattle-trap.' He turned to look appreciatively at Gloria's crisp print dress with its white collar and cuffs. 'By the way, how do you manage to look so pretty on the clothing coupons we're allowed?'

She blushed. 'I make my own. I've found a stall in the market where I can pick up remnants. It's nothing new for me, I used to do it in London. Usually there's only enough for a blouse or a little dress for Shirley, but sometimes I find a piece big enough to make a frock for me if I cut carefully.'

'You're a clever little thing, aren't you?' He smiled, his eyes on the road ahead. 'You haven't found a young man yet, then?'

'No.'

'I'm surprised.'

'The other girls and I go to dances sometimes at the village hall. The soldiers from Boothley camp come, but you hardly ever see the same fellers twice. It's no time to be getting fond of anyone, is it?'

He was silent for a moment and his eyes clouded, then he said quietly: 'No Gloria. It certainly isn't.'

'*Oh!*' She looked at him anxiously. 'Oh, I'm sorry. I wasn't thinking.'

He smiled his sudden, quick smile. 'It's all right, Gloria. I'm all over it now. You don't have to be careful what you say.' He pressed his foot down on the brake and turned right into a lane. 'We're almost there. The Wheatsheaf is just down here. I know you're going to like it.'

It was a long time since Gloria had eaten food like the lunch Tony bought for them at the Wheatsheaf. Succulent steak, garnished with crisp brown onion rings; golden chips and homegrown carrots and peas. It was followed by apple pie with thick cream. And because Tony was a special customer, the landlord had unearthed a bottle of his best Beaujolais from deep in the bowels of his cellar.

'How do they do it?' Gloria whispered, leaning across the table.

Tony tapped the side of his nose. 'Their son is a farmer – that and what we'll call careful management.'

He snatched up the bill quickly when it came, but not before Gloria had seen what she thought an outrageous figure in the last column.

'Please, let me pay my share. I'm earning good money now and –'

He held up his hand and frowned at her. 'Shhh. Do you want to get me a bad name? It'll be a black day when I can't buy a pretty woman lunch.'

Gloria felt decidedly tipsy when they left the pub and Tony suggested a walk to settle their meal and blow away the cobwebs. He parked the car by a copse of trees that led down to a stream and they walked in the lazy afternoon sunshine. To Gloria there had never been a more perfect afternoon. The air was warm and mellow, heavy with the scent of clover and buzzing with the sound of a thousand insects. They sat down on the bank of the stream and Tony said suddenly:

'Are you happy, Gloria?'

She looked at him in surprise. 'I suppose so. I haven't really thought.'

He pulled a long blade of grass from its sheath and nibbled at the sweet green stem. 'That's about it nowadays, isn't it? We don't get time to ask ourselves the important questions any more. Life slips past and half the time we don't know whether it's a living death or a dying life we're living.' He paused, then said: 'Did I ever tell you I had a son?'

'No.' She was shocked, and unsure of whether he was serious or not.

'Well, I have. He lives in America with his mother, Gillian Fane. Ever heard of her?'

Gloria's mouth dropped open. '*The* Gillian Fane? The one who was in *Song of Granada*?'

'That's the lady. Our marriage was all over a long time ago, long before I met Leonie. Gill and I were a couple of silly stage-struck kids at the time. It was never right. Marcus was just two when we parted. A beautiful little boy, and now he's almost a man.' He sighed wistfully. 'I still miss him, but I'm glad he's not old enough to be drafted into the army now that America has joined the war.' He smiled at her. 'Do you know, that's the first time I've spoken about him to anyone for – oh, I don't know how long.'

'Will you see him again – after the war perhaps?'

He shrugged. 'Who knows? I'm a stranger to him even now, so heaven knows what he'll make of me then. No, I suppose I have to face the fact that I've lost him.'

Gloria was moved by the wistful smile that she knew concealed his sadness. It seemed he was destined to lose all the people he loved. Sudden tears blurred her vision, intensifying the stream's glitter and the trembling of the leaves. The wine, the food and the mellow summer afternoon had loosened her inhibitions and she reached out instinctively to take his hand. 'You said you were over it – Claire, I mean – but you're not really, are you?'

His fingers curled warmly round hers. 'Not really, if I'm honest. But maybe I never will be, not completely.' He turned to look into her eyes. 'Dearest, sweet little Gloria. You understand, don't you?'

'Yes.' She swallowed hard. 'I should have been killed by rights,' she told him. 'One weekend when I came up here to see Shirl, the cinema where I used to work had a direct hit. I'd swapped fire-watching with another girl. She was killed.'

He put his arms around her shoulders and pulled her close. 'Poor Gloria. How terrible for you.'

'It seems like fate, doesn't it?' she said. 'Makes us see that there's a pattern to things somehow – that God hasn't finished with us yet.'

For a long moment they were silent, then Tony said: 'It's so restful, being with you. I can be myself and not what people expect me to be. People like you are rare, you know.' He kissed her lightly on the lips. 'You should be patented, made into pills for peculiar people – like me.' He glanced at his watch and sighed with regret. 'I suppose it's time we were getting back or I'll get the wigging of a lifetime from Nanny for keeping you out so long.' He got up and pulled her to her feet. 'Thanks for today, Gloria.' He looked at her, his head on one side. 'What is it that Shirley calls you – Glow?'

'Glor,' she told him, grimacing. 'Horrible, isn't it?'

'I like Glow better. It suits you. You're like a little glow-worm, shining in the dark; sweet and bright and comforting.' He drew her close and kissed her again, his lips lingering on hers and making her head spin in a way that had nothing to do with the wine. Then suddenly he was laughing light-heartedly and pulling her along with him through the trees and back to the car, leaving the sadness, the joy and the dreams behind with the willows and the shining water.

In the kitchen at Longueville Hall Shirley and Imogen were parading in their new school clothes for Jim. Gloria and Tony arrived in time to see Shirley in her hockey shorts. Using the kitchen table as a stage, she was strutting up and down, singing a chorus of 'Run, Rabbit, Run' and using the hockey stick as though it was a gun. Imogen, Molly and Jim applauded loudly when she took a final bow.

In the doorway Tony said to Gloria: 'That little girl of yours is very talented, you know.'

She blushed with pride. 'I know. I've always encouraged her. I used to think that maybe she could make a career of her dancing, but now I've changed my mind. If she gets a proper education she might go to college and make a teacher or something.' She smiled. 'Isn't it funny? If she hadn't come to Houlton – if it hadn't been for the war – she might never have had the chance.'

Tony looked thoughtful, the seed of an idea beginning to germinate in his mind.

'Where have you been, Glor?' Shirley was saying. 'We were ever so lucky. Imo and I got almost everything we needed at the school sale. They showed us round, too, and you should just *see* it. There's a big art room and a science lab; oh, and the biggest, *best* gym you ever saw, with wall bars and ever so much apparatus. It's a *really* posh school. We're to have dancing lessons too – folk dancing and ballroom and –'

'Wait!' Gloria laughed. 'Let Imogen get a word in. I'd like to hear what Nanny has to say too, if you don't mind.'

But Shirley paused only for breath before going on: 'Hey, you'll never guess – Tilly Marks was there with Mrs Phipps. Her mum wrote and said she wasn't to go to the high school but Mrs Phipps is sending her anyway. She's paying for all the stuff herself. She told Nanny, didn't she?' She looked at Molly, who drew down the corners of her mouth.

'Now then, Shirley, you mustn't gossip, it's not nice. Off you go upstairs and change now, both of you, while I get the tea. You can show Gloria the rest of your uniform after.'

When the girls had gone, Gloria looked at her. 'Was it true about Tilly?'

Molly nodded. 'The child's mother wrote back in answer to the letter about Tilly's scholarship, saying that she didn't want her to go. She said she couldn't afford the expense and that girls weren't worth educating anyway.'

'And Mrs Phipps was annoyed?' Tony put in.

'She certainly was. That girl has come along in leaps and bounds since she's had her,' Molly said. 'Such a poor little scrap she was when she first came to Houlton; dirty and scruffy – barely housetrained. And her *language* . . .' Molly raised her eyes to the ceiling. 'Edith Phipps has worked miracles on her. Mind you. I don't know that I approve of what she's doing over this school thing. Overstepping the mark, if you ask me. I mean, what'll happen once the war's over and Tilly has to go back to London? It'll be a rude awakening for the child then, all right.'

Gloria looked at Tony and saw that his thoughtful expression had developed into a gleam of excitement in his eyes. She raised an enquiring eyebrow at him, but he nodded towards Molly's back and frowned. Maybe he'd tell her later what was on his mind.

When she saw Shirley to bed later that night, Gloria asked her if she was happy.

'Oh, *yes*,' Shirley said as she snuggled down. 'There's so much to look forward to – the holidays, then the new school.'

'You love it here with Nanny and Imogen, don't you?' Gloria asked wistfully. Molly's remark about the way Tilly Marks would feel when she went back to London had reinforced her plan to settle down near here when the war was over. She didn't want Shirley feeling resentful at being made to go back to London.

'Yes.' Shirley was looking at her mother's pensive expression. 'It doesn't mean I don't love you, though, Glor,' she said softly.

'But you don't like being called my little girl any more, though, do you? And you never come into bed with me for a cuddle either.'

Shirley frowned. 'That's because I'm older,' she said gravely.

'Is it? Or is it because Imogen thinks it's soppy?'

Shirley shook her head. 'Imo's never had a mum like you. She thinks you're smashing. I bet she wouldn't mind have someone to cuddle. It's just that with you being away such a lot I've got used to *not* having you with me. And I don't want people to think I'm a baby, specially now that I'm going to the high school.'

'What about when we're alone?'

Shirley reached up her arms to pull Gloria down to her. 'It's okay then, I s'pose,' she said.

Gloria hugged her tightly, her heart full of gratitude. She hadn't lost Shirl after all. She was still her little girl, thank God; even if she wasn't allowed to say it.

'I'm going to make a documentary film about the evacuation.'

Gloria stared at Tony. 'But I thought all your films were about the fighting?'

'They have been, so far. But this is a kind of fight too, isn't it? One that's closer to home – and to all our hearts. It was Nanny talking about the Marks child that made up my mind; that and you talking about Shirley and the chances she wouldn't have had at home. So many children's lives have been changed. They've seen a side of life they might never had known existed had it not been for this war – both better and worse. It's almost the biggest social upheaval since the industrial and agrarian revolutions in the last century. It's going to mean that the next generation will be very different from the present one. More understanding and tolerant but also more thrusting and ambitious.'

By now he'd lost Gloria but, nevertheless, she could see that the subject might make an interesting film. 'Well, it'll keep you out of the firing line for a change,' she remarked.

He laughed. 'I have to admit that you have a point there. Now, the thing is, will you give me your permission for Shirley to take part?' He took in the look of doubt on Gloria's face and added quickly: 'She'll get paid, of course.'

160

'It isn't that,' she said quickly. 'I don't want her school-work interrupted.'

'I've thought of that. It'll be shot during these holidays, with a bit of luck,' Tony said. 'We don't have to shoot in sequence and I can get all the scenes with the kids done before they go back to school if I get on to it right away.' Already he was making mental notes. 'I'll need a first-class writer, someone who's used to working with kids and can get the emotional slant right. Mmm . . . Ben Maycox would probably do it. I'll ring him –'

'It isn't *just* that, Tony,' Gloria interrupted his flow of thought sharply.

'Oh?' He looked at her. 'What then?'

'It's what I was saying to you yesterday. Now that Shirl has this chance of a good education I'd like to get her mind off the stage. Now that I know she's capable of it I want her to grow up to a good job with prospects and maybe a pension at the end of it. Security.'

He pulled a face at her. 'It sounds deadly dull, Gloria. I doubt if you'll get a girl like Shirley interested in that kind of future. She'll make up her own mind when the time comes.'

'I can steer her, though. From what I can see of it, the stage is very insecure. You either make a lot of money or nothing.'

'That's not quite true,' Tony said. 'A lot of people make a reasonable living, and Shirley does have a natural talent.'

'Would you let Imogen take it up?' she asked quietly.

'If she wanted to, yes. Shirley has done a lot for Imogen. She's brought her out – given her confidence. She doesn't have Shirley's sparkle and vivacity, but if I detect the slightest hint of talent in her I'll encourage it for all I'm worth.'

Gloria said nothing. She felt slightly ashamed. It wasn't that she wanted to squash Shirley's ambition – the ambition that she herself had fostered. Just that since she herself had been earning better money she could see brighter horizons opening up for them. And since this new chance to better herself had come Shirley's way it seemed positively criminal to throw it away. But with Tony's background and hers being poles apart, she could hardly expect him to see that.

'Of course she can be in it if she wants to,' she said. 'She'd never forgive me if I said she couldn't. But you won't want her to begin work this week, will you? I'll be back at work on Monday and this is the only time I have to spend with her.'

'Good heavens, no. It'll be at least ten days before I can even get a team together.'

Tony's plans for spending time with Imogen went by the board as he spent hours on the telephone in his study talking to the Ministry of Information and to scriptwriters and producers, as well as his own crew, who were scattered around the country enjoying their few days' leave. Gloria found herself taking Imogen with her when she took Shirley for picnics and jaunts. Not that she minded. Tony's daughter was now Shirley's closest companion. She had changed; the sharp-tongued plain-featured girl had become more relaxed. She smiled and chattered instead of scowling and it was suddenly possible to see that the thin little face with its expressive grey eyes could very possibly develop into something close to classical beauty in a few years' time.

The week flew by and Gloria found herself waking on the morning of her last day. She was on the landing going down to breakfast when Tony waylaid her.

'How about having dinner with me this evening?' he invited. 'I feel I've neglected you all week.'

'You mustn't feel that. You're not here to entertain me,' she said.

'Nevertheless, I feel I owe you a thank you for taking care of Imogen while I was busy.' He smiled his engaging smile. 'Besides, I've missed you. You will come, won't you?'

She relented. 'Thank you. I'd like to.'

As they drove into town that evening he told her that everything was arranged and that shooting would begin on Monday.

'I'm using archive material of the children leaving London,' he explained, his eyes alight with enthusiasm. 'And I'm planning to dramatise the story of two children, slanting it in a positive way to show the brighter side. Most of our films have been used to boost morale and this will be no exception.'

'Thank you for not mentioning the film to Shirley.'

He turned to smile at her. 'I didn't want to divert her attention. I knew you wanted to enjoy as much time with her as you could and I didn't want to do anything to spoil that. As it was, you had to have Imogen tagging along.'

'Imogen is part of Shirley's life now.' Gloria sighed a little wistfully. 'I'll be gone this time tomorrow. I almost wish I could stay and watch the filming myself. The girls are going to love it.'

'I hope so. I imagine Shirley will need something exciting to help her not to miss you too much.'

'Thanks. It's kind of you to say so, but I'm afraid she'll hardly miss me at all.'

He had booked a table at a hotel on the outskirts of the town. The meal was not as good as the one they had enjoyed at the Wheatsheaf and for Gloria it was tinged with sadness because she knew it might be some time before she came to Houlton again. Maybe the next time Tony would not be there. All through her meal her thoughts persistently returned to the night they had spent together at the London flat – and the way he had kissed her on the first day of her holiday. Sometimes when she caught him off guard there was a sad, lost look in his eyes. It seemed to her that in spite of all he had, and the fact that he was enjoying his new work, he was often lonely. She longed to be able to make him happy again.

'You're not eating. Is it all right?' Tony was looking at her with concern.

'Oh yes, it's lovely.' Gloria applied herself to her sweet with a relish she did not feel.

'You're very quiet. Is it something I said?'

She made herself laugh. 'No. It's just that it's my last night.'

'Is it grim at the factory?'

'Oh, no. Hard work, yes, and boring sometimes, but we have fun too. We have lunchtime concerts once a month. Leonie came once. She toured the shop floor afterwards. Did she tell you?'

'No, she didn't. So, did she come and see you – have a word?'

'No,' She looked at her plate. 'But I dare say we all look the same in our overalls and caps.'

His mouth hardened. 'You're saying that she ignored you.'

'Oh, *no*. At least, not on purpose. There was a lot for her to see; so many people and –'

'That's typical.' Tony signalled to the waiter for the bill. 'Let's go. It's getting hot in here and you can't hear yourself speak.'

In the car she looked at him. 'I've made you angry. I shouldn't have mentioned –'

'Why not?' He turned to look at her. 'Leonie came from a similar background to you, you know, only she was from Birmingham, not London. Her father was a backstreet butcher and she's had no formal education at all. I first met her when she took part in a talent competition at the theatre where I was appearing.'

She looked at him in surprise. 'But – that's not what it said in that article in *Home and Beauty*.'

'No, it wasn't, and what I've said is strictly between you and me. I just thought you should know.'

Gloria was silent for a moment, digesting the fact that Leonie Swann had begun life just as she had. 'It just shows, doesn't it?' she said quietly. 'If you have talent you can go a long way.'

'With luck and a lot of help, you can,' Tony said with a hint of bitterness in his voice. 'Too far sometimes.'

'Maybe I shouldn't stop Shirley from going in for the stage, if that's what she really wants,' she said thoughtfully. 'But whatever she does I wouldn't like her to forget who she is or where she comes from. I think . . .' She glanced at him and bit her lip. Had the wine loosened her tongue too much? Would he think her presumptuous, voicing her own opinions just as though she was his equal? But he was looking at her. Waiting.

'Go on,' he invited. 'What do you think?'

'I think that . . .' She paused, searching for the right words to express what she felt – what she was just discovering that she felt. 'I think that what you are – where you start from is what makes you the kind of person you turn out to be. If you forget it and try to turn into someone different, you finish up . . .'

'One-dimensional,' Tony supplied, then substituted: 'A sort of cardboard cut-out of a person?'

A smile lit her face. 'That's right. That's *just* what I was trying to say.' The smile vanished from her face as she realised the gaffe she'd made. 'Oh – I didn't mean . . .'

'Don't apologise. You've hit the nail on the head.' He took her hand and pressed it warmly. 'But you're no cardboard cut-out, Gloria, thank God. You're real and human.' He drew her towards him. 'And very, *very* sweet.' He kissed her gently and drew her head down onto his shoulder. 'I'm going to miss you,' he said, his lips moving against her hair. She made no reply, unable to think of one, and after a moment he put his fingers under her chin and tipped her face so that he could look at her. 'That was your cue to say you'll miss me too,' he said softly. 'Or maybe you won't?'

'Of course I will,' she whispered.

'I'll be at Houlton for some time, shooting the scenes with the children,' he said. 'Is there any chance you might get over again – for a weekend, perhaps?'

She sighed, her heart heavy with regret. He wanted her. He actually *wanted* her. 'I wish I could, but the next weekend I get I'll have to go and see Ma and Pa. I haven't seen them for months.'

'Of course. I understand.'

She looked up at him, desperately anxious to let him know what being with him meant to her. 'Tony, what you were saying the other day – about the night I didn't go home. Ma still thinks I was up to no good. She never did believe my story about staying with a friend.'

'Oh, dear. That was my fault. I'm sorry I was so selfish.'

'You weren't. That part isn't important.' She bit her lip. 'It's just that it seems a shame – getting the blame for something that never happened.'

He searched her eyes for a long moment before he kissed the soft, eager mouth so invitingly uplifted for him. Then, very gently, he took both her hands in his and said: 'Darling little Gloria. I'm afraid I've given you too much wine to drink.'

'No.' She shook her head. 'I'm not tipsy, honest. If you want . . . I'd like to . . .' She trailed off as she saw him shaking his head.

'You might think you do now, darling, but tomorrow morning you'd hate me, and yourself too. I couldn't have that on my conscience.' He kissed her softly. 'But I do appreciate your sweet generosity.' He pressed the car's starter button. 'I'm taking you home now before we do something we'll both regret.' He glanced at her hurt face. 'While we're still friends, eh?' She nodded unhappily. 'Good. I value your friendship, Gloria. That's why I won't let anything spoil it.'

As he put the car into gear and moved forward, Gloria sank deep into her seat, misery and humiliation eating into her heart like acid. *I value your friendship*. He didn't want her after all. He never had. How could she have been such a fool?

Chapter Eight

Shirley and Imogen sat side by side in the darkened cinema with Molly and Jim on either side of them. As *Jenny and Joan*, the story of two evacuees, unfolded they held hands in delight at seeing themselves and some of their friends on the screen.

Tony's patient and skilful direction and an inspired script had brought about the most natural piece of amateur acting ever seen, so said the critics. And the story of the upheaval wrought on families by the outbreak of war, the emotive parting of parents and children and the triumphant emergence of two of the children in their new environment was both powerful and moving.

When the lights went up there were tears in Molly's eyes as she turned to Jim. 'Well! It was well worth all the weeks of having the film crew about the place, wasn't it?'

'I'll say it was.' Jim leaned across the look at the girls. 'What did you think then, seeing yourselves up there on the screen? Proper little film stars now, eh?'

It had been made clear from the outset that no fuss was to be made over the girls' appearance in the film. There was no cast list and no report in the newspapers. At the end of the film the only acting credit read: *Performed by the children of London, evacuated in September 1939*.

Shirley smiled with blissful satisfaction. 'It was smashing, wasn't it?'

All the way home on the bus she was silent. In her mind she was already an experienced actress. It was the only dream she had ever had, and now she knew for sure that it was within her grasp. When she was grown up she would ask Tony Darrent to give her a job. And of course he would. It was all out there, her glittering future – just waiting for her.

'Don't you want to act too, Imo?' she asked later when the girls were sitting on Imogen's bed drinking their bedtime cocoa.

Imogen frowned, her head on one side. 'I don't know. Probably not.'

Shirley stared at her in amazement. 'But you enjoyed being in the film with your dad, didn't you?'

'Ye-es, I suppose so. It was only a small part, though, and there was an awful lot of waiting about.' She smiled. 'I can think of something I'd like much better.'

Shirley, who couldn't imagine *anything* better than being a real actress, stared at her agape. 'What's that?'

Drawing her knees up and hugging them with both arms, Imogen said: 'I'd like to be married and have lots of children.' The grey eyes twinkled dreamily behind her spectacles. 'Just think. It'd be such *fun*.'

Gloria saw the film with her friend Jane and three of the other girls from the factory. She was intensely proud of Shirley, but apart from Jane, to whom she confided most things, no one knew that the child who played the leading part in the film was her daughter, Shirley. Leonie's snub and Tony's kindly meant but humiliating put-down had made her wary of such self-indulgence. Taking the respect and acceptance of others for granted was something she was rapidly learning not to do.

In the darkened cinema she watched, swelling with pride as Shirley acted out her part; appearing first as a sad and lost-looking little evacuee waif, progressing to the confident, healthy child who danced and sang in a Christmas concert. And finally the growing girl who emerged, radiant and triumphant in her high-school uniform, ready to begin the education that would prepare her for the opportunity-filled future awaiting her after the war. The character that Shirley played was based on Tilly

Marks, a fact which made Gloria vaguely uncomfortable. She knew that Ma would be less than pleased at her granddaughter's portraying a member of the feckless family she despised. She would just have to try to explain to her that it was only acting and what Tony called 'artistic licence'.

Since the summer holiday she had spent at Houlton, her dream of owning a cottage in the country had suddenly and unexpectedly become reality. Alf Martin, one of the foremen at the factory, told her casually one lunchtime in the canteen that an old aunt of his had died, leaving him her cottage and all its contents. He seemed to think it a bit of a liability and told her he intended to sell it.

Holding her breath, Gloria asked him what price he was asking.

He rubbed his chin thoughtfully. 'Well, it's only a little two-up, two-down job. There's no electricity or bathroom and all the water comes from a well in the back yard. Furniture's old-fashioned, too. My missus wouldn't give any of it houseroom.' He sucked in his breath noisily. 'Dare say I'd be lucky to get a couple of hundred for it – if that.'

Gloria's heart was beating fast. She had saved almost that much. Trying not to appear too excited, she asked: 'Would you let me have first refusal, Alf?'

He looked at her in surprise. 'Thought you were happy with your mates in the hostel?'

'I am. But it'd be nice to have a place of my own where I could have my little girl to live with me,' she told him. 'When can I see it?'

He scratched his head, looking at her doubtfully. 'Any time, duck, but I reckon you're in for a disappointment. It's not like London houses.'

She smiled. Alf had obviously never been to the East End. 'I'd like to see it just the same.'

'Right you are then. I'll take you round there soon's this shift's finished, if you like.'

Rook Cottage stood on the very edge of Boothley village, conveniently close to the one and only bus stop. It had a thatched roof, latticed windows and a stout front door almost hidden by a trellised porch covered in tangled clematis. Alf produced the key and opened the door. As they stepped inside Gloria found herself in a small, spotlessly clean front parlour. The floor was covered in oilcloth with a home-made rag rug spread before the fireplace. The high mantel shelf was draped with a red, bobble-fringed cloth and adorned with a pair of Staffordshire figures and a brass oil lamp. A horsehair sofa was flanked by two matching high-backed chairs and in the window stood a pedestal table holding a large aspidistra.

Alf studied her face. 'Told you it weren't no palace,' he said. He crossed the room and threw open a door. 'Kitchen's through here.'

Gloria saw a small living-room-cum-kitchen with a window overlooking the back garden. In the centre stood a deal table covered by a chenille cloth; four ladder-backed chairs were tucked under it. In a deep recess a range sat gleaming like ebony from years of black-leading. Under the window was a shallow stone sink and a wooden draining board with a blue-and-white-checked skirt enclosing shelves underneath. Her heart fluttering with excitement, Gloria preceded Alf through the door in the corner that opened immediately onto a narrow stair-case. At the top were two bedrooms. The front one, complete with brass bed, looked out over the porch, while to the rear a smaller room had a view of the back garden.

Alf pointed down to the well with its little slated roof and winding gear. 'They used to reckon that was the purest water in the county,' he told her. 'When I were a lad I'd stop off here on my way home from school for a drink. Cold as ice, it were. My, but it tasted good on a hot summer's day.' He looked at her, his head cocked enquiringly. 'Well, what do you think of it? Told you it weren't nothing special, didn't I?'

'I think it's perfect,' Gloria said with a smile. 'I love it. Would you take a hundred and seventy-five, Alf?'

His eyebrows rose. 'You sure, duck? Don't you want to talk it over with anyone?'

'No. I've made up my mind,' she told him. Already she could picture herself and Shirley living here, enjoying the ice-cold well water in summer, snugging round the parlour fire in winter, all cosy. It was just what she'd always dreamed of.

She kept the cottage as a surprise, not telling Shirley until all the formalities were completed and the place was hers. But when she took her to see the place for the first time she was to be disappointed.

'You mean you want me to come and *live* here?' Shirley stood in the little front parlour and looked around her with obvious distaste. 'But how could we? There's no bathroom and no lights, and you have to pull all the water up from that well thing in the garden. Besides, I don't want to leave Houlton.'

'I thought it would be fun.' Gloria was so disappointed she could have wept. 'Just you and me, Shirl. We'd be together again.'

'How'd I get to school?'

'The bus stops at the end of the lane. Oh, Shirl, say you like it. I got it for you – for us.'

'But we wouldn't see much of each other anyway,' Shirley argued. 'You work such long hours. I'd be here on my own a lot of the time.'

Gloria had to concede that she was right. 'We could always get a wireless – one with an accumulator battery,' she suggested hopefully. But already she knew that she was losing the battle. She should have thought – should have realised that Shirley had grown used to being with her friends; with Imogen and Molly and Jim Jarvis. She was accustomed now to the kind of luxury Longueville Hall had to offer. Perhaps she hadn't been fair, expecting her to move at the moment. *Later*, she promised herself. In another year perhaps, when she'd had electricity laid on and saved up enough to modernise the place a bit. Maybe then Shirley would want to come here. For a moment they stared at each other, each dismayed over the disappointment they'd unwittingly caused each other, then Gloria smiled and slipped an arm round her daughter's shoulders.

'Never mind, love. It was only an idea. You and Imogen could always come and spend weekends here with me, though – if you'd like to.'

Shirley heaved a sigh of relief. She hadn't wanted to hurt her mother's feelings. 'Yes,' she said. 'Perhaps we could. That'd be fun.'

But the weeks went by and Shirley never came for the promised weekend visit. Somehow she was always too busy with homework or other school activities. When they did meet she was full of all the exciting new things she was learning. They were teaching her French and Latin, it seemed. Gloria was vastly impressed: just fancy a daughter of hers being able to speak French! But as the weeks grew into months, Gloria's feeling that they were growing ever further apart intensified. She was glad that her daughter was getting opportunities that she herself had never had, but there were times when she wondered just how high a price she was going to have to pay.

She put off moving into Rook Cottage. She had toyed with the idea of asking Jane to share it with her, but with them both working awkward shifts she knew it would be neither economical nor practical. Alf had been right, she should have taken advice before deciding to buy. In the meantime the cottage remained empty and Gloria tried not to worry too much about her unwise investment.

Whenever her shifts allowed, Gloria would make a flying Saturday visit to Northampton and take the girls to the pictures and out for tea afterwards. She hadn't seen Tony at all since the summer before, and though half of her longed to see him again, the other half was glad to avoid him. She shrank from facing him, quite sure she would make a fool of herself if she did. What she saw as his rejection of her still hurt, though she blamed herself. It must have been the wine she had drunk that night that had made her ruin everything and humiliate herself like that. She was so ashamed that she hadn't even told Jane about it.

The United States Air Force had begun to make its presence felt. A base had been set up six miles from

Boothley at Melthorpe, a tiny hamlet on the Cambridgeshire border, and it wasn't long before the loose-limbed servicemen in their smart, expensive-looking olive-green uniforms were to be seen around the village mingling freely with the locals. They nodded and spoke politely to the older folk, carried shopping baskets for weary housewives and plied the schoolchildren, to whom each one was a glamorous hero, with packets of chewing gum and sweets, but they whistled audaciously at every passing pretty girl, delighting some and putting up the indignant hackles of others.

The news soon circulated round the shops and factories that on Saturday nights dances were to be held at the base. A flyer appeared on the hostel notice board announcing that American service vehicles would tour the villages, providing free transport for any girls who wanted to go.

At first the girls were wary of the open invitation, then some of the bolder, more adventurous among them decided to try it. They went at first in twos and threes, maintaining that there was safety in numbers, all of them curious to discover for themselves what these exotic creatures who spoke like film stars were actually like. When the first girls returned, telling of the sumptuous buffet suppers with the kind of food no one had set eyes on since before the war – whole hams, whipped cream and fresh fruit, not to mention free drink of every conceivable kind – eyes widened and mouths gaped disbelievingly. All the same, when the girls next appeared, wearing stockings made of the delicate new fabric called 'nylon' and proudly displaying bottles of perfume and lipsticks that the other girls would have happily given up a month's sweet ration for, the numbers attending the weekly dances began to creep up.

But while the others dressed up and flocked to Melthorpe on their Saturday evenings off, Gloria remained where she was, sewing dresses for Shirley or reading the true-romance magazines she loved to relax with. Those girls with the gossamer-fine stockings and make-up; what did they have to do to get them? she asked herself suspiciously. No. She would have nothing to do with it. No more humiliations. All that was behind her.

Oddly enough it was on one of her Saturday trips to Northampton that she met Billy. It was a February evening with the first hint of spring in the air and she was on her way back to Boothley on the bus. She was deep in thought about *Mrs Miniver*, the moving film about a wartime family she and Shirley had just enjoyed, and she didn't hear the polite enquiry until it was repeated.

'Excuse me, ma'am, is this seat taken?'

Looking up, she saw a young man with soft brown eyes looking down at her. He wore the familiar olive uniform and immediately she was on her guard. She had heard all about the brash way these Americans had of picking a girl up. 'Er, no.' She edged carefully along the seat. 'No, it isn't taken.'

'Thank you.' He sat down beside her and she was pleased and relieved that he kept carefully to his half of the seat. After a moment he glanced at her.

'I'd be obliged if you'd be so kind as to tell me when we get to Melthorpe, ma'am,' he said with studied politeness. 'You see, I'm kinda new around here.'

Gloria smiled in spite of herself. As if she hadn't guessed. 'I get off before we get there,' she told him. 'But it's the next stop after mine so you can't miss it.'

He laughed and she saw that he had strong white teeth and that this dark eyes crinkled attractively at the corners. 'Why do you English always say that?'

'Say what?'

'*You can't miss it*. They say it most every time. But I still do. Do you know that your English towns are the most difficult places to figure out?'

'In peacetime we have signposts,' Gloria told him. 'But they've taken them all down in case of an invasion.'

'Is that so? I thought it was just to confuse us GIs.' His eyes twinkled at her. 'One thing's for sure. If the Germans ever came here they'd sure give up and go home pretty fast. Never did know a place with so many twists and turns.'

'It's a very old country,' Gloria said. 'I suppose that's why.'

'Do you come from around here? You don't sound like the local folks.'

'I'm from London,' she told him proudly.

'From London? The capital city. Gee, I'd sure like to see that. They tell me that even after the bombing, it's still a beautiful place.'

'Oh, it is. The most beautiful city in the world. Everyone says so.'

'I'm Billy Landis.' He held out his hand. 'Sergeant Billy Landis, United States Air Force. Glad to know you, ma'am.'

After a slight hesitation, she put her hand into his. 'Gloria Rayner. I work at the aircraft factory at Boothley Bottom.'

'Hi, Glory.' He chuckled. 'That's another thing – these place names. They slay me. Where 'n the world did they get a name like *Boothley Bottom*?'

His laugh was infectious and Gloria found herself joining in. Then she noticed that the bus was nearing her stop. 'I get off in a minute,' she said.

He looked disappointed. 'Gee, that's a shame. Hey, listen, I'd get off with you but I only have a four-hour pass. Look, do you come to the base dances?'

'What? Oh, no. Sorry, I don't.'

'But you *should*. We have a great time. Why not try and make it next week, Glory?'

She was already standing up and trying to edge past him. 'Excuse me,' she said agitatedly. 'If I don't get up the driver'll go right past my stop.'

'Only if you promise to come to the dance.' The brown eyes teased her. 'I'll look out for you. Aw, c'mon, Glory. Say you will.'

Gloria glanced around her. In the seat behind a fat woman with a bulging shopping bag was glowering disapprovingly at her and two youths across the aisle were sniggering behind their hands. She shot them a disdainful look.

'Oh – all *right*,' she said, acutely embarrassed. 'I'll come. But please let me out now, will you?'

He swung his long legs aside and she edged past into the aisle. The woman behind muttered something about 'Yanks and brazen hussies' as Gloria pushed her way down the bus to the door. It was with great relief that she jumped down as the bus came to a standstill. Hoisting the strap of her bag onto her shoulder, she set off along the lane at a brisk pace but a moment later she was alarmed to hear hurrying footsteps behind her. She swung round and found herself face to face with Billy Landis.

'Oh, it's you. You shouldn't have got off here. I told you the *next* stop.'

'You *can't* miss it.' He laughed down into her eyes. 'I couldn't let you go like that, Glory. I said something back there that annoyed you, didn't I?'

She shook her head. 'No. It was just that I didn't want to miss my stop. Look, there isn't another bus for an hour. You'll get into trouble.'

But getting back late didn't seem to worry him. 'Why don't you like the dances, Glory?'

She sighed. 'I didn't say that. I just . . . don't go out much.'

'Well, you should. You're a swell-looking girl, real pretty.' He looked at her anxiously. 'It is okay to say that to a British girl, isn't it?'

She laughed, 'Yes, it's okay.'

He looked relieved. 'Only we all got issued with the little book, see. Seems there's a whole lotta words we use that you British folks get upset at.' He looked around. 'Say, is there some place around here we can get a drink – a coffee or something?'

'Only the Dog and Doublet.'

His eyebrows shot up. 'The *what*?'

'The pub.'

'Oh, I get it – a *bar*. Great.' He took her arm. 'Lead me to it. If you, er, want to, that is.'

In the village pub there was a log fire burning in the open hearth, taking the chill off the evening and scenting the air with the fragrance of woodsmoke. It was too early for most of the locals, but one or two men were leaning against the bar talking to the landlord over their pints of ale. When Gloria came in with Billy they stopped talking to stare at the pretty girl and the good-looking young American airman. Gloria felt awkward but Billy seemed oblivious to their obvious hostility.

'Hi there, guys,' he said cheerily. 'C'n I have one of those, please?' He pointed to the pints of ale on the bar. 'And for my friend . . .' He raised an eyebrow at Gloria. 'What's it to be, Glory?'

'Just a lemonade, please.'

Billy smiled at the two locals. 'Will you guys have another of those on me?' he invited.

The men looked at each other, then smiled sheepishly, accepting his offer and mumbling grudging thanks. As they carried their drinks to the far end of the room, Gloria said: 'You shouldn't do that, you know.'

'Do what?' Billy took an experimental sip of his ale.

'Buy their friendship. Country people can be so rude to strangers. They're not like that in London.'

'I'm sure glad to hear it. We're only here to help win the war, but to hear some folks, you'd think we were the enemy. Getting through to some of these people is like trying to nail Jell-o to the ceiling.'

Gloria laughed, saving up the expression to tell Jane later. 'I know. You should let them get on with it. It's only stubborn British pride. We don't like having to admit that we need help. You should hear my pa. But they'll come round eventually.'

He shook his head. 'We've been told – it's your country. So you get to have the last word no matter what. No getting into fights and arguments.' He peered into his pint mug. 'Say, this stuff wouldn't be too bad if it wasn't so darned *warm*.' He took another thoughtful pull at it. 'Even so, guess I could get to like it in time. Now – tell me all about yourself, Glory.'

'It's *Gloria*. And there isn't much to tell. I work at the aircraft factory and live at the hostel.'

'And you don't go out much. I already got that. What do you like to do, then?'

'I like to see my daughter when I can. She's evacuated to Houlton, about six miles away. Some Saturdays I take her into Northampton to the pictures. That's where I've been today.'

'I see.' He was trying to look at her left hand. 'So you're married?'

'No.' Gloria took a drink of her lemonade. That should cool any interest he had in her. It usually did. But when she looked up at him again he was still smiling.

'Wanna tell me about it?'

He deserved ten out of ten for persistence anyway. 'You wouldn't be interested,' she told him.

'I might. Try me.'

Somewhat taken aback by his directness, Gloria said: 'Well, it's the same old story. I met a bloke, fell for him and believed him when he said he loved me. Then, when it was too late, I discovered he was already married.'

'Gee, that's tough. But you kept the baby. How old is she?'

'Do you always ask so many questions?'

He shook his head. 'No, but then I'm not always this interested.'

'She's twelve years old – almost thirteen, and her name is Shirley.'

He smiled. 'That's a swell name for a little girl. Is she as pretty as you, Glory?'

She opened her mouth to correct him again, then gave up. 'I think I've got some photographs somewhere.' She opened her bag and produced the wallet of photos she always carried with her. There were some taken during Leonie's Christmas concert in 1939 and some more recent ones of Shirley in her new school uniform. 'That's her,' she said, pointing. 'That one there. She was in a concert, the first Christmas she was here. She was supposed to be Ginger Rogers and her friend there was Fred Astaire. Shirley loves to sing and dance. Everyone says she's a dead ringer for Shirley Temple.'

She handed him another snap. 'This one was taken when she started her new school. She won a scholarship to the high school.'

He looked puzzled. 'She needed a scholarship for that?'

'Oh yes. It's special you see. Only the best get in,' Gloria told him proudly.

He was smiling. 'She's a real little honey. I'd sure like to meet her.'

'Yes – well . . .' Gloria put away the photographs and looked at the clock over the bar. 'Look, we'd better go. You don't want to miss the next bus. There isn't another one till half-past ten.'

Billy downed the remainder of his ale. 'You c'n say that again. I'm gonna have to sneak in as it is. Lucky the guy on guard duty tonight is a buddy of mine.'

At the bus stop he held out his hand. 'It's been great meeting you, Glory. Will you come to the next Saturday dance? Aw, *please* say you will. I'd sure like to see you again.' He looked at her with those big brown eyes, appealing as a hopeful puppy in a pet-shop window.

The bus was coming; its dipped headlights could be seen rounding the bend in the road. In another minute he would be gone. 'All right,' she said impulsively. 'All right. I'll be there.'

'You *will*?' The eyes lit up in genuine delight. 'Say, that's great. I'll look forward to that.'

She watched as he leaped effortlessly onto the bus and waved to her from the platform. As she walked down the lane in the dusky, loam-scented evening, she reflected that she had told him almost everything about herself, yet she still knew nothing about him – except that he must surely be nine or ten years younger than her. Why on earth had she said she'd go to the dance next Saturday? She pictured Billy's laughing brown eyes; his annoying way of calling her 'Glory' and the disarming way he had of looking at her with that frankly admiring smile. And she discovered to her surprise that it was because she genuinely wanted to see him again.

★ ★ ★

Leonie sat in the drawing room of the Mayfair flat sorting through the pile of mail the caretaker of the flats had just handed her. Early that morning she had arrived back from a particularly exhausting overseas tour only to find, to her extreme annoyance, that the repairs to the latest bomb damage were still incomplete. There were still patches on the wall where the plaster had fallen off and the bedroom window was still boarded up. The caretaker of the block had apologised, explaining that bomb damage everywhere in London was being repaired in the same arbitrary fashion. It seemed they were only obliged to make the property what the Ministry of Works referred to as 'habitable' and, after all, it was the third lot of damage the flat had suffered since the bombing began. To Leonie's eye the flat wasn't in the least habitable and she had already decided not to stay in it for one minute longer than she had to. Roughing it in tents and huts on tour for the past weeks had made her long for peace and a little luxury. It didn't look as though she was going to get it here. She had already telephoned Molly Jarvis, telling her to expect her at Houlton the following day.

Molly's reaction had been one of delight. 'Oh, Madam, I *am* glad to hear that,' she said. 'Imogen will be so pleased to see you. It seems such a long time since –'

'I'm coming up for a *rest*,' Leonie interrupted sharply. 'I'm exhausted, Nanny. I can't tell you how rough it's been. I'm mentally and physically worn out.'

'Of course. You must be. I shan't let the children tire you,' Molly said. 'They're at school all day now anyway. They both love it at the high school.'

'Really? Well, I'm sure I'll hear all about it when I get there,' Leonie said. 'If I can contact Mr Darrent I might be able to persuade him to join me for a couple of days. We haven't seen each other for months.'

'Oh, that *would* be nice, Madam. I'll get the room ready, shall I?'

'Yes, I've no idea when Tony will be there, of course, but you can expect me some time tomorrow afternoon.'

As she spoke she'd been idly leafing through the pile of envelopes she had collected from the hall, which had been forwarded from the BBC. There used to be a secretary to sort them out for her and deal with the fan mail, but they were short-staffed now and it was down to the individual performers to attend to their own fan mail. It all looked perfectly straightforward; fan letters, requests for photographs, the usual requests for dates and even the odd proposal of marriage. They could go straight into the waste-paper basket. Then she came to the one with the Birmingham postmark and stopped, a feeling of dismay and annoyance bringing a sharp expletive to her lips.

'Shit! He's still writing, blast him.' She saw to her annoyance that he didn't even bother to mark the letter 'Private' any more. Tearing the envelope open, she scanned the smudgy scrawl that was her brother's handwriting.

Dear Eileen,

Thank you for sending the cheque. Not that it went very far. I'm surprised that you can be so mean when you're earning such pots of money, singing for the troops and broadcasting on the wireless – loved by all, no doubt. If only they knew. Or maybe you think we're not worth any more. Is that it, our Eileen? I meant what I said about writing to that magazine. On second thoughts, maybe I should come down to London. I'm sure your posh friends would like to meet your brother and hear about *my* memories of my little sister. The money what you sent would just about pay for the train fare. If you can find it in that kind heart of yours to spare something to help Mum and Dad, send it to me at the bank as usual. Hoping this finds you as it leaves me,
    your loving brother,
    Norman.

A chill went through Leonie's blood as she sat staring down at the sheet of flimsy paper. The amount of money she had sent in response to his regular demands mounted up to quite a substantial sum now, yet still he wasn't satisfied. How much longer could he go on demanding money in return for his silence? She should never have sent him anything in the first place. She should have ignored his first letter. If he'd gone to the magazine with his story she could have denied all knowledge of him, branded him an eccentric crank, trying to gain attention for himself. She chewed her thumbnail. What about her parents, though? If it were to get around that she had refused to help her aged mother and father, it wouldn't do much for her public image. Norman was threatening to come to London now. Of all the bloody cheek! Yet she daren't call his bluff. He could do her a lot of damage if he wanted to, a hell of a lot. She hadn't come this far only to let that whining little rat ruin it all for her. Suppose she went up to Birmingham and saw Mum and Dad for herself? She could smooth things over and make sure that they thought well of her – she could give them a couple of hundred in person. That should put a stop to Norman's little game. She looked at her watch. She could go now – this afternoon, she decided impulsively; stay at a hotel overnight and then go straight on to Houlton tomorrow as planned.

At Euston she was lucky; there was a train waiting and she was quickly on her way, travelling first class in her most inconspicuous grey suit, wearing a headscarf and a pair of dark glasses. Eager fans were the last thing she wanted at that moment. At New Street she tipped a porter to get her a taxi, but when she gave the driver the address he shook his head.

'Nothing left of Block Street now, missus.'

She frowned. 'Nothing at all? I knew it had been bombed . . .'

'More like flattened,' he said with a grim little laugh. 'Old property, you see. The bit what didn't burn fell down in a cloud of dust.' He peered at her. 'You ain't been up for some time then?'

'No. Tell me, the butcher's shop – Smith's – did that go too?'

'Told you. Nothing left – flat as a pancake.'

'Nevertheless, I'd still like to go there.'

He shrugged and started the engine. 'Up to you, missus. You'm payin'.'

When the taxi pulled up at what had once been the end of the street in which she had been born, Leonie saw that the driver hadn't exaggerated. There was nothing to see but a deserted bomb scar. The rubble had been cleared away long ago and tufts of grass were pushing up between the cracks in the rough ground. She was looking at a patch of wasteland. It was as though the street with its houses and shops had never been there. She paid the taxi and stood looking round her uncertainly. Maybe there was still someone nearby who knew what had really happened to the inhabitants.

Two streets away she found a small sub-post-office and shop that she remembered from her childhood days. She went in and enquired where there was a list of casualties that she could study. The elderly post mistress peered at her sympathetically through the grille.

'Was it someone from round here you were looking for, dear?'

'Yes. The Smith family from Block Street.'

The woman nodded. 'Ah, yes. Well, you can't be a relative or you'd have been notified. Mr and Mrs Smith were killed in the direct hit. The first week of the raids, it was. November 1940. A terrible night, that was. No one round here will ever forget it.' She frowned. 'Wait a bit, though. Now, if I remember rightly, their son was lucky. He was in the Rose and Crown – the pub at the end of this street. They all took cover soon's the bombs started to fall.' She shook her head. 'Came out next morning only to find his home and his poor mum and dad gone, poor feller.'

Leonie thanked the woman and walked out of the shop, fury seething inside her like a near erupting volcano. So her old home had been gone and her parents dead for two and a half years? No wonder Norman had asked to have the money paid straight in the bank. How dare he threaten to expose her? She'd write straight back to him, telling him she'd go to the police if he dared to ask for any more money.

At the end of what had been Block Street she paused. It was hard to believe that she had been born and grown up there. The space that had once held some thirty or so dwellings looked so small, not much bigger than the kitchen garden at Longueville Hall. She tried to feel sad about her parents, but she could feel nothing. She was barely able to remember what they looked like. Part of her was profoundly glad that all this was gone. Now no one could ever point to the mean little street where she had first seen the light of day and say it was where she belonged. Now she could truly belong to herself – to Leonie Swann, the new self that she had created. Now that the past had been erased for ever, she could settle into her new identity and look forward to a bright new future – once she had dealt with Norman.

She had no idea where he lived and she had no intention of finding out. The only address he had given was that of his bank, the reason for which was now painfully obvious. All her cheques had been paid into his account there. She fumed as she thought of the mounting balance in his account and the glee with which he would watch its accumulation, laughing at the power he held over her.

Checking into a hotel, she unpacked her overnight case and sat down to write him a letter, then she rang for a porter and asked him to take it round to the bank where she had sent the cheques. Wait till he read that, she told herself with satisfaction as she closed the door. That's that, she told herself with satisfaction as she closed the door. That would shut his grasping, whining little mouth for him once and for all.

Too shaken by her discovery, Leonie did not go straight to Houlton as planned, but back to the Mayfair flat, where she spent the night thinking. Norman could have contacted her when their parents were killed, but he hadn't done so. Clearly he had planned all this even then. He had been waiting, watching her climb to fame, until he felt that the time had come to strike. His greed and deviousness sickened her. Fame and success could be a lonely business, she reflected. She had letters by the sackful, declaring the undying love and admiration of unseen fans – people she would never set eyes on. But success made more enemies than friends among those closer to home. It generated envy, spite and resentment. Even Tony had turned against her, or so she sometimes thought. They hardly saw each other nowadays and when they did there was no light of love in his eyes anymore, not even the husbandly pride he had once shown when they were in company.

Next morning she shopped for presents; a silk scarf for Nanny, tobacco for Jim, gold cufflinks for Tony, embroidered handkerchiefs for Imogen and a record of Judy Garland singing 'How About You?' for Shirley. There had never been a time when she needed allies more than she did now.

That evening when she and Tony were alone she poured him a large whisky and sat beside him on the settee. Drawing her bare feet up under her, she linked her arm cosily through his, trying not to notice his slight withdrawal at her touch.

'It's so wonderful to be with you again, darling. You are glad to see me, aren't you?'

'Of course I am. That goes without saying.'

'Nevertheless, it would be nice to hear.' She paused. 'You haven't asked me why I wasn't here when you arrived yesterday.'

He sipped his drink. 'I suppose I'm used to you never doing what you say you'll do.'

She frowned. 'That's not fair. Actually I went up to Birmingham.'

'*Birmingham*? Whatever for?'

She was gratified to see that she had his full attention at last. 'I went to see my parents. I've never forgotten what you said about finding out whether they were all right.'

'It took you long enough.' He looked at her enquiringly. 'Well, are they – all right, I mean?

'No.' Leonie swallowed hard, turning her head away slightly. 'Block Street received a direct hit. They were both killed outright.'

There was a pause, then he said: 'It must have been a shock.'

'It was, rather.' She turned to him, his eyes brimming with the tears she found so easy to induce. 'It made me feel suddenly that I have no one.'

He slipped an arm round her shoulders. Her tears never failed to touch him. 'Don't be silly, darling. You have us – Imogen and me. You have your own family.'

'I know, darling.' She sniffed hard and fumbled for a handkerchief. 'But we've all grown so far apart since the war began. Besides, losing one's parents is like breaking a link in the chain.'

'But you hadn't been in touch with them for years.'

She took a deep, tremulous breath and peered up at him from under moist and sooty lashes. 'I never mentioned it to you, but I'd been sending them money. Now I wish I'd gone to see them. Knowing that I neglected them makes it so much worse. I'll never get the chance to put things right now.' She looked up at him and said with a little break in her voice: 'I feel so . . . lost and alone, Tony – so *sad*.'

He drew her close. 'I'm sorry, Leonie. I wish there was something I could do.' He looked down at her as she dabbed the tears from her cheeks. 'What about your brother – Norman, wasn't it?'

'He's gone too.' The lie tripped so easily from her lips. 'So you see, darling, I only have you now; you and darling Imogen, of course. If I lost you I don't know what I'd do.' She touched his cheek with her fingertips, her eyes wary. 'Is there anyone else in your life at the moment – anyone special, I mean?'

Tony shifted her weight from his shoulder. Since Christmas he had formed a relationship with the continuity girl from the unit. She was attractive, she clearly adored him and they had their shared interest in work in common. Sexually, too, they were more than compatible. It was an extremely satisfying relationship. He and Leonie had always been open about these things and he saw no reason why he should deny the affair.

'There is a girl, yes,' he said lightly.

She stiffened. 'I see. I thought as much. Who is she?'

'I don't think there's any reason why you should know. She isn't any kind of threat.'

She got up and walked across the room, pausing to take a cigarette from the box on the mantelpiece and light it. 'I'll never divorce you, you know.'

He looked up at her in surprise. 'No one is asking you to. There's no question of that. Look, Leonie, after Imogen was born you made it clear that you were no longer interested in me physically. I'm a normal man, you know. You surely didn't imagine I was going to become some kind of eunuch.'

'Of course not. And I've never made any secret of the fact that I couldn't risk another pregnancy. You always knew that was the only reason. But things are different now. Contraception is so much safer.' She turned to look at him. 'I've turned a blind eye to your affairs in the past, Tony. But now I *need* you. I need your help and support, your . . .'

'Love?' He almost spat the word at her. 'Please, Leonie, spare me that. You haven't the vaguest idea what it means to love another person, so don't pretend that you have.'

She ground out her cigarette furiously and rounded on him. 'You owe me a little respect and consideration at least, I think.'

He laughed bitterly. 'Owe you? *Owe* you? If it hadn't been for me you'd have stayed where you were – sitting at the cash desk in your father's butcher's shop. I've even given up the career I planned for myself to put you where you are. No, Leonie. I owe *you* precisely nothing.'

Leonie's face turned bright red. 'You recognised my talent, I'll give you that much, but you didn't hesitate to cash in on it, did you? If it hadn't been for me you'd have had none of this.' She threw her arms wide to encompass the lavishly furnished room. 'It was my talent that made you what you are today. Do you think anyone would have employed a washed-up old ham like you if you hadn't been married to me?' She stood over him, a sneer distorting her beautiful mouth. 'I'll tell you something, shall I? Peter only let you do that stupid Shakespeare because he didn't want to lose *me*.' She threw back her head and laughed derisively. 'Henry the sodding Fifth! If you could only have *seen* yourself in those *tights*. The laugh of London. Better than the Crazy Gang. No, darling *Mr Leonie Swann*, that's your only claim to fame. Yesterday's hero.' She laughed harshly, her temper as hot as fire. 'And I'll tell you another thing. I don't believe there's a girl, Tony. That's all a sham. You can't get it up any more, can you? Who'd have you any more? Even the army wouldn't take you with your flat feet and your flabby belly.'

His face white and pinched with anger, he sprang up from the settee and came towards her. The look of cold fury on his face sent a stab of fear through her and she stepped back, raising an arm protectively.

'Don't you dare touch me.'

He stopped in his tracks to stare at her with something approaching loathing. 'I wouldn't touch you with a ten-foot barge pole, Leonie,' he said, his voice low with tightly reined control. 'I hope I never have to touch you again. I wish you could hear yourself. I wish your devoted fans could hear their dream girl at this moment, screeching like some old fishwife. I'm afraid your background is showing, *Eileen*.' He walked to the door, then turned to look at her. 'I'll be leaving first thing in the morning. Good night.'

When he'd gone Leonie stood staring at the door for a long minute, waiting for her pounding heartbeat to quieten. The air still twanged with the vibration of his anger. How could it all have gone so wrong? she asked herself. She had set out to cajole him into a reconciliation. She had really meant to make it work and she had started off all right. It was his mention of that bloody girl that had sent it all spinning out of control. He must have known it would; he must have been baiting her all along – just waiting for an opportunity to start a row. She stamped her foot in frustration. How could she have let her temper get the better of her like that? She had gone too far this time. He'd never forgive those terrible emasculating things she'd said to him. Hell and damnation! She threw herself down on the settee, beside herself with fury. What had she done to deserve so much hate? She – Leonie, the woman every serviceman in England was in love with. If only they knew how alone and unloved – how despised she really was.

Molly Jarvis closed the kitchen door behind her quietly and looked across to where Jim was listening to the nine o'clock news and moving the flags on his war map. He had two pinned up on the wall. One of Europe, the other of England, where he kept track of air raids. As well as London, Coventry, Birmingham and Bristol, this year had seen the relentless bombing of the ancient cities of York, Bath and Exeter. It seemed that Hitler had turned his attention on England's historical and cultural heritage now. Sometimes he was horribly afraid there'd be nothing of the old England left by the time Hitler had finished with it. He'd been a lot happier since America had come into the war. With the help of the US Air Force maybe they could begin to strike back in earnest. It was heartening that at last things were beginning to look more hopeful. He looked up as his wife came in, her brow creased with anxiety.

'Hello. Something up, love?'

Molly sighed. 'It's them.' She jerked a thumb ceiling-wards. 'They're at it again. I really thought they might behave themselves this time, if only for Imogen's sake. If you ask me, they won't be together much longer at this rate.'

'Oh surely not? They've always quarrelled. I expect they'll have made it up by morning.' Jim smiled.

'Not this time.' Molly shook her head. 'He went off to bed in a blazing temper and I heard him say he'd be gone first thing in the morning.' She sank wearily into her chair by the range. 'I don't know, I'm sure. That poor child!

She'd been looking forward so much to having both her parents here for a few days. Such plans she'd made. Now he's off again. You'd think with the war and everything that people could try and be nice to each other, wouldn't you?'

Chapter Nine

Gloria stood uncertainly by the bar in the corner of the vast hall decked with flowers and coloured flags. The Stars and Stripes and the Union Jack were draped side by side over the dais at the far end where a band made up of American servicemen was playing. It was the kind of band Gloria had only ever heard in films before. Loud brass and melodious woodwind blended to perfection, filling the air with music that made her toes itch to dance in spite of her nervousness.

Jane nudged her. 'Stop looking so scared. You look smashing in the outfit. I wish I had your flair for fashion, Gloria.'

Gloria was wearing a made-over dress she had stayed up late the previous evening to finish. She looked down at the scarlet chiffon sleeves she had stitched into her three-year-old black dress and fingered the newly lowered neckline. 'You don't think it looks – well, too much, do you?'

Jane shook her head vigorously. 'No. Honestly, Glor, it's really nice and that red suits you a treat. You knock the other girls here into a cocked hat.' She looked towards the bar. 'Come on, let's go and get ourselves a drink. It'll give us something to do.'

But Gloria hung back. 'I don't know. I feel funny. I've never been to a place like this before.'

'Everyone's the same,' Jane said, pointing to the throng of giggling girls around the bar. 'Come on. Who's going to notice two more of us among that lot?'

But Gloria's eyes were anxiously raking the hall for Billy. There were so many people here – girls of all shapes and sizes and of course American servicemen, awesomely handsome in their exquisitely pressed uniforms, their hair slicked down and their tanned faces smoothly shaved. More men than Gloria had ever seen before collected together in one place, and every one looking like a film star – or so it seemed to her. Yet in all that throng Sergeant Billy Landis was nowhere to be seen.

The trip out to the base in the crowded lorry had been uncomfortable. Squashed in among so many chattering girls, Californian Poppy and Soir de Paris mingling sickeningly with female sweat. Gloria had felt her stomach churning with nausea. She'd been grateful when the lorry finally entered the gates of the base and they all tumbled out. Another minute and she was sure she would have disgraced herself and thrown up. Now they were here in this alien atmosphere of loud gaiety, surrounded by men from another country who seemed to Gloria to be looking them over as though they were so many pieces of meat in a street market. All she really wanted at that moment was to be back at the hostel listening to the wireless and doing her sewing.

'Well, I'm going to have a gin and orange,' Jane said, taking the initiative. 'I'll get you one too, shall I?'

Before Gloria could reply she had gone, elbowing her way through the dense crowd at the bar. Left alone, Gloria felt vulnerable. Standing back against the wall she tried to look as inconspicuous as possible as she watched the dancers on the crowded floor. Some couples were jitterbugging – something that was strictly barred in most English dance halls. These Americans seemed to excel at it, throwing their partners around with effortless dexterity. Flashes of thigh and lace-edged petticoat could be seen and sometimes even a glimpse of French knickers. Gloria bit her lip and swallowed hard, wondering what Ma would say if she could see them. Suppose one of them asked her to dance – and then expected her to do that? She'd die of fright.

'Hi there, Glory. You came, then.'

She turned to see Billy standing at her side. He looked so nice in his uniform, his black wavy hair brushed back over his ears. She felt a surge of relief. 'Billy. I thought you weren't here.'

He shook his head. 'I said I'd be here, didn't I? I've been looking for you. Guess I shouldv'e told you some place we could meet up.'

'It's all right.' She glanced around for Jane, who was nowhere in sight.

'I've been looking forward to seeing you again,' Billy went on. 'I was afraid that maybe you wouldn't come.' He took her arm and added almost shyly: 'You look swell, honey. What'll I get you to drink?'

'Oh, it's all right. My friend is getting me one.'

He looked slightly taken aback. 'Friend?'

'Yes, Jane. I didn't want to come on my own – just in case . . .'

'In case I stood you up?' He smiled and gave her arm a little squeeze. 'Gee, Glory, I wouldn't do a thing like that.' He bent close. 'I'm sure glad to hear it's a girlfriend, though. You had me worried there for a second.'

When Jane appeared with the two glasses, Gloria introduced her to Billy, after which he led them across the room to where he had a table earmarked. As they sipped their drinks, Jane glanced at Gloria.

'I'm not going to play gooseberry,' she whispered, leaning across. 'When I've finished this I'll make myself scarce.'

The band started up again and a tall blond airman materialised out of nowhere and asked Jane to dance. Billy took Gloria's glass from her and put it on the table.

'Dance?'

Dancing to the Air Force band, held firmly in Billy's arms, was the experience of a lifetime to Gloria. The music was uplifting and infectious. It gave her the heady feeling that she was taking part in a film. Billy was a good dancer; it was easy to follow him and their steps seemed to match perfectly. They danced the quickstep and slow foxtrot to some of Gloria's favourite romantic tunes; 'That Lovely Weekend' and 'A Nightingale Sang in Berkeley Square'. A little later, when the band got into its stride with the Glenn Miller number 'In the Mood', Billy persuaded her to try some jitterbugging, though, to her relief, he didn't attempt anything embarrassingly acrobatic. Halfway through the evening they stopped for supper and Gloria's eyes opened in disbelief when she saw the buffet laid out for them in an adjoining room. There was everything from ham, chicken and whole fresh salmon to ice cream and mountains of fresh fruit. There was real butter, golden and glistening on the crusty bread, and slices of real lemon and orange floating in the big bowl of punch in the centre of the table. It was the kind of food she hadn't seen, let alone tasted, since before the war. At last she could see for herself that it was all true what the other girls had said.

Billy made sure she had a generous helping of everything and they carried their heaped plates back to the table.

'You know all about me, but you didn't tell me anything about yourself, Billy,' Gloria told him when at last she had eaten her fill of the delicious food.

'Hey.' He looked up with a disarming grin. 'I guess that's true. I was more interested in you the first time we met. Well, I come from a place called Boulder, in Colorado. It's a beautiful part of America, very scenic. I guess you'll have heard of the Rockies?'

Gloria's eyes opened wide. 'Oh, yes. I've seen them – on the pictures.'

Billy smiled proudly. 'Boulder is a kind of health resort and folks come for miles just to take the mountain air. My dad owns the local garage and gas station. When I left college I worked with him for a while. I was going to engineering school, but then I enlisted instead.' He smiled at her. 'My folks were pretty upset at that, but I always wanted to fly and it seemed like a good chance.'

'And do you – fly, I mean?'

The smile left his face. 'I guess that's one dream that won't come true, Glory. I didn't make it through the training course. I turned out to be better at navigation so that's what I'm stuck with. Not that it isn't an important job,' he added quickly. He took a long pull at his glass of beer. 'I was disappointed first off, but I've gotten to like the job now.'

'Have you got any brothers or sisters?' Gloria asked.

'Two sisters. One older'n me. She's married. And one who's still in high school.'

'I wish I had sisters,' Gloria said wistfully. 'But I've got Shirley, of course.'

'I guess you must miss her.' Billy looked at her, his head on one side.

'Yes, but I do see her now and again. It must be harder for you, being so far away.'

He sighed. 'You know, I never thought I'd miss my folks as much as I do. Trouble is, no one knows when we'll get to go home again.'

'Tell you what,' Gloria said impulsively. 'You must come home to London with me some time. And to Houlton to meet my Shirl. You can borrow my family if you like.'

'I *can*? No kidding? That'd be real dandy, Glory.' He looked up as the band struck up again. 'If you've finished your supper we could dance again. I don't want to waste a second of this evening, Glory. I'm having the greatest time.'

At last the evening drew to a close and the last waltz was played. In the romantically dimmed lights Gloria floated round the floor in Billy's arms feeling as though her feet hardly touched the ground. His hair smelled so nice, spicy and clean, and his cheek was smooth and soft against hers. When he turned his face to smile into her eyes, brushing his lips softly against hers, it felt just right somehow, almost as though it was meant to happen. As they neared the doorway he whispered: 'Whad'ya say we sneak out now, before the rush starts? I'll walk you to the gate.'

Together they slipped out and Billy waited while Gloria got her coat from the cloakroom. Taking her hand, he walked out with her into the spring-scented evening.

'I'd like you to know that tonight has been real special for me, Glory,' he said as they stopped in the shallow of a wall. 'Wanna know a secret? This is the first time *I've* been to one of those Saturday dances, too. Some o' the other gals, they scare the pants off me. They're so – well, I guess they're only out for what they can get. You're not like that.'

'I should hope not,' Gloria said indignantly. 'They're the ones who get us all a bad name.'

He shook his head. 'Not that I blame them. You folks have had a real tough time, putting up with the bombing, the shortages and all. And a lot of those guys are no angels, I c'n tell you. They're out for what *they* can get too – if you know what I mean.'

Gloria nodded. 'Oh, I do.'

'But you and me – we're two of a kind, Glory. I could tell that right off.' He slipped an arm around her waist and drew her closer. 'I guess you know I brought you out here to kiss you good night. You're not gonna get mad at me, are you?'

'Well . . . I . . .' But Billy wasn't going to wait for an answer. Drawing her close he kissed her, gently at first, then deeper and more searchingly, gently probing her lips apart with his tongue. Gloria had never liked this kind of kissing before but she found to her surprise that with Billy she was stirred into an instinctive response. Although she couldn't have said in what way, Billy was different from all the other men she had met. Everything about him spoke of sincerity. Somehow she knew that he wasn't just trying to impress. He meant what he said.

She allowed her arms to creep around his neck and her head to fall back, relaxing in his arms and enjoying his kisses, but when his fingers began to unfasten the buttons of her coat she stiffened and drew back. He stopped at once and looked anxiously into her eyes.

'I'm sorry, baby.'

Gloria felt her throat tighten. 'No, *I'm* sorry, Billy. It isn't that I don't like – don't trust you. It's . . .'

'I know. You don't have to explain.' He drew her gently to him and kissed her. 'We'll play it by ear, honey. I know you got hurt before. I understand.'

And somehow Gloria knew that he did. She put her arms around his waist and laid her head against his chest. 'Not many men are so understanding,' she whispered. 'Once most of them know I've got a kid they think I'm fair game. They only want me for –' He stopped the words with a finger against her lips.

'Hush. Don't say things like that, honey. Look, I told you; back home I got two sisters and a mom. I hate the way some guys talk. It makes me want to throw up sometimes, just listening to them. I want you to know that I'm not like that.'

'I know you're not, Billy. I wouldn't be here now if I didn't know that.' She looked at him. 'But, look, I think you should know something. I'm older – a lot older than you. I'm twenty-nine.'

He smiled. 'So what?'

'So – how old are you, Billy?'

He nuzzled her neck and gave her earlobe a playful little bite. 'Hey, didn't your mom ever tell you, never ask a gentleman his age?' He chuckled, then grew serious. 'This is wartime, Glory. Years don't mean a thing in wartime, 'cos none of us knows how few we might have left. It's what we *feel* and what we can give each other – that's what's important.'

The increasing babble of assembled voices down by the gate told them it was time for the transport taking the girls back to Boothley to depart. Billy and Gloria walked across the compound hand in hand and he helped her up into the crowded lorry.

'Say, you will come again next week, won't you?' he called.

She bit her lip, suddenly remembering. 'Oh – I can't next week. I promised to go to London to see Ma and Pa.'

'I'll call you,' he shouted. 'At that hostel place where you hang out. I'll call you Wednesday night – okay?'

'Yes, all right – okay.' The gates opened and the lorry revved up and moved away. Gloria waved until she couldn't see him any more. Jane edged up to her in the semi-darkness.

'Well, did you have a good time after all?'

Gloria smiled dreamily. 'Oh, yes. Did you?'

Jane smiled. 'Smashing. I met this chap – I mean *guy*.' She giggled. 'Sounds funny, doesn't it? His name is Chuck. That's Charlie in our language. He's fun and ever so handsome.' She nudged Gloria. 'Here – what about that supper, then? I think I'll come again. Will you?'

'Yes,' Gloria said dreamily. *What we feel and what we can give each other, that's what's important*. Billy's words echoed inside her head. 'Yes, I think I'll be coming again,' she replied, but she didn't add that it wasn't the buffet supper she looked forward to.

'I suppose you think you're going to get the leading part in the play now?'

Linda Freeman, her hands on her bony hips, challenged Shirley as they changed for gym in the cloakroom. 'Just because you were in that soppy film you think you're Vivien Leigh or someone. Well, I can tell you, you've got another think coming. You weren't all that good, Shirley Rayner. In fact some people are saying you were rotten in it.'

Ever since word had gone round the school that Shirley Rayner was the girl who played the leading part in *Jenny and Joan*, she'd had to put up with every kind of teasing, from good-natured ragging to the spiteful baiting that Linda Freeman never seemed to tire of. Linda was a year older and had achieved some acclaim the previous year when she had played the part of Viola in the school's production of *Twelfth Night*. The thought of Shirley, a first-year girl, posing a serious threat to her prospect of pulling off another success was more than she could bear.

Shirley hitched up her navy-blue gym knickers and gave Linda a look of pure scorn. 'Tony Darrent said I was brilliant,' she said. 'And *he* should know better than a bunch of silly girls like you.' She sniffed disdainfully. 'If you want to act in the school play, you're welcome to it,' she added, with a disdainful toss of her auburn curls.

198

Linda changed tactics. 'Oh, I see, it's not good enough for *you* now you're a film star, is it?' She stood fixing her rival with a steely glint in her green eyes. 'So when is Tony Darrent going to make you his leading lady then, eh?' She laughed shortly. 'Some chance, I *don't* think.'

'Might be sooner than you think,' Shirley said rashly, her chin jutting. 'Then you'll laugh the other side of your silly face, Linda Freeman.'

'I see. So you wouldn't be in the school play if they paid you, I s'pose?'

'I'd be in it if I was asked,' Shirley said nonchalantly. 'Even if you are only a bunch of amateurs.'

'*Amateurs*, are we? Just wait till Miss Halgarth hears *that*.'

'Are you coming, Shirley?' Imogen, who had been listening, intervened quietly. 'Miss Green will be cross if we're late.'

Linda turned on her heel and flounced off, while Shirley pulled a face at her retreating back. 'Stuck-up cow,' she said, reverting to her native cockney. 'Thinks she's the bee's knees just because she was in last year's tatty old play.' She turned to her friend. 'Know what she said? She said that some people are saying I was rotten in *Jenny and Joan*. Dirty little liar.'

Imogen shrugged. 'Well, Daddy always says you can't please everyone,' she said blandly.

Shirley stared at her indignantly. 'What do you mean? I *was* good, wasn't I?' She looked into her friend's face, her confidence slipping a little.

'Of course you were. Everyone said so. But it doesn't do to brag about it. Nothing's worth having people hate you. I learned that.'

'*Who* hates me?' Shirley said, stopping dead in her tracks.

'Well, Linda for a start. And you only make it worse, arguing with her like that.'

'It's just jealousy,' Shirley protested. 'I can't help that, can I?'

'Perhaps not. It's the way you are with them, though,' Imogen pointed out. 'If you just laughed it off they'd soon get fed up and stop. They don't tease me.'

'You didn't have the leading part,' Shirley snapped.

'*See*? That's exactly what I mean.' Imogen touched Shirley's arm. 'Look, I was just like that once. Remember what a rotten time I gave you when you first came to Houlton? It was all because I thought I was better than anyone else. And it was *you* who taught me how silly I was to cut myself off from everyone.'

Shirley was silent. She felt suddenly deflated. She had to stand up for herself. She had always done that, it was her nature. But surely she wasn't behaving in the unbearable way that Imogen had – *was* she?

'Remember how the other kids at the village school used to rag me?' Imogen reminded her. 'And how you stuck up for me and made them let me join in at playtime? I was ashamed then, Shirl, because I knew I didn't deserve it. They'd have hated me for ever if it hadn't been for you. That's why I'm telling you this now.'

Shirley's throat tightened. 'I know. I don't really care what loopy Linda says. I don't want to be in the silly play anyway.'

Imogen peered into her friend's downcast face. 'You know you do, really. Come on, cheer up, misery. Miss Green'll skin us both alive if we don't get a move on.'

The school play was to be *A Midsummer-Night's Dream* and the auditions were to be held on the following Friday afternoon after school. The play was to be put on at the end of the summer term, performed in the open in the school grounds. Later that evening after tea, as Shirley was going upstairs, Imogen called out to her from her father's study.

'Hey, Shirl! Come and look at this.'

Shirley went into the oak-panelled room and saw that Imogen was reading a thick leather-bound book she had taken from one of the bookshelves.

'We're not supposed to touch things in here,' she said. 'What's that book?'

'It's Shakespeare,' Imogen said. 'I thought I'd have a look at the play they're going to do at school.' She looked up at Shirley, her eyes shining. 'There are lots of good parts in it. Let's take it upstairs and read it. Daddy won't mind. There might be a part you'd fancy auditioning for on Friday.'

Shirley pulled a face. 'Shakespeare's stuffy, isn't it?'

'No, not a bit. Daddy used to read it to me sometimes, when I was home for the holidays before the war. There are lots of funny bits in this one. They put it on at my old school,' she said. 'I was too young to be in it that time, but I enjoyed it because there are fairies in it.' She closed the book and looked at Shirley, excitement glinting in her eyes. 'What do you say we have a go at the auditions, Shirl? I can just see you as Puck.'

Her enthusiasm was infectious and Shirley nodded. 'Okay, I will if you will. It might be a laugh. What'll you try for, Imo?'

Imogen smiled ruefully. 'I'd like to play Titania, the fairy queen, if only I wasn't so ugly.'

Shirley stared at her indignantly. 'You're *not* ugly. Whatever makes you say that?'

Imogen tugged at one her thick brown plaits. 'Mummy thinks I am. I've heard her say so lots of times.'

'Well, *I* don't. With your specs off and your hair loose you look smashing.' She grasped her friend's hand. 'Come on, let's see.'

Upstairs in Imogen's bedroom Shirley unplaited her friend's hair and brushed it loose till it hung in shining waves over her shoulders, then she carefully removed the ugly wire-framed glasses and stood back to study her friend thoughtfully. 'Can you see to read without them?'

Imogen picked up the book and held it in front of her, blinking a little as she stared at the words. 'Not as well as I can with them, but it's not too bad.'

'You've got really nice eyes,' Shirley said, studying her. 'No one can see them properly behind those specs. Tell you what – do you think you could learn some of the words for when we do the audition? Then you needn't wear them.'

Imogen brightened. 'That's a good idea.'

With Shirley's help Imogen worked hard and by Friday she was word-perfect in Titania's wakening scene. Miss Halgarth, the English mistress, was impressed by the work the child had put into memorising her lines, and even more impressed at the improvement in her looks without the ugly spectacles. It was the first time she had seen her without her glasses and with her hair loose. With make-up and lighting she could look quite striking as Titania, she had just the right kind of elfin appeal. And after all, she reminded herself, the child was the daughter of a well-known actor and actress. If Imogen was in the play it was possible that the Darrents might even grace the opening night with their presence. If the word were to be discreetly passed round that Tony Darrent and Leonie Swann were to be there, it would be a big draw. Weighing up all the pros and cons, Miss Halgarth decided to give the part to Imogen. Linda Freeman got the part of Puck – Shirley, to everyone's surprise and her chagrin, was given the part of Bottom the weaver.

'Lots of hard work from now on, girls,' Miss Halgarth said from the platform, clapping her hands to silence the babble of excited voices. 'It's a very ambitious project and I want this to be our best performance yet. It may mean coming into school when you'd rather be out playing so I hope you're all quite sure you want to be in it.'

Imogen felt for Shirley's hand and squeezed it. 'I'm sure,' she whispered. 'Are you?'

Shirley pulled a face. 'I don't know. I never thought I'd be playing someone called *Bottom*. Apart from anything else, he's a feller.'

'It was because you read the part so well in the scene with me,' Imogen told her. 'It means we'll be acting together.'

'But I'll have to wear a donkey's head,' Shirley protested.

'Not all the time.' Imogen laughed. 'Oh, come on, Shirl! It's going to be such fun.'

Shirley grinned in spite of herself. 'Oh, well, there are some funny bits in it. It'll be a laugh, I s'pose.'

* * *

'A *Yank*, did you say?' Ma turned from the gas stove to stare incredulously at Gloria. 'I never thought a daughter of mine'd stoop to that kind of behaviour.'

'What kind of behaviour, Ma? Billy's a nice bloke. I haven't done anything wrong.'

Ma snorted in disbelief. 'That's as may be,' she said, returning to the dried-egg Welsh rarebit she was making for tea. 'It's not what people'll think when they sees you with 'im, though. I've seen the way these gels flaunt themselves with the Yanks. Short skirts an' made up like dog's dinners – brazen as you please. Need their arses tannin' if you asks me. If I was their mothers I'd do it for 'em.' She heaved a sigh. 'There's only one way for it all to end. Only after one thing, them Yanks. They'll be laughin' on the other side o' their painted faces when they finds themselves in the club.'

'Billy is a nice feller from a good hard-working family,' Gloria told her mother patiently. 'I'd've brought him home with me to meet you and Pa this weekend, only he couldn't get a pass. So I thought I might bring him when Shirl and me come at Easter.'

Ma sniffed. 'Well, I dunno, I'm sure. We'll 'ave to see about that. I'm not sure as your pa'll 'ave a Yank in the house after some of the tales we've been hearin'.'

Gloria said nothing. They both knew perfectly well that Pa would do exactly as Ma said in the end. He always did. 'Well, will you ask him?' she said at last. 'I know you'll both like Billy. He's ever so homesick and I – well, I said I'd sort of share you with him.'

'*Share us*?' Ma's eyebrows shot up. 'What a funny thing to say – without so much as a by-your-leave, too.' She looked at her daughter, her hands on her hips. 'I dunno about you, our Gloria. First it's a feller what's married, then that there Tony Darrent you had such a pash on. Now it's some Yank. Why can't you find yourself a feller what's *normal*?'

'Billy *is* normal. He's just like anyone else, you'll see. His dad owns a garage and he's got a mum and two sisters. He's not like some of those you've heard tales about, Ma, honest. If he was I wouldn't go out with him.'

Ma sniffed loudly. 'I'm not so sure about that. And how long've you known this walkin' miracle, may I ask?'

'A few weeks.' Gloria felt that the slight exaggeration was justified. She felt she'd known Billy for years, even though they'd only spoken twice and been together on that one evening.

He'd telephoned as he promised the previous Wednesday evening and, when she'd tentatively suggested that he might accompany her to London at the weekend, the disappointment in his voice had been plain to hear.

'Aw, Glory – I'd love to have gone with you, but there'll be no passes this weekend.'

A tiny stab of fear pierced Gloria's heart. 'Does that mean you're flying?'

'Can't talk about that, baby. You know the score.'

'Sorry. I shouldn't have asked.'

'But if you were to ask me again some time . . .'

'How about Whitsun?' Gloria asked. 'I'm hoping to take Shirl with me then. We could all go.'

'Hey, that'd be just dandy. C'n I let you know nearer the time?'

'Of course.'

'Being with you was just great last Saturday, honey,' he said quietly.

'I enjoyed it too.' She had lowered her voice and glanced around the crowded corridor to see if anyone was listening.

'I can't wait to see you again. How about the Saturday after next? Think you c'n make it to the dance?'

'I'll try.'

'Gee, honey, I sure hope you can. I miss you.'

'I . . . miss you too.'

'Don't sit there moonin'. Get a cloth and dry up some o' them saucepans.'

Jerked rudely out of her reverie, Gloria jumped up from the chair and began to help her mother, who glanced speculatively at her.

'I 'ope you ain't fallen for this Yank.'

'What? Oh, no. Nothing as soppy as that.'

'I should 'ope not. Don't want you slopin' orf to America. What would young Shirl make o' that?'

Gloria smiled. 'Shirl's growing up quick, Ma. Wait till you see how tall she is.'

Ma put the toast in the oven to keep warm and looked at Gloria. 'I been meanin' to 'ave a talk with you about Shirl,' she said. 'Pa's not the man he was, you know. The war and the ARP's taken it out of 'im somethin' shockin'. In another eighteen months or so Shirl'll be leavin' school. It's quieter 'ere now, so how'd you feel about her comin' 'ome to giv me an 'and in the shop so's 'e can take things easy?'

Gloria stared at her mother, horrified. 'Shirl won't be leaving school for *years* yet, Ma. She won a scholarship to the high school, remember?'

'But that don't mean she can't leave at fourteen.'

'No – but she *isn't*. I want her to go on and get all the education she can. She can stay at that school till she's seventeen, take her school certificate and matriculation – maybe go on to college. University, even.'

Ma stared at Gloria. '*University*? What's the good o' that to a kid like Shirl? Pretty girl like 'er'll be wantin' to get married before she's twenty. What good'll all that book learnin' be to 'er then?'

'But at least I want her to have the choice, Ma. I want her to have the chances I never had. She's got the opportunity now and she's bright. She can do it.'

But Ma was shaking her head, lips pursed. 'All mothers want the best for their kids,' she said. 'But you've got to cut your coat accordin' to your cloth.' She sniffed. 'Anyway, in the end it's what *they* thinks is best as counts. You're livin' proof of that, our Glor.'

'But that's what I mean, Ma. I don't want her making the same mistakes as I did.'

'You don't want 'er gettin' ideas above 'er station either, do you?' Ma went on. '*That* only ends in tears.'

'Shirley's clever, though. She can make something of herself if –'

'If you ask me, livin' with them Darrents has turned 'er 'ead.' Ma opened a drawer and took out a handful of cutlery. 'All this actin' in films and livin' the kind of life she ain't never been brought up to.' Her words were punctuated by the angry clatter of knives and forks as she flung them round the table. 'It's doin' the girl no favours, you mark my words.'

'But Ma . . .'

'No,' Ma turned to face her, red-faced. 'You let 'er leave school soon's she can an' come 'ome. Pa and me'll see 'er right. An' when we retires there'll be a nice little business 'ere for both o' you. Your Pa an' me've worked 'ard for this business all our lives. It may not be much but it'll give you an' Shirl more security than all your book learnin'. You see if it don't.'

Gloria was about to tell her mother of the money she was saving for after the war and the new opportunity-filled life that awaited them, but one look at her mother's face told her that there was no point in complicating the issue further. She sighed. 'Eighteen months is a long time, Ma. Let's just wait and see, shall we?' She looked up hopefully. 'And what about this Whitsun? Can I bring Billy home with me – if he can get a pass, that is?'

Ma shrugged her shoulders impatiently as she applied herself to dishing up the meal. 'Oh, all right then, if you must. But 'e'll 'ave to take us as 'e finds us. You c'n tell 'im there's no standin' on ceremony in Angel Row, Yanks or no Yanks.'

Although it was her parents' reaction to Billy that Gloria worried about, it turned out to be Shirley who caused her the most anxiety. Shirley had met Billy for the first time several weeks earlier when Gloria brought him to Houlton for a visit. From the moment they met she had made no effort to hide her resentment. He had arrived with gifts for everyone. Chocolates for Gloria, canned fruit and ham for Molly and cigarettes for Jim. When he offered the two girls candy bars and chewing gum, Imogen accepted delightedly, but Shirley shook her head.

'No, thank you. I'm not allowed to take sweets from strangers.'

Gloria stared at her in horror. 'Shirl! Don't be so rude. Billy's not a stranger, he's a friend.'

But Billy only laughed. 'I'm sure we'll get along just fine when we've had a chance to get to know each other. I'll just leave the candy here on the table for now,' he said tactfully.

When they were alone, Gloria took Shirley to task about her bad behaviour. 'What did you want to be rude to Billy like that for? I didn't know where to look.'

Shirley pouted. 'I thought it was going to be just you and me this weekend. And now you say he's coming home with us at Whitsun.' She pulled a face. 'Why do we have to have *him* tagging along?'

Angered, Gloria lashed out: 'Because I want him to come, that's why. And you can always stop here if you don't like it. You don't *have* to come with us. Half the time you've got no time for Ma and Pa any more anyway.'

Shirley was stung. Gloria never used to speak to her like that before she met this Yank. She was different since he had come along; always talking about the dances she'd been to and showing off the nylon stockings and perfume this Billy person kept giving her. Shirley knew all about the Yanks. The older girls at school often gathered in little knots in the cloakroom talking quietly and giggling together. When the younger girls tried to listen they shooed them away, but Shirley knew what they were talking about. Some of them had American boyfriends and they liked to compare notes and discuss what had happened when they went out with them. Catching their half-smothered snatches of conversation made her feel funny inside – a strange feeling she didn't understand, halfway between resentment and disapproval, with a good sprinkling of envy mixed in, though she refused to acknowledge that bit. Twelve was a rotten age, she decided. She wasn't a child any more. She understood a good deal more than the grown-ups thought she did. And yet she wasn't properly grown-up either. Now Gloria – her own mother – had one of these exotic creatures to show off and Shirley was determined that she wasn't going to be won over with packets of chocolate and chewing gum. Just because they had so much of everything they thought they could *make* everyone like them. Well, she wasn't going to be a pushover like all the rest. Even if Nanny and Jim fell over themselves to be nice to him, *she* wasn't going to, so there.

Billy had a weekend pass at Whitsun and the three of them travelled up to London together on Friday morning. To Shirley, who hadn't been home for some time, Angel Row looked down at heel and very much the worse for wear. There were glaring gaps in the street where some of the houses, damaged beyond repair, had been demolished. Some of the bomb sites were littered with piles of rubble, and the houses that still stood were shored up and looked frail and precarious. But though battle-scarred, the Rayners' greengrocery and fruiterer's shop was open for business as usual. The sign above the shop was faded and the woodwork was blistered and sadly in need of a coat of paint. But the produce in the window looked as fresh and appetising as ever, thanks to Pa's early-morning visits 'up the market' in Covent Garden. He never bought anything but the best and if there were any oranges or lemons about it was always Rayner's who had them in first.

In spite of her initial disapproval, Ma had been on her knees scrubbing for days and she had the place shining like a new pin for Billy's visit. Shirley and Gloria were to have their old room and Billy was to sleep on the put-you-up in the parlour. When Billy unloaded his bulging grip onto the kitchen table, Ma's eyes were round with disbelief.

'Now then, young feller, I'm not sure I c'n accept all this stuff,' she said warily. She picked up a tin of yellow cling peaches and stared at the label. 'Blimey, I ain't seen these for years; corned beef nor ham neither.'

Billy smiled. 'You're more than welcome to them, ma'am. Us GIs can't accept hospitality without taking along our share. Specially when we know how short of stuff you are.'

Ma bridled proudly. 'We manage all right. You don't want to bother yourself about us.' Her features softened as her eyes fell on the peaches again. 'Still – if you're sure.

It'd be a pity to waste it when you've brought it all this way.'

Shirley stood by the door. So far no one had even noticed her. As usual everyone was making a fuss of Billy. She pushed rudely past him. 'Did you see my film, Ma? Did you think I was good?'

'I'm not sure that I did, miss,' Ma said, looking down her nose. 'What was they thinkin' about, lettin' you be seen in them scruffy clothes at the beginning? I sat there ashamed. I don't mind tellin' you. When you went from 'ere in '39 you was as smart as paint and pretty's a picture.'

'It was only a film, Ma,' Gloria put in. 'And she was smart at the end of it in her school uniform.'

'Mmm – 'andsome is as 'andsome does,' Ma replied. 'We'll 'ave to see what goin' to a posh school and actin' in a film's done to your manners, won't we, my gel?'

Billy chuckled and gave Shirley a playful nudge. She glowered up at him crossly, her face scarlet. How could Ma embarrass her like that in front of *him*? Her resentment of him deepened to out-and-out dislike.

It was the next day that Ma started throwing out hints about leaving school and coming home to help in the shop. Shirley was horrified. Later, when she was alone with Gloria in the room they shared, she asked her about it.

'She won't really make me, will she, Glor?' she asked anxiously. 'You know I want to be on the stage when I leave. Tony says I'm a natural actress.'

'You don't want to take too much notice of what Tony Darrent says,' Gloria warned. 'He means well, I'm sure, but when he gets carried away with his filming he doesn't think. He's probably forgotten all about it by now.'

'Even if he has, *I* haven't,' Shirley said. 'As soon as I'm fourteen I'm going to leave school and get a job on the stage somewhere.'

'Oh no, you're not, my girl. You're going to stay on and take your school certificate. You've got a chance I never had and I'm going to make good and sure you take it. If you're not coming home to help Ma, then you're going on with your education and that's flat.'

Shocked, Shirley stared at her mother. Never in her life before had Gloria laid down the law to her like this. Here she was, held fast between two options, neither of which appealed to her one little bit. None of it would have happened, she was quite convinced, if it hadn't been for that Billy.

That evening Billy took Gloria Up West to Rainbow Corner, the American Forces Club he had been telling her about just off Leicester Square. Once again Shirley was to be left out. She was too young, she was told. Instead she had to be content to watch Gloria getting all dressed up. She took hours over her hair, pinning it up high in front to fall in curls to her shoulders at the back. It was the latest fashion and Shirley watched enviously, wishing she could do hers like that too.

'Where are we going tomorrow, Glor?' she asked wistfully. 'We haven't done anything together yet.'

Gloria turned from the mirror, her teeth catching her lower lip as she gazed remorsefully at her daughter. She and Shirl had done nothing but fall out this weekend. If only she'd try and make herself more pleasant to Billy. Heaven knows he tried hard enough to win her round.

'I know. I'm sorry, love. I'll try and bring you back something nice tonight. Billy says they have lovely doughnuts at the club. Like some of those?'

'No thanks.' Shirley shook her head, picking at a loose thread in the bedspread. 'I just want us to be together,' she said. 'Like we used to be.'

Gloria crossed the room and enveloped her in a perfumed hug. 'We will, love, I promise. What do you say we all go up to Hampstead Heath tomorrow? It won't be like it used to be before the war, but it'd still be nice. And Billy's never been there.'

'All right.' Billy, Billy – why was it always what Billy'd like?

Shirley sat in the kitchen with her grandparents downstairs after Gloria and Billy had gone. They listened to *In Town Tonight* on the wireless and later *With Love from Leonie* was on. Pa looked at her.

'She's got a good voice, I'll give 'er that,' he said, relighting his pipe. 'Not a patch on good old Marie Lloyd, o' course, but then no one ever will be, if you ask me.' He puffed till the pipe was well alight. 'Nice to you, is she – this Leonie?'

'She's all right,' Shirley said moodily. 'We don't see much of her, though. I like Tony best. He says I'm a natural actress. That's why I want to go on the stage.'

Ma and Pa exchanged meaningful looks. The sooner the child could be got away from influence like that, the better, Ma's eyes said.

After her favourite Saturday-night programme, *Music Hall*, was over, Shirley said good night to her grandparents and went upstairs. She didn't go straight to bed but amused herself by trying on some of Gloria's clothes and experimenting with her make-up. Then, climbing on a chair, she reached the top of the wardrobe and took down a selection of the magazines Gloria had collected over the years: *Picturegoer* and *Film Review* as well as *Vogue* and other fashion magazines. Shirley never tired of reading about the stars, their private lives and how their careers had started. Getting undressed and slipping into bed, she settled down to read, determined not to let herself fall asleep until Gloria got home.

They came home from Rainbow Corner in a taxi. It was amazing how easily Americans managed to get one. It seemed they only had to snap their fingers and a cab would appear out of nowhere, as if by magic. In the back seat Billy drew her close.

'Enjoy the evening, honey?'

'Oh, yes.' Gloria snuggled up to him in the darkness. Her head was still spinning with the gaiety of the club, the music, the dancing – she was getting quite good at jitter-bugging now – and the lavish food and drink. The club had been filled to bursting with glamorous people.

'I had a lovely time. I'm having a smashing weekend.' She glanced up at him apprehensively. 'I'm sorry about Shirl, though, I don't know what's come over her. She's usually such a good kid.'

211

Billy smiled. 'Forget it, honey. I guess she's a little bit jealous. After all, she's never had to share you with anyone yet, has she?'

'I suppose not, but still . . .'

'Shhh. Don't give it another thought. I can think of better things to talk about.' Billy's mouth covered hers and for the next few minutes she did indeed forget Shirley – and everything else too.

'Your mom and pop have been really great to me, Glory,' he said, settling her head on his shoulder. 'If it hadn't been for you and your family I'd have been dreadful homesick this weekend – my first Whitsun away from home.'

'I'm glad we've helped.'

'Helped? You've more than just helped, all of you. Even Shirl reminds me of home – fighting with my kid sister.' He looked down at her. 'Glory, I guess you know by now that I've fallen in love with you?' When she was silent he drew his head back to look into her eyes. 'Does that shock you?'

Her eyes glistened in the dimness. 'Shock me? Oh no, Billy. It's just – I don't know what to say.'

'Well, does it make you unhappy?'

'Oh, *no*.'

He cupped her chin and tipped her face up to his. 'Is it too much to hope that you might love me back – just a little bit?'

'Of course I love you, Billy.' She reached up to kiss him. 'It's just that I never thought I'd trust anyone enough to say that again.'

He kissed her. 'I wish I could get to see you more often, Glory,' he said. 'Just the two of us, I mean. We never really get any time alone, do we?'

For a long moment she looked at him. 'There's something I haven't told you, Billy.'

His eyes looked into hers, anxiously. 'Uh-oh. Is it something bad?'

She laughed. 'No. A while ago I bought a little cottage. I'd saved some money and got the chance to buy it cheap.

212

It's furnished and everything. I had hoped that Shirl and me'd live there together, but I should have thought . . . She's better off where she is at the moment.' She paused, looking at him shyly. 'I was going to ask Jane, my friend, to come and live in it with me, but that wouldn't really work either.' She moistened her suddenly dry lips. 'At – at weekends . . . when you . . . when we were both free, we could . . .'

He pulled her close and she felt his breath warm against her ear as he asked: 'Oh, honey – are you saying what I think you're saying?'

'It's only an idea,' she said. 'Only if you want to.'

'If I *want* to?' He held her away from him to look searchingly at her. 'Wait a minute. Are you sure it's what *you* want?'

She frowned. 'I wouldn't want you to think I was being forward – or cheap.'

'Oh, Glory, you could never be either of those. Don't ever say a thing like that again. I told you, I love you.'

'And I love you, Billy. If I didn't I'd . . .'

'I know, honey. I know.' He looked into her eyes. 'Look, we could get engaged if you like. I could buy you a ring.'

She shook her head. 'No. Let's just keep it to ourselves for now – our secret.'

He smiled. 'Okay, honey, just as you say. But some day, when the war is over, we'll get married, eh?'

'That would be lovely, Billy.'

'And I'll take you back home to Colorado – Shirley too.'

She buried her head against his shoulder. He was so sweet, so good to her. Billy might not be Tony Darrent, but he was here, he loved her and made her feel cherished and cared for. Suddenly everything that had ever worried her – Ma and Pa, Shirl, the cottage, and what was going to happen to them after the war – faded into insignificance. When the war ended she would marry Billy and everything would fall miraculously into place. It all seemed so simple.

It was half-past one when she crept into the little room she shared with Shirley. She undressed as quietly as she could and slipped carefully into bed beside her daughter to lie staring at the ceiling, her head full of dreams. With the blackout curtains drawn back, the room seemed to be lit by a million stars. It was a magic kind of a night – a night she'd remember for the rest of her life.

Suddenly there was a movement beside her.

'Glor, I'm still awake,' Shirley whispered. 'I've been waiting for you.'

Gloria turned to look at her daughter. 'Do you know what the time is? You should be asleep.'

'I've been reading some of your film magazines, Glor, and I've been thinking. There are special schools where you can go to learn about acting. If I stay on at the high school for School Cert like you want, can I go to one of them instead of college?'

Gloria turned over, sleep tugging at her eyelids. 'I suppose we could look into it,' she said. She could afford to be indulgent. After all, by the time Shirl left school they'd probably be getting ready to leave for America.

Chapter Ten

A sunbeam penetrated a chink in the curtains to tease Gloria's closed eyelids. She opened them and turned her head to look at the clock on the bedside table. It was only five o'clock. For a moment she lay savouring the feeling of languor. It was so warm and comfortable here in bed at Rook Cottage. No need to get up for hours yet.

Turning her head on the pillow, she looked at Billy. In repose, with his dark hair tousled and his mouth relaxed and soft, he looked so young. If it weren't for the morning stubble that darkened his jaw, he would look like a little boy. She longed to take him in her arms and hold him there safely till the war was over. Sometimes she felt that he, and so many others like him, had been thrust into manhood before their time.

The past year had been the happiest she had ever known. Ever since last spring she and Billy had spent every free minute here at Rook Cottage. It never seemed to matter to them that they had to light oil lamps and fires through the winter and draw all the water they needed from the well. They were ecstatically happy together. They would light the fire in the range to cook the little treats that Billy brought with him from the base, sharing the chores and the washing-up. It was all such fun – an adventure. They felt like two children playing house.

When Molly first heard about the cottage Gloria had bought, she unearthed some discarded curtains from the attic in Longueville Hall and gave them to her to make over for her new home. She thought it was a pity that

Shirley couldn't share it with her yet, but she agreed that the cottage was a good buy and would be something for them both to look forward to for after the war.

'It wouldn't really be practical for you to try and live there yet,' she told Gloria. 'But there's no reason why you shouldn't start making it nice.' She knew that Gloria spent some weekends there, but no one knew that Billy often joined her. Sometimes Gloria asked herself why she didn't feel guilty about it. But being with Billy, sharing a bed with him and loving him felt like the most natural thing in the world, so what was there to feel guilty about? They were totally committed to one another and as soon as the war ended they would be married. It was no one's business but theirs, she told herself.

The curtains Molly had given her provided several yards of sound, unfaded material. Gloria had made pink brocade curtains and a matching bedspread for the bedroom and a warm pair in wine-red velvet for the parlour. In the winter she and Billy had been so cosy in front of the fire. She would tell Billy tales of her childhood in the East End and he would describe Colorado and his family, planning the life they would share there after the war. Later they would snuggle up together in the big feather bed in the room above. In the warmth and delight of their love and their dreams for the future, the war and all its horrors seemed a million miles away.

Now that spring had come again, they were working on the garden; tidying and planting it for summer. Gloria had never had a garden before and she was planning to have all the old-fashioned flowers – cornflowers and holly-hocks, foxgloves and marigolds – looking forward to the riot of colour and perfume they would create.

The one thing she did feel guilty about was not spending more time with Shirley, but the child hardly seemed to notice her absence. She and Imogen were working on their School Certificate courses now and even though the examination was two years away they always seemed to be up to their ears in homework.

Playing Titania in *A Midsummer-Night's Dream* had finally made up Imogen's mind for her. She was to go to

RADA after school and study drama, hoping for a career as a classical actress. Shirley had taken it for granted that she would go too and this had caused a slight cloud to loom on Gloria's horizon. She hadn't yet mentioned to Shirley her intention of going to America once the war was over to marry Billy. She hadn't mentioned it to her mother either. But she was pretty sure that neither of them would receive the news well.

Billy opened his eyes and looked at her. 'Hi,' he said sleepily.

'Hi.' She slipped her arms around him. 'It's all right, it's early yet, only half-past five. No need to get up.'

'Mmm, good.' He settled himself more comfortably, pulling her close.

'Do you want a cup of coffee or anything?'

'I'd rather have the "or anything".' He laughed softly and began to kiss her.

As always their lovemaking was slow and tender, but no less passionate for that. Billy had known instinctively right from the first time just how to arouse her. Gently caressing her and covering her in tiny kisses, he would wait till he heard her breathing alter and felt the quickening of her heartbeat. He took his time, making sure that she received as much pleasure as she gave him. When he felt her climax approaching he hastened his own so that they reached the height of their passion together. Afterwards he lay holding her quietly till their breathing returned to normal.

'Honey,' he now said. 'Look, I've been putting off telling you, but this might be our last time at Rook Cottage for a while.'

Her eyes opened wide with alarm as she looked at him. 'Why?'

He shook his head. 'There's a buzz on. I can't say more.'

'An exercise?' she asked fearfully. 'Or the real thing?'

He pulled her close and buried her face in his neck. 'Honey, you know better than to ask questions like that.'

'I know, but . . . Oh, Billy, I get so scared sometimes.'

'Don't be. I've told you and now we won't mention it again. We'll make the most of what time we do have.' He sat up and stretched out his arms. 'Hey, it looks like it's gonna be a great day out there. Suppose we get up and make a start on that gardening?'

They ate breakfast together in the kitchen with the back door open so that they could hear the sound of the birds. Billy had taught her how to make the little pancakes that he called 'biscuits' for breakfast and they enjoyed them now with maple syrup he had brought with him from the mess. But as they ate, Gloria's heart was heavy. She couldn't help thinking about what he had said and wondering anxiously if it had anything to do with the 'second front' that everyone was talking about. The rumour was that it would start any day now. But then people had been saying that for months and everyone was weary with waiting. It was wonderful and exciting to think that the war might soon be over and won, but terrible to contemplate the lives that must inevitably be lost in bringing this about. If she lost Billy now . . . She put the thought from her mind and forced herself to smile at him as she rose and began to clear the table.

'Well, shall we put our wellies on and make a start then?'

It was on the morning of 6 June that Jim ran excitedly out to Molly as she hung out her washing in the kitchen garden.

'Molly, Molly! It's happened, love. It's started at last.'

'What's happened?'

'The second front. Our lads have landed in Normandy. We've invaded. It's the beginning of the end, love. We're going in for the kill at last.'

For the rest of the day he hardly moved from the wireless, till Molly got quite tired of moving him every time he was in her way. 'All those poor boys,' she muttered to herself. 'There'll be more broken-hearted wives and mothers tonight.'

When Shirley and Imogen came home from school they

were full of it too. 'Does this mean the war will soon be over, Jim?' Imogen asked.

Shirley was silent. Last month she'd celebrated her fourteenth birthday. Legally she could leave school this summer. Would the end of the war mean that she would have to go back to London before her education was complete? She couldn't help thinking about what Ma had said about her leaving school to help in the shop and the prospect dismayed her more than she could say.

'Of course it'll take time to finish Gerry off,' Jim said, one ear still on the wireless. 'It won't be over yet a while. I reckon it'll take a good twelve-month to clear up the mess old Hitler's made.'

Shirley heaved a sigh of relief.

That weekend Gloria joined them. She looked tired and pale. When the girls were out of the way she told Molly and Jim: 'Billy's gone. The whole unit went a week ago, but they were all confined to base for days before. Heaven only knows where they're headed. I can only guess.'

'We've got a lot to be grateful to those boys for,' Jim said. 'I knew as soon as they came in with us that we'd be all right. All those raids last year – Munich, Bremen, Berlin and the rest. Those Flying Fortresses must've knocked hell out of them; paid them back for what they've done to us. I know it meant a lot of civilians copped it, poor devils, but they never cared about our folks when they blitzed our cities, did they?'

Molly frowned at him and inclined her head towards Gloria. 'Try not to worry, dear,' she said, patting Gloria's shoulder. 'He'll be all right, I'm sure he will.' Later she scolded her husband: 'Haven't you got any sense, Jim Jarvis? Going on and *on* about bombing and killing when the girl's worried out her wits about the lad. Anyone with half an eye can see how fond of him she is.'

Early next morning Gloria was surprised to be wakened by Shirley slipping into her bed. She smiled. 'Hello, love.'

Shirley reached for her hand. 'You didn't sleep, did you? I heard you walking about.'

'Did I wake you? I'm sorry, love. I went down to make

myself some cocoa.'

Shirley peered into her eyes. 'It's Billy, isn't it?'

'Yes. I can't help thinking about him, wondering if he's all right.'

'You love him, don't you?'

Gloria blinked hard at the tears that threatened. 'Yes. Yes, I do.'

Shirley nodded. 'It's all right, Glor. I understand. I'm not a kid any more. I haven't been very nice to Billy and I'm sorry now. When he comes back . . .'

'We're going to be married, Shirl,' Gloria said. 'And after it's all over we're going back to America to live. You too, of course.'

'To *America*?' Shirley stared at her. 'But what about RADA?'

'I expect there are drama schools there too.'

Shirley's heart sank. Going to America was the last possibility she'd considered. 'What about Ma and Pa? Will they be coming too?'

Gloria shook her head, smiling a little. 'I can't imagine them wanting to, can you?'

'Not really.' She almost said that she didn't want to go either, but she stopped herself just in time. Gloria was worried about Billy. Shirley wasn't a child any more. She had begun to learn that one must sometimes put other people's needs before one's own, so she kept silent. After all, in Jim's opinion the war was going to last for quite some time yet.

'They haven't seen much of us over the last five years, have they?' Gloria was saying. 'It's not as if we've been together a lot. I don't think they'll mind all that much.'

'No.' Privately Shirley knew that they would mind. She was pretty sure that Gloria knew it too, but this wasn't the time to express such doubts. She thought about her grandmother's disapproval of her going on the stage. If she went to live in America with Gloria and Billy, at least she wouldn't be pressured into leaving school to go and work in the shop in Angel Row.

★ ★ ★

Leonie and her producer, Tim Manson, were having a serious discussion in his office on the top floor of Broadcasting House. He had sent for her after receiving a directive from the board of governors.

'They don't feel that sentimentalism is the thing any more,' he told her.

Leonie stared at him. 'Why ever not, for God's sake? What do they want me to sing, "Land of Hope and Glory"?'

Tim winced. He'd known she wouldn't agree with the board's decision. He wasn't sure that he did either. 'It's just that the War Office seems to think it might have a softening effect on the men; make them lose the will to win.'

Leonie snorted derisively. 'I have it on *very* good authority that both the Navy and the Air Force think my songs send the men off in good heart. You've seen some of the letters I've had, Tim. The boys request those songs over and over again: "Silver Wings in the Moonlight", "A Nightingale Sang . . ."'

'I know, sweetie. It's just the bods at the War Office. They think your love songs are bad for the Army's morale.'

'I've never heard such utter rubbish in my life,' Leonie said. 'So what do they suggest? Am I to stop broadcasting?'

Tim smiled wryly. 'I don't think even the War Office would dare to take *With Love from Leonie* off the air. There'd be a riot.'

'What, then?'

'Well, how about including some of the more rousing numbers in our next recording session? There are some quite good ones, you know. Jolly and forward-looking. "I'm Going to Get Lit Up When the Lights Go On in London", for instance.'

Leonie grimaced. 'I'll think about it,' she said reluctantly. 'Maybe I'll go along to the publisher's and see what's new.' She stood up. 'But I'm not promising anything, mind. And I'm not going to sing anything that isn't

221

me. It wouldn't be popular and it wouldn't do my image any good.'

'Of course not, darling. It's for you to decide in the end.' Tim stood up and went with her to the door. 'Are you doing anything for lunch?'

She adjusted her silver fox furs and turned to look at him. 'I'm meeting Tony, as a matter of fact.'

Tim tried hard not to show his surprise. It was rumoured that the Darrents were separating. They hadn't been seen together for months and all the gossips had it that there was an irreconcilable rift between them. 'Oh, he's in town then?'

'Well, I could hardly have lunch with him if he wasn't, could I?'

Leonie's razor-sharp tone made him wonder if she was nervous about the coming meeting. 'Well, have a nice time, then. And do give him my best wishes, won't you? I enjoyed his last film so much.'

'I'll tell him.'

Downstairs Leonie got the doorman to call her a cab. There was just time to go back to the flat and change. When Tony had telephoned asking her to meet him she'd been surprised. Ever since their cataclysmic row they had avoided each other. Their respective work made it difficult for them to meet anyway, but each of them had been careful to ascertain that the other would not be there when they arranged to visit Imogen at Houlton. After his unexpected telephone call it had crossed her mind that he might be about to ask her for a divorce and she had already made up her mind not to give him one – especially not if he intended to remarry. Quite apart from anything else, the publicity would be disastrous for her.

At the flat she changed into her most glamorous dress and a saucy little hat. Then she took them off and replaced them with a classic suit in a rose-pink linen set off by a screen-printed silk scarf. Her hair was freshly shampooed and set and she touched up her make-up with fresh lipstick and mascara. She'd show him that she could look blooming with or without him. She looked at her watch.

There was just time to call a cab and get to the club in comfortable time for their appointment.

She was just picking up her bag and gloves when the doorbell rang. Biting her lip with annoyance, she went to answer it. It was probably the caretaker with a parcel or a message. But when she opened the door her jaw dropped in shocked disbelief. Outside in the corridor stood her brother, Norman.

His sparse hair was plastered down with Brylcreem and he had grown a moth-eaten moustache since she last saw him almost eighteen years ago. He smiled, displaying crooked and nicotine-stained teeth. 'Hello, Eileen.'

'What do you want?' Leonie's heart was thudding with apprehension. It was almost a year since she had written the letter to Norman telling him she was on to his deception and warning him not to contact her again. Since then she had heard nothing and had quite thought that she'd dealt satisfactorily with the matter.

'Aren't you going to ask me in, our Eileen, after I've come all this way to see you?' Norman's whining nasal voice with its thick Birmingham accent grated on her raw nerves like a steel file. She was aware of the lift doors opening and the voice of her next-door neighbour speaking to a companion as she got out. Any second now they would come round the corner and run slap into Norman. Holding the door open, she said quickly: 'You'd better come in.'

In the hall Norman smiled at her again. 'Well now, isn't this nice?'

'Why are you here and what do you want?' Leonie snapped. 'I'm going out and I haven't got long, so you'd better make it quick.'

To her intense annoyance he ambled into the drawing room, looking around him with interest as he went. 'Nice place you've got here, Eileen. Must have cost you a bob or two, all this fancy stuff.'

'That's none of your business. Look, I told you; I'm going out.'

With maddening nonchalance Norman settled himself in an armchair, took out a tin in which he carried home-rolled cigarettes, and lit one up before looking at her. 'Oh, *dear*. Is that the way to treat your long-lost brother? I'll have you know it cost me thirty-five bob to come down to London to see you.'

Leonie wrinkled her nose at the acrid odour of the cheap tobacco. 'I don't remember asking you to come, actually,' she told him acidly.

'Oh, don't you – *actually*?' Norman mimicked her voice. 'Maybe not, but I'm here now so p'raps you'd better hear what I've got to say.' He picked a shred of tobacco from his lip and flicked it across the room.

'Then get on and say it.' Leonie looked pointedly at her watch. 'Come to the point, Norman. My husband is picking me up any second now. I don't think he's going to be very pleased to find you here.'

'Your husband, eh? I'd like to meet him. Maybe I'll save what I've got to say till he gets here. Shall we have a drink while we're waiting?' He eyed the cocktail cabinet, licking his lips.

Leonie fumed. 'No, we will not have a drink. Say what you've got to say at once or I'll have you thrown out.'

Norman's smile vanished and his pale eyes narrowed to a pair of spiteful slits. 'Don't kid yourself that you can scare me, Eileen, 'cos you can't. I've got you just where I want you. And I 'appen to know there's no husband coming. There was a cab downstairs waiting for you but I told him he could go, so you needn't worry.'

Leonie gasped. 'How *dare* you?' She bit her lip. What was she to do now? Short of going off and leaving him in the flat she was at a loss to know and she knew that he was well aware of the fact. 'I warn you – if you don't go at once I'll call the caretaker and have you removed,' she said.

He chuckled at her modified threat, 'Oh, I don't think you will. Think of the stir that'd cause. I wouldn't go without making a lot of noise and fuss. What would your posh neighbours say?' He recrossed his legs and flicked the ash from his roll-up onto the carpet. 'Okay, I'll tell you what I come for, Eileen. It's quite simple, I've run short of cash and I want some more. You can spare it so why not?'

Leonie's temper flared. 'Of all the bloody cheek! Look, you'll get no more out of me,' she said. 'I told you in the letter I wrote. I know that Mum and Dad died in the bombing. What you're doing is blackmail – demanding money with menaces. It's against the law, or didn't you know?'

'Okay, go to the police.' He leaped suddenly to his feet with a speed that had her stepping backwards in alarm. 'Put it this way: either I get the cash from you or from one of the papers. I don't give a toss either way. They'd pay generously to have the story of how you neglected your mum and dad after you made your name on the stage. The readers'd be all agog to read about the lies you told about your aristocratic family – about how your real mum and dad died in poverty without you caring a bugger about them.'

'Your word against mine. Who do you think would listen to a nobody like you?'

'Ah, but I've got photos.' He grinned up at her. 'A lovely one of you taken at Googe Street Elementary School, along with all the other Block Street kids.' He licked his lips, savouring the look on her face. 'Then of course there's the little matter of your police record.'

She stared at him. 'Police record? What are you talking about?'

'Surely you haven't forgotten the time you got caught for shoplifting in Woolworth's?'

'But – but I was only fourteen then. It was only a lipstick. Dad never used to give me any pocket money.'

'It was lipstick the time you got caught. There were all the other times when you got away with it. Rings and brooches, bars of chocolate. A common little thief – that's what Mum called you when she found out. Said she'd never be able to hold her head up in the street again.' He thrust his face close to hers and smiled evilly. 'Wouldn't go down too well with the fans, would it?'

She turned away in revulsion. 'You'd never prove any of this.'

He smiled triumphantly. 'Oh, but that's where you're wrong, Eileen. Our dad was a very methodical man, you see. He had a tin box with everything in it. Along with the gold watch Grandad left him and deeds of the shop, there was their marriage certificate, our birth certificates, the old photos I told you about – everything. It's all there – even the newspaper cuttings about your appearance in the juvenile court.'

'I don't believe you. The house was bombed – a direct hit.'

'The box was made of steel. It survived and I've got it put away somewhere safe. You pay up, Eileen, and you can have it lock, stock and barrel. If not, it goes to the paper that offers the most.'

'All right. What do you want?'

He paused, taking a last drag of his evil-smelling roll-up before flicking it into the fireplace. 'Five thousand'd see me set up for life. I could buy a little business. Yes, five'd do me nicely.'

'*Five thousand pounds?* You're mad.'

'No, *you'd* be mad to turn me down, Eileen. I give you my word. Pay up this time and it's the last you'll see of me – refuse and I go to the papers.'

Leonie's head was spinning. 'Look, I can't decide just like that. Anyway I don't keep that kind of sum in the flat. I told you, I've got to go out now. I'll . . . I'll have to think about it and let you know what I decide. Please – will you go now?'

He stared at her suspiciously. 'How long's all this thinking going to take? I warn you, I ain't hanging about for ever.'

She shook her head. 'Oh, I don't know. Give me till tomorrow.'

'I've got no money for London hotels.' He looked around him. 'I'll have to doss down here.'

She shuddered. '*No.*' Opening her bag, she drew out a five-pound note and thrust it at him. 'Here, this ought to be enough to get yourself a decent place.'

He pocketed the money. 'Okay. I'll see you tomorrow then – about this time. And you better come up with the right answers if you don't want to make front-page news by the end of the week.'

She let him out and stood with her back against the door. At least she'd got rid of him – for the time being. She waited until she was sure he'd be clear of the building, then went downstairs to call a cab. Tony would already have been waiting for fifteen minutes. She prayed he wouldn't have grown tired of hanging round and left. This time she really needed him.

Tony was waiting for her in the bar when she arrived. He looked handsome in a light-grey suit, his fair hair slightly longer than usual and gleaming with health and cleanliness. He sat on a bar stool chatting to the barman, a dry martini in front of him. When he turned and saw her, her heart skipped a beat as his face lit up in the familiar smile she hadn't seen for so long.

'Leonie.' He got off his stool and came to meet her, hands outstretched. 'Lovely to see you. It's been ages.'

'Yes. It's good to see you too. Get me a drink please, darling, a stiff one. I've had quite a morning.' She chose a table well away from the bar and Tony joined her there with the drinks. He took out his cigarette case and offered it to her; she took one gratefully, and lit it at the flame of Tony's lighter, drawing the smoke deep into her lungs and blowing it out slowly.

'Aah, that's better.'

He watched her as he put away case and lighter. 'Is something wrong?'

She made herself smile, shaking her head. 'Later. Tell me first what prompted this invitation.'

He looked surprised. 'Is it so surprising that I should ask my wife to have lunch with me on one of the rare occasions when we're both in town at the same time?'

Leonie sipped her drink. 'Let's face it, darling,' she said in an undertone. 'We haven't exactly been what you'd call *close* over the past couple of years, have we?'

'I know. And neither of us is going to pretend that there aren't faults on both sides,' Tony said. 'Maybe it's time we buried the hatchet, if only for Imogen's sake.' He smiled. 'Which brings me to one of the reasons I wanted to see you today. I had lunch with Peter and my old friend

Daniel Sherwood yesterday. Daniel's been on the examination board at RADA for the past couple of years. I was telling him about Imogen and how much she longs to study there, and he invited all of us to RADA's end-of-term production. It's on Tuesday and I thought it would be rather nice if we all went together.'

'You want me to put on a show – play happy families?'

Tony frowned at her acid-tongued remark. 'It would mean an awful lot to Imogen. Surely you wouldn't spoil things for her just because of our quarrel? Surely it's time we forgot about all that?'

For Imogen's sake. Nothing changes, does it? Leonie was about to make this bitter observation when she remembered Norman and her pressing problem. She tapped the ash delicately from the end of her cigarette and glanced up at him through her lashes. 'Of course I want to forget our past differences, darling. I'll be honest with you. I rather suspected that you'd brought me here today to ask me for a divorce.'

He laughed. 'Good heavens, no.'

'Your . . . little friend – she's gone, then?'

He lifted his shoulders. 'I can hardly remember her. So, what do you say about the play? I thought we might take Shirley along. I understand she's set on going to RADA too. I'm sure she'd enjoy it.'

'That's a good idea. I could go to Houlton and bring them both back. We could all stay at the flat.' She glanced at him. 'Where are you staying, by the way?'

'Peter put me up at Richmond. I'm only here on a flying visit. I had to come and see him about casting a film. I've been offered a job by the Rank Organisation. I'm hoping to direct a story about the RAF, set at the outbreak of war; fiction this time. We should begin filming in the autumn if everything goes to plan. It's rather exciting.'

He saw that she seemed rather preoccupied and paused. 'But that's another story. Tell me why you've had a bad morning.'

'Oh, Tim called me in. Something about the powers that be at the War Office objecting to sentimental songs.'

He laughed. 'You're joking.'

'I'm not. They seem to think that sentimental songs will turn the men into a bunch of fairies and make them lose the will to fight.'

'I'm sure you can talk them out of that,' Tony said. 'Surely that wasn't all?'

'No.' Leonie ground out her cigarette. 'I'm in trouble, Tony.'

'What kind of trouble?'

'You remember I told you that my parents had been killed in the Birmingham bombing – my brother too?'

'Yes.'

'Well, it appears that Norman is still alive.'

'That's good news.'

'Hardly. He's blackmailing me.'

Tony's eyebrows shot up. 'Blackmailing you? But why – and how?'

'That article in *Home and Beauty* – the one in which I . . . romanced a little about my background. He's threatening to spill the beans. He'll say I neglected my parents and didn't even know they'd been killed till two years later and – oh, God knows what else besides.'

Tony frowned. 'But you were sending them money, so how can he say you were neglecting them?'

Leonie bit her lip. She'd forgotten she'd told Tony that. 'All the time I was sending it, *he* was taking it,' she said quickly. 'I didn't know they were dead and he never told me.'

'But what made you think *he* was dead?'

She swallowed hard. It was getting complicated. 'B-because . . . I didn't hear from him again. I – just assumed. Then he suddenly appeared at the flat this morning, making all these demands and threats.'

Tony snorted. 'Despicable little rat. Let him do his worst, I'd say. It's his word against yours.'

'I can't afford to do that, Tony. He convinced me that he could make it stick. And you know what the papers are when it comes to a juicy bit of gossip. Think what they could make of it. In the eyes of the public I stand for caring and family ties. I'd be finished by the time Norman had done his worst.'

'So what do you intend to do?'

She gave him her wide-eyed appealing look. 'I was rather hoping you'd tell me.'

'Well, you can't give him any money. That would be putting your head in a noose. He'd be back for more.'

'He promises that if I pay up he'll stay away.'

He gave her a rueful smile. 'And you believe him? A man like that? It's what they always say.'

'I can't let him go to the papers.'

'I'd call his bluff,' Tony said. 'Why should anyone believe him, after all? Can he actually prove he's your brother?'

'Yes. It seems he has all the evidence he needs in a tin box my father kept. It survived the bombing. That's what he had for sale.'

'Have you seen it?'

'No.'

Tony shrugged. 'I doubt if it exists. Call his bluff, Leonie. At least stall him for a while and see what happens. He'll probably lose his nerve. His sort are always the same – all huff and puff and very little substance. The worst thing you can do is let him see you're worried.'

Leonie was far from convinced but she didn't press the matter further. They lunched and talked about their respective careers. Before parting they finalised the arrangements to attend the RADA play together, Leonie deciding to go to Houlton the following day to collect the girls. She would leave on an early train and kill two birds with one stone. When Norman arrived for her decision, she'd be gone. She'd leave a note for him with the caretaker, saying she'd been unavoidably called away and would get in touch as soon as she could. Maybe he would lose his nerve. But she doubted it.

When Leonie arrived at Longueville Hall she was somewhat dismayed to find Gloria there. It seemed that

Shirley's mother was taking a week's holiday and, be-cause Shirley was at school, had decided to spend it at Houlton.

Sensing her disapproval, Molly said, 'I hope you don't mind Gloria staying here, Madam. She does bring her own rations and she's a great help in the house and the kitchen.'

'Of course I don't mind, Nanny. It's just that I have an invitation for Shirley. I was going to take both girls to London for a couple of days, but now I suppose Shirley will have to miss the treat.'

'Oh, I see.' Molly watched helplessly as Leonie searched the wardrobe in her bedroom with mounting irritation, pulling out dresses and throwing them onto the bed. 'Can I help?' she offered.

'I was looking for the black Hartnell dress I had made last year,' Leonie said. 'The one with the matching jacket. I've only worn it once and I thought I might wear it to this show we're going to. They'll expect a bit of glamour. Ah, here it is.' Finding the dress, she drew it out of the wardrobe and spread it over the dressing-table stool. 'I'll try it on later, just in case I've put on weight.' She lit a cigarette and stood looking round her. 'You know, this room is beginning to look shabby, Nanny. If only re-decorating weren't so difficult.' Putting her cigarette down on an ashtray, she fingered the bed hangings. 'What do you think – do they need replacing?'

'You'd never get material like that nowadays, Madam,' Molly remarked, 'and wallpaper is unobtainable. I was only saying to Jim just the other day, that carpet in the drawing room –' She stopped, sniffing the air suspiciously. 'Something's burning.'

Leonie glanced round and gave a shriek. 'Oh, my God, it's my cigarette. It's fallen off the ashtray onto the dress.' She snatched up the dress and began to brush the ash from it. The dress itself was unmarked, but there was a hole burned right through the jacket. 'Oh, *hell!* It's ruined,' she wailed.

'Is anyone hurt? I heard someone scream.' Gloria put her head hesitantly round the half-open door.

'It's Madam's dress,' Molly told her. 'A cigarette fell onto it.'

'Oh, dear. Perhaps there's something I can do.'

Leonie shook her head impatiently. 'There's nothing anyone can do about a burn like that.' She thrust a finger through the hole and Gloria saw that it was right in the front. The watered silk material had burned quickly and irreparably.

She took the dress from Leonie and held it up. It had a beautifully cut flared skirt and a tiny backless bodice with shoestring straps. 'The frock itself is all right,' she said.

'But I couldn't wear it without the jacket,' Leonie said crossly. 'The two go together. It's an *ensemble*. It's a Hartnell – specially made for me. I'd set my heart on wearing it tomorrow. Oh, *damn!* Everything seems to be going wrong lately.'

Gloria and Molly exchanged glances as Leonie's eyes filled with angry tears. In Molly's opinion her work and the rift with Mr Tony were making her nervous and overwrought. She had seen her like this before.

'Madam was wanting to take the girls to London for two days,' she said awkwardly, by way of explanation. 'Seems there's something on at the Royal Academy of Dramatic Art.'

'But it's out of the question now that *you're* here, Gloria,' Leonie said bluntly. 'Obviously you'll be wanting Shirley to spend her time with you.'

All three women knew that Shirley would give her eye teeth to go to London. 'I wouldn't dream of standing in the way of a chance like that for Shirl, Miss Swann,' Gloria said quietly.

Leonie looked at her and felt a little ashamed. She really was behaving rather badly. The business with Norman had shredded her nerves and the accident to her dress on top of everything else seemed like the last straw. 'That's very generous of you, Gloria,' she said. 'I know Imogen wouldn't want to go without her.' She smiled. 'Shirley really has brought Imogen out, you know. She's quite a different girl nowadays.'

232

Gloria smiled. 'She's growing up, that's all.'

'While we're waiting for them to come home from school, why don't we go down to the drawing room and have tea together?' Leonie invited.

'Thank you,' Gloria held up the dress. 'What shall I do with this?'

Leonie waved her hand dismissively. 'Oh, just throw it down with the others. It's useless now. I'll send them all off to Mrs Churchill's Aid to Russia Fund or something.'

'Isn't there anything else you can wear?'

'I was counting on wearing that. Everything else I'd left here is hopelessly out of fashion now and I've no wretched coupons left to get something new.'

Gloria said nothing. Looking at the pile of expensive dresses heaped on the bed, she thought wistfully of what she could do with them. Some of her own clothes dated back to the beginning of the war and had been made over to keep up with current fashion again and again. What must it feel like to have a dress by the famous Hartnell specially made for you? But then with Leonie's wealth she supposed it was the kind of thing one would take for granted.

In the drawing room Leonie sank into the settee and gave a sigh. 'Be an angel and bring us some tea, Nanny.'

'I made a Madeira cake this morning,' Molly said. 'Made with real eggs from the farm – none of your nasty dried stuff. Would you like some of that too?'

'It sounds like sheer heaven.' Leonie looked at Gloria who was standing by the baby grand piano, fingering the Chinese silk shawl that was draped over it. 'Do come and sit down, Gloria.'

'I was looking at this,' Gloria glanced at her. 'It's beautiful material – pure silk.'

Leonie was lighting a cigarette from the silver box on the coffee table. 'Yes, I suppose it is. The colours are rather nice too.'

Gloria was looking at her, wondering if she dared voice the idea that was going through her mind. 'I wonder, would you miss it here on the piano?'

Leonie frowned as she inhaled the smoke from her cigarette. 'Why? Do you want it?'

'Oh, no – at least, not for me. It's just that I saw this article in a fashion magazine the other day; a little jacket designed by Steibel and made from Chinese silk. It had a nipped in waist and a cut-away front . . .' She described the style with her hands. 'It would set off your Hartnell dress beautifully and I'm almost sure there's enough material here.' She drew the shawl from the piano and let its silken richness slide sensuously through her hands. 'If you can spare the shawl – and you'd trust me enough to try . . .'

Leonie was on her feet, taking the shawl from Gloria and draping it across her shoulder as she looked into the gilt-framed mirror over the fireplace. The reds and golds of the rich pattern complemented her dark colouring dramatically. Her eyes lit up with pleasure. 'Oh – *yes*, I do believe you're right. It would look quite sensational. And no one else would have anything like it, would they?' She stopped, looking doubtfully at Gloria. 'But surely there isn't time? We'd have to leave here tomorrow mid-morning at the latest.'

'If I got to work straight away I'm sure I could have it finished in time.'

That evening Gloria measured, cut, pinned and fitted, pausing only to eat her dinner. She talked to Shirley as she worked, but the girl, excited about the coming trip, soon disappeared upstairs with Imogen to choose what they would wear. By the time Gloria tumbled into bed late that night, the little Chinese silk jacket lay over the arm of the chair in her room, basted and ready for machining. The following morning she was up at dawn, working away on Molly's old hand-operated sewing machine in the kitchen, and by the time Leonie came down to breakfast the jacket was ready for her to try on.

'Oh, Gloria, you're a *genius*.' Leonie turned this way and that in front of the mirror. 'I can't thank you enough for this. You really must let me pay you.'

Gloria shook her head. 'Oh, no. I enjoyed doing it. I love a challenge like that and the material was lovely to work with.'

'But I must give you something.' Leonie looked at her thoughtfully. 'I know: you must come to London with us,' she said. 'I'm not sure whether there'll be a seat for you at the play, but if not you could still do some shopping in the West End and stay with us at the flat. Oh, do say you'll come.'

Gloria nodded happily. 'I'd love to. Thank you.'

They travelled up on the mid-morning train and arrived in London early in the afternoon. The girls were excited at the thought of going to RADA and seeing the place where they both hoped to study. Leonie had telephoned their headmistress the previous day and arranged for them to have two days off.

As a special treat, Leonie took them all to lunch at the Savoy. In the River Room she told them that during the Blitz part of this very room had been used as a dormitory and that as well as underground shelters there had been a miniature hospital in the building for first aid.

'Thank God that's all over now,' she said to Gloria. 'Your parents must be relieved now that the second front has started. There's no likelihood of any more bombing now. They'll all be too occupied over on that side.'

'Are your parents still living?' Gloria asked.

Leonie hesitated. 'I'm afraid not.' She dabbed her lips with a napkin. 'They both died some time ago.' Suddenly her eyes lighted on a short, stocky man walking across the restaurant towards them and her cheeks flushed rosily. '*OH*! It's Noël Coward,' she whispered.

To her great delight he paused by the table, looking hard at her. 'Leonie, my dear. It's so long since we last met, though of course I'm a great fan of your delectable radio programme. How are you?'

'I'm very well, thank you, Noël. And you?'

'Positively blooming.' He took her hand and kissed it. 'You're looking even lovelier than I remember you. And I haven't forgotten that play I promised to write for you.'

235

'I'm looking forward so much to working with you.' She looked round the table. 'May I introduce my daughter, Imogen? And this is her friend, Shirley and her mother, Gloria Rayner.'

He gave them a brief nod, then returned his attention to Leonie. 'Tell that husband of yours he should be arrested for allowing you out of his sight looking so ravishing,' he told her with an impish smile. 'Do give me a ring some time and we'll have lunch.'

He moved away with a wave of his hand and Leonie gazed after him, her eyes shining. If it hadn't been for the war she'd have enjoyed a very different kind of popularity by now, she told herself wistfully. But then she couldn't really grumble. Her name was a household word, after all. She'd certainly take Noël up on that offer of lunch, though. Once the war was over there'd be no more need for her kind of request programme. Besides, she longed to embark on a more glamorous career in the theatre the moment the opportunity presented itself.

Tony had arranged to collect the girls from the flat after lunch and take them to RADA to be introduced to his friend Daniel Sherwood and given a guided tour. Leonie had taken both girls to the hairdresser's and they were still out when he walked into the drawing room. Finding Gloria there caused his eyes to widen.

'Gloria! What a surprise!'

She was dismayed at the sudden quickening of her heartbeat. 'I was staying at Houlton for a few days, so Leonie invited me along too,' she explained.

'I see.' He frowned. 'I'm afraid I only have four tickets for the show.'

'That's all right. I thought I might go over to Whitechapel this evening and visit my mother and father. Surprise them.'

He smiled. 'Ah, yes. Well, it's good to see you.'

'Yes. It's been a long time. I dare say we've both been busy.'

'You're still working at the aircraft factory?'

'Yes. I've seen all of your films. They were very good.'

'Thanks.'

'It's good of you to take Shirl along with you to this RADA play.'

'Not at all. I know she's planning to go there when she leaves school.'

'It's what she's planning, but it may not be possible. You see, I'm planning to marry and go to America when the war is over.'

His face broke into a smile. 'You've met someone and fallen in love? An American soldier?'

'Airman.'

'That explains the radiant look. It's wonderful, Gloria. I'm so glad for you. You deserve to be happy.'

Just for a split second Gloria knew a pang of disappointment. He so obviously meant what he said. He *was* happy. There wasn't even the smallest glimmer of regret in his voice. If he never saw her again, it clearly wouldn't concern him one bit. The knowledge hurt.

He sat down on the chair opposite. 'Tell me about him. I hope he's worthy of you.'

But to her relief Leonie and the girls returned before she had a chance to embark on a description of Billy's finer qualities.

When Tony, Imogen and Shirley had gone, Leonie looked at her. 'Now, I don't want any arguments. I've made you an appointment at André's. You're to have the full works – hairdo, manicure, facial and make-up. It's all paid for and it's my treat.'

'Oh, but I couldn't . . .'

Leonie laughed. 'Oh yes, you could.' She took a card from her bag and gave it to Gloria. 'Here you are. I've booked you with Monique. She's the best, I always insist on her. You'll feel and look like a new woman, I promise. Off you go now. It's in Park Lane – only five minutes' walk.'

When Gloria came out of the smart Mayfair beauty salon she felt like a princess. She had never been inside one of those places before and it was quite the nicest present

Leonie could have given her. Her blonde hair was piled high in a glamorous pompadour and her skin felt smooth and tingling after its massage. She glanced surreptitiously in every shop window she passed and enjoyed a little thrill of pleasure at the reflection that looked back at her.

Entering the building, she went up in the lift. To her surprise she found the door to the flat ajar and as she went inside she heard voices coming from the drawing room. Meaning to go quietly to her room so as not to intrude, she crept past the half-open door, but she stopped dead in her tracks as Leonie suddenly burst out loudly:

'I'll give you two thousand, Norman. Take it or leave it. It's all you're going to get. I'm not a millionairess in spite of what you think. And you're going to have to give me the box and all its contents for that.'

'What do you take me for?' Leonie's unseen companion chuckled in a way that sent cold shivers down Gloria's spine. 'Give me the two thousand if you like, but make no mistake, I'll be back for the rest. You can have the photos for that. Bring the cash to the address I gave you tonight. I'll hang on to the rest of the stuff – the birth certificate and the cuttings about your shoplifting. You can pay for them when you've had time to sweat a bit more – *if* I don't get fed up with waiting in the meantime.'

'I've a damned good mind to give you nothing.'

'Suit yourself. I told you before, it's no skin off my nose. I'll get the money one way or the other. Either you pay up or I sell the lot to the papers. I tell them that the beautiful Leonie Swann is my sister – who used to be a snot-nosed little kid from a butcher's shop in Birmingham, pinching stuff out of Woolworth's to try and make herself look like someone she wasn't. I'll tell them how this Darling of the Nation dropped her hard-working mum and dad when she made her pile, and made up a pack of lies about who she was and where she came from.' He chuckled sadistically, obviously enjoying himself. 'Why don't you admit it, our Eileen? I've got you right where you bloody well deserve to be, you tight-fisted bitch. I'm gonna squeeze you till you beg for mercy. By the time I'm done you'll be glad to pay me *ten* thousand quid, let alone five – just to be shot of me.'

'*Get out!*' Leonie screamed. 'Get out of my flat, you slimy blackmailing little toad!'

'Oh dear, oh *dear*,' the man mocked. 'I ask you – is that a nice way to speak to your brother?'

There was a crash as some heavy object was thrown across the room. Gloria slipped inside her room and closed the door. From behind it she heard the man's hastily retreating footsteps and the loud slam of the front door. After a pause she heard Leonie gasp and then begin sobbing as though her heart would break.

Chapter Eleven

For a moment Gloria stood listening to the harsh sobs coming from the other side of her door. Her mind went back to that day when Tony told her that Leonie Swann came from a background so similar to her own that they might have been sisters. Perhaps Leonie deserved the things her brother had said to her, but blackmail – demanding all that money in such a vile, cowardly way – she certainly did not deserve. For a moment Gloria stood listening to the sobs, then she made up her mind. She couldn't just stand here doing nothing. Suddenly Leonie was no longer the dazzling star, admired by millions, she was just another woman – a woman exactly like her. And at this moment she needed help. Opening her door, she stepped into the hall.

Leonie stood with her back to the door, one hand to her mouth in an attempt to stifle the sobs that racked her body; tears were streaming down her face.

Gloria took a step towards her. 'I didn't mean to eavesdrop but I heard him. I'm sorry, but I heard what your – your brother said.' As Leonie began to sob afresh, she held out her arms. 'Oh, please don't cry like that.'

Leonie almost threw herself into Gloria's arms, holding on to her as though she were a lifeline. 'Oh, God, what shall I do, Gloria? He'll finish my career. He'll blacken my name . . . *ruin* me.'

'It's no disgrace to come from an ordinary family,' Gloria said quietly. 'You've worked hard to get where you are. You're a success. Why don't you just let the papers have the story yourself? You could make it sound as though that other story was a mistake. You could make it sound like something to be proud of, which it is.'

Leonie shook her head. 'It's too late for that. Besides, there's all the rest – the things I can't be proud of.' She swallowed painfully. 'Shoplifting is hardly something to crow about.'

'There must be something you can do,' Gloria said. 'No one should have the power to hold you to ransom like that, specially for something that happened so long ago.' She led the trembling Leonie gently towards the drawing room. 'Come and sit down. I'll make you a nice cup of tea.'

In the room she saw the mess of broken china on the carpet. Leonie had thrown a large vase at Norman and it had shattered against the wall into hundreds of pieces. 'I'll get this cleared up before the others come back and see it,' she said.

By the time the room had been tidied and the tea made, Leonie had calmed a little. Sipping her tea, she told Gloria about her unhappy childhood and her ambition to be an actress, the way she and Tony had met and the blossoming of her career.

'I was only a child when I took those things,' she said. 'It was just a silly juvenile madness – a few cheap trifles. I'd almost forgotten about it. It's as though it happened in another life. And it isn't as though I didn't learn my lesson. I had my punishment when I was put on probation for shoplifting.' She put her cup down on its saucer, her hand trembling. 'But if it were all to come out now, think what the papers would make of it.'

'But people love you,' Gloria said. 'Surely your fans would be loyal?'

Leonie shook her head. 'No. They expect you to be perfect, you see. To them we're different beings – idols, up on a pedestal, above all normal human failings. Then there are the others – the people within our circle. You make many enemies in this business,' Leonie told her. 'There's a lot of petty jealousy and spite. The higher you

241

climb, the more they want to see you tumble, in spite of calling themselves your friends. But what worries me the most is that there's a lot of this that Tony doesn't know. And I'd do anything to stop him finding out.'

'I see.' Gloria looked at her. It was worse than she had imagined. 'So you're going to pay?'

'I don't have any alternative.' Leonie took a crumpled scrap of paper from her pocket and spread it out on her knee. 'He says I'm to take the cash to this address tonight. It's some lodging house in King's Cross. I'll have to go to the bank now. And when Tony gets back I'll have to tell him I can't go to the play with them. You can go in my place.'

'Won't he wonder what's wrong, though?'

Leonie drew a deep shuddering breath. 'I'll make up some story. I've no choice. I have to do it.' She grasped Gloria's arm. 'Will you promise me you won't say anything to anyone – especially Tony – *ever*?'

'Of course I won't.'

Leonie's shoulders slumped suddenly. 'I've been a bitch in my time,' she muttered. 'I've done and said some awful things. I've been cruel to Tony – and to Imogen.' She raised her eyes to look at Gloria. 'To you, too. That time I came to the factory where you work, I pretended not to know you. It was a despicable thing to do. I'm sorry.'

'It doesn't matter.'

'But it does, I deserve all I'm getting. I –'

'Look,' Gloria stopped her words, a hand on her arm. 'I've had an idea. *I'll* take the money. You go to the play with Tony and the girls as though nothing has happened and I'll take the money to this address and get the box for you. I'm supposed to be going to Whitechapel, but Ma and Pa aren't expecting me so no one need be any the wiser.'

Naked relief shone in Leonie's eyes. 'Oh, Gloria! But I couldn't let you do it.'

'Yes, you could. It's the obvious answer. You go now and get the cash. I'll do the errand for you, then you can destroy all the evidence and forget all about it.'

'But he – Norman will be expecting me. He'll suspect something.'

'Not when I give him the money. That's all he wants, isn't it?'

Leonie made a quick telephone call to her bank manager to make sure she'd be allowed to withdraw that much money in cash without notice, then she put on her coat and left. Half an hour later she returned and gave Gloria a fat brown envelope containing the money – more money than Gloria had ever seen in her entire life.

Gloria got off the bus and looked again at the address on the piece of paper; 128 Markham Street. Finally she found it, a run-down street at the back of the station. Grubby children played in the gutter and an old man with a brown wrinkled face was selling newspapers on the corner outside the public house, calling out his incomprehensible sales cry in a plaintive whine. Gloria tucked her handbag with its precious contents more securely under her arm and began to walk hesitantly down the street of four-storey Victorian houses, looking carefully at the numbers. She was grateful that it was still daylight. She would not have fancied walking here in the blackout.

Number 128 was obviously a lodging house. A rank odour floated up the area step from the overflowing dustbins at the bottom and the paint on the front door was chipped and faded to an indeterminate grey. Her knock was answered by a fat woman who stood wiping her hands on a greasy overall, one eyebrow raised enquiringly. In answer to Gloria's request for Mr Smith she jerked her head towards the stairs. 'First floor back. Number three,' she said abruptly and retreated once more into the dark recess beyond the staircase.

Her heart beating unevenly, Gloria went up the uncarpeted stairs, wrinkling her nose at the assorted stale cooking odours that pervaded the place. She found the door with a 3 painted on it and knocked. It was opened almost immediately by a short man with thinning mousy

243

hair and a straggly moustache. The look of eager anticipation he wore was quickly replaced by one of irritation.

'Wha' d' y' want?' he asked.

Gloria recognised the voice at once. Its accent had been strange to her and she would have recognised it again anywhere as the one she had heard earlier at the Darrents' flat. But the notion that this man was Leonie Swann's brother would otherwise have been unbelievable. 'Leonie sent me,' she said. 'I've brought – what you asked for and I'm to collect what you have for her.'

His expression changed again. Greed made his pale eyes glint in the dim light of the landing as he held the door open. 'Oh. You'd better come in, then.'

'There's no need,' Gloria said, eager to get away. 'Just give me the goods and I'll go.'

The man's eyes narrowed suspiciously. Sticking his head out of the door, he glanced up and down the landing, then grabbed her sleeve. 'Come in. Don't want the whole house listening, do we?'

The room was furnished with the bare essentials. Gloria vaguely took in a sagging bed covered by a faded folkweave bedspread, a table and one chair. The floor was covered in cracked linoleum and a pair of stained brown curtains hung at the window. She looked apprehensively at Norman.

'Where's the box?'

'Not so fast.' He peered at her. 'Where's Eileen? Why didn't she come herself and who are you?'

'She had an appointment. She couldn't get out of it so I offered to do the errand for her.'

'You still haven't told me who you are.'

'There's no reason why I should. It doesn't matter who I am.'

'Oh yes, it does. For all I know you could be . . .'

'The *police*?' She saw him wince. 'Well, I'm not. I'm just a friend, so hand it over and I'll go.'

Norman Smith licked his lips, clearly relieved. 'You've got the cash, you say?'

'Yes.'

'All of it?'

'All of it.'

'Let's see then.'

Warily and keeping a firm hold of her handbag, Gloria showed him the envelope. Loosening the flap, she allowed him to see the bundle of notes inside. 'It's all there. You'll have to take my word for it. I'm not handing it over till I get the box.'

Norman went across to the bed and bent down, drawing out a battered cardboard suitcase. Opening it, he lifted out a dented steel box with a stout clasp. Then, glancing warily at her, he placed himself between her and the door.

'This is it. Now give me the –' The rest of his words were drowned by an earsplitting crash somewhere quite close. The building gave a violent shudder and the door flew open, almost propelling Norman into her arms. Soot cascaded down the chimney and splinters of glass from the shattered window flew in all directions. Gloria turned away, shielding her face and head with her arms, but a long shard of glass sliced into Norman's scalp. He let out a piercing yell as blood began to stream down his forehead and into his eyes.

'Oh, God! Oh, Christ, I'm bleeding.' Dropping the box with a clatter, he clutched his gashed head.

The landing outside was already jammed with the tenants of the other rooms. There was a babble of raised voices as they jostled each other in a mad scramble for the rickety staircase. Someone shouted: 'It's started again – the bloody Blitz is back.' Outside in the street a woman's hysterical screaming could be heard; somewhere a baby was crying and a man's voice boomed stridently, ordering everyone to take cover.

Gloria staggered backwards, falling onto the bed as Norman pushed past her to elbow his way to the door joining the mass of people heading for the shelters. As Gloria watched him disappear, the wound in his head was still bleeding profusely.

For a moment she stood in the sooty and glass-strewn room, rooted to the floor with dazed shock. Then it was as though some force outside her own control took over, galvanising her into action. Scooping up the steel box from the floor, she hastily wrapped it in a scarf she found hanging behind the door and ran down the staircase of the now empty house. The street below was deserted and suddenly uncannily silent. Papers scattered from the abandoned news stand on the corner fluttered silently among the drifts of broken glass. She half ran, half stumbled along the pavement, not stopping till she got to the corner, when a low roaring overhead made her stop and look up.

A plane, the like of which she had never seen before, was passing overhead. It had flames coming out of the tail and as she watched the engine stopped abruptly and the flames went out. Staring at it in fascination, Gloria saw the plane glide heavily onwards, swaying perilously from side to side. For one horrific moment it seemed to be heading straight for her. As she watched, mesmerised, it dipped, then seemed to straighten up and sailed on over her head to take a sudden dive behind the houses of the next street. There was a deafening crash and a rising plume of smoke; then came the force of the blast, which lifted Gloria off her feet and threw her against the wall, knocking all the breath from her body.

When she got to her feet she was smothered in dust and shaking violently. What in God's name was it? Were the Germans sending pilots on suicide missions now? Hastily dusting herself off and making sure she still had the metal box, she hurried on as fast as she could. As she ran she thought about the Darrents and Shirley, praying that they were safe. She thought about Billy – her sweet, dearest Billy, God only knew where, fighting to free them from horrors like this. But her most immediate and urgent thought was to put as much distance as she could between herself and Norman Smith in the shortest time possible. The strange crashing aeroplane, sinister and frightening as it was, had done Leonie Swann the biggest favour of all time – just as long as Gloria could get herself back to Mayfair without getting herself killed.

She got as far as the Underground station on foot, taking cover in doorways three times on the way. The pattern was always the same. The strange-sounding aircraft would roar overhead, its engine would splutter and then cut out; it would glide unsteadily in eerie silence for several minutes, then plunge abruptly into its deadly, devastating dive.

Down in the Underground rumours were rife. The planes were piloted by prisoners of war drugged into compliance, or by men with terminal illnesses snatched from their hospital beds. The most bizarre rumour was that they had no pilots at all. No one could swallow that one. Clutching her priceless prize, Gloria waited anxiously for things to quieten. At last the trains began to run again and she boarded the first one she could, changing at Baker Street for Green Park. She was on her way, her mission accomplished. It was only as she sat there in the train on the last leg of her journey that she remembered the bulging envelope still in her handbag. A smile of delight spread over her grime-smudged face. She had done even better than she thought: she'd got the money *and* the box.

To her relief Mayfair seemed relatively untouched by the evening's bombing. Letting herself into the flat, she looked ruefully at herself in the mirror, remembering the pleasure she had taken in her appearance just a few short hours ago after the beauty treatment. Now the carefully groomed hair hung about her face in sooty strands, and dirt streaked what had been a perfectly made-up face. Never mind, she told herself, it was in a good cause. She was just thankful to be still in one piece. She changed out of her dust-covered clothes, had a bath and washed the dirt – and the expensive style – from her hair.

When Shirley, Imogen and the Darrents arrived home safely at half-past ten, Gloria felt a surge of relief. The girls ran to her in the drawing room, full of enthusiasm for the play they had seen and telling her how it had been interrupted halfway through for the air raid. To them it had only added to the excitement. Tony looked at her white face curiously and asked if she was all right.

'You're looking rather shaky, Gloria,' he said. 'Where were you when the raid started?'

'I was . . . on my way home,' she said, half truthfully.

'To Whitechapel? Did you get there?'

She shook her head. 'No. I came back here as soon as I could.' Out of the corner of her eye she could see Leonie looking at her anxiously. As soon as she could, Gloria excused herself and went to her room. After a few minutes there was a tap on the door and Leonie slipped inside, turning the key in the lock.

'Thank God you're all right. I've been sick with worry,' she said. 'Everyone was saying that the King's Cross area was badly hit.' She looked at Gloria. 'I take it you didn't see him.'

'Yes, I did.' Gloria opened her wardrobe where she had stowed the box. 'I think this is what you want, isn't it?'

'Oh – oh, you got it. Thank God!' Almost weak with relief, Leonie wrenched the box open and searched anxiously through the contents, making sure that everything was there.

'The raid started soon after I got there,' Gloria told her. 'Your brother was cut by flying glass. He made a dash for the shelter along with everyone else in the building. He was very frightened, so much that he forgot all about me – he even forgot this.' She opened her bag and took out the envelope.

Leonie stared disbelievingly at the package, then at her, her eyes round with astonishment. 'The *money*? You've saved the money too?' She threw her arms round Gloria and hugged her hard. 'You risked your life for this.'

Gloria shook her head. 'No, I didn't. You wouldn't have got me into a shelter along with a man like him. No, to tell the truth I was almost home before I remembered the money was still in my bag.'

'Nevertheless, I'll be in your debt for a very long time. If ever I can help you in any way, just let me know,' Leonie said, 'Anything you need – any time, Gloria. Just ask.'

* * *

Gloria and Shirley managed a brief visit to Whitechapel the next morning before their return to Houlton. They found Ma in a belligerent mood.

'I thought we'd done with bombs,' she complained. 'Now it seems that 'itler's gone and thought up something else to chuck at us. I 'ope 'e rots in 'ell when the Allies catches up with 'im.'

'Well, I'm just glad you're both safe and well,' Gloria told her. 'Why don't you and Pa come and live in my cottage till it's over and done with? Can't be all that long now, can it?'

Ma looked scandalised. 'Leave 'ere now? Never. We've stuck it out this long and we'll see it through to the end.'

Gloria looked appealingly at her father. 'What do you say, Pa?'

He shook his head, sucking hard on his pipe. 'Ma's right. Besides, they're going to need experienced ARP wardens again if these new attacks keep on.'

Ma looked at Shirley. At fourteen she was as tall as her mother. Her red-gold hair fell in curls to her shoulders and she was wearing a smart new dress that Gloria had made her. 'Well, miss?' Ma pursed her lips. 'Quite the young lady now, ain't you? Leavin' school this term?'

'No, she isn't, Ma. I told you,' Gloria said. 'She's staying on. Anyway, if Mr Butler gets his way, seems like they'll all be staying on till they're sixteen.'

Ma pursed her lips. 'Not in *my* lifetime, I 'ope. Not for gels leastways.'

'But I won't be able to stay on if the war ends and we go away, will I, Glor?' Shirley looked at her mother. Surely Gloria was going to tell Ma and Pa about marrying Billy. Wasn't that what they'd come for?

Ma looked from one to the other, her eyes narrowing as she asked: 'What does she mean – go away? What's goin' on? Come on then – out with it.'

Gloria licked her lips, wishing Shirley had kept quiet about it. 'It's just that I . . . might be going to America when the war is over,' she said. 'Billy has asked me to marry him.'

Ma's jaw dropped as she stared in stunned silence at her daughter. '*Marry* him?' she said at last. 'But 'e's only a kid. He must be at least ten years younger than you.'

Gloria coloured. 'Of course he isn't – not that much anyway. He's old enough to fight, isn't he? You make me sound like Methuselah, Ma.'

Ma's mouth tightened into a tense line. 'So you're goin' off to America with 'im, are you? That's the last we'll see of either of you, I s'pose.'

'I expect we'll come back for holidays,' Shirley put in.

'Holidays? Do you realise how far away it is? It ain't Margate you're goin' to, you know. It's the other side of the bleedin' *world*.'

Gloria sighed. She'd known there'd be a fuss. She looked at her father in mute appeal. Taking his pipe out of his mouth, he said mildly:

'It's your life, love. You must do what makes you happy.'

'Oh, that's right,' Ma said bitterly. 'You just tell 'er to go off. Tell 'er not to give a thought for the ma and pa what've stood by 'er through thick and thin.'

'Please, don't let's fall out over it.' Gloria kissed Pa, then turned to her mother, but Ma had already turned away to walk into the shop. As they left she was serving a customer. She didn't say goodbye or even look up.

Shirley looked at her mother as they walked together down Angel Row. 'Sorry, Glor. I shouldn't have said anything about America, should I?'

Gloria shrugged. 'She had to know some time. She's got to learn that she can't live our lives for us for ever.'

'Do you think the war'll be over soon?' Shirley was thinking of RADA and all the exciting things she'd seen and heard the previous day. She couldn't bear the thought that she might never get the chance to go there.

'I don't know,' Gloria said wearily. 'What with this new spate of bombing and everything, who can say? Sometimes I think it'll never end.'

Shirley bit down hard on the relief that made her want to smile.

* * *

London soon learned that the new robotic flying bomb was officially called the V-1, but it wasn't long before it was irreverently rechristened the 'doodlebug'. The V-1s rained down relentlessly on London till September, when a newer, more sinister flying bomb joined the onslaught. The V-2, more like a giant rocket than a plane, fell indiscriminately and without the V-1s warning, exterminating everything in its path. London was once again in the grip of bombardment; just when everyone had been buoyed up with the euphoria over the second front. Mothers and children once again left London for the comparative safety of the countryside, once more crowding into villages and market towns.

With Billy gone, Gloria no longer felt peace at Rook Cottage, so rather than allow it to stand empty she let it to a young woman from Woolwich whose husband was in the Navy. She and her two small boys were grateful to find a place they could have to themselves in the quiet and safety of the country, while Gloria spent more of her weekends with Shirley at Houlton.

Letters came from Billy. They were few and far between, short and scrappy with little or no information, but Gloria was glad to get them just the same. As days came and went with news of bitter fighting, she worried constantly about him. She worried about Ma and Pa too. If only she could get them out of London. Ma had always been difficult and uncompromising, but there had always been a strong bond between them for all that, and Gloria hated the unhealed rift that had opened between them. At Christmas Leonie suggested that she invite them to Longueville Hall, which she did, but Ma wrote back in her careful, spidery handwriting, declining the offer in frigidly polite tones.

It was a beautiful Christmas, bitterly cold but bright and sunny. A hard frost laid a veneer of silver on the lawns and decorated the trees with diamond spangles. Imogen and Shirley were in the village pantomime and Gloria took Jane with her to see them. They laughed till they cried at the wartime jokes and slapstick comedy, and

Gloria was so proud of her beautiful daughter playing principal girl to Imogen's handsome principal boy.

At Longueville Hall they played charades and enjoyed the sumptuous dinner that Molly managed to provide in spite of shortages and rationing. From his depleted wine cellar Tony still managed to produce bottles of Mosel and claret to drink with it and Jim had carefully stored away apples and pears from the orchard.

In spite of the new spate of V-2 bombing everyone felt that the end of the war was at last in sight. Weary Londoners looked upon it as Hitler's last-ditch attempt and no one seriously thought he had a chance of winning now. It was just a case of sitting it out and waiting. Life gradually became easier in many small ways. That winter the blackout had been relaxed to a 'dim-out'. After all, the latest 'bombers' had no pilots to see. To Jim's secret regret, the Home Guard had been disbanded. He had risen to the rank of sergeant and had come to enjoy his evenings drilling the men, the monthly church parades and his nights on watch at various sites around the village.

Over the holiday Tony and Leonie managed to put on a convincing performance, each playing the role of loving spouse. Leonie had remained silent about Norman's failed blackmail attempt. She allowed Tony to believe that she had taken his advice – and that Norman had caved in when she had called his bluff. Tony had been busy with rehearsals for the film he was to make, the shooting of which had been delayed until the New Year. To Leonie's dismay he showed no inclination to share a bedroom with her at Longueville Hall, but slept in his dressing room, fuelling anew her simmering feelings of resentment.

On New Year's Eve they gave a party. Most of the village was invited. Jim cut down a ten-foot fir tree from the grounds, which Imogen and Shirley trimmed with the glass baubles and decorations purchased before the war and carefully preserved and used every year since. With her usual resourcefulness and ingenuity, Molly provided a tasty buffet complete with mince pies and punch, and the hall was cleared for dancing to gramophone records. It was halfway through the evening that Gloria found herself dancing with Tony.

'You're looking especially lovely tonight, Gloria,' he said as he smiled down at her.

Gloria blushed with pleasure. It was a long time since she'd been close to Tony like this. She had never forgotten the summer of 1941 when they had shared a short holiday here at Houlton – the way he'd kissed her and the things they'd talked about. She hadn't forgotten either, the way she had ruined it all by throwing herself at him, or his polite but humiliating refusal. The memory still made her curl inwardly with shame. All she hoped was that *he* had forgotten – as he surely must have done, with the exciting life that he led.

'What are you thinking about?' he asked, lifting her chin with his forefinger. 'Whatever it is, it's making you blush delightfully.'

'It's nothing,' she said. 'It's a bit warm in here.'

He swung her round and pulled her arm through his. 'Let's got into the conservatory,' he said. 'It'll be cooler there and I'll get you a glass of lemonade.' He laughed. 'You see, I haven't forgotten your favourite tipple. There isn't much that I forget, if the truth is known.'

In the conservatory they sat side by side in the basket chairs. Gloria sipped her lemonade and wondered exactly what he meant about forgetting.

'Now tell me all about this American of yours,' Tony invited as he lit a cigarette.

'There isn't much to tell. He's overseas at the moment. He went last June at the time of the Normandy landing.'

'You must miss him.'

'Yes, I do.'

'And when he comes back?'

'We'll be married – I suppose.'

'You don't sound very sure.'

Gloria shifted restlessly in her chair. Ever since Ma's disapproving reaction, she had been doing some serious thinking. 'Sometimes knowing Billy seems a bit like a dream,' she said.

He smiled. 'War's like that. We live life in a series of cameos.'

'My mother wasn't too happy when I told her I was going to marry Billy.'

'It's your life, not your mother's.'

'I know, but she did have a point. There's something else, you see.'

'Which is?'

'Well, he's younger than me.' She glanced at him. 'Quite a bit younger.'

'Do you think it bothers him?'

'It's not that so much.' She bit her lip. 'I wonder sometimes if I wasn't kind of – well, a substitute for his mother.'

Tony laughed. 'I very much doubt that.'

But she shook her head, her eyes troubled. 'Would it be fair, though? Has he thought about it enough? And what about when he arrives home with me – me *and* Shirl – what will his family think? Will I be what they want for him?'

'Surely it's what you and Billy want that's important.'

Gloria shook her head. 'I don't know. There's Shirl, too. She's got her heart set on going to RADA with Imogen. I know she doesn't really want to leave England.'

'You could always leave her here with us.' When she didn't reply he asked quietly: 'Do you love him, Gloria?' He took her chin in his hand and made her look at him. 'Well – do you?' His eyes searched hers.

'Yes, but . . .'

'But *what*? There should be no buts if you love him, Gloria. You must know that.'

'It's just that I wonder if it's the right *kind* of love.'

'How many kinds are there?'

She shrugged, lowering her eyes from his.

'Only one kind that I know of, between a man and a woman,' he said quietly.

The conversation was getting too involved for her liking. How could she tell him that the memory of his kiss – a kiss that meant less than nothing to him – would always stand in the way of any new love that might come her way? Billy was sweet and good and yes, of course she loved him. Who wouldn't? But he was so young – he had his whole life before him. He deserved better than second-hand; second-best. He was worthy of someone who could give him her heart, whole and untouched. She looked at Tony, making herself smile.

'Can we dance again? Listen, someone has put on "Where or When?" It's my favourite.'

He nodded and reached for her hand. 'You're a very sweet person, Gloria,' he said softly. 'A very special person. You once saved – well, if not my life, then certainly my sanity. I'll always be grateful to you for that. Please don't spoil your life. Listen to your heart and do what will make you happy. You owe yourself that.'

They went back to the party and danced in silence. The words of the hauntingly romantic song seemed to hold a message for her as they circled the makeshift dance floor. What she had felt then, she still felt as powerfully as ever, but Tony inhabited another world, and he was married to a woman who had become her friend – a woman with whom she shared a secret. Tony could never in a thousand lifetimes belong to her. She repeated his words inside her head. *You saved my sanity. I'll always be grateful to you for that.* His gratitude was better than nothing, she supposed. And that night – the night when he heard that Claire had died – it had been to her that he turned. The suffering she had shared with him that night would always belong to them; it was a memory no one else could share. At least she could cherish that.

As the clock struck midnight they all raised their glasses and wished each other a happy New Year. Everyone linked arms and Leonie led them in singing 'Auld Lang Syne'. Then Tony proposed a toast, the first of the newly begun year.

'Here's to 1945. The last year of the war,' he said, holding his glass aloft. 'The beginning of the end.'

Glasses were raised and everyone drank, reiterating his toast: 'The beginning of the end.'

* * *

'I think it went rather well, don't you?' Leonie was taking off her make-up at the dressing table.

'Yes. I'm sure everyone enjoyed themselves.'

She looked up at him through the mirror. 'I was glad to see you being so nice to Gloria tonight.'

'Is there any reason why I shouldn't be nice to her?'

'None at all. Every reason that you should.'

He looked at her. 'You've changed. There was a time when you were as patronising as hell to her. Now you treat her almost like a human being.'

Leonie swung round on the dressing-table stool. 'That's unfair. Gloria's been a good friend to me. I've a lot to be grateful to her for.'

He turned to look at her, one eyebrow raised in surprise. 'Grateful – you? Oh, for the silk jacket she made for you out of the shawl?'

She hesitated, wanting to confide in him, to have him on her side again. Since the business with Norman she had felt a desperate need of warmth and reassurance. 'More than that,' she said. 'I've got to know Gloria a great deal better over the past few months and it has been good for me. She's like the personification of all the people out there who listen to my programme.'

Tony's lip curled slightly. Now she sounded more like the old Leonie. 'You mean she's that strange phenomenon, the woman in the street?' he said cynically. 'A member of your adoring public.'

She ignored the jibe. 'No. Tony. She's a woman, Full stop. A warm, kindly, generous woman. I discovered that when – when she did me a great favour.'

'Did you a favour?' He paused in the act of removing the studs from his dress shirt. 'What favour?'

Getting up, she went to him. 'Tony, there's something I didn't tell you. You remember I told you last summer that Norman was trying to blackmail me – threatening to go to the papers.'

'Yes.'

'Well, I didn't tell you that he came back. I tried calling his bluff, but I could see that it wasn't going to work. I'd no choice but to pay.'

He stared at her. 'You actually gave him money? You fool, Leonie! Why didn't you tell me?'

'There wasn't time and anyway I . . . didn't want to involve you. The thing is that Gloria was there. She overheard everything he said. She was such a help and support, Tony. She promised to keep all of it secret, but not only that, she offered to take the money to him and get the evidence for me.'

He was frowning. 'Wait a minute, when was all this?'

'At the flat, last June. On the day we took the girls to the RADA play.'

'The night of the first V-1 raid?'

'That's right.'

'She offered to take that risk – for you?'

'No one knew there was going to be a raid.'

'You're not telling me that you actually let her do it?'

'She *insisted*, Tony. And really I had no choice. You were due back with the girls any minute. We were going to the play and –'

'How much did you pay him?'

She licked her dry lips. She had expected him to sympathise with her dilemma. It wasn't going as she'd hoped. 'Five thousand.' As his eyes widened in shocked surprise, she hurried on: 'He promised that he wouldn't ask for any more. I *had* to pay it. Listen, I'd seen Noël at the Savoy only that lunchtime. It reminded me how important it is for me to plan for my future career now that the war is almost over. So when Norman threatened to ruin things for me, I had to agree to pay. But I couldn't get the money, go all the way to King's Cross with it and be back before we were due to leave for the play.'

'So you let that girl go across London with all that money on her, to do your dirty work for you while you got dressed up and went to the theatre?'

'It wasn't *like* that. I didn't ask her, Tony. She could see the hopeless tangle I was in and she offered to help. But listen, you haven't heard the best part. They were just doing the exchange when the raid started. Norman panicked and ran off to the shelter. Gloria came back with the evidence – *and* the money. Wasn't she wonderful?'

Tony was shaking his head. 'I saw her later that night, after the raid. She looked like death. She couldn't stop trembling. Now I know why. You let her risk her life just so that you could hang on to that stupid myth about your family background. Christ, Leonie, I knew you were self-centred but this borders on megalomania.' He looked at her. 'And make no mistake, he'll be back for that money. He'll be biding his time but he'll certainly be back. Blackmailers never let go. You realise that, don't you?'

'But don't you see? He can't. I've got the evidence now. He can't hold anything else over my head.'

'What evidence? Where is it?'

'I burned it.'

'Burned what? What was there?

'My birth certificate, some photographs. All in a tin box thing.'

'What interest could rubbish like that possibly be to a newspaper?' He grasped her by the shoulders. 'I can't believe that you let Gloria risk her life for something so trivial. Sometimes you make me sick, Leonie. You and that vastly inflated ego of yours. I believe you'd sell your own grandmother if you thought it'd get your photograph on the front page of some magazine.' He pushed her from him in a gesture of disgust. 'This just proves to me how selfish and shallow you are.'

'Tony, *no*. Listen.' She ran to stop him leaving the room. 'There's more – other things I haven't told you.'

He sighed wearily. 'No more now, Leonie. I'm tired. I want to go to bed.'

She held tightly to his arm, biting her lip. She was losing his sympathy. Should she tell him the rest – lay her soul bare for him? Should she take the gamble? 'There was something else, Tony. Something serious that I never told you about.'

He looked at her sceptically. In this mood he could never quite tell when she was acting and when she was on the level. 'What? Come on, then, are you going to tell me or aren't you?'

She swallowed hard. 'When I was in my teens, I . . . stole some things from a shop. Damn silly things, rubbish really. But I was caught and charged – put on probation. It was only a childish prank, but because of it I have a police record. That's what Norman was going to tell the papers. He had proof, too. Can you imagine what it would look like?'

He groaned. 'Why on earth didn't you tell me this before?' He looked at her, suddenly seeing her through new eyes. Was this the woman he had sacrificed his career as a classical actor for? A shallow, egotistical, jumped-up nobody who'd step on any face to get where she wanted to be? She had never loved him anyway – simply used him just as she'd used Gloria and everyone else she had ever come into contact with. Suddenly he felt he hated her – hated and pitied her both at the same time.

He stood up. 'So you got away with it? You sent Gloria to do your grubby little deal for you and she pulled your chestnuts out of the fire – *literally*, as it happens. Well, all I hope is that you get what you want. God only knows you've put enough necks on the line for it.' At the door he turned. 'I'll be leaving tomorrow – or rather today. We start filming again next week and there's a lot to do. I don't know when I'll see you again. Good night, Leonie.'

'Found yourself another slut, have you?' she screamed at him. 'I hope you don't fool yourself that they chase you for your sex appeal. Can't you see that they're just cheap little gold-diggers, on the make – out for what they can get?'

He paused in the doorway to look pityingly at her. 'Well, you'd know all about that, wouldn't you, Leonie? I've been married to the queen of all gold-diggers for the last sixteen years, and I'm sick to the back teeth of you. It's warmth and sincerity that I have to look elsewhere for.'

'*Swine!*' She snatched off one of her feathered mules and hurled it after him, but it hit the closed door and fell harmlessly to the floor. Throwing herself across the bed, she pushed her fist into her mouth in anguish. 'Go to hell then,' she spluttered, beside herself with tears of rage. 'Bloody well go to *hell*! I hate you, Tony bloody Darrent. *I hate you*. I hope you burn in hell.'

* * *

That spring term Shirley and Imogen worked extra hard at school. Because of overcrowding in the school, a handful of particularly bright students had been chosen to take the School Certificate one year early and both girls were among that number. Shirley was especially pleased. If she had to go to America, she could leave with her education complete. A cloud hung over the prospect of her leaving. She and Imogen had become as close as sisters and they could not imagine being apart.

The hardness of winter gentled into spring. Gloria was a regular weekend visitor now that Billy was no longer with them. Shirley worried about her mother. She was quiet and withdrawn much of the time. Unlike the old Gloria, who had always been eager and ready for a trip to the pictures to see her favourite stars, she spent a lot of time in the kitchen, chatting to Molly, or walking by herself, her face closed and preoccupied. Shirley wondered sometimes whether she was as keen on going to America as she made out to be. She had asked her once, but Gloria flared up at her.

'*Want* to go? Of course I want to go. Why? Are you trying to throw a spanner in the works now, like Ma?'

Shirley had stared at her, taken aback by the fiery reaction to her innocent question. 'I only asked, Glor. You seem so quiet sometimes; so far away, that's all.'

Gloria had stared at her for a moment, then bitten her lip, her face crumpling. 'I'm sorry, love,' she'd said tearfully. 'I didn't mean to snap at you. It's just the worry.'

'Billy'l be all right, Glor,' Shirley said, stroking her mother's hair. 'I know he will. The war's nearly over now.'

Gloria was silent. She longed to tell Shirley she wasn't going to marry Billy – wasn't going to America – but she couldn't. Not until she had told Billy himself. And the prospect of telling him was eating away at her heart, making her sick with anguish. How could she hurt him? How could she bear the hurt herself? Because she knew that sending him away would tear her heart out. 'Of course he will,' she muttered, squeezing Shirley's hand. 'Take no notice of me, love.'

Jim still sat by the wireless at every news bulletin. He got especially excited at the news that Allied troops had crossed the Rhine.

'We're nearly there now, love,' he told Molly. 'Won't be long now before we're hanging out the flags.'

Aware of the rift between Gloria and Ma, Shirley wrote to her grandparents every week. It was hard to know what to write about. Ma had made it clear that she didn't approve of too much schooling and she had no interest in the country. Neither did she approve of Shirley's theatrical ambitions or the lifestyle she led here at Houlton. But somehow, in spite of it all, Shirley managed to fill a couple of pages with assorted titbits of news. In return Ma wrote back. The doodlebugs and buzzbombs seemed to have stopped now. There wasn't too much damage around Angel Row, thank goodness. The shop had taken a bit more battering, but London County Council had promised to put it right as soon as they could. The business was still doing well and Pa still made his early morning trips 'up the market'. It was nice to think that Gloria and Shirley would soon be home to help out. She and Pa weren't as young as they used to be. There was news about the neighbours, of marriages and deaths and births. In fact, Ma's letters contained much more news than Shirley's. Sometimes when she was reading them she wondered how she had ever lived in Angel Row. Before the war seemed so long ago – another life, which she only barely remembered. It was a whole world away. And going back to live in it again, as Ma seemed to expect, was totally inconceivable. But she and Gloria would be going to America, so there was no chance of that anyway.

In late March, Peter Jason sent for Leonie. The anticipation of peace filled the London air with a special kind of excitement, as fresh and fragrant as the scent of the daffodils in the flower-sellers' baskets.

Peter had moved back into London now, renting a temporary office in Old Bond Street. Leonie climbed the two flights of narrow stairs, complaining bitterly to Peter when she was shown into his office.

'Really, darling, I'd have thought you'd try to get a place with a lift. After all, you have some very successful clients on your books now.'

Peter smiled. 'All in good time, Leonie. We'll have to take this rehabilitation business one step at a time.'

'So . . .' Leonie settled herself in a chair and smoothed her skirt. 'What have you got for me?'

'A play. I think you're going to like it.'

'By Noël?' Her eyes lit up. 'I knew he'd keep his promise to me. Did I tell you I saw him at the –'

'It's not by Noël,' Peter interrupted. 'This is by a new young playwright called Paul Winspear. He was invalided out of the army after being wounded at El Alamein and he's been writing ever since. I think he's going to make quite a name for himself.'

Leonie was clearly disappointed. 'I'm not sure that I want to commit myself at the moment,' she said. 'Noël did promise and I don't want to find myself too tied up to accept, do I?'

Peter shook his head. 'I wouldn't turn this down if I were you. When you read the script you'll see what I mean. And there's a whisper that a film might soon be made of one of Noël's most popular plays. I'm keeping you in line for a leading part in that – if you're interested, that is.'

'Interested? Of *course* I'm interested. So what is this new play about?'

Peter pushed a bound manuscript across the desk towards her. 'It's called *Joy in the Morning*.'

'And do I play Joy?'

Peter frowned at her. 'It's a serious play, Leonie. A drama about a couple struggling to readjust to normal life after the trauma of war.'

Leonie looked at him. 'No music? No songs?'

Peter sighed. 'Your voice won't last for ever, you know. This is a chance to get into the legitimate theatre.'

Leonie was leafing impatiently through the scripts. 'I know, but isn't this all a bit depressing? There's a character here who actually comes home blind.'

'I know – and you play his wife. It's a very strong part, Leonie. She's a selfish, pleasure-loving woman who finds a new strength through her husband's disablement.'

But Leonie was shaking her head. 'What will my fans think, Peter? They'll come expecting me to be the Leonie Swann who was in *Sunshine Sally* and *Prince of Hearts*; the girl who sang their favourite songs for them and encouraged them all through the war. Now that it's almost over –'

'When the war is over, the struggle will begin for many of us here at home,' Peter pointed out. 'That's the message of the play. Read it, Leonie. Reserve your judgement till you've read it.'

Leonie was doubtful, but she took the manuscript back to the flat, poured herself a stiff drink and curled up in a corner of the settee to read. It was past midnight when she finally laid the script down, having read it through twice. In a state of suppressed excitement she undressed and took a bath. She had never been so impressed by anything in her entire life. The couple in the play were just like herself and Tony. She wanted more than anything else in the world to play the part and she knew with a profound certainty deep inside her that she could make a success of it. Peter had been right: it was *her* part. She had always tried to be close to her fans and in this play she would have the opportunity to show them that she was really *like* them – could weep and suffer and love, just as they did. It would give her a chance to show Tony that he'd been wrong about her, too. She wasn't shallow. In playing this part she would have the chance to reveal the true depths of her character; the warmth and sincerity he had accused her of lacking. She would make him eat his words if it was the last thing she ever did.

When she was comfortably settled in bed, she lifted the telephone and dialled Peter's number. After several rings he answered sleepily.

'Jason here.'

'Peter. I've just finished reading the script of *Joy in the Morning*.'

He gave an audible groan. 'Christ, Leonie, is that all? It's the middle of the night. Tomorrow morning would have been quite soon enough to tell me that.'

She laughed. 'Don't be such an old grouch, darling. It's not that late. I had to ring because I knew you'd want to know that I absolutely *adore* it. I can't wait to play the part and I'm longing to meet the man who wrote it.'

'Then you'd better come along to the office on Friday,' he said. 'He's coming in to see me at eleven o'clock. You can meet him then. And now, Leonie, do you mind very much if I get some hard-earned sleep?'

She put down the telephone, switched off the bedside light and slid down under the bedclothes. Every inch of her tingled with a feeling of excitement that was almost sexual. She had the strongest feeling that she had reached an important turning point, both in her career and her life.

Chapter Twelve

When it came, the news took them all in different ways. Gloria heard at her bench at the factory. A great cheer went up when the announcement was made, and Jane grasped her round the waist and began to whirl her round.

'It's over,' she sang excitedly. 'It's actually *over*. Can you believe it?'

But Gloria felt numb. They had all been waiting for so long that now it had finally come, the news left her oddly unmoved. Her immediate thoughts were of how changed life would be now that they were at peace. To begin with, she would be out of a job. Ma and Pa would expect her to go home, while Shirley would have to stop on at Houlton at least until after her exams. Then there was Billy. She hadn't had a letter from him now for almost ten weeks. It wasn't unusual or surprising, considering all that had been happening. Many of the girls with husbands or boyfriends serving abroad didn't hear for weeks. Now she found herself dreading the immediate prospects of having to tell him of her decision not to marry him.

At Longueville Hall, Jim received the news with quiet satisfaction.

'Well, old England's done it again, love,' he told Molly, looking up from his seat next to the wireless set with moist eyes. 'The Hun has surrendered at last. Surely they'll know now that they can't keep us British down, no matter what the odds. There'll be a lot of changes now. You mark my words.'

'Changes – how?' Molly asked, stopping only momentarily from doing the ironing. 'I can't see how it'll affect us.'

Jim shook his head. 'I reckon we'll be having a change of government for a start. Winston's all right for wartime but when the lads come home they'll be looking for a better world.'

'Well, why shouldn't we get it with Winnie?'

'Why? Because he's against most of the reforms. Beveridge wants this new health plan of his passed, and the sooner the better if you ask me. Better medical attention for everyone, not just those that can afford it. Then there's Butler's education act to be put into practice – properly, not just half-measures.' He shook his head. 'No, things've got to become better now than they were before the war, otherwise they'll likely have a revolution on their hands.'

Molly sniffed disapprovingly. Men! They were never happy unless they were stirring things up. 'I'd have thought people'd be only too happy to let things be as they were before the war,' she said. 'You'd think they'd be glad to be done with fighting.'

'Ah, but now we've got to fight for ourselves,' Jim told her. 'For a better way of life for ordinary folk. No more poverty. Decent housing. I reckon as a nation we've earned that much at least. And if it's to be had with a fresh government, then that's what folks'll vote for.'

'Well, I think it's downright ungrateful,' Molly said, outraged. 'After all Mr Churchill has done for us, are we going to cast him aside like – like an old sock or something?'

Jim smiled. 'I dare say he won't be too sorry to sit back and put his feet up for a change,' he said. 'He's no chicken, after all. The war must've taken it out of him even more than the rest of us – all that responsibility. No, give the younger men a chance, that's what I say. Let Winston retire gracefully and take a well-earned rest.'

At the high school the girls were allowed out early after the headmistress had assembled the school to make the announcement. As they came out into the May sunshine, they saw that the Union Jack had been run up the flagpole to flutter triumphantly in the fresh spring breeze.

'I suppose you and Gloria will be off to America soon now then,' Imogen said glumly as they waited for the bus.

'I don't know.' Shirley looked doubtful. 'Glor doesn't exactly seem excited about going. If I mention it she snaps my head off. Sometimes I wonder if she's gone off the idea.'

'I asked Daddy if you could stay with us,' Imogen said. 'He said it would be up to you and Gloria – that I wasn't to try to influence you either way.'

'You never told me.'

Imogen smiled. 'Just think, if you stayed we could be going to RADA in the autumn, you and I.' She clutched Shirley's arm and squeezed it tightly. 'Oh, Shirl, you won't go to America, will you? You know you don't want to.'

Shirley lifted her shoulders helplessly, torn both ways. 'I don't know, Imo. I'll just have to wait and see what happens.'

'I bet there'll be some fun in town this evening,' Imogen said, cheering up. 'What do you say we take the bus into town later and see what's happening?'

Leonie was at the theatre where a rehearsal of *Joy in the Morning* was in progress. The stage manager called her during a break to say that there was a telephone call for her. She took it in the prop room, which was nearest to the stage.

'Leonie Swann speaking.'

'Leonie, it's Tony. You've heard the news?'

'News?'

'Germany has surrendered. It's all over.'

'Oh, that? Yes, I heard.'

'I thought we might go up to Houlton this evening, celebrate with Imogen, Shirley and the Jarvises. I'm free from now. I could come and pick you up from the theatre.'

'Oh. Well, of course that would have been lovely, but I'm afraid I can't.'

'Why not? Your first night is weeks away yet.'

'There are some snags with the script. Paul is going to have to do some rewriting and Gerald wants me to be here to discuss it with them both.'

'But not tonight, surely? It isn't every day we win the war.'

'You go,' Leonie said. 'Somehow I don't feel much like celebrating anyway, not when I think of all the lives that have been lost – all the heartbreak.'

Tony was silent at the other end of the line. He was frankly taken aback. Leonie – concerning herself with other people's broken hearts? It sounded most unlikely. 'Even so, it would be nice if you could make it,' he said.

'Tell them I love them all very much and I'll get up to see them as soon as I possibly can. Have a lovely time, all of you. I'll have to go now. Gerald will be anxious to get on again. Goodbye, darling. Oh, and I suppose I should wish you a Happy Peace or something.'

'Thank you, Leonie. The same to you,' he said dryly.

Leonie replaced the receiver. From where she stood she could just see Paul Winspear as he stood talking to the director, Gerald Bates, on the side of the stage, and her heart gave the lurch that was becoming so familiar to her. The moment they had met for the first time in Peter's office that Friday morning six weeks ago, something amazing had happened. For Leonie it was like a sudden flash of lightning, a charge of electricity passing between them, taking her totally by surprise with its shocking intensity. In the intervening weeks during the preliminary read-through, discussions and early rehearsals, Paul had never once given her the slightest hint that he reciprocated the powerful attraction she felt, but an almost primeval instinct told her without a shadow of a doubt that it was as powerful for him as it was for her. It was just a question of breaking down his iron reserve – the deeply rooted discipline that had made him such a good soldier – to get to the simmering passion that she sensed lay beneath his calm veneer.

Taking a deep breath, she began to walk towards the two men. Seeing her approach, Gerald turned.

'Ah, Leonie. I've just been saying, we'll call it a day now, as it's something of a special occasion. I dare say the crowds are going to thicken as the afternoon wears on, and some of the cast will be wanting to get home before it gets impossible. I've called the next rehearsal for ten thirty tomorrow morning. Is that all right with you?'

'Fine.' As he walked away to tell the rest of the cast, she looked at Paul. 'It'll take you hours to get out to Teddington. Come back to my flat. You can work in peace there.'

Paul looked older than his thirty-five years. He was a tall man with thick dark hair and the gaunt, almost haunted look of a man who has seen war at its worst. His face was craggy, his eyes the dark, lustrous brown of mahogany, but there was a certain vulnerability about his mouth that made Leonie's bones ache with the urge to kiss him.

'I can only work effectively when I'm alone,' he was saying. 'And as I have a lot of work to do on Act II before tomorrow, I think I'd better try to get home.'

'Oh, but I'll be going down to Houlton,' she lied. 'I'll take you to the flat and get you something to eat before I leave, then it's all yours till tomorrow.'

He smiled, the long, slow smile that turned her knees to water. 'Thank you, Leonie. That's very thoughtful. I must admit it would be a marvellous help.'

Even as they made their way down Shaftesbury Avenue and across Piccadilly, people were beginning to gather, laughing and jostling each other good-naturedly. It was obvious that there was little chance of getting a taxi. Everyone seemed to have stopped work for the day, eager to get out on the streets and celebrate. By the time they had walked as far as Mayfair, they were both breathless. As Leonie unlocked the door and let them into the flat, she turned to him with a smile.

'Well, at least we made it without being stampeded in the rush. I'll make some tea. What would you like to eat?'

269

He shook his head. 'Don't bother about me if you want to get off. It won't be easy getting to the station. I'm quite capable of looking after my own needs if you'll just show me where everything is.'

Leonie knew that Paul's wife had left him soon after he came out of the army, though she didn't know any details about the split. He had been on his own now for some time and she guessed that he didn't bother too much about cooking himself proper meals when he became engrossed in his writing. Never before in her life could she remember feeling the urge to take care of a man – not till now. But there was something about the way Paul's hair curled into the nape of his neck for want of cutting, and the slightly frayed shirt cuffs, that brought out a maternal instinct she had never known she possessed.

'It won't take me any time at all to rustle you up a quick meal,' she said. 'Eggs and bacon with a few chips perhaps? Men usually like that.'

He rewarded her with the slow smile. 'That sounds very nice. But what about your train. You'll never get a taxi and if those crowds get any thicker . . .'

'I'll manage. Don't worry. Now, I'll show you where everything is.' She showed him the bathroom and where he might sleep, then to the room that Tony used as a study, where she suggested he might work. After that she disappeared into the kitchen to don an apron. Twenty minutes later she called him to a neatly laid table.

'I thought you wouldn't mind eating in the kitchen.'

'Not at all. It looks delicious. Aren't you joining me?'

She shook her head. 'No. I'd better go and see if I can get a taxi now. Enjoy your meal – and the peace and quiet. See you tomorrow morning.'

At a small restaurant on the corner of Maddox Street Leonie ordered chicken salad and a glass of white wine. She followed it with a pot of coffee, over which she lingered for the next half-hour, smoking and listening to the increasing volume of the singing and babble outside in the street. It was eight o'clock when she paid her bill and left.

Outside, Regent Street was now completely filled with people, dancing, singing, letting off fireworks and generally enjoying themselves. Struggling against the tide, which seemed to be making its way down to Piccadilly, she pushed her way back to the flat and made her way up in the lift. Letting herself in quietly, she heard the sound of the typewriter tapping in the study and smiled to herself. In the bedroom she changed into a black skirt and a clinging cream silk blouse and went back into the kitchen to make coffee.

Gloria arrived at Houlton at half-past five. Getting off the bus outside the post office, she set off on the walk up to Longueville Hall, but she hadn't gone more than half a mile when she heard the hooting of a car horn behind her and turned to see Tony pulling up in the smart blue Humber Snipe he had recently acquired. Reaching across, he released the passenger door for her.

'Gloria! Good to see you. Jump in.'

She settled herself gratefully in the deep leather seat beside him. 'Thanks a lot. I wasn't looking forward to the walk.'

'Wonderful news, eh?' He turned to smile at her. 'We had the same thought – to spend this memorable day with our daughters?'

She nodded. 'Yes, though somehow I can't get very excited at the moment. Perhaps it hasn't sunk in yet.'

'Funny, Leonie said much the same thing. I rang her as soon as the news came through. I thought she might join me here to celebrate with Imogen, but she's too tied up with rehearsals to come.'

'That's a pity.'

'Never mind. At least you're here. What do you say we take both girls into town this evening to mingle with the crowds and see the lights go on?'

'If you like. I dare say it's what they'd like.' She wondered if perhaps she might catch the mood herself if she went into town and mingled with the crowd; whether it might help her snap out of the gloom that seemed to have descended on her. So preoccupied had she been that she had even forgotten to bring the new blouse she'd made for Shirley.

'It's a historic occasion, after all,' Tony was saying. 'Something to tell their grandchildren about.' He looked at her. 'You don't have to get back tonight, do you?'

'I'm afraid so, though I did ask Jane, my friend, to cover for me if the buses stopped running and I didn't make it. It's probably anybody's guess what will happen tonight.'

'That's all right. No need to worry. I can run you back.'

'Thank you, Tony.'

He glanced at her pale, drawn face. 'I suppose this means that the time of decision has arrived for you,' he said quietly.

'Not really,' she told him wearily. 'I've already decided, that's the trouble.'

But although he waited she did not offer to tell him more and he did not press her.

That evening Tony, Gloria and both girls packed into the car and drove into town to join in the festivities. Molly and Jim were invited too, but they preferred to stay at home and listen to the celebrations in comfort on the wireless. At ten o'clock they drove back to Houlton and, after the girls had been packed off to bed and they had drunk the cocoa Molly insisted on making them, Tony and Gloria set off for Boothley. As they drove, Gloria was silent.

'You're very quiet, Gloria. Is anything wrong?' Tony asked.

'Nothing that time won't put right,' She turned to him. 'Tony, would you do something for me?'

'Of course, anything.'

'It's just – I made a blouse for Shirley and forgot to bring it with me this morning. If I go and get it, will you take it back for her?'

'Of course.'

As they drew up ouutside the hostel she looked at him hesitantly. 'I'd ask you to come in, but . . .'

He laughed. 'It's all right. I'll wait here.'

'You're wise to.' She smiled wryly. 'You'd probably get mobbed. Some of those girls – especially this evening if they've been celebrating.' She jumped out of the car and went into the building. Hurrying along the corridor to her room, she pushed the door open. Jane was standing by the window. She swung round, startled, as Gloria came in.

'Gloria. I wasn't expecting you back tonight . . .' Her voice trailed off, she looked flustered and her eyes seemed unable to meet Gloria's. 'As a matter of fact I was just thinking about ringing you at Houlton. I . . . didn't quite know what to do.'

'Why? What's happened?'

Jane picked up a folded sheet of paper from the dressing table. 'This came this morning. I didn't get it till we came back from the shift. You'd left by then. It's from Chuck . . .' She paused, seeing from Gloria's face that she'd already guessed that the letter held bad news. 'I think you'd better sit down, love.'

Gloria shook her head. 'Just tell me. Get on with it.'

Jane swallowed. 'It's Billy, Gloria. I'm so sorry, love, but he was badly wounded at the Rhine crossing. He died of his wounds a few days later.'

Gloria sat down suddenly on the chair by her bed. The colour had drained from her face, leaving it deathly pale. 'The Rhine crossing? But that was weeks – *months* ago.'

'I know. Chuck's letter's dated April the tenth. All the mail has been delayed. He knew that you and Billy were sort of engaged but that there was nothing formal so you wouldn't be informed through the usual channels. He . . . felt you should be told.' Jane took a tentative step towards her friend. She was disturbed by the way she had taken the news. Apart from her deathly pallor, it was almost as though she hadn't taken it in. 'Gloria, are you all right, love? Is there anything I can do?'

Gloria shook herself as though trying to rouse herself from a deep sleep. 'No. No, I'm all right.' Getting up, she opened the dressing-table drawer and took out the blouse she had made for Shirley. Very slowly and meticulously she wrapped it in a sheet of tissue paper, then turned to her friend. 'I'm going back to Houlton,' she said calmly. 'I only came back for Shirley's blouse. I'll see you tomorrow, Jane. Good night.'

Jane stared at her, open-mouthed. 'Going back? But how will you get there?'

'Tony – Mr Darrent is waiting for me in the car. If I'm not back tomorrow, tell them . . . something – anything you like. Will you?'

'Of course I will, but . . .' Jane watched helplessly as Gloria hurried out of the room.

Climbing back into the car, Gloria said: 'If you don't mind, Tony, I'd like you to drop me at Rook Cottage. It's on the edge of the village. It's not out of your way. I've decided to stay the night there.'

She pushed the parcel containing the blouse into the glove compartment. 'Give that to Shirl, will you? Tell her I hope she likes it.'

As he drove, Tony could feel the tension emanating from her. He knew that something had happened to upset her, but she didn't volunteer to tell him what was wrong and he didn't know how to ask her. As he drew up outside the little thatched cottage he said: 'I've never seen this cottage of yours. You wouldn't care to invite me in for a nightcap, would you?'

She paused. 'You can come in if you like,' she said. 'But there's nothing much to see and I haven't got anything to offer you in the way of drink.'

'That doesn't matter.' Tony was already getting out of the car. He waited, standing in the porch, while she unlocked the door, then followed her into the little parlour. Taking out a match, she lit the oil lamp and drew the curtains. It was when she turned her face towards him and he saw her expression that his fears were confirmed. He took a step towards her. 'Gloria – something's wrong, isn't it?'

She stiffened and crossed her arms over her breast, hugging herself defensively. 'Billy's dead,' she said flatly. 'Isn't it stupid? I was worried sick about telling him I couldn't marry him and all the time I needn't have been, because . . . because he was dead.'

'When did it happen?'

'It was at the Rhine crossing – weeks ago. All this time I've been eating my heart out for – for *nothing*.' Her shoulders began to shake. Her face crumpled and she seemed almost to disintegrate before his eyes. Tears welled up in her eyes and streamed down her cheeks.

Profoundly moved, Tony stepped forward and put his arms round her rigid body.

'Oh, Gloria. Oh, my dear, I'm sorry – so sorry.' He held her while she sobbed, great racking sobs that sounded as though they would tear her slender body apart. They tore at him too. He felt helpless, able to do nothing but hold her and mutter the useless phrases that had become vacuous from overuse during the past six tear-drenched years.

At last he felt some of the tension go out of her as she sagged against him. He held her away from him, fumbling in his pocket for his own handkerchief and dabbing at her cheeks. 'Let me get you something – a cup of tea. I don't suppose you've got any brandy?'

'No.' She shook her head. 'I – don't want – anything.'

'Let me help you upstairs them. You should try to get some rest. I'll go to the pub and see what I can get.'

He helped her, protesting, up the narrow stairs and into the front bedroom with its big brass bed. She lay down, but when her head touched the pillow she caught the faint scent of the hair cream Billy had used and began to tremble uncontrollably.

'Don't – go,' she stammered between clenched teeth. 'I – don't want to be alone – please.'

He sat down on the bed and took her hand.

'All these past weeks – all I could think of was how to send him away,' she said. 'And all the time he was lying there badly wounded – needing someone he loved to help him. And now he's dead and it's too late. He was so young, Tony. Too young for me. But he gave me more love than I've ever had in my whole life. And all I could think of was how to tell him something I knew would hurt him. How can I live with that? How can I ever forgive myself?'

'But you *didn't* hurt him,' Tony said, stroking her hair. 'It didn't happen. He loved you and I'm sure you gave him so much back.' He looked around the room. 'Did you bring him here?'

She nodded. 'We were so happy here. I can still feel him here, Tony. Still see him. I can even *smell* him.'

'I know. I know.'

She looked up at him, remembering. 'Yes. You *do* know, don't you? I'd almost forgotten. Tony, do you still think of her – Claire? Does it still hurt? Does it ever get better?'

He squeezed her hand. 'Yes. It does get better, I promise you. After a while the hurt begins to soften at the edges. It stops cutting you and only probes gently at the memories. You'll want to keep those memories, won't you?'

'Oh, yes.'

'We can't – wouldn't ever want to forget, not really forget. The trick is to let time wash the memories clean of sadness.' He smiled at her. 'Will you be all right now while I go to the pub to get you something to help you to sleep?'

She held on tightly to his hand. 'Don't leave me – not yet.'

She was still shivering and he pulled the eiderdown up round her, then, after a moment's hesitation, lay down beside her and held her close. 'Do you remember the time you did this for me?' he whispered. 'You were so wonderful to me that night. You'll never know what you did for me. Do you know, if it hadn't been for you I think I might have been tempted to end it.'

'*Don't*.' She shook her head at him. 'Don't talk of dying, Tony. I don't want to think of death any more.' She shuddered and reached out for him. 'Tony . . .'

'Yes, darling?'

'Will you stay with me till morning, please?'

'Of course I will.' He held her close, her tears wetting his face, trying to warm and strengthen her with his own body; held her till he felt the tension slowly ebb out of her; till her breathing deepened and he knew that she slept, emotionally exhausted. It was then that the memory of Claire came back to him as vividly as the day he last saw her; the day they said goodbye. Closing his eyes he saw again her fair hair, lifted by the sea breeze; her beautiful expressive eyes, full of love and sadness; her arm lifted in farewell. And from under his closed eyelids the hot tears crept to scald his cheeks and mingle with Gloria's as the sky outside began to lighten.

'When Gerald first told me that Leonie Swann was to play the part of Janet Freer in my play, I must admit that I had reservations.' Paul sat in the drawing room sipping the coffee Leonie had made.

She smiled at him. 'Is that a polite way of telling me you were appalled?'

'I wouldn't put it as strongly as that.' He smiled. 'A little fearful, shall we say? I couldn't see a woman who was a popular singer and musical-comedy star playing a serious dramatic role like Janet Freer.'

'I see. So what is your verdict now that we've started rehearsals?'

'I wouldn't be telling you any of this if I wasn't one hundred percent delighted with the way you're interpreting the role,' he told her. 'In fact I wouldn't even be here in your flat.'

'I think what you're saying is that you'd have moved heaven and earth to have had me kicked out if I hadn't come up to scratch.'

'I'm afraid I might have.'

'You might just have had a problem there.' Leonie lit a cigarette, taking her time and blowing the smoke out languidly. 'After all, as you've just said, I am a star – and you are . . .'

'An unknown? A raw newcomer?' He smiled. 'That is something I intend to remedy as soon as I can,' he told her. 'Which is why I would never have tolerated an actress who was wrong for the part. I'd rather have sacrificed the play.'

Leonie put on a mock-horrified expression. 'Good heavens! We must all thank our lucky stars that I wasn't too dreadful then, mustn't we?'

He looked at her thoughtfully over the rim of his cup, deciding to ignore the sarcasm in her voice. 'I'm so sorry you didn't manage to get your train, but it's been a bonus to have had this opportunity to talk,' he said. 'I expect you'd like me to leave now.'

'Not at all. If you've finished the reworking of Act II why don't you try it out on me? Or are you completely satisfied with what you've done?'

He smiled wryly. 'Oh, dear. Did I sound as overconfident as that?'

'Not in the least. We all need to be sure of what we're doing. I admire a man who can recognise his own talent and knows his own worth. And I happen to think you're a very talented writer, Paul.'

A smile lifted the corners of his mouth. 'In that case I shall fetch the script and read it to you.'

They read the reworked act together and Leonie agreed that the adjustments he had made were just what was needed to strengthen the dialogue.

'It makes the relationship between Janet and her husband, Ivor, much more poignant. They are two people who have outgrown one another,' she said. 'Who in normal circumstances would have parted, but Ivor's war injuries – his blindness holds them together. Somehow they each have to come to terms with the fact that he is now totally dependent on her and she is obliged to overcome her inherent selfishness.'

'That's right.' Paul leaned forward, his eyes alight. 'And it's only when their roles have reversed and she realises that *she* is the dependent one that their relationship becomes whole again.'

'It's a wonderful play, Paul.' She paused. 'Forgive me for asking, but was it written from your own experiences?'

'I suppose it was – in a way. But we all have to draw on our own experience to a certain extent, don't we?' He looked at her with his direct dark gaze. 'And you? You play the part with such perception that I confess I've wondered . . .'

'The same thing?' She laughed. 'My marriage to Tony and our reasons for staying together are very complex. Other couples marry for love. You could say that we married for a property. My talent. That was what Tony saw and wanted when we met. He developed it, nurtured it and benefited from it in many ways. But now he despises it because he believes that it deprived him of his own career.'

Paul frowned. 'That sounds very cynical. There must have been love too, surely?'

Leonie drew hard on her cigarette, then stubbed it out firmly. 'No. We were both dazzled. And when you're young that is often enough. Success is a great aphrodisiac.'

He smiled gently. 'You talk as though you're old. You can't be more than – what – thirty?'

Leonie smiled enigmatically. If that was what he thought, then let him. 'I'm only just beginning to realise that I've never known real love,' she said softly. 'I've never missed it – till now.'

There was a pause, then he stood up. 'I must go.' He looked at his watch. 'I wonder if the trains are running normally.'

'I doubt it.' Leonie stood to face him, her eyes holding his.

'Teddington is a very long way to walk. Why don't you stay here?'

He took a step closer. 'I think you know why, Leonie.'

Her heart was hammering so hard in her breast that it was difficult to breathe. She said: 'Stay, Paul. Why not? It's what you want, isn't it? It's what we've both wanted since that first day in Peter's office.' She stepped closer and lifted her hand to trail her fingers down his cheek. 'I'm right, aren't I?'

He stood perfectly still. 'Of course you're right. But I don't make love to other men's wives in their own homes.'

'Home?' She let her head drop back and chuckled softly. 'This hasn't been Tony's home for a very long time.

When he isn't away on location or with one of his women, he stays at a hotel.'

'He's unfaithful to you?'

'To me – and to all the others. Amoral would be a better word for what Tony is.'

With one long, sensitive hand he cupped her chin. 'Are you very unhappy, my darling?'

'No. It isn't a case of getting my own back, Paul. It's not a game I'm playing. Until now I've never felt there was anything missing from my life. I've been content to put all my emotional energy into my work. I've never wanted another man; never felt – what I'm feeling now – for anyone.' She lifted her arms and let them creep around his neck, her fingers lacing into his hair, raising her face to his.

For a brief moment he looked deep into her eyes, then his arms closed round her, crushing her close, and his mouth was on hers, kissing her hungrily. Leonie was shaken by the sudden violence of his kiss and the desperation of his hands on her body. She felt her own smouldering desire burst into flame, raging through her like a forest fire. Murmuring helplessly, her lips never leaving his, she pulled off his jacket and began to unbutton his shirt, thrilling to the sensation of his hands on her skin as he slipped the blouse from her shoulders and unhooked the lacy bra beneath.

His lovemaking possessed her totally. For the first time in her life she was not in control – nor had she any desire to be. He overpowered her gloriously both in mind and body; stripping her of all pretensions, charging her emotions, stirring every nerve and sensation till she cried out with the force of a climax that was exquisitely painful and brilliant and terrible. Then, ignoring her pleas for him to stop, he went on and made it happen all over again.

Gloria wakened with the singing of the first birds. At once the realisation of Billy's death hit her like a hammer blow. She turned her head and saw that Tony still slept. She raised herself on one elbow to look at him. He had stayed.

He could easily have crept away once she was asleep, but he'd stayed. Gratitude filled her heart, making the tears prick at her eyes. She touched his cheek, finding it rough with morning stubble, and her heart twisted to see that he no longer appeared as he had when she had first seen him in those early films. He was beginning to look his age, though for her the streaks of grey in his hair and the tiny lines at eyes and mouth only made him even more attractive. Had he been very unhappy all these years with Leonie? she wondered. How many women had there been since Claire died? A good many, she guessed. But none who had captured his heart as Claire once had. As she watched, he opened one eye, then both, gazing up at her bemusedly, temporarily disoriented by his surroundings. He blinked and roused himself.

'Gloria. What time is it?'

'Half-past five.'

'How are you feeling?'

'I'm all right. I'll be fine.'

He sat up and ran a hand over his jaw. 'My God! How do I go anywhere looking like this?'

'Don't worry. I've got a razor and things. I kept them here for Billy. He had an electric shaver, you see, and there's no electricity here. I'll go down and get some water.' She made to get out of bed but he took her arm.

'Not yet. Plenty of time.' He smiled at her. She looked frail and innocent, almost waiflike with her hair tumbled and skin devoid of make-up.

'I'll never be able to thank you enough, Tony,' she said.

'For what?'

'For last night.'

He shook his head. 'I'm so glad I was there.' He drew her down into the crook of his arm and she lay for a moment with her head on his shoulder. She turned her face up towards him and it seemed the most natural thing in the world to kiss her. A brushing of lips deepened into a full-blown kiss, both of them aroused by the emotion of the previous night's happenings and the need that each of them felt. Tony looked into her eyes.

'This is the second time we've slept together all night with all our clothes on,' he said. 'Who would ever believe it?' He slipped one hand into the neckline of her crumpled dress to stroke the warm, soft skin of her shoulder. 'Once, a long time ago, you made me the sweetest, most generous offer,' he whispered. 'And I've regretted ever since that I didn't accept.'

'Why didn't you?' she whispered.

'Because I knew it would have meant so much to you. It would have been taking an unfair advantage,' he said. 'Perhaps that sounds conceited and pretentious, but it's true.'

'Because you knew I'd have given myself to you sincerely – while to you it would have meant nothing. Is that what you mean?'

He winced. 'You make it sound so cold and heartless. Believe me, Gloria, it wasn't. It was because I like and respected you too much that I resisted.' He smiled wryly. 'It's not something I'm noted for, I'm sorry to say.'

She was quiet, occupied with her own thoughts. If he had made love to her that night, things might have been so different. Who could tell where it might have got them by now?'

He smiled. 'If you were to make the same offer now I'd be afraid you were only offering out of gratitude.'

'And you'd be wrong. I think I've grown up a bit since then,' she said thoughtfully. 'And I dare say a great many people have turned to each other during the war years out of sheer need of warmth and comfort.' She raised her eyes to his and he saw the raw, irresistible need in them.

'We've always had a special relationship, you and I, haven't we, Gloria?' he said as he drew her closer. 'A deep understanding that very few men and women share.' His lips took hers gently at first, but her eager response aroused him quickly to passion.

Their lovemaking was brief and fiery and sweet and when it was over Gloria felt at peace. Lying quietly in his arms, she wondered what he would say if she were to tell him that her love for him was the reason she hadn't been able to marry Billy. She guessed that he would be appalled, even embarrassed, so she kept quiet. Instead she looked up at him and smiled, stroking his cheek.

'You'd better get up now and have that shave. The Jarvises will be wondering where you've got to.'

'Will you be all right, darling?'

'I'll be fine.'

He kissed her forehead. 'When will I see you again?'

She shook her head. 'Who can say? We both know this was just the once, Tony. It was like I said, for warmth and comfort. Don't let's pretend it was anything else. We'll see each other from time to time, I expect. But you belong to a different world from me. We'd never have met if it hadn't been for the war and now that it's over we'll be going our separate ways.'

'I don't want us to lose touch,' he said.

'But we *will*, dear.' She kissed him softly. 'Don't spoil it. Don't make promises you'll regret. Get up now, Tony. I'll get you some water for shaving. It's time to go, time to say goodbye.'

He began to protest, then looked into her eyes and stopped. He knew that she meant it. And he knew that, sadly, she was probably right.

It was two weeks later that the letter came. Gloria was working out the last week of her notice at the factory and she came off the early shift to find the blue air letter waiting for her in the rack. Puzzled, she turned it over. She couldn't think of anyone who would be writing to her from overseas. The address of the sender was printed in capitals on the back; Mr and Mrs H. Landis, Bluebird Garage, Boulder, Colorado, USA. Billy's parents? With mounting curiosity Gloria tore the air letter open, unfolded it and began to read.

My dear Gloria,

We have never met but my family and I feel we know you from all we have heard of you through Billy's letters. You will know by now that we lost our dear boy just a short time before the end of the war. As you can imagine we have all been totally devastated by his loss. Billy was always such a joy to his father and me, right from the day he was born. We know, dear, that you meant a very great deal to him and he would have wanted us to get in touch with you. We would dearly love to meet you and if you will allow it, we will send the fare for you to come over and visit with us – just as soon as you can. Do *please* try to come, my dear. It would mean so much to be able to talk with the dear girl who shared Billy's last days and who obviously made him very happy. Let me know if you will accept our heartfelt invitation and we will cable the fare to you right away.

For now, God bless. Our love to you,

Louise and Hal Landis.

Gloria read the letter through twice more before the contents completely registered. Billy's parents wanted her to go to America to stay with them, to talk about the relationship she had shared with their son. How could she do that when she had been planning to let him down? It was out of the question. She pushed the letter into her pocket and walked around with it for the whole of the next day, refusing even to think about how she would reply.

It wasn't long before Jane sensed that Gloria had something on her mind. They were having their evening meal together the following day when Jane said suddenly:

'What's worrying you, Gloria? You've been miles away ever since yesterday. I keep speaking to you and you don't even hear me. Is it anything to do with that air letter you had yesterday?'

Without a word Gloria took the crumpled letter out of her pocket and passed it across the table to her friend. Jane read it slowly and carefully.

'You'll go, of course,' she said when she had finished.

Gloria shook her head. 'How could I let them send me all that money when I wasn't gong to marry Billy? If he'd lived I'd have sent him home unhappy. I'm not what they think, Jane. I don't think I could face them.'

284

'You made Billy happy and, as his mother says here in the letter, you were the one he spent his last days with. I think you should go for their sakes, Gloria. You need never tell them about your decision, need you?'

'But what will they think when they see I'm so much older?'

Jane laughed. 'Anyone'd think you were ninety instead of thirty-two. You've always looked younger than you are, Gloria. You don't *look* that much older than Billy. Anyway, I don't think age has anything to do with it.'

But Gloria was still unconvinced. 'I'd be a terrible disappointment to them.'

'Why do you always put yourself down so?' Jane grasped her arm. 'You could never be a disappointment to anyone, Gloria. You're a kind, sensitive, compassionate person. Look at it this way, since Billy was killed you've been feeling bad, thinking you let him down by not wanting to marry him. Well, this is one way you can make up for that. Go and see his folks. Share your memories with them. Tell them what a smashing boy he was and how much you thought of him. You'll feel better for it and so will they. Do it, Gloria. You'll always regret it if you don't.'

'You really think Billy would have wanted me to go?'

'I know damned well he would. And so do you.'

Gloria flew out of Northolt Airport bound for the USA on the day that Shirley and Imogen sat their School Certificate examination. Two weeks later Pa Rayner collapsed at the supper table and was taken to hospital suffering from a severe stroke. Soon after that, Gloria began to suspect that she was pregnant. Little did any of them realise just how much the events that followed in the days and weeks to come would alter the course of all their lives. Nothing was ever to be quite the same again.

Chapter Thirteen

Shirley dragged another sack of potatoes through from the store room to the shop. It was half-past three on the afternoon of Christmas Eve and quiet after the rush, but there still might be a last-minute panic, so best be prepared.

Christmas this year would be a miserable affair. Since Shirley had been back at the shop in Angel Row, Ma had been too busy nursing Pa to bother with much else and Shirley had been working far too hard in the shop to think about making many preparations for the festive season.

Since Pa's return from hospital, the daily routine had had to be altered drastically to allow for the constant care he needed. The shop was now the responsibility of Shirley, helped by Dave Green, a young man with a gammy leg who had been badly wounded in the North African campaign. Dave was glad of the work. He'd been on the dole since his discharge from the Army. Every morning at the crack of dawn he took the horse and cart to Covent Garden to do the buying and on his return saw to all the heavy work. The shop itself was left to Shirley.

Standing behind the counter in the lull between customers, she looked down at her hands. They were chapped and sore, rough and ingrained with the soil from the potatoes and root vegetables. The fingernails she had taken such a pride in were broken and rimmed with dirt. But her fingernails were the least of her worries. The chief cause for her concern and resentment was her mother. When Pa was taken ill, Gloria had been notified by cable.

But Ma had followed it up immediately by an air-mail letter, telling her not to come home precipitately. Pa was in good hands in hospital and there was nothing she could do. After the Landis family had sent all that money, it was only right that she should stay out her time with them, she wrote. She would get Shirley home to help her. So, on the day that Shirley and Imogen left school for the last time, Shirley had packed all her things and come home to Whitechapel.

She hadn't minded at first. It was an emergency after all, and it was only meant to have been temporary. Gloria should be back from America in plenty of time for Shirley to take the entrance exam and go to RADA in the autumn as planned. But Gloria hadn't come home. She had written once or twice from Colorado, saying that she was having a good time and that Billy's family had made her very welcome. But after her leaving Colorado there had been a long lapse in correspondence. Eventually she wrote to say that she had met some English people in the USA who had offered her a temporary job as a house-keeper in Yorkshire, which she had accepted. She would only be away for about a year and she was sure that Ma and Shirley would understand.

Ma had certainly not understood. She was vociferous in her anger and resentment.

'Why 'ave folks turned so selfish since the war ended?' she demanded. 'First it was the election – they ditched Mr Churchill after all 'e done for us. Now it's people. There's no *carin'* no more. It's a case of I'm all right, Jack, bugger you. Even me own flesh an' blood.' She went about her work tight-lipped with disapproval of Gloria's behaviour. Although she didn't really mean to, she took out her pent-up anger on Shirley simply because the girl was there. Inside she felt hurt and let down by the daughter she had loved and stood by. Gloria had known for some time that her father was desperately ill, yet she had never tried to come home and see him, even after her return to England. It was true that Pa was now out of danger and at home, but his stroke had robbed him of his speech and his left side was completely paralysed. It would have meant a lot to him to see his only daughter. Although she would not admit it, Ma felt suddenly old and lonely and afraid.

Shirley couldn't believe it was happening. It was like a bad dream. Gloria had always had such high hopes for her. She had worked so hard and sacrificed so much when Shirley was little to send her to dancing classes and make sure she always had nice things to wear. And she'd been so proud when Shirley had won a scholarship to the high school. She had never stopped saying how determined she was that Shirley would have a better start in life than she'd had, and Shirley had always believed her. Yet Gloria had gone off to this new job without a thought for the sorrow and hardship, the heartbreak of Shirley's missed opportunity. It was unbelievable.

To make matters worse, Shirley heard, just two days before the atom bomb was dropped on Hiroshima and Japan surrendered, that she had passed her School Certificate with credits in five subjects. She had pushed the letter into her pocket without even bothering to tell Ma, who had no use for such things anyway, especially not at this time. A fat lot of good it was going to be to her now, she told herself bitterly.

In September Imogen had written to say she had passed her entrance exam for RADA and would be starting there shortly. Shirley was consumed with envy and bitterness at the thought of her friend doing all the things they had planned to do together. It was so unfair. She had sat down that very night and written to Gloria, pleading her disappointment and begging her to come home. In her letter she described how hard life was at the shop, how much she missed Imogen and the Jarvises and of course Gloria herself, begging her to try to come home at least for Christmas. But all she had received in return was a brief letter from Gloria saying that she was truly sorry that Shirley had to be disappointed but that it could not be helped. She would make it up to her as soon as she possibly could. She ended the letter with a vague promise to come home soon, but saying that she would be needed there for Christmas. What could make these people she was working for more important to her than the family that needed her so desperately? Shirley asked herself again and again. How could she be so uncaring and selfish? Shirley wondered whether perhaps her mother had met another man. But if that were the case, why didn't she say so?

Imogen came to see her unexpectedly one busy afternoon in late November. She looked radiantly happy, attractively dressed in the latest fashion, a Jaeger dirndl skirt in striking red-and-black-checked wool with a smartly cut black jacket to match. Shirley, who was wearing an old cardigan and soil-caked mittens to keep her hands from freezing, greeted her with a scowl.

'Come to gloat, have you?' She glanced through the window to where a little sports car stood at the kerb, surrounded by children, all gazing curiously at its gleaming red bodywork. 'Who's that you've got with you?'

'It's Charles Morgan,' Imogen said. 'His father's Sir James Morgan, the High Court judge. Charles is almost eighteen. He's in his second year at RADA but he'll be leaving soon to do his National Service. He's really nice, Shirley. Do come and say hello to him.'

'Like this?' Shirley held out her dirty hands. 'I suppose it's Lord Snooty's idea of a bit of a lark, is it – *slumming*? Can't you see I'm up to my neck in it? Another time do you think you could let me know when you're thinking of dropping in for tea and cakes?'

Imogen was clearly stung by Shirley's tirade. When she had left, apologising and going away with a sad, hurt look in her eyes, Shirley had felt close to tears. Why had she been so beastly to her best friend? It wasn't Imogen's fault that she was in this impossibly awful situation. It was all Gloria's fault. After Shirley had closed the shop, she had gone up to her room and written a letter to Imogen, apologising for her churlish behaviour and trying to explain the reasons for it. A few days later she received a reply. Imogen said she would come round to see her the following Saturday evening when perhaps they could talk.

289

When she arrived Shirley took her upstairs to the room she and Gloria had once shared.

'I'm sorry it's not very nice,' she said apologetically as she closed the door. 'I'll switch on the electric fire. It'll soon warm up.'

Imogen took both her hands. 'Shirl, what's the matter? You look so tired.' She looked down at the roughened little hands. 'Where is Gloria?' she asked. 'Why is she leaving you to do all this alone? Is she staying on in America for good?'

'No. She's got herself a housekeeping job up in York-shire,' Shirley told her. 'It must be a bloody good job; she isn't even coming home for Christmas.'

Imogen frowned. 'That's not like Gloria. Are you sure there's nothing wrong?'

Shirley shrugged. 'What could be wrong? Maybe going to America has made her feel fed up with us all. She sounds happy enough with her new job when she writes. It's just as if she's finished with all of us – doesn't give a damn.' Shirley swallowed hard. 'It doesn't look as if I'll ever get to RADA now.'

'Look, why shouldn't you study in your spare time? I could find out the names of some drama teachers for you if you like, so you wouldn't be too far behind when you do start.'

Shirley gave her a rueful smile. 'You've got no idea, have you? Look, I'm up at six to help Ma and get the shop ready for opening. After we close at six in the evening there's the copper to light for all the washing. Pa's what they call incontinent, which means he wets the bed. He needs several pairs of clean sheets and pyjamas every day. There's the ironing and the housework, not to mention the cooking and washing-up. Ma does as much as she can but she needs to spend so much time with Pa. She can do with all the help I can give her. On top of that there's all the cashing-up and going to the bank – the books, the shopping. There's no such thing as spare time here, Imo.'

'I'm sorry. Oh, poor love!' Imogen glanced at her friend. 'I was going to ask if you could come home with me for Christmas, but I can see there's no chance of that. Maybe things will look up in the New Year. Why don't you apply for the entrance exam so that you can take it and start as soon as Gloria comes back?'

'I'll see,' Shirley said wearily. It was only too clear that Imogen still didn't fully understand her situation. 'I'll have to see what happens, Imo. It wouldn't surprise me if she never came back.'

'I'm sure she will. And soon too.' Imogen looked at her. 'You won't lose touch with me, will you? I'd hate that.' She took Shirley's hands again. 'Oh, Shirley, I can't tell you how much I miss you. RADA's wonderful but it isn't the same without you. We were going to have such a good time there together.'

'I know. I miss you too.' Tears sprang to Shirley's eyes. 'I miss you and Nanny and Jim and the house and school. I miss Houlton and the fresh air and the fields. Oh, Imo, I *hate* it here! It's smelly and dirty. There's no bathroom or indoor lav and the place is falling to bits from all the bomb damage that's never been fixed properly. It's cold and damp. There's no one to talk to or laugh with. Pa's illness is so awful, Imo. He can't eat properly and he can't talk. He just makes noises and he dribbles. I try to love him like before, but it's so hard. It's as though he's gone away and there's this – this *thing* in his place.' She looked at Imogen with brimming eyes. 'I expect you think I'm awful, saying a thing like that about my own granddad.' She turned away, gasping and fumbling in her pocket for a handkerchief. 'I – I thought when the war was over it was going to be so wonderful, but it's not. It feels like hell here sometimes, Imo. Just like *hell*.'

Imogen put her arms around her friend and they wept together. Imogen out of love and pity for her friend; Shirley out of weariness and disillusionment and sheer agonising frustration.

'I'm sure your grandmother appreciates all you've given up for her,' Imogen said quietly. 'I'm sure she's grateful.'

Shirley rubbed her knuckles angrily across her tear-stained cheeks. 'No, she isn't. She just thinks it's my duty,' she said. 'She never did hold with my going on the stage anyway. She didn't even want me to stay on at school. Well, she's got her way now, hasn't she?'

'I'm sure she doesn't think of it like that. She must have been proud of how well you did in the School Cert. You got more credits than I did.'

'She doesn't know about it.' Shirley sniffed hard. 'I didn't bother to tell her. What's the point?'

Christmas Day came and went. Ma spent most of it sitting upstairs with Pa while Shirley sat on her own listening to the wireless in the kitchen behind the shop and trying not to think of the happy time they would all be having at Longueville Hall.

On the afternoon of Boxing Day there was a knock on the back door and she opened it to find Dave Green standing there. He wore a shiny blue serge suit, his unruly brown hair was plastered down with Brylcreem and his worn shoes gleamed with polishing. He drew a brown-paper parcel from behind his back and grinned shyly.

'I thought you might like this, Shirl,' he said. 'And I wondered if you'd like to come out for a walk.'

Inviting him into the kitchen, Shirley unwrapped the parcel to find a box of chocolates inside. She was surprised and touched at the thoughtful gesture. A box this size must have taken up all his sweet coupons for a whole month.

'Thank you, Dave,' she said, giving him her best smile. 'I'm sorry – I haven't got you anything.'

He shrugged. 'That's all right, I didn't expect it.' He looked at the floor and shuffled his feet bashfully. 'Well, er, would you like to come out, then?'

They walked the deserted streets in the thin winter sunshine, gazing into shop windows and making careful, polite small talk. Shirley discovered that Dave was twenty-two and that his family had all been killed in the Blitz. Since his discharge from the Army he had lived alone in a bed-sitting room two streets away, eking out a meagre living on the small wage that Ma paid him.

'What did you do before the war?' Shirley asked him.

'I was apprenticed to a painter and decorator,' he told her. 'No chance of going back to that with this leg of mine. Can't climb up and down ladders no more.'

Shirley was silent. Maybe she'd been selfish, thinking about the chance she had missed. There were other young people far worse off than she, and poor Pa couldn't help being ill. Next year she might get another chance, but for Dave and thousands of others there would be no second chance.

'You're quiet,' Dave said. 'A penny for them.'

She turned to him with a smile. 'I was just wondering if you'd like to come back to our place for tea,' she said. 'The Christmas cake is only a bought one this year, but it's quite nice, and there's home-made trifle. I made it myself. Will you come?'

Dave's grey eyes lit up delightedly and she suddenly saw that he was quite nice-looking. 'Thanks very much, Shirl. I'd love to,' he said.

Shirley's life grew no easier with the New Year. Pa was no better and Ma continued to spend most of her time caring for him. The work seemed even harder and that winter was especially cold and bleak. The icy draughts found every crack in the little house in Angel Row and it didn't matter how much coal she heaped on the fire or how much oil she burned in the paraffin heater – the temperature never seemed to rise more than a couple of degrees. All through January she got up each morning to find the pipes frozen, and standing in the shop serving vegetables and fruit made her hands and feet numb and painful with chilblains.

But the one bright spot in every day was the sight of Dave's smiling face. He always managed to cheer her up, however bad things looked. He was always around to help in any way he could, far above and beyond the duties he was paid for. And he was always ready with a laugh and a joke in spite of the pain Shirley knew his crippled leg caused him when there was frost.

Saturday night became their regular night for going to the pictures and Shirley began to find herself looking forward to it all week. Dave always arrived on time, dressed in his best suit, his face freshly shaved and his shoes polished. He always saved up his sweet coupons so that he could buy her some sweets, liquorice allsorts or sherbet lemons, which he knew were her favourites. They sat in the two-and-nines and both enjoyed exciting thrillers with Humphrey Bogart or romantic dramas with Ingrid Bergman or Margaret Lockwood. Sometimes they chose a musical and Shirley would sing the songs to herself later in her room as she got ready for bed. Her throat would tighten with nostalgia as she remembered the shows that she and Imogen had taken part in during the war and the career she had looked forward to so confidently.

Shirley had wondered at first if Ma would object to her friendship with Dave. After all, she still had four months to go before her sixteenth birthday and Dave was a good six years older. But surprisingly Ma had raised no objection. She liked and trusted Dave and, although she would never have admitted it, she felt a little guilty about the way Shirley had to work. With Pa as he was, this was no place for such a young girl. It wasn't really fair to expect so much of her. But with Gloria away she'd had no option but to enlist Shirley's help and to take her away from the life she knew she had planned. It was bad enough without making the child resent her position too much. Without Shirley's youth and strength she and Pa would be in a mess and she recognised the fact only too well. What she thought of her daughter, she kept strictly to herself, but whenever Gloria's name was mentioned her lips tightened and her back stiffened. After the shame she had brought on them when Shirley was born; after they way they'd stood by her and all they'd done for her since – to go off like that when her father was ill and she was so badly needed. Ma would never forgive her; never as long as she lived.

Shirley and Dave had been going out regularly for two months before he attempted to kiss her. At first he took her hand in the darkness of the two-and-nines. Then his arm ventured along the back of her seat to drop gently around her shoulders. The week after that, as they said goodnight outside the back door of 10 Angel Row, he slipped his arms around her waist and drew her to him.

'Would you let me kiss you good night, Shirl?' he asked shyly.

'All right then, go on.' She raised her face to his, closing her eyes as he pressed his lips gently to hers. She opened her eyes to look at him, surprised that there was no more to it than that. In the pictures they seemed to feel much more – eyes closed and heads thrown back in apparent ecstasy. Perhaps they hadn't done it properly. She put her arms around him and hugged him tightly, raising her lips to his for a second kiss. This time Dave seemed to lose some of his inhibitions. His lips pressed and moved excitingly against hers and his arms tightened round her. When the kiss came to an end he was slightly breathless.

'Oh, Shirl, you're so lovely,' he said, hugging her close and burying his face in her auburn curls.

She waited for whatever would happen next, but he released her and took a step backwards. 'I – I better be off now,' he mumbled. 'It's getting late. Your ma will be getting anxious about you.'

Shirley took a step towards him. 'Why should she? She knows where I am and who I'm with.'

'That's just it,' he said.

'I don't know what you mean.'

'Look, Shirl, I'm a lot older than you. You're just a kid, really – and yet. . . .'

'And yet what?' She put her arms around his waist and laid her head against his chest. 'Don't go yet, Dave. It's nice out here, just you and me.'

'Better not. I'd better go.'

She looked up at him. 'Wasn't it nice, kissing me? Are you saying that I'm too young for you, that you'd rather have an older girl? Is that it?'

'What I'm saying is that you don't know what you do to me, Shirl,' he said, his voice husky. 'I'm not made of stone. Go on, get indoors now, there's a good girl.' He paused and stepped forward to kiss her once again briefly. 'Of course it's nice, kissing you, silly. *Too* nice, if you want to know. As for me wanting an older girl. . . .' He put his lips against her ear and whispered; 'I wouldn't swap you for Rita Hayworth, Betty Grable and all the others rolled into one.'

That night as she lay in bed, Shirley went over and over what Dave had said. She knew of course perfectly well what he had been getting at when he spoke of 'what she did to him' and the thought that she had the power to arouse him excited her. But at the same time it disturbed her too. Dave was nice. She liked him a lot but she didn't love him. She didn't intend to stay here at the little shop in Angel Row for the rest of her life, God forbid. Sometime in the future she would be leaving – going to RADA or finding some other way into a stage career. She was determined to do it, even if it took her a long time. So she didn't want to get too involved. She didn't want to hurt Dave, yet she didn't want to lose him. She turned over, punching her pillow. What should she do? Who could she ask for advice? She couldn't ask Ma, that was for sure. Try as she would, she couldn't imagine Ma ever being in the same situation. If only Gloria were here! But Gloria's letters spoke of her job, the beauty of Yorkshire, the weather – everything except coming home.

Shirley and Imogen met fairly regularly. It was usually on Sunday mornings when they were both free. Their favourite meeting place was a milk bar in Shaftesbury Avenue quite close to the Lyric Theatre, where Leonie was appearing. One Sunday at the beginning of March Imogen took her to see the photographs of *Joy in the Morning* displayed outside. Leonie looked unusually domesticated in various scenes from the play, which Shirley thought looked dramatic and interesting.

'It's doing awfully well,' Imogen told her. 'They say it's set for a really long run. I went to the first night with Daddy. Mummy is frightfully good. It's a very sad story, about a man who comes home from the war blind. She was about to leave him because they weren't happy together, but of course she has to stay when he comes home helpless.'

'It's not a very glamorous part, is it?' Shirley asked, studying the photographs carefully. 'Doesn't she sing any more?'

'She hasn't given it up,' Imogen told her. 'But the critics have given her such wonderful reviews that she may stick with legit acting from now on. Look, that's Paul Winspear, the man who wrote the play.' Imogen pointed to a portrait of a lean man with dark hair that fell forward over his forehead. He wore an open-necked shirt with a cravat at the throat. 'Isn't he handsome? He looks like those pictures of Lord Byron, doesn't he?'

'Yes, a bit. How's your dad?'

'Oh, he's still busy making a film about the war. You'd think people would have had enough of it, wouldn't you?'

'I might just about get to see that when it comes out.' Shirley looked wistfully at the photographs and wished she could see Leonie's play. She felt so far removed from the glamour of the live theatre since she'd moved back to Whitechapel. Everything had changed so. Even the way Imogen spoke sounded different. Since she started at RADA she had developed what to Shirley seemed a slightly affected way of speaking; clipped and precise, her words almost too perfectly enunciated. She used words like *frightfully* and *awfully* a lot too. It irritated Shirley and made her lapse perversely into her native cockney just to annoy. The meetings with Imogen depressed her. The other girl looked so grown-up. Her long-legged, coltish awkwardness had gone and she moved gracefully now. Tall, poised and sophisticated, she looked much older than her fifteen years. She made Shirley feel like a brash little cockney sparrow hopping about, pecking crumbs out of the gutter.

'I'll never get to study acting now,' she said gloomily as they sat over their milk-shake and sandwich lunch. 'I'll never have a real stage career like you.' She shredded the discarded crust from her ham sandwich. 'You know, sometimes when I lie in bed at night I can see it going on and on like this for ever. I'll probably end up marrying Dave. We'll run the shop together and bring up a horde of kids and I'll probably never even *see* the inside of a theatre again.'

Imogen looked at her wistfully. 'You won't believe me when I tell you that I'd quite like that kind of life.'

Shirley shot her a sharp, angry look. 'No, I bloody well wouldn't,' she said bluntly. 'You don't know you're born, Imo. You think it's like something off the pictures, don't you? All walkin' 'and in 'and into the sunset. Well, it ain't.'

'I only meant that having a husband and children would be nice,' Imogen said. 'I know how hard you work, Shirley, but it won't always be like that. Your Dave sounds so nice. Having a husband who loves you, and babies – that would be lovely. Surely it would make up for the rest?'

'No, it *wouldn't*. You don't know what you're talking about. We just don't live in the same world any more, Imo. No use pretending we do, so just put a sock in it, will you?' Shirley glanced up at the clock on the wall. 'Look, I've got to go now. See you again soon, eh?' She got up and walked quickly towards the door, Imogen hurrying after her.

'I'll walk with you to the bus.'

They walked in silence for a while, Imogen afraid to touch on what was obviously a sensitive subject again. At the bus stop she said:

'Look, Shirl, I've got the name of an acting coach. She used to be quite a well-known actress and now she's retired she gives lessons. She coaches for RADA and LAMDA exams. I saw her name in *The Stage*. That's the paper that we –'

'I *know* what *The Stage* is,' Shirley snapped. 'I'm not *that* out of touch.'

Imogen sighed and took a cutting from her handbag. 'Well, anyway, here it is. I cut it out for you. It's not all that far from where you live. If you could just manage one lesson a week it would help.'

'I suppose you think I've let my accent go to pot again.'

Imogen smiled. 'I know you only do it to annoy me. Actually, I love it. It reminds me of when we were kids.' She smiled at Shirley, her eyes twinkling, and Shirley's good nature got the better of her bad mood. She began to chuckle and the two soon found themselves giggling helplessly.

'Do you remember when I used to give you lessons?' Imogen said. 'In return for you teaching me how not to be a stuck-up little prig.'

Shirley nodded. 'Oh, Imo. I *do* miss you,' she said. 'I'm sorry I was so touchy. We'll always be friends, won't we?'

Imogen hugged her as the bus drew up beside them. 'Of course we will, silly. See you soon.' And as Shirley climbed aboard the bus she called out: 'And don't forget those lessons.'

'I won't,' Shirley called, tucking the cutting into her purse.

On Shirley's birthday in May Dave took her Up West for a meal and to the pictures afterwards. They saw *Meet Me in St Louis* with Judy Garland and Shirley came out of the cinema with stars in her eyes. It was such a beautiful, romantic story of growing up and teenage love, and Tom Drake was so handsome, he made her feel all gooey inside. He wasn't all that unlike Dave to look at, she reflected, looking sideways at him as they rode home on top of the bus. She slipped her arm through his and cuddled up to him affectionately.

'Thanks for taking me out tonight, Dave,' she said. 'I've had a lovely time. You shouldn't have spent so much money, though. It must have cost you a fortune.'

'That's all right,' he said shyly. 'I've been saving up. You're worth it.' He gave her arm a squeeze.

They saw the ambulance standing at the kerb in front of the shop as soon as they turned the corner of Angel Row. Shirley began to run, with Dave limping after her as fast as he could go. As they reached the shop, Ma came out wearing her outdoor things. Her face was white and drawn.

'Thank God you're 'ome,' she said. 'It's Pa. He 'ad another stroke an hour ago. They're taking 'im into the London Hospital again.' She clutched at Shirley's arm. 'He's real bad this time, Shirl. I'm afraid 'e won't get over this one, love.'

'Oh, Ma! I'll come with you,' Shirley said. 'Dave'll stay on here till we get back, won't you, Dave?'

They sat by Pa's bed for most of the night watching the still, ashen face, cruelly distorted by the latest stroke. Although Ma held his hand and talked to him constantly, he never regained consciousness. It was four thirty and beginning to get light when a nurse came to check on his condition. Ma had nodded off in the chair next to the bed, but Shirley was awake and alert. She watched the nurse's face as she leaned over Pa and knew from her expression that it was all over.

'I'm sorry, dear,' the nurse said in answer to the question in her eyes. 'It was very peaceful. He must have just slipped away.' She nodded towards Ma. 'Shall I wake her and break it to her or will you?'

'I'll do it,' Shirley said.

Ma took the news philosophically. 'Well, I did all I could for him,' she said wearily, taking a last look at her husband's face and automatically straightening the sheet. 'He was a good 'usband and father and 'e done all 'e could for 'is country. It's just a pity 'e had to go all through the Blitz just for this.'

'Come home and get some sleep now, Ma,' Shirley said, taking her grandmother's arm. 'We won't open the shop tomorrow. Dave'll help me make the funeral arrangements and I'll send Gloria a telegram.'

Ma's tired eyes flashed and her mouth set in the determined line that Shirley knew so well. 'You'll do no such thing, my gel,' she said. 'She couldn't come when 'er father needed her. There's no call for 'er to come running now 'e's gone, sheddin' crocodile tears. It's too late for all that.'

But Shirley did send a telegram first thing the following morning. Ma wasn't thinking straight at the moment, she told herself. She must surely want Gloria to know and to come home for the funeral.

The funeral was arranged for the following Friday, when the shop was closed and the blinds drawn respectfully. Molly and Jim Jarvis sent a sheaf of spring flowers from the garden at Longueville Hall and wrote Ma a sympathetic letter to say how sorry they were for her sad loss. The Darrents sent a beautiful wreath of gold and white roses. Imogen came in person, bearing a posy she'd made herself from pink and white carnations and delicate ferns. Pa's colleagues from the ARP carried his coffin. There being no other family mourners, Dave escorted Ma and Shirley into the church and it was only as they followed the coffin out at the end of the service that Shirley saw Gloria standing at the back. Ma saw her too; Shirley knew she did by the sudden tightening of her hand on Shirley's arm, but she walked straight ahead, refusing to look at her daughter or give her any sign of acknowledgement.

At the graveside Shirley sensed rather than saw Gloria standing on the fringe of the little group of mourners, but once the interment was completed she whispered to Dave to take Ma and Imogen home in the funeral car, telling him she would join them soon. She ran after Gloria, who was already walking briskly away along the path.

'Glor . . .' she gasped breathlessly, catching at her arm. 'Glor – I'm glad you came. You're coming back to Angel Row, aren't you?'

Gloria looked across the churchyard towards Ma. 'Will she want me to?'

'She'll be all right once she sees you,' Shirley said. 'She's just a bit upset that you never came before, but better late than never, eh?'

Tears welled up in Gloria's eyes and she pulled Shirley to her and hugged her hard. 'I'm sorry, Shirl,' she said. 'I let you all down, didn't I?'

'No – 'course you didn't,' Shirley said, a lump in her throat. 'Everything'll be all right now you're home again.'

She peered into her mother's eyes. 'Why didn't you come when Pa was ill, Glor?'

'I couldn't. It wasn't possible. First I was in America and then . . . then there was this job I was offered. It was on the plane on the way home. It was too good an opportunity to turn down, Shirl. I couldn't afford to. I'd have come to see Pa if I could, love.' She turned to look at Shirley. 'You do believe that, don't you?'

'Of course I do. Yorkshire's a long way away, isn't it? And good jobs aren't easy to find these days, are they?'

Gloria swallowed hard and composed herself. 'It must all sound like a lot of feeble excuses, I know. But it isn't. It's a long story and I'll tell you all about it some time.'

'I know. Shall we go then?' Shirley linked her arm through her mother's and began to walk. The churchyard was empty now. Dave had done as she asked and taken Ma home in the funeral car without waiting, but it wasn't very far to walk. She glanced at Gloria and thought how thin she looked, wondering if it was the black coat she wore that drained the colour from her face, making her look so pale and drawn. 'I've missed you so much, Glor,' she said, hugging the arm she held. 'Last winter was terrible. You don't have to go back to Yorkshire tonight, do you?'

'No. I've left there now.'

'Oh, the job's over, then?'

'Yes. It was only temporary.'

'I see. Are you back in London to stay then?'

Gloria shrugged. 'It all depends.' She looked at Shirley. 'I'm sorry about RADA, love, I know how much it meant to you.'

'It's not too late,' Shirley said eagerly. 'I could still take the entrance exam and go in the autumn.'

'I'm afraid there's no money for it now, love.' Gloria was biting her lip hard. 'The trip to America took most of my savings.'

Shirley's face fell. 'I thought Billy's family paid your fare?'

'They did, but there were other expenses. I couldn't let them pay for everything.'

Shirley was shaking her head in bewilderment. 'But what about this job you've had?'

'It was good but it didn't pay anything like what the aircraft factory paid. The fees for a place like RADA are out of my reach, I'm afraid, love.'

Shirley was devastated. When she had seen Gloria standing there at the back of the church she had fondly imagined that all her dreams were about to be revived. For a moment they walked in silence, then she remembered something. Looking hopefully at her mother, she said: 'Glor – there's the cottage. You don't live near enough to use it any more. It's standing there empty. You could sell it and. . . .' She broke off as she saw Gloria shaking her head.

'I've been advised not to sell the cottage,' she said. 'Property prices are going to go up and if I could have the place modernised. . . .'

'Modernised? Where would you get the money from to do *that*?' Shirley asked, her voice sharp with resentment.

'I'll have to save it, and there is some talk of the new Labour government giving grants for places with no bathrooms and so on. All property is at a premium now and will be till they start a rebuilding programme. I'll be looking into that. Once the place is more up to date I'll get a better price for it. It all takes time, though.'

Shirley fell silent. Gloria was oddly different since last they had been together. Being in America and Yorkshire seemed to have changed her in some subtle, indefinable way. It was as though an invisible barrier had come down between them. Gloria was the same – and yet she wasn't. It was like talking to someone who only *looked* like her. But now was hardly the time to probe the mystery. And disappointed though she was, she recognised the fact that it was no time for arguments about money.

Ma had laid on tea and sandwiches for a few friends and neighbours back at Angel Row and when Shirley slipped into the kitchen she found her grandmother busy brewing up the tea, a clean pinny over her black crêpe dress.

'Ma,' she said, slipping an arm round her grandmother's waist. 'Guess who's in the parlour?'

Ma stiffened, her corsets creaking ominously as she straightened her back and turned to stare unblinkingly into Shirley's eyes. 'If you're talkin' about our Gloria you needn't bother,' she said grittily. 'I saw 'er in the church, but I've got nothin' to say to that young woman. Anyway, I thought I told you not to let 'er know.'

'I had to, Ma. She would have come before if she'd been able to get away. You know Glor better than that.'

'I thought I did.' Ma poured boiling water into the big blue enamelled teapot and turned to Shirley. 'I told your mother years ago that this shop was for you and 'er. It's what 'er pa wanted and it's what we both worked for all these years – all through the Blitz an' all – to give the two of you security for the future, so don't tell me she 'ad to go up to Yorkshire to get a job when there was one 'ere for 'er all the time. A home *and* a job. Not just a job either but a nice flourishin' little business.'

'She's back now,' Shirley said. 'Oh, Ma, you will be nice to her now she's here, won't you?'

'Nice to 'er?' Ma turned steely, outraged eyes on her granddaughter. '*Nice* to 'er – when she turned 'er back on 'er own flesh and blood and chucked a lifetime of 'ard work back in our faces? No, my gel. That's somethin' I *won't* forgive in a hurry.' Ma snorted explosively and picked up the tray, sweeping out of the kitchen without another word.

The sandwiches and tea were partaken of in an atmosphere that was fraught with tension. It was clear to everyone that Gloria's presence at the small gathering had cast a cloud on the proceedings and as soon as they decently could the friends and neighbours made their excuses and drifted away. Even Dave could see that the family needed to be alone and left quietly, kissing Ma's cheek and telling Shirley that he would see her in the morning. When only Imogen remained, Shirley rose and motioned to her.

'Imogen and I will do the washing-up now, Ma,' she said. 'Then you and Gloria can have a talk.'

Ma's back stiffened. 'I'm sure there's no need for us to keep Gloria any longer,' she said stubbornly. 'No doubt

304

she'll be wanting' to get orf and catch a train or somethin'.'

'No, Ma. I'd like to talk,' Gloria said. Her face was deathly pale and Shirley saw that her hands were clasped so tightly in her lap that the knuckles showed white. Quietly she collected up the used cups while Imogen took the sandwich plates, and the two of them went out of the room, closing the door behind them.

In the kitchen, as Shirley ran water into the sink and began to stack the crockery, Imogen said:

'What's wrong with Gloria? She looks terrible. Has she been ill?'

Shirley shook her head. 'I don't think so but I don't really know. I haven't had a chance to talk to her yet.'

Imogen picked up a teacloth and began to dry. 'Your grandmother doesn't seem too happy to see her.'

'She can't forgive her for not coming home to see Pa when he was ill. She'll come round, though,' Shirley said, though she wasn't at all sure that Ma would come round.

They were putting the best china away in the dresser cupboard when the sound of raised voices from the parlour made them exchange glances. Imogen said:

'Perhaps I'd better go now, Shirley. It's family business. I'm only in the way.'

But Shirley laid a hand on her arm. 'No. Come in with me. They'll have to stop if you're there.' She took Imogen's hand and drew her unwillingly through into the parlour where Ma and Gloria stood facing each other on opposite sides of the room.

'Gloria's leavin' now,' Ma said, her mouth drawn into a thin, determined line. 'She's 'ad no use for us over the past twelve months and now we've got no use for 'er.' She glared at Gloria. 'I want you to know, my gel, that from now on as far as I'm concerned I ain't got no daughter. What I 'ave got is a good granddaughter. Our Shirl 'as stood by me like a good 'un while you was orf gallivantin'. She's been a better gel to me than you ever was and I want you to know that this business is 'ers now. I'm 'anding everything over to 'er. When I'm gone Rayner's Greengrocery and all Pa and me 'ave worked for all these years will belong to Shirl. After the way you let your pa down, you ain't welcome in this 'ouse no more, Gloria. And that's flat.'

White-faced, Gloria turned without a word, picked up her coat and handbag and prepared to leave. Appalled, Shirley stepped forward and grasped her grandmother's arm. 'Ma! Ma! *Don't*. Don't let Gloria go like this. You're upset. You don't know what you're saying.' She turned to Gloria. 'Don't go. She didn't mean it.'

But Gloria was already at the door. 'Oh yes, she did, Shirley,' she said quietly. 'I know Ma. She's never in her life said something she didn't mean.' She gave Shirley a sad little smile. 'Don't worry, love. You stay. She needs you. I'll be in touch when I've found a job and somewhere to live.'

Through the sleeve of her grandmother's dress, Shirley could feel her trembling. She shot Imogen a pleading look. 'Go after Glor for me, will you?' she whispered. 'Make sure she's all right. I can't leave Ma like this.'

'Of course. I'll be in touch, Shirley. Bye.' Imogen quickly gathered up her things and left. As the street door slammed behind her, Shirley carefully helped a trembling Ma into a chair.

'Why did you want to upset yourself like that, Ma?' she admonished gently. 'Gloria would have come home sooner if she could. You do believe that, don't you?'

'I believes what I sees,' Ma said stubbornly. She looked up at her granddaughter and squeezed her hand. 'Make us another cuppa, there's a good gel.' She drew a deep, shuddering breath. 'Oh, my Gawd, what a day! I don't mind tellin' you, I'm just about done in.'

In the kitchen Shirley filled the kettle and set it to boil on the gas stove. The row with Gloria on top of Pa's illness and death had taken its toll of Ma. In the parlour just now she had looked every day of her sixty-two years. Shirley's heart was heavy as she recalled her grandmother's words to Gloria. *I'm handing everything over to her. Rayner's Greengrocery will belong to Shirley*. She was trapped. She'd never get away now; never get the chance to make that stage career she had dreamed of. Gloria would never come back to Angel Row while Ma was here. That much was certain. And Ma would be totally reliant on her for everything from now on.

'Gloria! Please wait.'

Gloria was walking fast, as though she couldn't get away fast enough. Imogen had to call twice before she heard, but when she realised that the breathless cry was directed at her Gloria hesitated, turned, then stopped to wait for the girl to catch her up.

'I'm sorry you had to witness all that,' she said as Imogen drew level with her. 'I'm afraid my mother is a very hard, unforgiving woman.'

'I'm sure she'll be sorry once the strain has worn off,' Imogen said. 'She's had a very hard time of it these past months, what with your father's illness and everything.' She paused. 'And so has Shirley.'

'D'you think I don't realise that?'

'Have you got time for a cup of tea or something?' Imogen asked. 'There's a café over there.'

They crossed the road and went into the café. Gloria sat down at one of the oilcloth-covered tables while Imogen bought two cups of tea at the counter and brought them across.

'I would have come when Pa was ill, really I would,' Gloria said. 'But it just wasn't possible. After I'd been to visit Billy's family I got this housekeeping job, you see. I lived in and only had one day off a week. There wasn't time to come all the way down to London and back in a day. And when Pa was taken ill this last time there wasn't even time for me to get here.'

'It's been very hard on poor Shirley,' Imogen said. 'She isn't used to working so hard and she was looking forward to RADA so much. It's a lot of talent going to waste, Gloria.'

'I know, *I know*. You don't have to tell me.' To Imogen's dismay two tears slipped down Gloria's cheeks and dripped onto the table. 'I can't afford to send her now, Imogen. I just can't *afford* it. I haven't even got a job now and all my savings have gone. No one knows what it does to me to have to say no to her – to see all her dreams go out of the window. It's all I've ever wanted and planned for her, ever since she was a baby. It's my dream too, Imogen.'

Imogen watched as Gloria fought back the tears, rummaging in her handbag for a handkerchief. She wanted to ask why Gloria hadn't thought of Shirley before she agreed to go to America. And also why she agreed to take on a job in Yorkshire when she already knew her father was ill. But pity for the woman's obvious distress prevented her. She reached across the table to touch Gloria's hand. 'Look, you said you were looking for work. I know you get along well with Mummy. She thinks very highly of your talent for sewing. She's not happy with her present dresser and she's looking for someone to take her place. Would you like me to ask her to bear you in mind for the job?'

Gloria looked up. She badly needed a job but work for Leonie – where she might run into Tony almost every day. . . . 'Oh, well – that would be marvellous, Imogen, but I'm not sure. . . .'

'Mummy would jump at the chance to get someone she knows well and who is as clever with her needle as you are.' Imogen gave Gloria a wry smile. 'I'm not going to pretend it would be all honey. Mummy can be difficult sometimes.' She paused. 'You probably don't know that she and Daddy have unofficially separated.'

Gloria felt her heart miss a beat. 'No, I didn't know. I'm sorry.'

'Yes, so am I. I hardly ever see Daddy nowadays. He's away on location so much of the time. Anyway, as I said, Mummy isn't the easiest person to work for. She'll pay you well, but you'll certainly earn it.' She smiled. 'But you've got a calmness about you which is just what she needs. Shall I tell her you're available and ask her to get in touch? Can she contact you at Angel Row?'

'No.' Gloria bit her lip. 'I'm afraid not. You heard Ma. She chucked me out – no ifs or buts.'

Imogen stared at her. 'You mean you've actually got nowhere to stay?' Gloria shook her head. 'Not even tonight?'

'I've still got Rook Cottage. I was going to get the train and go up to Boothley.'

'But you can't do that. It's too far away if Mummy wants to see you. Look, you'd better come back with me. I've only got a one-bedroom flat in Earls Court, but you're welcome to sleep on the settee in the living room. Will that do?'

'Thank you, if you're sure it wouldn't put you out.'

Imogen looked at her watch. 'If we hurry I might just catch Mummy on the phone before she goes to the theatre, then you can pop along in the morning and see her.'

As they travelled on the Underground, Gloria looked at the self-possessed young women at her side and wondered why she wasn't living with one of her parents. Poor girl! For all the wealth and privilege she'd had she'd been short of love all her life. If their situations had been reversed, Gloria would have been only too delighted to have her daughter with her. She allowed her thoughts to dwell on the Darrents and wondered what could have happened to bring about their separation. Their marriage had never been happy but she'd been under the impression that they stayed together because of their public image. Had the war changed all that? She sighed wistfully, wondering briefly if she should shoulder any of the blame. She'd made such a mess of everything; was she responsible for this too? The way things looked now, her dreams for Shirley would never come true. They would never even know the pleasure of sharing a home again – and she was afraid that Shirley would never forgive her. In the years to come the chasm between them would widen and widen, forcing them further apart. If only there were something she could do about it.

Chapter Fourteen

Gloria sat in the star dressing room at the Lyric and watched as Leonie took off her make-up after the Saturday matinee. Leonie had made the bare little room with its green-painted brick walls as cosy as possible, bringing in her own furniture, carpet and lampshades to give it a homely feel. As she said to Gloria, 'When one spends so much time in a place it's essential to create a warm and relaxed atmosphere.'

Gloria was reminded nostalgically of the time she had gone backstage to see Tony when he had appeared in *Henry V*. It all seemed so long ago now – a lifetime.

'I must say it's the most marvellous stroke of luck, your being free to take this job just when I need someone so desperately,' Leonie was saying. Her voice was slightly distorted as she grimaced into the mirror in order to get the last vestiges of greasepaint off. 'I really need someone who knows me – who can anticipate my needs and not wait to be *told* all the time. The last woman was absolutely clueless. She had one of those voices that grate appallingly when one wants to be quiet just before curtain-up, and she was always putting out the wrong costume and letting things get tatty. When can you start, darling?'

'Well, if you think I'll suit –'

'*Suit?*' Leonie almost screamed the word. 'You'll do more than suit. You're like a gift straight from heaven. There's no one – absolutely *no one* I'd rather have.'

'Well, I suppose I could start fairly soon if you like. Whenever your present dresser has worked out her notice, I suppose.'

'Oh, never mind that.' Leonie waved a dismissive hand. 'I've already paid her off and let her go. Damned glad to see the back of her.'

'I still have one or two things to sort out, including somewhere permanent to live,' Gloria said. 'That could be difficult in London at the moment.'

Leonie glanced around at her. 'Oh? I naturally assumed you'd be living at home with your mother and Shirley.'

'I'm afraid my mother is still angry with me for not managing to visit while my father was ill. She isn't speaking to me at the moment.'

'Oh, dear. I'm sorry to hear that. I was sorry to hear about your father too, of course – and your American friend.' Leonie shook her head. 'You've had a rough time of it lately, haven't you? And families can be sheer hell at times, can't they?' She swung round to face Gloria. 'We both know how *I've* suffered in that particular area.'

'You've had no more problems with your brother, I hope,' Gloria said, lowering her voice.

'No, thank God. And if you don't mind, Gloria, I'd rather we drew a veil over that particular little episode. It's strictly between you and me.'

'Yes, of course.'

'So – you're homeless? Well, we must do something about that, mustn't we? You must come and stay at the flat.'

'Oh, but I couldn't,' Gloria said. 'When you leave here you must want your privacy.'

Leonie screwed the top back onto her jar of Leichner removing cream and began to put on her street make-up. 'Actually it can get rather lonely sometimes, going back to an empty flat.' She glanced at Gloria. 'Tony and I are no longer living together, you know. I'm surprised Imogen didn't tell you. I'm sure it's no secret that our marriage has been on the rocks for some time. The war and the long separations it brought about didn't help.' She etched in her eyebrows with quick, deft strokes. 'Tony has never been short of female company – I'm sure you know all

311

about that.' She cocked a newly defined eyebrow at Gloria through the mirror, making her blush hotly. 'His ex-wife, Gillian Fane, has been over to make a film. They've been seen around together, then since she left he's taken up with some chorus girl or other, or so I hear. His love life is none of my business any more.' She applied her lipstick and smiled. 'Actually, now that we're apart we get along much better than we have for years. Everything has been amicably sorted out. As for me. . . .' She turned to look at Gloria, her eyes shining. 'Strictly between ourselves, Gloria, I'm in love – I truly believe it's the real thing and I *couldn't* be happier.'

Gloria smiled back. 'Oh. I . . . I'm very glad for you.'

'If you're to stay at the flat it's as well that you know the situation. He sometimes stays over, you see. It's Paul Winspear, the man who wrote this play.' She sighed. 'He's so *wonderful*, Gloria. It was love at first sight – so romantic. He has the most adorable, warm, melting brown eyes and the moment they met mine it was just like fate.'

'Oh, then will you – I mean are you and Tony. . . ?'

'Getting divorced?' Leonie shrugged. 'Who knows? It's difficult. Paul is married too, you see. Oh, she left him soon after he came out of the Army, so it wasn't me who broke things up between them. For the moment we're taking things a step at a time.' She looked at Gloria. 'So what do you say? Would you like to be my dresser-cum-confidante? There's no one I'd rather have and I know I can trust you to be discreet.' She laughed suddenly. 'Oh, how *silly* of me! I haven't mentioned money. How would eight pounds a week and rent-free accommodation suit you?'

Gloria gasped. 'That's extremely generous, but I couldn't impose on you at the flat permanently.'

'You wouldn't be *imposing*, darling.' Leonie's dark eyes flashed and there was a slight edge to her voice as she added: 'Naturally I'd expect you to do a little light housework in return for food and lodging. It's quite impossible to get a reliable maid these days. And the place is quite big enough for us not to get in each other's way.'

'I see. Yes, of course.' The implications were only too clear. Gloria cleared her throat. 'In that case, would you mind if I sometimes went away for the weekend? I still have my cottage at Boothley and I'd like to make sure it's in order.'

'Naturally. You'll want to take Shirley there, I suppose.' When Gloria declined to answer and lowered her eyes, Leonie smiled. 'Ah – you're blushing. Am I to take it that you've found a new man friend then?'

'I . . . you could say that.'

'Well, of course your Sundays through till Monday evenings will be your own free time to do with as you please.' Leonie rose and slipped off her wrapper to reveal a pair of black satin and lace camiknickers. 'Hand me the dress from the hanger over there, darling, will you?'

At that moment the door opened and a man walked in. Leonie launched herself into his arms.

'Paul, *darling*! I wasn't expecting you this afternoon.'

'I know. I thought we might have tea together before the evening performance.' He took her chin in one hand and kissed her possessively. It was only as he was raising his head that he noticed Gloria, who had been standing awkwardly, half hidden behind the door, Leonie's dress over her arm. He frowned at Leonie. 'Oh – why didn't you tell me you had a visitor?'

Leonie laughed. 'You didn't really give me a chance, did you, darling? This is Gloria Rayner. She's a very old friend and she's going to be my new dresser. I'm so lucky that she's looking for a job just when I need her. She's a positive *genius* with her needle. You wouldn't believe how talented she is. Gloria, this is Mr Paul Winspear.'

'Pleased to meet you, sir.' Gloria didn't know whether to offer her hand or not, but apart from a dismissive sweep of his dark eyes, Paul made no attempt to acknowledge her. She cleared her throat. 'Well, I'll er . . . be off now,' she said, edging towards the door. Paul's glowering expression made her feel distinctly unwelcome.

'You can move your things into the flat whenever you like,' Gloria said with a wave of her hand. 'I'll tell the caretaker to expect you. He'll let you in. And don't worry about the job. You'll soon slip into the routine. I'll see you soon.'

The last Gloria saw as she closed the door was Paul Winspear enfolding Leonie in an embrace that looked both passionate and demanding. There was something about the man that she had disliked on sight. The eyes that Leonie saw as warm and melting seemed to Gloria dark and enigmatic, and there was something cruel, almost predatory about his mouth that sent a chill through her. But she told herself it was none of her business whom Leonie chose to associate with. She had given her a much needed job and a place to live and that was her most immediate concern.

Number 127 Manderville Road, Stepney, was the last house in a terrace of shabby Regency villas. Once an elegant town house, it had now been converted into four flats, its stucco façade chipped and its paint peeling. The little wrought-iron balconies that embellished the first-floor windows were rusting and perilously rickety and the railings that had once protected the shallow area had been taken at the beginning of the war.

Magda Jayne occupied Flat 1 in the basement, where she also had her studio. Shirley stood looking down the short flight of steps that lead to a red-painted door bearing a sign that said: 'Stage Coach, Actors' Studio.'

Now that she was here she was nervous. It would use up most of her weekly wage to take two lessons a week, which, according to the advertisement in *The Stage*, was the minimum Miss Jayne accepted. Could she persuade her to accept her for one weekly session? Well, she would never know until she asked, she told herself. Straightening her shoulders she walked down the steps and knocked on the door.

The woman who answered her knock must have been about fifty. She was tall and willowy with abundant dark hair streaked with grey, which she wore smoothed back into a loose knot at the nape of her neck. She wore well-cut slacks and an exotically patterned Chinese silk tunic. But it was her eyes that made the greatest impact on Shirley. They were an unusual hazel-green colour and deeply penetrating. Shirley felt as though they could see right through to all the doubt and insecurity she was feeling. As the woman raised an enquiring eyebrow, Shirley cleared her throat nervously.

'Oh, hello. I – I've seen your advert in *The Stage* and I've come to enquire about acting lessons.'

The woman held the door open. 'Please come in.' Her voice had a deep and impressive resonance that told Shirley that she was in the presence of a seasoned actress.

The narrow hallway was dim but the moment Miss Jayne opened a door to her right, glowing colour seemed to leap out at Shirley from every direction. The walls were painted plain white and on them hung a number of modern paintings, some of them abstracts, each a riot of brilliant colours and bizarre patterns. Over the fireplace was an eye-catching life-sized nude with waist-length raven hair that drew Shirley's eyes like a magnet. She thought it extremely beautiful. Against the wall facing the door stood a divan covered in a red-and-white-striped cover. On it were heaped jewel-coloured cushions, their hand-woven covers embroidered with glowing silks and dotted with tiny pieces of mirror and sequins, and above it hung a Persian wall hanging in luscious shades of gold and wine. The floor was of plain polished boards with a fringed oriental rug in the centre. By contrast to all these sensual assaults, a businesslike desk stood in the window recess, one chair behind it, another to one side. Magda Jayne indicated one of these.

'Will you have a seat, Miss . . .?'

'Oh – Rayner,' Shirley said, trying hard not to stare about her at the exotic room. 'Shirley Rayner.'

'What a pretty name. You want to enrol, Shirley?'

'Well, yes, I'd like to.' Shirley decided to come straight to the point. No use wasting the woman's time. 'The trouble is I don't think I can afford two lessons a week.'

Magda smiled. The smile seemed to light her eyes from within. It relaxed and warmed Shirley like sunshine on a

315

cold day. 'Well, before we talk about money, suppose you tell me a little about yourself. To begin with, would you like to tell me what makes you want to take acting lessons?'

Before she knew it, Shirley was pouring out her life story to this woman – this magnetic stranger she had only just met. All the time she was talking, Magda was watching her shrewdly, the perceptive hazel eyes taking in every detail of her speech and mannerisms. When she had finished, Magda said:

'But what do *you* want, Shirley? It seems to me that you've been heavily influenced by those around you: your mother, your friends and now your grandmother. Have you ever really asked yourself what *you* want?'

'I want to be an actress,' Shirley said firmly. 'It's what I've wanted ever since I can remember. Gloria – that's my mother – would never have pushed me into something I didn't want to do. In fact, she's not as keen on it as she used to be. When I got a place at high school I think she had visions of me being a teacher or a doctor or something. But I still want to act more . . . more than anything else in the world.'

Magda looked at the slender, work-roughened hands that twisted nervously at the strap of the cheap little handbag, then up into Shirley's shining blue eyes. 'I charge twelve pounds a term. That is twelve weeks – twenty-four lessons. Could you manage that?'

Shirley bit her lip. 'I'm not sure. I wondered if I could have one lesson a week . . .' She trailed off, watching as Magda opened a drawer and took out a book. Opening it, she passed it across the desk to Shirley.

'Read that for me.'

Shirley saw that it was a poem by Swinburne, one that they had studied in English-literature lessons at school.

'Just read me the first verse,' Magda prompted. 'Don't worry about it. Take your time.'

Shirley took a deep breath and began: 'When the hounds of spring are on winter's traces, The mother of months in meadow and plain . . .' She loved the poem, and the lush, singing phrases soon made her forget her nervousness. Her enjoyment came out in her voice and her eyes as she read, going on without being prompted to the second verse, after which she stopped, suddenly embarrassed that she had read more than was asked of her.

'Thank you.' Magda was smiling. 'How old are you, Shirley?'

'Sixteen.'

'You do realise that your voice is very nasal and that your breathing is all wrong, don't you?'

Shirley blushed. 'Imogen, my friend, tried to teach me to speak properly, but since I came home again I've let it slip.'

'Don't worry. Once you get into the right habits it won't be possible to let it slip, as you put it,' Magda said. 'It will come as second nature.' She pulled a desk diary towards her. 'So, when do you want to begin?'

Shirley caught her breath. 'Well, as I said, I don't know if I can afford . . .'

'Would half-price suit you?' The hazel eyes were in deadly earnest as they looked into hers.

'Two lessons a week for . . .?'

'For six pounds,' Magda said. 'Children are usually half-price, aren't they? And you are scarcely more than a child. Now, what time of day would suit you best?'

It was arranged that Shirley would go to Magda on Mondays and Thursdays after the shop closed at half-past six. From the beginning she had told Ma where she was going. Although she knew her grandmother would not approve, she was determined not to give way.

For her part, Ma said nothing. She knew better than to argue or try to stop Shirley from following her dream, however silly and futile she considered it. She relied heavily on her granddaughter now that she had fallen out with Gloria and she was alone in the world. She was all too aware that the girl could get a job anywhere. If things got too awkward for her, she would probably go off to live with her mother, and where would Ma be then? Obliged

317

to sell the shop and move, that's where. More than likely she'd end up in some home for old people. She had seen such places: old folk shuffling about aimlessly like a lot of zombies, waiting to die. An ice-cold fear clutched at Ma's heart whenever she thought about it. *No*, she didn't want that. If only the girl would drop this stage fad and take a real interest in the business. But common sense told her that if Shirley was prevented from doing what she wanted, she'd fret for it all the more. Let her get it out of her system, she told herself. When she was a bit older she'd come to realise that a good established business was worth more than all the glitter and tinsel.

Shirley adored the lessons with Magda, looking forward to Mondays and Thursdays – counting the days as though she were waiting for a special treat. In the early weeks she learned things she had never imagined she would need to know – about the anatomy of the respiratory system, the mechanics of the chest, lungs and throat and all the muscles employed in voice production. 'You wouldn't dream of operating a machine without first learning how it worked, would you?' Magda said. Shirley learned how to breathe correctly, controlling her ribs and diaphragm, and how to project her voice and enunciate her vowels, ridding herself of the offending nasal tones. Every day she would get up early and do her breathing exercises in front of her open bedroom window. She would gargle to keep her throat healthy and faithfully perform her voice exercises, steadily elongating the vowel sounds, controlling the sound from a thin whisper to a full-throated, rounded, steady flow, trailing off again evenly to a whisper. As she practised she visualised the sound as Magda had suggested – seeing it as a brightly coloured ribbon flowing from her mouth.

Magda was encouraging. She told Shirley that she had a good lung capacity and a strong larynx, no doubt due to singing from an early age. She promised that as soon as they'd ironed out her vowels they could go on to some poetry and maybe a scene from a play. With this end in view, Shirley worked as she had never worked before.

Downstairs in the kitchen Ma would raise her eyes to the ceiling and shrug helplessly. Gloria hadn't known what she was starting when she put all those highfalutin notions into the child's head. Shirley'd be far better off using her spare time to encourage young Dave. It was plain to anyone with half an eye that the poor feller was hopelessly sweet on her. She could do a lot worse than marry a good steady chap like Dave who'd be a good hubby and only too happy to run the shop with her. Having a gammy leg, he wouldn't be likely to stray either. It was an ill wind, Ma told herself with satisfaction. But then again, she'd noticed that things were very different since the war. The men demobilised from the services were still restless, and the women had got it into their heads that they could have the same freedom that men had. Both sexes seemed to feel that there was more to life than settling down to marriage, a home and children. If they were to ask Ma, she would have told them that it would all end in tears. But no one did ask her.

Dave always went to meet Shirley after her drama lessons. They'd walk home through the streets on the warm summer evenings. As the light evenings shortened and winter drew on, they would sometimes stop off at the Prince of Wales, Dave's favourite pub, for a drink on the way. Shirley passed quite easily for eighteen and there was never any question about her right to be there; nevertheless, she never mentioned it to Ma, who would have been annoyed with Dave for taking her there.

Christmas came once more – a happier and more relaxed one this year, though Ma missed Pa badly. In spite of her announcement to Gloria about the shop being Shirley's, the situation at Angel Row remained the same. Shirley still found herself in the position of employee and received what she considered a meagre wage. But whenever she complained about this, Ma threw out heavy hints that she had changed her will and that Shirley was the sole beneficiary of all her worldly goods, including the shop. Everything would be hers in the fullness of time.

★ ★ ★

Dave never knew what mood he would find Shirley in after her lessons with Magda Jayne. Sometimes she would be elated and animated, at other times pensive and preoccupied. He never minded; her mood swings were all part of the excitement. To him she was the most mysterious, magical creature in the world and just as long as he could be with her he didn't care.

Saturday was the day he looked forward to most. On Saturday evenings she was all his. After the shop closed they would go Up West, have tea at Lyons Corner house in Leicester Square and then on to the pictures. Dave looked forward all week to holding Shirley's hand in the dim warmth of the cinema, to breathing her fragrance and tasting the sweetness of her lips when he held her close. He knew that she was young and had great plans for the future; plans that clearly did not at the moment include him. But he refused to look too far ahead or think too deeply about that. If he could make her love him enough, perhaps she would forget her dreams of the footlights and stardom.

Once a month on a Sunday Shirley met Imogen. It was from Imogen that she had learned about her mother's employment with Leonie and that she was living at the Mayfair flat. She deeply resented the fact that Gloria had made no attempt to get in touch or to find out if Ma was well and recovering from losing Pa. Gloria's behaviour since the end of the war was something she would never understand or come to terms with.

Now that she was studying drama at last, she had something to tell Imogen when they met. She felt equal to her again. Just as they had in the old days, they could swap notes and dream about the golden future awaiting them both.

'You never ask me about Gloria,' Imogen remarked one Sunday afternoon when they had taken sandwiches to Hyde Park instead of eating at the milk bar. 'She misses you an awful lot, you know. She's always asking about you whenever I see her.'

'She knows where I am; why doesn't she write to me?' Shirley said, her chin lifting stubbornly. 'I've never heard a word from her since Pa's funeral. Sometimes I think she doesn't give a damn about Ma and me any more.'

'Mummy keeps her pretty busy, I'm afraid,' Imogen said.

'What's wrong with Sundays? She has them off, doesn't she? If she doesn't want to come home she could easily meet me somewhere, but she's never even tried to.'

Imogen sighed. 'I wish you and she would make it up,' she said. 'I always used to envy the close relationship you two had. She's always been my idea of a real mother. She told me she had written to you but you didn't reply.'

'She *what*? That's a laugh. I never got any letters.' Shirley sniffed. 'She's just saying that to make herself look in the right.'

'As for Sundays, she goes to Boothley most weekends,' Imogen said.

Shirley frowned. 'Boothley?'

'Yes. To the cottage. I'll bet she'd like you to go with her some time. It would be so nice if you could spend time together. Oh, Shirl, if only you'd meet her halfway! This thing between you – it's gone on far too long. I'm sure she'd be thrilled to hear all about your drama studies.'

Shirley put down her sandwich and looked at her friend. 'Look, Imo. Glor and I used to be really close, as you said. I'd have done anything for her and I know that all she ever wanted was me. But when Billy came along she changed. I understand that. She's still quite young and he was nice. But after she went to America to meet his family she just turned into another person. I can't think why she didn't stop there. She let me down, Imo. All those years of building me up and then she let me down flat. She let Ma down, too – landed us both in it and went away without even trying to help.'

'Your grandmother was pretty definite about not seeing her again,' Imogen reminded her. 'She said some very hurtful things. I was there, remember?'

''Course she did. She was hurt,' Shirley said defensively. 'She'd just lost Pa. Gloria treated both of them badly. You couldn't blame Ma for being angry. Oh, don't let's talk about her now,' she said suddenly. 'We'll be arguing in a minute and she's not worth it.'

'How's Dave?' Imogen asked after a small silence.

'He's okay.'

'He's awfully nice, Shirley. Are you planning to get engaged?'

Shirley stared at her friend. '*Engaged*? At my age? I've got a better future in front of me than that.'

'I only thought . . .'

'Well, *don't* if you can't think of anything better than that,' Shirley snapped. 'Do *you* want to give up everything just to be someone's wife?'

'I might if I fell in love,' Imogen said dreamily.

'Oh, honestly!' Shirley brushed the crumbs from her skirt and stood up. 'Let's go and feed the leftovers to the ducks before I strangle you, Imogen Darrant. You're the most maddening girl I know.'

When they met the following month, Imogen produced a letter from Gloria. She gave it to Shirley as they sat at their usual table in the milk bar.

'Gloria asked me to give you this,' she said. 'She said she wouldn't risk the post again.'

'Oh, thanks.' Shirley pushed the envelope into her pocket and it wasn't until she was undressing for bed later that night that she found it. Sitting on the bed, she tore open the envelope and unfolded the sheet of paper inside.

Dear Shirley,

Imogen tells me you never received any of the other letters I wrote you. I can only guess at what might have happened to them. I hope you're well, love, and that you've managed to find it in your heart to forgive me for the way I let you down. I honestly couldn't help it and one day you'll understand.

Imogen tells me you're having drama lessons and that you're doing really well. I'm sure you'll make that stage career one day, love, and no one will be prouder of you than I will. I have a good job here with Leonie Swann. It's quite exciting working at the theatre. I get a lot of sewing jobs to do but I like that as you know. I can get you a couple of complimentary tickets if you'd like to come and see the show. I'm sure you could come backstage after if I asked Leonie's permission. I know it would interest you. Let me know if you'd like that, love.

At the moment I'm living at the flat in Mayfair. I have a nice room and my pay is quite good, though I have to work quite hard for it. Leonie makes sure she gets her money's worth. But don't tell Imogen I said that, will you?

I miss you more than I can say, Shirl, and I'd love to see you more than anything in the world. If you'd like to fix something up just drop me a line, or you could ring me at the flat in the mornings. I hope Ma is well and that she's quite recovered now from poor Pa's death. I'd like to see her too, but I'm afraid she won't forgive me for a long time yet – perhaps not ever.

Take care of yourself, darling. I love you.

Gloria.

Her throat painfully constricted, Shirley read the letter through twice, tears blurring her vision till the words swam together. Over the past months she had tried hard to convince herself she didn't care about Gloria's apparent rejection, but it was no use, she cared very deeply. She missed her too. She had felt abandoned when Gloria hadn't got in touch. But she had told Imogen that she'd written, and repeated it here in the letter. Why should she say it if it wasn't true?

Ma was out visiting a sick friend down the street and Shirley crept into her bedroom and began to open the drawers of her dressing table. She hated doing it but she had to satisfy herself that Ma hadn't done what she suspected. It was in the bottom one, where she kept what she called her 'papers' in an old chocolate box, that she found them. Everything was there: identity card, ration book, clothing coupons. There was a copy of Pa's will and her own various insurance policies. Right at the bottom lay a bundle of five or six letters, unopened and addressed to Shirley in Gloria's handwriting. Ma obviously couldn't bring herself to destroy them – or to read them either. She had simply tucked them away out of sight and closed her mind to the deceptive act. After a moment's thought, Shirley put them back where she had found them and closed the drawer. Pa's maxim had always been, Least said, soonest mended. And in this case she reckoned he was right.

Gloria soon found herself acting as cook and housekeeper as well as dresser to Leonie. Sometimes she wondered if she couldn't be described as her nanny, too. She was required to comfort and soothe, to boost Leonie's flagging confidence, to flatter and cajole – and, on the evenings when Paul Winspear accompanied Leonie back to the flat, simply to merge into the background and disappear completely. The agreement about her hours, which were supposed to fit in with opening hours at the theatre, had completely gone by the board. They now seemed to extend from dawn till bedtime. The one thing Gloria had managed to remain firm about was her time off on Sunday and Monday when she would take the train to Northampton and then the bus to Boothley Bottom to exchange her hectic weekday job for the comparative peace and quiet of the countryside.

She had been with Leonie almost twelve months before she saw Tony again. It was a Monday morning and she was busy with the housework while Leonie was out seeing Peter Jason, her agent. Leonie hated the housework being done while she was in. She said the vacuum cleaner brought on her migraine, so Gloria found herself doing the work during any odd moments she could snatch. Leonie was always forgetting her key and Gloria was in the habit of leaving the door on the latch for her if she was in.

Unable to make the doorbell heard above the roar of the vacuum cleaner, Tony had let himself into the flat. When he touched her shoulder Gloria gave a cry of alarm and spun round. But her flushed face paled when she saw the man who stood smiling at her elbow.

'*Tony*! Oh, my God, you made me jump.'

'I'm sorry if I startled you, Gloria. I did ring but I couldn't make you hear. The door was on the latch so I just came in. You shouldn't do that, you know. There are some funny people about.'

'So I see.' As she unplugged the cleaner, Tony laughed.

'I suppose I asked for that.' He perched on the arm of the settee. 'It's wonderful to see you again. How are you?'

'I'm fine, thanks. I'm afraid Leonie's out and she won't be back for a while. She's gone to see Mr Jason.'

'Yes, I know. He told me she was going in to the office this morning. I heard from Imogen that you were here so I came early, hoping to catch you.'

'Catch me? For what?'

He laughed. 'Just for a chat. No need to look so suspicious.' He took out his cigarette case and offered it to her. She shook her head. 'I must say I was surprised to hear you were working for Leonie. How are you finding things?'

'I'm very grateful to have a job and a place to live.'

He looked up from lighting his cigarette and gave her a wry smile. 'That's not what I asked you.'

Gloria sighed. 'Look, Tony, this is an awkward situation. If you're hoping to draw me . . .'

He held up his hand. 'Good heavens, Gloria, hasn't Leonie told you that we're on quite amicable terms? I was only asking as a friend, strictly between ourselves. I've been married to Leonie for a long time, remember? I do know what she can be like. I just hope she's not exploiting you.'

Gloria pushed back a strand of hair. 'I don't know what you mean.'

'Come off it. You're supposed to be her dresser and I find you doing the housework. I wouldn't mind betting she has you cooking and rinsing out her smalls too. Strictly off the record, how much does she pay you?'

'Please . . .' Gloria blushed. 'She pays me enough.'

'Well, I hope you're right.' He smiled suddenly. 'So –
tell me your news. How did you get on in the States?'

'Very well. The Landis family were very kind to me.'

'You weren't tempted to stay?'

'No. I'm a Londoner born and bred. I got homesick. I
was ready to come home when the time came.'

'And since?'

'I worked in Yorkshire for a few months – for some
people I met on the plane coming home.' She hesitated,
looking at him. 'Then . . . then my father died.'

'Yes, Imogen told me. Shirley's helping out at the shop,
I hear, and taking part-time drama lessons.'

'I felt bad about her not going to RADA but it couldn't
be helped. My mother and I quarrelled. It's all a bit . . .'

'I understand. So now you're here, working for Leonie.
I'm glad we're all still in touch, Gloria. I've missed you. I
mean that.' Tony got up and went to the cocktail cabinet.
'For God's sake put that bloody duster down and have a
drink.'

Gloria shook her head. 'No, I couldn't. Besides, it's too
early.'

Tony looked at his watch and replaced the decanter of
whisky in the cabinet. 'Perhaps you're right. How about
some coffee then?'

Over the coffee, which they drank sitting at the kitchen
table where Gloria felt more comfortable, Tony told her
about his ex-wife's visit to England to make a film for the
company he worked for.

'It was great to see Gill again. She brought my son,
Marcus, with her too. You should have seen him, Gloria.
He's twenty now. Such a tall, handsome fellow. He's at
Yale, reading history and English literature. He hasn't
decided yet on what he wants to do but he's done quite a
lot of acting with his college drama group and Gill says
he's good.' He sighed. 'It made me feel damned old, I can
tell you. He reminded me so much of myself at that age.'
He drew hard on his cigarette. 'Seeing him made me feel
I'd missed an awful lot, too. He's my son and yet I don't
really know the first thing about him. He doesn't even

have my name any more. Gill had his name changed to Fane.'

'I'm sorry, Tony. And I know what you mean.' She looked thoughtfully at him. 'I haven't seen as much of Shirley as I'd have liked since the war. We used to be so close once. Life is full of surprises – and regrets,' she added quietly.

He reached across the table to touch her hand. 'We are still friends, aren't we, Gloria?'

'Of course. Why do you ask?'

'You're – I don't know – different. I get the feeling that you're holding me at arm's length.'

'Perhaps I am. We did say goodbye after . . . that last time, didn't we?'

He looked into her eyes for a long moment as though trying to read what was hiding in their depths. 'How are you, Gloria?' he said at length. 'How are you *really*, I mean?'

'I told you. I'm all right.'

'No new man in your life?'

'No. I hear you have someone new, though.'

He frowned. 'Who told you that?'

She blushed. 'Leonie said something about a chorus girl.'

He looked puzzled for a moment, then threw back his head and laughed. 'Trust Leonie. I was seeing Pat Burnette for a while, but she's a rising musical-comedy star, not a chorus girl. As a matter of fact she reminds me a lot of Leonie at that age – ambitious, full of youthful enthusiasm, a bit brash. She was much too young for me, of course. I had a distinct impression that she only went out with me because she thought I might help her career along.' He smiled wryly. 'The story of my life, eh? And just between ourselves, she had the intellect of a fruit fly. I admit it did my ego good, being seen around with a lissom young blonde on my arm, but after a while even that gets tedious.' He chuckled and squeezed Gloria's hand. 'I can't *tell* you how good it is to see you, Gloria. You and I have always had something a bit special, haven't we? You always make me fccl so relaxed. Have dinner with me one evening?'

Very gently she withdrew her hand from beneath his. 'I'm always busy at the theatre in the evenings.'

'Not at the weekends, surely?'

'I always go away at the weekends.'

'Lunch, then?'

'I don't think so, Tony.'

He cocked an amused eyebrow at her. 'Are you giving me the brush-off by any chance?'

'Let's face it, it would make life very difficult. Much better leave it.'

He sighed. 'I don't agree, but if you say so. . . .' He stubbed out his cigarette. 'I'm here to talk to Leonie about selling Longueville Hall,' he confided. 'We hardly ever get up to Houlton nowadays. Anyway, it's time we made things official and started divorce proceedings. I think she'll agree.'

'Sell Longueville Hall?' Gloria was shocked. 'What will happen to Jim and Molly Jarvis if the place is sold?'

He frowned. 'That's the one thing that bothers me. We could pension them off, of course. Or maybe they'd like to come and work here, looking after Leonie. It'd take some of the pressure off you – you look positively shredded. Or maybe she and this Winspear character will buy a house together, who knows? Things are all very fluid at the moment.'

'What will you do?' She looked at him.

'I've got a couple more films to make under my present contract. When they're in the can I'm planning to form a Shakespearean company – touring England first, then Canada. It's still at the planning stage, I'm in the process of working out the details with Peter. I've had enough of making films about the war. I'm even tired of flying.' He smiled wryly. 'I rather suspect I might be getting old.'

She smiled back at him. 'You know you don't really believe that.'

'Taking Shakespeare on tour is what I've always wanted, Gloria. I can't wait to get into rehearsal.' His eyes shone at the thought. 'I'm going to play Macbeth and Hamlet, Richard II – all the roles no one else would ever let me play. I might even have a go at Lear.'

'Well, good luck with it.'

'Thanks.' He leaned towards her, touching her hand. 'You're always so good for my ego, Gloria. You and I go back a long way, don't we? If you change your mind about that dinner I'd be more than pleased. I mean that.'

They heard the front door slam and Gloria got up from the table and began to clear the cups into the sink. 'That's Leonie. You'd better go and see her.'

When he had gone she sat down again at the table and tried to examine the whirling vortex of her emotions. It was still there, what she had always felt for Tony. It always would be; she admitted it now. Hearing about his latest affair, however trivial he protested it was, had given her pain. The fact that he cared so little about it somehow made it worse. No one had been able to stir his emotions as deeply as Claire once had and she guessed that no one ever would, least of all she. There was a bond between them, yes, but Tony clearly had no idea how strong it was, or how deep it went with her. And that was the way it must always stay.

She turned towards the sink and began to run hot water onto the used coffee cups. Thank God he would soon be going out of her life permanently. It would be less painful that way.

As Shirley's course of lessons with Magda progressed, a strong relationship developed between them. Magda often made tea for Shirley when she arrived hot and out of breath after a long day in the shop. She was watching a very promising talent develop before her eyes month by month and it buoyed up her spirits and excited her. When they were talking together over the teacups, she soon recognised the trap the girl had fallen into at home and sympathised with her predicament. In her turn she told Shirley of her own disappointment. She had been at the height of a promising career when the war began. Joining

ENSA, she had gone abroad with a repertory company. On the voyage back from Egypt, the ship on which they were travelling was torpedoed. Magda lost a lung and several ribs and was adrift in a boat for days. Her injuries meant the end of her stage career.

'I tire too easily,' she told Shirley. 'And my voice gives out after about an hour's work.' She smiled. 'But I can still teach, and students like you, my dear, make all the heartache and disappointment worth while. I see a great future for you if you continue to work hard.'

Shirley meant to work hard. She had begun to memorise speeches from Shakespeare now, and this evening she could hardly wait to perform Juliet's poison speech, which she had worked hard all weekend to perfect.

'"Farewell, God knows when we shall meet again . . ,"',She lost herself in enacting the scene. Magda watched, seeing herself as a very young girl, aching for the hope and innocent naivety she saw in front of her. When Shirley had finished and seated herself again at the desk, she asked:

'Do you have a boyfriend, Shirley?'

'There is someone, yes.'

'Have you know him long?'

'About a year and a half, I suppose.'

'And do you love him?'

Shirley was taken aback. What was Magda getting at? What did boyfriends have to do with anything? She'd been hoping to hear what she thought of her performance. 'Well – not really,' she said. 'I'm too interested in acting. Too busy to be bothered with stuff like that.'

'You mustn't shut out life, though. Acting is all about living. You mustn't forget that. Your technique is coming along very well,' Magda said. 'But to play the great dramatic roles you need emotional experience. Juliet was deeply in love. To play her you need to know that anguish, to feel the longing and the pain as well as the joy of being loved in return. You haven't really lived until you've been truly in love.' Magda put her hand against her breast and closed her eyes.

Privately Shirley thought it was nonsense. After all, what was acting if not pretending? 'Oh, so if I wanted to play a murderess, would you expect me to go out and kill someone?' she asked dryly.

Magda opened her eyes and stared at Shirley for a moment. 'Don't be facetious, Shirley,' she said sharply. 'Don't belittle the finer emotions. They are the grist to the actor's mill. You're such a pragmatic child. Learn a little softness. Learn how to weep – how to feel your own sorrow. A good actress must be a little selfish in order to live, but she must also sacrifice and suffer in order to give pleasure. In other words, darling, you need to experience life – to *live*.' She looked at Shirley's crestfallen face and leaned forward. 'Don't look so downcast. Living is something we can't escape. It happens to us all. It will come.'

'I suppose so,' Shirley said glumly.

'Listen, dear, there is something I want to talk to you about,' Magda said. 'The London Academy of Music and Dramatic Art hold examinations three times a year. The next date will be in November. I would like to enter your name. If you pass the exam you will be awarded a bronze medal. You could then go on to take a silver and a gold. Are you interested?'

Shirley's eyes shone. 'Oh yes, please. What would I have to do?'

'You would perform two set pieces in full stage make-up, but without costume or props. You would also be required to read a piece from sight. You would be marked on things like stage presence, business, voice production and stage make-up.' She opened a drawer and drew out a leaflet. 'I already have the syllabus, so if you are agreeable I could obtain the scripts and we could begin preparing next week.'

Dave found Shirley quiet as they walked home together that evening. Her mind was full of the bronze-medal exam and the other things Magda had said. She meant to pass that exam, and pass it well.

'Penny for them?' Dave said, bending to look into her eyes. 'You're miles away tonight. Lesson go well, did it?'

'Oh, yes.' Shirley linked her arm through his and hugged it. 'Miss Jayne is entering me for an exam in the autumn. I'll have an awful lot of hard work to do. It's for a bronze medal.' She looked up at him. 'Dave, how would you like to go to the theatre – Up West?'

Dave looked nonplussed. 'I don't know. I've never been to the theatre. What would it cost?'

'Nothing. Gloria – my mum – is dresser to Leonie Swann, the actress. She's in a play at the Lyric. She'd get seats for us if you'd like to go. What do you say?'

Dave looked unsure. 'You want to go, don't you?'

'Oh, I'd love to, Dave.' She gave his arm a squeeze and smiled up at him. 'So will you come with me?'

His heart twisted inside him as he looked down into those wide blue eyes. It was impossible to refuse her anything when she looked at him like that. He drew her into the shadow of a doorway and kissed her. 'Okay then, of course I'll go if it'll make you happy,' he said, hugging her tightly to him.

Shirley snuggled against him. Dave really was nice and being kissed and cuddled by him made her feel all relaxed and safe. Perhaps it *was* love she felt for him, though she couldn't help feeling that there should be something more – something magical and exciting. If only all this emotional experience – this *living* that Magda talked about – could be hurried up a bit.

That night Shirley wrote to her mother. She didn't give away Ma's secret but said the letters must have gone astray. She told Gloria about her drama lessons and the coming exam. She wrote a few snippets of news about the shop, Ma and Dave too. She ended by telling her how much she had missed her and said that she and Dave would love to accept the tickets to see Leonie in *Joy in the Morning*, possibly going backstage afterwards.

When she had finished the letter and sealed it into its envelope she sat on the bed for a long time, her eyes misty and far away. She'd dreaded her third winter at Angel Row; the finger-and-toe-numbing cold in the shop day after day and the draughty little house with all its uncomfortable inconveniences, but now that she had something to look forward to it hardly seemed to matter. Soon she would escape to a wonderful new life, to success and fame and a dream come true. It was all going to happen for her. She could feel it opening like a beautiful flower inside her. All she had to do was to work hard and wait.

Chapter Fifteen

When Tony had come to the flat to discuss divorce with Leonie, it had shaken her. She had never seen him so positive and determined. He clearly meant business. And as far as she knew there was no other serious love in his life. He had even talked of selling Longueville Hall. Not that she minded that; she was tired of the place anyway. It held too many unwelcome memories. Now that the war was over and she had made her name in the legitimate theatre; now that she had met Paul, her life had changed totally. Why cling to a past that was dead? Tony and she had fallen out of love long ago. Attitudes were changing too. It was no longer a ruinous scandal to be divorced, even for people in the public eye. Too many marriages, entered into impulsively during the war, had failed to withstand the changes that peace had brought.

Yet to Leonie divorce still smacked of failure, especially when neither partner wished to remarry. In a way it was burning one's bridges. She'd stalled Tony that morning at the flat, telling him she would think about it and let him know. She had continued to stall him ever since, but to keep him quiet she'd agreed to let him go ahead and put Longueville Hall on the market. Even Imogen hardly ever went there any more. When she wasn't working hard at RADA she was having fun with the young man she had taken up with. The place was simply sitting there eating money. It made sense to let it go.

Tony had mentioned the Jarvises, asking if she could perhaps offer them employment at the flat. She had rejected that idea out of hand, suspecting him of planning to get them to spy for him – report back all that she was doing with a view to divorcing her on grounds of adultery if all else failed. If she allowed that, she would no longer be a free woman in her own home. Tony knew about Paul, of course, but as yet he had no proof that they were sleeping together. If she was going to agree to a divorce it would be on her terms. She would not be forced into it and neither did she wish to see her private life sordidly reported in the gutter press. Her future as a straight actress was still tenuous. If they were going to do it, it must be done quietly and discreetly.

Her relationship with Paul kept her on her toes, the adrenalin flowing. It was exciting in its sheer unpredictability. He was moody – light-hearted and devil-may-care one day, gloomy and irritable the next. Negotiations were taking place on the sale of film rights of *Joy in the Morning* and he was writing a new play with her in mind for the leading part, but so far he had refused to let her read any of it. When he was working he was taciturn to the point of rudeness. He would shut himself away for days at a time, then turn up in the small hours of the morning elated and amorous, sweeping her off her feet, flatteringly eager to make love. Leonie had long since given up trying to understand him but his mercurial personality thrilled and excited her, and she was convinced that his brilliant talent was going to take her to worldwide stardom. Although she would not admit it, she stood in awe of his superior intellect and feared the quick, explosive temper that even surpassed her own.

On the Saturday night that Shirley was due to come backstage, Leonie was at her best. The show had gone well. The audience had been especially receptive and appreciative and she had responded as she always did, with a deeply emotional performance which, instead of draining her, left her almost incandescent.

As she came down from the stage after the last tumultuous curtain call, Gloria was ready with fresh hot coffee, hot water and a change of clothes. When Leonie burst into the dressing room she was breathless, her eyes shining with elation.

'Did you *hear* them, Gloria? I don't think I've ever had such a rapturous audience, even before the war on the night *Sunshine Sally* opened. Five calls, we took, and even then they were still calling for another.' She threw herself into a chair and kicked off her shoes. 'Oh, I *wish* Paul could have been here to hear it. It was for him as much as for me.' She stood up, turning to let Gloria unzip her dress. 'Did I tell you he's gone down to Cornwall to look at locations for the film?'

'Film – of this play?' Gloria asked, helping Leonie on with her wrapper.

'Yes. Isn't it exciting? The cinema is where the real stars are made. One can reach a much wider audience. It's all still very hush-hush so of course we mustn't say too much yet, but it's been confirmed that the Rank Organisation has bought the film rights of *Joy in the Morning* and with luck filming should begin early next year.' She sat down at the dressing table and began creaming off her make-up. 'I wish Paul would let me read the new play. It sounds even better than *Joy*.' She glanced up at the clock. 'Oh – I've just remembered. Shirley was in front this evening, wasn't she? What time do you expect her round?'

Gloria was examining Leonie's costumes for damage and loose buttons before putting them away on hangers. 'I told them to give us half an hour.'

'Oh, good. It'll be so lovely to see darling Shirley again. She and I always got along so well. You have a very talented little daughter, Gloria. I hope you realise it.'

'Oh, I do. And she's not so little any longer.'

'I can't wait to see how she's grown up. It must be almost two years since I saw her last.'

'I believe it is.' Gloria poured hot water into the washbasin and drew the screen around it for Leonie to wash. Continuing to tidy up the dressing room, she listened to Leonie's continuous chatter mingled with splashing from behind the screen. 'It's such a pity she couldn't

336

have gone to RADA with Imogen. Those two were so inseparable – more like sisters than friends. I suppose your mother couldn't find someone else to help her in the wretched shop, could she? Old people can be so selfish?'

'It isn't just Ma,' Gloria said. 'I couldn't afford to send her now.'

Leonie emerged from behind the screen and sat down at the dressing table again. 'I'd have thought you could have managed it. You don't spend your money on anything else, do you?'

You don't give me the time to, Gloria wanted to say. 'I – have the cottage to maintain,' she said instead, turning away.

'*That* place? I don't know why you don't sell it and let Shirley have the benefit of the money.' Leonie applied her lipstick and ran a brush through her hair, then she stood up and held out her arms for the dress Gloria held ready for her. 'Making a talented child like Shirley miss her opportunities for the sake of a run-down greengrocer's shop in the East End is just plain *criminal* if you ask me. You should speak to your mother – put your foot down.'

Gloria bit hard on the retort she wanted to make. Nobody *was* asking Leonie. It was none of her business. It was all very well for her to talk. She hadn't any idea what it was like to be hard up. If she only knew . . .

At that moment there was a hesitant tap on the door and Gloria opened it to find Shirley standing outside, a reluctant Dave hovering in the background. Shirley wore a suit of soft violet wool. She had saved hard for it, keeping an eye on the shop window for weeks and praying that no one else would get there before her. It was cut in the new Dior style they were calling the New Look. The skirt was calf-length and flared and the jacket had a tiny nipped-in waist and flaring peplum which enhanced the gentle curve of her hips. A tiny stand-up collar framed her face. Her hair was brushed into a shining halo of auburn curls and her only make-up was a hint of pink lipstick. Dave stood behind her, looking acutely uncomfortable in his best blue suit. His face shone with recent shaving and his newly cropped hair was severely disciplined with hair cream.

'Come in, both of you.' Gloria held the door wide.

Shirley said: 'Thanks. This is Dave, Gloria.'

'How do you do, Dave.' Gloria held out her hand. 'I hope you enjoyed the show.'

'Oh yes, Mrs – er, Rayner.'

'It was *wonderful*,' Shirley cut in excitedly. 'Leonie was just terrific. She got *ever* so many curtain calls.'

'I'm so glad you liked it.' Leonie appeared, smiling, from behind the door and threw out her arms theatrically to Shirley. '*Darling* – it's been so *long*.' She kissed Shirley on both cheeks and then held her at arm's length to look at her. 'My goodness, how you've grown up! You were always pretty but you're positively *beautiful* now. Come along in and tell me all about those drama lessons you've been taking. What did Gloria say that actress's name is? Is it anyone I know, I wonder?' Her arm around Shirley's waist, she drew her into the room, leaving Dave standing awkwardly by the door. Gloria smiled at him.

'Would you like a cup of coffee? Take no notice of those two. Shirley was evacuated to Leonie's house when she was nine, so they're old friends.'

'Yes, I've heard all about it,' Dave said. He nodded towards the coffee, laid out on a tray. 'A cup of coffee would be very nice, thanks.'

Leonie listened with rapt attention to Shirley's news, giving every appearance of sharing in her excitement as she bubbled over with the news about the bronze-medal exam she was to take in November.

'So you're not too disappointed about RADA then?'

'Not so much now that I'm at Stage Coach,' Shirley told her. 'I still see Imo. And we have so much more to talk about when we meet.'

On the other side of the room Gloria tried her best to entertain a tongue-tied Dave, who was clearly wishing himself a hundred miles away from this alien environment. Talking to him, Gloria discovered that she had been at school with his oldest sister, Ida, sadly killed in the

Blitz. She knew other members of his family too, but she didn't like to engage him in conversation about his family in case it was painful.

They had been talking for about twenty minutes when the door opened and Paul Winspear walked in. Leonie gave a cry of delight and leaped up from her chair.

'*Paul*, darling! You're back. I wasn't expecting you till tomorrow.' She kissed him so extravagantly that Dave flushed with embarrassment and turned his head away. 'Oh, I *wish* you'd been in front tonight. It was quite the best reception we've had since the beginning of the run.' Remembering her guests, she turned. 'Darling, I'd like you to meet Shirley Rayner. She's Gloria's daughter and she grew up with Imogen at Houlton all through the war. She's planning to be an actress. The young man is her friend, er, Geoff.'

'Hello, Geoff.' Paul nodded briefly towards a blushing Dave, who opened his mouth to correct the mistake and then closed it again as Paul turned his attention to Shirley, who had stepped forward, mesmerised by this tall, striking man. Paul was much better-looking in the flesh than in the photographs Imogen had shown her outside the theatre. The camera could not capture the mysterious light in his dark eyes or the sheer dynamism that emanated from him. She held out her hand and smiled up at him shyly.

'I enjoyed your play very much, Mr Winspear.'

Paul took the hand she offered and looked into the violet-blue eyes. 'Why haven't I met this enchanting creature before?' His words were addressed to Leonie but his eyes never left Shirley's face. 'I thought you said she was a child?'

Leonie gave an uncertain little laugh, noticing for the first time the firm curves of Shirley's figure and her long, shapely legs. 'She *is*. What are you now, darling – fifteen?'

'Seventeen,' Shirley corrected.

Paul smiled. 'So you're Gloria's daughter? How extraordinary. Tell me what you liked about the play.' His hand still held hers and Shirley was sharply aware of its pulsing warmth. Her own hand tingled as though she were being charged with a force – a magical energy that made her feel alive and excited. As she began to tell him what she had enjoyed in the play, the words seemed to come so easily that she surprised herself. It was almost like listening to someone else talking. All that Magda had taught her about the appreciation of drama seemed suddenly to gel and take form.

Paul's eyes widened. 'You're very perceptive. Where are you studying – at RADA?'

Shirley shook her head. 'I'm taking private tuition with an actress called Magda Jane. She has a studio in Stepney. It's called Stage Coach. I'm taking the London Academy's bronze-medal exam in November.'

His lips twitched with amusement. 'Well, you certainly seem to have learned a lot. Stepney – is that where you live?'

'No, I live in Whitechapel. I help my grandmother run her shop.'

'Whitechapel, eh? And not a hint of an accent. Ten out of ten to Miss Jayne, whoever she is.'

Shirley withdrew her hand – the heady spark of confidence he had ignited in her suddenly gone. Was he laughing at her? She looked at Leonie. 'I, er, think we'd better go now. Thank you for the tickets and the coffee. We've enjoyed it so much.'

Leonie, who had been watching with mounting fury, switched on her smile again. 'Not at all, angel. You must come and see me again some time.'

Gloria escorted Shirley and Dave through the maze of backstage corridors. 'Maybe we could meet some time, Shirl,' she said as they reached the stage door.

'Our hours clash, though, don't they?' Shirley said. 'There's only Sundays and Imogen says you go to Boothley at weekends.'

'That's right,' Gloria said unhappily.

Shirley looked pointedly at her mother, waiting for her to suggest a weekend together at Rook Cottage. When she didn't, she said shortly: 'Well, obviously your weekends are all booked up. If you get an evening off some time, just drop me a line. Thanks for arranging this evening for us. Good night, Gloria.'

'Good night, love. Please keep in touch, won't you – and give my love to Ma.'

'I will. Come on, Dave.'

Gloria caught Shirley's arm and drew her back to kiss her cheek. 'Take care, darling. God bless.' Shirley held herself stiffly and Gloria felt her aloofness like a barrier between them. She smiled at Dave. 'It was nice to meet you. Good night.'

''Night, Mrs, er, Rayner. And, er, thanks.'

In the dressing room Leonie glared at Paul. 'Did you *have* to look and speak to the child like that? It's very unkind to pretend to be interested in a girl as young and impressionable as Shirley.'

'Unkind? To whom?' He laughed and sank languidly into an armchair. 'And you can take it from me, that was no child, my dear. The delicious Shirley may not be fully aware of it yet, but she's a highly sensuous young person. And very definitely *all* woman.'

Leonie's heart began to beat faster as she felt the anger swell to almost uncontrollable passion in her breast. 'You were practically *undressing* her with your eyes,' she said, her eyes flashing. 'Hanging on to her hand, looking at her as though you were about to *eat* her. Honestly, Paul, it was so obvious. So – so *blatant*. Right under her mother's nose, too.'

He looked up at her, one eyebrow raised cynically. 'Oh, I see, it's Gloria you're worried about, is it?'

'Well, she *is* an employee of mine. Naturally I don't want to see her offended.'

'I'd no idea you were so solicitous.' Paul stood up, his dark eyes dangerously bright. 'In that case we'd better be a little more discreet in future, hadn't we? Perhaps I shouldn't come to the flat quite so often – certainly not to stay the night. We mustn't upset your dresser's high moral standards, must we?'

Leonie looked at him sharply, a prickle of fear stirring in the pit of her stomach. 'You know I didn't mean that.'

'Then just what *did* you mean?' His voice was hard. 'I hope you're not the jealous type, Leonie. If there's one thing I can't stand it's a possessive woman.' He stared at her. 'I believe that's one of the most tiresome things I can think of, Leonie; not to say boring. You're not jealous, are you?' He took a step towards her.

'No – no, of course I'm not. I've never been jealous in my life.' Her heart quickened. She hated it when he looked at her like that. She backed away from him till her back was pressing hard against the wall, flinching slightly as his hands descended heavily onto her shoulders. He bent swiftly and kissed her hard, bruising her mouth and biting her lips painfully.

'Good. I've always felt that you and I are kindred spirits, Leonie,' he said softly as he unbuttoned her dress. 'And that means each of us recognising that the other must be free. If I look at another beautiful woman it doesn't mean I want you any the less.' His hand was inside her bra, the long sensuous fingers caressing her breast. 'And you are completely free to do the same.' As he pressed his body against her she felt the familiar churning in her stomach, the weakness that buckled her knees.

'You know – I'll never want – any man but you, Paul,' she whispered.

He bent and swept her up into his arms, but she shook her head wildly.

'No – not here – not now,' she murmured breathlessly. 'Gloria will be back any minute.'

He paused, then let her go abruptly. 'Just as you please,' he said coldly. 'I made a special effort to come back early to be with you this evening, Leonie. I was actually looking forward to seeing you and telling you all about the film locations I've chosen. I thought we might spend the weekend together, but you don't seem to be in the mood for anything but picking a quarrel.'

'Oh no, that's not true. I hate quarrelling with you, Paul. It makes me miserable.' She caught at his hand as he turned away. 'A weekend together would be lovely. Don't be cross, darling. I've missed you so much.'

'You've missed me and yet you can push me away when I want you. That's not exactly the action of a woman burning with desire, is it?'

'I'm not pushing, it's just . . .' Biting her lip, she went to the door and turned the key in the lock. 'There – just in case,' she whispered as she went into his arms.

As Gloria walked down the corridor a few minutes later, she heard smothered sounds coming from the dressing room. Trying the door gently she found that it was locked. Standing outside for a moment or two, she listened to Leonie's muffled cries and knew what was happening. She'd been awakened by the same cries during the small hours sometimes on the nights that Paul stayed over and she knew that they were not born of ecstasy. As Leonie's dresser she could not help seeing the bruises Paul had inflicted on her body. Clearly he was a brutal lover and equally clearly Leonie needed and wanted him – and what he could do for her career – so much that she was prepared to put up with his sadistic tendencies. She sighed and shook her head. Maybe Leonie had taken on more than she could handle this time, she told herself.

All the way home Shirley's head was in the clouds, her mind on the play. She was busy committing to memory every detail of Leonie's dressing room; storing it all up to fantasise over later when she was alone. One day she would be in her place, she told herself. *She* would be on the stage, receiving all that applause and adulation; *she* relaxing and receiving guests afterwards in her luxurious dressing room. When Gloria had opened the stage door for them, a little group of autograph hunters had stepped forward eagerly, hoping for the emergence of one of the stars. They'd fallen back, disappointed, when she and Dave stepped out. But one day they would greet her with hopeful, adoring eyes, she promised herself.

She thought about Paul, too. No man had ever looked at her like that before, or held her hand in that special, meaningful way. He was Leonie's new man, she had gathered that much from Imogen, though she didn't seem

343

entirely happy about the situation. The way he had looked at Shirley made her tingle all over. Did he really love Leonie? Surely a man in love did not look at other women like that? But she was learning fast that you never really knew with men. There were the nice, safe, dull ones, like Dave, who never put a foot wrong; and the dangerous, exciting ones like Paul who broke all the rules and got away with it. Yet with either there was always the possibility of the unexpected.

When they reached Angel Row she relaxed in Dave's arms and tried to enjoy his kisses, but deep in the secret recesses of her mind the image of Paul Winspear still lurked. She found it impossible not to wonder what it would be like to be kissed by him. With a little frisson of excitement, she guessed that his kiss would be like a powerful drug: once taken, she would be hopelessly addicted. Just one date with him would be an experience. It would provide some of that *living* that Magda was always talking about. She smiled wryly to herself, guessing that just one date with Paul would not be enough. It would provide a one-way ticket to heartache, but there was little need for her to worry. The chances of Paul Winspear asking her out were about as remote as her landing the lead in a West End play.

Neither of Imogen's parents had mentioned to her that Longueville Hall was going to be sold. It was only when she decided on the spur of the moment to go to Houlton for a weekend visit that she discovered the fact.

'But why didn't anyone tell me?' she asked Molly. 'Don't I have a say in *anything* any more? First they plan to divorce, now they're selling my home, and all without a single word to me about it.'

Molly smiled. 'I'm sure they meant to,' she said awkwardly. 'I dare say each of them thought the other had said something to you. Anyway, I doubt if it'll sell quickly. People don't want places the size of this nowadays.' Inwardly she ached for the girl. Her childhood had been insecure through her parents' constant quarrelling, and now that she'd left school to study they seemed to think that she was a completely independent adult with a life of her own – that they no longer needed to be responsible for her welfare. Molly knew different. Inside Imogen craved love and security as much as ever, and once Longueville Hall had gone, once she and Jim were no longer here to provide a safe haven for the girl, where would she go? Who would provide the stability she needed so desperately?

'Never mind. You'll always be welcome in our home, dear,' she said soothingly. 'And this place really is a waste of your parents' money nowadays. It's far too big and neither of them ever comes to stay any more.'

'But I love it so. All the memories. We had such fun here during the war, you and Jim and Shirley and me. Where will you and Jim go?'

'Don't you worry about us, my pet. We're not as young as we used to be and we're quite happy to retire. Your daddy has been very generous and we've saved a bit over the years. We've decided to buy a little house in the village. It's all settled. We were lucky to find it, what with the housing shortage and everything.'

Imogen bit her lip as a thought occurred to her. 'Gloria still has her cottage over at Boothley, Nanny. Do you ever run into her?'

Molly shook her head. 'No, dear, why?'

'She comes up most weekends, according to Mummy, but she never brings Shirley. I think she's planning to get a grant, modernise the cottage and sell it.'

'She hasn't been to see us,' Molly said noncommittally.

'Nothing's the same since the war ended,' Imogen said gloomily. 'People don't seem to care about each other as they used to. I thought it would all be so marvellous when it was over, but look at us. We've still got food rationing, coal and petrol shortages; houses and flats are almost impossible to find.' Her face brightened. 'I think I'll bike over and see if Gloria's at home. It's ages since we had a good natter. Maybe she can talk Mummy out of selling. I certainly mean to nag Daddy into changing his mind.'

The Jarvises exchanged glances. They'd heard the many rumours that had circulated about Gloria and the child, cared for at Rook Cottage, but neither of them had the heart to mention it to Imogen. Jim fetched her old bicycle from the stables and dusted it off, giving the chain a spot of oil and checking the brakes before he pronounced it fit to ride. Then they watched, feeling guilty at their inability to help her, as she cycled hopefully off down the drive.

Rook Cottage looked the same as the last time she had seen it. The tiny front garden appeared a little neglected, full of fallen leaves from the tall elms in the churchyard close by, but that wasn't surprising with Gloria only there at weekends. As she walked up the front path, Imogen wondered how she coped with the inconveniences of the place after the luxury of the Mayfair flat where she lived all week. No indoor sanitation and no electricity or water must come as a hardship in this day and age especially in winter. She knocked on the door and waited.

When Gloria opened the door she looked startled to see Imogen standing in the porch. The colour drained from her cheeks and her eyes widened in shocked surprise.

'Imogen! What are you doing here?'

'I'm over for a weekend at Houlton. I thought it would be nice to bike over and see you.'

'Oh.' Gloria peered out into the lane as though she were afraid someone might be watching. 'Well, you'd better come in then, I suppose.'

Imogen shook her head. 'If I've come at an inconvenient time it's all right. I should have let you know, only there wasn't time and you're not on the telephone.'

Gloria bit her lip. 'I'm sorry, Imogen. I didn't mean to sound rude. It's lovely to see you. Was there something you wanted – something special, I mean?'

'Well, yes. I wanted to talk to you about my parents selling Longueville Hall. Did you know about it?'

'I had heard, yes.'

At that moment the gate creaked and Imogen turned to see a young woman wheeling a pushchair up the path. 'Oh, you've got a visitor. I'll go.'

The young woman unstrapped a fair-haired toddler from the pushchair and carried him into the house past Gloria. Imogen stepped sideways to let her pass. 'Well, I'll go . . .'

'No. Come in.' Gloria held the door open. 'Now that you're here, we might as well have that talk.' She turned to the woman with the child. 'Take Michael through and give him his milk, will you, Margaret?'

The little parlour was chilly and Gloria apologised as she indicated a chair. 'Do sit down. I'm sorry if it's a bit cold but we don't light the fire in here till the afternoon.' She looked at Imogen. 'I'd be obliged if you'd keep this visit to yourself, Imogen – as far as your parents are concerned, I mean.'

Imogen nodded uncomfortably. 'Of course. Perhaps I . . . shouldn't have come. If . . .'

'You'll have gathered that Michael is my child,' Gloria went on.

'Look, you don't have to tell me –'

'No. It's time I told someone,' Gloria said. 'I can't keep it to myself for ever.' She looked at Imogen. 'I'm not asking you to keep it a secret. That wouldn't be fair.'

'I won't tell anyone anyway,' Imogen said. 'Why should I?'

But Gloria seemed not to have heard. 'I discovered I was expecting when I was in America,' she said. 'It was a terrible shock. I came home sooner than I should have done because of it. On the plane I got talking to a woman who told me she'd been to America for special treatment at a clinic. She told me it was her last chance of having a baby. She'd been married ten years and tried everything. The American doctors had told her the treatment wouldn't work in her case and she was terribly depressed. I told her that I was pregnant but couldn't keep the child.' She looked at Imogen. 'You'll have guessed the rest.'

'She offered to adopt the baby?'

347

'Yes. It seemed like a wonderful stroke of luck, meeting her. They were obviously well off and they'd have done anything to get a child of their own. You can imagine how relieved I was. Well, she and her husband lived in Yorkshire and by the time we landed in England it was arranged that I would go straight there and live with them until the baby was born.'

'So what happened?' Imogen asked.

Gloria paused. 'It was a difficult birth – six weeks premature. Then, when he was born, Michael almost died. He had to stay in the hospital and while he was there they did tests. They found that he had something wrong with his heart.'

'Oh, Gloria, how awful! I'm so sorry.'

'The adoption fell through, of course. The Hensons wanted a perfect child and who could blame them? I couldn't abandon my little son when he was sick and needed me. I'd loved him from the moment he was born, anyway. So . . .'

'You brought him back here?'

'I was lucky. I met Margaret in hospital. Her husband was killed right at the end of the war and she'd lost the baby she was expecting, too. She's got no family of her own and she badly needed a fresh start and someone to love. I offered her a home and a job looking after Michael here.' She looked around her. 'It's not much of a home, but we keep it as warm and cosy as we can and I've put in for a grant to make it better – put in proper plumbing and everything.'

'And what about Michael – is he getting better? Can he be cured?'

'There's an operation for his problem now, thank God. And he can have it under this new National Health Scheme,' Gloria explained. 'It's to widen a valve in his heart that isn't working properly. He's not too bad now while he's so little. He was late walking and he's small for his age. But when he gets more active the problems will start. He mustn't exert himself or get overtired, you see. He needs constant attention.'

Imogen was silent. At the back of her mind something was nagging. 'But surely,' she began, 'surely if Billy's family had known you were carrying their grand-child . . .' She stopped. Billy had left the US Air Force base at Boothley almost a year before the end of the war. Michael couldn't possibly be his child. She smiled apologetically at Gloria. 'I'm sorry.'

Gloria nodded. 'Now you see why I didn't want to tell anyone,' she said. 'As you know, I never married Shirley's father. Ma would have gone mad if she'd known I'd made the same mistake again. She was so good to me. How could I land her with the same problem again, especially with Pa so ill?'

'Shirley really misses you. You used to be so close. She'd understand if she only knew. Couldn't you tell her?' Imogen asked.

Gloria shook her head. 'I can't, not yet anyway. She'd be bound to tell Ma.' She smiled wryly. 'I can imagine some of the things Ma says about me. Shirl wouldn't be able to stop herself from blurting it out. I know her. I can't provide Shirl with a home under the circumstances. In our separate ways we both rely on Ma. Better to leave things as they are, at least for the time being.'

Imogen was silent, remembering the harsh, uncompromising things old Mrs Rayner had said to her daughter on the day of her husband's funeral, imagining how deeply they must have hurt. 'So you let them go on thinking the worst of you? Let them believe that you're selfishly thinking only of yourself, when all the time . . . ?' Imogen shook her head. 'Gloria, maybe I shouldn't ask but – couldn't the baby's father . . . ?'

'That's out of the question,' Gloria said firmly. 'He must never know.'

Imogen was silenced by Gloria's firm tone. Clearly, for reasons best known to herself, she was determined not to pursue that course. She considered for a moment, then her face brightened. 'Why don't you tell Mummy? I'm sure she'd help. She'd give you a rise in wages for a start. I know she seems thoughtless sometimes but –'

'*No.*' The word was so positive that it stopped Imogen in mid-sentence. 'This is *my* problem, Imogen. It's nobody's fault but mine. I got myself into it and it's up to me and no one else to sort it out. I don't need help, advice or handouts from anyone.'

'I'm sorry. I wasn't trying to interfere. I shan't tell anyone, Gloria,' Imogen said, chastened by Gloria's firm determination.

'As I said, I'm not swearing you to secrecy. I'm not ashamed of having Michael, and eventually everyone will know. But as things are, it's better this way for the time being.' She smiled. 'Thanks for trying to help just the same, love. I appreciate your concern.' She moved to a chair and sat down, an indication that the subject was closed. 'Now – you came here to talk to me about the sale of Longueville Hall.'

Imogen shrugged. 'My problem seems trivial compared to yours. I just thought you might try to persuade Mummy not to sell. I love the place so much. It's the only real home I've ever had. Shirley and I were so happy there. I hate the thought of it belonging to someone else.'

Gloria nodded thoughtfully. 'Change always is painful.' She looked around her at the simple little room. 'This place is full of memories for me. I bought it so I could have Shirl to live with me. If she hadn't been so happy with you at Longueville Hall my life would have taken a completely different turn.' She pulled her thoughts back to the present and Imogen's problem. 'What will Molly and Jim do when the house is sold?'

'They seem to be quite looking forward to their retirement. They've even found a little house for sale in the village.'

Gloria smiled. 'See? You won't have to stop coming to Houlton just because your parents don't own a house here. If I know Molly she'll always keep a bed ready for you.'

Imogen nodded. 'Sometimes Molly and Jim feel more like family than Mummy and Daddy,' she said wistfully. 'Before I go, can I see Michael?'

Gloria looked pleased. 'Would you really like to? Wait there a minute and I'll fetch him.'

She left the room to reappear a moment later carrying the little boy. Imogen thought him the prettiest baby she had ever seen. He was a lot like Shirley, with the same wide blue eyes and softly curling red-gold hair. She reached out her arms to him.

'Hello, Michael. Are you going to let me hold you?'

He regarded her for a moment, then smiled and held out his arms. She took him from Gloria and he put his arms around her neck and pressed his little face against hers.

Gloria smiled. 'He likes you. He's quite shy usually. He doesn't see many people.'

Imogen was enchanted. 'Oh, Gloria, he's a darling. I'd like to take him home with me.'

'You'd soon bring him back.' Gloria laughed. 'He's not so enchanting when he wakes up at three in the morning.'

'I wouldn't mind. I've always wanted babies.' Imogen hugged the little boy. 'Can you talk yet, Michael?' She looked into the baby's face. 'Can you say Imo-gen?'

Michael watched her mouth, concentrating on its movements, but he didn't attempt the name for himself.

'He's a proper little parrot. I bet he'll say it as soon as you've gone.' Gloria took the child back. 'Come and see me again when you're in Houlton, won't you, Imogen? It was good to see you – and talk.'

'Yes, it was,' Imogen said. 'But I wish you'd talk to Shirley. I know she'd love her little brother. It seems so sad that she doesn't even know about him.'

'Believe me, it's better this way for the time being,' Gloria said.

'Molly was wondering why you hadn't been over to visit her and Jim,' Imogen said. 'What shall I tell her?'

'Tell her I'm busy keeping the cottage aired. I only have Sundays off from work. There really isn't time for visiting. All that's the truth, as you know.' She smiled ruefully. 'Believe me, Imogen. There's nothing I'd like better than to see Molly, and I will eventually. One day soon I'll make it all up to everyone. I just have to get Michael sorted out first. You do understand, love, don't you?'

Imogen understood but she felt uneasy that she was the only member of their circle to have stumbled on Gloria's secret. Her main concern was Shirley. They had never had secrets between them before and now she found herself unwittingly in possession of this intimate piece of family knowledge that Shirley had far more right to know about than she.

Shirley put the finishing touches to her make-up and closed the box with its sticks of Leichner greasepaint. Over the past weeks she'd been collecting them one by one. Numbers five and nine, white number twenty for highlighting, carmine for her cheeks, lake and brown liners and the little pots of blue and green eye shadows. Powder and cotton wool, orange sticks and a big pot of removing cream completed the kit, all stowed away in an old cigar box of Pa's she had found. Now she was ready and she sat nervously awaiting her turn in the back room of the church hall where the exams were being held, taking deep measured breaths just as Magda had taught her to control the thudding of her heart. She had come here on the bus, alone. It was a Friday afternoon and Dave was standing in for her at the shop. Ma hadn't said much, but her tight-lipped expression made it more than adequately clear what she thought of the whole thing.

The door opened and the previous student lurched in, leaning against the wall and blowing out her cheeks in exaggerated relief at getting the ordeal over.

'What was it like?' Shirley asked.

The girl pulled a face. 'Terrible. I forgot my lines and had to be prompted twice. Then I rubbed my eye and smudged all my make-up.' She peered at herself in the mirror. 'God almighty! Just look at me. I look like something the cat dragged in.'

'But did you pass?'

The girl gave her a rueful glance. 'What do you think?' Anyway, I don't know what *you're* getting worked up

352

about. You look smashing and I bet you're ten times better than me anyway. Look at the pathetic marks I got.' She held out her card, but before Shirley had had time to look at it properly a woman opened the door and called her name.

'Shirley Rayner. Will you come this way, please?'

The stage had been fitted with proper stage lighting and Shirley looked out, shielding her eyes from the glare of the footlights to where the examiner sat at a table halfway down the hall.

'You may begin.' The voice reached her clearly and she hurried to her position, took a deep breath to steady her voice and began the first piece.

Once she had begun she lost herself in the acting, enjoying herself thoroughly and quite forgetting that she was being examined. At the conclusion of the second piece she read the passage from a script the examiner handed to her. It presented no difficulties to her and she read it smoothly and with as much expression as she could. When she had finished there was a pause as the examiner continued to write. Shirley held her breath. After a moment he said, without looking up at her:

'Thank you. Will you come down here, please?'

He was still writing when she reached him. She waited, then he put down his pen and looked up at her with a smile.

'Well, Miss Rayner, you have given me a very nice performance. You have a good presence, and your acting has both spirit and sincerity.' He handed her the card. 'You can read my remarks at your leisure, but I can tell you now that I have passed you with honours and I hope I'll be here to give you an equally good silver medal next year.'

In a euphoric haze Shirley thanked him and walked from the hall. She felt oddly unreal, as though she floated, her feet hardly touching the ground. She was on her way. Someone who *counted* had actually said she was good. It had to be the happiest moment of her life.

In the dressing room the other girl waited. Her face was now cleaned of the smudged make-up and she had her coat on, ready to leave. She looked inquiringly at Shirley.

'Well?'

'I . . . I passed – with honours.'

'*There*. What did I tell you?' the girl said without a hint of envy. 'I knew you would, just looking at you. I've never been any good at this, perhaps they'll let me stop trying now. But you – you're a born actress if ever I saw one.'

Outside the dull, cold November day seemed to melt into spring. Shirley danced rather than walked along the pavement. She felt that everyone was looking at her – as though she were taking the star part in a film. Surely nothing could ever make her feel so happy?

Suddenly she was aware of a car horn hooting persistently behind her and she turned to see Imogen, hanging out of the window of a red sports car.

'Hey, Shirley! Hang on. We've come to pick you up.' Imogen laughed up into her face. 'No need to ask you how it went. Your expression is enough.' She jumped out of the car and hugged Shirley warmly. 'You passed?'

'Yes. With honours.'

Suddenly they were clinging to each other, half laughing, half crying. 'That's *wonderful*,' Imogen said. 'Congratulations, darling. I knew you'd do it. Look, Charles is home on leave and he's offered to take us both out to a nightclub to celebrate. How about that – are you on?'

Shirley's spirits rose. It would be wonderful to celebrate her success. Ma had seemed far more interested in Princess Elizabeth's wedding during the past few weeks than in her exam, in spite of her suspicious grumblings about where all the clothing coupons were coming from for the sumptuous dresses. 'I'd love to, Imo,' she said hesitantly, 'but I've nothing to wear.'

'That's all right,' Imogen said. 'We'll all go back to the flat and you can borrow something of mine.' She tugged impatiently at Shirley's arm. 'Oh, come *on*, Shirl! You can't just go tamely home after passing your bronze. It's a once-in-a-lifetime thing.'

Shirley thought of Ma's lugubrious expression as she had left this afternoon, leaving her to cope with the Saturday afternoon rush at the shop. She was sure to put a damper on her news if she went straight home now. 'Okay, why not?' she said rebelliously. Suddenly her heart quickened, excited at the prospect of an evening's extravagant fun.

At Imogen's flat Shirley chose a swirling cocktail dress of black lace over taffeta. It was quite severely cut, with a boat-shaped neckline; a large pink rose tucked into the waistline was its only decoration.

'You look fantastic in black,' Imogen said, leading her out into the living room where Charles waited patiently with a gin and tonic in his hand. 'Doesn't she, Charlie?'

Charles nodded appreciatively. 'An absolute knock-out.' He looked at his watch. 'Shall we go now? I've booked a table at the Café Romano for eight-thirty. I can't think what you girls do that takes so long.'

Shirley had never been anywhere like the Café Romano. Its plush decor, the soft, warm lighting and glittering chandeliers combined to heighten her glow of achievement and happiness. She ate things she had never tasted before at dinner. Never in a million years would she ever have imagined that she would enjoy snails. Then there was asparagus with its distinctive flavour, delicious breast of wild duck en croûte followed by a wickedly rich chocolate pudding that was redolent of brandy. They drank champagne, Charles and Imogen toasting Shirley loudly so that the other diners turned to look at the pretty auburn-haired girl in black, with indulgent smiles at the uninhibited gaiety of the group of young people.

The band was good. It had played all through dinner in a discreet, unobtrusive way, but now it struck up with more vigour, tempting the replete diners to take to the dance floor. Charles asked Imogen to dance and she glanced at Shirley.

'Do you mind? Will you be all right?'

Shirley laughed. 'Of course, silly. I'm perfectly happy just sitting here watching everyone.'

She watched, fascinated, as couples gradually filled the small floor, swaying gently to the music in the limited space. She had never seen so many handsome men and beautiful women gathered together before, or such high fashion, brilliant colours and luxurious, shimmering fabrics. Gloria would have been bewitched by it all. The music was infectious and Shirley's feet itched to dance too, but she knew she would have to wait her turn to dance with their shared escort. Suddenly she felt a hand on her shoulder and heard a voice say:

'Dance with me?' She looked up to see Paul Winspear's dark eyes smiling down at her.

Her heart did a somersault in her breast as she heard herself reply: 'Oh, thank you, I'd like to.'

His eyes swept over her with undisguised admiration as she rose from the table and went with him to the floor. When he put his arm around her waist she felt a thrill like an electric current course through her veins and it was all she could do not to shiver with delight.

'I've never seen you here before, Shirley.' When she didn't reply he looked down at her. 'It *is* Shirley, isn't it?'

'Yes, it's Shirley. I haven't been here before. My friends brought me this evening. It's a celebration.'

'Oh? Birthday?'

'No. I passed my bronze-medal exam this afternoon.'

'Well, congratulations.' He pulled her a little closer. 'No wonder you're looking so radiant. So what's next?'

'A silver medal, then a gold. Maybe then I'll be able to audition for a job somewhere.'

'I'm quite sure the world will be your oyster. Producers will beat a path to your door.'

She glanced up at him. 'I think you're laughing at me.'

'Oh, no. Believe me, I'm not laughing.' He held her eyes with his for a long moment and she was acutely aware of his long hard fingers on her waist and the hand that held hers in the same pulsating grip she had experienced the first time they met.

'Shall I tell you something, Shirley?' They were right in the centre of the floor now, their bodies pressed close and almost at a standstill among the crowded dancers. Mesmerised, Shirley shook her head. 'Ever since that evening when we were introduced in Leonie's dressing room I haven't been able to get you out of my mind,' he said quietly.

'But – but that was ages ago.' Shirley's heart was beating fast.

'I know. You can't imagine how much I've wanted to see you again. And now suddenly here you are. It's as though I'd conjured you up, just by wishing. Do you know what I'd like to do? I'd like to whisk you away from here – have you all to myself. Will you come?'

'I can't. I . . . I'm with friends.'

'I know. I saw. But not an escort, I think.'

'No, but just the same . . .'

'Where is the young man you were with at the theatre?' Shirley shook her head. 'I don't know. He's just a friend. He works for my grandmother.'

'So you're a free agent, Shirley? Footloose and fancy-free, as they say. No suitors jealously guarding your honour?'

'No.' She laughed. 'I don't want any. I've got ambitions. There are too many other things I want to do before I settle down to all that.'

He bent to brush his lips across her cheek. 'I can see that we're two of a kind, Shirley.' His breath tickled her ear tantalisingly. 'So if I can't tempt you away tonight, when can I see you again?'

Her heart was pounding so hard she felt sure he must feel it. 'Oh, I don't know. I mean . . . what – what about Leonie?'

'Leonie?' He smiled down at her bemusedly. 'What about her?'

'Well, aren't you and she . . . ?'

'Leonie and I are like you, footloose and fancyfree. We have an understanding. We each live our own lives. I write plays and she acts in them. But even that could change if either of us finds something we like better – either personally or professionally.'

'Oh.'

The music came to an end and Paul gave her a little squeeze. Slipping his hand into his inside pocket he produced a card and pressed it into her hand. 'My address and number. Give me a ring if you'd like to have dinner some time,' he said, smiling into her eyes. 'I'll be waiting for your call, Shirley. I have a strong feeling it's no accident that we met like this tonight. I don't believe we should try to cheat fate, do you?'

When she returned to the table Imogen was looking anxiously at her. 'Do you know who that was you were dancing with?'

'Yes. Paul Winspear. I met him at the theatre when I went to see Leonie in his play.'

Imogen leaned closer, lowering her voice. 'Be careful of him, Shirley. I've never liked him and I've an idea Gloria shares my feeling about him.'

But Shirley was in no mood to listen to warnings or criticisms. She was almost eighteen; old enough to take care of her own life. She and Paul had a very special rapport. She sensed it and she was sure that he did too. She was certain that he was destined to play an important role in her life. And she could hardly wait for the curtain to rise on it.

When Charles's sports car roared to a stop outside 10 Angel Row it was one-thirty. Shirley crept round to the back yard and let herself in quietly. Taking off her shoes, she crept through the kitchen into the hall and began to climb the stairs in the dark. She was halfway up when the light was suddenly switched on, temporarily blinding her.

'What the 'ell bleedin' time d'you call this, my gel?' Ma stood at the top of the stairs, fearsome in steel curlers and voluminous flannel nightgown. 'Start this kinda caper an' you'll find yourself up the stick like your mother did. I won't 'ave it. D'you 'ear me? *I won't bloody well 'ave it.*'

Shirley stood blinking up at her grandmother, the pleasure of her success and her beautiful evening suddenly crushed. Angry resentment at Ma's thoughtless cruelty flared up inside her.

'Why do you have to spoil everything?' she shouted indignantly. 'I've had enough of slaving behind a counter for you. I'm sick and tired of this dump; being treated like a kid and working for next to nothing. As soon as I can I'm getting another job and leaving here.'

Ma's shoulders slumped and the fire went out of her eyes. 'Yes, my gel,' she said. 'You might *'ave* to do that – and sooner than you think, too.'

Chapter Sixteen

Leonie pulled her fur coat more closely around herself, shivering in the teeth of the icy Atlantic wind coming off the sea. Cornwall in spring was supposed to be balmy and picturesque but she found the rugged coastline gloomy and depressing and as for the weather, they might as well have been at the North Pole.

All week they'd waited here on the cliffs at the edge of the moorland for the rain to stop so that they could shoot the suicide-attempt scene that had been written into the screenplay. The leading man had caught a cold and the director's temper had gone from tetchy to downright explosive. If they didn't get the weather they wanted soon, they would be severely behind schedule.

Filming was a bitter disappointment to Leonie. As a stage actress she found it impossible to get used to shooting scenes out of sequence. It went against everything she had ever learned about leading up to the climax of a role. The hotel was draughty and inconvenient; she hated the interminable waiting about and found the hasty *al fresco* lunches provided by a dubious firm of caterers totally unpalatable. But worst of all was her disappointment over Paul's absence. She had naturally assumed that he'd come on location with them and it had only been on the night before they left London for St Ives that he had told her he wasn't coming.

Although he had been asked to write the screenplay of *Joy in the Morning*, he had declined. He was working on something new and was quite happy to pass the work on to an experienced screenwriter. Privately Leonie thought the man had ruined it and she blamed Paul. Once he had been paid the enormous sum he had received for the film rights, he seemed to have lost interest in the project. But when she angrily accused him of this he had lost his temper. They had parted on bad terms and she'd been uneasy and preoccupied ever since filming had begun, a fact which had hampered her performance. It had hardly endeared her to the director either, who made no secret of the fact that he thought her a whining, uncooperative bitch.

A sudden fresh surge of rain lashed icily into her face as the shower increased to a torrent. She swore ferociously under her breath and glared at the lowering grey sky as she hurried for the shelter of the car once more. Sitting behind the rainwashed windscreen, she loosened her coat and lit a cigarette. She felt distinctly sorry for herself. Everyone seemed to have deserted her. After Paul had left in a temper the night before she left London, she'd been so lonely and desperate that she had even rung Tony, but he was about to leave on location work too, shooting the last film of his contract somewhere up in Yorkshire.

Even Gloria had not accompanied her on location. She had made it clear that she did not want to go so far away. Apparently there was some kind of family crisis and she said she would rather take her holiday while Leonie was away. Being without her had made Leonie realise for the first time just what a treasure Gloria was; always at hand with hot drinks, aspirin or a warm coat; impervious even to her blackest moods; seeming to anticipate every need without being told. The dresser provided by the film company wasn't in the same league; a plain, sullen woman with bad breath who couldn't even make a cup of coffee without spilling half of it in the saucer and who wouldn't have recognised a needle if she'd been impaled on one.

Leonie's thoughts returned as always to Paul, wondering what he was doing while she was away. Was work his only reason for not wanting to come with her? She was plagued constantly by jealousy and suspicion. Did he have someone else? Was he perhaps even at this moment with another woman? Someone younger? When they were out together she often caught him looking at other women, most of them in their early twenties or even younger. It hurt unbearably, but she knew better than to reproach him.

She adjusted the car's rear-view mirror so that she could see herself in it. God, she looked awful! Damn this godforsaken hole. The relentless sea winds were drying her skin and turning her hair into a salt-caked haystack. And now, to add to the horrors, she could see fine but unmistakable lines forming around her eyes and mouth. Depression set in, settling like a chunk of lead in her chest as she reminded herself that she had recently turned thirty-eight. Another two years and she would hit forty. What then? Downhill all the way. She shuddered, pushing the thought away. Paul thought she was five years younger, the same age as him, but at this rate he would soon guess that she had deceived him.

Thinking about it, she was fairly sure that he would marry her if she made it clear that this was what she wanted. After all, they were a good team professionally. Their work was complementary, and they had been together for three years now. That must count for something. His own divorce had gone through some time ago. Hers would have, too, if only she hadn't foolishly clung to her dead marriage. She made up her mind there and then: the moment she got back to London she would contact Tony and tell him to go ahead with the divorce. There would be no need for grounds now that they had been apart for so long. Even the public had grown used to not seeing them together. And then – she smiled to herself, savouring the thought of their reconciliation – then she would tell Paul she wanted them to be married and watch his face light up. She'd make it clear that it needn't tie them down, of course. They would still both be free. Paul's freedom meant a lot to him and she respected that. But if they were married he'd be hers no matter what.

Other women would know it. He'd probably appreciate that. It would stop anything too heavy developing. On second thoughts she wouldn't wait to get back to London, she'd telephone Tony in Yorkshire tonight.

A tapping on the car window startled her out of her reverie. It was Deborah, the director's assistant.

'Rain's stopped, Miss Swann. We're ready to shoot the scene now if you are.'

Leonie dragged herself stiffly out of the car. What a bloody bore. All she really wanted was a hot bath, a good meal and bed. The sooner she got this film over with, the sooner she could go home and get on with her life. All she hoped was that the notices would make it all worth while.

When Ma showed Shirley the official-looking letter she'd had from the council, she'd been stunned to see that it had been written the previous November, almost four months ago.

'Why didn't you tell me about this before?' she asked.

Ma shook her head. 'Never mind that, just read it,' she said, slumping into a chair at the kitchen table.

Shirley read through the letter, then went back to the beginning and read it again to make sure she understood. There was no mistake. In a way it was the answer to all the wishes she'd made when she first came home to White-chapel. But on reflection she saw that it could have disastrous side effects too. She looked across the table at her grandmother's stricken face.

'Didn't you answer it?' she asked.

Ma shook her head. 'I thought they'd change their minds. I thought there'd be an outcry – tryin' to take folks' 'omes off 'em like that. But I 'ad some bloke round from the council last week about it. 'E said it'd 'appen whether I said yes or not. Tried to tell me it'd all be for the best.'

'He could be right, Ma,' Shirley said gently, sorry for the friction that had developed between them since her outburst on the night of her exam. 'The street was badly damaged in the Blitz. Half the buildings have gone any-way. It'll never be the same as it was before the war. And a nice new flat in the block they're planning to build – just think, no more draughts, a proper bathroom and constant hot water . . .'

'But this is my *'ome*,' Ma wailed. 'Your grandad brought me 'ere when we was first married nearly forty years ago. This is where we worked together all our married life, brought up Gloria an' you; stuck it out all through the Blitz. We was 'ere after the worst of the docklands raids when the King and Queen come round theirselves to see the damage. Mr Churchill 'imself shook Pa's 'and when 'e come down the ARP post that day. You an' Glor was both born in that room up there.' She looked up at the ceiling and Shirley saw with dismay the tears that filled her eyes. She'd never seen Ma cry before, not even when Pa died. 'This place ain't just bricks and mortar, it's my life, Shirl,' Ma said dejectedly. 'Pa an' me 'ad a good life 'ere. We never asked for much. A drink and a sing-song down the pub on a Saturday night an' a seat at the Hackney Empire now and again as a special treat.' She fumbled in her apron pocket for a hanky. 'If they pull it all down they might as well knock me on the 'ead too, 'cause I'll be finished.'

'Oh, Ma, don't take on like that.' Her throat tight, Shirley rose to put her arms round her grandmother's shaking form. 'I'm sorry for all the nasty things I said. You know I didn't mean them.'

Ma dabbed roughly at her eyes, annoyed with herself for displaying weakness. ''Course I know that. Listen, will you do somethin' for me, gel?'

''Course I will. Anything.'

'Get our Glor to come round. I want to see 'er. Will you do it for me?'

'Oh, Ma.' Shirley smiled through her tears. 'Of *course* I'll get her. I'll ring her right away.'

'Tell 'er I ain't on the warpath no more,' Ma added. 'All the fight's gorn outa me since this letter come.'

When Gloria heard Shirley's voice on the telephone she was surprised and pleased. But when she heard that her mother wanted to see her, she was apprehensive.

'What's it about, Shirl?' she asked cautiously. 'She's not ill, is she?'

'No. She's had this letter. They're going to pull the street down. For redevelopment, it says in the letter. They're offering her compensation – what they call "compulsory purchase" – and they'll be rehousing her temporarily till they've built this new block they're planning in the place of Angel Row. She'll get a brand new council flat then.'

'It sounds very fair,' Gloria said.

'Not to Ma, it doesn't. She's really upset, Glor. That's why she wants to see you. You will come, won't you?'

'Look, if you're really sure she wants me I'll come and stay for a few days,' Gloria said. 'I've got some holiday due. Leonie's going away on location with the film company. I want to spend some of it at Boothley, but I'll come home first. All right?'

'Oh, thanks, Glor. Ma wants you all right. I've never seen her so down.' She paused, then added: 'I'll look forward to seeing you too. I . . . I've missed you.' She was about to ring off when Gloria said:

'I heard how well you did with your exam. Imogen told me. I was so proud of you, love.'

'Oh, thanks. I meant to ring you and tell you.'

'I wish you had.'

'I'm sorry. I've been so busy what with the shop and my lessons. I take my silver in the summer.'

'I'll hear all about it when I come, eh? I'll be with you the day after tomorrow, love, if that's all right.'

As Shirley walked back from the telephone box she felt relieved. The responsibility of Ma's predicament weighed heavily on her young shoulders. Surely the time had come to let bygones by bygones? But apart from practical matters, it would be nice just to be with Gloria again. It was so long since they had enjoyed the relationship that had always been special to them. Although in a way she enjoyed the secrecy of her meetings with Paul, she felt uneasy, too. Deception was not part of her nature. She longed to unburden herself to someone she could trust.

She had waited for five weeks before giving in to the temptation of telephoning Paul. Ever since the night they had met at Romano's, the card he had given her had lain at the bottom of her handbag. Every time she caught sight of it she felt a little thrill of excitement at the prospect of what might happen should she pick up a telephone and dial that number, but every time she made up her mind to do it, her nerve failed her.

She and Dave had continued to share their free time, though Dave had been peeved that she had gone off with Imogen and Charles on the night of the exam without even coming to tell him the result. She had argued with all the indignation of one who knows herself to be in the wrong, irritated by his assumption that he should have been the first to hear her news.

'You don't own me, Dave Green,' she had shouted, then been instantly ashamed at the hurt in his eyes.

It had taken a lot of courage to ring Paul. Perhaps by now he would even have forgotten who she was. She pictured his cool response, his handsome brow furrowed as he racked his brain to fit a face to her name. If that happened all her illusions would be shattered along with her confidence. She wasn't sure that she could take it.

She finally rang him one wet Monday evening on her way back from the post office. Her knees trembled as she stood in the phone box, her finger shakily poised over button 'A' as she waited for him to answer the ringing tone.

He had not forgotten her. His response to her hesitant opening was enthusiastic and encouraging: 'Shirley! How wonderful to hear you! I've waited so long for you to ring. I quite thought you'd forgotten me. How are you, darling?'

Her relief was almost overwhelming and his use of the word *darling* had her cheeks glowing with pleasure. 'I'm fine. How are you?'

'Working hard – longing for a delicious diversion like you. When am I going to see you?'

'Oh, I don't know.'

'Tomorrow evening? Dinner?'

It hadn't been easy. Not only did she have to explain to Ma where she was going, there was Dave too. In the end she used Magda. She was taking an extra lesson, she told them – because of the coming exam. She was surprised how easy it was. They believed her implicitly.

It was with mingled feelings of guilt and triumph that she set off to meet Paul that first time. He had arranged to meet her at a hotel in Marble Arch, but she had lost her way slightly and was late. When she arrived hot and breathless in the hotel foyer, she found to her dismay that he was nowhere to be seen. She sat for a while in the reception hall, but the young man at the desk kept looking suspiciously at her. Perhaps he thought she was a lady of the streets, touting for business. Finally she went across to the desk and asked for Paul by name. Immediately the man smiled.

'Ah, you must be Miss Rayner. Mr Winspear asked me to give you a message. I would have passed it on before if only you'd asked, miss. You're to meet him in the bar.' He pointed. 'Just through those doors over there.'

He came to meet her with outstretched hands, waving away her apologies and confused explanations. They had dinner and talked – about Paul's work, a new play which he was having some problems with; about Shirley's classes. Paul complimented her on her appearance and on her voice, which he said was maturing. He could detect a great improvement in its depth and timbre since the last time they'd met. After dinner they sat in the hotel lounge and Paul held her hand as they talked some more. He was so easy to talk to, so sympathetic. He understood her dreams and ambitions as no one else ever had. At ten-thirty he took her all the way home in a taxi. In the back of the cab in the dark he had drawn her into his arms and kissed her. Never in her life had anything made her feel so wonderful. She felt like a glass of sparkling champagne, a Catherine wheel on firework night, a skylark soaring high above the clouds. Lying in bed later that night she relived every minute of their date, savouring the feel of his lips on hers, his powerful arms around her, the masculine scent of his expensive clothes. As they parted he had clung to her hand and said:

'Ring me again soon – promise?'

'I will,' she'd replied breathlessly. Where would they go next time? she wondered. What would he say and do? She couldn't wait to find out.

She had to wait a week, though. She couldn't push her luck. One extra lesson a week was all she could expect Ma and Dave to swallow.

The next time, Paul took her back to his flat after dinner. It was a nice flat, small but comfortable, furnished in a rather austere, masculine style with leather armchairs and muted colour schemes. He gave her brandy to drink, which made her feel pleasantly drowsy. Then, after they had talked a while he stood up and held out his hands to her, calmly announcing that he was taking her to bed. She laughed, not taking him seriously at first, but when he picked her up and carried her into the bedroom she hadn't been laughing. Her heart thudded against her ribs with a mixture of apprehension and anticipation.

She trembled as he slowly undressed her, feeling shy and embarrassed as he examined her body as though it were a priceless piece of porcelain. But her shyness melted in the warmth of her mounting desire as he caressed her sensuously with long, sensitive fingers. Soon every nerve in her body sang. Her heartbeat quickened and her limbs grew languid as they sank together onto the bed. But when he began to kiss her all over she felt her body take on a surprising life of its own, arching towards him convulsively as the torment within her became unbearable.

Having aroused her he undressed swiftly and when he rejoined her and she felt his naked flesh warm next to hers and his hardness against her thigh, she gave herself up willingly and eagerly to his lovemaking. Never in her life had she wanted anything with such feverish intensity.

The pain of his first entering was soon forgotten as their passion mounted. His initial gentleness was overtaken as his need increased and he pulled her this way and that, his face contorted with pleasure as he whispered hoarse instructions, telling her what to do to get the utmost pleasure out of their lovemaking. Urged on by this new-found delight, she became his willing pupil, obeying him until at last she was rewarded by a height of sensation never before imagined. She stiffened, her body arching and her breath suspended in her throat as the soaring waves of ecstasy shuddered through and through her. Then she heard Paul cry out and opened her eyes to see him arch above her, possessed by a powerful, pulsing climax that made his eyes appear opaque and the veins in his neck stand out like rope. Then he released his breath in a sigh and collapsed on top of her, burying his face between her breasts and murmuring her name over and over.

Shirley lay cradling his head, her fingers tangled in his thick hair, savouring the new delicious tingling in her body, relishing this new heady achievement, feeling like a real woman for the first time. Now she knew what Magda meant by *living*.

'I was your first,' Paul whispered as his breathing returned to normal. 'Your first lover. That makes me very proud.' He kissed her. 'It's a tremendous compliment.'

Shirley smiled dreamily. 'I've never wanted to with anyone else,' she said. 'And now I never will.'

Since then they had met three more times. Once a week was all she could manage, but she counted off each day. Never had the weeks seemed so long; never had she longed so much to be with one person, to see, kiss and hold him. Nothing was more important than what she felt for Paul. Even her valued drama lessons took second place. Now she knew what love and living really was.

Gloria arrived the following evening, just after they had closed the shop. Shirley took her through to the kitchen and for a moment she watched as her mother and grand-mother stood staring speechlessly at each other. Then Gloria put down her overnight case and took a step forward, opening her arms wide.

'Ma! Oh, *Ma*, I've missed you so.'

They were clinging to each other, both of them weeping, each of them too full to speak. Shirley turned away and filled the kettle. They'd have a lot to talk about. And if she knew them both, they'd need a large pot of tea to get them through it. She made the tea, put out the cups and left them to it.

When Gloria came up to bed she was able to tell Shirley that Ma seemed resigned to the changes that were inevitable in her life.

'I managed to make her see that she'd soon have to retire anyway,' she said as she undressed. 'She deserves a rest. She should take life easy. The compensation money will be a nice little nest egg and there'll be every convenience at the new flat.'

Shirley moved closer to her mother as she joined her in the bed. 'Good. So she's happier now, then?'

'Yes. She and I are going to the council offices tomorrow to sort everything out.' Gloria turned to look at Shirley. 'All she's worried about now is not having anything to leave to us,' she said. 'I soon put her mind at rest on that one. Told her we just want to see her comfy in her old age.'

'Good. Thanks for coming, Glor. It's been awful without you all this time.'

'I know, love. It wasn't what I wanted, though.'

'But you never came when Pa – I thought you might have asked me to go to Rook Cottage with you. Then even last Christmas you never . . .' Shirley shook her head. 'Oh, never mind. You're here now.' She snuggled up to Gloria. 'Glor, there's something I want to tell you.'

'Me too, Shirl. It's something I should have told you a long time ago, but now seems like a good time.' She paused, summoning up all her courage. 'Shirl, I've got a baby.'

Shirley caught her breath and sat up, staring at her mother. 'You've *what*?'

'I've got a baby. A little boy. He's called Michael and he's two years old.' Gloria put out her hand as Shirley began to speak. 'No, love, hear me out. Don't say anything yet.' She unfolded the story of Michael's birth and his sickness, the failed adoption plans and her hopes for the operation that would allow him to grow up to a normal life. When she had finished Shirley lay down beside her with a sigh.

'Oh, Glor – why didn't you tell me all this? Now I can see why you behaved as you did. So many things are clear now, but why didn't you say? I mean, I can see why you didn't tell Ma – but why not me? He's my brother. He's two years old and I've never even *seen* him.' She looked into Gloria's face. 'Who looks after him when you're working?'

'Margaret, a friend I met in the hospital. She's a widow. She's a good sort, Shirl, and marvellous with little Michael. I applied for a government grant for the cottage when they were first announced. It came through and the builders started a couple of months ago. We're having electricity laid on, and proper plumbing – a bathroom built on behind the kitchen. You wouldn't know the place. Next winter we'll be really snug and cosy. You'll have to come and see when it's finished. Should be soon now.'

'Did you tell Ma tonight – about the baby?'

'No.' Gloria sighed. 'I can't yet. She's got enough to worry about at the moment.'

They were both silent, knowing that telling Ma was the biggest hurdle Gloria had to face. Then Shirley asked the inevitable question: 'Glor, is he Billy's?'

'No. It was after . . . after I heard that Billy'd been killed.'

'I see. Then who . . .?'

'I'm sorry, love, but that part's still secret. It might always have to be. It's not the way it seems either. He – Michael's father is – was very special.'

'And . . . you loved him?'

'Yes. I loved him – long before Billy. I always will.'

'Then why isn't he taking care of you both?'

'Because he doesn't even know about Michael himself.'

371

'Doesn't *know*? But he might want to help. Surely he should be told?' Shirley was silenced by Gloria's expression.

'It's out of the question, love. Too many lives would be affected by it.'

'He's married, you mean?'

'Just leave it, love. Don't ask me again.'

'All right, I won't.' Shirley switched off the light. 'It's late. We'd better go to sleep now.'

After a moment Gloria said drowsily: 'I'm sorry, love, what was it you were going to tell me?'

Shirley sighed. There had been enough surprises for one day – enough emotional unburdenings. 'Oh, it'll keep,' she said sleepily. 'Tell you tomorrow, eh?'

But long after Gloria was asleep she lay thinking. So Gloria had a baby son – her half-brother. A few months ago she might have been shocked and disappointed, but now that she had met Paul and fallen in love herself, she understood. Poor Gloria! How it must hurt not to be able to be with the man she loved; not to be able to tell him she had given birth to his son. She longed to see little Michael and tried to picture what he would look like. But she dreaded to think what Ma's reaction to this new grand-child would be. Would it cause a new rift between her and Gloria – just when the old one looked like being healed? And then there was the question of her own part in the change in their situation. When the street was demolished and Ma moved, what would become of her? Not only would she lose her home but her job too. And with no wage coming in, how would she be able to afford her drama lessons? Finally there was the problem of Dave. Some time soon she would have to tell him about Paul – just as he was about to lose his job, too. She turned over with a sigh and tried hard to put it all out of her mind for a while and sleep. The future looked full of gaping uncer-tainties and unwelcome prospects. The one thing she was sure of – shining like a star through her clouded future – was her love for Paul.

* * *

Dave called for her as usual on Saturday evening and they went out, leaving Ma and Gloria to talk. They'd been to see the housing officer the previous day and it had been arranged for Ma to go into a bed-sitting room for six months until the new flat was ready for her. It wasn't ideal but Gloria had assured her that it would only be temporary and that the time would soon pass. So far no one had mentioned Shirley's plans and she hadn't liked to ask what was to become of her. As they walked down Angel Row she told Dave about the redevelopment.

'I know about it,' he told her calmly. 'Luckily the street where I live doesn't come into the plan as yet, so I'll be all right. It won't affect me.'

'But it will in one way. You'll lose your job, Dave,' Shirley said impatiently.

'I've been offered another,' Dave said. 'Quite a good one if it comes off, managing a busy grocer's shop on Hackney Road. The owner's retiring, going to live down in Kent, but he doesn't want to sell the business.'

'I'll not only lose my job but my home too,' Shirley said.

Dave looked at her. 'Won't you still live with your grandmother?'

'Don't see how I can in a bed-sitting room.'

'Oh.' Dave considered for a moment, then his face lit up in a smile. 'Well, the answer's easy. We'll get married.'

Shirley's mouth dropped open in dismay. 'Oh, Dave, don't be silly.'

'Why is it silly?' He stopped walking to look at her. 'It's the obvious solution, Shirl. There's even a little flat over the shop we could have. We'd get married eventually anyway – wouldn't we?'

Shirley shook her head. 'No, we wouldn't. Look, Dave, you know I'm training for a stage career. Besides, didn't it ever occur to you to ask me if *I* wanted to get married?'

He looked crestfallen. 'I love you, Shirl. I just assumed . . .'

'Yes, well, you assumed wrong. I don't want to get married for years yet – perhaps not ever.' Carried away, she almost added: *and certainly not to you*, but stopped herself just in time as she noticed his wounded expression. Taking his arm roughly, she said: 'Oh, come on, let's go and have a drink and talk it over properly. And for heaven's sake take that miserable look off your face.'

It was still early and they found a quiet corner in the pub and settled down with their drinks. Shirley knew that it was now or never but she didn't look forward to hurting Dave even more. He'd been good to her when she needed a friend. She was fond of him, but she couldn't allow him to go on thinking of her as his. She crossed her fingers tightly, hoping she could do this without making life too hard for them both.

'Look, Dave, things are changing. All around us life is starting to look different. We can't stand still. We've no choice but to move with it.'

He looked at her over the rim of his beer mug. 'What are you trying to tell me?'

She took her courage in both hands. There was no other way but to give it to him straight. 'I've met someone else, Dave.'

He looked at her steadily. 'I'd guessed – had my suspicions for a long time, but I didn't want to believe it. All right, who is it?'

'No one you know. No one from round here.'

'Someone well off, I suppose?'

'What do you take me for, Dave? I'm not a gold-digger.'

'Someone who can help you get on then – someone to do with the stage?'

That much she couldn't deny. She shook her head. 'It doesn't matter who he is, Dave. The thing is, I . . . I love him.'

'I see. And he loves you?'

'Of course he does.' For the first time Shirley realised that Paul had never actually said he loved her. But surely actions spoke louder than words, didn't they?

'No doubt he hasn't got a crippled leg like me,' Dave said bitterly, putting his glass down heavily on the table.

'Oh, Dave, don't say things like that. It wouldn't make any difference if I . . .'

He stared at her, his eyes dark with pain, knowing she'd been about to say, *if I loved you*. 'You've let him, haven't you?' he said quietly.

'What do you mean? Let him what?' Shirley felt her cheeks colouring.

'You know what I mean all right. You've slept with him.'

'That's none of your business.'

'All this time you've been going out with both of us. Seeing me at weekends and – and sleeping with him in between.' He swallowed hard. 'Is it him who's been giving you these *extra lessons*?' He laughed bitterly. 'Huh! That's a good one. What kind of lessons, I'd like to know.' He pushed his glass away from him, spilling some of its contents onto the table as he stood up. 'That's that then. I wouldn't have you now if you went down on your knees to me. I worshipped you, Shirl. Now I find you're nothing more than a little slut. Tell your grandmother I've given in a week's notice, will you?' And with as much dignity as he could manage he hurried towards the door.

Shirley got to her feet and went after him. Outside in the street she tried to take his arm.

'Don't go like that, Dave. I'm sorry. I never meant to hurt you.'

'What did you think it'd do to me, eh? Give me a good laugh?' He shook her hand off, his eyes bright with unshed tears. 'Look, you've had your say, now just leave it, will you? I don't want to talk about it any more so just do me a favour and let me go.'

She stood watching helplessly as he walked down the street, his head high, trying hard not to limp. Her throat ached with remorse and pity. She was fond of Dave. She'd have done anything rather than hurt him, but she couldn't have let him go on thinking she would marry him. She imagined them running the grocer's shop together and living in the flat above, going on year after year until they were old. Ending up like Ma and Pa. She shuddered, suddenly needing the comfort of Paul's arms. Turning, she headed for the Underground station.

When Paul opened the door to her she saw that he was unshaven. He wore an open-necked shirt and slacks and his hair was rumpled. He gave her a smile.

'Darling! What a nice surprise! Come in, you're just what I need. I've been working but it isn't one of my better days.'

The flat was a mess. Paul had been working at his desk in the window and the floor was littered with crumpled sheets of paper. Every flat surface seemed to be covered in used coffee cups and there was a plate bearing the remains of a meal in the middle of the floor.

'Sorry about the pigsty,' Paul said, sweeping aside a pile of books so that she could sit down. 'My daily treasure doesn't come in at weekends and I've been too busy to tidy up.'

'That's all right. Let me.' She began to pick up some of the litter but he took her hands.

'Leave that and come here.' He drew her close and kissed her lingeringly. 'Mmm, you taste so good. But why are you here, darling? Everything's all right, isn't it?'

She shook her head. 'No, not really. At least – nothing that need bother you. I just wanted to see you suddenly, that's all.' She looked up at him. 'Paul, do you think we could go to bed, please?'

He laughed, raising his eyebrows at her in mock surprise. 'Good heavens, Miss Rayner, such abandonment! I'm not sure that I should let you corrupt me like this.' He rubbed his jaw. 'Shall I shave first or can you stand a face like sandpaper?'

She slipped her arms around his waist. 'I love you just as you are; besides, I can't wait that long.'

The bedroom was as chaotic as the rest of the flat but she didn't care. She undressed hurriedly and fell unheedingly into the unmade bed to make love to Paul with an urgency generated by her bruised emotions, letting her heightened senses erase the memory of the painful scene with Dave. Later, as they lay blissfully satiated in each other's arms, she said:

'I told Dave this evening that I couldn't marry him; that there was someone else.'

Paul shifted his position slightly to look down at her. 'That might not have been a good move.'

She frowned. 'Why not? I couldn't let him go on thinking I was his girl.'

He sat up and took a cigarette from the box on the bedside table. 'None of us can afford to make enemies, though, can we?'

'Dave will never be an enemy,' she said. 'But I couldn't string him along like that. It wouldn't have been fair.'

He lit the cigarette thoughtfully and looked down at her. 'You didn't tell him about me, did you?'

'Not by name, no.'

'Thank God for that.' He exhaled a cloud of smoke. 'I don't want irate, rejected suitors coming round here, making sordid scenes on the doorstep.'

Shirley felt a pang of disappointment. 'I thought you'd be pleased that I'd given him up for you,' she said.

His eyes narrowed as he looked at her through the cloud of smoke. 'Let's get one thing quite clear, darling. You don't have to give up anything or anybody for me. We're both completely free to live our own lives and to see anyone we wish to. Neither of us is committed in any way. We're good friends, okay? We amuse each other and –'

'*Amuse?*' The colour draining from her face, Shirley sprang up from the bed. 'Is that all it is to you – an amusement? You make me sound like . . . like a toy – some cheap thing you buy from Woolworth's and throw away when you're tired of it. I'm not here for your *amusement.*' Grabbing up her clothes, she strode towards the bathroom, but Paul got there first and threw his arm across the doorway, barring the way. His mouth was curved and his eyes gleamed with amusement as he looked down at her.

'Do you know that your eyes flash like ice when you're angry? Your cockney accent comes back too.' He struck a pose and mimicked her voice: 'Sam cheap fing yer buy from Woolwurf's.' He threw back his head and laughed. 'Just like one of those stallholders from the Portobello Road.'

Almost blind with wounded pride and fury, Shirley raised her hand and slapped him hard across the cheek, the wiry black stubble stinging her palm. Paul caught her arm and twisted it swiftly behind her back, making her cry out in pain.

'Little spitfire. You like to play rough games, don't you?' he said, his face close to hers. 'I've always suspected it.' Kicking the clothes she had dropped out of the way he forced her down onto the floor. 'Let's see if we can make you say you're sorry for that lapse of control, you little cat,' he breathed into her ear.

'Paul – no, *don't!*' She struggled, suddenly afraid of the glint of sadistic excitement she saw in his eyes, but he pinned her body to the floor with his own weight. His mouth closed on hers, crushing her lips mercilessly against her teeth, shutting off her breath until she thought she would suffocate. Striking out frantically at him, she pulled free and scrambled to her feet. Gathering up her scattered clothes, she ran into the bathroom, slammed and locked the door. Leaning against it, her legs trembling, she allowed the tears of hurt and humiliation to stream down her cheeks. How could he love her one minute and treat her like that the next?

He was in the kitchen making coffee when she came out. He wore his dressing gown and turned to smile calmly at her as though nothing had happened. 'Ah, there you are, darling. Coffee?'

'No, thank you. I'm going home.'

He turned to her, reaching out to touch her face. Seeing her flinch, he frowned and said: 'Ah. I went too far. It was your fault, though. You shouldn't have hit me. I misread you – I thought you wanted . . .' He smiled down at her. 'Some women like a little horseplay. Forgive me?'

She looked at her feet. 'You . . . you scared me. You hurt.' She fingered her bruised mouth.

'Darling, I'm sorry.' He pulled her close. 'Sometimes I forget that you're just a baby.'

'No, I'm not.'

'You're thinking that your nice Dave wouldn't have done that to you, I expect.'

'I'm not.'

He tipped up her chin to look into her eyes. 'Oh, dear, do you hate me now?'

Slowly she shook her head and he smiled.

'Good. Kiss me then.'

After a moment's hesitation she raised her lips to his and he kissed her with surprising tenderness. 'There. All better now?'

'You said . . . you said that we could both see anyone we wanted to. That hurt because I don't want anyone else, Paul.'

'Nor I, darling – for the moment. But you're very young. I wouldn't dream of trying to tie you down. It wouldn't be fair. I'm your first lover and that's always special, but believe me, I won't be your last.' When she looked unconvinced, he added: 'Don't you see that the greatest gift I can give you is freedom?'

'I – I suppose so.'

'I've got a surprise for you,' he whispered. 'What would you say to a part in the play I'm working on? It's perfect for you. I wrote it with you in mind. Would you like to read it?'

'Oh, Paul, I'd *love* to.' Her eyes sparkled up at him, the incident in the bedroom almost forgotten. 'Oh, but I've got to go now. Can I take the script home with me? Can I come back tomorrow and –' A sudden ring at the doorbell silenced her and she looked up at him. 'Who's that?'

He smiled. 'Not having my crystal ball handy, I'll have to wait till I've opened the door.'

'Don't go.'

'I must. It might be important.'

She held out her hand. 'Oh, but . . .' Before she could stop him he had walked out into the hallway and opened the door. Standing behind the kitchen door, Shirley was horrified to hear Leonie's voice say:

'Darling – surprise, *surprise*! Filming is all over. Isn't it bliss? I couldn't bear another second down there in that dead and alive hole. I just had to drive straight back to London – and you.'

There was a pause during which Shirley could hear the sound of enthusiastic kissing. In the silence she could hear her own heart thumping away in her chest. The voice went on: 'You must have known I was coming – waiting for me hopefully in your dressing gown.' She giggled. 'Oh, darling, I've missed you so *much*. I thought the wretched film would never be done with. I've got such plans for us both. Just wait till you hear.' Shirley held her breath as she went on: 'I drove all the way up from Cornwall without stopping once and I'm simply *dying* of thirst. That coffee smells marvellous. I'll just help myself, shall I?'

Shirley looked around her frantically but there was no escape. The kitchen door was thrown open and the next moment she found herself looking straight into Leonie's surprised eyes. Her dark hair hung loose about her shoulders and her unfastened fur coat revealed a clinging cream silk dress. At the sight of Shirley the smile vanished from her face and her jaw dropped.

'Shirley?' She turned to stare challengingly at Paul, who stood behind her looking unconcerned. 'What's *she* doing here?'

'I came to read Paul's play,' Shirley said quickly. 'There's a part in it for me.'

Leonie stared at her for a moment, then flung her head back and hooted with derisive laughter. 'Oh, my *God*. Don't tell me you fell for that old chestnut.'

'I don't know what you mean.'

'It's the oldest trick in the book, darling. *You?* Take part in a West End production? It's ludicrous, you're just an amateur. He's stringing you along, darling, trying to seduce you. Didn't you see through it?' She took a step towards Shirley, her eyes narrowing as she took in her bruised lips and slightly dishevelled appearance. 'Or maybe you're not as naive as you look. Perhaps he already has and this is your way of blackmailing him.'

With a shocked gasp, Shirley pushed past her into the hall. Paul put out a hand to stop her, but she shook him off and ran out, through the door and down the stairs into the street, not stopping till she was well clear of the building.

Clearly his relationship with Leonie was as strong as ever. Her head spun. This *freedom* he talked about – she didn't understand it. When you loved someone you weren't free anyway – you didn't want to be. All you wanted was that one person and no one else. Tears almost choked her as she hastened her slowed pace to catch a bus just pulling up at a bus stop. This was the worst night of her life. It was like a nightmare. Nothing could ever possibly be as agonising as this. All she could think about was getting home to Gloria, pouring it all out to her and having her mother comfort her as she had in the far-off prewar days of childhood.

When Gloria answered a knock on the street door to find Dave standing on the doorstep, she was surprised.

'Hello, Dave. I thought Shirley was with you.'

'She was, but . . . Can I come in, Mrs Rayner?'

'Of course.' Gloria held the door open for him. 'There's nothing wrong, is there?'

'No.' Dave stood in the narrow hallway, looking unhappily down at his feet. 'I just wanted to talk to you, if you don't mind.' He licked his lips nervously. 'Is your mother about? I mean, if you like we could go to the pub.'

Gloria smiled. 'It's all right, she's in bed. She decided to have an early night.'

'Oh. It's not that I don't want to see her . . .'

Gloria touched his arm reassuringly. 'Don't apologise. I understand. Come through to the kitchen, Dave. The kettle's on.'

Sitting at the kitchen table, his hands round a mug of hot tea, Dave told Gloria about Shirley's confession that she was in love with someone else. 'I don't want you to think I'm running to you with tales,' he added. 'It's just that I'm worried about her. She won't tell me who this bloke is and I've got an awful feeling she might be heading for a packet of trouble. I didn't know what to do with myself after we parted. I bought an evening paper and decided to go on a bit of a pub crawl. I thought I might get drunk. It's what blokes usually do when they've been chucked, isn't it? But drinking just seemed to make me feel worse. So then I thought if I came and talked to you . . .'

'I might talk her out of it?' Gloria shook her head. 'I'm sorry but I've no idea who her new boyfriend is either, Dave. We haven't been very close over the last couple of years. I can't make her change her mind, I'm afraid. I can't promise to do anything, but I will talk to her and try to get to the bottom of it.'

'Thanks, Mrs Rayner. I'd appreciate that. At least I know you won't let her go and do something she might regret.' He stood up. 'I'll go now before Shirl gets back. I wouldn't want her to know I've been here.' He looked at her. 'You won't tell her, will you?'

'No, of course I won't.' She went with him to the door and saw him out, shaking her head as she walked back into the kitchen. He seemed a nice young man. What a pity it was that all the nice people of this world seemed to get the rough end of the stick while the ones who didn't give a damn got off scot-free. Was it this new man in her life that Shirley had tried to tell her about on her first night at home? She wished now that she'd listened. Maybe she could have done or said something to help avoid Dave's misery.

It was only as she was clearing the table that she noticed he'd left his newspaper behind. A copy of the late edition of the London *Evening News* lay on the chair where he'd been sitting. When she picked it up and unfolded it, the black front-page headline screamed up at her:

FILM DIRECTOR BADLY INJURED IN AIR CRASH.

Underneath the story ran:

Tony Darrent, film-director husband of actress and singer Leonie Swann, was badly injured this afternoon when the plane he was piloting back to London after the completion of his latest film crashed over the Yorkshire moors. He was pulled clear of the burning wreckage seconds before it exploded and taken to Leeds Royal Infirmary, where he is being treated for third-degree burns and other injuries. A hospital statement gives his condition as 'serious but stable'.

Then followed an account of Tony's career that read ominously like an obituary.

The kitchen swam sickeningly before her eyes and Gloria clutched the back of a chair for support. 'Tony,' she murmured. 'Oh, Tony, my love! Oh, dear God, don't let him die.' Pulling herself together, she looked at the clock. It was just after eleven. She'd pack her things and go straight to the station now. Wait, though – which station? As she ran upstairs and began to throw her clothes into her overnight bag, she tried to organise her confused thoughts. Leeds, the paper said. That would be either St Pancras or King's Cross. She'd find out which when she got there.

She crept quietly downstairs and scribbled a hasty note for Shirley, propping it against the cooling teapot on the table, then she let herself out of the street door. Maybe if she was lucky she'd catch a cruising taxi in the main road. There was bound to be a night train. If not, she would sit it out till the first one left tomorrow morning, because no matter what anyone said or did, one thing was crystal clear. She had to go to Tony, to be with him now – as soon as possible. It could be the only chance she'd ever get to tell him that she loved him – that she always had and always, always would.

When Shirley arrived home, Gloria had been gone a little over half an hour. She found the note, hastily scrawled on the back of a used envelope: *Sorry, love, called away urgently. Couldn't wait for you to get home. Don't worry, I'll write soon. Love, G.*

Shirley dropped the note on the table and sank into a chair. She had never needed Gloria as badly as she needed her tonight. But obviously someone else needed her more. Was it Michael? She hadn't said. He had priority in her life now and who could grudge a sick child the loving care of his mother?

383

A tear slipped silently down Shirley's cheek and she lowered her head onto her arms. Now that Paul had proved himself to be false, she felt there was no one in the world who really cared about her.

Chapter Seventeen

It was midday when Gloria arrived at the hospital. She had missed the last train to Leeds the night before and sat all night in the waiting room, snatching what little sleep she could on one of the hard benches. On enquiring at the hospital reception desk, she was directed up to the surgical ward, but there she was told that Tony was allowed close family visitors only.

'But I've come all the way from London specially,' Gloria said wearily. 'I'm an old friend. I sat up all night, waiting for a train. Please don't tell me I can't see him.'

The nurse looked at her tired face sympathetically. 'His daughter is with him at the moment,' she said. 'If you'll just wait here. What name is it?'

'Just tell her it's Gloria, she'll know. We've been friends for years – please . . .' Gloria watched as the nurse rustled her way back down the corridor and disappeared through a door. Moments later she reappeared and beckoned to Gloria.

'Just five minutes,' she said. 'I'd better warn you, you may be shocked by his appearance, but try not to show it. He's very weak, so please don't excite him in any way.'

As she entered the small side ward, Imogen rose from her chair by the bed. She looked tired and deathly pale.

'Gloria! How good of you to come.' She crossed the room and hugged Gloria briefly. 'I've been here since last night. They telephoned me and Charles drove me up at once. How did you know?'

'The paper. It was in the evening editions.' Gloria was looking past Imogen at the figure in the bed. Tony seemed to be swathed in bandages. 'How is he?' she whispered.

'He's asleep at the moment. His leg was badly crushed and they operated on that last night – inserted steel pins. He's still drowsy from the anaesthetic.' She turned towards Gloria, her face fearful. 'He has dreadful burns to his face and hands, too. The surgeon tells me that they'll do skin grafts later, so it'll be a long job.' She tried to smile. 'But the good news is that his eyes are all right, and his flying helmet saved him from more severe head injuries. We have to thank God for that.'

'Will he . . . will he be disfigured?'

Imogen shrugged. 'God only knows, Gloria. All I really care about is that we still have him.' Her voice broke and Gloria took her hands.

'You look so tired, love. Why don't you go and get some sleep?'

Imogen shook her head. 'I want to be here when he wakes.'

'Does Leonie know?'

'I tried to locate her,' Imogen said. 'I left messages everywhere I could think of. I'll just have to hope that one of them reaches her.'

Gloria nodded. 'The nurse said only five minutes.' She went hesitantly up to the bed and looked down at Tony's still form. She couldn't see much of his face. It was hard to believe that this heavily bandaged person was the vital, talented man she loved. As Imogen said, it was a miracle that he was still alive. They must hang on to that for now – take things a day at a time. She wondered about his future career. When he knew the nature of his injuries he would be devastated. He would need all the help, all the love and support they could give him. She hoped that somehow she would be allowed to give him hers.

The nurse looked in. 'I'm sorry. I'm going to have to ask you to leave now.'

Imogen reached for Gloria's hand. 'Where are you staying?'

Gloria shrugged. 'I haven't even thought yet. I suppose I'd better find somewhere.'

'I'm staying at the Great Northern. I've got a double room. If you don't mind sharing you can come with me.' Imogen rummaged in her handbag for a pencil and paper. 'I'm in number twenty-three. I'll write them a note. Why don't you check in and have a bath and a sleep? Then you can come back and take over from me if you want to.'

Gloria was asleep when Imogen returned to the hotel. She shook Gloria's shoulder gently.

'Gloria, it's me – Imogen.'

Gloria opened her eyes and gazed round at the unfamiliar room as consciousness seeped back. She sat up. 'Imogen. Tony – how is he?'

Imogen smiled. 'He's awake. He's going to be all right, Gloria. He's still under heavy sedation for the pain, but he was able to say a few words to me.'

'Can I see him? Did you tell him I came?'

'I did, and he seemed pleased.' Gloria made to get out of bed but Imogen put out her hand. 'Don't get up. Rest a bit longer. They want Daddy to rest now until this evening. The surgeon will be in to see him this afternoon.' She took off her coat and sat down.

'You look all in, Imogen,' Gloria said. 'Why don't you get some sleep now?'

Imogen shook her head. 'I still haven't located Mummy. I can't think why I haven't heard from her. After all, if you saw it in the papers, surely she must have seen it too.'

'Isn't she filming in Cornwall?'

'Yes, but they were almost finished last week. She could be on her way home.' She got up and went to the telephone. 'I'd better try ringing round again.'

Half a dozen phone calls later, Imogen was still no nearer to locating Leonie. She had tried the Mayfair flat twice on the off chance that Leonie had gone home for the weekend, but the number seemed to be out of order. Little did she know that Leonie was in fact there all the time, heavily asleep after taking the telephone off the hook and swallowing two strong sleeping tablets.

Her row with Paul after Shirley had left had been fiery and spectacular. Finding Shirley at the flat had shaken her badly. Her own dresser's daughter! She couldn't believe that Paul could be so indiscreet, or so lacking in discernment. Finally, vowing never to speak to him again and promising all kinds of retribution, she'd stormed out of his flat and taken a taxi to Mayfair.

When she arrived at the flat the telephone was ringing. Thinking it would be Paul, she snatched up the receiver.

'I don't want to speak to you, you two-timing sod – '

'Leonie, it's me, Max.'

She stopped, biting her lip with annoyance. What the hell did the director of the film mean, calling her at this hour? Couldn't he let her have a weekend in peace? Trying hard to keep the irritation out of her voice, she said breezily: 'Max. Sorry, darling, I thought it was someone else – someone who's been – '

'Look, I've been ringing your number for hours. I'm afraid it's not good news, Leonie,' Max interrupted. 'I've just finished looking at the final rushes of *Joy in the Morning*. It's a sheer bloody disaster.'

'Oh, surely you're wrong, Max,' she said tartly, her temper still smouldering. 'In fact you'd better be. If I've wasted my valuable time on a flop, I warn you, I'm going to be extremely angry.'

'*You're* going to be angry?' Max's voice thundered down the line at her. 'Listen, Leonie, the film drags from beginning to end. It lacks sparkle. It lacks interest, suspense, conflict – everything that makes a film stand out. In fact, for my money it's pure dross. And the reason I'm ringing you is because I attribute all this to *you* and you only. You've been obstructive and downright bloody-minded all along. There's hardly a member of the cast or crew who you haven't upset. If the film flops – and I'm very much afraid that it will – you'll have only yourself to blame.'

'You're just trying to cover your own back, aren't you, Max?' Leonie hissed into the receiver furiously. 'For instance, wasn't the cretin who wrote the screenplay a friend of yours? Couldn't any of it possibly be *his* fault?'

'Everyone knows about your relationship with Paul Winspear, Leonie,' Max said evenly, 'and that you'd have liked him along to pander to your every whim. The screenwriter I chose is an experienced professional. I've worked with him countless times and in my opinion he made a damn good job of it – unlike you. Look, Leonie, a lot of good actors have given their best for this film – banking on it for their future careers. You've let them down with your carelessness and your arrogance. You've let us all down. I want you to know that I shall make it clear to everyone who matters that I will not consider working with you again.'

'You're wrong, Max. The film *will* be a success,' Leonie said stubbornly. 'You're underrating my popularity. People will come to see it on the strength of the play's good notices – they'll come to see *me*.'

He gave a laugh that sounded more like a growl at the other end of the line. 'I sincerely hope they don't, for your sake, Leonie. If they're counting on seeing a good performance from you, they're in for a *big* disappointment.' He rang off abruptly, leaving her trembling with rage.

She slammed the phone down and poured herself a large gin, which she swallowed at a single gulp. What a night! One bloody awful thing after another – and none of it her fault. She had always said that the screenplay made rubbish of Paul's play. And who would have thought that Shirley Rayner, the child she had taken in to save her from the Blitz, and for whom she'd done so much over the years, would turn out to be nothing better than a scheming little tart? Just wait till she saw Gloria again. She'd have something to say to her about her daughter.

Lighting a cigarette and puffing furiously at it, she paced the room, but try as she would she could not rid herself of the vitriolic anger that churned her stomach and made her head pound. Finally, making up her mind, she ground out her cigarette and went to the bathroom. Taking a bottle from the cabinet, she shook out two sleeping tablets. Back in the drawing room, she took the receiver off its rest and laid it on the table, poured herself another generous measure of gin to wash down the tablets and went to bed.

Sitting at the bedside alone, Gloria was able to give way to the emotion she'd had to hide while Imogen was present. Watching over the sleeping Tony, she allowed the tears to flow. His eyes were closed; he'd been asleep ever since she arrived. She longed to touch his face or hold his hand, but it was out of the question. She looked at the heavily bandaged hands that lay outside the covers and wondered just how serious his injuries were and whether the doctors would tell her – a mere acquaintance – the truth if she asked. Then, as she was watching and speculating fearfully about the future, he suddenly opened his eyes.

'Gl-Gloria?' His lips moved with obvious difficulty and she could only just make out the whispered word.

'Darling, I'm here. I came as soon as I knew. Don't worry. Don't try to talk. Everything will be all right.'

His eyelids fluttered. 'You . . . won't go? Won't leave . . . me?'

'No, I'll stay.' She leaned forward. 'I wish I could hold your hand, darling. I wish I could put my arms around you.'

He narrowed his eyes in the semblance of a smile. 'Me . . . too. Soon – eh?'

'Yes. Soon.'

'Gloria, the doctor is here.' Imogen's hand was on her shoulder. 'He wants to examine Daddy. Shall we go and have a cup of coffee while we wait?'

She hadn't heard the girl enter the room and now she turned to see Imogen standing at her side. The ward sister and a doctor were just coming into the room. Gloria stood up, then, with a last look at Tony, followed Imogen out into the corridor.

In the visitors' canteen they faced each other across the table. Gloria took a sip of her coffee and looked at Imogen's thoughtful face.

'You've seen the doctors. Have they said how he is?'

'So far, so good, apparently. But he has a big ordeal to face – a lot of painful treatment before he's well again. Even then they can't guarantee that he won't always be badly scarred. When he's a little better they're going to transfer him to a special burns unit in London.' Imogen hesitated, then said: 'Gloria, I don't know whether you know. Daddy wrote to me last week to tell me that Mummy had been in touch to say she'd agree to a divorce if he still wanted one.' She glanced up at Gloria. 'I don't know what the situation is between them at the moment. Do you know?'

'I think they're still on friendly terms.'

'Did you know he wanted a divorce?'

'He mentioned it, yes. But I thought your mother was set against it.'

'Is it – is it for your sake he's asking?'

'Mine?' Gloria's eyes opened wide. 'No, of course it isn't.'

'How could you bear to work for her when all the time. . . ?' Imogen broke off, shaking her head. 'I'm sorry. I've no right. It's just that . . .' She licked her lips and looked at Gloria. 'Your child – Michael. He's Daddy's, isn't he? I couldn't help overhearing you just now, and seeing the look on your face when you thought you were alone with him. Suddenly it all fell into place. It's been going on for some time, hasn't it?'

Gloria looked at the pain in the girl's eyes and felt herself shrivel up inside. 'Imogen, please don't look at me like that. It isn't the way you think. We . . . he was only unfaithful to your mother with me once. It was when I heard that Billy had been killed. I felt so bad. Your father was kind and caring. It just happened.' She reached blindly for the girl's hand, tears running down her cheeks. 'I've loved him for years, Imogen. I loved him long before I met him – through his films. My bedroom at Angel Row was covered in pictures of him. If it hadn't been for the war we'd never have met, and when we did he was even more wonderful than I could ever have imagined. How could I not love him? Once, a long time ago, I was able to help him through a particularly bad time. It made a sort of bond between us. But I would never have done anything to break up your family. I never wanted to hurt you or to end his marriage.'

'You couldn't have anyway.' Imogen's fingers curled round hers and squeezed tightly. 'He and Mummy hadn't been happy for years. As long as I can remember they've quarrelled. Sometimes when I was at home in the holidays, when I was little before the war, I'd lie in bed and hear them shouting at each other. It used to frighten me. I felt so lonely, guilty too, wondering if it was somehow all my fault – if they'd both go off and leave me. Mummy never wanted me, you know. I suppose she blamed us both for spoiling her life. And I always knew that Daddy had his little flings.' She shook her head. 'Poor Daddy! I asked him once if they only stayed together because of me. He said it was because of their public image – the scandal a divorce would cause. So I knew that at least it wasn't my fault they continued to live together, making each other miserable.'

'And now you say Leonie has agreed to divorce him?' Gloria said. 'She must have decided very recently.'

'I expect she was missing Paul Winspear.' Imogen bit her lip. 'Gloria, there's something I think you should know. I hate telling tales, but did you know that Shirley has been seeing him?'

'Paul Winspear?' Gloria looked up in surprise. 'No I didn't.'

'I warned her,' Imogen said. 'I don't trust Paul. There's something about him – I don't know, a cruel, predatory streak. I couldn't bear to see Shirley hurt.'

Gloria's mind was working fast, remembering the night that Shirley had tried to tell her something, but never got round to it. And now she had broken with Dave and told him there was someone else. It all fitted with what Imogen was telling her. 'But he's years older than her,' she said lamely.

'He's a womaniser,' Imogen said. 'His wife left him. He can't resist a pretty face and the younger and more vulnerable they are, the better. I've seen the way he looks at them. He even tried to make a pass at me once.'

'Oh, God.' Gloria was picturing Shirley coming home the previous night and reading the note she had left. After the break-up with Dave, she'd have been desperate to talk; she would have needed her. And once again Gloria had failed her. But even if she were to go back to London now, there was Michael. He, too, needed her. She'd have to get back to him soon – she couldn't leave everything to Margaret. And now it appeared that Leonie – who paid her salary and provided her with a home – would be back in London any day and needing her too. She felt torn in all directions. To whom did she give priority, her children who needed her or the woman who employed her?

'Does Daddy know?' Imogen was saying. 'About Michael, I mean.'

Gloria sighed and shook her head. 'No. I didn't want to complicate his life any further.'

'Will you tell him now?'

'This hardly seems the time.'

'I don't know; maybe it is. It could be just what he needs to help him over the ordeal to come.'

Gloria looked uncertain. 'I don't know. I'll have to leave tomorrow anyway, Imogen,' she said. 'I can't possibly stay any longer, much as I'd like to. Especially now that your mother has finished filming.'

'Of course. I'll have to go too. But once Daddy's been moved to London it'll make things easier.' She looked at Gloria. 'Will you tell him before you leave?'

'Perhaps. I'm still not sure it's the right thing. Imogen, there's something I'd like to ask you to do for me.'

'Of course, anything.'

'When you get back to town, will you see Shirley for me? Talk to her about Paul Winspear. She'll listen to you. I'm so afraid for her.'

'Of course I will, Gloria. By the way, does she know about Michael?'

'She knows about him, but she's never seen him.'

Imogen nodded. 'As long as I know.'

393

Gloria made one more visit to Tony before leaving. Sitting beside his bed she talked brightly to him about his war films, all of which she'd seen and enjoyed; about her work with Leonie and the theatre; about Shirley's drama lessons and the redevelopment plans for Angel Row. Everything, in fact, except the one thing Imogen had urged her to tell him. Something at the back of her mind kept telling her this was not the right moment. When that moment came – if it ever did – she would recognise it instinctively.

When it was time to go she leaned over him and touched her lips softly to his in a kiss that was no more than a butterfly's touch.

'Goodbye for now, darling,' she whispered. 'Once you're back in London I'll come as often as I can. I'll be thinking about you all the time. God bless.'

Tony's eyes swam with tears and his lips formed the words: 'I'll miss you.'

At the door she turned to wave, her heart as heavy as lead within her.

Imogen had written Shirley a note, asking to meet her at their usual place on Sunday afternoon. She hadn't received a reply to the note, but she was there early, in the hope that Shirley would come. She'd been waiting for about ten minutes at a table close to the window when she saw her coming in through the milk-bar door. She waved, then watched Shirley threading her way through the tables. She looked older, more sophisticated and yet sad, her eyes hurt and wary. When she reached the table she smiled apologetically.

'Hello, Imo. Sorry I didn't have time to answer your note.'

'It's okay. Don't bother to get a coffee. I've got a pot and two cups.'

Shirley sat down. 'It's awful about Tony, Imo. How is he?'

'Making progress. They'll be transferring him to one of the main London hospitals soon, for skin grafts.'

'Is it bad?'

'Bad enough.' Imogen sighed. 'I imagine it's the end of his acting career. He was taking a Shakespearean company to Canada, you know.'

'I heard that.'

'It's still going ahead. Everything's in place for the tour. It's scheduled to begin next month.' She paused. 'Actually he's asked me to go instead of him.'

Shirley's eyes widened. 'Oh, *Imo*! What a chance.'

'I know. I can't actually take his place, of course. He was to have directed and played some of the major roles. Other people will take over that side. I'll only be going along to represent him, really – as another Darrent. But I'll be playing a few small parts, and it'll be wonderful experience and enormous fun.'

Shirley smiled wistfully. 'I really envy you. What about your boyfriend, Charles?'

'He's going anyway. He applied for a job as an assistant stage manager some weeks ago and got the job. It's the lowest of the low, general dogsbody, but he'll be able to learn a lot. He wants to be a director eventually, you see.' She leaned forward. 'Between the two of us, he's asked me to marry him, Shirley.'

'I guessed he would soon.' Shirley smiled. 'And will you?'

'I'm tempted. He's a lovely person. I do adore him, and you know how much I've always wanted babies.'

'But your career?'

Imogen shrugged. 'I've seen at close quarters what ambition can do to a marriage – and a family. I'll never repeat that, God willing.' She reached out to touch Shirley's hand. 'Shirley, are you still seeing Paul?'

Shirley stiffened and withdrew her hand. 'No.'

'I see. You quarrelled?'

'Not exactly. If you really want to know, your mother came back from Cornwall and found us together at his flat. You can imagine the scene. But even before that it was beginning to go wrong.'

Imogen searched her eyes. 'Darling, I'm sorry for you, of course, but I can't pretend I'm not relieved. I've never liked Paul. You're not hurt, are you?'

'I hate myself, Imo,' Shirley said thickly. 'I should have seen what kind of person he was. I was just so stupid, blinded by love, I suppose – or infatuation. The worst thing is that I hurt Dave, the best friend I've ever had – apart from you. Now he's gone, Gloria's gone, soon Ma and Angel Row will be gone, and now you too. I . . . I feel I'm gradually losing everything and everyone, Imo. It feels as though life is giving up on me.'

'I'm sorry, darling. Something nice will happen for you soon, just you wait and see. I'm sure of it.'

'I wish I was.' Shirley shook her head. 'Do you remember the fun we had at Houlton during the war, Imo?' she said wistfully. 'The concerts we were in; our Fred and Ginger act? We had such plans, didn't we? Life was going to be so marvellous, so full of opportunities for us after the war, when we were grown-up.'

'I know. They were good days, weren't they?'

'Ever since Gloria went off to America things have gone from bad to worse. When she came home last week it was almost like the old days, but then she just took off again – quite suddenly and without any real explanation. She didn't even say where she was going.'

'Oh, I thought you knew. She went up to Yorkshire – to see Daddy in hospital. She shared my room at the hotel for a couple of days and she told me a lot of things while we were there together.'

'Did she tell you about Michael?'

'I knew anyway,' Imogen confessed. 'I found out quite by accident. I was staying with Molly and Jim at Longueville Hall for a weekend and I cycled over to Boothley to see Gloria. It was quite a shock. He's a lovely little boy, Shirley. Have you seen him?'

'No. I want to go to Boothley as soon as I can, though. I can't believe I've got a half-brother I've never set eyes on. Until I've seen him for myself it won't seem real.'

'I wanted Gloria to tell Daddy before she left, but I don't think she did,' Imogen said.

Shirley looked puzzled. 'Why should she tell *him*?'

Imogen bit her lip. She had assumed that Shirley knew who Michael's father was, but by the look on her face she clearly did not.

'Michael's his – Tony's, isn't he?'

Imogen sighed. 'She should have told you. I wish she had.'

'I'm always the last to know things,' Shirley said.

There was an awkward silence between them, then Imogen asked: 'Where will you go when you have to move out of Angel Row?'

'I don't know. I suppose I'll find a bed-sit or something.' She sighed. 'Life's pretty dreary at the moment. If I could only get a job in rep or something I'd be off like a shot, but according to what I've heard all the small theatres in the provinces are closing through lack of business. Everyone's buying television sets and staying at home to stare at them.'

Imogen squeezed her hand. 'Poor Shirl. I'm sure things will soon start looking up for you.'

'I hope you're right.' Shirley smiled ruefully. 'But with my luck I wouldn't bank on it if I were you.'

Leonie stepped out of her taxi outside the hospital. She wore her fur coat and her favourite 'disguise' of headscarf and dark glasses. She paid the driver and walked into the hospital.

'I'm Leonie Swann,' she told the girl on the reception desk. Taking off the glasses, she said, 'Mrs Tony Darrent, in other words. I'd like to see my husband, please.'

The girl looked up, her face pink with surprise at being suddenly face to face with a famous actress. '*Oh*! Miss Swann, I mean Mrs Darrent. Of course, I'll get a porter to take you straight up.'

In the lift the porter, slightly less impressed than the receptionist, eyed Leonie's expensive fur coat and sniffed appreciatively at the waft of French perfume that filled the lift.

''Ad to come far, 'ave you?' he enquired chattily.

Leonie gave him a withering look. 'From London. I've been away filming on location. No one thought to inform me of my husband's accident till yesterday.'

She had finally learned of the plane crash on the day after her return, when she had tried to contact Tony in Yorkshire in order to pour out her troubles to him. Getting no reply at his private telephone number, she had rung the location office number only to be told of the crash.

'Everyone's been going frantic, trying to get hold of you, Miss Swann,' the office girl told her. 'Your daughter, the hospital, and Mr Jason, your agent. Thank goodness you've rung in at last.'

Leonie had poured herself a large brandy and sat down to assimilate the impact of the shock. Tony badly injured – *burned*, they said. How ghastly! And just when she had decided to divorce him. Now everyone would think she was dumping him because of his accident. What rotten timing!

She telephoned the hospital to enquire about him and was relieved to hear that he'd come through surgery well and was improving. At least he wasn't going to die. It would have looked so bad if she hadn't been at his side. Now her first priority had better be to get up to Yorkshire as soon as she could.

She'd awakened to find her temper had cooled and she began to review her situation with Paul. After sleeping on the previous night's row she had decided that he was merely having a little fling with Shirley while she was away. It couldn't possibly be serious. She had behaved like a jealous schoolgirl, losing her temper like that when she should have played the scene with cool detachment. Paul's new play was almost finished and if the film did flop, as Max feared it would, she would need a new vehicle. A good one – and quickly, if her popularity was to be sustained. As for Shirley, maybe Leonie could use her influence to get the girl out of the way.

Another brandy and a pot of coffee later Leonie's thought processes had moved into overdrive. It was an astonishing stroke of irony that this accident of Tony's had placed her in an almost identical situation to that of the character she had played in *Joy in the Morning*. What marvellous publicity it would make for the film once the papers got hold of the angle. It was just possible that what Max had feared would be a hopeless flop might be turned into a success after all. She wondered briefly if Tony would be out of hospital in time for the premiere. If she could be photographed arriving at the cinema on his arm, it would cause an absolute sensation. She could already see the headlines: BRAVE ACTRESS'S TRUE-LIFE TRAGEDY, LEONIE SWANN HIDES HER ANGUISH BEHIND A SMILE . . . She got up from the table and headed for the bathroom. There was no time to be lost. She must start preparing for the role of attentive, loving wife immediately.

When she first saw Tony, the shock was like a kick in the stomach. No one had prepared her for what he would look like. If she had been unexpectedly confronted with the man propped up in the bed, she would not have recognised him as her husband. Her stomach churned unpleasantly and for a moment she thought she was going to be sick. The nurse with her touched her arm.

'Are you all right, Mrs Darrent?'

'Yes – yes, I'm all right.' She forced a smile onto her face. 'Tony, *darling*. I hear you're quite the star patient. You're doing *so* well, I'm told. Moving back to London soon, too. Won't that be nice?' She looked at the bandaged hands lying on the coverlet and was overcome with relief that she had a good excuse not to touch him. The sight of the blistered, blackened facial skin made her want to gag. She swallowed hard and looked at the nurse, who'd been watching her with unnerving closeness. 'Thank you, nurse,' she said brusquely. 'I'd like to be alone with my husband now, please.'

When the nurse had withdrawn, she pulled up a chair and sat down beside the bed. Tony was looking at her in a way that set her teeth on edge. It was impossible to assess what he was thinking with that blank, expressionless look.

'How are you, Leonie?' he managed to say.

'I'm fine. The film is in the can, as they say. It should be released in a couple of months' time. I think the premiere will be at the Leicester Square Theatre.'

He turned his head slightly to look at her. It was typical of Leonie that she had placed herself where he could not see her without painful movement. 'You must be glad you decided to go ahead with the divorce now,' he said.

She caught her breath theatrically and gave him a reproachful look. '*Darling*, how can you be so cruel? Of course I won't divorce you now that you need me so badly. What wife could be so heartless?'

'It shouldn't be too difficult – for you,' Tony said emotionlessly.

'You're bitter. It's understandable. Our marriage has hit some rough patches in the past. We've both been selfish. But you know I've always loved you, darling, no matter what. You surely can't have doubted that. I want you to get well just as quickly as you can and come home to me. I'm going to take care of you. I'll be the perfect nurse. You'll see.'

Something suspiciously like a groan escaped Tony's lips. 'Leonie,' he said. 'I'm sorry but I'd like you to go now, please.'

She hesitated. Was he feeling ill, or was he giving her the cold shoulder? It was impossible to tell. She would have to give him the benefit of the doubt. She stood up. 'All right, darling. But I'll be back. I'm going to give you all the attention you deserve – make up to you for all the years we've lost together.' She forced herself to bend closer. 'I won't kiss you. It would probably hurt, wouldn't it?'

'Yes, it probably would.' As the door closed behind her he groaned again. Christ! What had he done to deserve this? He felt like some poor defenceless animal caught in a trap. Leonie as the devoted wife and nurse was one role she'd never sustain. If only he felt strong enough to tell her that all he wanted was that she should go away and leave him alone.

* * *

Whan Ma heard of Shirley's quarrel with Dave, she was furious.

'What are you thinkin' of, my gel, turnin' down a steady young feller like Dave? You could go a lot further and do worse, y'know.'

'But I don't want to get married just for a job and somewhere to live,' Shirley protested. 'Life has to have more than that to offer.'

Ma sniffed in loud contempt. 'You're still 'ankerin' after the stage, ain't you? Time you woke up to life an' got them stars outa your eyes, my gel. Blokes like Dave don't come along that often you can afford to kick 'em in the teeth. You'll be sorry for what you done. You mark my words.'

Gloria returned to pay them a flying visit, and, seeing that there was animosity between her mother and daughter, she invited Shirley to go with her to Boothley for a visit. She explained to Ma that the girl looked peaky and needed a break. Shirley was torn between a desire to go and guilt about leaving Ma to cope with the shop alone.

'I'll go and have a word with Dave,' Gloria promised. 'I'm sure he'll come and help out for a couple of days. Anyway, the shop'll be closing soon for good. I can't see that it'd make much difference if it closed now.'

Dave agreed to help out and two days later Shirley and Gloria set off for Boothley. Once they were on their way, Shirley told Gloria that she had seen Imogen and heard about her visit to Leeds to see Tony.

'You and he have always been friends, haven't you?' she said, glancing at her mother.

'We've always got along well together, yes,' Gloria said guardedly.

'Imo seemed to think you should have told him about Michael,' Shirley ventured. 'I don't see why she should have thought that would help him.'

But Gloria made some noncommittal reply and turned to look out of the window, refusing to be drawn.

At Boothley, spring was in evidence everywhere. The trees were bursting into leaf and the cottage gardens were full of daffodils. At Rook Cottage a smiling Margaret was ready for them with a meal. Little Michael sat in his highchair with his bib tied on in readiness. When Shirley saw him she fell instantly in love with him and insisted on sitting beside him at tea and taking him up to bed later.

'He's so lovely,' she told Gloria later. 'But I can't believe you kept him from me for so long. I wish you hadn't, Glor. I've missed all his babyhood.'

'I had my reasons,' Gloria said. 'Some day soon maybe you'll understand.'

'He looks so well. I can hardly believe he's ill.'

'Margaret tells me she took him for his check-up at the hospital this week,' Gloria told her. 'They think they might be able to operate within the next six months or so.'

Shirley looked at her. 'When he goes into hospital, will you let his father know?'

Gloria turned away. 'I don't know. I'll see.'

Rook Cottage had improved beyond all recognition. A new bathroom extension had been built on at the back with an extra bedroom above it. The kitchen had been modernised and they now had the benefit of electricity. Margaret had decorated most of the rooms and the whole place shone like a new pin.

'We're going to re-plan the garden this summer, now that the workmen have finished,' Gloria told her. 'We thought we'd make a feature of the old well. Have it thatched, and have a wooden top made so that Michael can't climb up and fall in. We can stand pots of geraniums on it.'

'Do you ever see Nanny and Jim Jarvis?' Shirley asked.

Gloria shook her head. 'I haven't seen them for years. I wish there was time, but there never is. When I come it's usually a flying visit.'

'So they don't know about Michael?'

'Not from me, though they've probably heard about him.'

'Glor – you're not ashamed of him, are you?'

'Of course I'm not. What a silly thing to say,' Gloria was stung into replying. 'It's just that it'd be awkward, trying to explain. I'm not in a position to tell them – or anyone else – what they'd obviously be curious about.'

'I can't see Nanny or Jim asking awkward questions or pointing fingers at you,' Shirley said. 'It's not their style. And I know Nanny would love Michael.'

'That's as maybe,' Gloria said. 'But at the moment I'm not planning to put them to the test.'

Gloria had intended to broach the subject of Paul Winspear with Shirley; to ask her whether Imogen had managed to speak to her about him. But try as she would she could not summon up the courage to bring up the subject. Who was she to preach to Shirley about men? she reasoned. Shirley would probably be quick to point out to her mother that she'd made a big enough mess of her own life. She thought nostalgically of the days long ago before the war and the close relationship they'd all had and she couldn't help wishing they could be as they'd been then – knowing with a deep sadness that they never would.

The two-day visit to Rook Cottage was over all too soon and Shirley reluctantly kissed little Michael goodbye and accompanied Gloria back to London. They parted company at Euston Station, Shirley to Angel Row and Ma; Gloria to Mayfair and Leonie. Over the past few days she had been thinking hard and now she had come to a firm decision. All that remained now was to deliver the news to Leonie.

Leonie was in the blackest of moods. On her brief visit to Yorkshire she had found Tony less than enthusiastic over her plans to nurse him back to health, then on her return to London she had found Paul's response distinctly cool. He had refused to discuss the new play. Things were not going her way, but she was determined that she would make them, come hell or high water.

She greeted Gloria's arrival at the flat with sarcastic surprise. 'So there you are. I've been wondering when you'd do me the honour of coming back to work.'

'My holiday doesn't actually end till Monday,' Gloria reminded her. 'I've come back to give you my notice, Leonie. I'll be leaving in two weeks' time.'

'*Leaving*?' Leonie stared at her, taken aback by this new blow. 'But you can't. I need you. Just look at the state of this flat.' She seemed oblivious to the fact that she'd created most of the mess herself. 'I take it you've heard about poor Tony's dreadful air crash?'

'Yes.'

'I've just been up there to see him. I've decided not to go ahead with the divorce after all; I'll bring him home here and nurse him back to health. I'll be busy soon with a new play, so of course I'll need you here to care for him.'

'*Me*?'

'Of course. *I* can't take on the role of nurse, can I? Not that I'd be any good at it even if I had the time. You should see his face, it's the most *frightful* mess.' She shuddered delicately. 'I've always been squeamish when it comes to things like that. Poor Tony, his days as a heart-throb are decidedly over.' She lit a Turkish cigarette and peered at Gloria through a cloud of perfumed smoke. 'He doesn't want to come. Can you believe that? You'd have thought he'd have been grateful to me under the circumstances, wouldn't you?'

'I don't think he has all that much to be grateful to you for, Leonie,' Gloria said, her heart thudding with anger. 'He made you a star, gave up his own career for you, and you've treated him with contempt for as long as I've known you.'

'How *dare* you? Don't be so bloody impertinent,' Leonie snapped. 'Tony should consider himself lucky. No one else will want him now, that's for sure. He's just being a fool. If he plays his cards right we can capitalise on this accident of his – make it work for us. Being seen together at the premiere of *Joy in the Morning* will give both our careers a tremendous boost.'

Gloria felt sick. She could hardly believe that even Leonie could stoop so low. 'You'd actually use Tony's disfigurement to get publicity?' she said incredulously. 'I can't believe it. Don't you care *anything* for his feelings?'

'Oh, don't be so po-faced.' Leonie tapped off the ash from her cigarette. 'Tony would have been the first to appreciate the opportunity himself a few years ago. Publicity is everything in our business. But he's gone soft in his old age.' She looked at Gloria. 'He's forty-seven now, you know. He's not the handsome, dashing young matinee idol he was before the war. Those days are gone for ever.'

'We're *all* older,' Gloria said.

The remark stung Leonie far more than anything else Gloria could have said. She peered curiously at her pale face, the anxiety of the past few days clearly etched about her mouth and eyes. 'You're in a strangely waspish mood today, aren't you, Gloria? I know you once did me a little favour, but that doesn't give you the right to such familiarity.' She lit a new cigarette from the stub of the last one before crushing it out. 'Anyway, in my opinion you should be more worried about that daughter of yours. I caught her behaving like a little tart with Paul Winspear when I came back from Cornwall. It's patently obvious that they're sleeping together. It's *her* you should be worrying about.'

'I'm quite capable of taking care of my own family. Which is what I intend to do from now on,' Gloria said, her stomach churning sickeningly. 'And I'm sorry but I still intend to leave.'

Leonie opened her mouth to argue, but one look at Gloria's expression told her that she'd be wasting her time. 'Oh, suit yourself then, Gloria,' she said with a wave of her hand. 'You're not indispensable. Dressers are ten a penny, and I can always get an agency nurse in for Tony.'

In the weeks that followed, Shirley attended every audition she saw advertised. They ranged from the chorus of a Drury Lane musical, where she joined a long line of hopeful young girls at the stage door and queued up for hours, to auditions in a Camden Town church hall for a female juvenile lead for a northern repertory company. The producer was an old friend of Magda's and she'd promised to put in a good word for her, but the weeks went by and when Shirley heard nothing she had to admit that she wasn't going to get a job easily, however talented she might be.

Ma made no secret of her relief. 'No good'd come of it,' she said with a sniff. 'Say what you will, it ain't steady work. You get yourself a nice job in a shop, my gel. Do what you know.' She pulled an envelope out of her pocket. 'Look, I got this this mornin'. They've found me a little two-room flat, so you c'n move in with me when we leave 'ere. You won't mind sharin' a bedroom with your old Ma, will you?'

Shirley's heart sank. She thought of Imogen, going off with Charles on the Canadian tour with Tony's newly formed company. It wasn't fair. If it hadn't been for her famous father she'd never have got a job like that straight out of drama school. Imogen wasn't really all that dedicated to the theatre either. It wasn't that Shirley grudged her the chance, of course, but she couldn't deny that she felt envious and a little resentful.

Dave had already moved on to take up his new job. Shirley had hardly seen him since their row and when she ran into him two months after he'd left Whitechapel she was surprised and impressed by his improved appearance. He looked well groomed, almost handsome, with his hair cut in a fashionable, slightly longer style. He wore a new suit too, with a longer jacket and drainpipe trousers that accentuated his slim build. She'd been to Stepney for her drama lesson and was getting off the bus when she saw him walking towards her. At first she wondered whether to look the other way. Being snubbed by Dave was the last thing she needed and she wasn't sure whether he'd want to speak to her or not. But while she was still hesitating he spotted her and smiled.

'Hello, Shirl.'

'Hello, Dave. What are you doing over this way?'

'Just came to pick up one or two things I left with my old landlady,' he told her, falling into step beside her. 'On your way home?'

'Yes.'

'Got time for a drink?' He glanced uncertainly at her. 'Only if you want to, I mean. Don't feel you have to.'

'No – yes, I'd like to.'

In the pub he looked at her. 'You okay, Shirl? You've lost weight.'

She shrugged. 'Ma and I have moved into a two-room flat. There isn't really room for me. We have to share a bed and Ma is so restless. I don't get much sleep. I've been trying to get a job, but no luck so far.'

'That's a shame.' He took a sip of his beer. 'I, er, thought you might be planning to get married.'

She looked away. 'That's all over, Dave. And anyway there were never any wedding plans.'

'I see.' He paused, clearing his throat. 'Look, there's a vacancy at my shop. I know it's not what you're looking for but the money isn't bad.'

She glanced at him with a rueful smile. 'Is there really a job? Or do you mean you'd make one?'

'Oh, nothing like that. I'm still answerable to the owner. No, one of the girls is leaving soon – she's expecting.' Shirley said nothing and he went on quietly: 'I'm not saying I wouldn't make room for you if I could, though, Shirl. My feelings haven't changed. I might as well admit it. I still feel the same about you. Reckon I always will.'

She sighed. 'Oh, Dave. You make me feel awful. I never wanted to hurt you, honestly.'

He looked at her. 'As long as you're not with – with *him* any more, could we see each other now and again? I mean, no strings or anything. What do you say?'

She looked at his hopeful eyes and melted. 'Oh, all right them, why not?'

His eyes lit up. 'That's smashing. You must come and see the shop, Shirl. I've reorganised it all and I've got the flat upstairs. Three rooms, a bathroom and kitchen. I've never had such luxury. And that job's still there if you want it, remember. Think about it and let me know.'

'Okay, Dave. I will.'

Shirley took her silver-medal examination two weeks later and passed, once again with honours. But her triumph was marred by what she read weekly in the theatrical paper, *The Stage*. Television was what the public wanted now. Small provincial theatres were closing down one after another through lack of business and because of it the valuable practical training ground where generations of young actors had traditionally learned their craft was vanishing fast.

Finally, through sheer necessity, Shirley was forced to admit defeat and accept the job Dave had offered. And soon after, much to Ma's delight, they fell into a regular habit of going out together once a week. It was over a drink one Saturday evening in June that Dave passed her a copy of the London *Evening News*.

'Isn't that your friend's mum?' he asked, pointing to a picture on the front page.

Leonie was pictured arriving at a West End cinema for the premiere of *Joy in the Morning*. Dressed in a shimmering black evening gown, she clung to the arm of Max Forsythe, the film's director. Underneath the picture the caption read: 'BEAUTIFUL SAD LEONIE ATTENDS PREMIERE. The brilliant, multi-talented star of *Joy in the Morning* takes time off from her vigil at the bedside of sick husband Tony Darrent to attend the premiere of her strangely prophetic first film.'

'She sounds a really devoted wife,' Dave remarked. 'And they've been together for twenty-two years, so the paper says. Just shows. Some of these show-business marriages work okay, don't they?'

Shirley, who knew better about the Darrents' marriage, said nothing. Dave went on: 'Shirl, now that you've settled down in the job and you and I get along okay again, you wouldn't like to get engaged, would you?'

Shirley bit her lip. 'Oh, Dave . . . I don't know.'

'It makes no sense,' he said, 'you and your gran squashed into that tiny flat, sharing a bedroom, when I've got all that space. We get on all right, don't we? I mean, I know you don't feel as strong for me as I do for you. But I know I could make you happy. What do you think?'

Shirley had an audition in two days' time. It would be the twenty-eighth she'd taken this year. When she started working with Dave she had given up her drama lessons with Magda and decided not to try for any more stage jobs, but deep inside a stage career was still her dream and when she'd seen the audition advertised in *The Stage* last week she'd had a really strong hunch about it. She hadn't mentioned it to Dave. Luckily it would take place on their half-day closing so she wouldn't have to ask him for time off. She'd have just one more try, she promised herself. And if she didn't get the job this time, she'd definitely give up.

'Just give me a few days to think about it,' she told him. 'I'll let you know at the end of next week.'

It was even worse than usual. There was only one vacancy in the company, another rep, this time in the Midlands where live theatre still seemed fairly healthy. Twenty hopeful girls took turns to stand on the stage in the dimly lit theatre and perform their carefully rehearsed audition pieces. But afterwards there wasn't even the hope of waiting for a telephone call or letter. The director made his choice there and then; a tall dark girl who reminded her of Imogen and who had already had two years' experience of repertory work. Once again Shirley came away with her hopes shattered.

At the shop she let herself into the side entrance and climbed the stairs to Dave's flat. He was doing the books at the kitchen table and looked up in surprise when she walked in.

'Shirl? What are you doing here?'

'I just came to tell you that I'll marry you, Dave,' she said. 'If you still want me, that is.'

Instantly he was on his feet, his arms around her, hugging her close. 'Still *want* you? Oh, God, Shirl, if you only knew how much.' He kissed her, holding her so close that she could feel his heart beating against her own. She knew she had made him happy and as she rested her head on his shoulder she tried to feel glad and to share his happiness. There would never be anyone who loved her more, she told herself. He'd make a good husband. She was a lucky girl. But there was a huge lump in her throat and deep inside her heart ached for the dream that would never now come true.

Chapter Eighteen

When Leonie learned that Tony was finally fit enough to leave hospital, it came as a shock. Since Gloria left her she'd had a string of maids, none of them any good. They all wanted endless time off and a wage that was ridiculous. And of course none of them was likely to be the slightest use when it came to caring for an invalid. She'd tried hard to get Gloria to come back, but to no avail. In spite of all Leonie's enticements Gloria had remained adamant. Paul's new play was about to go into rehearsal any week now and she didn't see how she was going to cope with that *and* with having Tony at home. It was all too tiresome for words.

'But I've tried to tell you, Leonie,' Tony explained for the hundredth time when she outlined her difficulties. 'I don't *want* to come back to the flat. It's all arranged. When I leave here I'm going to Houlton – to Longueville Hall.'

'But Longueville Hall is up for sale and Nanny and Jim have left. The place is empty,' Leonie said with studied patience. Since his accident she had developed a ponderous, patronising way of speaking to him as though he were a retarded five-year old and it tried his patience so hard he could have screamed at her.

'Leonie, I've already told you, I've had the place taken off the market and Nanny and Jim are going to move back in with me until I can find another housekeeper. There's absolutely no need for you to worry. I'm not an invalid. And I've absolutely no intention of being a bloody nuisance to anyone.'

'But I wanted you to be in London,' she complained. 'You've already missed the film's premiere. If you're worrying about people seeing you, I'm sure there's no need. They'll soon get used to your appearance just as I have. How do you expect to pick up your career again if you hide yourself away from everyone?'

Tony sighed, his tolerance stretched to its limit. 'I'm not hiding myself away, as you put it. And I think you're talking about *your* career,' he said. 'No, Leonie. You've had all the mileage you're going to get out of my accident, so why don't you just agree to the divorce now and leave me alone?'

Tony's skin grafts had healed well. The surgeon had done all that he could, but in spite of the infinite care he had received, Tony was still scarred. The first time they had allowed him to look into a mirror he had been totally devastated. The face that had looked back at him, with its unnatural-looking shiny pink skin and slightly lopsided expression, seemed to him that of an ugly stranger. But gradually over the months the improvement of his appearance and his acceptance of it met somewhere in the middle and he finally came to terms with the reflection that the mirror offered him each morning. He was getting back the mobility of his facial muscles so that the stiff, expressionless look was softening, and, most important of all, he was learning to smile again.

Talking to the doctor and other patients in the burns unit where he had received his treatment, he had realised how lucky he was to have got off as lightly as he had. The rest of his body functioned perfectly normally. There was no reason why he should not pick up his career as a director again. His hands, though scarred and misshapen, still worked so that he'd be able to drive and attend to his own needs. Leonie's concern, he quickly realised, was more for herself than for him. She had basked in the 'faithful, devoted wife' image and now she was afraid of the adverse publicity a divorce would create.

'I'll make sure it's all done with the minimum of fuss,' he promised. 'I'll do my utmost to keep it out of the papers or at least to make clear that the decision is mine. Let's face it, Leonie, no one knows better than you that our marriage is dead. You and I are the only two people it really matters to. Why not just let it go?'

For all Leonie's protestations that she cared only for his welfare, Tony knew that if he agreed to return to the flat he would regret it deeply. Sometimes he was sure he detected a gleam of triumph in her eyes when she looked at him. The fact that his good looks had gone for ever gave her the edge over him. She would like to have him dependent on her; to be able to trundle him out as living proof of her selfless devotion whenever it suited her. But he was determined that it would never happen. He would not be subjected to that kind of humiliation. He had done enough to boost the career of Leonie Swann. Now he was determined to pick up the threads of his own life and make a fresh start.

'You know, one of the other burns patients said something to me the other day,' he told her. 'Something that hadn't occurred to me before. He said: Everyone's looks go in the end. There's no escaping that. We all change as the years go by. With us it's just happened suddenly instead of gradually. In a way we're lucky because we know where we are. Those who really love us will love us whatever we look like.' He smiled wryly. 'He was right, wasn't he? No surer way of finding out who your true friends are than getting your looks ruined.'

Leonie shuddered. The real irony of his words failed to reach her, but they probed uncomfortably at her chilling dread of passing time, something she was becoming increasingly aware of. 'Oh, Tony – *don't*.'

'So you won't want me around as a living reminder of life's cruel folly, will you?' He smiled his rueful, lopsided smile and she turned away, pulling on her gloves.

'All right, Tony. Joke about it if you must,' she said stiffly. 'If that's the way you want it, go to Houlton. And you can put the divorce plans into motion seeing that you're so determined. I can see now that all my concern for you has been wasted.'

* * *

413

All through the long and painful months of recovery Gloria had visited Tony whenever she could. When she left her job with Leonie she had gone to live with Margaret and Michael at the cottage in Boothley. It was wonderful to be able to spend more time with Michael and she'd managed to get a job behind the bar of the Dog and Doublet. Ever since Ken Doubleday, the landlord, had lost his wife he'd been short-staffed. She and Margaret helped him in shifts, turn and turn about. During her week of evening shifts, Gloria travelled up to London to spend a day visiting Tony. She put in a flying visit to Ma too and saw Shirley whenever she could. She looked forward very much to seeing Tony and watching him improve, both physically and mentally, week by week. They would walk together in the hospital grounds and she would tell him all her news. He learned of Shirley's failure to get work in the theatre and of her engagement to Dave Green, and of Gloria's worry concerning her mother and what she would do once Shirley had married, leaving her alone.

Imogen wrote twice-weekly letters to her father, describing in detail everything that happened on the Canadian tour. She seemed happy and was obviously learning a lot and enjoying herself. Having little news of his own to tell, Tony would read Imogen's letters to Gloria and together they would look at the photographs she sent.

'You must be terribly disappointed not to be there with them,' she said. 'The Darrent Shakespearean company was your dream, wasn't it?'

He smiled resignedly. 'Some dreams just aren't meant to come true, Gloria. As we get older, that's one of the realities we have to face.' He touched his cheek thoughtfully with one forefinger. 'When something like this happens to you, life takes on a different perspective. I can't grumble. I made a success of my war films and I've done a lot of the things I set out to do. I'm only just beginning to realise how lucky I am.'

'Lucky?' She looked at him.

'Luckier than many. You only have to look around you.' He smiled and took her hand. 'Other dreams take the place of the broken ones. And sometimes they're even better. For instance, if this hadn't happened to me you wouldn't be here with me now. You really meant it when you said goodbye to me, didn't you?' He took both her hands. 'I can't tell you what your visits to me have meant, Gloria. I look forward so much to seeing you and hearing your news.'

'I just wish you were nearer,' she said, 'so that I could see you more often.'

'Me too.' He squeezed her hands. 'Which is why I've made up my mind: when I leave hospital I'm going to Houlton, to Longueville Hall.'

She smiled delightedly. 'Oh, Tony, that's wonderful. I'll be able to visit you every day – if you want me.'

'Of course I want you. I fact . . .' He glanced at her speculatively, 'How would you feel about coming to keep house for me?'

She caught her breath. 'At Longueville Hall? Oh, Tony, I'd love to but I don't think I could.'

He looked crestfallen. 'I thought you'd be pleased. Why not?'

'Well, to begin with, what would Leonie have to say about it?'

'Nothing. I believe that if the truth were known she'd be relieved that someone else was taking on the responsibility. She's agreed to a divorce at last. I'm starting proceedings as soon as I can see a solicitor. Leonie's not a problem.'

'There's another reason,' Gloria said, frowning. 'I'm not exactly free to do as I like, Tony. There's someone else I have to consider.'

'Not Shirley? She has her own life now.'

'No. Not Shirley.'

'Your mother? You feel you should move back to London and live with her?'

'No.'

'Then who?' He was looking at her intently. 'Someone you've met? A man?'

Gloria smiled. 'I suppose you could say that.'

415

He sat back in his chair, letting out his breath slowly. 'Ah – I see. Well, it was bound to happen, wasn't it? You're a very attractive woman, Gloria. You still have your life ahead of you.'

'Tony . . .' She touched his hand. 'Tony, I'm talking about my small son. He's two and a half and his name is Michael.'

He turned to look at her. 'Your *son*? You have a child – two and half years old?' His eyes widened incredulously as they looked into hers. 'Gloria, is he . . . is he. . . ?'

'Yes, Tony.'

For a moment he stared at her, too stunned for words, then he was out of his chair. Pulling her to her feet, he held her close. 'My God, Gloria, why did you never tell me before? Why haven't I *seen* him?'

'At the time it seemed better not to,' she said. 'It would have caused so much trouble for so many people. I was in America when I found out I was pregnant. It was a shock. I decided to have the baby adopted. I intended to come back with it all behind me. But he was born with a heart defect, and anyway, once I'd seen him I couldn't have parted with him.'

'A heart defect?' He held her away from him. 'What is it? Is it serious – can it be cured?'

'Yes. It's a heart valve that isn't functioning as it should. At one time there would have been no cure, but now they can operate.'

'We must get another opinion. We must see that everything is done for him – and as soon as possible. Oh, Gloria, when can I see him? I can't believe it! I have a *son*. It's like being given another chance to make a go of life.' He looked at her. 'As soon as my divorce is through we'll be married. My son must have my name. Michael Darrent.' He said the name experimentally. 'It has a fine ring to it, doesn't it? Do you think he'll grow up to be an actor?'

Gloria laughed. 'He'll be himself, whatever that may be. But I know you'll love him, Tony.'

'Of course I will.' He looked into her eyes. 'I love you too, Gloria. You do believe that, don't you?'

'I believe it,' she said happily.

'Now I've got something to live for again – something to look forward to,' he said.

Gloria held him close, gratitude filling her heart. At last she'd been able to admit to Michael's existence. She'd felt so guilty about keeping him hidden away from all the people who mattered most, especially his father. It was almost as Shirley had once said – as though she were ashamed of him. Now she felt as though a great burden had been lifted from her shoulders. 'Tony,' she said softly. 'You don't have to marry me because of Michael, you know. If you really want it we can have his name changed to yours, but I'd never hold you to anything. That was partly why I've kept it to myself all this time.'

Tony held her away from him to look gravely into her eyes. 'Gloria, listen. I want you to know that I'm asking you to marry me because I love you, not just because of the child. And for the same reason you mustn't feel obliged to agree. If you don't feel you could love me in return, or if you can't face life with me, crocked up like this, I'd understand. I wouldn't blame you.'

She placed her fingers over his lips, her heart full. 'Tony, *Tony*, don't say things like that. Of *course* I love you.' She swallowed hard at the lump in her throat. 'I've always loved you and I always will. To me you're just the same person that you've always been and I can't think of anything I want more than to be married to you.' She stood on tiptoe to kiss him tenderly.

An ironic little smile drifted across his face as he looked down at her. 'It's funny, I used to dread getting old. I was always peering into the mirror, looking for grey hairs and wrinkles, worrying about going bald or putting on weight. Now none of that matters any more.'

'It never mattered – not to me,' she told him. 'And I'm not trying to flatter you when I say that to me you look as good as you've always looked.'

'Bless you.' He kissed her. 'All these months you've been the one person who has come to see me because you really wanted to and not out of a sense of duty. We've always had something special and you've proved to me the value of what we have.'

It was strange, the way good could come out of bad, Gloria reflected. If it hadn't been for the war she and Tony would never even have met. And if it hadn't been for his terrible accident he would never have known he had a son. They might have gone their separate ways for ever.

Leonie considered Paul's new play, *Give Me Yesterday*, even better than *Joy in the Morning*. Her own part was that of the widowed mother of a wayward daughter who was growing up to an awareness of herself as a woman. Both women fell in love with the same man, a feckless young American artist who was totally unable to cope with the situation and who finally destroyed all three. It was a powerful drama that required strong, emotional acting from both the older and the younger woman. At the first read-through it became clear that the actress who had been cast as the daughter was totally unequal to the demands of the part. Afterwards, over a drink at a nearby pub, Paul expressed his fear that a serious mistake had been made in the casting.

'Never mind, darling,' Leonie said. 'I'll ring Peter Jason after lunch. I'm sure he'll have someone on his books who'll fit the part nicely.'

But Paul was shaking his head. 'I still think Shirley could do it.'

Leonie stared at him. 'Shirley? Shirley who?'

'You know perfectly well who I mean. Shirley Rayner.'

She stared at him, trying to conceal her annoyance. 'You can't be serious. The girl has absolutely no experience.'

'She's had training and she has talent, Leonie. She has that spark of vitality that the part needs.'

'Paul, you're a brilliant playwright,' Leonie said placatingly, 'but you have absolutely no idea when it comes to acting. Shirley would never cope with a role like that. She isn't ready for the West End theatre, or any other theatre either if it comes to that. It just isn't in her.'

'I happen to believe it is,' he said stubbornly. 'She's young, but she's eager to learn.'

'Oh, I've already gathered that,' Leonie said sarcastically. 'Anyway, it isn't your job to cast the play. You should leave it to the production team. You'll make yourself unpopular if you try to interfere.' She took in his brooding expression, and, reading the danger signals, reached out to touch his arm. 'Darling, why don't you let me get Peter to send round some girls to audition? I'm sure he has plenty of talented young actresses with experience on his books who'd jump at the chance.'

'Where *is* Shirley these days?' he asked, shrugging off her hand.

She frowned. 'I've no idea. They pulled down the street where the family used to live. I haven't a clue where she is now.'

'You know where her mother is, though. You could find out.'

Leonie swallowed her anger. How dare he ask her to do his errands for him – go looking for his past floozies? If she hadn't been so afraid of his temper she'd have told him where to go in no uncertain terms. But she had to tread carefully with Paul these days. It had taken a lot of ingratiating to get back on his right side. His temper was explosive and unpredictable, especially when he was thwarted. Nowadays it took more than an hour or two in bed to assuage it. Sometimes she wondered if persuading him to move into the Mayfair flat with her was a good idea after all. Living with him was like sharing a cage with a half-tamed tiger at times.

'Give me Gloria's address and I'll get in touch with her myself,' he said.

Leonie looked at him warily. On second thoughts maybe it would be better to handle this herself. Already an idea was beginning to form in her mind. 'Don't worry, I'll fix it, darling. If that's what you really want.'

Later that afternoon she knocked on the door of Magda Jayne's studio in Stepney. When the drama teacher opened the door, she was astonished to find Leonie

Swann standing on her doorstep. Leonie was graciousness itself as she sat drinking tea with Magda in the studio.

'I've heard so much about you from Shirley Rayner that I felt I really must come and pay you a visit,' Leonie said chattily. 'Shirley stayed with me all through the war, you know, at our country house in Northamptonshire. I flatter myself that it was I who first awakened her interest in the theatre.'

'I've heard all about the wartime concerts,' Magda said. 'Shirley is extremely talented. The poor girl has tried so hard to get her foot on the first rung of the ladder, but I'm afraid she hasn't had any success. It's a very tough time for young actors trying to break into the business. I know that if things had been normal in the theatre she'd have been well on the way to a brilliant career by now, but with so many small theatres closing up and down the country it's become almost impossible to get a job.'

'I know. Do you know where she is nowadays?' Leonie asked casually.

'Sadly, no.' Magda spread her hands helplessly. 'She isn't with me any more, I'm sorry to say. She was so disappointed after the last audition that she lost heart and decided to give up trying. She's working in a grocery shop in Hackney now, I believe.'

'What a sad waste! Has she auditioned many times?' Leonie asked.

'A great many. She'd set her heart on the last one. It was with a rep in Birmingham. They were looking for a girl to play juvenile leads.'

'Really? Do you know who the producer was?'

'Gerald Maddox, I believe.'

'Gerald?' Leonie beamed. 'He's a very old friend of mine. We worked together before the war. I'm sure that he'd find a place for darling Shirley if I were to give him a ring.' She stood up. 'Thank you, Magda. It was so nice meeting you. I've been promising myself a visit to you for some time. I try to keep up with what the young hopefuls are doing and help wherever I can. After all, they are the theatre's future, aren't they?' She began to pull on her gloves. 'Goodbye. It's been so nice having this little chat, and if I can put any students your way you can be sure I will.'

All the way home in the taxi Leonie hugged the information to herself. What luck that it should have been Gerald Maddox who last auditioned Shirley. He owed her a favour from the time she'd got him the job of assistant stage manager on *Sunshine Sally* – his first foot on the ladder. She'd be sure to remind him of that. The moment she got back to the flat she put through a call to the Mask Theatre in Birmingham. This way everyone would be happy, she told herself contentedly as she listened to the ringing tone. And Birmingham was such a nice long way from London, too.

'How are you, Ma?' Gloria looked round the cramped little flat that her mother shared with Shirley and wondered how they could tolerate it. Rook Cottage was small but at least they could get out into the fresh country air whenever they wanted to. Here, opening a window only filled the room with air polluted by carbon monoxide from the constant stream of traffic on the busy road below.

'Have you heard yet when you'll be moving into the new flat?' she asked as she took off her coat.

'No. Sometimes I wonder whether I'll live to see it 'appen,' Ma said gloomily. 'When Shirl gets married next month I'll be stuck 'ere with nothin' to do but twiddle me thumbs all day. It won't even be worth cookin' meself a meal with no one to share it with.'

'Surely it won't be that bad?' Gloria said. 'You've still got your friends and your whist drives to go to.'

Ma shook her head. 'It ain't the same as it used to be. Since the war Whitechapel ain't a patch on what it was. Half the old streets've gone, people scattered 'ere there and everywhere – them as weren't killed in the Blitz. The 'eart's gone out of the place. It's the end of the good old life we knew. Them days won't never come again. Sometimes it don't feel like we won the war at all.'

Gloria looked at her mother. She'd never seen her quite this depressed. Since moving from Angel Row she had aged. The loss of the little shop that had been her life for more than forty years had left an irreplaceable void in her life. There was no longer anything to get up for in the mornings, and Gloria could see that when Shirley left Ma would miss her badly. There'd be no one young and lively coming home in the evening; no link with the outside world. If only she could get her to move closer so that she could keep an eye on her.

'Ma, look, now that I'm so far away it isn't convenient for you, living here. I can't come up to visit you as often as I'd like to and Shirley will be too busy to come often when she's married, what with the shop and a husband too. Won't you think again about coming to live in Boothley?' Seeing her mother's features beginning to set in the familiar stubborn lines, she went on hurriedly: 'Listen, I've got something to tell you, Ma. It might come as a shock. I'm getting married.'

Surprise took the place of stubborn discontent on Ma's face. '*You* are?' Her eyes opened wide. 'Who to?'

'To Tony – Tony Darrent.'

Ma's mouth was a startled O. '*"im*?' she barked. 'But 'e's already married – to that there Leonie Swann.'

'They're about to be divorced. He's coming out of hospital soon and going to live at Longueville Hall. I'll be going there to look after him.'

Ma folded her arms and her mouth into uncompromising disapproval. 'I don't 'old with divorce. Never 'ave. You know that.' She eyed Gloria suspiciously. 'You've always been stuck on 'im, 'aven't you? Well if you asks me you're 'eadin' for trouble, bitin' off more than you can chew. D'you think 'e'd marry the likes of you if 'e 'adn't been disfigured in that there accident? Course 'e wouldn't. Can't get no one else to look after 'im, that's what it is. That Leonie won't want 'im no more. That's the only reason 'e's asked you.'

'That's a very unkind thing to say, Ma. And it's not true.'

Ma shook her shoulders. 'Well, time'll tell, gel. That's all I got to say. Thank God young Shirl's seen some sense at last. Marryin' young Dave Green is the best thing she could do. I been prayin' it'd 'appen.'

'Ma, there's more – something else I have to tell you.' Gloria was surprised to discover that her heart was beating faster at the prospect of what she was about to reveal. It was incredible that at thirty-five she still feared her mother's angry disapproval. Clearing her throat, she went on: 'I . . . I've got a little boy, Ma. Michael. He's three and a half. He's Tony's son. Very few people have known about him till now. Not even Tony himself. Margaret Jeffs, a friend I met in Yorkshire has helped me bring him up at Rook Cottage since he was born. He was the reason I couldn't come home when Pa was ill; the reason I stayed away when you needed me. I'm sorry.'

A variety of startled expressions chased themselves across Ma's features. For a moment or two she seemed to have lost her power of speech, then she folded her arms across her bosom and said: 'Well, since the goin's-on in the war nothin' surprises me no more. Always flung yourself at that feller's 'ead. It was bound to 'appen, I s'pose. Still, I'm glad to 'ear 'e's doin' the decent thing. That's somethin', I s'pose.'

Relief surged through Gloria. 'So will you at least pay a visit to Boothley to see Michael, Ma?'

'Dunno. I'll 'ave to think about that. I'm not sayin' I approve of any of it. I don't want you to go thinkin' I do.'

'He'll be going into hospital soon, for a heart operation,' Gloria told her. 'It's something he was born with. But they can operate now.'

This made Ma sit bolt upright in her chair, riveted. 'Why didn't you tell me before? Poor little mite.'

'The doctors say he'll be all right. He's quite a tough little thing.'

'All right – when he's got 'eart trouble? That's it then.' Ma's eyes shone now with the determined glint Gloria hadn't seen in them since she waged her one-woman war with Hitler. 'I reckon you're goin' to need some 'elp, our Glor. What with a feller gettin' over an accident an' an invalid child. I know me duty. I'll not see you strugglin'. I'll come.'

423

'You *will*? Oh, that's marvellous. You can have Rook Cottage, Ma. Margaret, my friend, has been courting Ken Doubleday from the Dog and Doublet for the past year. I think they'd like to get married as soon as they can. That'll leave Rook Cottage empty. Oh, Ma, just wait till you see it. You'll love it now that it's been modernised.'

'Well, that's as maybe.' The light in Ma's eyes belied her stern expression. 'I've never liked the country as you know – all them smells.' She sniffed, wrinkling her nose. 'But I dare say I'll get used to it in time. Most important thing we've got to do is look after that child.'

Shirley and Dave were to marry at the local register office. The date was set for 4 August. It would be the Saturday before the bank holiday so they'd be able to go away for a long weekend. Dave had booked a room at a guesthouse in Southend.

He'd been counting the days, crossing them off the calendar in the kitchen at the flat. He had bought a new suit to wear for the ceremony and he'd been busy for weeks redecorating the flat ready for Shirley to move in with him after the wedding.

Shirley, on the other hand, grew more apprehensive as the day drew nearer. Each week, as she received letters from Imogen, she studied the postmarks: Toronto, Ontario, Quebec. They sounded so far away, so exciting. Imogen wrote of full houses and ecstatic receptions. They were well received everywhere they went, it seemed. She wrote of the small parts she was playing while understudying larger ones, and of all that she was learning, far more than at drama school, she said. She made it all sound so exciting and such fun, relating anecdotes, mentioning the comradeship of the other members of the company and the team spirit they enjoyed. In every letter she mentioned Charles and their growing relationship. The most recent one was full of the news that they planned to marry on their return to England in the spring. She sounded so fulfilled and happy, so in love with Charles and with life. Shirley couldn't help envying this ecstatic happiness that had somehow eluded her.

424

Am I doing the right thing? she asked herself again and again. Can I really settle down with Dave? Can I really give up the idea of a career in the theatre? Am I being fair to him – to either of us? On the other hand, she did not have Imogen's opportunities, her entrée to all the right people and places. At the very best all she could expect was a small part with a touring company that would last perhaps six weeks before she'd find herself back on the dole, auditioning for jobs again.

Once again everything around her was changing. Ma was about to move to Boothley to live in Rook Cottage. And although she would never admit it, she was delighted at the prospect. An ecstatic Gloria was to marry Tony and move into Longueville Hall with him and little Michael. It seemed there was no place in their plans for her. Dave was all she had. He was kind and safe and he loved her. She was lucky and she really should be grateful. She went Up West alone to buy her wedding dress. She would have liked Gloria's help in choosing it, but, knowing how busy she was, she didn't ask.

To Ma's horror she chose green. 'Couldn't've picked a more unlucky colour,' she exclaimed with a shake of her head. 'I dunno, I'm sure,' she grumbled. 'I always dreamed my girl'd 'ave a white weddin'. Gloria never 'ad one at all, an' now you're gettin' hitched in one o' them registry offices – in *green* of all colours. I tell you, no good'll come of it – even if it do go with your new name.'

That was another thing, Shirley reflected as she hung up the apple green two-piece. Shirley Green sounded so ordinary. Shirley Rayner had always sounded as though she just *might* have become someone special. But Shirley *Green* – never in a million years could she achieve fame with a name like that.

On the evening before the wedding Shirley washed her hair and packed her clothes into two large suitcases, ready to move to Dave's flat. Ma had decided to go to a whist drive with a friend so that she could have the flat to herself. It was a warm evening and she sat at the open window, drying her hair in what breeze there was. Looking down into the street, she saw the telegram boy enter the building and a few minutes later there was a tap on the door. Pulling her dressing gown round her, she went to open it.

'Telegram for Miss Rayner,' the boy said, handing her the small orange envelope. Shirley's heart plummeted. Telegrams meant bad news. Everyone knew that. During the war parents and wives had dreaded the sight of the telegram boy in his blue uniform. But who in the world could be sending a telegram to her? And what would it say?

'Better open it, 'adn't you?' the boy prompted cheekily. 'In case there's a reply.'

With trembling fingers Shirley ripped open the envelope and unfolded the sheet of paper inside. The printed strips read: FURTHER TO RECENT AUDITION, VACANCY FOR JUV. ACTRESS. NOTIFY IMMEDIATELY IF ACCEPTABLE. The sender was GERALD MADDOX. THE MASK PLAYERS. BIRMINGHAM.

The words danced a crazy jig before Shirley's eyes as she read them over and over. Could it be true? Was someone playing a joke on her?

'Well?' The boy was still waiting.

'Oh, er, no reply, thanks.' Shirley closed the door and went to sit at the table. Spreading the telegram out in front of her she read it yet again. How ironic that her chance should come now, when she was unable to take it. Now she would never know if she'd have been a success – a star, even. If only – oh, if *only* she were free to accept the offer! She could have been travelling to Birmingham tomorrow, starting work as a real professional actress instead of marrying Dave and turning into plain Mrs Shirley Green.

Suddenly she made up her mind. Jumping up from the table, she ran to the window and leaned out, calling to the boy who was just leaving the building. 'Hey, boy! Can you come back up here, please? I've got to send a reply after all.'

She scribbled her acceptance on a scrap of paper and paid the boy, then she dressed hurriedly. When she was ready she took Ma's pad of lined notepaper and a packet of cheap envelopes out of the sideboard drawer and sat down at the table. Biting the end of the pencil she searched her mind for the right words. The notes to Ma and Gloria weren't so difficult. It was the one to Dave that was really hard. Poor Dave. He didn't deserve to be jilted and she felt dreadful about it, but she couldn't help herself. This was probably the only chance she'd ever get to do what she had always wanted to do. She *had* to take it. If she didn't, she'd regret it for the rest of her life and probably resent him too. Somehow she must try to find the words to temper the deep wound she was about to inflict with understanding.

At last the three sealed envelopes lay on the table. She stood up and put on her coat, then, picking up the suitcases she'd packed earlier, she walked out of the flat and down the stairs.

Gloria stepped down from the bus and headed for Mason's Stores, reflecting as she had before what a good position it had. With its double windows stacked with pyramids of tins of fruit and packets of custard powder, it stood right in the middle of the little shopping centre close to a bus stop.

Inside there were plenty of customers and as she waited she looked around appreciatively at the improvements Dave had made since he took over as manager. Wearing a spotless white coat, he was serving at the provisions counter, deftly slicing bacon with a shiny new electric machine as he made pleasant conversation with his customer. When he looked up and saw her, he smiled in surprised recognition.

'Mrs Rayner. Good afternoon. What can I get for you?'

'I'd like a word, please, Dave,' she said. 'I know this isn't the best of times but I'm only up from Boothley for the day.'

'It's okay. I was just about to take my lunch break anyway. We can go upstairs to the flat if you like.' He wiped his hands on a clean cloth and called to one of his assistants. 'Mary. I'm taking my break now. Take over here, will you?'

Gloria followed him through a storeroom at the rear of the shop, piled high with cartons and boxes; through a door and up a flight of stairs to the flat. As he closed the door she looked around approvingly. It was bright, the walls freshly distempered and brand-new linoleum on the floor. Dave opened the door to a tiny kitchen.

'Come in. I'll put the kettle on.'

'Don't let me stop you having your meal,' Gloria said.

'It's okay. I only have a sandwich and a cuppa midday. I usually get it ready before I open up in the morning. I cook myself a proper meal after closing.'

'You seem very well organised,' Gloria said, looking round at the smart blue and white paintwork.'

'A case of having to be,' Dave said ruefully.

'Dave, I've been meaning to come and see you for weeks. I expect you know why I'm here.' Gloria looked at him. 'What Shirley did – it was unforgivable. I want you to know that neither Ma nor I knew anything about it before you did.'

Dave shrugged helplessly. 'I won't pretend I wasn't gutted when I got her letter that morning, Mrs Rayner. In fact, that would be putting it mild. Getting chucked on your wedding day's no joke.'

'I know, Dave. And believe me, we were terribly upset too. I tried to get in touch with you that Saturday, but . . .'

He shook his head apologetically. 'I know. I'm sorry. After Mrs Rayner sent Shirl's letter round I just shut myself away up here all over the bank holiday; didn't answer the doorbell or the phone. I couldn't face anyone.'

All the colour had drained from his face and Gloria bit her lip in anguish. She hadn't come here to make him relive the trauma. Perhaps she should have left well alone. For the hundredth time she asked herself how Shirley could have done this to him. 'In a way I blame myself,' she said painfully. 'Ever since she was a baby I've encouraged her to want a stage career.'

Dave poured out two cups of tea and took the cover off a plate of sandwiches, which he passed to Gloria. 'Do sit down and have one, Mrs Rayner. They're the best ham.' He grinned wryly. 'One of the perks of the job, you could say.' 'He took the chair opposite. 'You mustn't blame yourself,' he said. 'Shirley's a born actress. I always knew that. If she'd let that chance go by she'd have regretted it for the rest of her life. I can see that now. She might even have come to hate me if she'd given up everything she wanted to marry me. She's got talent – got what it takes, as they say. And to be fair, I think it hurt her too, doing what she did to me. She's not a selfish girl at heart.'

'I hope she realises how much pain she caused us all,' Gloria said angrily. 'I was upset when I found out what she'd done, but Ma was devastated. It hit her really hard. She thought the world of you, Dave. In her eyes Shirley was a lucky girl and she's convinced that she'll rue the day she let you down.'

'No.' Dave shook his head. 'Like I said, it'd probably never have worked out anyway. I'll go and see the old lady some time and try and explain that to her. I always liked her too. She'll be lonely now that Shirl's left.'

'Not for long. She's coming to live nearer to me,' Gloria told him. 'I'm getting married myself soon and going to live in Northamptonshire.'

'That's good news. I wish you luck,' Dave said.

'Look, Dave, if there's anything I can do.' She bit her lip. People always said that. It had such a hollow ring. 'I mean – look, don't be lonely, will you? I know you've got no family of your own.' She took a scrap of paper from her handbag and scribbled the address of Rook Cottage on it. 'Here, this is where Ma will be living, and I won't be far away. If ever you want to come and see us – stay for a weekend, or longer – you'll be more than welcome.'

Dave took the paper and folded it carefully. 'Thanks a lot, Mrs Rayner. I'll remember.'

'And good luck with the shop. It all looks very nice. I'm sure you'll make a great success of it.'

'Thanks. I'll do my best.'

Outside in the street, as she waited for the bus, Gloria asked herself again whether what had happened was her fault. Since Shirley had jilted Dave she'd asked herself the same question time and time again. She hadn't been a good mother to Shirley; she hadn't had the chance to be a mother to her at all, really. But that was largely the fault of the war and their enforced separation. If Shirley had grown up at 10 Angel Row, Whitechapel, would she be the same young woman she was today? Would *any* of them be the same? Gloria knew that war had changed them all. They were the helpless victims of fate. Her dream for Shirley had been fame and fortune, but everything has its price, and sometimes dreams have a nasty way of rebounding on you in unexpected ways.

Since Shirley's departure, one letter had arrived at Rook Cottage. It bore a Birmingham postmark and it was brief. She begged to be forgiven for walking out and leaving Gloria and Ma to pick up the pieces. She said she had found a nice room and was enjoying her job with the Mask Players. She had signed a three-month contract and was earning eight pounds a week.

A three-month contract. She had given up security and broken the heart of the man who loved her for the chance to be an actress for three months. Gloria only hoped that she wouldn't regret it. She hoped that the pain she had caused wouldn't return to haunt her.

She made several attempts to reply to the letter, but she couldn't find the words to say what she really felt. Half of her blamed herself and sympathised with Shirley's all-consuming obsession for the stage, while the other half could not forget the thin young man with the pale, earnest face who had loved and wanted her so much. For her it brought back a poignant reminder of the unbearable ache rejection and unrequited love brought. She knew from bitter experience that that ache would live in Dave's heart for the rest of his life. In the end she did not reply at all.

A week before Tony was due to leave the hospital, Molly and Jim moved back into Longueville Hall to get everything aired and ready. Gloria had been to see them to make arrangements as soon as she had a date from the hospital. She found Molly there alone and, sitting in the cosy little living room of the Jarvises' cottage over the first fire of the autumn, she told her of the Darrents' impending divorce and of the marriage plans she and Tony were making. Then, taking her courage in both hands, she told Molly about Michael. The older woman received the news without surprise.

'We knew there was a little child.' She reached out to touch Gloria's hand. 'My dear, you can't live in a rural community like this and keep things like that to yourself,' she said. 'You can't stop the rumours spreading either. Local folks have speculated about little Michael ever since you first brought him here as a baby.'

'What are they saying?'

Molly smiled. 'Everything except the truth, as it happens. But gossip isn't important. What *is* important is that the three of you are going to be together at last.'

'Imogen knew before anyone else. She paid me a surprise visit.'

Molly nodded. 'I know. I tried to stop her coming but I couldn't think of an excuse. To the girl's credit, she never breathed a word.'

'She guessed later, after Tony's accident, that he was Michael's father.' Gloria looked at Molly. 'It wasn't me who broke up the marriage, you know.'

'Bless you, love, I know that. Jim and I used to hear the rows.' She raised her eyes to the ceiling. 'Some of the things she used to say to him. She's no lady, you know, for all the glamour. Her lack of breeding used to come out when she lost her temper. We always knew she made him miserable. I always guessed that you and he had a soft spot for each other too. And after all that's happened he deserves some happiness.'

'So you're not shocked?'

Molly smiled. 'Knowing the truth – all the facts, *and* the people concerned – how could I be?'

'Ma was, till I told her about Michael's illness. That seemed to alter everything for some reason. I didn't tell you; I'm planning to bring her to live in Rook Cottage.'

Molly smiled. 'What a good idea! You can be sure we'll make her welcome here,' she said. 'I'll get her to join the WI and the Mothers' Union.'

Gloria laughed. 'Well, you can try,' she said. 'Since Princess Elizabeth got married, her main interest is the royal family. She's even made a scrapbook and she cuts out all the pictures she can find of the royal couple and little Prince Charles.' She smiled. 'Between ourselves, I think she identifies with the Queen now that she's a grandmother. She says the royal family don't let you down even if your own does.' Gloria smiled. 'But I'm hoping that Michael will help her settle down here. I'm sure he'll make her feel useful and at home again.'

Tony finally came out of hospital one Friday afternoon towards the end of October. Gloria collected him and they travelled by hired car to Houlton. It was late afternoon when they arrived at Longueville Hall and as they drove up the drive Gloria reached for Tony's hand.

'Welcome home, darling.'

'This really feels like coming home,' he said. 'Now that you're here with me.' He turned to look at her. 'Will Michael be there?'

She nodded. 'Yes. Margaret said she'd bring him so that he was here to meet you.'

'Will he know who I am?'

'I've been telling him for weeks that he's going to meet his daddy.'

Tony's eyes clouded. 'When he sees me, he won't be . . . frightened of me, will he? It's the one thing I've been dreading.'

Gloria pulled his arm through hers and hugged it. 'Of course he won't. A little shy perhaps, but not frightened. Why should he be?'

Tony rubbed his jaw. 'Because of this. I'm no oil painting any more.'

432

'You are to me,' she whispered. 'As for Michael, he's never seen you before. Children have a way of accepting people at face value.'

He turned to smile at her. 'Face value. What an apt expression.'

Molly had the front door open as the car drew up. She stood there on the threshold with Jim beside her.

'Welcome home, Mr Tony.' She held out her arms as they came up the steps and Tony hugged her warmly.

'It's good to be home, Molly. Thank you both for all you've done.'

Jim carried in the bags and they all went through to the kitchen. Sitting on the floor in front of the Aga, playing with his toy cars, was Michael. Tony stood in the doorway for a moment, looking at him, his eyes apprehensive. He took a step forward.

'Hello, Michael.'

The little boy looked up. 'Hello.' He got to his feet and walked across to where Tony stood and stared up at him for a long moment, his blue eyes assessing. 'Are you my daddy?' he asked, glancing at his mother and then back at Tony.

'Yes, I am. Is that all right?'

Michael studied him for a moment, then he said: 'Do you want to play with my cars?'

'Thank you. I'd love to.'

Gloria watched as Tony got to his knees on the hearth-rug and began to play with his son. As he reached out for one of the cars, Michael tentatively touched one of his misshapen fingers.

'You've got a poorly hand,' he said with some concern.

'I did have, but it's all right now,' Tony told him gravely.

'Did the doctor make it better?' Michael asked.

'Yes.'

'Did it hurt?'

'No, not much.'

'The doctor's going to make me better soon too,' Michael told him.

'I know, and after that you're going to come and live here with me. Will you like that?'

Michael glanced up at Gloria. 'Can Mummy come too?'

'Of course she can.' Tony looked up with a smile. 'All three of us together. Won't that be fun?'

Gloria swallowed hard and turned to Molly. 'I think I'll go upstairs and unpack for Tony,' she said.

Molly nodded understandingly. 'You do that, love, and I'll put the kettle on,' she said. 'I'm sure you'll all be wanting your teas.'

Ma moved into Rook Cottage a fortnight later. Most of her luggage was sent on ahead and Gloria went up to London to fetch her and one suitcase of essential things. All the way in the train she listened to her mother's complaints, tolerating them because she knew they were the product of her anxiety and apprehension.

'If I don't like it, our Glor, I'm comin' straight back,' Ma said at least a dozen times. 'London might've changed, but at least it's what I *knows*. If it wasn't for you needin' me I'd've stopped where I was, y'know.'

'I know, Ma,' Gloria said. 'And I really appreciate it. But just give it a chance, that's all I ask. See how you get on. No need to stay if you don't like it.'

Ma grunted and stared moodily out of the window. 'All them years of gropin' about in the blackout, an' now, just when they've switched the lights back on, 'ere I am goin' where they ain't never 'eard o' street lights.'

'We're going to get them soon, now that we've got the electricity laid on,' Gloria told her. 'And you must admit you won't miss the noise and the traffic, now will you?'

'Will folks be friendly, though?' Ma muttered, thwarted at having her argument shot down. 'Country folks don't understand us Londoners. I'm warnin' you – I'm not stoppin' where I ain't welcome.'

All through the journey she found fault with every-thing, but once she arrived at Boothley and met Michael all thoughts of returning to London seemed to fly out of the window. The moment they met, Ma and her grandson formed an instant rapport and within minutes it was as though they had always known each other. As for Rook Cottage, the place surprised and delighted her, though she would have died rather than let anyone see it.

'Mmm, don't seem too bad,' she said grudgingly, looking round her. 'It don't seem to be damp, even if it is in the country.'

'Wait till you see your room, Ma,' Gloria said. 'I've given you mine. I'm moving in with Michael until we move to Longueville Hall. It overlooks the garden. It's not much to look at now, but you wait till spring. You never know, you might even find that you like gardening yourself,' she added optimistically.

Ma soon made the little room with its pink-striped wallpaper and flowered curtains her own personal territory. Pa's photograph took pride of place on the dressing table, but the big studio portrait of Shirley, taken when she was five in her best Shirley Temple frock and ballet shoes, had been banished from sight on the day that Shirley had jilted Dave. Her name hadn't passed Ma's lips since.

When Gloria saw that her mother had set out her brush and comb and hung her clothes in the wardrobe, she heaved a sigh of relief. It was a sure sign that Ma had given the place her seal of approval. She had decided to stay.

Margaret was married quietly to Ken in late December. Gloria and Tony shared their first family Christmas with Michael and Ma at Longueville Hall. Molly and Jim joined them too and it was almost like old times, except for the fact that Imogen and Shirley were missing. Nevertheless, it was still a happy time for them all as they watched Michael's eyes grow round with joy and wonder at the glitter and presents. Then, in the first week of the New Year, Gloria was notified by post that Michael was to have his operation at last.

She and Tony drove up to Great Ormond Street with him on a cold blustery day in late January. Unaware of the coming ordeal he and his parents faced, he chattered

435

happily to them all the way, while Gloria tried to hide the cold fear that clutched her heart. Had fate smiled too kindly on her these past months? Was she about to pay the price of happiness yet again? Tony was beside her now to share the anxiety. But she wasn't sure that even that would be enough to sustain her if she lost Michael now after all they'd both been through.

Chapter Nineteen

Give Me Yesterday had enjoyed good business in the West End. They had played to packed houses ever since opening night, but the theatre was booked for a new production and already the management was faced with the decision either to find a new venue or take the play on tour.

As usual at this stage, Paul had lost interest. He was well into writing a new play and utterly absorbed in his work. Leonie too was becoming bored and restless. The legitimate theatre was all very well but she missed the acclaim that her wartime singing had brought her. Peter Jason had recently received an exciting offer for her to tour Australia. There would be a series of concerts at which she would revive her recorded wartime favourites and a couple of guest appearances on TV shows. She hadn't done any TV before and she was tempted to accept. The only thing that stopped her was Paul. When he was working he neglected himself terribly. Since they'd been together she'd discovered things about herself that she had never suspected before. She actually liked looking after him and organising his disorganised life, soothing him when he was tired and frustrated and making sure he got enough to eat. Ever since they had parted during the filming of *Joy in the Morning*, she had been trying to persuade him that it would be a good idea for them to marry, but Paul simply laughed the idea off, refusing to believe she was serious. She was pretty sure there was no one else and he still insisted that Shirley had meant nothing to him. She was fairly confident that she was the only woman in his life and that he needed her. For the moment, she told herself, that would have to be enough. Part of Paul's attraction was his unpredictability. If she were to go on the extended Australian tour, however, things might well be different. And so Leonie kept the tour offer to herself. It might yet prove to be an effective trump card.

The news that Tony was to marry Gloria and, furthermore, that they had a child had shaken her to the core. How could that common little slut have worked for her; lived in her flat and accepted a salary from her when all the time she'd been sleeping with Tony behind her back for years? They said that the quiet ones were the worst, but really – Gloria of all people! She had always known that Tony had questionable taste, but she could only imagine that he'd been feeling particularly deprived when he'd taken that little guttersnipe to bed. Apparently the child they had spawned had something the matter with it – probably the result of a botched abortion attempt. Well, it was no more than the pair of them deserved. Clearly he would never have considered marrying her if it hadn't been for his accident, she told herself with a bitter little smile. The way he looked now he was lucky that even Gloria was willing to take him on. They were just a couple of panic-stricken people, clutching desperately at their last chance.

But although Leonie was unaware of it, there was trouble brewing. Paul was far from happy or contented with their arrangement and her complacency was about to suffer a severe setback. It was on her birthday, the last day of January, that things came to a head between them. She had instructed Paul to pick her up at the theatre after the show and take her out to dinner. When he was not in her dressing room when she came down after the final curtain, she rang the flat but there was no reply. Thinking that he must be on his way, she changed and waited. By the time an hour had passed with no sign of him and still no reply to the telephone, her temper was simmering dangerously.

She went home in a cab only to find Paul sitting in the study tapping away furiously at the typewriter. A cigarette dangled from the corner of his mouth and the ashtray on the desk overflowed with stubs. He wore his dressing gown and there was twenty-four hours' stubble on his face.

Standing in the doorway, she unleashed her fury. 'So *this* is where you are. Do you realise that I've been sitting waiting for you this past hour? We had a table booked at the Café Royal for ten thirty.'

Unruffled, Paul glanced at his watch. 'God, is that the time? I'll get ready. They won't mind if we're a bit late.'

'A *bit late*? By the time you're ready it'll be after midnight. I've been ringing till I'm blue in the face. Why didn't you answer the phone?'

He shrugged. 'You know what I'm like when I'm working. I didn't even hear it.'

'Well, if you think I'm going out now you can think again.'

'Act III is coming along so well that everything else just went out of my head,' he said coolly. 'So if you really don't want to go out, I'll carry on. After all, we can go tomorrow, can't we?'

'No, we can't,' she snapped. 'I'm sick and tired of taking second place to your work, Paul. I wait on you hand and foot, care for your every need, yet you can't even put yourself out for me on my birthday.'

He sighed. 'I've said I'm sorry. I can't do more. Make up your mind, but don't stand there nagging like a fishwife. It's tedious and boring.'

His calm, unrepentant attitude infuriated her. Coming into the room, she slammed the door behind her and stood facing him, her eyes flashing. 'Tedious and *boring*, is it? Who the bloody hell do you think you are? I've had about enough of playing mother to you, wiping your nose, bolstering your inflated little ego and telling you a hundred times a day that you're a sodding genius. You don't seem to realise that I have a career too. I wasn't going to tell you, but I've had the offer of an Australian tour. Peter keeps asking me when I'm going to make up my mind. All that's holding me back is *you*.'

His expression hardened. 'Wait a minute, let's get this straight, Leonie; I'm not holding you or anyone else back. You know damned well that ever since my divorce my maxim has been; Travel light, travel free. It was only at your insistence that I moved in here with you. Now, if you've had a good offer, then for Christ's sake take it. I don't want you for ever whining on about all you gave up for me, like some snivelling suburban housewife.'

'I *see*. So that's all the thanks I get, is it?'

'I think it's fair enough. We've been good together a lot of the time. I've written good parts for you. You've played them well. Some of the time it's even worked, our living together. But there comes a time when things get too demanding – claustrophobic. If you want to know, I think the time has come for a break.'

Leonie stared at him, sitting there so calm and so cold, this man she had given so much of herself to – her mind, her body, her compassion – far more than she'd ever given Tony. And now he was tossing her aside with as little thought as he'd give to a page of his writing that hadn't worked. After all the time they'd been together, how could he be so casual about breaking with her? Suspicion stirred in the back of her mind. Was it possible that he had someone else? Had she perhaps been here tonight – under her own roof? Was that why he hadn't been available to answer the phone? 'All right, Paul, who is she?' she demanded. 'Don't tell me there isn't anyone. I know you better than that. You can't do without a woman in your life. When I was away on location you even took up with that child half your age.'

'There's no one. And who's this *child* you're talking about?' He began to laugh, heating her temper to boiling point. 'I must say, this is the first time I've been accused of child molesting.'

'You know bloody well who I'm talking about.' She hissed at him like a feral cat, the hair on the back of her neck prickling as it rose. 'And even after that night when I

440

found the two of you together it wasn't over, was it? You'd have put her in the play – you'd have risked your reputation – everything to have the little tart around. You'd have done it too if she hadn't gone off to the job in Birmingham.'

He spun round, his brows meeting in a fearsome frown. 'Do you think I don't know it was you who engineered that, Leonie? Do you really imagine that I haven't been onto your manipulative, devious little mind right from the first? I knew you'd wangled Shirley that tuppeny-hapenny job in rep to stop her getting the part I wanted her to have.'

Her mouth dropped open. 'You knew – how?'

'Never mind. It doesn't matter now.' He laughed wryly. 'And even if I were second-guessing you've just confirmed it for me, haven't you? Sometimes you're not as clever as you think you are, Leonie.'

She stepped away, biting her tongue for allowing herself to fall into his trap. 'I was only saving you from making a fool of yourself,' she said scathingly. 'You'd been seen together. People were beginning to talk. Someone had to get you out of her clutches.'

'Out of hers and into *yours*, is that what you're saying?' Suddenly his temper got the better of him and he sprang to his feet to grasp her by the shoulders. 'All this is down to sheer, raw jealousy, isn't it? You were jealous of her youth, her looks and her vitality – *and* her talent, of course.' He shook his head. 'Who do you think you're kidding, Leonie? You're as transparent as a pane of glass.' He stared down at her, his eyes like burning coals. 'This birthday you're making such a fuss about, which one is it, eh?' he taunted. 'You'd have me believe it's your thirty-fifth, but it's really your fortieth, isn't it? And you thought you'd fooled me about that, too. I'm surprised you actually wanted to celebrate it.'

The colour drained from her face. 'You *bastard*! You cruel bastard.' She squirmed in his grasp, wincing as his fingers bit deeper into her flesh. 'Let me go, you swine. You're hurting.'

441

'First tell me how you fixed it. Come on, let's have it, Leonie. It'll be interesting to see if you can be straight for once.'

'I went to see that drama teacher of hers,' she said between clenched teeth. 'Magda Jayne or whatever the woman's ridiculous name is. She told me Shirley had had an audition with Gerald Maddox, but that he hadn't given her a job. Gerald owed me a favour from way back, so I asked him to make her an offer. Is that so dreadful?'

'I see. I made it easy for you, didn't I?' He let her go abruptly. 'You told me she had no talent, that she wasn't ready to appear in any theatre. If you really thought that, why saddle Maddox with a dud actress?'

'So as not to spoil your play, of course,' she said, rubbing her bruised shoulders. 'I did it for you. Because at the time you were too damned stupidly besotted to judge properly.'

'Oh, how *kind* and thoughtful,' he said sarcastically.

'Anyway, I hear that Shirley's still with the Mask Players and doing quite well. I probably did her a favour.'

'Don't kid yourself. She'd have had her name in lights by now with my help and you know it. But you weren't going to risk that, were you, Leonie? You got her a piddling little job in the provinces, one you knew she'd jump at. You put her on the road. Well, now I'm putting *you* on the road.' His voice was as cold and sharp as steel. 'You can go off on your Australian tour – or a tour of hell for all I care. I want you out of my life just as soon as you like.' He got up and slammed the cover onto his typewriter, then he strode out of the room. Crestfallen, she followed him into the bedroom, where he had begun to throw his clothes into a suitcase.

'Paul, wait – don't be so hasty. I was only thinking of you. I meant it for the best, honestly. Sleep on it. We can work something out.'

'I've already worked it out,' he said.

'You won't get far without me,' she flung at him. 'You'll never make it on your own. Who's going to make sure you eat properly and see that you have clean clothes to wear?

442

Who's going to chase away unwanted visitors so that you can work in peace? You'll soon find out how hard I've worked for you.'

He spun round to look at her and she shrank from the look of sheer dislike in his eyes. 'If you really want to know, Leonie, I'm sick and tired of being treated like a pet poodle and told what to do and having my friends chosen for me. It's *over* – understand? Neither of us is suited to sharing our lives. I need freedom and space, you need to stifle and possess, like – like a bloody boaconstrictor. We're incompatible. It's time you faced it.'

In the hospital waiting room Tony sat holding Gloria's hand. The sister on the surgical ward had begged her to go home and get some rest, assuring her that they would telephone the moment Michael was out of surgery, but she was adamant. She wanted to stay, to be as near as possible. 'He might need me,' she said over and over. 'If he asked for me and I wasn't here, I'd never forgive myself.'

Tony felt helpless. He didn't know what to say to her, and in a way he felt left out. He was anxious, too. Only now did he realise what Gloria had been through during the past four years and how much the child meant to her. Because of the war she had missed much of Shirley's childhood and circumstances had forced her to allow someone else to bring Michael up. She'd missed so much of his precious babyhood. It would be too cruel if he were to be taken from her now. The surgeon had assured them that although a valvotomy was a delicate procedure, it had so far proved effective and successful. Michael was a strong child. He saw no reason for concern, he kept telling her. But in spite of Tony's repeated attempts to comfort her she seemed far away, unreachable as she sat next to him, staring into space. Even the contact of their hands was not enough to bridge the gulf between them.

The hours ticked by. He left her to go to the canteen and brought back a tray of tea and toast for her, which she left untouched. Finally, unable to bear it any longer, he said, 'Gloria, for heaven's sake, let me in. Don't shut me out like this. He's mine, too, remember. It isn't my fault that I haven't known him from birth.'

She turned her head to look at him, almost as though she were noticing him for the first time.

He took both her ice-cold hands in his. 'Gloria, I've only known Michael for a few weeks, it's true, but the bond is there between us. It was there from the very first moment. I love him. I love you too. It's the kind of love I thought would never come to me again. I couldn't bear it if anything happened to take that love away from me now.'

For a moment she stared at him, then her face suddenly crumpled and she was in his arms, sobbing out all the tension she had held in. 'I'm sorry, darling. It's just that I've been on my own so long. Everything I've gone through, I've gone through alone. Putting up a wall of defence has grown to be a habit.'

He held her close. 'It's a habit you can drop from now on.'

'I've been thinking about Shirley such a lot lately,' she confessed. 'I wish now that I'd answered her letter. I should have tried harder to understand what she did. I feel partly to blame – and I miss her so *much*, Tony. But she's gone from me now, perhaps for ever. She's a grown woman with a life of her own. She doesn't need me any more.'

'You have me now,' Tony said quietly. 'And Michael.'

She looked at him. 'I know, darling. I'm so lucky to have you. You'll never know how grateful I am.'

'I want to be a comfort to you – to share it all,' he said, stroking her hair. 'The worrying times, the sadness as well as the happiness. That's how it's going to be from now on, I promise you. Michael will come through, you'll see. He *has* to.'

She found that his cheeks were wet too and she held him close as their tears mingled. He'd been through so much himself, and now he was suffering again for Michael – as much as she was. How could she have been so thoughtless? 'Of course he will,' she whispered.

He held her away from him to look into her eyes. 'The moment he's fully recovered we'll be married,' he said. 'Let's set a date here and now. It'll give us something positive to look forward to and work towards – a goal.'

'All right.' She smiled. 'May? Michael should be fine by then, surely. The first of May. I love the spring.'

He kissed her. 'May Day it is. And I'll –' He stopped as the door opened and Sister came in.

'Mr Harvey-Moreton will see you in my office if you'd like to come this way.'

Gloria gasped and rose shakily to her feet, her heart thudding in her breast. 'Michael – is the operation over? Is he all right?'

'Please don't be worried.' Sister smiled. 'The operation is over and everything went to plan. But Mr Harvey-Moreton would like to tell you all about it himself, so if you'd like to come with me . . .'

It was through Imogen that Shirley heard of her half-brother's successful operation. Apparently she had received the letter on the last leg of the Company's tour of America and had written straight away to Shirley to say how pleased and relieved she was that Michael could begin to live the normal life none of them had dared to hope for.

I was so sorry not to be able to visit him, or to accept your invitation to the wedding on 1 May. It's sure to be a happy occasion and I know that Daddy and Gloria will be happy together. Best of all is that it makes you and me members of the same family. Have you realised, Shirley – we share a little half-brother and Daddy is now your stepfather? Isn't that fun? We've always been close, but now we can actually call ourselves sisters – well, stepsisters anyway. By the way, my other half-brother, Marcus, came to see me the other day. We got along well together but it was strange to think that we'd never set eyes on each other in all these years. You must write and tell me all about the wedding –

every detail, since Charles and I won't be able to attend. . . .

Clearly she had no idea that in spite of the letters she'd written, Shirley hadn't heard of her mother's impending wedding or of Michael's operation either.

Shirley had been with the Mask Players just ten months. Her original contract had been extended at the end of the initial three months. When Gerald Maddox had asked her into his office one morning the previous November after the morning rehearsal, she had been dreadfully afraid she was going to be given notice, but to her relief Gerald had begun by telling her how pleased he was with her work.

'I must admit that I had reservations when Leonie Swann asked me to give you a break,' he said. 'I know her of old and she's a devious woman. I had an idea that there was some ulterior motive behind her insistence that you should be given a chance to prove your ability.'

Shirley stared at him. 'Leonie asked you? I had no idea.'

'But you do know her?'

'Oh, yes. I was evacuated to her country house during the war. I grew up with her daughter Imogen, but I wouldn't have thought . . .' She trailed off, remembering that the night Leonie had walked in on her and Paul, he had mentioned a part for her in his play. She began to see the obvious reason for Leonie's assumed altruism.

'Well, perhaps she's mellowed with age, or perhaps I'm maligning her unfairly,' Gerald said. 'Whatever her motive, she did both of us a favour. You've worked really hard and now I'd like to offer you a twelve-month contract with the company. Bernice Selby is leaving, which means you'll take her place and I'll engage another ASM.' He smiled. 'All those juvenile leads and character parts you've been longing to tackle will fall to you now, and of course it will mean a small salary increase too.' He looked up at her. 'Well, how does that sound to you?'

'It sounds wonderful.' Shirley felt herself flush with pleasure. 'Thank you, Gerald, I'll do my best. I promise I won't let you down.'

'I know you won't and I'm looking forward to seeing you blossom as an actress.' Gerald smiled at her and held out his hand. 'Welcome as a permanent member of the Mask Players, Shirley. And good luck.'

It was the proudest day of her life and Shirley reflected later that if only it hadn't been for the rift with her family she would have been completely happy. However, she knew now, as she always had, that she had done the right thing in not marrying Dave. She had written to him again, apologising for walking out on him but pointing out that it was the best thing she could have done for both of them. He had replied promptly, generously forgiving her and agreeing with her that their marriage would probably never have worked. It was a friendly letter, full of news about the shop and his job. He ended by saying that he would be pleased to see her whenever she was in London and that he wished her the best of luck.

In view of this she could see no good reason for Gloria to stay angry with her. She'd written to her at Rook Cottage several times, but never received any reply. It was so unfair. She could understand Ma's disapproval. She'd never been in favour of her taking up a career in the theatre, but Gloria had steered her towards it from baby-hood, so why was she so angry now that she'd achieved her aim? She longed for her mother to see her play a major role – yearned for her approval and pleasure. Once they'd been so close, but now they had grown so far apart that it seemed almost impossible to remember the special relationship they had once shared. She'd even had to find out through Imogen that Tony was Michael's father.

When Gerald Maddox scheduled a run of R. C. Sherriff's all-male play *Journey's End* for the last two weeks in June, the female members of the company knew that they would be getting a week off. It did not take Shirley long to decide what she would do with her holiday. She would go to London and try to get herself an agent. She would see the latest West End plays, too – as many as she could squeeze in – and, if she could summon up enough courage, she would go to Whitechapel and try to make her peace with Ma.

During her ten months in Birmingham she'd had little on which to spend her money. She had saved quite a bit and she booked herself into an inexpensive hotel in Woburn Place for the week. It was close to the Underground and not too far from the heart of things. On the first morning she went to see Peter Jason. He was the only agent she knew personally, having met him a couple of times when he had visited Tony and Leonie at Houlton. She climbed the stairs to his office in Charing Cross Road and asked the receptionist somewhat hesitantly if he would give her a few minutes of his time. The girl went away and, to Shirley's surprise, came back to say that Peter would see her. He stood up and greeted her warmly when she was ushered into his office.

'It's Shirley, isn't it?' He smilingly indicated a chair. 'I'd never have known you, of course. The last time I saw you you were just a little girl.'

Shirley felt at ease with the kindly grey-haired man at once and when he agreed to represent her she could not disguise her delight. 'Thank you very much, Mr Jason. I must admit that I thought it would be quite hard to get an agent to take me on,' she confessed.

Peter smiled at her. 'You're getting a good grounding with the Mask Players,' he said. 'I'm sure I'll be able to get you plenty of work once your contract there expires.' He rang through to the outer office for coffee and sat back in his chair, regarding his delightful new client with interest. 'Tell me, how did you get the job with Gerald Maddox? An audition?'

Shirley smiled. 'Yes, I did an audition for him.' She did not tell him that Leonie had engineered the job offer. After all, she had proved her own worth since.

'I expect you'll be going to see *Give Me Yesterday* while you're in town. It's still playing, though with an almost entirely different cast. Leonie has gone on an extended tour of Australia, but I expect you've heard all about that.'

'No, I hadn't, actually. I'm a bit out of touch since I've been in Birmingham.' She glanced at him. 'Have you seen anything of Tony?'

'Tony Darrent?' He smiled. 'I was at the wedding, of course. He seems to have got over his accident extremely well and he looked very happy with his new bride.' He frowned. 'Wait a minute – aren't you related to her?'

'She's my mother.'

Peter looked surprised and a little embarrassed. 'Oh. But you . . .'

'I wasn't invited to the wedding,' Shirley put in quickly. 'When I took the job with the Mask Players I upset my mother by walking out on the man I was to have married.'

'I see. Well, it happens in the best of families,' he said dismissively. 'I'm sure it will blow over.'

'Is Tony working again yet?'

'Oh, yes. He's doing quite a lot of radio drama now. The Third Programme are planning a classical season and he's been very much involved with that.' The receptionist came in with coffee and as she withdrew Peter said: 'As you're family, so to speak, I'll let you into a little secret; I've offered Tony a partnership with this agency. I think it might be something he'd enjoy. He's still thinking about it as a future possibility but I feel confident that he'll accept eventually.'

Shirley smiled. 'That's wonderful.'

'Completely selfish motives as far as I'm concerned,' Peter said. 'I've only a few more years to go before I retire and I'd like to think there'd be someone like Tony to carry on. He knows most of our clients personally and an agent who is also an actor is a tremendous bonus.'

When they'd finished their coffee Peter noted all Shirley's particulars and enclosed them in a file along with the photograph she'd brought. 'I'll make the trip up to Birmingham to see you work,' he said.

Shirley's eyes sparkled. 'Will you really?' She opened her handbag and eagerly searched for a programme of the

Mask Theatre's forthcoming attractions. 'We're doing *The Corn Is Green* in three weeks' time,' she said, passing it across the desk to him. 'I'm playing Bessie Watty. We start rehearsals next week. I'm really looking forward to that.'

Peter smiled at the refreshing glow of enthusiasm in the youthful face opposite him. 'Then that's when I'll come,' he said, making a note on his desk diary.

Outside in the street Shirley felt as though she walked on air. She had an *agent*. One of the best agents in London, too. Now she was really on her way.

At the shabby apartment house in Whitechapel she was told by a neighbour that Ma had left some months ago.

'Can you give me the address?' Shirley asked. 'Has she moved to the new block? She was promised a flat there.'

The woman shook her head. 'Bless you, no, love. She's gone to live in the country with 'er daughter. Some village in Northamptonshire, or some such place. I'd a nice card from 'er at Christmas. Seems she's got 'er own place – a real thatched cottage. Roses round the door an' all, I shouldn't wonder. All right for some, ain't it?'

So Ma had gone to live at Rook Cottage? All the people she loved were together now. Only she was left out. Hurt sat like a sharp-edged stone in Shirley's chest, depressing her deeply. She went back to the hotel, determined to enjoy the rest of her short holiday in spite of it all.

She went to see Magda, who insisted on making coffee and sitting her down to relate all that she'd been doing. The studio Shirley had once found so exotic now looked shabby and vaguely pathetic. But the welcome was warm and Magda was delighted to hear all her news, especially that she'd been promoted to a permanent place in the company.

'You remind me so much of myself at your age, Shirley,' she said. 'There'll be no war to ruin your career before it gets off the ground, please God. I shall watch your progress with great interest and pride. You won't lose touch with me, will you?'

Shirley kissed her. 'Of course I won't. If it hadn't been for you, none of it would have been possible.'

That afternoon she paid a brief visit to Dave. She had to steel herself for the visit, half afraid that seeing her might upset him. Yet she was loath to go back to Birmingham without trying to put right the wrong she'd done him.

When she walked into the shop the staff eyed her with a mixture of curiosity and resentment. Most of them had been working there when she was, and they returned her greeting with hostile, challenging eyes. But Dave was his old self. When he saw her his eyes lit up in the familiar smile and he lifted the counter flap and called to Mary to take over for him. Upstairs in the flat they were to have shared he made tea for her, asking about her new life and her budding career with genuine interest.

'Now, tell me what you're planning for your week off. I expect you'll be off to Houlton to see your mum and gran.'

She looked at her hands. 'No. There's still bad feeling between us, Dave. They were very angry with me for going off as I did. I've written to Gloria several times but she hasn't replied. Seems she can't forgive me.'

He looked troubled. 'I'm sorry to hear that, Shirl. I'd no idea.' There was an awkward pause, then he pushed a plate of chocolate biscuits towards her. 'Come on, eat up,' he urged her with a smile. 'So, have you been to the theatre?'

'I'm going every night,' she told him, seizing the chance to change the subject.

'And Hampstead Heath? The funfair – are you going there too?'

She shook her head. 'Fairs are no fun by yourself. Besides, there are so many plays I want to see. The rest of my days are going to be full.'

'Oh, but you can't go back without a visit to the fair,' Dave said. 'What are you doing on Saturday?'

'Well . . .'

'You'll be cross-eyed with staring at a stage by then. Come up the Heath with me – just for old times' sake?'

She looked at him with new eyes. He had developed a new assertiveness since he'd been his own boss. Once he'd have been tentative and shy about asking her, especially after what had happened. Now he looked as though he could take her refusal in his stride with no ill feelings. This new attitude took her off guard and she laughed. 'Okay then. Thank you, Dave. I'll look forward to it.'

He smiled. 'Good. So will I. I'll pick you up at your hotel about six. I've got a little car now. It's only second-hand, but it gets me around. We'll have a bite to eat first.' Again it was a positive statement rather than a question.

As he let her out of the rear entrance of the shop, she looked at him and said: 'You've changed, Dave.'

His eyebrows rose in surprise. 'I have? In what way?'

She lifted her shoulders. 'I don't know. You're more grown-up. I think *sophisticated* is the word I'm looking for.'

He laughed. 'Sounds much too grand for me. You've changed too, Shirl.'

'Have I?'

'Oh, yes. You've developed a kind of gloss.' He nodded towards the shop. 'The girls in the shop saw it. Didn't you see the way they looked at you?'

'I thought that was resentment.'

'Envy, more like. One look at you and anyone can see that you're confident – fulfilled. You look as though you know who you are and where you're going.' He smiled a little wistfully. 'I could never have made you look like that.'

She bit her lip. 'Dave . . . I . . .'

He held up his hand. 'No, don't say it. That's all over, no reproaches. Now we're both free to enjoy being friends.' He opened the door for her. 'Enjoy the rest of your holiday, Shirl. See you on Saturday.'

During the months she'd been away, London had lost its tired look. Clearly much hard work had been put into making the city bright and clean again. Many of the bomb sites were still there, but they'd been tidied up and fenced off and new buildings had begun to spring up to take the place of those that had been bombed.

She spent the rest of the week going to the theatre, in some cases twice in one day; queuing for the gallery to make her spending money go as far as possible, she saw all the latest West End productions. Sitting on her hard seat high up in the 'gods', she took notes and learned as much as she could from the performances of all the actors, male and female, old and young alike. On her last evening she treated herself to a ticket for the upper circle at Wyndham's to see Paul Winspear's play *Give Me Yesterday*. She enjoyed it very much, taking special interest in the actress who played the part she imagined that she herself might have played. It was a very good part and, as the play progressed, part of her hated Leonie for doing her out of it. But on deeper reflection, she realised that playing in the West End so early in her career might easily have led her down a blind alley. At the Mask Theatre over the past year she had learned much about the theatre in general. She'd had to turn her hand to many other things as well as understudying and playing walk-ons. She'd made coffee and swept up; she'd helped with stage management and props, sat in the prompt corner with the script, even done a little scenery painting. Once she'd assisted the electrician when his lad was ill with flu. Most important of all, she had learned how very *little* she knew. If she'd gone straight into Paul's play she might never have developed the humility that every true performer needs. She might have grown conceited and cut herself off from much valuable knowledge and experience. Maybe Leonie had inadvertently done her a favour after all.

When the curtain came down on the last act, she hung back in the auditorium after the audience had filed out, drinking in the atmosphere of the theatre with its traditional gilt and plush decor. Maybe one day she would be appearing here herself, she told herself with a little frisson of excitement.

She was just walking out into the corridor when the pass door leading to the backstage area opened. Out of the corner of her eye she saw a tall man in evening dress, and when she heard him call her name she turned.

'By all that's wonderful – *Shirley*.'

She turned to see Paul Winspear coming towards her, a smile on his face. It was too late to escape so she decided to face out the unwelcome confrontation as coolly as she could. 'Hello, Paul.'

'What are you doing here? I hope you're not "resting".' He grasped both her hands.

'No, I'm not resting. As a matter of fact I'm a permanent member of the company now.'

'At the Mask?'

'Yes. I had a week out so I came up to see some shows and to get myself an agent.'

'And were you successful?'

'I certainly was. Peter Jason has taken me on.'

His eyes widened. 'Peter? My word, you won't regret that. He's one of the best.'

She couldn't be sure that he wasn't mocking her – stringing her along. 'He's coming up to see me working in a couple of weeks' time,' she said. 'We're doing *The Corn Is Green*. I'm playing Bessie.' She was suddenly aware that she sounded like a bragging juvenile and felt her cheeks redden embarrassingly. 'Look, I'm sorry, I've got to go now.' She turned but he took her arm.

'Hang on. Don't run off like that.' His eyes swept over her, taking in the slender figure in the stylish black suit with its pencil-slim skirt and nipped-in jacket, the skilful subtlety of her make-up and the new short, crisp hairstyle. He had thought her attractive before but now she was positively beautiful. 'You haven't told me what you thought of the show yet.'

'Oh, I enjoyed it very much, Paul. It's even better than *Joy in the Morning*.'

'I'm glad you thought so. Look, have you got a dinner date?'

She hesitated. 'Well, er, yes,' she lied, peering at her watch. 'I'm sorry. I'll have to run. It was nice seeing you, Paul – bye.'

'Goodbye, Shirley.' He watched her go thoughtfully. 'Or should that be *au revoir*?' he added quietly.

Hampstead Heath was sheer delight. Shirley and Dave dined at a little Greek restaurant first, then drove out to

Hampstead. It took Shirley back to her childhood when she saw the coloured lights twinkling in the trees and felt the infectious excitement of the throng of people making their way towards the funfair. They walked around, looking at everything, and tried their hands at various sideshows. Dave won a giant teddybear at the rifle range and a box of chocolates at dart throwing. They saw a young girl packed in a coffin filled with ice, and ate candyfloss and toffee apples with childish enjoyment. Then there were the rides: the breath-taking Big Dipper, and the Dragon ride. Dave seemed to have endless energy, throwing himself enthusiastically into the spirit of the fairground, till at last Shirley had to beg for a break. He looked at his watch.

'Good heavens, I hadn't realised how the time had flown,' he said. 'You're right. It is time we took a break.'

Although there was a stall nearby, selling coffee and doughnuts, he led her towards a café on the edge of the fairground with umbrella-shaded tables around it. 'This looks just the place,' he said, pulling out a chair for her at one of the tables. 'Sit there and get your breath back while I get the coffee.'

She sat looking round her. The dusk was deepening now, and the brightly coloured lights that were strung everywhere glittered and shone. The funfair was coming into its own special magic time of day. Shirley drank it all in; the brassy music and the lights, the colour, the noise, laughter and screams of delight from the more daring rides. She breathed in the scent of sawdust, toffee and frying onions. Almost *anything* could happen on a night like this, she told herself happily. She was so glad she'd agreed to let Dave bring her. It was the perfect ending to her week's holiday.

Suddenly she looked up to see a strange man standing in front of her. He was smiling. 'Hello, Shirley. It's good to see you.'

'Oh – I'm sorry but . . .' She half rose, apprehensively, then something in his smile froze her blood. It was *Tony*. She hadn't seen him since his accident. She knew he'd been burned badly and had plastic surgery, but she hadn't been prepared for a change like this. The handsome features that had claimed the hearts of millions of film- and theatre-goers were blurred and distorted, altering his expression completely. If he had not spoken to her she would never have recognised him. Quickly she gathered her control. She mustn't let him see how shocked she was. Apart from his scars he looked well and happy, and infinitely pleased to see her. She smiled and held out her hands.

'Tony! What a surprise! How lovely to see you after all this time.'

The hands that grasped hers were scarred and cruelly misshapen, but they were warm and pressed hers with genuine affection. 'How are you?' she asked him. 'And what are you doing here?'

'I'm here with my family,' he said proudly, turning slightly to look behind him.

Shirley followed his gaze to where Gloria stood on the fringe of the tables. She was holding the hand of a small boy who was hopping excitedly from one foot to the other. Shirley let go of Tony's hands and walked slowly across to them, her eyes fixed on the two figures, almost afraid to blink in case they disappeared. 'Gloria,' she said, her throat tight. 'Oh, *Glor.*'

Gloria dropped the child's hand and gathered Shirley into her arms. 'Oh, Shirl, love, it's so good to see you. I've missed you so *much.*' They looked at each other, almost too full for words. Tears shone in Gloria's eyes as she said: 'Just look at you. You look so grown-up and so lovely.'

Shirley laughed shakily. 'And you look happy. You and Tony are married, I heard about it from Imo. And little Michael had his operation.' She bent to hug the be- wildered boy. 'Hello, Michael. Remember me?' She looked at Gloria. 'Is he really all right?'

'He's fine. Just fine, thank God.'

'Oh, Glor – why did you stay so angry with me? Why didn't you answer my letters?'

Gloria frowned. 'Letters? I only got the one – just after you left. I'm sorry, love but I didn't know how to answer it. I hoped you'd write again, but . . .'

'But I *did*. I wrote several more, to Rook Cottage. I tried to –' Shirley broke off, remembering the other time when Gloria had failed to contact her. The same person must be responsible for intercepting the letters. They looked at each other, both arriving at the thought simultaneously. In unison they said: 'Ma.' And both burst out laughing.

They shared a table. Dave brought a tray of coffees and a lemonade for Michael, who was preoccupied with the teddy Dave had won. They toasted each other, laughing and talking, trying confusedly to catch up on all their news at once. Then Shirley said:

'I can't get over the coincidence of meeting you here like this.' She broke off as she saw Gloria and Dave exchange glances. 'Dave – it was you!' She looked at Dave. 'You fixed it all.'

He held up his hands. 'Guilty, I'm afraid. I couldn't let it go on. I knew there had to be some kind of misunderstanding. I telephoned Gloria at Houlton and arranged for us all to meet here this evening.'

'Tony was already up in town, making recordings,' Gloria explained. 'We'd been promising Michael a trip to Hampstead Heath and this seemed a good opportunity. Tony stays at his flat in Earls Court when he's recording. I brought Michael up by train this morning.'

Shirley pulled the little boy onto her lap. 'It's a late night for you. Aren't you tired?'

He shook his head, grinning up at her with wide blue eyes. 'I went to bed this afternoon, so I can stay up all night now.' He treated her to his most winsome of smiles. 'Can I have this teddy, please?'

'Of course you can.' Shirley hugged him. 'If I'd known I was going to see you I'd have brought a present for you anyway.'

'When do you have to go back?' Tony asked. 'Can you come back to Houlton with us for a couple of days?'

Shirley shook her head regretfully. 'I must go back tomorrow. Rehearsals start on Monday. It's my first big part.'

'But you'll come home soon?' Gloria said eagerly. 'Just as soon as you can – please. Tony is away a lot and I get a bit lonely at times. It'd be lovely to have some time together again, just you and me.'

'I'll come. But you'd better prepare Ma,' Shirley warned. 'She might not want to see me.'

'After what she did with those letters she can hardly argue,' Gloria laughed. 'I hardly see her myself nowadays. You wouldn't believe it, but she's become a real countrywoman. She's joined the WI and the Mothers' Union and she's become a keen gardener, too. Rook Cottage has never looked so pretty.'

'I'm glad she's happy,' Shirley said. 'Maybe she'll find it in her heart to forgive me.'

The four said good night at the park entrance. Michael rode on Tony's shoulders, thumb in mouth and heavy-eyed with sleepiness, still clutching his teddy. Shirley stood on tiptoe to kiss him and ruffle the curly hair.

'Night-night, darling. See you soon.'

He gave her a sleepy smile and took his thumb out of his mouth briefly to answer her. 'Night-night.'

There were hugs all round, then they went their separate ways, promising again to get together just as soon as they could.

In the car Shirley looked at Dave. 'Thank you for tonight, Dave. It was a wonderful surprise.'

He grinned. 'It's not often I get the chance to play Santa Claus. I enjoyed every minute.'

'You're a good man, Dave.' After a moment's silence she said: 'Dave – are you happy?'

He turned to look at her briefly. ''Course I am. I've got a good job, better than I ever expected to get. My own home with all mod cons –'

'You know what I mean,' she interrupted.

He smiled. 'If you're asking me if I still carry a torch for you, as they say, the answer's no. I'll always admire you,

Shirl. I'll always be here as a friend for you, but as for the past – well, it's the past. As a matter of fact Mary and I are talking about making a go of it. She's a good girl. She likes the business and she's worked hard to help me. I reckon we're well suited to each other.'

'Didn't she mind about tonight?'

He shook his head. 'She trusts me. Besides, she knew I was planning to get you back together with your mum. She's all right, Mary.'

'You love her?'

'You know I've never been one for flowery talk, Shirl, but since you ask, yes, I love her. Best of all, she loves me – in a way that no one ever has before.'

Shirley blinked as tears filled her eyes. 'I'm glad. You deserve it, Dave.'

Looking out at the starlit summer sky she felt suddenly wistful. She had achieved her goal; she had her foot firmly on the first rung of the ladder of success. She was about to embark on her first major role, the chance she had prayed for to show her talent at its best. And tonight she had been reunited with her family. All her dreams were coming true. But seeing the way Gloria looked at Tony, clearly loving him now with all his scars as much as she did when he was acclaimed the most handsome man in the English theatre, and hearing the hidden emotion in Dave's voice when he talked about his Mary stirred an unfulfilled longing deep inside her. 'You haven't really lived until you've been truly in love,' Magda had once said. Shirley had thought she'd discovered love with Paul, but she knew now that what she had thought of as love had been purely physical. Their relationship had been ill-advised and had ended in hurt and betrayal. All she could say of it was that it had been useful experience to her as an actress. The real, true love that other people had was still as elusive to her as a will-o'-the-wisp.

But as she gazed out of the car window at the star-studded, velvet night she thought how wonderful it must be to love and be deeply, unselfishly loved in return. Would she ever know that love? Or must she resign herself to finding fulfilment in her career alone?

Chapter Twenty

Sitting in his seat in the front stalls of the Mask Theatre, Marcus Fane gazed up at the cast of *The Corn Is Green* as they lined up for the final curtain. But his eyes were on one member of the cast alone; the young woman who had played Bessie Watty. Not only had she given a captivating performance, but he thought she was quite the most beautiful girl he had ever seen. As the leading man led her forward to take a final bow, she seemed to smile straight into his eyes. He applauded enthusiastically, glancing at his companion.

'Wasn't she just great? I can't wait to meet her. Do you think you can fix it for me?'

'I should hope so,' his elderly companion replied with a smile. 'After all, I am her agent.'

Shirley took a last bow along with the rest of the cast before the curtain came down. It was Saturday night and the last performance of *The Corn Is Green*. She had enjoyed rapturous receptions every night and had loved the part of Bessie Watty, the brash cockney teenager. As she made her way to the dressing room she shared with Frances Moss, the middle-aged character actress who had played Miss Moffat, Jack Brown, the stage doorkeeper, stopped her in the corridor.

'There's a feller to see you, Miss Rayner,' he said. 'He says he wants to see you on business, but y'know what some of 'em are. Tell you any old yarn to get in.'

'Did he give a name?' Shirley asked.

'Yeah, but you know what my 'earin' is, I didn't catch it properly.' The little man frowned. 'Jacobs, Jansen – summat like that.'

Shirley's heart quickened. All week she'd been expecting Peter Jason to come and see the show, but he hadn't put in an appearance. By Saturday's matinee she had resigned herself to the fact that he hadn't been able to make it. 'Jason,' she said excitedly. 'Was it Jason?'

Jack nodded eagerly. 'Reckon that was it, miss.'

'He's my agent, Jack. Don't keep him standing at the stage door.'

'Sorry, miss. What d'you want me to tell 'im?'

'Ask him to give me ten minutes to change, then I'll meet him in the green room.'

'Right you are, Miss Rayner. Ten minutes it is.' He hurried off and Shirley turned and went into the dressing room.

Her fingers trembled as she took off her make-up and changed into cream slacks and a black corduroy shirt. Frances, watching shrewdly from her side of the room, cocked an enquiring eyebrow.

'Got a date, ducky?'

'My agent was in front,' Shirley said. 'He wants to see me. He promised he'd come up to see the show but I thought he'd forgotten.' She paused to look at herself in the mirror, suddenly besieged by doubts. Suppose it was bad news? Suppose he hadn't liked her performance and wanted to break it to her that he couldn't represent her after all? She turned to look at the older woman. 'Tell you what, Frannie, why don't you join us?'

'You and your *agent*?' Frances laughed. 'You must be joking, lovie. Neither of you will want an old ham like me hanging around mucking things up. He's probably about to make you the offer of a lifetime.' She had changed into her outdoor clothes and was hanging up her costume. Placing the wig she wore for the play carefully on its stand, she gave it a final tweak. 'Well, that lot can go back to Wardrobe. It's goodbye to old Moffat, poor old cow.' She began to put on her coat. 'I'm off,' she said. 'My landlady has invited me to supper. She says she's making steak-and-kidney pie and it's my favourite, so I mustn't be late.' She winked. 'When you get to my age the promise of a plate of steak-and-kidney pie is often the only thing that gets you through a performance by the last show, Saturday night.' She picked up her bags of shopping, done between shows, and bustled out of the room. 'Have a nice weekend, ducky. And break a leg with your agent. See you on Monday morning.' She paused in the doorway. 'It's a ten-o'clock call, Monday. Don't forget.' She said this every Saturday night without fail and Shirley smiled indulgently.

'I won't. Night, Frannie. Enjoy your steak-and-kidney.' High on adrenalin, and with the applause still ringing in her ears, Shirley wondered if she would ever get as blasé about her work as Frances. The older actress was brilliant at character parts like Miss Moffat and seemed to put so much of herself into her performances, yet the moment she was off stage she was herself again – grumbling about her landlady or planning a visit to the laundrette. It was as though she took off the character along with the costume.

Applying a dash of bright lipstick, Shirley picked up her bag and was about to leave the dressing room when there was a tap on the door. She opened it to find Peter Jason standing in the corridor.

'Peter. I was just on my way to meet you in the green room. Didn't Jack give you my message?'

'Yes, he did, but I'm not alone and there's something I wanted to ask you first.' He smiled at her. 'I enjoyed the show very much, Shirley. And I thought you were very good indeed.'

Shirley blushed with pleasure and relief. 'You *did*? I'm so glad. You can't go wrong with a play as well written as that, though, can you?'

Peter shook his head. 'Oh yes, you can,' he said. 'She's a flamboyant, character, the easiest of parts to overplay, but you played it with just the right balance. You never fell into the temptation to burlesque.'

'Thank you, Mr Jason.'

'Peter, please.' He peered round her into the room. 'May I come in, or is someone in there still changing?'

'Oh, no.' She held the door open, blushing at her own thoughtlessness. 'Do please come in. I'm afraid I can't offer you a drink.'

Peter shook his head. 'We'll go up to the green room in a moment. As I said, there's someone waiting to meet you. I just wanted to have a word with you first.'

Shirley swallowed hard. It sounded ominous. Perhaps his compliments had been the sugarcoating for a bitter pill he was about to hand her.

Peter sat down in the chair she pulled out for him. 'I'll come straight to the point. You know Paul Winspear's play *Give Me Yesterday*?'

'Yes, I saw it in London.'

'It has been decided to take the show on a tour of the provinces, but most of the cast have other commitments. How would you like to play the part of Jessica on that tour?'

'Oh!' Shirley stared at him with wide eyes. 'Oh, Mr Jason – er, Peter, I'd love to, but . . .'

'It's all right. I checked. Your contract here will have expired before the first rehearsal date. But anyway, I know Gerald would have released you.'

'When do you want me to come and audition?'

He smiled. 'We can dispense with that. As a matter of fact Winspear himself put your name forward. I believe you and he knew each other slightly.'

'Yes.'

'He tells me he met you through Leonie and that you met again briefly when you went to see the play in London the other week.'

'That's right.' A sudden thought struck Shirley and she looked at him apprehensively. 'How much will Paul have to do with the production?'

'Nothing. He's working on a new play at the moment, and when it goes into rehearsal he'll be very much involved with that.'

'Is it Paul you've got with you?'

Peter laughed. 'Good heavens, no. As a matter of fact it's a very eager young American actor called Marcus Fane, over here to get some stage experience. He's going to take over the role of Jason Hamilton, the young artist in the play, so you'll be working together. That's why I invited him to come up with me. He enjoyed the show enormously. I think I can safely say that he's already a fan of yours and he can't wait to meet you.'

'Oh, that's nice,' Shirley said inadequately. She felt slightly unreal, as though she were dreaming it all. She had waited so long for something like this to happen; prayed and fantasised about it, but now that it had she couldn't seem to react as she should.

Peter stood up. 'Right then, that's settled. I'll draw up a contract for you and make all the necessary arrangements with the management. I'll send everything to you for signing in due course.' He held out his hand. 'Right, shall we go up to the green room and have a celebratory drink? If I know Marc, he'll be getting restless by now.'

Upstairs in the green room Peter led the way across the crowded bar to where a tall, loose-limbed young man sat on one of the stools at the bar. 'Marc, I'd like you to meet Shirley Rayner,' he said. 'Shirley, this is Marcus Fane.'

He wore casual clothes, slacks and a white polo-neck sweater under a cinnamon-brown corduroy jacket. He uncoiled his long length from the bar stool and turned a pair of startlingly blue eyes on Shirley.

'Hi, Shirley.' He held out his hand. 'Great to meet you.' His voice was deep and musical, with an attractive hint of a West Coast accent. 'I enjoyed the show very much.'

For a moment she was taken aback, sure she had met him somewhere before. There was something about those eyes and the way he smiled that struck a familiar chord, but she could not place it. She took the hand he offered.

'Hello, Marcus. How nice to meet you.'

'I thought you were just great tonight,' he said enthusiastically. 'And Peter tells me you might be touring in Paul Winspear's play with me.' He looked at Peter. 'Did you get her to say yes?'

464

'I certainly did.'

The blue eyes blazed their delight.

Shirley smiled and shook her head. 'I still haven't quite taken it in. It's very exciting. I can't wait to begin rehearsing.'

'Me neither – especially now.' His eyes held hers, making no attempt to disguise the admiration in them.

Peter was watching them, a slightly amused expression in his eyes. 'Look, why don't you two grab that corner table over there,' he suggested. 'I'll get the drinks and bring them across.'

As they sat opposite each other, Shirley said: 'You know, it's the strangest thing, but when I first saw you I felt sure I knew you from somewhere.'

Marcus laughed. 'Hey, that's supposed to be my line. Matter of fact, I do happen to be English. I was born here; I still have an English passport. I'm only American by adoption, I guess you could say. My father lives here.'

'Really?'

'It's true. He and my mother were divorced when I was a kid and she had my name changed to hers. I've only actually met him once since then. Mom and I came over about five years ago, soon after the war ended. His name is Tony Darrent and he's an actor too. He was injured in a plane crash a while back. I haven't seen him but . . .' He stopped speaking, puzzled at the smile on her face. 'I guess I talk too much. What is it – did I say something funny?'

'I'm sorry. No. It's Peter. He's laid all this on deliberately. You see, I know your father very well. I was evacuated to his country house when war broke out. I lived there all through the war and grew up with your half-sister, Imogen.'

His eyes widened in amazement. 'Imogen? But that's amazing. I made the trip up to Vancouver specially to meet her when the Darrent Shakespeare Company played there some time back. It was she who suggested I should contact Peter when I came over to England.'

'Did she tell you that your father was married again?'

'Sure, she seemed very pleased about it.'

'But you wouldn't know that it was my mother he married?'

He sat back to stare at her in astonishment. 'Say, what do you *know*?' He grinned at her. 'Peter sure kept all of this up his sleeve.'

At that moment Peter joined them with the drinks. 'No need to ask if you two have been getting to know each other,' he said with a smile.

Shirley looked at him reproachfully. 'You knew about the family link between Marc and me all the time and you never said a word to either of us.'

'I wanted it to be a surprise,' he said. 'But I did have other reasons for not telling either of you. I didn't want you to prejudge each other. And I wanted to be sure you were going to get along together. A twelve-week tour can be absolute hell playing opposite someone you can't stand the sight of.'

'Well, that's one problem you can put out of your mind.' Marc addressed Peter but his eyes were on Shirley. 'Shirley and I are going to get along just fine. You can bank on it.'

'What brought you over here?' Shirley asked. 'Apart from wanting to meet your father again, I mean. Is it hard to find work in the States?'

'It's not too bad. I've done a lot of summer stock since college. It's great experience. The trouble back home is that once people get to know who Mom is I never can tell whether I'm getting a job because I'm good or because of my name. When you've got a well-known parent it's hard to go places on your own merit. Over here no one knows who I am and that's the way I aim to keep it.' He smiled at her. 'But that's enough about me. So your mom and my dad got married?' He shook his head. 'I can't get over it. What does that make us? Stepbrother and sister, I guess.'

'I've been trying to find the time to go to Houlton one weekend. Would you like to go with me? It would be a marvellous surprise for Tony.'

He picked up his glass and took a drink, looking at her doubtfully. 'I'd love that, Shirley, but not yet. I'm here to

466

make it on my own and that's what I mean to do. I've even sworn Peter to secrecy, so I'd be obliged to you if you'd keep all this to yourself.'

'Of course, if that's the way you want it, Marc.' She smiled at him ruefully. 'It does seem a shame, though. I'm sure he'd love to see you.'

'Oh, I'll go and see him, eventually. I've promised myself that.' He paused, twisting his glass in his hands. 'It's always been a big regret of mine that I never got to know my dad.'

'I know what you mean. I never knew my father either,' Shirley told him.

'I never had much family life at all,' Marcus said. 'I wasn't much more than a baby when Mom and I went to the States for her career. I had a whole string of nurse-maids till I went to school. Guess I was kind of a lonely little kid.'

'It was the war that broke up my family,' Shirley told him. 'Before the war there was just Gloria, she's my mother, and my grandparents, but we were close and happy. Then the war split us all up and life was never the same again for any of us.'

He put his hand over hers. 'Guess we've got a lot in common, Shirley.'

She looked up at him. That sudden, dazzling smile reminded her of his father. Her first fleeting impression that they'd met before had been in that smile. His resemblance to Tony as he'd been all those years ago when she'd first known him was quite uncanny. He had the same clear, expressive blue eyes and the finely sculptured features, cruelly devastated now for Tony since his accident. 'Marc,' she said quietly, 'your father was badly scarred in that plane crash. When you do go to see him you should be prepared for quite a change in his appearance.'

'I guessed that. But he's still my dad, isn't he? The only one I've got.'

On a sudden impulse she turned her hand over and curled her fingers round his, returning their pressure. 'I'm glad we're going to be working together, Marc,' she said simply.

'Me too.' His eyes still holding hers, he said: 'Hey, look. I'm not busy this weekend. Why don't I check into a hotel in town? We could spend some time together. You could show me the town – if you're not doing anything.'

'I'm not doing a thing.'

'I brought the script of the play with me. We could try out some of our scenes together.'

Peter cleared his throat noisily. 'Well, I think I'll be off now. I've got a long drive in front of me and it looks as though I'm going to have to make it on my own.'

Marc looked concerned. 'Hey, Peter, I'm sorry. If you'd rather I came back with you . . .'

Peter laughed. 'No, you stay and get to know each other. I'm not quite so decrepit that I need someone to hold my hand.' He tossed back the last of his drink and stood up. 'Besides, I can see that you two are planning to do a lot of talking and, er, rehearsing.'

As he made his way out of the theatre, he smiled to himself. He had a hunch those two young people were destined for great things together – and not all of them to do with acting.

Insisting that the night was young and that meeting up with a stepsister warranted a celebration, Marc consulting the green room's barman and discovered the name of the city's ritziest night spot. Before Shirley could catch her breath he had telephoned to book a table. She had to beg him to let her go home and change first. They took a taxi to the street where she had her small two-room flat and Marc came up with her and waited while she changed into a dress of indigo taffeta with a romantic swirling skirt and stand-up collar. The rich dark colour accentuated the creaminess of her skin and the golden lights in her hair. When he saw her Marc gave a long, low whistle.

'Wow, you look a knockout, Shirley.' He fingered the neck of his polo-neck sweater, looking slightly doubtful. 'Say, d'you think they'll refuse to let me in, dressed like this? I didn't bring any other clothes. I wasn't really figuring on stopping over.'

Shirley laughed. 'Don't worry. The moment they hear your accent they'll fall over themselves. It's been like that ever since the war.'

'Well, okay, if you say so.' He offered her his arm. 'Let's go on the town.'

Shirley couldn't remember enjoying herself so much. Marcus was such good company and it turned out that they really did have a lot in common, sharing the same ambition and taste in plays. They ate and drank, talked nonstop and danced till two thirty in the morning. Finally Marc hailed a taxi, where she dozed against his shoulder all the way home, feeling relaxed and slightly light-headed.

It was only when they reached her flat that he remembered that he hadn't booked a room. 'Darn it. It went right out of my head. Never mind, I guess I'll find a motel somewhere,' he said with a shrug.

Shirley looked at him. 'Not here, you won't. We don't have motels over here. You can get almost anywhere in England in one day, so there's no need.' She looked at her watch. 'And you won't get a hotel to take you at this time of night – specially without any luggage.' She pushed the door open. 'Nothing for it but to stay here.'

He followed her into the flat. 'Look, Shirley, I hope you don't think I've done this on purpose. I wouldn't want to . . .?'

She turned and looked him gravely in the eye. 'If I really thought for one moment that you had, I'd give you the address of the local Sally Army hostel.' She laughed at his expression. 'I'll find you a pillow and a couple of blankets. The settee is quite comfy.'

Neither of them slept much that night. Shirley lay staring into the darkness, deeply aware of the close proximity of Marcus a few yards away on the other side of the thin partition wall. She was remembering all the things they talked about during the evening, and the way his eyes shone when he talked about the theatre and his fierce determination to make a name for himself on his own account and without help from either parent. She thought of the little dimple that appeared at the corner of his mouth when he smiled, which more than once she had caught herself itching to touch; of the lock of hair that would keep falling across his brow. She thought of the easy, magical way their steps had matched when they danced together and how good his arms felt around her.

Marcus, lying on the settee in the living room, was blessing his luck at meeting such a fantastic girl – not only meeting her but discovering that they were to work together for the coming twelve weeks. When he closed his eyes the bright, vivacious face with its violet-blue eyes and halo of red-gold hair was still there. He could still feel the delicious sensation of her slender body in his arms when they danced. He bit his lip hard and turned over. If his friends back home knew that he was wasting an opportunity like this, they'd never let him forget it. They'd brand him as the biggest idiot under the sun not to take advantage. But he knew that he and Shirley needed to take things a step at a time. What they were about to share was too important, too good to rush. It would happen, there was nothing surer than that. And when it did it was going to be out of this world. It was going to mean something very special for them both.

On Sunday they read through the script of the play together, their heads close over the shared manuscript. Then they went out to lunch at the pub round the corner. Marcus was keen to soak up the atmosphere of one of the traditional English pubs his mother had told him about. After lunch they walked in the park and talked some more before returning to the flat for tea.

'What time does your train go?' Shirley asked.

He shook his head. 'I don't know. I guess there'll be a pretty good service from here to London, though.'

Shirley laughed. 'You don't know British Rail on a Sunday.'

'You mean there aren't any trains?'

She began to put her coat on. 'There are, but you have to take pot luck. They're always repairing the lines or something. I'll come to the station with you.'

He was secretly disappointed to find that there was a fast train due in ten minutes. On the platform they looked at each other. Marcus said: 'When will I see you again, Shirley?'

'When we start rehearsals, I suppose.'

He took both her hands. 'I can't wait that long. I have to see you again before that. Can I come up here again – soon?'

'Of course, if you really want to. But I'm sure there are lots more exciting things for you to see in London.'

Still holding her hands he drew her close. 'Not for me. You're the most exciting thing that ever happened to me, Shirley. But I guess you already figured that out.' His lips found hers. He kissed her lightly, then looked down at her inquiringly. 'So, do I get to come back next weekend?' His eyes searched hers, desperately trying to read a response in them.

Shirley was trembling. His kiss had been light and brief but it had affected her like a glass of champagne on an empty stomach. She gave him a quick hug and said as light-heartedly as she could: 'Of course you do, Marc. I'd love you to come. I'll look forward to it.'

She more than just looked forward to it, counting the days till the following weekend. But her time was too busy to make the time drag. Playing in the current production and rehearsing for the next, she tried hard not to let thoughts of Marcus ruin her concentration. On the contrary, anticipation gave her performance a new edge. There was a new sparkle in her eyes and a lightness in her step. Frances was one of the first to notice it.

'Anyone would think you'd fallen in love,' she said teasingly. 'It wouldn't be anything to do with a certain young American, would it?'

'I haven't the slightest idea who you mean,' Shirley said, turning wide, innocent eyes on the older woman. They laughed together, both knowing that with her usual perception, Frances had hit the nail squarely on the head.

Marcus was sitting right in the centre of the front row when the curtain went up on Saturday evening. The moment Shirley made her entrance at the beginning of Act I she spotted him immediately. Her heart skipped a beat but she didn't allow it to throw her. Later, however, when Frances had tactfully withdrawn, leaving them alone in the dressing room, she admonished him for it.

'When I came on and saw you sitting there I almost forgot my first line,' she said.

He laughed. 'Not you. I wouldn't have done it if I didn't know you're a pro right down to your fingertips.'

It was the nicest compliment he could have paid her and she forgave him at once. Standing on tiptoe she kissed him lightly. 'Well, what are we going to do?'

He looked into her eyes for a long moment. 'I'm better organised this time. I've hired a car, so we can drive out of town. I guess we're going to eat first,' he said. 'Then dance a little, then . . .' He drew her close and kissed her – deeply this time, putting into his kiss all the longing he had endured during the past week. 'I've missed you, Shirley. I thought Saturday would never come.'

'I've missed you too,' she said.

They dined and danced, barely moving on the postage-stamp-sized floor, their arms around each other, cheeks softly touching. The longing they both felt affected them like sweet, heady wine until Marcus whispered:

'I guess it's time to go, Shirley.'

She looked up at him. 'It's such a shame to have to say good night.'

He frowned, affecting mock distress. '*Darn* it, would you believe I went and forgot to book a room again?'

They looked at each other for a moment. 'Well,' he said, nuzzling her ear. 'Do I get the address of the Sally Army hostel or will you take pity on a poor homeless waif?'

Her eyes shone softly in the dimmed lights. 'I suppose I'll just have to take pity on you,' she said.

Neither of them spoke much during the drive back. Together they climbed the stairs to the flat and the moment the door closed behind them they were in each other's arms. In the darkness they clung to each other. To

Shirley it was like being suspended in time and space. Their lips met and met again in hungry, searching kisses that left them both breathless and spoke more vehemently of what they both felt than any words. Then Marc lifted her in his arms and carried her into the bedroom.

Shirley knew right from that very first time that she was in love; this time the deep, true love that Magda had spoken of. This was being alive – this was the *living* that made the very meaning of her being crystal clear. This was what she had been born for. Best of all, it would last for ever – and beyond. At the height of their lovemaking she was aware of calling out his name, of saying 'I love you' over and over. With anyone else it would have been reckless and ill-advised. With Marcus, she knew instinctively that saying what was in her heart was intrinsically right.

Afterwards, as they lay in each other's arms, still dazed with the wonder of what they had experienced, Marc said:

'Do you believe in destiny, Shirley? Do you believe that some people are meant to meet – and love? Drawn together by some irresistible power?'

'I never have, till now,' she said dreamily. 'But when I look back, everything that ever happened to me seems as if it was pointing me in your direction.' She looked at him. 'Do you feel that too? Is that what you mean?'

He drew her close. 'That's exactly what I mean,' he said with a contented sigh. 'Oh, Shirley, now that I've found you I'm never going to let you go. I love you so much. You're so . . . so perfect.'

'No.' She stirred uneasily. 'I'm not perfect, Marc. No one is perfect.' She twisted her head to look at him. 'You don't really know me at all,' she said. 'I've got faults just like everyone else. Maybe when you've had time to get to know me better you'll change your mind.'

'Never,' he said happily. 'Nothing you could do could ever make me feel any different.' He grinned at her. 'What could you possibly have done that's so terrible?'

For a moment she looked into his eyes. Was this the time for confessions – for telling about the selfish things she'd done, her bad points as well as the good? *Of course it isn't*, a small voice in the back of her head told her. A moment like this was too precious, too tenuous to spoil by putting it to the test. It was a new beginning, a rebirth, not to be tarnished by the mistakes of the past. She grinned mischievously. 'Well, there was the bank robbery, of course.'

'Is *that* all?' He laughed and kissed her. 'Oh. well, I think I can live with that.'

Gloria could not remember being so happy. Since Michael's successful operation and her marriage to Tony, life had been so wonderful that sometimes she had to pinch herself when she woke in the mornings, just to make sure she hadn't dreamed the whole thing. But as the summer passed and Tony began to work normally again, two problems arose. First, Tony's radio work took him away from home more and more frequently. Most weeks he stayed at the London flat and came home at weekends. Then, in early September Michael started nursery school and she found herself spending most of the day alone.

Soon after the wedding they had decided that Longueville Hall was far too big for the three of them. Since the war, few women seemed to want domestic work any more and there were far too many rooms for their requirements. The house was sold early in August and they bought Hindley Lodge, a pretty little Georgian villa next to the church.

Gloria had occupied herself happily for weeks, planning the decor and colour schemes, making curtains and other soft furnishings. But once it was all done and Michael had started school she found herself once more with time on her hands. She was used to working, to occupying her days with something more useful than housework, and she felt restless and bored, living only for the weekends when Tony, Michael and she could be together.

Tony was sympathetic and suggested she invited friends to stay. Margaret came to see the new house and stayed the night, but life at the Dog and Doublet in Boothley was busy and with the shortage of staff she couldn't be spared for more than one night. Gloria had hoped that Shirley might visit more, but with her working till late on Saturday evening there wasn't time. She wrote regularly and promised to come for a few days as soon as she could, but all that seemed a long way off.

She invited Jane. They had kept in touch in spite of the fact that they'd hardly seen each other since the wartime days at the aircraft factory. Jane was married now to a civil servant and lived in Gloucestershire. The two of them had a wonderful time, reminiscing and catching up on all their news. But when she went away the days seemed longer than ever. Michael was growing up fast. He had his friends to play with and seemed to need her less and less now that he was fit and well.

Talking things over, she and Tony agreed that to return to London permanently would not be fair to Michael. It was healthy for him here in the country. He was growing into a happy, sturdy little boy, who loved the freedom of the country lanes and fields. It was where he belonged. Then there was Ma. Having persuaded her to move, it would hardly be fair to leave her high and dry. It seemed that, for Gloria, there was nothing for it but to settle to a life of waiting for weekends.

It was when Imogen and Charles came home at last at the end of October that the idea first came into being. They had been quietly married in America towards the end of the company's extended tour and Imogen was already pregnant. But although Tony was disappointed not to have been at his only daughter's wedding, he forgave her when he saw how happy she and Charles obviously were. Imogen was positively radiant over the coming baby. At last she was to start the family she'd always longed for.

'So far we're keeping it to ourselves,' she told Gloria as they unpacked together in the guest room at Hindley Lodge. 'At least, I'm not mentioning it to anyone in the company. I want to go on working as long as I can. The

DSC is to tour this country now. We've got a couple of weeks out and then we're off to Brighton to start the tour. I'm looking forward to it so much and I've never felt so well in my life.' She pulled a face. 'My only problem is my costumes. They're all so tight and if I ask Wardrobe to let them out they'll probably guess.'

'If you can get them to me, I'll do them for you,' Gloria offered.

Imogen's eyes lit up. 'Oh, would you, Gloria? That would be marvellous.'

The following weekend Imogen smuggled the costumes home with her on the pretext that she wanted to have some photographs taken. In Gloria's bedroom she paraded in them.

'See what I mean?' she said, standing sideways in front of the cheval mirror.

Gloria laughed. 'You look as slim as a wand to me, but I dare say you might be feeling a little uncomfortable round the waist. I can easily let them out if there's enough material. Let's have a look.'

But when Gloria turned the costumes inside out she could see that they would allow only the barest half-inch of adjustment.

'They're dreadfully tatty,' she said, sitting back on her heels and fingering the material. 'The hems are frayed and the trimmings are tarnished and split. Most of the seams are beginning to go, too. If I start altering them I'm afraid they'll probably fall apart.'

'I know. We've all complained about it,' Imogen said. 'They were second-hand when we got them – prewar, I shouldn't wonder. But commissioning new ones would cost the earth. We've been told we'll just have to make do. Luckily they don't look too bad under stage lighting.'

Gloria said nothing. An idea was taking shape in her head. It was making her eyes sparkle and Imogen was quick to pick up her excitement.

'Gloria, what is it? Are you thinking what I *think* you're thinking?'

Gloria laughed. 'That sounds Irish, but yes, I believe I am. I could make the company a whole new set of

476

costumes. It'd take a little time, but I'd love to do it. You'd have to bring me photographs of all the ones you've got . . .' She stopped, looking up at Imogen doubtfully. 'Oh – but maybe your producer wouldn't trust me to do it.'

'*Trust* you? After the miracles you worked on the costumes for those wartime concerts? All you had then was some butter muslin and a few bits of tinsel, yet you created sheer magic. And I've still got the photographs to prove it.' She stopped, suddenly remembering something. 'I've also got that little Chinese jacket you made for Mummy. She gave it to me and I still wear it. That proves how clever you are, if anything does.' She threw her arms round her stepmother. 'Oh, Gloria, when I tell our producer this piece of news he'll forgive me anything – even getting pregnant.' She grasped Gloria's hands. 'We could go up to Wardour Street together and get everything you'd need from the theatrical costumiers. You must read all the plays and I'll lend you my collection of historical costume books. And when I have to give up work because of the baby, I could help you with it – do all the boring bits so as to leave you free to design and create. We could work on it together.'

Gloria's eyes shone with anticipation. 'Oh, Imogen, this is just what I've been wanting. It'll be my contribution to the DSC. After all, I'm a member of the Darrent family now.'

'Leave it to me,' Imogen said. 'I'll get it all laid on.' As she was changing back into her own clothes, she said suddenly: 'Talking of families, have you heard anything from Marcus?'

Gloria looked puzzled. 'Marcus?'

'Marcus Fane – Daddy's son by his first marriage.'

'No. Should we have heard from him?'

'He came to see me when the company was in Vancouver,' Imogen told her. 'He said he was coming over to England to get some stage experience. I gave him a letter to take to Peter Jason. I just thought he might have been in touch.'

Gloria shook her head. 'Not as far as I know. Peter is still urging Tony to go into partnership with him. They see each other regularly. I'm sure he'd have mentioned it.'

Imogen shrugged. 'Oh? Well, maybe he thought better of the idea.' She smiled. 'It was the first time I'd met him. I liked him a lot. I think you would too.'

'It's sad for Tony that his son grew up without knowing him.'

'Well, he's made up for it with Michael.' Imogen laughed. 'I've never seen a father and son so besotted with each other. They're inseparable.'

'I know. And it means so much to me, Imogen, after the years when I was struggling to bring him up alone. I'm so very lucky. I have a healthy little son and a husband who adores us. It's just that sometimes I feel a bit guilty about Shirley.'

'You made it up with her, though, didn't you? She wrote and told me all about your meeting at Hampstead Heath and she seemed happy with the Mask Players.'

'Yes, but I don't think she really looks on Tony and me as her family,' Gloria said. 'Sometimes I think she's keeping away so as not to intrude. Yet I don't want her to feel duty-bound to come here.' She sighed. 'Maybe we've drifted too far apart. Sometimes I wonder if it's too late to mend things properly between us. Ma still doesn't mention her name much, but I know that secretly she'd give anything to see her again.'

'Maybe Daddy feels a bit like that about Marcus,' Imogen said thoughtfully. 'Except for him I suppose it *is* too late. They're total strangers. Two grown men with completely separate lives.'

Shirley took her leave of the Mask Players the first week in October. The company gave a party for her. It was an emotional parting. Gerald Maddox made a little speech and presented her with a cream leather vanity case the company had bought her as a parting gift. The only thing that spoiled it for her was that Marcus wasn't there. He had sent a telegram at the last minute to say he couldn't make it, but would meet her at the station the following day.

On the Sunday she travelled to London. They were to begin rehearsals in a week's time. In the meantime she planned to show Marcus her London – all the places the tourists never saw. She was looking forward to it so much. After their break there were to be two weeks of intensive rehearsal before the tour opened in Manchester, but she had been studying her part and already knew her lines almost perfectly.

Marcus was waiting to meet her train. Since their first meeting he had spent every weekend except this last one in Birmingham and they had both looked forward to the time when they would be working together. Marcus had the use of a flat in Smith Square that belonged to an old friend of his mother and it had been arranged that Shirley was to stay there with him until the tour began.

As she got down from the train at Euston Station and walked down the platform, her heart lifted. She saw him at once, standing there at the barrier, tall and handsome in the casual clothes he loved to wear. Now their life and their shared career could really begin. He saw her and lifted his arm in greeting. She waved back and hurried towards him.

In the taxi she chattered eagerly, telling him about the party the previous night and showing him her present, which she carried with her. She was too excited to notice his air of aloof preoccupation.

The flat was comfortable and spacious. Shirley walked from room to room while the taxi driver helped Marc to carry up her luggage. When they were finally alone she held out her arms to him.

'Oh, darling. I can't believe I'm here at last. The last few days have seemed like an eternity. I was so sad you couldn't come to the party.' She stood on tiptoe to kiss him but instead of his arms encircling her, they hung unresponsively at his side. She looked into his eyes, sensing for the first time that there was something wrong. Standing back to look at him, she said: 'What is it? You *are* pleased to see me, aren't you?'

He smiled, but it wasn't the joyous, spontaneous smile she loved. 'Of course I'm pleased to see you. Now, what'll you have to eat? I've got –'

She caught at his arm, stopping him in mid-sentence. 'Marc, what's wrong? Don't tell me it's nothing. Something's upset you, I can see that.'

His eyes clouded and he drew away from her to walk to the window. 'I wasn't going to say anything. I'd made up my mind not to let it make any difference.'

'*What*, Marc?' She went to him, her heart thudding with fear and uncertainty. 'If something's happened I want to know about it – please.'

He turned to look at her, one hand brushing back his hair in the familiar mannerism. 'I met Paul Winspear,' he said quietly. 'Peter took us both to lunch at the Garrick Club and Winspear and I stayed on to talk about the play after Peter went back to the office. I disliked the guy on sight, but I wasn't prepared for what he'd say. He didn't know that you and I had become close. He . . . said things about you; things that made me want to smash his face in. If he hadn't been who he is I believe I would have.'

Her heart sank. 'Oh, Marc.' Taking his hand she led him to the settee and drew him down beside her. 'I don't know what he told you, but I'll tell you the truth and I hope you'll believe me. Paul and I had an affair. I thought I was in love with him. I was pretty naive, I suppose. I knew that he and Leonie Swann had been together for some time and I should have realised that he was just amusing himself while she was away on location. When she came back to London he dropped me like a hot potato. What did he tell you?'

He didn't look at her. 'He told me what a good pupil you were – in bed. That he was your first lover. He described how you couldn't get enough of him.' He turned away from her. 'It made me feel sick, hearing you spoken of like that.'

'Oh, Marc. I should have told you before. How could he?'

'He went on to tell me how you jilted some other guy – walked out on the eve of your wedding. He seemed to think you did it because you couldn't forget him. Is that true too?'

'*No*. At least . . .' She swallowed painfully. How dare Paul talk about her like that – twisting the truth in such a vicious, devious way? But having her own past held up to her like this, especially by Marc, hurt more than Paul's lies and betrayal. It made her sound so hardboiled and self-centred. She touched his arm. 'Yes. It is partly true, but it wasn't the way Paul tells it. I'd known Dave for a long time. He was – *is* a good man. He asked me to marry him at a time when I was vulnerable, when I felt a failure and needed someone badly. Deep down I always knew that it wasn't right. Then the offer from the Mask Players came, right out of the blue, and I had to make the decision.'

'So you walked out on the guy?'

'Yes, I walked out. I got the telegram offering me the job the night before the wedding and I knew that I just couldn't turn it down. It was everything I'd longed for. It was like standing at a crossroads, Marc. And seeing the right way all brightly lit and signed for me.' She looked at his face and was suddenly afraid. 'Dave and I are still good friends. He understands and agrees that what I did was right. We'd have made each other unhappy. He's found someone now who suits him down to the ground. And I've found *you*, Marc. So I did make the right decision, didn't I?' She looked at him beseechingly, but the eyes that looked back at her were dark with doubt.

'If you ever did that to me . . .'

'But I *won't*.'

'I've never fallen for anyone the way I fell for you, Shirley. I've seen so much of this kind of thing all my life. Mom was always dating some new guy and bringing them home. As a kid I was always finding some strange guy in her room and it still hasn't stopped. As soon as I was old enough I moved out. Recently she's been dating younger and younger guys – some of them are even younger than me. How do you think it made me feel, hearing folks make crude jokes about her – hearing my own mom referred to as an ageing nymphomaniac?'

She went to him. 'I didn't know. I'm sorry, darling. But I'm not like that. I never could be. Surely you don't believe . . .?'

He turned away. 'How can I be sure of that now?'

'How can any of us be sure of *anything*?' she asked desperately. 'I know I love you, Marc. I believed you loved me too. But if you can doubt me like this, if you can't trust me, then perhaps we should . . . we should stop seeing each other.'

He paced the floor angrily, avoiding her eyes. 'How can we not see each other when we're supposed to be working together?'

'I could find myself somewhere else to live,' she said quietly. 'We don't have to share this flat.' When he didn't reply, she added: 'Are you saying you'd rather I gave up my part in the play?'

'No. There's no need for that.' He shook himself angrily and turned to face her. 'I've already decided to fly back to the States on the first flight available. I'll be letting Peter know first thing in the morning.'

She stared at him, her heart freezing. 'You're going home? But why?'

'I have to. I'm so mixed up over all this, I can't think straight any more. They want guys my age for the army – this war in Korea. Maybe I'd better enlist. At least that way I'd be doing something worth while.'

'Marc – no!' She went to him and grasped his arm, her distress turning to frightened anger. 'Marc, listen. What Paul told you – it happened before I met you. Didn't *you* ever make a mistake? Have you gone through life being perfect? For all I know there are things in *your* life that *I* wouldn't like.'

He stared coldly down at her. 'Well, you can think yourself lucky that you'll never have to go through the trauma of hearing about them as I did.' He turned on his heel and walked out of the room.

Shirley sank onto the settee, her heart numb with disbelief. It was like the worst kind of nightmare. How could Paul have done this to her? How could Marc believe him and not her? It was so unfair. Reaching for the telephone she put through a call to Houlton. Gloria answered:

'Houlton 234.'

'Gloria. It's me – Shirley.'

'Shirley! How lovely to hear you. We heard from Peter that you're going to tour with *Give Me Yesterday*. Are you going to come and see us first?'

'I'd like that,' Shirley said. 'But there are a couple of things I have to do in London first. I'm ringing to ask you a favour. The thing is, I had arranged to stay with . . . with a friend, but it's fallen through. Can I stay at Tony's flat in Earls Court, or is he using it? It'll only be for a couple of days, till I can fix something else.'

'Of course you can. Tony's here with me. He says stay as long as you like. He'll telephone the caretaker and tell him to let you in.'

'Thanks. I'll ring you again tomorrow and let you know when I'm coming up to Houlton. I'm longing to see you all.'

'Do try to come this week, Shirl. Imogen and Charles are here at the moment.'

'I will. I promise.' She said goodbye, then rang for a taxi, collecting her luggage together and waiting with it on the landing. When the taxi came, Marc still had not reappeared.

At Tony's flat she busied herself finding sheets in the airing cupboard and making up the spare bed, then she made herself a strong cup of coffee and sat down to think. Inside her heart was still cold with shock. How could Paul name her for a part in his play one minute and deliberately try to ruin her life the next? In the spare room she lay down on the newly made bed fully clothed and let her frozen heart thaw into tears of despair. How could life be so cruel? Must this hammer blow fall just when everything looked so bright and promising?

She fell into an exhausted sleep after a while. When she awoke the sky outside was dark, but her mind was crystal clear. She knew exactly what she had to do. Sitting up, she reached for the telephone. Paul should not be allowed to get away with this. Maybe losing Marc was her fault. She should have told him about Paul and Dave in the first place. But she had to make Paul see what he had done. She had nothing to lose. She had already decided to give up her part in the play and she'd lost Marc anyway. Nothing could hurt her as badly as that.

The phone rang several times before he answered. 'Hello, Paul Winspear.'

'Paul, it's Shirley Rayner.'

'Shirley, darling. How nice to hear from you. All ready to begin rehearsals?'

She ground her teeth at his mockingly jocular tone. 'Paul, I have to see you.'

'What a delightful prospect! Perhaps we could have dinner one evening next –'

'*Now*, Paul. I'm at Tony's flat. I want you to come round here now. It's important.'

There was a pause, then he said: 'It all sounds rather ominous. As a matter of fact, you only just caught me. I was just going out.'

'I must see you. As soon as possible.'

'May one ask what it's about?'

'I said *now*, Paul.' She slammed down the receiver and sat thinking. Her heart was pounding and her hands and feet were like ice. She must calm herself before he arrived or she wouldn't be able to say what she planned to say effectively. Getting up, she washed her face and applied a careful make-up, then she went into the living room and poured herself a large whisky from Tony's cabinet. By the time the doorbell rang she felt more in control of herself.

When she opened the door he looked at her imperiously. 'I had to cancel an appointment to come round here, Shirley. I hope it really is important.'

'It is,' she said succinctly, turning and walking into the living room. He followed and looked pointedly at the drinks cabinet. She ignored his tacit request and went straight to the point. 'I hear you've been telling some rather unpleasant stories about me.'

'Really? Who can have told you that?'

'I think you know perfectly well who it was, Paul. Marcus Fane and I met some weeks ago. We fell in love and everything was fine – until you started pouring poison into his ears.'

He affected surprise. 'Me?'

'Yes, you. What you told him upset him so much that he's decided to fly back to the States tomorrow. He's even talking of enlisting in the US Army.'

'How very melodramatic,' he sneered. 'It sounds suspiciously like emotional blackmail to me.'

'I think you should know that I'm not prepared to take part in *Give Me Yesterday* without him.'

He stared at her, clearly taken aback. 'You can't back out. You're under contract.'

'I don't care.' She walked towards him. 'If the management wants to sue me, let them. I'll tell them how you slandered my character to another member of the company, making it impossible for me to work.' Her words had clearly shocked him at last and she went on: 'Why did you do it, Paul? You put my name forward for the part. You want your play to be a success, so why sabotage it? You hurt me once for no reason. Wasn't that enough?'

'All this fuss about a couple of innocent man-to-man remarks. How was I to know that you and he had a thing going?' He was blustering now. 'All I said was –'

'I *know* what you said,' she interrupted. 'The damage is done. I'll be going to Houlton tomorrow, taking a long rest with my family. I'll ring Peter and I'll write a letter of explanation to the tour manager.' On trembling legs she walked to the door and opened it. 'Now I'd like you to leave, please.'

Paul hesitated, then he walked purposefully to the door and closed it firmly. 'Listen, Shirley, I'm sorry for what I said. I certainly didn't mean for all this to happen. What I said to young Fane was said jokingly.'

'Well, I'm afraid the joke has misfired, Paul. Marc didn't see the funny side, and neither do I.'

He sighed. 'All right. It was vindictive of me. I admit it.'

'But why, Paul – *why*?'

He turned away and lit a cigarette, drawing deeply on it before he went on: 'Oh, I don't know. There he was, all eager, virile youth, raring to go and lusting after you. Every time your name was mentioned his eyes lit up like a bloody pin table. I could almost hear the bells ringing inside his head.'

'I see. So you had to smash his happiness, like a spoilt child.'

He stubbed out the barely smoked cigarette. 'Yes – *yes*, all right. It was sheer spite. Now are you satisfied?'

'Satisfied? When you've just ruined my life *and* my career? I'll never forgive you, Paul – never.'

He looked again at the drinks cabinet. 'Oh, for God's sake give me a whisky and listen to me for a minute, will you?'

'Why should I?'

'Look, I'm not trying to make excuses for what I did, I'm just saying that it isn't entirely my fault.' He looked at her. 'Well, are you going to do me the courtesy of hearing me out?'

Silently she splashed some whisky into a glass, added soda and handed it to him, then she sat down and looked at him. 'All right, I'm waiting.'

He took a deep gulp and winced as the fiery liquid scalded his throat. 'You know that I was badly wounded in the war,' he began. 'It was a head injury. I lay in hospital for weeks, unconscious. I think they thought that even if I pulled through I'd end up like a vegetable. Eventually I came round, but for months I didn't know who I was – didn't remember a thing. Well, to cut a long story short, I was lucky. In spite of the fact that I still had bits of shrapnel floating about inside my head, too deeply embedded for them to risk removal, I made a full recovery. But the man I had been was gone for ever. When I came home my wife said my personality had completely changed. My temper was unpredictable. It would flare up without warning. A couple of times I actually struck her, which was why she eventually left me.' He looked at her ruefully. 'No doubt you remember my flashes of violence. I do inexplicable things too at times; irrational, cruel things such as speaking to young Fane like that about you.' He paused to light another cigarette, studying her face and trying to assess her reaction over the flame of his lighter. 'Do you think I'm proud of myself, Shirley? The one good thing in all of it is that I can still write. Without that I think I'd just put an end to it all. One of these days one of those pieces of junk will pierce something vital in my brain and that'll be my final curtain anyway.' He drew smoke deep into his lungs and let it out slowly. 'I don't know if you've heard, but Leonie and I split up before she went to Australia. Again, it was my fault. I more or less kicked her out in one of my black moods. The trouble is that now she's gone I miss her like hell. Now that I've lost her too, I realise that we were right for each other. I really believe that we brought out the best in each other, for whatever that's worth.' He looked at her. 'It was feeling bitter about my own damned stupidity that made me want to spoil young Fane's smug satisfaction, I suppose, though I know that can't be of much help to you now.' He stubbed out the cigarette he'd just lit. 'I've made up my mind, Shirley. Once I've got my new play off the stocks I'm flying out to Australia and I'm going to try to get her to take me back. If she wants to be married, then that's what we'll do. I know now that I can't live without her.'

Shirley sank slowly into a chair. 'I hope you'll break it to Peter first that it's you who messed up the tour of *Yesterday*,' she said bleakly. 'Not to mention what you've done to two people's lives.' She choked on the last word. She hadn't known about Paul's war injury and subsequent illness. It explained a lot, of course, and now she couldn't even blame him for what had happened. She was left as always to take all the blame herself. It was a bleak prospect.

'I'm sorry, Shirley,' he said quietly. 'I'm really sorry. If there's anything I can do . . .'

'There isn't.' She turned away so that he wouldn't see the tears only barely held at bay. 'Just go. Just leave me.

Maybe it's for the best. After all, if Marc was willing to believe . . .' She heard the door bang shut as Paul made his escape.

On his way down in the lift he drew a long breath and let it out slowly. He'd got out of that very nicely. Thank God for his creative powers and his ability to think on his feet. She'd change her mind about giving up her part in the play once she'd calmed down. Shirley's career was too important to her for her to pass up a good chance when she saw one. After all, she'd thrown one bloke over for it. He smiled to himself. Funny – women were always a soft touch when it came to war wounds, though he'd pushed his luck a bit far this time. Amnesia *and* embedded shrapnel was stretching it a bit. Still, she'd swallowed it all right. A good thing no one had access to his discharge papers. Shooting yourself in the foot while cleaning your rifle wasn't nearly as romantic as amnesia. The bit about wanting Leonie back hadn't been invention, though. He only wished to God it was. Even if she did take him back they'd probably make each other's lives hell, but he hadn't any option. Life without her wasn't life at all any more. He only hoped she felt the same.

Shirley was up early next morning. She hadn't slept and she wanted to get the business of cancelling her contract over as soon as she could, then go to Houlton. Her first visit was to Peter Jason's office. When she told him she was pulling out of the tour, he stared at her incredulously.

'What's wrong?' he asked. 'What's happened to bring about this sudden decision?'

'Marcus and I – things have been said about me. Marcus believed them and we . . .'

'Are you telling me that the two of you have had a row – a lovers' tiff?' Peter sighed and shook his head.

'It's more than that.'

'It damn well better be.' Peter's normally mild face was dark with annoyance. 'If you ask me to get you out of this contract at this stage in the proceedings you'll have to find yourself another agent. And you might not find that easy.

I've got a dozen young actresses on my books who'd give their eye teeth for a chance like this. You got this part on the author's recommendation, without even an audition. Let them down at the last minute and the word will spread like wildfire.' He leaned towards her. 'Unreliability, unprofessionalism – they're the worst labels any actor can acquire. You might never be offered a decent job again.'

To his dismay Shirley burst into tears. Fumbling in his pocket for a clean handkerchief, he passed it across the desk to her.

'Oh, come now, there's no need to upset yourself like that,' he said gruffly. Reaching across the desk, he patted her shoulder. 'Come on, dry those tears. I'll ring for some coffee and you can tell me what this is really all about.'

Shirley swallowed hard, deeply embarrassed by her own lack of control. 'You mean you . . . you haven't heard?'

'Heard – from who?'

'From Marcus. He's flying back to America.'

Peter's eyebrows shot up. 'Him too? This is the first I've heard of it. What the hell is going on? Is everyone going mad? When?'

'Today. As soon as he can get a flight, he says.'

She poured out the whole story to him, including the story Paul had told her the previous evening about his war injury. Peter did his best to hide his impatience with Winspear's capriciousness and the folly of young love and forced himself to be as understanding as he could.

When Shirley had finished her story and been calmed by a cup of coffee, he said soothingly: 'Look, I'll tell you what – why don't you go off and spend a couple of days with your mother and Tony? It'll do you the world of good and I know they'll be pleased to see you. I'll be in touch tomorrow or the next day. If Marcus is going home, I don't see why you should turn down your part. This could be an important step in your career, Shirley. Don't throw it away for a mere whim.' He smiled indulgently. 'At this moment you think your heart is broken, I know. But I promise you it isn't. And even if it was, I can assure you that work is the very best therapy.'

Deep inside she knew he was right about work, though she had to make herself ignore the way he made light of her pain. She promised him she would take his advice and rethink her decision, then she dried her eyes and left. It seemed to her once more that she was destined to have either career or love, never both.

She telephoned the time of her train before she left the flat and when she arrived at Castle Station in Northampton Tony was waiting on the platform. He hugged her and took her case.

'I can't tell you how excited everyone is at the prospect of seeing you,' he told her as they drove up Marefair towards the town centre. 'Gloria is dying to show you the new house and all she's done to it and Michael didn't want to go to school this morning in case he missed something. Gloria did tell you that Imogen and Charles are home with us at the moment, didn't she?'

'Yes, she told me. It'll be lovely to see Imo. It seems ages.'

'She's expecting a baby in May.' He turned to smile at her. 'I'm going to be a grandfather. A couple of years ago that would have panicked me. Now I can hardly wait.'

Shirley smiled tremulously. 'Imo's always wanted children. I'm so . . . so happy for . . .' She swallowed, suddenly overcome with emotion.

Tony glanced at her. 'Everything is all right, isn't it?'

'Yes, yes, of course.'

'I was delighted to hear about the tour.'

'Yes. Thanks.' She watched as the familiar streets flew past, the landmarks so dearly familiar to her and so little changed: All Saints' Church, Abington Square, the Racecourse and Kingsley Park. Although she was a Londoner, born and bred, this town was where all her happiest memories were. This was where she had grown up. It felt more like home than London ever had. As the shops and houses gave way to the Northamptonshire countryside, leafless now in its austere winter beauty, her thoughts went back to the warm September day when she had seen Houlton for the first time. How strange and alien it had all seemed then, so green and quiet! How scared she'd been, lying in bed, listening to the strange country sounds; how homesick for her family and the bustle and grime of the city. Her heart was full of the same nostalgic longing now – the feeling of being uprooted and torn apart. But this time it was a deeper emotion, one that would not be so easily soothed and dispelled.

Tony broke into her thoughts: 'Your grandmother is coming to lunch.' He smiled wryly. 'Just thought I'd better warn you.'

Shirley looked at him, her reminiscences momentarily forgotten. 'Ma? Oh, dear. I'd hoped to go and see her tomorrow – on my own.'

Tony laughed. 'Can you imagine her being left out of the reunion? The moment she knew you were coming she invited herself. I think she's secretly dying to see you again.'

'If I know Ma she'll be planning to give me a piece of her mind. I'll be lucky to get away without a thorough telling-off.'

'You might be pleasantly surprised,' Tony said. 'Your grandmother has mellowed since she's moved to Boothley. Believe it or not, she's become a confirmed countrywoman. She's made the garden at Rook Cottage look a perfect picture and she's quite revolutionised the WI ladies.' He laughed. 'She's even joined the church choir.'

Shirley stared at him incredulously. 'Ma? With her voice?' She laughed. 'Pa always used to say it was made for selling coal.'

'I'll say this for her, no one dozes off in the back pews while *she's* singing.'

As they drove through the village, Tony pointed out the sign above the door of the post office. 'See that?' He slowed the car so that she could read it.

Shirley read aloud: 'Postmistress Matilda Jane Marks. *Tilly?* She stayed on, then?'

'She certainly did. One of the youngest postmistresses in the country, so I'm told. The Phippses are so proud of her.' He looked at her. 'Remember the film we made? Your character was modelled on Tilly.'

'I remember.' She smiled. 'The war must have been the luckiest thing that ever happened to poor Tilly. It's a funny world, isn't it?'

He nodded. 'It certainly is.'

At Hindley Lodge Shirley was welcomed warmly. Gloria and Imogen came out into the drive to hug her, while Charles stood somewhat shyly in the background. They went into the house together and Shirley found herself standing in the square, oak-panelled hall with its polished floor and glowing Turkish rugs.

'The house has a lovely warm, welcoming feel,' she said. Then, looking round, she whispered: 'Where's Ma?'

Gloria laughed. 'She's waiting for you in the drawing room. Sitting in state like a duchess, ready to give you an audience.'

'A good wigging, you mean.' Shirley took a deep breath and squared her shoulders. 'Oh, well, I'd better go in and get it over with.'

Gloria led the way to a door on the right of the hall. 'Don't let her manner put you off. She's longing to see you, really,' she said. 'You know Ma. She always has to have her say.'

The drawing room was square and perfectly proportioned, decorated in pastel colours. Softly draped, rose-coloured velvet curtains hung at the windows and the floor was covered by an Indian carpet in soft greens and pinks. In the hearth of the white marble fireplace a basket of flowers filled the room with perfume. Ma sat straight-backed in a chair by the long window that looked out over the garden. She turned as Shirley came in and looked her up and down sternly.

'So – you've condescended to come 'ome at last, 'ave you?' she said. 'An' about time too, you bad girl you.'

Shirley crossed the room to her, surprised to see that Ma looked much smaller than she remembered her. She looked well, but milder and less forbidding in spite of her tone of voice and the disapproving set of her mouth.

'Hello, Ma,' she said. 'I've missed you. I hope you've forgiven me.'

Ma folded her arms across her bosom. 'Not sure as I 'ave, my gel. What about that poor feller you jilted them, eh?'

'Dave's forgiven me,' Shirley said. 'He's marrying a girl who really suits him. I think I probably did him a favour, Ma.'

'That's as may be.' Ma sniffed. 'Be all the same if you 'adn't, though. Fat lot *you* cared, goin' orf like that without so much as a by-yer-leave. Made me ashamed, you did. That a granddaughter of mine should –'

'I *did* care, Ma.' Shirley drew up a stool and sat close to Ma's feet. 'It wasn't an easy decision. And if it makes you feel any better, someone . . . someone very special has just done the very same thing to me.'

Ma looked at her for a long moment, her eyes softening, then she bent forward to take Shirley's face between her hands. 'Someone's 'urt you? Yes, I can see it in your eyes. So you know now. Not that I'd ever wish that for you, love.'

Shirley swallowed. The last thing she wanted was sympathy. She could just about cope with Ma's abrasiveness, but kindness would be the undoing of her. 'I'm all right,' she said, swallowing hard. 'At least I will be now that you and I have made it up.'

Ma bent and kissed her. ''Course we 'ave. You know your old Ma's bark is worse than 'er bite. Life's too bleedin' short to bear grudges. I've missed you somethin' rotten, gel. Many's the time I've 'oped you'd send me a letter, but you never did, you naughty gel.'

'I thought you wouldn't want to hear from me,' Shirley said. 'I did send you my love, though; in the letters I wrote to Glor at Rook Cottage.'

'Oh – yes.' Ma coloured guiltily. 'I did wrong to 'ide them letters. But I did it because I didn't want you getting round Glor. She's as soft as grease – anybody's for a few soft words. That's 'ow she got 'erself into so much trouble. Still, I shouldn't'a done it. I was just too stubborn to admit it at the time.' She looked at Shirley. 'We both done wrong, you 'n' me, but all that's over now, eh?'

Shirley knew this was the closest Ma would ever get to an apology. She smiled and squeezed her hand. 'Of course it is.'

Ma peered at the clock. ''Ere, come on, it's dinnertime and I dunno about you but I'm starvin'.' She got to her feet and took Shirley's arm. 'Y'know, I just *can't* remember to call it lunch. There's a lot of things I have to remember now Glor's gorn up in the world. But I tell them they'll 'ave to take me as they find me or not at all.'

Shirley laughed. 'No one in their right mind would ever want you to change, Ma.'

Lunch was a festive occasion with Jim and Molly Jarvis especially invited as a surprise for Shirley. Afterwards Gloria and Imogen showed her their costume project. A large room at the top of the house had been converted to a sewing room. On a rail under a muslin shroud several finished costumes already hung. Shirley exclaimed at the bright jewel colours and the luscious textures of the satins and velvets, specially made for theatrical work. She admired Gloria's skill in creating dresses that looked as though they had stepped straight out of a bygone age. Her mother seemed so happy and fulfilled here with her husband and child, she reflected, and now this new occupation which Imogen was to share during the later stages of her pregnancy. Later, when she and Imogen were alone together in her room, she implied wistfully that she felt she no longer had a place in the family.

'You're not the only one,' Imogen surprised her by saying. 'I always have felt odd-man-out, I've been away so long now that Mummy has gone to Australia and Daddy has remarried I feel I don't really belong anywhere.' She smiled quickly at Shirley. 'Not that I'm not happy for Daddy. Gloria is the best thing that ever happened to him. He's so relaxed and happy and he's come to terms with his disfigurement more contentedly than I'd ever have dared to hope.'

'But you have Charles now. And soon you'll have your baby too. As for me . . .' Shirley's eyes filled with tears.

Imogen touched her arm. 'Shirl, darling, something's wrong, isn't it? I've known it ever since you arrived. Can't you tell me about it?'

'Oh, why is it that we can't love the right people?' Shirley burst out. 'If only I'd been able to love Dave as he loved me, none of this would have happened.'

'Life is rarely that simple,' Imogen said gently. 'What is it?' Her brow creased into a frown. 'It's not Paul Winspear again, is it?'

'Not in the way you mean.' Shirley hesitated. Marcus had said he didn't want his family to know he was here until he had made a success of his career. But Imogen had been the one who advised him to come. And anyway, by now he was probably on a plane, somewhere over the Atlantic. 'I met Marcus,' she said. 'Your half-brother. Peter introduced us. He was to have taken the part of Jason Hamilton, the young artist in Paul's play.'

Imogen's face broke into a smile. 'So he *did* come over? But that's wonderful news. I liked him a lot. You and he would make a perfect couple. It would be –' She broke off as she saw the distress on Shirley's face. 'What went wrong?'

'Oh, *everything*. We've been seeing each other for weeks. He'd been coming up to Birmingham, spending every weekend with me. It was all going to be so marvellous, being together on tour, working. Then Peter introduced him to Paul Winspear.'

'And . . .?' Imogen took both of Shirley's hands. 'Tell me, darling. Come on, get it off your chest.'

'Paul told him that he and I had had an affair – with salacious details, by the sound of it. He also told him how I walked out on Dave the night before the wedding. He said I did it for love of him.'

'Oh, no.' Imogen frowned. 'The *rat*. And Marc actually listened – and let it ruin things between you?'

'It hit him hard,' Shirley told her. 'It seems that his mother was quite promiscuous. She had a lot of men in her life. Marc had a traumatic childhood. Now he thinks I'm the same kind of woman.'

'Didn't you make him listen to the truth?'

'It wasn't easy. Paul had twisted things so. And the trouble was, I couldn't actually deny any of it. My explanations weren't enough, Imo. He's totally disillusioned with me. He's given up his part in the play and gone back to America.'

Imogen watched with helpless dismay as the tears slipped down Shirley's cheeks. 'Oh, darling. I'm so sorry. If only there were something I could do.'

'There's nothing anyone can do,' Shirley said. 'Except that I want you to promise me you won't tell Tony or Gloria. I promised Marc that I wouldn't tell them he was over here and I don't want him to think I let him down in that too.'

When Michael came home there was a special tea, then they all played together till his bedtime. He insisted that Shirley went to read him a story and proudly showed her the teddy she had given him at Hampstead Heath.

'He guards my bed for me when I'm at school,' he told her, hugging the bear. They had a long talk all about school and his friends after she'd finished reading to him. 'I like having a sister like you,' he said sleepily. 'You won't go away again, will you?'

She smiled. 'I have to, darling. I can only stay for a couple of days. I'm going away on tour soon, you see. But we'll be bringing the play to Northampton in a few weeks' time, so I'll see you then.'

'Oh. That's good.' He was having trouble keeping his eyes open but he sat up suddenly, remembering something. 'Shirley, do you know what Imogen told me?'

'No, darling, what?'

'She says that when her baby is born I'll be its *uncle*. Won't that be good? I'll be the only boy in my class who's an uncle.'

Shirley laughed. What a complex family they'd become, the Darrents and the Rayners. Their lives seemed to become more and more entwined. Briefly she wondered how Michael would get along with his American stepbrother, Marcus. It seemed doubtful that he'd ever get the chance to find out now. And it was probably all her fault.

At last Michael couldn't keep his eyes open any longer and she was able to tuck him in snugly and creep quietly away. Downstairs in the drawing room the rest of the family were watching television. Now that there was a station close enough to Houlton, Tony had bought a set.

'This is the medium to aim for,' he told Shirley as she sat down beside him. 'It won't be long before this takes the place of the cinema.'

Gloria shook her head. 'Surely not? People will always enjoy going to the pictures,' she said, remembering her happy days as an usherette at the Adelphi. 'They'll always want big stars to look up to and copy. I'd hate to think the cinema would ever die.'

Tony nodded. 'I agree with you, of course, but TV is closing the repertory theatres. I'm afraid it's only a matter of time before cinemas go the same way. It's called progress and I'm afraid the period of adjustment is always painful.'

At nine o'clock Ma began to yawn and Tony got ready to drive her home. Shirley went along too and was shown round the new-look Rook Cottage.

'I've got runnin' water *and* a bathroom,' Ma told her proudly. 'The well's still in the back garden, but I don't use it any more.' She snapped a switch and the room was flooded with light. 'There y'are,' she said triumphantly. 'I never thought things in the country could be more modern than London, but everythin' 'ere is better than what I 'ad there – includin' nice clean air to breathe. Can't think why I didn't want to come before.' She smiled wistfully. 'Pa would've loved it 'ere. I often think I was selfish not to move when 'e was alive. 'E always fancied a little place in the country where 'e could grow 'is own vegetables when we retired.'

'But you're not lonely. You've made friends?' Shirley asked.

Ma shrugged. 'Oh, yes. I 'ave now. Some of 'em was a bit stand-offish at first, but I soon let 'em know what's what. Now they knows they can take me or leave me.'

'So they take you?'

'Most of 'em. Them as don't ain't worth botherin' with anyway.' Ma kissed her. 'Take care of yourself, duck. And don't forget to write an' tell me 'ow you are.' She bent forward to whisper in Shirley's ear. 'As for this geezer oo's broke your 'eart – just you forget 'im. Get on with what you've worked 'ard for. It's taken a lot of guts to get where you are, so don't you let nuthin' 'appen to stop you now.'

Shirley hugged her. 'I won't, Ma. Good night and take care of yourself.'

Her short stay came to an end all too soon and it was time for her to leave. Tony was due to go up for a one-day recording session at the BBC so they travelled down to London together. Sitting opposite him in the train, she suddenly realised to her surprise that she had forgotten all about his scarred face. It was because he was so happy, she decided. Since his accident and his marriage to Gloria he was so much more relaxed. He wasn't obsessed with his looks any more. He smiled a lot – that same dazzling, bright-eyed smile that Marc had. It tugged painfully at her heart every time she saw it. Feeling her eyes on him, he looked up from his newspaper.

'All right?'

'Yes, thanks.'

'Are you happy, Shirley?'

The question took her by surprise. 'Happy? Yes, of course.'

'I know this part is a big chance for you, but your mother is afraid you're nervous about it.'

She laughed. 'Nervous? Well, yes, of course I am, but not unhappy.'

'I probably shouldn't tell you, but she's worried that there's something wrong. Is there – in any other area of your life, I mean? I heard what your grandmother said about a broken heart.'

'There has been an . . . emotional upset,' she told him. 'But it's nothing that time won't heal. Ma's advice was the best I've had: to put all my energy into my work and forget what happened. That's what I intend to do.'

Tony smiled sympathetically. 'Well, you know we're here whenever you need us, don't you? You know we're your family and we love you?'

She nodded. 'I do – now.'

Rehearsals for *Give Me Yesterday* were to take place in a church hall in Islington. Shirley had spent the weekend at Tony's flat concentrating on her lines and as she travelled to the first rehearsal she was fairly confident that she was word-perfect. She had rung Peter as soon as she was back in London, to reassure him that all was now well and she had regained her composure. He had reminded her of the schedule and also that John Gerard, the director, was a stickler for punctuality. 'He's a prickly devil,' he said. 'He has a short fuse but a good sense of humour and he's a positive genius for getting the best out of actors. Try and get on his right side. If he likes you and your work you'll find him quite tolerant.'

She arrived at the hall with five minutes to spare and hung up her coat in the cloakroom. Most of the cast had already assembled and stood warming their hands on the radiators or talking to each other. They seemed quite a pleasant, friendly crowd. Shirley introduced herself to an attractive older actress with red hair, whose name, she discovered, was Lesley Fraser. She told Shirley that she was taking the part Leonie had created.

Suddenly the door at the end of the hall flew open to admit a draught of icy air and a stocky man with longish hair. He wore a cracked leather jacket and carried a tattered, bulging briefcase. Lesley muttered: 'That's John Gerard.' Shirley looked at him with slight apprehension. 'He's impatient and impossibly eccentric, but quite brilliant,' Lesley went on. 'I've worked with him before. He certainly knows his stuff.'

Shirley watched as the perceptive, needle-sharp eyes swept the room, taking in the material he was to work with. She could well imagine that he had an explosive temper.

Striding to the stage at the end of the room and dumping his briefcase on a chair, he clapped his hands as though they were a crowd of unruly children.

'All right, everyone. I'm your director, John Gerard, the bloke whose guts you're going to love to hate for the next few weeks,' he said. 'Now I'd just like to ascertain that I have a full cast. I'll tick you off from the cast list so as to put faces to names.' He began to read out the names of the characters, looking up as the actors answered with their own names. When Shirley replied he glanced up at her, his dark, penetrating eyes assessing her shrewdly.

'Ah, yes, Shirley Rayner,' he said enigmatically, ticking her off and leaving her to imagine what he might have heard about her. Had Paul been talking to him too?

She was last from bottom of the list, the last character being Jason Hamilton, the part Marcus was to have played. When he read out the name there was silence. The other members of the cast glanced inquiringly at each other. John Gerard read the name again, his voice a shade louder. He looked up, his dark eyes flashing impatiently.

'Oh, for Christ's sake. Look in the gents, someone. We haven't got all bloody morning to hang about.'

One of the men went off and Shirley, quaking in her shoes, took a step forward. Surely Peter should have let him know, but as it was partly down to her that they were one short she'd better try to offer some kind of explanation.

'Excuse me, Mr Gerard.'

He looked up with an irritated frown. 'The name's John,' he snapped. 'No formalities, for God's sake. This isn't an insurance office.'

'No – sorry.' Shirley cleared her throat. 'I . . . I was just going to say that . . .' She felt a cold draught on her back again and turned to see that someone had just opened the door. He pulled it shut behind him and turned. She stared at him, her heart leaping in her chest as the cry burst from her: *'Marc!'*

John Gerard looked up from his clipboard. 'Yes, you were saying? Marc who?' He broke off to stare in amaze-

500

ment as the girl and the newcomer flew into each other's arms and clasped each other in a passionate embrace.

'I couldn't go. I couldn't leave you,' Marcus whispered. 'I know he must have been lying – I knew it all along, really. I must have been crazy to risk losing you like that. I'm sorry, darling.'

Shirley shook her head and clung to him, her heart too full to speak. She was oblivious to the astonished faces all round her. *Marc was back*. He hadn't left her after all. It was a miracle.

'Oh, bloody *hell*, this is all I need.' Gerard flung his script in the air. 'I know I said no formalities but this is ridiculous. It's going to be one of *those* tours, is it?'

To his astonishment and Shirley's acute but happy embarrassment, the rest of the cast burst out laughing.

March 1950

Imogen ushered her father and Gloria along the corridor of the New Theatre and into the box she had booked for them. 'I got the prompt side for you, Daddy,' she said. 'I know you hate being able to see into the prompt corner.' She was almost eight months pregnant now and had been living at Houlton, helping Gloria with her costume collection, since Christmas. Planning this evening had given her so much pleasure and excitement, though she had let Gloria in on the secret.

'I can't think why you chose Monday night to book for us,' Tony complained. 'You know the first night in a new theatre is always tricky. I'd have preferred to wait till they settled down and got their bearings.'

'I had my reasons,' Imogen said enigmatically, with a wink at Gloria. 'Shirley will join us after the show, which is why I got a box. She can slip in through the pass door. It's just along the corridor from here.'

They settled themselves on the blue upholstered chairs and Tony looked down into the rapidly filling auditorium. It was a large theatre with white and silver decor and seats in royal-blue plush, a theatre normally used for variety or musical shows. Tony shook his head.

'I'm glad to see they're getting a good house for their first night,' he remarked. 'Though I must say that this theatre hasn't really the intimate atmosphere needed for a straight play.' He glanced round. 'Did anyone think to buy a programme?'

Imogen laughed. 'What did your last servant die of?' She handed him the programme and waited, looking at Gloria in anticipation, but to her disappointment he put it to one side with only the briefest of glances.

The orchestra pit filled with musicians who began to play a medley of popular light music. Then the lights dimmed, the music faded and there was a soft swish as the blue and silver curtain rose on Act I. Tony leaned forward with interest, while Gloria felt nervously for Imogen's hand in the darkness.

Shirley was good. Gloria hadn't seen her act professionally till now and she was astonished at how far she had come. Her movements were graceful and easy, her voice strong and musical and she played the part with a wisdom and emotional power far beyond her years. As Gloria watched her daughter there was a lump in her throat. Shirley had made it. She'd done it by herself, in spite of all the obstacles and disappointments she had encountered along the way. She had exceeded all the dreams and hopes she'd had for her. She was a daughter to be proud of.

Act I was almost halfway through when Marcus made his first entrance. Tony, who had been leaning forward, his arms resting on the box's ledge, suddenly sat up straight. For a few minutes he watched, then Gloria saw his hand reach out for the programme. She nudged Imogen, who bit her lip excitedly, holding her breath as she saw her father scan the cast list. Finding the name he was looking for, Tony dropped the programme and leaned forward again, peering intently at the handsome young man playing the part of Jason Hamilton.

Imogen quietly moved from her seat to sit next to her father. 'Now you see why I wanted you to come tonight, Daddy,' she whispered.

He turned to look at her and she saw that his eyes were very bright. 'You *knew*? Why didn't you tell me?' he whispered. 'No one told me he was an actor. I didn't even know he was in this country. Why hasn't he been in touch?'

'He wanted to wait till he'd had a chance to prove himself,' Imogen said. 'He didn't want help or special influence. He wanted to make it by himself.'

'Well, he's done that all right,' Tony said. 'He's good. Damned good.'

The curtain came down on the first act to loud applause and Tony sat back in his seat, looking round incredulously at his wife and daughter. 'You *both* knew about this,' he said as he caught sight of Gloria's face. 'And neither of you breathed a word. Peter must have known, too. Did Shirley know when she came home last November?'

Imogen took his hand. 'That's another surprise, Daddy. Marc and Shirley are engaged. Peter Jason introduced them when the tour was first cast and they fell in love almost at once.'

'Shirley and Marcus? Well, I'll be . . .' Tony beamed with pleasure as the house lights began to dim again and the curtain rose on Act II.

All three watched, enthralled, as the rest of the play unfolded; then it was over and the cast lined up to take the curtain calls. Shirley, aware of the special party in the box, looked up with a smile as they responded to the enthusiastic reception. The curtain fell for the last time and the audience began to file out.

'We're to wait here,' Imogen said excitedly. A moment later the door at the back of the box opened and Shirley stepped in, still in her costume and make-up. She was followed by a bewildered-looking Marcus. Imogen got up to greet him.

'Marc, how nice to see you again. I enjoyed the play so much. I thought your first night here would be a great opportunity for a family reunion, so I arranged one. This is Gloria, Shirley's mother. And I don't think I need to introduce this gentleman.' She stood aside and Marcus and Tony came face to face. For a moment they looked at each other, both lost for words, then Tony said:

'Congratulations – to both of you. You were very good indeed.' He shook his hand. 'But I wish to God someone had told me what to expect this evening. It would have given me time to think what to *say*.' The tension was broken as they all laughed. Marcus stepped forward, holding out his hands to his father.

'Me too. Who ever heard of a speechless actor? All I can think of right now is, it's great to see you again – Dad.'

In the excited conversation that followed, Tony looked at the two vibrant young people. They brought with them into the small space of the box the very essence of all that was close to his heart: the scent of greasepaint, the throbbing pulse of excitement that had epitomised the theatre and the life he had loved ever since he could remember. Just for the briefest of moments he envied them, feeling a deep nostalgic yearning sweep through his veins for all that he had lost. But it was only for a split second. At that moment, as though she read his thoughts, Gloria turned to him and reached for his hand, giving it a reassuring squeeze and smiling the special smile that told him without words how much she loved him. He was lucky. He had survived an appalling accident and been reborn to a new and better life. He had his new career in radio and the promise of a partnership with Peter. He had the love of a loyal wife and a beautiful little son. And if all that wasn't enough, here was Marcus, handsome and talented, treading in his footsteps and looking for his father's approval. He had so much – so very much to be thankful for. He was luckier than he could ever have hoped.

Later that evening the five of them drove back to Houlton together. In the back seat of Tony's Bentley Shirley sat between Imogen and Marcus.

'I can't wait to show you the village where I grew up,' she told Marcus, squeezing his arm. 'I can't wait for you to meet Michael and Ma and Charles. Isn't it great that we actually share the same family? They're all such special, unique people.'

'*We* are, you mean,' Imogen said and laughed. 'We're wonderfully, hopelessly entwined.' She smiled as Marcus slipped an arm around Shirley and drew her close. 'And getting more so by the minute,' she concluded happily, turning to look out of the car window.

Above them a new moon pierced the spring sky and a handful of stars twinkled brightly.

This Year, Next Year

Part One

Chapter One

Amy knew that the nightmare was about to begin but there was nothing she could do about it. She tried hard to wake up, but it was as if she were frozen – sucked down into a vortex of fear, destined to re-live the terror once again.

She and Mark were walking out onto the pavement when the car stopped a few yards down the road. Before she had time to recognise its occupant it suddenly began to reverse at speed. Alarmed, she snatched Mark up into her arms and jumped back against the hedge to avoid the back wheels as they mounted the pavement.

It was then that she saw him.

Leaving the engine running, Alex leapt from the car and grabbed the child from her arms, pushing him into the back of the car. Then he grasped her roughly by the collar of her coat and bundled her unceremoniously into the front passenger seat. A moment later, they were roaring down the street at speed.

Rigid with terror, Amy hardly dared to look as they careered into the main road without stopping, narrowly avoiding a passing car and tipping a cyclist on to the pavement.

'Alex, for God's sake be careful! What's the matter with you?' Gritting her teeth, she held tightly to the sides of her seat as the car wove perilously in and out of the traffic. 'Why are you here? What's wrong?'

1

'*What's wrong?*' he mimicked. 'You might well ask.'

She glanced at him, alarmed by his grey-green pallor. There were beads of sweat on his forehead and his lips were drawn back from his teeth in a menacing travesty of a smile. Alone in the back seat, baby Mark was being thrown about like a shuttlecock by Alex's erratic driving. He was wailing loudly with fear and crying out for her. Turning in her seat, Amy tried to comfort him.

'It's all right darling. We'll soon be home.' But the child's wails drowned her soothing. She turned again to Alex. 'Please stop. You've been drinking. You don't know what you're doing . . .'

'I know what I'm doing all right.' He threw her a look of pure hatred, so ferocious that it made her recoil. 'Of course I've been drinking, you bitch – driven to it by you. Why didn't you tell me you'd taken a job? Half the bloody country knew before I did. That must have given you the best laugh of all.'

She bit her lip. So that was it. 'I'm sorry, Alex. I should have told you. I meant to. It was just that . . .'

'That you knew I'd put a stop to it, right?' He turned to glare at her with bloodshot eyes. 'Well, if you want to make a fool of yourself, do it. I don't give a damn any more. You're a selfish little cow and always were. But I won't have you farming my son out to some idiot stranger. I told you what would happen if you ever did that again, and by God I mean to see that it does.'

Panic quickened her already racing heartbeat as she remembered his threats. In this mood he was capable of anything. 'Alex, *don't*. It's not like you think. You can't imagine how lonely I've been – how frustrated, alone in the house with you away all the time. It's wonderful to be working again. And it's not doing Mark any harm . . . *Oh!*' She gasped as he swung the car across the road directly in the path of an oncoming lorry. Its brakes screeched and the driver leaned out of his cab to hurl abuse at Alex. There was a thud, followed by a scream as Mark fell off the back seat onto the floor.

'Alex! For God's sake. You've hurt Mark now.'

But the child's cries only served to anger him more. As the car lurched forward again he rounded on her furiously.

'*I've* hurt him? That's rich. It's *you* who've hurt him. If he's crying it's because of what you've done to him – to Chloe's child. He's all I have left of her, but do you care? Dumping him like a parcel of rubbish anywhere that suits you. You've done it on purpose, haven't you? To get back at me – at us – at me and Chloe. But you shan't have our child. *We won't let you!* Do you hear?'

Cold with terror, Amy stared at him. What was he talking about? His eyes were wild, the pupils dilated. He was completely out of control; living in some fantasy nightmare of his own making in which she was the enemy. How could she reason with him in this state?

They were speeding through the tree-lined streets of the estate now. Children were playing outside after school. A ball rolled into the road in front of them and a little girl ran out from between parked cars to retrieve it. Amy screamed, clenching her fists and closing her eyes as she waited for what seemed inevitable. But the child jumped back in time and the accident was miraculously avoided. Next time – oh God, next time they wouldn't be as lucky.

She turned and pleaded with him, her voice trembling. 'Please, oh *please*, Alex. You must stop and listen to me. We can talk this out quietly at home. I can make you see if only you'll calm down. Please – please stop before you kill someone. If not for me, then for Mark. He's hurt. Can't you hear him?'

They had turned into Willow Drive now and suddenly he stood on the brakes. The tyres shrieked and the car shuddered to a halt, throwing Amy forward so violently that her forehead met the windscreen with a dizzying thud.

'Get out,' he snapped. 'Go on, get out – *now*, before I throw you out.'

Her head still spinning with pain, she opened the door and got out of the car on trembling legs, almost weeping

3

with relief. Thank God he'd listened to reason at last. She reached for the handle of the rear door to get Mark, but before she could open it Alex had slammed the car into gear and revved the engine. With a screech and a grinding of gears the car leapt forward, gathering speed as it roared down the road.

In a blind panic she ran after it, her arms outstretched, oblivious of the blood trickling down her face from the cut on her forehead. In vain she screamed for him to stop. She could see Mark standing on the back seat looking out of the rear window as the car sped away. His little face contorted with terror, he held out his arms to her as the distance between them lengthened. Then the car rounded the corner and disappeared from view.

Amy staggered to a stop. Her legs gave way beneath her and she sank to her knees in the road, tears streaming down her cheeks.

'Mark – Mark, my baby! Oh God – *God* what shall I do?'

Shocked neighbours who had witnessed the harrowing scene from their windows were running out to help, but it was Addie Shaw who was first at her side, enfolding her in motherly arms and murmuring soothing words.

'There, there, luvvie, it'll be all right, you'll see. You come home with me. Jack's already rung the police. They'll catch him, never fear. I'm here now.'

Amy surfaced, dragging herself up from the depths only to find that Addie had turned into her mother. She closed her eyes, then opened them again. She was still there – watching – waiting. *Mum* . . . after all this time.

Chapter Two

It was in 1906 that fourteen-year-old Sam Leigh went to work for Jacob Feldman at his clothing factory in Ox Lane, Hackney. The job had been secured for him at the orphanage where he had grown up. He was hired to run errands and to make himself generally useful until he was older and strong enough to get himself a labouring job. But Jacob's shrewd eyes picked up the boy's potential almost immediately. Slightly built and small for his age, Sam was bright and quick to learn. He was willing and eager to please, too, and seemed to blossom under his employer's attentive eye. Until now he had been a mere face in a crowd. A number with a body attached. A child of no importance. Being noticed and called by his name was a new and heady experience to Sam and he responded to it encouragingly.

The more Jacob saw of the boy the more he liked him. His wife Esther had died giving birth to his only child, a daughter, Rachel, who was the apple of his eye. With the help of a daily woman, nineteen-year-old Rachel had kept house for him since leaving school and, being blessed with a gift for figures, had lately taken over the book-keeping side of the business; something which was a great source of pride to Jacob. She also visited the outworkers once a week to pay them.

Young Sam learned quickly and when he had been with Feldman's Clothing for a year Jacob decided that the boy should become an apprentice. He would teach him all he knew about the clothing trade, just as he himself had learned from his father, and perhaps with luck, by the time he was ready to retire, Sam would be able to manage the business for him.

He decided that he must first remove the boy from the spartan lodgings found for him by the orphanage and take him into his own household. But before doing so, Jacob tried to discover something about his protégé's origins. His enquiries at the orphanage were met with indifference. All that anyone knew about him was that he had been abandoned as a newly born infant on the steps of the workhouse, apparently by some servant girl who had given birth to her illegitimate child in secret, but as time went by Jacob became more and more convinced that the boy had Jewish blood. His dark good looks and his aptitude for business certainly pointed in that direction.

Gradually Sam's pinched, waif-like little face filled out and his body developed bone and muscle. By the time three years had passed and he had reached the age of seventeen he had grown into a tall, handsome young man. His dark hair curled glossily and his brown eyes shone with health and a zest for learning. Jacob felt blessed, happy that his judgement of the boy had proved well-founded. He felt sure that the good Lord had sent him Sam as a substitute for the son he had never had. It was up to him to bring out the boy's full potential.

When he approached Sam on the subject of religion he found him willing and as eager to embrace the Jewish faith as he had been to learn the business. Since living with Jacob and Rachel he had already become accustomed to their food and customs. Why not join them in their acts of worship too?

After approaching the Jewish religious authorities, the Beth Din, Jacob himself undertook Sam's instruction and found him a delight to teach. Once he had been taught something he never forgot it, and to Jacob's delight Sam was finally judged ready to be accepted into Judaism by the Jewish rabbis – the dayanim.

Rachel watched her father's preoccupation with Sam with mixed feelings. All her life she had been first in her father's affections, though she recognised that like all fathers he had always wanted a son. She liked Sam. Who could fail to like the cheerful, good-natured young man who had come into their lives? As he grew to manhood she was far from impervious to his physical attractiveness, too. Although he was five years her junior, he was already as mature as she was, and he was as keen and dedicated to the business as she and her father. On her visits to the factory she had seen him at work. Already he was an expert cutter; the maintenance of the machines gave him no problems at all, so that Jacob had been able to dispense with the services of the repair man. The female machinists loved Sam with his ready wit and cheerful manner. He encouraged them to sing as they worked, leading them with his pleasant baritone voice in all the current popular songs, so that the workshop rang with the sound of singing mingled with the whirr of machinery. With his charm he could twist them around his little finger, effortlessly getting twice the work out of them. A delighted Jacob had already made him workshop foreman.

As Rachel watched and saw how things were progressing, it became clear to her that to fall in with her father's plans and to re-establish her prior entitlement to her father's affection there was only one thing for it. She must marry Sam Leigh and give her father a grandson.

When she went to Jacob and shyly confessed her wish he was overjoyed. He was also relieved. Rachel was twenty-four. Most Jewish girls were married long before this. If her mother had been alive she would have seen to it that her daughter met the right young men. She would have entertained friends with sons of a suitable age, sifting through them until the right one was selected. Jacob had neither the time nor the necessary social skill for this. His life had been dedicated to his business, his home and his child. There had been no time in his busy working schedule for socialising except, of course, at the synagogue. Also, if he were to put aside his natural paternal prejudice he would have been obliged to admit that Rachel was not the prettiest of girls. True she had inherited her mother's fine dark eyes and abundant hair, but working long hours over the ledgers had made her short-sighted, which necessitated the wearing of ugly wire-rimmed spectacles. For the same reason, she had also developed a slight stoop, and truth to tell she was inclined to be a little on the heavy side for current tastes. If her mother were alive she would doubtless have known how to alleviate these problems, Jacob told himself, stroking his beard wistfully. Though he had never yet met a man who had complained of a good build in a wife. Broad child-bearing hips were surely a definite advantage. And she could cook like an angel. Her honey cakes melted in the mouth. Jacob smiled, nodding to himself. Yes, Sam was particularly partial to them, as he was to her other culinary accomplishments.

He broached the subject with Sam one evening as they walked home from the factory together.

'Tell me, Samuel, what do you think of Rachel?'

The young man looked surprised. 'Rachel? I like her, of course. She's a very clever young woman and a good cook.'

Jacob cleared his throat. 'Ah, but – have you ever thought of her in an – er – affectionate way at all?'

Sam considered. 'Since I have lived with you she has been like a sister. She has been very good to me.'

Jacob frowned. Was the boy really so naive or was he deliberately misunderstanding him? He decided to take the bull by the horns. 'I'm asking if you have ever thought that she might make you a suitable wife, Samuel,' he said. 'After all, you'll be needing to marry soon, won't you? A man is not complete without a wife.' He spread his hands. 'And there is my Rachel – needing a husband. What could be better – for either of you?'

Sam's cheeks coloured scarlet. It was totally unexpected.

He'd never seen Rachel as anything but Jacob's daughter. Never actually *looked* at her properly. And certainly never thought of her as a potential wife. That Jacob was actually offering his beloved only daughter to him was the most tremendous compliment; he recognised that, and yet . . . He tried to speak, but his voice seemed to have deserted him. He slipped a finger inside his collar to loosen it. Jacob smiled indulgently and shook his head.

'Ah, I see I have overwhelmed you. No need to answer now,' he said. 'Just think about it. I can tell you in confidence though that Rachel is very fond of you. And if you were to approach her I know she would not rebuff you. Ask her out to the theatre, why don't you? Buy her a little gift – some flowers or sweetmeats to show her that you admire her. You have my permission – and my blessing,' he added hopefully.

Alone in his room later, Sam weighed the situation and found it heavily loaded on the side of marriage. He was already one of the Feldman family in all but name. He liked his job and the comfortable life he had with the Feldmans. Already he had embraced their religion as his own. He felt happy and established with it, so why not complete the conversion? At the back of his mind the possibility that Feldman's might one day pass into his hands occurred to him fleetingly. But he thrust the thought aside, dismissing it as mercenary and unworthy. He had been so lucky. Jacob Feldman had been like a father to him and he liked and respected Rachel. They were the only family he had ever known, so why not repay them in this way if it was what they both wanted?

On Jacob's advice he invited Rachel to go to the theatre with him. He chose the music hall. Over the past few years it had become more respectable. It had even been rumoured that this year's Royal Command Performance was to include some music hall acts. But Sam had a particular reason for taking his prospective bride there. He wanted to see if she could actually laugh. In all his years in the Feldman household he had seldom seen her smile and had certainly never seen her rather serious face relax into a full-blown laugh. He wasn't at all sure that he could commit himself for life to a woman who never laughed.

They went to the Hackney Empire where Marie Lloyd was on the bill. Sam could see right away that Rachel thought Marie's saucy songs and suggestive manner vulgar, and he was just beginning to feel he'd made a mistake in bringing her when the comedian came on; a little man with a white face and outsized boots in which he performed a fantastic dance. Halfway through the little man's act Sam heard a strange spluttering noise from the seat beside him. He turned to see that Rachel's face was contorted and that she was holding her handkerchief to her mouth. Full of concern, he laid a hand on her arm and asked if she was all right. Lowering the handkerchief, Rachel turned to him, her dark eyes swimming with tears.

'Oh, Sam,' she spluttered. It was only then that he realised that she was not ill but actually convulsed with laughter. 'Oh, *Sam*, I don't know when I've enjoyed myself so much.'

It was a swift courtship. Rachel had already known that she intended to marry Sam, but once they began to spend time in each other's company and she discovered what a fascinating companion he was, she was even more determined to become his wife. To her surprise she found that with Sam she felt relaxed as never before. He brought her a kind of happiness she had never experienced. He made her laugh. With his quick, light-hearted wit he made her see things in a totally different light, so that suddenly people and life were fun. And the first time he kissed her the sudden and explosive revelation that she had actually fallen in love struck her like a bolt from the blue.

Jacob was ecstatic. He had never seen his daughter look so happy. Sam had achieved wonders; he had transformed Rachel from a plain girl into a radiant woman. Her eyes shone (she now wore the ugly spectacles only when she was working), her hair gleamed and she began to take more interest in her appearance. She bought new clothes and held herself in a new, upright, proud way that actually made her look slimmer.

They were married in November 1911, just before the festival of Chanukah, which Jacob felt was most appropriate. God had sent a miracle into his life and he gave thanks for it every day.

The wedding was a quiet affair. Jacob had only one sister, Naomi, who had emigrated to America back in the nineties. When he knew that Rachel was to be married he had written to Naomi, inviting her and her husband Aaron to the wedding. Naomi had replied, saying that they could not afford to make such an expensive journey, but that she longed to see her brother again and if Jacob could pay his passage he would be more than welcome to come to New York and stay with them for a holiday.

At first he dismissed the idea as out of the question. The business was doing well and he could easily afford to go. But in all his years in London he had never taken so much as a day off. Rachel tried to persuade him to accept her Aunt Naomi's offer.

'You've never even taken a day off for illness, Father. You deserve a holiday. Sam and I can easily manage the factory.'

Sam too did his best to persuade his father-in-law to take the trip. Secretly he looked forward to having his new wife the house and the factory to himself for a few weeks. He was eager to prove both to Jacob and to himself that he was competent and to establish himself properly as Rachel's husband. Although Rachel was now married, Jacob could not quite relinquish his hold on his daughter. He still seemed to feel that he and he alone knew what was best for her. It was for this reason that neither of them had told him that Rachel was almost certainly pregnant. If he knew there was a baby on the way nothing on earth would persuade him to leave the country.

At last, between them Sam and Rachel managed to

convince Jacob that a trip to America to see his only sister was an opportunity not to be missed. And, once the idea had established itself in his mind, he became quite excited at the prospect and began to look forward to it, making plans to look at new fabrics and machines while he was in America. Because as well as enjoying his stay he meant to make it work for him.

It was on a dull grey February afternoon that he came home in a state of high excitement to tell his daughter and son-in-law that his passage was booked. Taking out his wallet he waved the steamship ticket at them.

'I sail from Southampton on April the tenth. And it's to be on a brand-new ship too,' he told them proudly. 'The one we've been reading about in all the newspapers. It will be her maiden voyage. They say she's a miracle of engineering – impossible to sink. Can you imagine?'

As the boat train pulled out of the harbour, Rachel stifled a sob and Sam put a protective arm around her.

'Don't cry, sweetheart. Your father deserves a good holiday. He's really looking forward to it, and think what a joyful reunion he and your aunt will have. He tells me it's over twenty years since they last set eyes on each other.'

But Rachel was sobbing on his shoulder. 'But it's such a long way, Sam. He's never been away from me before.'

'But you have *me* now, darling,' he reminded her, slightly hurt. 'Please don't upset yourself. You'll harm the child.'

Rachel took a deep breath and put away her handkerchief. 'We should have told him, Sam,' she said. 'If anything were to happen . . .'

He laughed and tipped up her chin with his finger. '*Happen*? My silly girl, what can possibly happen? He couldn't be sailing on a more up-to-date vessel. And think of the lovely surprise we'll have for him when he comes home. Can you imagine his face?'

Rachel smiled, imagining the joy on her father's dear

face when they told him he was to be a grandfather. The thought cheered her.

But little did Rachel know that she had said a final goodbye to her father, or that he would never know the joy of holding his grandson in his arms. It was just five days later that he succumbed along with fifteen hundred other passengers when the SS *Titanic* sank in the icy waters of the North Atlantic.

On 20 November 1912 Rachel gave birth to a baby son. It was a painful and protracted birth. The highly qualified midwife Sam had engaged finally admitted after Rachel had suffered three days of agonising pain that she could not deliver the child without the help of a doctor and Jacob's old friend Doctor Epstein was sent for. Thanks to his skilful ministrations the child was safely delivered, but Rachel was severely weakened by her ordeal. The months of grieving for her father and the complicated birth had taken all her strength. Her life hung in the balance for several worrying days and the doctor informed Sam gravely that Rachel would bear no more children.

At first she seemed to have lost the will to live. Even Sam, who sat tirelessly at her bedside, urging her to get better, failed to rally her. But eventually the sound of her child's pitiful cries and the thought of leaving him motherless seemed to give her the necessary strength to revive and she began, slowly, to pull round.

The little boy was named Marcus Jacob in memory of his grandfather. But even after a month had gone by and the time arrived for the boy's redemption ceremony, Rachel was still too weak and ill to leave the house.

When the elderly daily woman who had served the Feldmans since Rachel was a baby announced her retirement, Sam engaged the services of a younger woman to help her in the house. Sarah Brown was a young married woman, one of Feldman's outworkers, whom Rachel had known for some time. Until recently she had been obliged to work at home, bound to the house in nearby Crimea

13

Terrace by her invalid mother-in-law. But now that the old woman had died Sarah was looking for a better paid job. Although she was not Jewish, Sarah was a clean woman of good character who was used to caring for invalids. Rachel had always liked her and Sam felt it would be good for her to have a woman of her own age at hand, someone to talk to as well as to help her during his long hours of absence; for now that Jacob had gone Feldman's was Sam's responsibility alone and he was busy at the factory and in the office all day and often late into the evening.

Jacob had left his entire estate – the business, factory and house – intact to his daughter, Rachel. Sam had tried hard not to show his shock and disappointment when the will was read. His late father-in-law had indicated at the time of their marriage that on his demise the house was to go to Rachel, the business to him. Although of course as husband and wife they would naturally share everything, to have been left nothing in his own right, after all the years of hard work and loyalty, seemed hard and hurtful to Sam.

Rachel, sensing his hurt, had assured him that it was only Jacob's way of looking after her future – that it was only hers on paper, which meant nothing, because she could never manage any of it without his help.

Little by little Rachel grew stronger. Sarah Brown was a strong, competent worker and the two women became good friends. Sarah was good with Marcus, too. He was a beautiful child but strong-willed, like his mother. Sarah could always manage him, however. She seemed to have the knack and the patience that Rachel lacked. Truth to tell, as time went by and she regained her strength and energy, Rachel was bored. She missed her visits to the factory and outworkers, and the satisfaction she had always had from keeping the accounts and balancing the books. She saw so little of Sam, and when he was at home all his time seemed to be devoted to playing with his baby son. If she were to help him in the business, she told herself, he would have more time to spend with her.

By the time Marcus was a year old Rachel decided that she was sufficiently recovered to return to her duties and take an interest in the business once again. Sam was a good manager, but he was clearly struggling on his own. His talent lay in organisation and with managing the workforce. He lacked the business skills that Jacob had, and which Rachel herself had inherited. She decided that she could do much of the work at home, while Sarah took care of Marcus and the housework. But when she put the idea to Sam he was shocked.

'There is no need for you to work, my love. I am your husband, your provider. You are needed here, caring for our home and our son.'

'But I want to help just as I helped Father,' Rachel protested. 'Sarah can manage Marcus much better than I, and see to the housework, too. It is our business. Yours and mine.'

Sam frowned moodily. 'It's yours, you mean. You're saying that you can't trust me to manage it properly.'

'No, no, darling,' Rachel soothed him. 'You're better even than father was at getting the best out of the workers. Why not concentrate on that and let me take care of the books and the orders as I did before?' Sidling up to him she rubbed her cheek against his handsome, newly grown beard and slipped her arms around his waist. 'Please let me take my share of the work, sweetheart,' she wheedled. 'I want so much for us to share everything, and I can do most of the work right here at home while Marcus is little. And I shall still cook your meals. You can be sure I shall not neglect either of you.'

As always, Rachel got her way. She was determined to make her rightful contribution to the business again. She was good at it, and although she would die rather than remind Sam of the fact, it was hers. Why should she relinquish it just because she had become a mother?

On 30 June 1914 the newspapers were full of the assassination of the Archduke Ferdinand in Sarajevo. Soon it seemed that all Europe was inflamed and in turmoil. A month later it was reported that Germany had invaded Belgium in contravention of the Treaty of Neutrality, drawn up in 1839. Sam sat over the breakfast table shaking his head over his copy of the *Daily Chronicle*.

'It's beginning to look serious,' he said. 'The Kaiser is riding roughshod over poor Belgium. It says here that he dismisses the Treaty as a mere scrap of paper. I can't see Britain standing for it.'

Rachel put down her teacup. 'You don't mean we might go to war, surely?'

'It could come to it.'

'But what will that mean?'

Sam glanced up at her. 'It needn't worry you my dear. It's a long way off. It won't affect us much, I daresay. Imports and exports might be affected, though. There could be shortages if it lasts long.'

'And men killed.' Rachel shuddered. 'I hate the thought of it.'

'The general opinion seems to be that it'd be over in a few months. The idea is that the French will be able to contain it, but Kitchener doesn't agree.' He pointed to the paper. 'According to this article, he's planning to assemble an army of a hundred thousand volunteers. Can you imagine that?'

Rachel paused, her cup halfway to her lips. 'A hundred thousand men?' she said thoughtfully, trying to visualise the number. 'A new army will need uniforms, Sam. Maybe it's something we should look into.'

By Christmas life for the Leighs and the Browns had changed drastically. When war was first declared, Sam, stirred by patriotism, had longed to volunteer.

'The whole of the Empire's in it now, my love,' he told Rachel, reading to her from the newspaper. 'Australia, New Zealand – even Africa. Look, it says here that Russian soldiers have landed on their way to France.'

But Rachel argued that there was valuable work for him to do at home. Thanks to her quick action and careful costing, Feldman's tender for making uniforms for Kitchener's new army had been accepted. In just a few months the Leighs' income had increased dramatically. Feldman's Clothing had moved to larger premises, acquired new machines and taken on more workers. With so many of the men going off to war there were plenty of women wanting work. Already, far-sighted Rachel was planning to make good use of their new equipment by going in for tailoring once the war was over. Off-the-peg suits, perhaps. And she had her eye on an elegant little Regency villa she had seen for sale on Hackney Road. There was a garden at the back in which little Marcus would be able to play – a place where washing could be hung out to dry in the fresh air instead of dripping from the rack in the dismal basement kitchen as it did now.

For the Browns, life was not so rosy. Sarah's husband Alf was one of the first to respond to Kitchener's jingoistic rallying call. Kissing Sarah, now pregnant with their first child, goodbye he marched off to France full of patriotic euphoria, to be killed within the first weeks, along with many others at the retreat from Mons. He was never to see his baby girl, Maryan, born the following January.

Rachel comforted Sarah as best she could, promising to give her whatever money she needed to pay the rent and keep a roof over their heads until she was fit to return to work. In private Rachel thanked the Lord that she had managed to persuade her own man to stay where he was and work for the country in other ways.

By the time the war ended Crimea Terrace was full of war widows, all struggling to bring up their families on pitifully inadequate incomes. They helped each other, sharing what little they had in good times and bad. While Maryan was a toddler, all Sarah could manage by the way of paid work was the rough work and washing, which Miss Rachel allowed her to do whenever Sarah could get Cissie Jessop next door to look after the baby for her. A widow like Sarah, Cissie eked out a living for herself and her two young sons by assisting at confinements and layings-out. Soon Maryan began school, so that her mother could accept the job of housekeeper that Miss Rachel had offered her, with a substantially increased wage now that they had moved to the smart house in Hackney Road. With Maryan attending school full-time Sarah could put in longer hours. Eight-year-old Tom, Cissie's youngest, could be relied on to make sure she got home safely. He was a good boy, running errands for the neighbours for coppers and looking after the younger kids.

Sarah was deeply grateful to Miss Rachel for her help and compassion through the hard war years. She'd known her ever since they were both girls and Rachel had called weekly to pay her wages for the outwork she'd done. She'd been a good and generous friend to them when times were rough, passing on clothes she had done with, some of them hardly worn. Sarah often thought wistfully that if young Marcus could only have been a girl, Maryan would have been the best dressed kid in the street.

Nowadays Rachel often let Sarah take home the leftovers from the dinner parties she had started to give since Feldman's had become so prosperous. Rachel would never allow anyone else to use her kitchen, insisting on preparing everything herself, however busy she was. But Sarah loved to watch her employer cook, fascinated by the way she prepared her meat and the various taboos and rituals of her religion. Maryan would await her mother's homecoming eagerly, her blue eyes round with anticipation as she waited to see what succulent delicacy there would be for supper that night.

As the years passed life became easier. In spite of the slump, Feldman's Clothing – now renamed Feldman Fashions – flourished. As the twenties dawned Rachel shrewdly foresaw a new demand for cheap copies of couture fashions. The war had brought a lot of changes for women and more were working. Now that they had the vote they were a new breed, energetic and independent.

Young working women had more money to spend on clothes and they would want to be wearing something fashionable but affordable. With this in mind, she took herself off to some of the shows given by top fashion houses and made sketches, later simplifying the latest in line and trends and adapting them for everyday wear. With her collection of sketches and made-up samples she approached the buyers at all the big West End department stores and came away with orders that rendered an admiring Sam speechless.

'My wife is a marvel,' he said throwing up his hands. 'A wonder already. What can I do to reward her?' He kissed her. 'What would you like, sweetheart? A ring – a bracelet?'

But practical Rachel shook her head. 'Take on a dozen more machinists,' she said. 'Let's just deliver on time. Give them good value for their money and maybe they'll order more from us.'

They did. And Feldman's went from strength to strength. Over the years that followed the business expanded again and Feldman Fashions grew to be a respected name in the trade.

Rachel refurnished the house and had electric light installed. She revolutionised the kitchen, organising the removal of the old cast-iron cooking range and replacing it with one of the newest gas stoves. She even bought an electric iron and a vacuum cleaner. Sarah viewed the changes with deep mistrust and suspicion. Every time she plugged in one of the appliances she feared electrocution, and the hissing, popping gas rings terrified her. But once she conquered her fear of the modern gadgets she was surprised and delighted by the time they saved and the way they lightened her workload.

Marcus was sent away to an expensive boarding school when he reached the age of eight. This saddened Sarah. He seemed so young to be going away from his home. Rachel too was sad. She confided to Sarah that Sam had insisted on the best education they could afford for the boy. It was a good investment, he said. And boarding school would teach him to stand on his own feet and make his own decisions.

When Maryan was ready to leave school Sarah asked Rachel if Sam would consider giving her a job. In Sarah's eyes the girl could do no better than work for the Leighs, whom she saw as her benefactors and providers. Ever since she could remember they had provided security for her. But when she told Maryan what she had arranged for her, the girl seemed less than grateful.

'I'm not sure that I want to be a machinist,' she said.

Sarah stared at her. 'Then what *do* you want to do, miss?'

'I don't know. Maybe work in a shop – or an office.'

'*Office?*' Sarah looked at her daughter contemptuously. 'What makes you think anyone'd give *you* a job in an office? You need to be able to typewrite and such. That means more schoolin', my gel. We ain't got the money for that kinda high-falutin' nonsense.'

'I could go to night school,' Maryan suggested.

Sarah shook her head. 'Ideas above your station is what you're gettin'. What good would you be for work, sitting in some stuffy classroom half the night?'

'But I want to better myself, Mum,' Maryan wailed. 'I don't want to stay in Crimea Terrace for the rest of my life.'

'Hard work is the only way for the likes of us to better ourselves,' Sarah said. 'Mr Sam is the livin' proof of that. Look at what he's done for 'imself.'

'He married the boss's daughter,' Maryan said under her breath. Mercifully her mother didn't hear the remark.

'That business has more'n doubled in size since old Mr Jacob died. Did I ever tell you that Mr Sam was a poor boy who started life with only the clothes he stood up in?' In actual fact Maryan had heard the story countless times. 'He's not proud neither,' Sarah went on. 'Not Mr Sam – told me that himself, he did. Proud of it. No, you stick with Feldman's, my girl, and you never know, you might end up as rich as what they are some day. In the meantime, we needs the extra money, so just you get yourself round there Monday morning, eight o'clock sharp, and don't let me 'ear no more about no office.'

Maryan had no choice but to accept what her mother said. The work at Feldman's was undemanding and she liked her workmates well enough. She'd grown up with most of them. But she knew instinctively that it would never lead to riches as it had for Mr Sam, whatever her mother said.

As she grew older and observed the lives of those around her, it angered her the way that everyone in Crimea Terrace accepted that they were destined to a life of poverty. They were born to it and would die with it. In between they would make what they could of life, living hand-to-mouth and struggling from one pay day to the next. Why should it be like this? she asked herself. Why should some have so much whilst others, like her and her mother, had next to nothing? She'd seen the inside of the Leighs' house when she occasionally went along to help her mother wash up after a dinner party. Thick, soft carpets and glittering crystal. Fine china and velvet curtains. The first time she saw it her eyes had almost popped out with the sheer luxury of it. She'd heard how her father, along with a good many others, had laid down his lives for his country. What good had it done them? Mr Sam, nice and kind though he was, had not laid down *his* life. Instead he had made a fortune out of making uniforms for men to get killed in. But when she dared to express these views, her mother was furious.

'Don't you ever dare let me hear you say such things again, you wicked girl. We owe everything to Feldman's. The Leighs have been good to us. Many's the night you'd have gone to bed with an empty belly if it hadn't been for Miss Rachel and don't you ever forget it.'

But Maryan turned away sullenly. Her mother was like all the others in Crimea Terrace: content to feel inferior, to take handouts from those better off – people who could shut the door in their faces without a second thought if it suited them. Maryan wanted something better – independence; a better life; never having to grovel and be forever thankful. She often spoke to her friend Tom Jessop about it. He agreed with her, though he didn't see how they could make things any better.

'We don't get the chance to be educated like they do and what can we do without education?' he said. 'Look at that Marcus Leigh. He's eighteen, the same age as me. But is he out looking for work – standing in the dole queue? No, he's at some posh school or other. And when he's done there he'll probably go off to Cambridge University or some other posh college. He'll never know what it is to struggle, will he? He'll just step into his dad's business and start raking it in like they do.'

Maryan was silent. The last time she'd seen Marcus Leigh had been at his Bar Mitzvah celebration five years ago, when she'd gone to help her mother lay the tables and wash up after the celebration party. She'd been surprised on that day to see how tall and handsome he'd become. His hair was dark and curly like his father's and he had the most stunning brown eyes. Ten-year-old Maryan had been quite smitten. She and Sarah had listened to him making his speech from behind the kitchen door. His voice was already deep and strong and he'd looked much older than his thirteen years in his smart new suit. From her place behind the kitchen door Sarah had almost burst with pride in the boy she had known from birth and cared for as a baby.

'A proper young gent,' she'd remarked. 'A credit to his mum and dad, he is. No mistake.'

Reminded of the occasion, Maryan wondered briefly what he was like now.

She picked up the job easily. By the time she had been at Feldman's a year, Sam had declared her a fully fledged machinist and she was allowed to work on their best lines. Talking to older girls, some of whom had worked elsewhere, she realised that she was privileged to work at Feldman's. Some other clothing factories she'd heard of in the East End were nothing more than sweat shops where the owners worked their girls long, gruelling hours for pitifully low wages that were docked for the smallest discrepancy, and where illness meant arbitrary dismissal. The Leighs were fair and considerate employers. As long as you pulled your weight and didn't take advantage of their kindness you could rely on being treated properly; which was why many of their employees had remained loyal workers from leaving school until retirement. Yes, Maryan was happy enough at Feldman's – for the time being. But although she still didn't quite know how, she was determined to better herself someday. She was confident that her chance would come, somehow. And when it did she would seize it with both hands.

It was in July 1930 that Marcus left the school where he had spent the best part of his eighteen years. His parents had discussed his future long and hard. Rachel wanted him to go to university, but Marcus had had enough of full-time education. He wanted to come straight into the business.

Sam was proud of his only son. He felt he was a chip off the old block. The boy seemed to have been blessed with the best attributes of all three of them. He had his father's good looks, his mother's quick, creative brain and his grandfather's shrewdness and good nature. In Sam's opinion he was ideally suited to the business.

Rachel argued that he should go to commerce college. Sam said he could do no better than learn as he worked, just as Sam himself had done – from the bottom upwards.

'It won't harm the boy to know how it feels to be a shop floor worker,' he argued. 'That is how good employers are born.'

Rachel was scandalised. 'You'd have him sweeping *up* and running *errands*?' she squeaked. 'My son? After all that expensive education?'

'And why not?' Sam argued, stubborn for once. 'It was good enough for me.' For once he did not intend to let Rachel override him. 'He might have had a better education than I ever had, but he's still my son.' Finally they decided to compromise and put it to Marcus himself. Rachel was certain that her cultured son would be as appalled as she was, and she was speechless when the boy calmly agreed.

'If I'm to manage the business on my own one day I'll have to know how everything works, Mother,' he said reasonably. 'I think Dad's right.'

And so it was that on a sunny August morning in 1930, just a year and a half after she had begun work at Feldman's herself, Maryan found herself showing Marcus Leigh how to thread up a machine on his first morning at the factory.

Over six feet tall and broad-shouldered, Marcus towered over Maryan, yet he was almost humble in his eagerness to learn. It amused Sam to put his son in her charge. He chuckled to himself as he watched from the window of his office. The slightly built little blonde girl, taking it all so seriously, and his tall, grown-up son with his thick dark hair and laughing eyes. Two such extremes. He was so proud of the way Marcus mixed with the factory workers, acknowledging that in this, their trade, they knew all and he nothing. In spite of his matriculation certificate and his fine intellect he had the right attitude, and when the time came, he would make a fine business-man, Sam told himself with satisfaction.

But Rachel still had misgivings. It offended her to think of her son working in the factory. He would learn coarse language and rough ways. It irked her to think of the attention she had paid to bringing him up to be a gentleman only to have him spend his days with uneducated artisans. To try to make it up to him – and much against Sam's better judgement – she bought him a sports car for his birthday that year. When he came home from the factory with his father that grey November afternoon a shiny red MG Midget was standing at the kerbside outside the house.

'Go on, did they really buy you a car? A brand-new one, all to yourself?' Maryan gazed at Marcus with wide blue eyes. It was the last week that they'd be working together. Marcus was to move on to cutting the following week, working with Jim Harris, Sam's head cutter. He'd be sorry to move. He'd enjoyed working with the girls, his shirtsleeves rolled up, singing all the popular songs along with them as the machines whirred merrily. Maryan had taught him the words of 'Tiptoe Through the Tulips' and 'Stardust' and, much to the delight of all the girls, he'd even attempted harmonising with them in his pleasant baritone voice.

'Yes, they really have, though I don't think it was Dad's idea. I could tell he didn't approve.'

'Why not? You've worked hard. You deserve it,' Maryan said stoutly. Somehow she didn't resent Marcus's good fortune. He didn't lord it over them like some would have, and he was good fun. He'd make a good boss one day just as long as he didn't change.

'I'm going to miss you next week,' Marcus said.

Maryan laughed as she raised the foot of her machine and turned her material deftly. 'Go on with you.'

'No, really. For one thing, Jim isn't as pretty as you are. I won't be able to sing along with him either. Have you heard his voice? He sounds like a cat with its tail shut in the door. A tone deaf one at that.'

Maryan laughed and Marcus watched with pleasure as the dimple in her cheek twinkled and her blue eyes shone. It struck him suddenly that she was a very pretty girl indeed. Before long someone would marry her and she'd turn into a drudge like the others he'd seen, down at heel as they pushed their second-hand prams in Hackney Market on Saturday nights, looking for bargains; harassed and worn out with poverty and childbearing before they were thirty. His heart suddenly full of tender compassion, he reached out his hand to touch her arm. 'Maryan – tell you what, let me take you for a spin this evening?'

Her smile vanished and she stared at him, her eyes round with astonishment. 'Me?'

He laughed. 'Yes, you. Well, I have to have someone to show off to, don't I?'

They arranged to meet at Whitechapel, outside the Underground station. Somehow keeping it secret made it all the more exciting, and the tacit understanding not to mention it to anyone was taken for granted. It would not be popular among the other girls and they both knew without actually voicing the thought that Sarah would disapprove of their meeting outside working hours as much as Rachel. If Sarah assumed that her daughter was with Tom Jessop, as she often was, Maryan was content to let her. After all, it was just this once.

She'd never been in a car before and as she slipped into the passenger seat her heart quickened with excitement at the feel of it. The scent of new leather and hot oil filled her nostrils. It was the smell of adventure. Marcus told her that he had learned to drive from one of the day boys at his school whose father had bought him a car and let him drive it to school. Maryan tried to assimilate this information. Fancy a schoolboy having a car. As Marcus drove off she caught her breath and held on tightly to the sides of the seat. They went so *fast*; faster than she had ever travelled before, even on a bus. And she felt as though everyone was looking at them. It was terrifying and wonderful all at the same time.

But although Maryan had expected to be taken out only once, it turned out to be the first of many outings. As the New Year came in and winter turned to spring, the trips became regular weekly treats. One Saturday afternoon Marcus drove her out into the Kent country-side and for the first time in her life Maryan saw fields full of baby lambs, and fruit trees bowed down with frothy blossom. They passed pretty cottages that had gardens full of daffodils and nodding tulips, children playing in the fields and people out walking dogs on leads. To a wide-eyed Maryan it was a whole new world.

During the drives they got to know one another. Marcus felt he could talk to Maryan as to no one else. He confided to her his secret ambition to be a designer.

'One day I'd like to make Feldman's a proper fashion house,' he said. 'What I really want is to go to Paris and study haute couture.' He glanced at her uncomprehending face. 'That's French for high-class fashion.'

'Can you really speak French?' Maryan asked him in awe.

'Yes. German and Latin too,' he told her. 'But art is what I was always best at. I want to design clothes that will be recognised all over the world. The kind of clothes that film stars and aristocratic women will give their eye-teeth for.'

'I bet you'll do it, too,' Maryan said, catching some of his enthusiasm. 'You can do what you want when your mum and dad are rich,' she added wistfully. 'I'll never get the chance to do the things I want.'

Marcus took her hand and gently squeezed it. 'And what are they?' he asked.

She shrugged. 'Oh, I don't know. I'm not clever enough to get a better job than what I've got now. I thought I'd go to night school once and learn typing and shorthand, but it's too late now, I suppose. I just know I'd like to have a better life. To talk like you do and – you know – *be* someone.' She looked at him, shaking her blonde head, suddenly embarrassed. 'I expect that sounds silly to you.'

'No, it doesn't,' he said gravely. 'It's not surprising you want to get away from a place like Crimea Terrace.'

Immediately Maryan was defensive. 'It's not a *slum* you know,' she told him warmly. 'All the folks who live there are respectable. They've got their pride, same as anyone else. They're clean too, as far as they're able to be.' She saw his indulgent smile and turned away crossly. 'Oh, what's the use of telling the likes of you? You don't know nothing about it. You don't know you're born, Marcus Leigh.'

'Oh yes, I do,' he told her firmly, taking her shoulders and turning her to face him. 'I appreciate all that my parents have done for me, but my dream is as far away as yours. They are so short-sighted. They can't see how I mean to take Feldman's on to better things. They're dead against my going to Paris. Can you imagine how frustrating that is?'

Maryan looked at him. But she wasn't trying to imagine his frustration. She was thinking how grateful she was to the Leighs for keeping Marcus close to home. And to her.

On Whit Monday Marcus took her to Southend. Maryan had never seen the sea before and she gazed in wonder at the vast expanse of water, sparkling in the sunlight. They walked along the promenade and ate ice cream. Marcus even persuaded her to go for a ride along the sands on a donkey. On the way home they bought fish and chips and Marcus parked in a quiet lane so they could eat them.

'What would your mum say if she could see us now?' Maryan asked suddenly as she rolled up the empty paper.

Marcus coloured suddenly. His mother had become curious about his outings in the car lately and he'd had to make up an old schoolfriend who lived in Surrey. Recently she'd begun to give dinner parties for friends with daughters and he was fairly sure she was trying to pair him off with one of them before he could make a doubtful choice. 'Why should she say anything?' he said a little too brightly. 'After all, your mother and mine have known each other for a long time.'

But not as equals, Maryan thought. Mrs Leigh doted on her only son. She had great plans for his future. Plans that obviously would not include the daughter of her charwoman. But she couldn't quite bring herself to voice the thought. Instead she said: 'She'll be hoping for a Jewish girl for you. Soon we'll be hearing of your betrothal.'

Taken aback by her perception, Marcus paused for just a fraction too long. Then he turned to her with the smile that always melted her heart. 'That's not for ages yet. Till then we can have a good time, you and me, can't we?'

Maryan shrugged and looked away, wounded by the

implication that he was using her to pass the time. 'I don't know. P'raps we should stop.'

He took her hands. 'Why do you say that?'

'You know why. Because you're upper class and I'm working class.'

He threw back his head and laughed. 'Rubbish. Dad started life in the workhouse. He's always telling me that. He's proud of the fact.'

'It's all right to be proud of it when you've made your fortune.'

'He's worked hard, that's all. My parents are as working class as yours.'

Maryan shook her head. 'You know as well as I do that it's not the same,' she said. 'Besides, you're Jewish and I'm not.'

'Who *cares*?' He drew her into his arms and held her tightly, but she struggled free.

'*They* will, Marcus,' she said, her eyes full of tears. 'Your mum and dad. You know they will.'

He looked down at her for a long time. Her brimming eyes moved him more than words could express. 'All I know is that I love you, Maryan,' he said at last. 'I think you love me too.' He cradled her face between his two hands. 'You do, don't you?'

Maryan swallowed hard. Of course she loved him. She'd die for him if she had to. But she'd been brought up to know that there were things she couldn't have. *No use cryin' for the moon*, her mother was fond of saying. Marcus Leigh might as well have been the moon. 'Even – even if I do, it isn't any use,' she said unhappily. 'We never should've started this, Marcus. I've told lies and I expect you have too. It was bound to end in tears.'

'It *won't*. Trust me. I won't let it,' Marcus said fiercely. 'Oh, Maryan, I want you so much. Don't say we have to end it now.' Before she could reply he pulled her to him and kissed her. For a moment she tried to resist, but his arms, strong around her and his mouth on hers were too much. Her arms crept around his neck and she gave herself up to his rising passion.

'Oh, Marcus. We mustn't – we shouldn't – I . . .' But her muttered words were lost in kisses. Their breath quickened and their passion rose to a fever as desire overcame all reason – all caution.

'I'll speak to them tomorrow. I'll make them see that there'll never be anyone but you in my life.' Marcus sat with Maryan's head on his shoulder. How long they'd been there neither of them could say, except that the moon had risen since they first parked there.

Chapter Three

On the night when she'd given herself to Marcus he had
made all kinds of promises. They would be married. He'd
make his parents see that they were made for each other.
Together they would make the name of Feldman's great.
He would design beautiful clothes for her and she would
be his model. They would travel and she would be the
most glamorous, the most talked-about woman in the
world. His wife. Mrs Marcus Leigh.

The following day everything had changed. He didn't
come to the factory that morning. When it was time for
her lunch break she went outside to eat her sandwiches in
the yard at the back of the factory. It was warm and the
sun was shining, but already the feeling of foreboding
that had been with her since waking that morning was
making her heart heavy. Then she saw him coming towards her. At first, when she saw the expression on his
face she was relieved. Obviously he had good news. She
needn't have worried. It was going to be all right after
all. But she could not have guessed what his good news was.

'Maryan, you'll never guess.'

'No – what?'

'I'm going to France.'

The smile that had begun to lift the corners of her
mouth froze. 'To *France*? But – I thought your parents
were so against it. I thought – you said you'd tell them –
about us.'

'I was going to. I was all set to begin.' He took both her hands and held them tightly. 'And I will darling, I promise you I will. In a way this is the beginning of our dream coming true. There I was, you see, with my mouth open ready to begin, when Mother suddenly came out with it. She said she and Dad had been talking and they thought it would be best if I went to France to study design after all. She said I'd proved myself at the factory and they felt I was ready.' He grasped her hands and swung her round. 'Isn't it *wonderful*? Oh, say you're pleased for me.'

'But, Marcus – *France*. You said . . .'

He caught her to him. 'Oh, please don't be sad, sweet-heart. Don't you see, when I come home I'll be in a much better position to ask for what I want. We'll be married then, I promise. I'll only be away for a year.'

'A year? A whole *year*.' To Maryan it might as well have been a century. It was over. She knew it as well as if he had told her bluntly. After a year away, the excitement and adventure of living in a foreign land, of doing the thing he so passionately wanted to do, he would have forgotten her. She was beaten and she knew it. *No good cryin' for the moon*. Her mother's voice echoed mockingly in her brain. She should have known that dreams like that would never come true for the likes of her. She swallowed hard. 'When do you go?'

'At the weekend. Mother is booking my passage on the cross channel ferry for me this morning. There is so much to do, getting my passport, packing and so on. That's why I didn't come in this morning. But I made an excuse to come out. I had to tell you.' He raised her hand to his lips and looked earnestly into her eyes. 'You will wait for me, won't you, Maryan? You won't forget me and marry someone else?'

She shook her head, smiling wistfully. 'Of course I'll never forget you. You know that. Especially not after . . .'

'I know darling.' He drew her close. 'We belong to each other for ever now, Maryan. You're my own dear

32

girl and always will be. I'll write. You will write back, won't you?'

She nodded miserably. Once he read her letters he'd know how far apart they truly were. She'd never be able to put on paper what she felt inside. It was hopeless.

By the time Marcus had been gone two months Maryan knew with dreaded certainty that she carried his child. She was frantic. There was no one she could go to. No one she dared confide in. She felt so ill too. In the early morning and at intervals throughout the day she was violently sick. The girls at the factory began to nudge each other and exchange knowing looks as she fled past them on her way to the lavatories.

It was one rainy evening in August when Tom Jessop heard the sound of weeping coming from the outside lavatory the two houses shared. He was on his way home from doing a late shift at the furniture factory. He paused, walked on a little, then returned to tap gently on the door.

'Are you all right in there? Can I do anything? Are you ill?'

The sobbing stopped and a muffled voice that he recognised at once said: 'I'm all right. Go away.'

'Maryan? Is that you?'

The door opened and Maryan emerged, her eyes red and swollen in her chalk-white face. He gasped with shock at her appearance and reached out a hand to grasp hers.

'What's happened? You look like death.'

For a moment she stared at him, then she fell against him, tears pouring down her cheeks. 'Oh Tom – Tom, I don't know what to do.'

He supported her gently. 'Look, come indoors with me. You don't want the neighbours seein' you like this. Mum's out. She's gone to help with a confinement in Rosedale Street. Chances are she'll be gone most of the night, so we can talk – if you feel like it, that is.'

In the Jessops' living kitchen Maryan sat by the range

and tried to control her sobs. She'd held them back for so long and now that she'd finally given way to them they wouldn't seem to stop, hiccupping uncontrollably in her throat till her chest hurt. Tom made a pot of tea and pressed a warm mug into her hands.

'Here, drink that. I reckon you'd better tell me about it, eh?'

She shook her head. 'I can't, Tom. Not you.'

'Well, if not me then who *can* you tell?' he asked, pulling his chair up close. 'We've known each other long enough. And one thing's for sure you gotta tell someone or go barmy by the looks of you.'

Maryan swallowed the tea and felt a bit better. Tom was right. She had to tell someone, though she couldn't see that there was anything to be done about it. She looked up at him. Kind Tom who had wiped her nose and dried her tears on her first day at school. Tom, with his earnest grey eyes and his floppy brown hair.

'Oh, Tom, I don't know what you'll think of me,' she said with a shuddering sigh. 'I – I'm having a baby.' It was out. She'd said it. The relief was so enormous that she began to cry again, quietly this time, and with a despair that wrung Tom's heart.

'Oh – poor kid. Poor little Mar,' he said, rocking her gently. 'Who was it? Just you tell me who did this to you. I'll kill the bastard.'

She shook her head. 'No, Tom. It wasn't like that. He doesn't know and he never must.'

'Oh?' He looked questioningly into her eyes. 'And why's that?'

'Don't ask me, please. I'm never going to tell anyone. I couldn't.'

'I see. He's married then?'

'No. But it was all a mistake. It was just the once and it never should've happened. It'd ruin his life.'

'Pity 'e didn't think o' that before. And what about *your* life?'

'That's my problem, isn't it?' She looked up at him with wide terrified eyes. 'Don't you dare say nothing to

34

Mum – your mum either.' she grasped his hands. '*Promise* me, Tom.'

''Course I won't. Not if you say so. But I don't see how you're gonna keep a thing like that secret.'

Maryan took a deep breath and clamped her teeth over her lower lip. 'I've heard about this woman. Down by the docks. She knows how to – to sort it out. I thought I'd . . .'

'No.' Tom was on his feet in an instant. Holding her hands tightly, he pulled her to her feet. '*No*, Mar. Them women are dangerous – evil old witches who don't know what they're doing. I've 'eard Mum talk about them. You'll kill yourself. Promise me you won't go an' do nothing like that. *Promise me.*'

'What else can I do?' she wailed. 'I'll lose my job. Mum might even lose hers too if it gets out. I don't know which way to turn.'

He looked deep into her eyes. 'Just tell me one thing, Mar. This bloke – would he marry you if you was to tell 'im?'

She shook her head. 'I told you – I can't tell him.'

'You sure, are you?'

'Certain.'

'Then there's only one thing for it.'

'What?'

'Marry *me*.'

For a moment she stared at him, relief almost overwhelming her. Then guilt and her inborn sense of decency took over and she shook her head. 'I couldn't let you do a thing like that, Tom.'

'Why not? It's what everyone expects anyway. We've always been together, you'n me, ever since we was nippers.'

'I know. It's not that.' She turned away, shaking her head. 'I'm – you know – *spoilt*. When you marry a girl you'll want to be the first. And anyway people will know soon enough that there's a baby coming.'

'So? They'll just think it's mine. And we'll be respectably 'itched by then anyway.'

'I couldn't do it to you, Tom. It's not fair. It'd be living a lie.'

He grasped her by the shoulders and turned her to face him. 'Look. If you say yes, it'll be nobody's business but ours, Mar. Yours and mine. It don't matter what anyone else thinks in the end, does it? What matters is that you're having a baby and you need someone to take care of you. I'm asking you to let it be me.'

'But why? Why should you, Tom?'

'Because I love you. I always 'ave, Mar. You know that. Blimey, if you don't, then you should do by now.' He tipped up her chin to look into her swollen eyes. 'Come on, gel, say yes and be done with it. Let's get things moving before any more time gets wasted.'

'You might be sorry tomorrow, Tom,' she said. 'Let's sleep on it, eh?'

He pulled her into his arms and held her tightly. 'I shan't never be sorry, Mar,' he said huskily. 'I ain't never wanted no other girl but you.'

She hid her face against his chest, tears beginning again. 'I've let you down, Tom. I feel ashamed. Not many men would do what you're doing.'

'Not many blokes got my common sense,' he told her with a grin. 'I know when I'm onto a good thing all right, don't you worry. Listen, you made a mistake, that's all. Everyone makes mistakes. God knows, plenty of blokes makes the same 'un. Difference is, they usually gets away with it.'

'Well – if you're really sure . . .'

'You mean you *will*?'

'All right then, Tom – yes.'

Tom was so happy. The delight shone out of his grey eyes like the sun on a spring morning. He couldn't wait to tell everyone, his mother, his brother and sister-in-law. He wanted to shout it from the rooftops. Maryan's mother was pleased too, when he went to ask formally if he could marry her daughter. She'd already guessed that Maryan might be pregnant, but knowing that it was Tom was a relief. She'd always looked forward to having him for her son-in-law. Such a good, steady lad. She couldn't ask for better than the son of her good friend and neighbour, Cissie.

Deep in his heart, Tom was more than happy, he was grateful. As Maryan had grown up and blossomed from a skinny little girl into a lovely young woman, he'd begun to think she'd grown out of his reach. She'd been clever at school and she was always saying that she wanted something better from life than her mother had been content with. Surely she'd be planning for something better than marrying a carpenter and setting up home in a two-up two-down, shared with her mother in Crimea Terrace. Perhaps it was these very aspirations that had led to her alliance with this mystery man who had betrayed her. Perhaps he was well off and upper class and that was why he couldn't marry her. Although Tom knew that Maryan was fond of him, in his heart of hearts he suspected that she would never have contemplated marriage with him had it not been for her unplanned pregnancy. But he wasn't going to probe too deeply into that theory. Maryan's past was behind them, and that was where it would stay. She had assured him that she wanted to forget it. She was to be his, and that was all he cared about.

The letters that Marcus wrote, telling of the exciting things he was doing and seeing, gradually dwindled and stopped when Maryan failed to respond to them. She continued to work at Feldman's and she and Tom let it become known that they were to marry. The girls clubbed together to give her a little wedding present, a pretty glass jam dish in a chromium-plated holder. Mr and Mrs Leigh also gave her a gift when they heard from Sarah that she was to be married. Mr Sam called her into the office on the Friday before the wedding.

'Mrs Leigh and I would like you to have this, with our best wishes,' he said, passing a prettily wrapped parcel across his desk.

Blushing, Maryan had unwrapped it to find a beautiful

little china jug nestling on blue velvet in a shiny black box. 'Oh, it's lovely. Thank you, Mr Leigh,' she said, backing away in embarrassment. 'And please – thank Mrs Leigh too, won't you.'

'I will, my dear. I will. And the best of happiness to you both.' Sam had smiled as she escaped, clutching her present. He'd always liked the girl and he didn't really understand that strange tightening of his wife's mouth and her look of disapproval at the mention of her name. After all, she and the girl's mother had known each other since girlhood, and Sarah had been a loyal servant to them for the past twenty years. But then who really understood women? Rachel had been adamant in her refusal to allow Marcus to study design in France. She wouldn't even discuss the idea. Then suddenly, almost overnight and for no apparent reason she'd changed her mind. He sighed and lifted his shoulders. Such mysterious creatures. But wonderful. Ah, yes, wonderful for all that.

The wedding went off quietly. There was a small celebration at the Prince of Wales pub in the evening. Sarah had made sure of that, pawning her mother-in-law's old sewing machine to pay for the treat. The whole street gathered to drink the health of the young couple in the customary fashion, with much good-natured ragging and jibing. The sing-song was in full swing when Maryan and Tom left, grateful to escape the smoky atmosphere and the ribald remarks and breathe in the comparatively fresh night air.

The month was September, but the season of mists and mellow fruitfulness was much like any other season in Crimea Terrace. It was a short street, one of a warren that made up the friendly community that Tom and Maryan had known from birth. The backs of the houses gave onto the mews housing the horses and wagons used by the brewery and other local traders, and the air was always redolent of dung and sweating horseflesh. When they reached number eight Maryan opened the door and they went inside.

They were to live with Sarah until they were on their feet and could afford a place of their own. In the meantime, they would share Maryan's bedroom over the parlour, which looked out onto the street. Sarah had prepared it specially for them, moving her own double bed into it and making it up with her best sheets, the ones Miss Rachel had given her when she bought new. The large brass bedstead dominated the small room, leaving only just enough room to move round it, but Sarah had baulked at moving out of the room she had shared with her Alf. Although he had been killed almost twenty years ago, she still felt that while she slept within the four walls she had shared with him he was not entirely lost to her.

1931 wasn't the best time to be starting married life. Already there had been bitter riots over the unemployment that was sweeping the country. But at least Tom had his job with the furniture factory at Bow. And Maryan's job at Feldman's would last for as long as she could still fit behind her machine. Sarah's job as housekeeper to the Leighs was secure, too. So with three wages coming in they were a great deal better off than most.

A door in the corner of the kitchen opened onto the steep, narrow staircase, which they ascended in single file. In the front bedroom Maryan opened the window. The singing from the pub reached her on the still night air. They'd got to the sentimental stage now, and she could hear full-throated snatches of 'I Can't Give You Anything But Love – Bay-bee'. She shook her head, wishing her mother hadn't spent her hard-earned money on booze for the neighbours. Heaven only knew there were better things they could have done with it. She turned towards Tom who was removing his specially bought tie and celluloid collar with obvious relief.

'They're well away. Just listen to them.'

He grinned ruefully. 'Just s'long as I don't 'ave to be there, I don't care what they do. Thank God I can take that thing off. Fair chokin' me, it was. Cuttin' right into my neck. Look at that.' He peered into the mirror, rubbing at the red wheals the rigid collar had left on his neck. Seeing her wistful expression he put down the collar and moved to where she stood at the window.

'Not regretin' marryin' me, are you, love?'

Her eyes filled with tears. 'Oh, Tom. How can you ask me that? By rights it should be me asking you. You deserve better than what you're getting.'

He held her at arms' length and looked into her eyes. 'I couldn't never get no one better than you, Mar. You know I've always wanted you. I just – just wondered if you was thinkin' of *him* today. Wishin' it was him standing beside you 'stead of me.'

She shook her head firmly. 'I told you, Tom. That's all over. It was a mistake, and I never want to talk about it again.'

'You're sure you don't want to tell me . . .?'

'No. Better you don't know, Tom. I know you've got every right to ask, but I'd rather we forgot it.' She looked at him in anguish. 'Oh, it isn't fair, is it? Expecting you to father another man's child. I shouldn't have let you . . .' He stopped her words with a kiss.

'Shhh. It'll be *your* child, Mar,' he said softly. 'That's good enough for me. And we've got all the time in the world to 'ave kids of our own. But I'll always love this one just as much as ours. I promise you that.'

Maryan laid her head against his shoulder with relief. No one must ever know the identity of her baby's father. Not even Marcus himself. But as for forgetting him – that was something she would have to learn to come to terms with by herself in secret.

As they lay side by side in the big brass bed Tom asked her: 'Well, how does it feel to be Mrs Jessop?'

'It feels safe, Tom,' she whispered. 'It feels like nothing can ever hurt me again.'

Christmas came, the happiest Maryan had ever known. The Browns and the Jessops gathered together for the occasion: Tom's brother, Bill, his wife, Maggie, and their small son, Johnny; Tom's mother, Cissie, and of course, Sarah. The seven of them squeezed round the table for

Christmas dinner at Sarah's and again for tea on Boxing Day at Cissie's. There were crackers and games and everyone was jolly.

For the Leighs the season was less jolly. It was the very first Chanukah since Marcus was born that the three of them had been apart. As they went to the Synagogue to pray; as they lit the candles and put the Chanukah lamp in the window, they thought of their son and missed him sadly, though privately Rachel told herself it was for the best. She had done the right thing in giving in to her son's wish to travel and study. She had never told Sam about the evening she had been visiting a friend in the London Hospital and had seen Marcus pick up Maryan in his car outside the Underground station at Whitechapel. In the radiant smiles the two young people had exchanged Rachel had recognised the danger signals. She had kept the discovery to herself and given a lot of thought to the situation. Finally she came up with what she considered to be the right solution. She did what had to be done, and the pain of missing her beloved son would be a worthwhile sacrifice. As for Sam – better he knew nothing.

Since their wedding Maryan and Tom had saved hard and managed to put away a bit towards their own home. Maryan's health had improved as the months of her pregnancy progressed, and by the end of December she was blooming, despite the awkwardness and discomfort of her widening girth.

At the end of January she was finally forced to give up work. She could no longer sit comfortably at her machine for hours at a time, nor get close enough to work accurately. Sam promised to keep her job open for her for a few weeks at least. Cissie had promised to care for the baby for her so that she could go back and work for a few hours each day. When she was called out to a confinement or a laying out they could come to some arrangement between them, she assured Maryan.

It was on the 9th of February in the small hours of the

morning that Tom wakened to find Maryan tossing restlessly beside him. He reached out to touch her arm.

'What's up? Are you all right, love?'

She turned to him. 'It's the pains. I think it's the baby, Tom.'

He was out of bed in an instant and knocking on Sarah's bedroom door. Half an hour later the two of them were in the kitchen, Tom stoking the range whilst Sarah filled her largest saucepan and the kettle, setting them both on to boil. Tom had already fetched Cissie, who was upstairs, examining Maryan. Presently she appeared at the open door to the stairway, rolling down her sleeves.

'She'll be a few hours yet. Go up and talk to her, Tom. Keep her mind off it while Sarah and me get things ready.' She looked round the kitchen. 'Glad to see you've got plenty of water on the boil. Don't want no nasty infection settin' in do we?' she grinned. 'Besides, I reckon we could all do with a cup of tea.'

Dawn was breaking when Cissie turned her son out of the bedroom at last, announcing that it was time for things to start happening.

'There's little enough room in 'ere for me and Sarah,' she grumbled. 'We don't want no clumsy great bloke under our feet, do we, darlin'?' She bent over Maryan and wiped the sweat from her brow. 'Come on, luvvie, we'll soon 'ave that baby 'ere for you,' she said gently. 'Not much longer now.'

But it was almost midday before Maryan was finally released from her suffering. For four long hours she had strained to push her child into the world. Gritting her teeth and pulling on the towel Sarah had tied to the bedrail, she bore down with every ounce of strength she possessed. The two older women had worked tirelessly, encouraging and reassuring, Cissie pressing down on Maryan's abdomen with every pain to aid the passage of the child. She was used to such scenes of suffering. Painful birth was a matter of routine to her, but Sarah had never seen a baby born before and she was terrified.

She felt sure she was about to lose her daughter and the child with her. How could such a frail body endure such toil and agony?

'Shall I go for the doctor?' she asked anxiously for the third time.

Cissie shook her head. 'No sense in lettin' yourself in for a bill you can't afford to pay,' she said brusquely. 'Take it from me, Sarah, she's doin' all right – no worse than most and better'n a good many. Couple more pushes and we'll 'ave it born. I c'n see the head already.'

Sarah bit her lip and looked on helplessly at her exhausted daughter.

Cissie shook her head at her. 'Oh come on, gel. Surely you can remember when you 'ad her. Two days an' nights you took. I was with you, remember?'

Reassured, Sarah turned back to Maryan. 'Cissie's right, love,' she said. 'You're doin ever so well. Not long now. Almost over.

And Cissie proved to be right. Ten minutes later the child was born. Yelling lustily, Maryan's little girl was delivered into Sarah's waiting hands. Cissie worked quickly, tying off and cutting the cord. She made a perfunctory examination of the baby, then bundled her into a towel and handed her to Sarah.

'Well, she's all right, thank Gawd,' she said. 'Everything in its right place and lungs on 'er as'd put a costermonger out o' business.' She turned to Maryan with a smile. 'Right, me luvvie. You got a healthy baby. All over bar the shoutin' now.'

Sarah stood by the window, hugging her tiny grand-daughter to her bosom, tears of relief coursing down her cheeks. Thank God it was over and they were both alive.

When the baby was put into Maryan's arms she looked down at her in wonder. So much pain and hard work for something so little. It had been worth it though. Very tenderly she touched the soft head with its covering of dark downy hair. The huge dark blue eyes looked up, unfocused, at her and love coursed through her veins like some powerful drug.

She's mine, Maryan told herself. All mine. My flesh and blood. Her eyes scrutinised every detail of the tiny features, searching for a likeness – to herself. And, if she were honest, to Marcus. In a way she hoped the child would not resemble him. She did not want a daily reminder of her folly. This child belonged to her – and to Tom. It was the least she owed him. But on one thing she was determined. Her daughter would never know that she had been conceived out of wedlock. She would grow up to hold her head up high – to think of herself as someone special. Somehow or other Maryan meant to make sure of it.

'What are you going to call her?' Cissie asked when she looked in next morning.

Too excited to sleep, Maryan had spent most of the night thinking about this. In the early hours when she had wakened to feed the child she had remembered something she had read in a film magazine Tom had bought her. Some months ago an American film actress had married an exiled Russian nobleman among great publicity and fuss. Recently she had given birth to a baby daughter and had named her Amethyst. The name had stuck in Maryan's mind. It had such an exotic sound. Surely no one with a name like that could grow up to be ordinary.

'I'm going to call her Amethyst,' she told her mother-in-law.

Cissie stared at her, her round face a mask of amazement. 'That's a funny old name,' she said bluntly.

'It's a jewel,' Maryan told her. 'It's unusual, isn't it – a bit special?'

'It's *that* all right.' Cissie thought about her son and how proud he had been to announce his daughter's birth to his workmates at the factory. They'd have a good old laugh when he told them her name was to be *Amethyst*. It sounded more like a race horse or a new kind of fruit off a barrow down the market. Besides, Amethyst *Jessop* didn't sound right somehow. Poor little mite. Oh well, never mind. I expect she'll get called Amy anyway, she told herself as she tucked the covers in round the sleeping baby.

From the very first moment he set eyes on her Tom Jessop adored his little daughter. There was no doubt about it. She was his child. He refused even to think of her as anything else. There was nothing he liked better than to nurse her, loving the sweet, wriggly feeling of her little arms and legs inside the shawl as he held her in his arms, and the trusting way she looked up at him with her big blue eyes. When Maryan stopped feeding the child herself he would delight in giving her a bottle; sitting patiently with her until every drop had gone, then putting her against his shoulder as he'd seen Maryan do, to bring up her wind. He even enjoyed changing her nappy, getting enormous satisfaction out of making her all comfy and sweet-smelling again. And, in spite of the amusement and even catcalls he received from other men in the neighbourhood, he was proud to walk her out in her pram on Sunday afternoons while Maryan put her feet up for an hour. The only thing he would not do was to call her Amethyst. To Tom she was Amy from the day of her birth. And nothing Maryan could do or say would induce him to call her anything else.

When she was old enough she would wait at the window each evening, watching for him to turn the corner of the street. Then she would run to the door, calling '*Daddy – Daddy*,' until Maryan or Sarah opened it for her to run out into his arms.

Maryan had gone back to work at Feldman's when Amethyst was two months old. She hated handing her baby over to her mother-in-law each morning, but they needed the money if they were to afford a place of their own. But when Amethyst was a year old Cissie met with an accident. She was stepping down from a tram when she slipped on a patch of ice and fell heavily. At the hospital she was found to have broken her leg in two places. As well as being in plaster from thigh to ankle, she would have to remain in hospital for several weeks.

The family had a hurried conference. If no one else could be found to care for little Amethyst during the day there was nothing for it but for Maryan to give up her job. Everyone looked at Maggie, whose small son Johnny had recently started school. Flushing, she reminded them that she had just started work again herself.

'I'd like to 'elp, honest, but we really need the money,' she said plaintively. 'I ain't worked since Johnny was born and Bill's been put on short time. I was lucky to get this job down the canning factory. If I give it up I'll never get nothin' else.'

Resigned to being reduced to only Tom's wage, Maryan looked at her mother. Sarah was looking tired and pale. The long hours she put in at the Leighs were beginning to tell on her. 'Tell you what, Mum. Could we take it in turns to look after baby?' she asked. 'Do you think Mrs Leigh would let me take on your evening work? After all, there's no cooking. It's only washing up and such. And you could do with working shorter hours.'

Sarah nodded. 'I think that's a very good idea – split the money between us. Long as I earn enough to pay the rent and buy my bit of food I'm quite content. You need it more'n I do. I'll ask Mrs Leigh first thing tomorrow.'

Rachel agreed that Maryan should replace Sarah on two evenings a week when she was entertaining. She did it with some reluctance. She and Sarah were used to each other's ways and when Sarah was there to help everything went without a hitch. True, Maryan had often been along to help at larger dinner parties, and the girl was pleasant and willing enough. A fleeting vision of Maryan getting into Marcus's car returned, but she pushed the thought aside. Marcus looked set to stay in Paris for some time to come. He wrote enthusiastically of all he was learning and how much he loved his life there. There were parties and a gay social life as well as hard work. He would certainly have forgotten his little fling with Maryan by now. And anyway, the girl was married and settled, with a child to support. Surely she would have put impossible girlish dreams behind her now that she had the realities of life to face.

The new arrangement worked out well enough, though with less money coming in Maryan and Tom had to abandon their plans for getting a place of their own. It would only be temporary, they told each other. Once Amethyst was at school Maryan would get a full-time job again. By then the slump would surely be over and things would be looking up for all of them. But they had reckoned without the demise of the furniture factory where Tom worked. The following January it went into liquidation and the fifty-two men employed there found themselves joining the ever lengthening dole queues.

Amy was the one person to be glad her father stayed at home all day. At two years old she was too young to realise the despair of the situation. She had her beloved Dad to play with all day. Wrapping her warmly in her woolly scarf and hat against the winter cold and fog, he would take her down to the docks to watch the big ships or to the mews behind their street to feed the big, gentle drayhorses with carrots. Sometimes they would go to the market last thing Saturday nights to buy leftover veg before the stallholders packed up. But whatever they did, it was always fun. To innocent Amy they were halcyon days, to everyone else they were bleak and desperately worrying, especially when Sarah went down with a severe bout of influenza which left her with a bad chest that stubbornly refused to clear up.

Maryan temporarily took over her mother's job at the Leighs' until the doctor finally diagnosed chronic bronchitis. Sarah's job was far too arduous for her, he warned. Unless she gave it up for something less taxing she would be in serious danger of contracting consumption. The answer was obvious. Maryan would take over her job completely.

Rachel accepted the change with a good grace. Maryan was used to the household routine now. Keeping her on was preferable to training someone new. Besides, Marcus had indicated in his letters that he would be home in a few months' time and she was already planning to entertain extensively for his benefit. Both she and Sam agreed that it was high time he took a wife. And Rachel meant to see to it that he chose wisely and well.

Maryan admired and resented the Leighs' home in equal measure. Rachel's tastes in furnishing and colour were superb. Ever since she had first been inside the house as a young girl she had promised herself that this was the kind of house she would have one day. But as the years passed the possibility grew fainter and fainter. Like Sarah, she watched Rachel cook and picked up tips on how to present food attractively, though the kind of food consumed in the Leigh household was far beyond anything she could ever afford. Rachel, knowing of their enforced poverty, allowed her to take home the leftovers, just as she always had. Some nights they feasted like lords, on chicken and asparagus, while on others they made do with bread and margarine. But at least they got by without having to apply for Public Assistance; a humiliation they all dreaded.

When Cissie first came home from hospital she tried to go back to her old job and even managed to attend the occasional confinement, but her leg was badly crippled. It hadn't healed well and she was in constant pain. Eventually she went to live with Bill and Maggie. Sarah, too, was feeling the effects of her illness. Taking care of the child and managing the housework tired her, although she would rather die than admit it, and Maryan could see the lines of exhaustion on her mother's face at the end of a long day. But there was little she could do about it. She was now the only provider. She worked such long hours herself that she hardly ever saw her child. In the early months it was bearable. There was always the hope that Tom would get work, but as week followed week and nothing materialised for him, he began to sink into depression.

From the good-natured, considerate boy that Maryan

had married, he degenerated into a sour, embittered man before her eyes. Grey-faced and round-shouldered with despair, he gave up looking for work. He gave up hope, and with it, his zest for life, until it seemed that the only thing he lived for was his little daughter.

To Maryan, coming home tired after a hard day's work, he appeared ungrateful, lazy and resentful. He blamed her for everything, goading her until she snapped back angrily at him, accusing him of letting her do everything; reminding him that she was the breadwinner. At which he would fling out of the house and stay out till late at night, accepting beer from better off pals who felt sorry for him, and coming home in the small hours the worse for drink.

Lying awake, waiting to hear his stumbling footsteps coming up the stairs, Maryan would weep tears of frustration, angry with the hand life had dealt her. Why should they have to live like this, while people like the Leighs lived in luxury? What had they done to deserve it?

She voiced these thoughts to her mother one day.

'Don't you go bitin' the 'and that feeds you,' Sarah admonished. 'I don't know where we'd be today if it hadn't been for the Leighs. Miss Rachel has been a good friend to us, my girl, and don't you ever forget it.'

'I'm not likely to with you to remind me,' Maryan said waspishly. 'Anyway, it's paid her to be reasonable with us, hasn't it? We've slaved our fingers to the bone for her, specially you. Look at you with your wheezy chest and rheumaticky knees. You're an old woman and you're not even fifty yet. What do you owe your wonderful Miss Rachel when all's said and done?'

'Friendship, that's what,' Sarah said stoutly. 'I'm proud to have been her friend – since your gran was alive – since before you was born. Ever since we was both gels.'

'You've been her *servant*, Mum. Nothing else. Her servant.' Maryan turned away, her lip curling. 'That's how she sees you and always has. If you don't believe me, just ask her. She don't invite *you* to her posh dinner parties, does she?'

'Of course she don't,' Sarah said. 'I wouldn't expect her to.' She took her daughter by the arm and looked into her eyes. 'Listen to me, Maryan. I've lived longer than you and I know what's what. The likes of us is all right so long as we knows our place and keep to our side of the fence. It's when folks starts getting above themselves that all the trouble starts.' She smiled in an attempt at reassurance. 'Things'll get better by 'n by. We was happy before. We'll be happy again. Don't get bitter, there's a good gel. There's no good'll come of it.'

But Maryan wasn't convinced. If she wasn't happy with the way things were there must be others who felt the same, who noticed how some people had made money out of the war, whilst others had died horribly in the trenches, leaving wives and children to manage as best they could. And now there was all this unemployment. The men and women who were rioting, *they* felt as she did – that something should be done to make things fairer, more equal; to bring about the Land Fit For Heroes that they'd been promised. Tom might have given up but she wouldn't. She might not be able to put the world to rights, but if she could do something for herself and her own family, then she would.

She was taking off her coat in the Leighs' basement kitchen the following Monday morning when Rachel appeared in the doorway.

'I'd like you to make a start on the downstairs rooms this morning, Maryan,' she said. 'Mr Marcus arrived home in the early hours and he's still asleep.'

At the mention of his name Maryan's heart skipped a beat. 'Just as you say, Mrs Leigh,' she said, trying to make her voice matter-of-fact. 'I didn't know he was due home.'

'He wasn't,' Rachel told her. 'At least, not yet. It was quite unexpected. But he isn't going back. He's had enough of life on the Continent, so I'm afraid we'll have to put up with having him at home again.' The smile on her face belied her words. She was obviously pleased and excited to have her son home again, whatever the reason.

'I've got to go down to the factory this morning,' she went on, putting on her hat and coat, 'but I'll be back around eleven. I want Marcus to have his sleep out so perhaps you could leave upstairs till this afternoon just this once.'

'Of course, Mrs Leigh.' Rachel went about her work, washing up the dinner dishes from the night before, scrubbing the front steps and cleaning the brasses on the street door. She had just carried the ashes from the drawing-room grate out to the dustbin and was about to lay the fire when she heard footsteps on the stairs. Looking out into the hall, she saw Marcus coming down the stairs wearing his dressing gown. When he saw her he stopped in his tracks.

'*Maryan*. What are you doing here?'

'I work here now. Didn't your mother tell you?'

He laughed. 'She's hardly had time to tell me anything yet.'

Acutely aware of her dishevelled appearance, Maryan wiped her hands on the coarse apron she wore and brushed away a stray lock of hair with the back of her hand. 'I see,' she said. 'What brought you home so unexpectedly?'

He sighed and stroked his cheek ruefully. For the first time she noticed a long scar that ran down from his temple to below his left ear. 'It's a long story. Do you think you could make me some breakfast? Then perhaps we can have a little talk.'

'Of course.'

Her hands trembled as she filled the kettle and began to cut bread for toast. It felt so strange – almost dreamlike – to be standing here, making breakfast for Marcus. He was as handsome as ever. A little heavier perhaps. Taller and broader than she remembered, but apart from that life seemed not to have touched him as it had touched her. She wondered about the scar on his cheek, and whether he would tell her about it.

'Mother wrote and told me you were married.'

She looked up, startled. 'Did she? I wonder why.'

'Maybe she thought I'd be interested,' he said, looking at her quizzically. 'Why didn't you write – answer my letters?'

She blushed. 'I – there wasn't anything to say.'

'Really? I'd have thought there was quite a lot.'

There was a moment's silence between them, then he said cheerfully: 'So, what's he like, this husband of yours?'

'Tom? Oh, he's just ordinary, like me,' she said. 'We've known each other since we were kids.' She set the plate of bacon and eggs before him. 'I've – we've got a little girl. She's called Amethyst.'

He stared up at her. 'A child? Well, you don't waste any time, do you? It seems hardly any time at all since you and I . . .'

'It does to me,' she interrupted quickly. 'You've been away a long time – almost three years, isn't it? We were just a couple of silly kids. Better we forget it, eh?'

'If you say so.' She made to leave, to get on with her work, but he put out his hand to stop her. 'Don't run away. Stay and talk to me, Maryan. It's all right. I'll clear it with Mother if you haven't finished your work.'

Reluctantly, she slid into the seat opposite and watched him eat. 'What – happened to your face?' she asked.

Again he touched the livid scar and his mouth hardened. 'I thought I'd like to visit Germany before I came home,' he told her. 'I meant to stay for a few months. But they aren't very partial to Jews in Germany at the moment.'

'You got into a fight?'

'You could call it that, I suppose. A pretty one-sided one, though. I tried to break up what I thought was a brawl. Some youths were beating up an old man. A woman had accused him of trying to steal her purse. She attracted the attention of some drunken thugs.'

'Had he stolen her purse?' Maryan asked. Marcus shook his head.

'No. He was a harmless old Jew on his way to the synagogue. Anyone could see that. And that was the real reason he was getting beaten. If I hadn't intervened they would have killed him. One of them drew a knife on me. That's how I got this. I don't doubt they would have liked to kill me too.'

Maryan gasped. There were certain people who were prejudiced in England, but not to this extent. 'But why?'

'Haven't you heard of Adolf Hitler?'

'I've read about him in the papers. He's the new German President, isn't he?'

'*Fuehrer*, he calls himself. He wants everyone in Germany to be of pure blood. He's telling the people that he's trying to create what he calls a Master Race. He's encouraging the German people to hate gypsies, blacks, anyone who isn't pure German. But Jews in particular, because there are more of them. Do you know that we are banned from public places and dubbed "sub-human"?'

'That's terrible.' Maryan shook her head. 'That's why you came home?'

'Partly. The old man I rescued had had enough. It wasn't the first time he'd been set upon in the street. He wanted to come to England. His son lives here in London. I offered to escort him. I'd seen more than enough myself.' He leaned forward earnestly. 'He has to be stopped, Maryan. Hitler, I mean. If someone doesn't do something about him soon he'll get worse. He's amassing the most enormous fighting force; men, weapons. How our Government can sit back and ignore it . . .'

'What could he do, though?' Maryan asked.

'Invade us. Take us over, Central Europe first, then us. We should be arming too. Hitler is a madman. Hungry for power. Nothing will stop him once he's allowed to get a hold.'

'*Don't*.' Maryan shuddered. 'You're frightening me. It's not long since we had a war with Germany. My dad got killed in it. We beat them that time. Surely they wouldn't start another.'

He looked at her wide, frightened eyes and his mouth softened into a smile. Reaching out he touched her hand reassuringly. 'I'm sorry, Maryan. Of course it won't happen. It's just my over-active imagination.'

She let out her breath on a sigh of relief. Men were always talking about war. She might have known it was all talk. 'Are you going back to work for your father now then?' she asked.

He nodded enthusiastically. 'In a way, yes. I'm hoping to persuade him to let me try out some new ideas. I've learned so much while I've been away, Maryan. I've worked with top designers and couturiers. It's a whole different world over there. You'd love it.'

'I daresay.' She was silent, wistfully remembering the promises – how she would wear his designs and travel with him, be his model. Ridiculous nonsense. The stuff of childish dreams.

Oblivious of her thoughts, Marcus was buttering a piece of toast. 'Tell me about this husband of yours. And the little girl – what did you say she's called?'

'Amethyst.'

He smiled. 'Very exotic. Sounds like a model. Is she pretty – like you?'

She blushed, imagining what she must look like, with her hair awry and streaks of soot on her face more than likely. 'She's not like me at all, really. Her hair is dark and curly and she has big blue eyes. More a dark violet really, like pansies.'

'She sounds a real charmer. Does she have your dimple?'

'Two,' she said proudly.

'And her father?'

For a moment she stared at him, then, realising that he suspected nothing, she said quickly: 'Tom lost his job twelve months ago. And Mum's been poorly too with her chest, which is why I'm working here now.'

He looked concerned. 'Poor Maryan. Life must be hard for you.'

She summoned a smile. 'Oh – we manage well enough.

Your mum is very good to us,' she added, despising herself for the echo of her mother she could hear in her ingratiating tone.

'She would be. Mother's a good sort.' Marcus wiped his mouth on his napkin and stood up. 'Well, I'd better have a bath and shave and make myself presentable before she gets back. I'll be seeing you a lot from now on, Maryan. Better get used to my clutter around the place. I'm hoping Mother will let me have the boxroom for a studio. I mean to start work on my designs immediately.'

Rachel lost no time in organising a busy social programme for Marcus. He tolerated it with a mixture of amusement and irritation.

'She's matchmaking,' he confided to Maryan. 'She won't rest until I've got a wife and three children. She's set her heart on it and when Mother sets her heart on anything there's no putting her off.'

'And will she get her way this time?' Maryan ventured. They were moving the collection of clutter out of the boxroom. Marcus put down the brass-bound portmanteau he was carrying and looked at her, one eyebrow cocked. 'Between you and me, Maryan, no. But don't breathe a word of it to her. I'm not ready to settle down yet. I want to become established as a designer first. A wife and all that marriage entails would only encumber me.'

Maryan turned away to pick up a stack of old newspapers, relief lightening her heart. Although she would not admit it, even to herself, deep in her heart she still loved him. Her work had been lighter since his homecoming. She actually looked forward to coming to Hackney Road each morning, because he would be there. There was the way he treated her too – as a friend instead of his mother's servant. She looked forward to their easy, relaxed conversations, storing them up to think about later when she was alone. He could never be hers, she acknowledged that, but until he belonged to someone else she still felt free to indulge in a little secret dreaming.

The dinner parties meant she often had to work late. There was extra work to do, too: silver to clean and glasses to polish, extra dusting and cleaning. On the evenings the Leighs entertained she would stay late to help serve the meal and then wash up afterwards. She didn't grumble because Mrs Leigh was generous with extra money, but things were difficult at home. Tom complained constantly and unreasonably that she was hardly ever there.

'I can't be in two places at once,' she told him tetchily. 'And heaven only knows we can do with the extra cash.'

'Oh, that's right. Rub it in,' he shouted. 'Do you think I sit here on my backside all day for the fun of it?'

'No, I don't. So why can't you help Mum a bit more instead of drinking with that bunch of layabouts down the Prince of Wales? You always seem to have the price of a pint, I notice.'

'You'd grudge a bloke the only bit of pleasure he gets, wouldn't you?' he snapped bitterly. 'You used to be a kind-hearted woman, Maryan. Now you're nothing but a bloody nag.'

'A bloody nag, am I?' Stung, Maryan rounded on him, close to tears. 'Ever asked yourself why, Tom Jessop? Sometimes I wonder why we're married, you 'n me.'

He gave a harsh laugh. 'You *wonder*, do you? Only one reason why you ever married me. And we both know what that is, don't we?'

Maryan stopped, her mouth dropping open with shock. She'd known he was bitter about losing his job, but she had no idea he bore a grudge about the reason for their marriage. Chastened, she went to him, her arms outstretched.

'Tom. Oh, Tom, love, don't say that.'

He turned from her. 'It's true though, isn't it? You never really wanted me.'

'No. No, it *isn't* true. You love Amethyst as much as I do. And she adores you. You're her dad.'

'In name, maybe. And what about you?' He turned to look at her and she saw that tears stood in his eyes.

'What about the kids you 'n me was gonna 'ave, Maryan? Seems I can't do nothin' on my own account. Not even be a real father.'

'Tom, you know as well as I do that it's just as well with the way things are. Another baby would put an end to me working, and then where'd we be?'

'Yes – *where*? You're already married to a no-hoper, aren't you? You've got an invalid mum and a kid to support too. No wonder you take such good care not to have kids.'

She stared at him. 'I don't do anything to stop it, Tom. It just – hasn't happened.'

'No, not likely to either when you've got no time for your husband any more, is it? I might as well be married to a bloody nun.' Before she could stop him he flung out of the house.

Maryan sank into a chair, her heart heavy with despair. She felt torn several ways at once. What was she supposed to do? How many people could she hope to please? And how much more worry could she take?

It was two weeks later that the Weiss family were invited to dinner with the Leighs. They too had a clothing factory and the two firms had been friendly rivals for some years. As usual Maryan worked hard. Rachel had taken special care with the meal. The house was decked with fresh flowers and all day wonderful smells had drifted up the stairs from the kitchen. Maryan's mouth watered as the various aromas tantalised her nostrils. There was roast chicken in a wonderful spicy sauce with a variety of vegetables, and for dessert Rachel had made one of her special strudels, rich with fruit, nuts and cinnamon. Maryan hoped the guests would not be too hungry so that there would be some left over.

While the two families were having drinks she washed and changed into the black dress and lace apron Rachel had provided, then, at the signal from Rachel's little bell, she carried the first course upstairs to the dining room where the Leighs and the Weiss's were seated.

It was a small party tonight. Mr and Mrs Weiss had just the one daughter, Jessica. As Maryan served the soup, she couldn't help looking at the glamorous young lady in the bead-embroidered white evening dress. Jessica was about nineteen, and quite exquisite. She wore her glossy black hair in the latest style with a heavy wave falling forward over her brow and she had the largest, most expressive brown eyes that Maryan had ever seen. She could see that Marcus too was mesmerised by the girl's beauty. As the meal progressed his eyes hardly left her face. Placed side by side, they talked incessantly, totally engrossed in each other's company. At her end of the table Rachel, dressed in regal blue, beamed her approval. Sam looked on benignly, happy that his wife and his business colleagues were happy; and Mr and Mrs Weiss seemed delighted with everything.

Washing up alone in the kitchen later, Maryan pictured the scene upstairs. Mrs Leigh had looked especially handsome this evening. Her thick hair, beginning now to grey, waved in attractive silver wings against her head; her tightly corsetted figure was upright and proudly held in her blue velvet dress; and her white hands were adorned with rings. Maryan compared her to her own mother, picturing the face lined with years of struggle, old before its time; the straggling grey hair, crudely sawn off with the household scissors; and the drooping, shapeless body, rarely clad in anything but a fraying print overall. What had Sarah to show for a lifetime of gruellingly hard work? Was that to be her fate too?

But it wasn't the prospect of that bleak future that dampened Maryan's spirits and dragged at her heart as she carefully put away Rachel's fine china. Far worse was the knowledge that this evening marked the end of her few months of innocent happiness. Jessica Weiss was clearly Rachel Leigh's trump card – her chosen daughter-in-law. If it came off it would be the perfect alliance of family and business. Now she saw why Rachel had gone to such endless pains with this evening's meal. Whether he knew it not, Marcus's bachelor days were rapidly nearing their end.

Chapter Four

Amy's first days at school were traumatic to say the least. To begin with, because of her February birthday she started after the Easter holidays and she seemed to be the only new girl. Everyone else appeared to have been at school for ever. Then Mum had told her she must only answer to her proper name.

'You're a big girl now and you're entitled to be called by your real name. Amethyst is a very special name, so don't forget.'

As she'd always been called Amy she wasn't at all sure that she liked her real name. It felt strange and funny, but she meant to try. After all, it was special. Mum said so. No one else was called Amethyst.

It was Tom who took her along on that first morning and when he kissed her briefly at the school gates and left her with a request to 'be a good girl for Dad' she felt her lower lip tremble. She felt bleak and lonely. Why couldn't she have stayed at home with Dad and Grandma like always? Already she hated this bewildering, unfriendly red brick building filled with noisy, rough children.

When the bell rang she was herded inside with all the others, jostled and pushed into a big cloakroom where a kindly bigger girl took pity on her and showed her where to hang her coat. Then, borne along on the tide, she found herself in a classroom. It had a big blackboard and rows of desks, each with a sloping lid and an inkwell and a little groove where you put your pencils. And it smelled funny: a mixture of socks and chalk and the stuff Grandma put down the drain.

The teacher was tall with grey hair and glasses and a very stern face. Towering over Amy like an avenging angel, she took her by the arm and steered her to a desk in the front row.

'I am Miss Vickers,' she said in her strange, deep voice. Her face was so close to Amy's that she could feel her breath on her forehead. It smelled of peppermints. 'You are to call me Miss.'

Then she went and sat at a tall thin desk in front of the class and began to call out all the children's names one by one. Everyone said 'here, Miss', but when it came to Amy's turn she said nothing. Miss Vickers peered over the top of her glasses at Amy in the most ferocious way.

'Amy Jessop, you are to say "here, Miss" like the others,' she told her.

'Not till you say my proper name,' Amy said, wagging an admonishing finger and using the tone her grandma used when reminding her to say please.

Miss Vickers' indignant eyebrows shot up. 'You are a very impertinent little girl. Remember your manners and answer properly when you're told.'

Amy's cheeks blazed. She didn't know what "impertinent" meant but she was sure it wasn't nice. 'Mum said I 'adn't got to answer to nothing but my proper name,' she protested, close to tears.

'Which is?' The teacher stared down at her register. The child's father had come to enrol her. Amy Jessop was the name he'd given.

'Amethyst,' the small voice piped up.

There was a moment's silence then some of the children began to giggle.

'*Silence*.' Miss Vickers thundered. 'I will not have levity in my class.' She glared at Amy. 'I think it would be best if we were to call you Amy,' she said. 'Amethyst is a very outlandish and difficult name. The other children

61

will find it awkward. You will be called Amy whilst you are in school. Do you understand?'

Amy's mouth tightened into a stubborn pout. 'No. *Amethyst*. Mum said. It's a special name and you got to call me it.'

'I do not intend to discuss it with you. While you are here, you will be Amy.'

Amy tried again to protest but the teacher ignored her, descending from her lofty perch to give out reading cards and proceeding with the morning's lessons. But the little scene had set a precedent. If the truth were known, Amy would have preferred to be called by her familiar name, but after Miss Vickers' arbitrary put-down her mind was made up. She would be called Amethyst or she would not respond. The battle was on.

Amy's first month at school was spent mainly standing in the corner. She was as determined as Miss Vickers. Either she was called by her proper name like Mum told her, or she would do nothing. She had her legs slapped, she was deprived of her playtime and she was made to stand in the corner for whole lessons, but still she would not answer to Amy.

When she did go out to play she had to suffer the taunts of the other children. They considered that she put on airs and graces, but it wasn't only on account of her name. Amy was by far the best dressed child in the class. Most of the others came from large families and wore garments that had been handed down so many times that they were tattered and worn almost beyond recognition. By contrast Amy's clothes were crisp and new, which to the other children was a source of bitter envy and resentment. In actual fact, Amy's clothes cost nothing. They were lovingly made by Sarah, run up on the ancient sewing machine that had belonged to her mother-in-law out of leftover scraps of material that Feldman's employees were allowed to buy occasionally for a few pence a bundle. But of course Amy's schoolmates were not to know this. Dancing round her they would taunt her with cries of 'swank-pot' and 'show-off'. They also delighted in chanting their own crude, humiliating version of her name: 'Amy-pissed. Amy-pissed.'

Miss Vickers, who in spite of her strictness was a compassionate woman at heart, witnessed Amy's increasing disquiet with some concern and in the end decided to wait by the school gate one afternoon and have a quiet word with the child's father.

When they got home that afternoon Tom questioned Amy about her defiance.

'Miss Vickers is very worried about you. Why are you being so naughty? You could be having a nice time with the other children. You want to learn, don't you?' he said. 'You don't want to grow up a dunce, not able to read and write.' Amy hung her head. 'Well, *do* you?'

'No, Dad.'

'Then why are you behaving like this? You've always been Amy. Don't you like your name no more?'

'Yes, Dad.'

'Then what's it all about?' Tom asked.

'Mum *said*,' Amy muttered, hanging her head. 'Mum said I wasn't to answer to nothing but my proper name. I was on'y doing what she said.'

Exasperated, Tom pulled her into his arms and hugged her tightly. 'Oh, you silly girl, Mum didn't mean you hadn't to do the lessons unless . . .' He broke off. 'Look – what do *you* want to be called?'

Amy's lip began to quiver and two fat tears dripped onto her cardigan. 'I want to be like all the others,' she hiccupped. 'I don't want to be kept in and stand in the corner while they all laugh at me. I want to go on being called Amy like always.'

'Then you shall.' He kissed her. 'Just you tell the teacher tomorrow. Tell her your Dad says it's all right, eh? And don't you worry about it no more. All right?'

'Yes, Dad.'

He took out his handkerchief and mopped her face. 'Dry them tears then and off out to play with you.' Under his breath he muttered: 'Wait till she gets 'ome. I'll Amethyst her.'

When Tom took Maryan to task about the incident there was a row. Maryan was tired as usual and inclined to be truculent.

'Fancy puttin' the kid through all that. I always said it was a stupid name to give 'er,' Tom complained. 'She was always bound to get ribbed about it. Why the 'ell did you 'ave to insist on it? It's made the poor little kid's life a misery.'

'I can't see what's wrong with having a nice name. It's unusual, that's all.' Maryan took off her coat and hung it behind the kitchen door. 'I suppose *you'd* like her to have been called Ada or Elsie or something equally common. Why shouldn't she have a classy name?'

'Because she don't belong to that class of people,' Tom argued. 'We're ordinary folks, you an' me, Mar. Yes, all right, *common* if you want to call it that. But you can't make a silk purse out of a sow's ear.'

Maryan rounded on him. 'Oh, that's typical of you, Tom Jessop. No ambition and never have. You never look no higher than the gutter. When she was born I made up my mind she'd 'ave something better than what I've 'ad. Calling her Amethyst was part of it.'

Tom sighed. 'It don't do to try and be somethin' you're not, Mar. We're workin' class and Amy's ours. She'll be like us. What's wrong with that?'

'*You* might be working class, but how do you know what class *she* is, eh?' The moment the words were out of her mouth she regretted them. The hurt in Tom's eyes wounded her and she reached out her hand. 'Tom – Tom, I'm sorry. I didn't mean that the way it sounded . . .' But this time he wouldn't be won over. Her cruel reminder that he was not Amy's father had cut him to the quick.

'You'll throw that in my face once too often,' he muttered as he pushed her aside and barged out through the back door. 'I'm goin' down the Prince. An' don't wait up for me. As if you *would*.' As he went he almost knocked Sarah off balance as she came through the door with a basket of washing. The older woman, who'd overheard the heated exchange from the yard, put down her basket and looked sceptically at her daughter across the kitchen table.

'You'll drive that feller away with your sharp tongue, my gel.'

White-faced and defensive, Maryan shook her head. 'He's so touchy. And he thinks he's the only one who knows what's best for Amy.'

'He's practically brought her up,' Sarah reminded her, beginning to fold the clothes. 'And how do you expect him to be anything else but touchy, the time's he's been out of work? A man's got 'is pride.' She looked at her daughter sideways. 'What did you mean when you said he didn't know what *class* Amy was?'

Maryan's tightly reined temper exploded. 'Oh, why don't you mind your own bloody business for once, Mum? I slave myself silly for all of you, and what thanks do I get? I've got ideas above my station. I don't treat my husband right. I'm making my kid miserable because of the name I gave her. Seems I'm nothing but the bloody villain round here. Well I'd like to know where the 'ell you'd all be without me, that's all.' She turned and pulled open the door to the stairs. 'There's no bloody privacy in this hole either – always someone with their ear stuck up against the keyhole. I'm *sick* of it.'

Upstairs in the room she shared with Tom she collapsed onto the bed and let the tears flow. She was tired and fed up with the way they were forced to live, but that was only half the reason for her misery. She was used to the inconvenience and discomforts of Crimea Terrace. She was used to being tired too. But she was strong and healthy. A good night's sleep usually put her to rights again. It was mental anguish that took its toll of her spirits and ground her down relentlessly.

Marcus had married Jessica Weiss eighteen months ago. The wedding had been a grand affair. The ceremony had taken place at the synagogue at Golders Green, where the Weiss family lived. It had been for family and Jewish friends only, of course. In contrast to the small

Leigh family, there seemed to be hundreds of Weiss's – cousins and aunts and uncles, nieces and nephews by the score all of whom were invited to the ceremony and to the reception afterwards at a smart hotel. But to mark the occasion of their only son's nuptials Sam and Rachel had given a party for the staff at Feldman's a few days before the wedding. Maryan and Sarah had been invited, and Rachel had insisted that Tom and Amy were to come too.

It was to be an evening that Maryan would never forget as long as she lived. The hall that had been hired for the party was decked with coloured streamers and flowers and she watched the happy couple as they circulated among the guests. It was sheer torture for her. They were so happy, so obviously head over heels in love. The way Marcus looked at his bride-to-be tore at Maryan's heart 'till she thought she would die of the pain. When they reached the table at which she sat with her family, Marcus shook hands with Tom, kissed Sarah's cheek, then bent to look at Amy.

'So this is the little angel I've heard so much about,' he said. 'Don't you think she's pretty, Jessie?'

Jessica bent down and took Amy's little face between her hands. 'She's sweet.' She smiled at Maryan. 'You must be so proud of her. I'm hoping for a big family,' she confided. 'I love children. I want at least four. Six if possible.'

Marcus laughed and squeezed his wife's tiny waist. 'I'm marrying a woman with plans, Maryan. She intends to be very busy.' He let his fiancée go and watched with pride as she drifted on to the next table. Bending, he whispered in Maryan's ear, 'What do you think of her dress?'

Maryan had already admired it. Made of rose-pink lace, it had a close-fitting long bodice which ended in petal-like points over the hips. The skirt, made of chiffon in a softer shade of pink, hung in handkerchief points that swirled about Jessica's shapely legs as she walked. 'It's lovely, really beautiful,' she said.

Marcus looked pleased. 'One of my first creations,' he told her, watching appreciatively as the skirt followed Jessica's graceful movements. 'And there couldn't be a more exquisite model for it, could there?'

He couldn't have had the least idea of the hurt his remark inflicted on her. Clearly he remembered nothing of the closeness they had shared, the plans, the promises they'd made to each other.

The two firms were to amalgamate. Weiss's had always made industrial clothing, whilst Feldman's served the fashion industry. The two families formed a board of directors and decided that it would make economic sense to sell the two smaller factories and buy one larger building. Fortunately it was in Hackney that a larger factory was found, which proved a great relief to most of Sam's staff and workers.

Marcus was working hard on the newly formed board to get them to let him try a few of his couture dresses on the market. At first they'd been dubious, but after he'd done the rounds of the West End stores with his samples and persuaded one or two of them to order for their 'model gowns' department, the Leighs and the Weiss's gave in and agreed to give it a trial.

Jessica's father had bought them a pretty little town house in Highgate for a wedding present. The spacious attic had already been converted into a studio with a huge south-facing window, from which, as Marcus told Maryan, he had a view of Hampstead Heath. In spite of his resolve to remain single he was ecstatically happy and deeply in love. And all she could do was to stand by, watching and suffering in silence.

It had been a blessed relief when the wedding was over and the couple had departed for a honeymoon in Venice. When they returned they would move into the little house that lay in readiness for them, to begin their life together, Marcus to his designing career, Jessica to the babies she looked forward to so much.

Occasionally they came to dinner at 124 Hackney Road. Maryan, dressed in her black dress and apron would wait on them, her mouth set in an expression of resigned subservience as she watched the loving glances the couple exchanged. She couldn't help noticing the way their hands met frequently during the meal: it was as though they couldn't resist touching each other. And once, when she dropped her serving napkin and bent to pick it up, she saw Jessica's bare foot secretly caressing Marcus's calf under the table. The sight had given her so much pain that she had left the dining room at the first opportunity, to be physically sick in the downstairs cloakroom. Her love and longing for Marcus was more powerful than ever. It overwhelmed her like an illness, an incurable disease that ate at her heart and soul until she thought it must surely kill her.

Only one thing seemed to mar the young Leighs' perfect marriage. After a year and a half had passed Jessica still had not become pregnant. Maryan knew she should be ashamed of the stab of triumph it gave her. But why should they have everything they wanted? What had they done to deserve to have every one of their wishes granted? It was only fair that they should have some disappointments. It gave her a feeling of secret satisfaction, knowing that, although no one else would ever share her knowledge, she had been able to give Marcus what Jessica had not.

But only this morning that one small bubble of compensation had been burst. Mrs Leigh had come into the kitchen with a broad smile on her face.

'Maryan, I'd like you and Sarah to be among the first to know: Mr Leigh and I are to become grandparents. Isn't it wonderful news?'

Maryan forced a smile. 'Yes – wonderful. Congratulations.'

'I didn't say anything before,' Rachel went on confidentially, 'But poor darling Jessica had two miscarriages last year. Such a bitter disappointment to them. As you know, they want a family so badly.' She clasped her hands together ecstatically. 'But this time the doctor assures them that everything will be all right. He's taking extra special care of her, and of course Marcus is treating her as though she were made of Dresden china.'

'Of course.'

Rachel prattled on. 'Of course the other grandparents are delighted too, but it isn't the first for them. They already have four other grandchildren. For Mr Sam and me it's very special.'

'When is it due?' Maryan made herself ask.

'November. She's booked into a nursing home in Kensington. Very exclusive. Private rooms and a nurse to every patient. Just think – hardly any time at all to wait,' Rachel said happily. 'It's July already, so there are only four more months. They didn't tell us this time, you see. They wanted to be quite sure, though I must say I had my suspicions. We mothers have an instinct for that kind of thing, don't we?'

Four more months. The words echoed in Maryan's ears as she lay on the bed. She shut her eyes, hating herself for the resentment she felt. So they were to have their dearest wish after all. If only she could be happy for them. If only things could have been different. If only . . .

She must have fallen asleep, exhausted by her emotional turmoil, and it was an hour later when Sarah touched her shoulder.

'I've brought you a cup of tea. Come on, love. Sit up and drink it. It's nearly nine o'clock and you've had nothing down you since breakfast.'

Maryan hauled herself into a sitting position and took the cup. 'Thanks, Mum. I did have a bite at the Leighs', dinner time, but like you say, it was a long time ago.'

Sarah sat down on the edge of the bed. 'I had a nice supper ready for you. Neck o'mutton with plenty of veg. You like that. It's still 'ot if you fancy it. I kept it on the hob for you.'

'Thanks, Mum. Where's Amy?'

'In bed and fast asleep in my room, bless 'er.'

'Tom?'

Sarah shrugged. 'I wish you 'n 'im wouldn't get across each other so. He does appreciate what you do, you know. Just as I do. But he don't want 'is nose rubbed in it all the time.'

'Then he shouldn't blame everythin' on me, should he?'

'He don't mean to. He worries me some times, moochin' round with nothin' to do. And he worships you and Amy, you know.'

Maryan bit her lip. 'I know, Mum.'

'Try 'n be nicer to him, eh?' Sarah said.

'Yes, Mum. I will.'

It was late when Tom came home. Maryan wakened as he slipped into bed beside her. She could smell the beer on him, but she knew he wasn't drunk or he would have made more noise on the stairs. As she felt the bed dip she reached out her hand.

'Tom . . .?'

'You still awake?'

'Yes. You all right?'

He moved closer and put his arms round her. 'Better than all right, love. I been offered a job.'

Her heart leapt. 'Tom. That's good news. What kind of job?'

He nuzzled her neck. 'Never mind it now. Tell you in the morning.'

'Tom – I'm sorry. About earlier, I never meant . . .'

'I know, love. You were tired.'

'Yes. I didn't mean what I . . .'

'I know you didn't.' He kissed her gently. 'Are you tired now?'

His hands had begun to caress her and she knew what the question meant. 'No. I'm not tired now.'

'Oh Mar. I love you so much, you know that. Amy too. I'd do anything for you both, you do know that, don't you?'

'Course I do, Tom.'

She submitted to his lovemaking, but inside her head the hateful images of Marcus and Jessica tormented her. Tears squeezed out from under her closed eyelids and soaked into the pillow. Tears for herself and for Tom. He deserved better. He was a good man; a better person than she was. If only this open wound of her love for Marcus would heal so that she could be free of its endless torture. He reached his climax and rolled away to lie still beside her, his breathing steadying.

'It'll be all right for us from now on, love,' he said, stroking her cheek. 'I can feel it in my bones. Just you wait 'n see. When I get back again everything'll be fine.'

'Get back?' Suddenly she was wide awake and alert. 'Back from where? Where is this job then?'

He raised himself on one elbow to look at her. 'Spain.'

'Spain? But that's abroad. What job can there be for you there?'

'They got a war there, love. A civil war. Ain't you read about it in the papers?'

Maryan shook her head. 'But that's got nothin' to do with you – with England. Why would you be going there?'

'Well – there was this bloke in the pub, see. He was talking about what's goin' on there. This new government they all hate so much. It's all about gettin' rid of people like Hitler. Fascists, they're called. Remember what the Leighs' son told you when he came back from Germany?'

'But that wasn't Spain,' Maryan argued. 'And it was to do with the Jews, not Spanish people.'

'No, *no*. I never said it was. Look, it's complicated. I'll explain proper tomorrow. The thing is, this bloke was recruiting for something called the International Brigade. They need all the 'elp they c'n get, from every country who'll join. It's a good cause, love. There's even blokes from universities givin' up their studies to go 'n 'elp, so it *must* be right.'

'You'd have to fight, though. It'd be dangerous.'

'Nah. Nothing to it. This bloke reckons that a lot of it will be mendin' the roads that've been blown up so's the proper soldiers can get their tanks on the go.' When he saw the doubt and anguish in her eyes he grasped her shoulders. 'I want to go, Mar. Don't you see? It's a proper man's job. Something worthwhile. I'll be able to hold my head up again.'

'How long would you be gone?'

'I dunno. This bloke reckons if everyone 'elps, all the other countries, it'll be over in no time. And maybe by then there'll be jobs goin' 'ere again.'

'We'll miss you, Tom.'

'Get on wi' you. Glad to have me out from under your feet, I shouldn't wonder.'

She put her arms around him and held him tightly. 'Oh, *Tom*. I might get onto you sometimes, but I do love you.'

It seemed no time at all before Tom was gone. Maryan had visualised him going off to Spain, smart in some kind of uniform, but he left home in his best suit and cap, carrying a cheap, newly purchased suitcase containing a few essentials. She wanted to go with him to the station to see him off, but he told her that they were all to meet at a rallying point, so she had to be content with going with him to the end of the street, where he kissed her and Amy and set off to catch the tram. Maryan watched him go with a bleak feeling of helplessness. Tears thickened her throat. He looked shabby and vulnerable, yet he carried himself erect, proud to be part of something which would restore his pride. Suddenly her heart was flooded with love and pity and a sadness she could hardly contain.

'Oh, Tom. Come back safe,' she begged inwardly. 'If you only come back safe I'll put all those impossible girlish dreams out of my head and be a good wife to you.' Beside her, Amy wept noisily.

'I want my dad. I don't want him to go away,' she wailed.

Autumn came early that year. By mid-September it was already cold and wet. Each morning they wakened to fog, swirling and clammy, trapping all the city fumes and odours so that it became as noxious and choking as poisonous gas. Sarah's chest was bad. The damp weather always brought on her cough and made her joints painful. Amy seemed to have an almost permanent cold and Maryan put it all down to the rising damp the little house was prone to. If only they had somewhere better to live.

There had been only two short letters from Tom: one to say that he had arrived at a place called Aragon, and another several weeks later to say that they were now bound for Madrid where the worst of the fighting was. The letters told very little. Tom's education had been even sketchier than Maryan's and he was no letter writer. His hastily scribbled notes gave nothing more than the barest facts, but they always ended with the words: *I love you. Kiss Amy for me. Your loving husband, Tom.* Never before had she read the newspapers so avidly. At the Leighs' she searched the pages of *The Times* and the *Daily Express* for news about the Civil War in Spain. Recently she had read something that seriously alarmed her. The British Government had decreed that men who enlisted on either side in the Spanish conflict would be liable to two years' imprisonment on their return. Would Tom return only to disappear inside for two years? It seemed so unfair when he was only trying to help.

She arrived early one morning at 124 Hackney Road and let herself in at the area door with her key. The kitchen felt chilly and it was soon evident that the boiler had gone out. Maryan took off her coat and rolled up her sleeves, setting about the clearing and re-lighting of it. Mr Sam would not be happy if there was no hot water for his bath at eight o'clock. It struck her as odd as she fetched coke from the bunker in the yard. Normally Mr Sam attended to the boiler himself before retiring. He must have forgotten last night.

It wasn't long before she had the fire alight and the kitchen warm again. The kettle boiled and she made the tea, setting the early morning tray and putting on a clean white apron, ready to take it upstairs. But before she had time to fill the pot the door opened and Rachel stood on the threshold in her dressing gown. Maryan took one look at her face and felt the blood chill in her veins. Something was terribly wrong. Mrs Leigh never came downstairs in her dressing gown. She always dressed as soon as she got up. But what Maryan found so alarming was the expression on her employer's face. Since yesterday she seemed to have aged ten years. Her eyes were red and swollen with weeping and her whole face seemed to sag dejectedly. Maryan put down the tray and went to her.

'Mrs Leigh – come and sit down. Whatever is the matter?'

Rachel walked past her into the kitchen and sank heavily into a chair. 'Sit down, Maryan,' she said quietly. 'I'm afraid I've got some very bad news to tell you.'

Maryan did as she was told, her heart quickening with apprehension.

'Last night Jessica went into premature labour,' Rachel said. 'Marcus telephoned his father and I around midnight and asked us to go to the nursing home. He said that he just wanted us to be with him, but we guessed from his voice that there was something seriously wrong.'

'Oh no.' Maryan put out her hand instinctively. 'Not the baby – is it . . .?'

'It was a little boy – stillborn.' Rachel bit her lips in the effort to keep the tears at bay. 'Jessica died an hour later. They're both dead, Maryan. We've lost our daughter-in-law and our grandchild.' As she said the words her control left her and she dissolved into a helpless torrent of weeping.

Rigid with shock, Maryan sat for a moment, longing to help and yet unsure of what to do. She'd never seen her employer lose control like this. She was such a strong woman. It was terrible to see her distress. The older woman's face crumpled and distorted with grief as the passionate sobs seemed to tear her apart. Rising, Maryan went round the table and put her arms awkwardly around Rachel's heaving shoulders.

'Oh, Mrs Leigh – if only there was something I could do,' she said. 'If only I could help you. Oh, please don't cry like that. Don't take on so.' Hastily she poured a cup of the fresh tea she had made and put the cup in front of Rachel. 'Here – drink that,' she urged. 'It'll make you feel a bit better.'

Rachel drank the tea and, with an enormous effort, regained control of herself. 'Th-thank you, dear,' she said hoarsely. 'I'm so sorry. I'll be myself again in a moment.'

'What happened?' Maryan whispered. 'Were there – complications?'

'It was her heart,' Rachel said. 'The doctor told Marcus afterwards that Jessica had a heart condition. The pregnancy had already worsened it and the labour was more than she could stand. He'd told Jessica early in the pregnancy but she refused to let him tell Marcus. It seems now that she'd had the condition from birth. She should never have tried to have children. But no one told Marcus. Can you imagine how he feels?'

Maryan was stunned. 'But – didn't her parents know?'

'Of *course* they did,' Rachel said angrily, her colour returning. 'They knew, but they never told Marcus – never mentioned a word about it to any of us. They let her marry him and try to have children and they knew all the time what it might do to her.'

Maryan shook her head. 'I don't understand. Their own daughter. How *could* they?'

Rachel dabbed at her eyes. 'We went straight to their house last night and faced them with it. I couldn't rest until I'd spoken to them.'

'And what did they say?'

'Apart from being upset at losing Jessica they were quite calm. They'd been expecting it since she was a small child, so unlike us, they were prepared. They said they never told her about her heart. They wanted her to have what happiness she could from life while she lived. They said that she'd had more happiness in the past two years than most people have in a lifetime. And they thanked us. Can you believe that? They actually *thanked* us for giving her our son. My poor Marcus. My poor, poor boy.' Rachel began to weep again, silent, hopeless tears that slipped down her cheeks unchecked. Maryan took both her hands and pressed them warmly, tears filling her own eyes.

'Mrs Leigh, I know how you must feel, but I can see what they meant,' she said gently. 'I expect they only did what they thought was best for their daughter. But they should have considered you too. And poor Mr Marcus.'

'If you could have seen him last night,' Rachel said, shaking her head. 'He's devastated – sick with grief. I don't think he'll ever get over it. All he could say was that he wanted to die too.' Rachel clasped her hand to her mouth. 'My own dear boy – and there's nothing I can do to ease his pain.'

'Look – would you like me to go home and bring Mum?' Maryan said suddenly.

Rachel's face brightened. 'Sarah? Oh, I would like to see her. The Rabbi will be coming later to say the Kaddish with us, but it would mean a lot to me to be able to see Sarah in the meantime.'

'Of course, I'll go at once.' Glad to have something positive to do, Maryan was already putting on her coat.

All the way to Crimea Terrace all she could think about was the way she'd wanted the bright bubble of happiness that Marcus shared with his lovely Jessica to burst. How could she have been so spiteful? Now he'd lost his wife and the child they'd both longed for, and she felt partly responsible, almost as though she had caused the tragedy through the power of her evil jealousy.

When Sarah heard the news she was stunned. 'Oh my dear lord. What a terrible thing to happen. Of course I'll come. My poor Miss Rachel,' she said, shaking her head. Eager to help, she moved quickly. Changing out of her working clothes, she donned her best coat and hat and hurried back to Hackney Road with Maryan to give what comfort she could to her old friend and employer.

In the dining room Sam ate his breakfast sad-faced and alone, an hour and a half later than was normal. He hardly touched the omelette Maryan made for him, toying only with a piece of toast. As he rose to leave the table Maryan put out her hand.

'Mr Sam. I'm so sorry – about – poor Mr Marcus's wife.'

Sam shook his head slowly from side to side. 'Sometimes when things like this happen it makes us wonder why,' he said. 'If only the child could have lived, he would at least have had something left of her. As it is . . .' he shook his head again. 'It seems so cruel.'

'Is he upstairs in his old room? Can I do anything for him?' Maryan asked. 'Take him something to eat – a drink?'

Sam shook his head. 'Oh no, my dear. He isn't here. He will remain with dear little Jessica until she is laid to rest.' He smiled gently at her shocked expression. 'That is our custom, Maryan. It's usual. There is something you can do for me though, if you will?'

'Of course. Anything.'

'Go to the factory for me and tell them what has happened. I shall not return for a week. Jim Harris will understand. Tell him I want him to take charge for me.'

The weeks of mourning that followed were bleak, but gradually the Leighs returned to normal, at least on the surface. The two familes spent much of the mourning month of shloshim together. After much talking they came to terms with Jessica's death and her parents made the Leighs understand, at least in part, the motives for their deceit. They had loved their daughter, wanted so much for her to be happy for what little time she had. She had been so in love with Marcus that they were afraid to tell him in case he was daunted by the thought of her illness. They had hoped against hope for some miracle to come out of that love.

For Maryan it was a depressing time. No more letters came from Tom and although she knew he was no letter writer she began to grow anxious. She thought of him in October when she read of the men who marched all the way from Jarrow to London with their petition. Tom would certainly have taken part had he still been here. When would all the trouble and hardship end?

Marcus was rarely seen. Unable to face the house in Highgate without Jessica, he had returned to his parents' home permanently, but he spent most of his time either at the factory or locked in his old studio at the top of the house, sometimes even taking his meals there. On the occasions when Maryan did see him she hardly recognised the gaunt, hollow-cheeked man as the carefree, debonair Marcus Leigh she had once known, and she wondered how she could have thought that the better off were immune to suffering. Tragedy could strike anywhere, on rich and poor alike, she told herself.

Amy still missed her dad. But life at school was better. Once the controversy over her name had died down she began to enjoy her lessons and Miss Vickers soon discovered that she had a quick and able pupil in Amy Jessop. At first the endless questions from the little girl with the bright blue enquiring eyes and soft dark curls, sitting at the desk directly beneath her, caused her irritation. She could barely get out half a sentence before the child was asking the whys and wherefores of the subject, but soon the two grew used to each other and learned to come to a compromise.

'If you will only wait until I have finished speaking, Amy, you will probably find there is no need to ask your question,' she said patiently. 'But if there is when I have finished, I will answer it for you.'

So Amy would wait with barely concealed impatience until Miss Vickers had finished speaking; during which time she would store up, not one question, but half a dozen.

That Christmas they put on a play. It was based on Cinderella and, to her great delight, Amy was given the part of the fairy. Sarah made her a spangled costume and every night either Sarah or Maryan would hear the lines for her before she went to bed. She was so proud and excited.

'Will Dad be home in time to come and see me in the play?' she asked repeatedly. But Maryan could not say.

It was now almost five months since she had heard from Tom and although she said nothing to her mother, the worry of it was eating at her constantly. Searching through the discarded newspapers for news of the Spanish conflict at the Leighs', she read about the bombing and the fierce fighting that was raging there. Tom had made it sound like a mere skirmish, yet it seemed to her like a dangerous, full-scale war. The papers spoke frighteningly of many casualties and some even had pictures of wounded and bandaged men. It was all very worrying.

But in early December something happened that took everyone's mind off their immediate problems. The new, uncrowned king abdicated in order to marry a divorced woman.

Everywhere people were talking about it. Mrs Leigh let Maryan come up to the drawing room to hear the abdication speech on the wireless. By the time it was over Maryan was in tears and Rachel's eyes were suspiciously moist. Sarah had been tight-lipped and uncompromising in her view; she was adamant that he shouldn't do it. He was letting his family down, deserting the destiny he was born to, neglecting his duty. But as Maryan listened to the young king's speech, so clearly painful for him to make, she thought she understood. He could not go on – could not face the duties of being king without the woman he loved at his side. Poor man. Poor, lonely man. It was true, sadness was not the prerogative of the poor and lowly.

The school play was a great success. Cinderella and her 'Prince Charming' sang the hit song of the year – 'Just the Way You Look Tonight' – with Miss Vickers at the piano and brought the house down. And Amy looked so dainty in her spangled frock as the fairy, remembering to wave her wand at exactly the right moment and not forgetting her lines once. Maryan was so proud of her. After the play was over she and Sarah helped her change out of her costume and brought her home, tired out but still chattering excitedly. After a cup of cocoa she was packed off to bed and Maryan and Sarah sat down to drink a last cup of tea before going to bed themselves.

The sudden knocking on the street door startled them both. Sarah looked at her daughter.

'Who can that be, this time o' night?'

Maryan stood up. 'I'll go, Mum. I expect it's one of the neighbours.'

But when she opened the door she found a man standing outside. He wore a raincoat and cap and he was leaning heavily on a stick.

'Mrs Jessop?' he enquired. 'Mrs Maryan Jessop?'

'That's right.' Maryan was mystified. Not only was the man a total stranger but he had a strange accent too. He wasn't even a Londoner. Yet he knew her name.

'I wonder – could I p'raps come in a minute?' The man said, swaying a little. 'I came round earlier, you see, and you weren't in. I got a bad leg injury in Spain and . . .'

At the word *Spain* Maryan instantly felt a stab of alarm. She held the door open. 'Of course, come in, Mr . . .'

'Bell,' the man said. 'Frank Bell.'

In the kitchen Maryan introduced her mother. 'This is my mother, Mrs Brown. Mum, this is Mr Bell. He's been in Spain.' She looked at the man. 'There's tea in the pot. Would you like a cup?'

He removed his cap. 'Thank you. That'd be right welcome.' He sat on the chair Maryan pulled out for him, shuffling his feet a little and staring into the fire.

When Maryan went through to the scullery to refill the kettle, Sarah said quickly: 'Is it 'er Tom? Has something happened to 'im?'

The man looked up at her. Biting his lip, he nodded briefly.

'Then tell her quickly,' Sarah said. 'Don't keep 'er hangin' on.'

'Where are you from, Mr Bell?' Maryan asked as she came back.

'Yorkshire. A little place called Bedale.'

'And you came all this way to see us? To – to see – me . . .' Maryan looked from Sarah to Frank Bell and back again. She'd known instinctively the moment she opened the door that the man was the bearer of bad news. Now she couldn't put off the dreaded moment any longer. She put down the teapot and sat down at the table. 'What is it, Mr Bell? Is it Tom?'

Frank Bell stood up, folding and refolding his cap nervously. 'Tom was a mate of mine,' he said. 'We were together all through the fighting. He were a good mate. A fine chap.'

'You say, *was*? Are you trying to tell me he's . . .?'

'I'm sorry, Mrs Jessop. It were at Madrid, about two months since. I came to find you as soon as they sent me home. We both promised each other we'd do that, you see – if anything 'appened like.' He moistened his lips, looking anxiously from one to the other. 'It were right quick, Missis. He must've died instant-like. A shell, it were. I got me leg smashed and Tom . . .' He broke off as Maryan crumpled before his eyes, sinking into a chair with a groan. Sarah rose quickly and saw him to the door.

'Thank you for coming, Mr Bell. It was good of you. But for you God knows when we'd have heard. It can't have been a nice thing for you to 'ave to do.'

In the kitchen she gathered Maryan to her and rocked her gently. 'There, there, luvvie. I know how it feels, believe me. He did what he felt he had to do, just like your dad. He died fightin' bravely for something he believed in. One day, when you feel better, you'll be proud of 'im. You'll be glad he gave his life tryin' to 'elp folks.'

On the dark stairs behind the closed door Amy shivered in her thin nightdress. Alone upstairs in the little truckle bed in the room she shared with Grandma she'd been unable to sleep. The words she'd had to say in the play were still going round and round in her head and every time she shut her eyes she could see the sparkle of the lights on her pretty frock and hear the music Miss Vickers played on the piano. It had all been so exciting, the applause and the laughter, the gasps of delight when she made her entrance in the sparkly dress with real wings at the back and waved her magic wand. She wished they could do it all again tomorrow. Perhaps if she went downstairs again Mum and Grandma wouldn't be too cross, just this once. Maybe they'd let her talk about it all some more – maybe even make her another cup of cocoa.

She'd been halfway down when she heard the man's voice and stopped, deciding to wait till he'd gone. Sitting down on the stairs she pulled her nightie down over her knees till it reached her ankles, to keep her legs warm. It was cold here on the stairs but it'd be warm in the kitchen. She pictured it: the range fire, glowing red under the high mantel with the china dogs; the red chenille cloth on the table with its fringe of bobbles that she loved to play with; Grandma's chair with the squashy round crocheted cushion on it. Then suddenly her attention was caught by something the man was saying. *Tom was a mate of mine – a good mate – a fine chap. He must've died instant-like.*

So – Dad wasn't coming home after all. He was dead. Very slowly she got up and crept back up the cold oilcloth-covered stairs and into bed. Slipping under the covers and shivering in the darkness, she tried to absorb what she'd heard the man say. *He must've died instant-like.* She didn't know what 'instant-like' meant, but Kenny Jackson's dad had died in hospital last summer so she knew what that meant. She'd asked Grandma at the time and she'd said it meant he'd gone to live with Jesus in heaven and wasn't ever coming home no more. Suddenly she felt afraid and small and lonely. 'I want my dad,' she whimpered plaintively into the darkness as the tears ran down her cheeks and into her mouth. It was Mum's fault, she decided. Mum had made him go away. Amy had heard their quarrels even if they thought she hadn't; all those times when they thought she was asleep or not listening or didn't understand. She was sure Dad only went because he hadn't got a job and Mum made him feel bad about it. And now he was dead and never coming home – and they'd never, *never* see him again. And it hurt so much that she didn't know how to bear it.

Chapter Five

'There, is that better? Can you see now?' Marcus hoisted Amy up onto his shoulders.

'Oooh, yes. I can see lovely now.'

With her head high above the crowd, Amy could see clear along the Mall all the way to the Palace. 'And they're coming – they're *coming*,' she squealed delightedly'. Marcus pushed Maryan in front of him so that she too could see the coronation procession as it passed. Everyone cheered as the golden coach carrying the new King George and his pretty queen drew nearer. Amy waved the little Union Jack that Marcus had bought her from the man selling them at Hyde Park Corner. Her eyes were round as she watched the scarlet-clad Yeomen of the Guard who flanked the coach and the splendidly liveried postilians. Then came the Guards in their plumed helmets, riding on proudly stepping horses, the light flashing on their polished golden breastplates and their spurs jingling. As the coach itself passed she leaned forward to get a better view of the figures inside. She glimpsed crimson and purple velvet robes, trimmed with snowy ermine; she caught the flash of a diamond tiara and, very briefly, glimpsed the profile of the King himself, his thin face sober and dignified.

'I saw them, Mum. I *saw* them!' she yelled, jumping up and down with excitement.

'Steady on, you'll have me over,' Marcus laughed as he

swung her down to the ground again. 'There – that's all for now.' He looked at Maryan. 'It'll be a couple of hours before they're back from the Abbey. Do you want to stay here and keep your place, or would you like to go to the park?'

Maryan shook her head. 'I think Amy has had enough for the time being. Maybe we should go and have something to eat. It's been a long time since breakfast.'

The three of them had been up since dawn, travelling up to Buckingham Palace from Hackney in Marcus's car. He had left it at a friend's house in Knightsbridge and they'd walked the rest of the way to get a good position from which to watch the procession. But even at that early hour the pavements had already been crowded. Some people had been there all night, camping out to get a better view. Whole familes were there, frying breakfast on camping stoves, passing round mugs of tea, singing and joking merrily. All of them were oblivious to the cool weather and determined to make the most of the historic occasion. And now, after their long wait, they had finally been rewarded. The splendour, the pomp and ceremony had thrilled everyone. But for now there was a lull and people were moving off – some to take up new positions; some, like Maryan, Marcus and Amy, to find a place where they could snatch an hour's respite.

They walked across into St James's Park and found a bench under the trees. There, Maryan unpacked the picnic they had brought with them. Mrs Leigh had insisted on providing the lunch, but it had been Maryan who had made the sandwiches, filled the flasks and packed everything into the specially equipped hamper Rachel had lent. Amy's eyes were round as she accepted a chicken sandwich and a ripe tomato and glimpsed the other delicacies awaiting them in the basket.

'It's very good of you to bring us like this,' Maryan said, passing the sandwiches to Marcus.

He smiled. 'Not at all. We couldn't let Amy miss seeing a piece of history in the making, could we?'

Maryan took a bite of her sandwich and chewed

thoughtfully. 'I couldn't help feeling sorry for them. They never wanted to be king and queen, did they? I mean, it was Edward who was brought up for it. They do say that King George is very shy and has difficulty with his speech, poor man.'

Marcus shrugged. 'We none of us know what's in store for us, do we?' he said ruefully. 'We just have to get on with life and play the hand it deals us the best we can. I daresay he'll do his best just as we all have to.'

Maryan stole a sideways glance at him. It was eight months now since Jessica's death. For the first four he had hardly spoken to anyone, remaining in his room and working long hours, often far into the night. When they passed on the stairs or in the hallway he would nod to her as though she were a stranger. She longed to help him, but this cold, gaunt stranger seemed so distant, so remote that she didn't dare to approach him. Mrs Leigh had been at her wits' end, fearing for his health. But in the early spring of this year he had launched his first fashion collection. It had been a great success and now the orders were rolling in. His success had cheered him and he'd begun to look more like his old self. Gradually he'd become more approachable. He'd even begun to smile occasionally. And then he had astonished Maryan one morning a few weeks ago by offering to take her and Amy to see the coronation.

She'd been working on the top floor one morning when he suddenly emerged from his studio, making her jump.

'Oh – Mr Marcus. I thought you were out this morning.'

He laughed. '*Mr* Marcus? For heaven's sake, Maryan, don't call me that. It makes me feel like an old man, and it makes *you* sound like a faithful old retainer. We're still friends, I hope.'

She'd blushed. 'Of course. It's just . . .'

'That my mother employs you? Well, as if that makes any difference.' He took a step closer and touched her arm, his eyes serious. 'Maryan, I want to apologise for not speaking to you before. I've been meaning to for months; to say how very sorry I was to hear about your husband.'

She averted her eyes. 'Oh, thank you, Mr – er – thank you, Marcus.'

'Believe me, I know all too well how you must be feeling. Losing the person you love is the very worst thing that can happen to you. And when it's your husband – and you have his child to bring up alone . . .'

'*Don't.*' She stopped him with a shake of her head. Not, as he thought, because it was too painful for her to speak of, but because talking about it in this way still made her feel guilty. She'd been fond of Tom, of course. She had grieved over his death, and it was certainly true that she missed him. But Amy wasn't Tom's child, and Tom wasn't, and never had been, the man she loved. Not in the same way that Marcus had loved Jessica. Nothing, not even his death, could alter that. Talking about their respective bereavements in the same breath seemed wrong somehow. It made her uncomfortable.

'I'm sorry, Maryan,' he said. 'I understand how difficult it is to talk about it. I just wanted you to know that I do feel for you.'

'I know. Thank you.' She made herself look at him. 'It's good to see you looking better.' He *did* look better. Leaner and older, perhaps. He had grown a moustache, too, which gave him a more mature appearance, but the light was back in his eyes again. He had, as his relieved mother had put it, 'come back to them'.

'I've been thinking,' he went on. 'How would Amy like to go and see the coronation?'

She stared at him in surprise. 'Well – I'm sure she'd love it. I was trying to think of some way we could get there.'

'Then think no more. I'll take you. We can go up in the car, early in the morning before the crowds get too thick. Perhaps we could take a picnic. Make a day of it.'

'I'm sure she'd love that. It would be a real treat. But

are you sure you won't have better things to do – other people to spend the day with?'

'Who better than you and Amy?' He laughed. 'To tell you the truth it's a good excuse for me to go and see it myself. I'm just a big kid at heart.' He sighed. 'And I seem to have lost touch with most of my friends these past months. So – if *you've* nothing better to do on May the twelfth?'

So here they were. At first Maryan had had doubts about whether she should have accepted his offer. What would Mrs Leigh think about it? Would she feel it was beneath her son to take his mother's servant and her child out for the day? But Rachel had seemed as pleased as Marcus at her acceptance, even offering to provide a picnic lunch for them all.

'It's so good to see him taking an interest in something again,' she said as they made a list of what to buy for the picnic. 'And it's so like him to think of those less fortunate than himself. Did you know he'd become interested in underprivileged children lately?' Somewhat deflated, Maryan admitted that she didn't.

'Oh yes,' Mrs Leigh went on. 'He's become very interested in charity. He was saying only yesterday that he might organise a fashion show and give the proceeds to Jewish refugee children. There are so many fleeing from Hitler's tyrany in Germany.' She smiled at Maryan. 'And they do say, don't they, that charity begins at home?'

It was only then that Maryan realised that far from viewing her as a contender for Marcus's heart, Mrs Leigh saw her son's gesture as purely altruistic.

When they had finished their lunch and Amy had fed her crusts to the clamouring ducks, the clouds that had been gathering all morning suddenly fulfilled their promise of rain. As Maryan took out the Mackintosh cape she had brought with her Amy began to whine.

'I don't want that on. It makes me feel all hot and sticky.'

Maryan shook her gently. 'Don't be awkward. You're

showing us up in front of Mr Leigh – when he's been so kind to us too.'

Seeing that the child looked tired, Marcus said: 'What do you say we collect the car and go for a run in the country? I think perhaps we've all had enough of crowds for one day.'

Amy brightened. 'Oh, yes, please. Can we, Mum? I want to see some cows and horses.'

So Maryan gave in. Driving out into the green of the countryside brought back poignant memories. It seemed strange to her, sitting beside Marcus as he drove, unaware that the child in the back seat was his own flesh and blood. She shut the thought out quickly. She had promised herself when she married Tom that no one else should ever know. It could do no good now that he was dead. All the same, she couldn't help fantasising a little as they drove along; imagining what it might have been like, had things turned out differently; if they could have been a proper family.

'Where are we going?' Amy asked.

'I'm going to show you something.' Marcus turned to Maryan. 'I don't suppose my parents have told you that they're building a house in the country?'

'No.' She shook her head, a little alarmed. 'They're thinking of moving then?'

'Not yet. It's for their retirement really. And perhaps weekends and holidays in the meantime.' He glanced at her and lowered his voice. 'And of course if there's a war they'll be safer out of London.'

She felt a chill run through her veins. War was something she refused even to let herself think about. 'There won't be, though, will there? Surely, after last time . . .'

He shook his head. 'I'm afraid it looks more and more as though Hitler will have to be taught a lesson by someone. I can't think why the Government are so complacent over it. We should be arming – showing him our might instead of trying to placate him.' He sighed. 'But let's not talk of war today of all days. Look, this is the place I've brought you to see. It's called Hazelfield.'

They were driving into a pretty village. It nestled in a green hollow in the leafy Essex countryside. In the centre was a large pond surrounded by emerald grass. Cottages were ranged above it on all sides, some with thatched roofs. On the hill on the farthest side a little church perched, its tower just visible above the tall trees of chestnut, elm and oak that were bursting into new green leaf.

'Oh, isn't it pretty?' Maryan exclaimed. 'Amy, isn't this a nice place?"

'Look – more ducks,' Amy said delightedly. 'Can I go and feed them? There are still some crusts left in the basket.'

When the ducks had had their fill Marcus took them to see the Leighs' partly built house. It was on the fringe of the village, not far from the church, which Marcus told them was called St Peter and St Paul. Built in the fashionable mock-Tudor style, the house was almost finished; only the interior had yet to be completed. They walked about in the empty shell and Amy enjoyed herself by trying to guess what the unplastered rooms would be.

'There are to be five bedrooms and a housekeeper's flat over the garage,' Marcus told them. 'They decided on five so that Jessica and I could have a permanent nursery here, with room for a nursemaid too.'

'I see.' Maryan glanced at him apprehensively. She had carefully avoided mentioning Jessica to him, but he spoke her name almost casually.

'But there, I always say you can't have too many bedrooms,' he went on brightly. 'You never know who you might want to invite. Everyone loves a country house party.'

'When are they thinking of retiring?' Maryan asked. 'I'd have thought your father had plenty of time yet.'

Marcus smiled. 'Not for ages, I daresay. Dad likes to be in charge at the factory, as you know. I daresay he'll keep on for as long as he's able. But they couldn't resist buying this plot of land when it came on the market. If there's a war building will probably stop, so they thought they'd better build their dream house while they still could.' He looked at her, one eyebrow raised. 'If you're worried about your job, don't be.' He laughed. 'Anyway, you'll have married again long before then.'

'Marry again? Oh no.' Maryan shook her head. 'I'm not sure I'd want to.'

He nodded. 'Nor me.'

'Anyway, who'd have me?'

'Anyone who wasn't blind, I'd say,' Marcus said, his eyes twinkling. 'You're pretty and still young – what, twenty-one?'

'Twenty-three now.' Maryan was silent as they walked back to the car. She had enjoyed the day, but in a way she wished it had never happened. When Marcus had invited them to the coronation her hopes had foolishly risen again. Perhaps he had asked her because . . . Maybe it might still be possible . . . She had quickly squashed the hope, admonishing herself – telling herself it was out of the question. Marcus would never look at another woman, let alone her. What they had shared six years ago had been a mere childish fling – nothing more. Certainly nothing to compare with the love he had had for Jessica.

Amy was quiet on the drive back to London and, turning to look at her, Maryan found she had fallen fast asleep on the back seat.

'Tuck the rug round her,' Marcus said. 'We don't want her to catch cold after such a perfect day, do we?'

Maryan did as he suggested. 'Thank you for everything, Marcus,' she said. 'Today has meant a lot to Amy. It'll be something she'll never forget. I daresay I wouldn't have managed to take her on my own.'

'Not a bit of it. I've enjoyed myself tremendously. And, like you, I wouldn't have come on my own, so you've done me a favour.' For a moment he was silent, his eyes on the road ahead, then he said: 'Maryan, can I tell you something?'

'Of course.'

'In confidence, I mean.' He glanced at her. 'I'm not even telling my parents.'

She shifted anxiously in her seat. What disclosure was he about to make? 'Are you sure you want to tell me?'

'Yes. I need to tell someone, just in case ...' He glanced at her. 'I'm going to Germany again in a couple of weeks' time. Ostensibly it's a trip to Paris for the summer collections. But afterwards I'm going on into Germany.'

Remembering his experiences there three years before Maryan felt her blood run cold. 'But – what for?'

'My brother-in-law, Harry Weiss, is going with me. The Weiss's have relatives over there. They're trying to help them get out before they're interned. At the moment they're still free to leave, but they aren't allowed to take their money or valuables out of the country.' He glanced at her. 'So we're going to smuggle out what we can for them.'

She turned to look at him. 'But how will you do that?'

'There is a friend who is a dealer in precious gems. He will convert the money into diamonds for them. Harry and I will arrange it and bring the stones back with us. We'll sell them over here and bank the money ready for when they get away.'

'But – won't it be dangerous?'

Marcus shrugged. 'Frankly, Maryan, I don't much care one way or the other.'

Shocked, she touched his arm. 'Please – don't say that.'

He sighed. 'Everything I lived for is gone. I might as well use what's left of my life helping others.'

'If your mother heard you say that ...'

'You mustn't tell her. You promised.'

'Of course I won't. But you must think of them, Marcus. They love you. You're all they have. If anything happened to you ...'

He shook his head. 'There are so many desperate people in danger over there. Others are risking their lives every day to help their friends. I've been so lucky all my life. I've had so much happiness, Maryan. Maybe my time has already run out, who knows? But what's my one meaningless life when there are so many at risk?'

Later that night, lying in bed with Amy sleeping soundly beside her, Maryan thought about their day together. And of the secret Marcus had confided to her on the way home. In some ways she wished he hadn't. He could have no idea how much the prospect of what he was about to do worried her. The weight of it lay heavy on her mind. What he proposed to do was madness. If he were caught . . . She shuddered at the prospect. One read in the papers about how Hitler's cruel regime was persecuting Jewish people. It seemed one needed only the remotest blood tie to be labelled Jew and made to wear the star of David on one's clothing and be jeered at in the streets. She had read even the mothers of little babies were made to display the star on their prams. Closing her eyes she whispered a prayer that he might be kept safe, wishing that there were more that she could do.

I saw the King and Queen in their golden coach. I went in a big car, all the way there an' back, and we went for a drive in the country after and we 'ad a picnic an' fed some ducks on a pond.'

'You never. You're makin' it up again. You're a great big liar, Amy Jessop.'

Amy stood in the playground surrounded by her disbelieving schoolmates.

'No I ain't then.' She stood firm, her hands on her hips and her chin thrust forward. 'I *did* go, s'there.'

'Whose car did you go in then?'

'Mr Leigh's. It's big, with lovely soft seats and it c'n go ever so fast.'

'Don't b'lieve yer. Why'd Mr Leigh take *you* to see the coronation?'

''Cause – 'cause . . .' Amy cast around in her mind for a really watertight reason. ''Cause he's gonna marry my mum,' she said with a sudden burst of inspiration.

This revelation silenced her tormenters, apart from a

girl called Lily Smith, a little older and more streetwise than the rest. She elbowed her way to the front of the group and stood challengingly in front of Amy.

'Bet 'e ain't,' she said scathingly. 'Bet yer tellin' whoppers again, Amy Jessop. Anyway – you ain't so clever. You missed the street party. We had a lovely time. We 'ad jelly an' cake and we all got a mug with a piksher of the King's 'ead on it.'

'Mr Leigh bought me a flag. *We* 'ad chicken sandwiches an' salmon ones an' cream cakes an' lemonade an' *pop*,' Amy retaliated.

'You *never*.'

'We *did*. Ask my mum.'

'You're a show-off, Amy Jessop. I '*ates* show-offs.'

Amy took a step towards her accuser, her hand reaching for one of Lily's scrawny pigtails, but before the two girls could resort to fisticuffs the bell went for the end of playtime and they all trooped back into school. Behind the lid of her desk Amy put out her tongue at Lily Smith, a gesture to which Lily responded with her best grimace, carefully perfected after long hours of practice at the mirror. It consisted of pushing up the tip of her nose whilst pulling down her lower eyelids with the fingers of the other hand. It made her look like a bulldog. Amy treated it with the contempt it deserved, tossing her head disdainfully and wrinkling her nose.

After Tom's death Amy had become what her grandmother called 'disagreeable'. She seemed to bear a grudge against her mother and she became uncommunicative, clamming up and refusing to talk. Sarah said they should ignore it. She was sure that Amy's truculence would pass, but as the weeks went on and the situation worsened, Maryan grew anxious. Why did Amy treat her as though she'd done something wrong? Her patience gradually wore thin and finally, after one of Amy's worst attacks of awkwardness she lost her temper and became downright angry. It was almost as though the child deliberately tried to goad her into anger.

'What's the matter with you, Amy?' she demanded,

shaking her by the arm. 'Your Grandma and I do every-thing we can for you. Why are you so naughty all the time?' When Amy turned away with a toss of her head and refused to answer, Maryan's temper snapped and she lashed out, grabbing Amy and slapping her legs.

'You naughty girl. You don't know how lucky you are,' she shouted. 'You're a horrid, ungrateful little girl.'

'I'm not. *You're* horrid.' The angry tears sprang from Amy's eyes and her face grew red as she said: '*You* sent my dad away. You didn't love him and you don't love me. You never take me out like he did. You never play with me. Nothing's nice no more. I – I *hate* you.' The tears grew into noisy sobs and she flung herself face downwards onto the floor.

The outburst frightened Maryan. She'd always known that Amy was fond of Tom, and she knew she missed him, but she'd had no idea that she actually held her to blame for his going away. Sinking to her knees beside the sobbing child she touched her gently.

'Amy – Amy love. Don't take on like that. I did love Dad. And I love you too. It hurts me when you behave like you do.'

Amy stopped crying and looked up at her, her huge blue eyes swimming with pain and bewilderment. 'You – you were always nagging him. I heard him say so. You wanted 'im to go away. I want Dad to come 'ome again. I – I want my Dad,' she whimpered.

Moved to tears herself, Maryan gathered the child to her and held her close. 'Amy – don't cry like that. You're too little to understand. Grown-up people don't always mean what they say. It wasn't like you think. Dad went away because he wanted to do something good. To help people. But he can't come home again, love. You know that. And we've got to try to get used to it as best we can.' She took out her handkerchief and wiped Amy's tears away. 'I do love you, Amy. Now that Dad's gone you're all I've got. You're the most important person in my life. But I need you to help me. I get sad too.' She sat in her mother's chair close to the range and pulled Amy onto her lap. 'Look, I'll spend more time with you from now on. We'll do all the things you like together. How's that?'

Amy nodded, still hiccupping a little. 'Can – can we go down the market, Sat'day nights?'

'Yes, if you like.'

'An' – an' feed the 'orses round the mews? Take 'em sugar and carrots?'

'Course – anything you like.'

'An' – an' will you stop at 'ome with me all day like Dad did?'

Maryan sighed. 'I can't do that, love. I have to go to work at Mrs Leigh's to earn some money for us all. To buy us food and pay the rent.' She gave Amy a hug. 'Listen, I'll make you a promise. One day it'll all be different. We'll go and live somewhere really nice and have nice clothes to wear.'

'When, Mum – when?' Amy looked at her with round eyes. 'How will we do that?'

'I don't know when or how. It might not be very soon. But I just know that one day we will. You're special, Amy. You've always been special to me since the day you were born. That's why I called you Amethyst.'

Amy frowned. 'I don't wanna be called Amethyst.'

'Not now, maybe. But one day you will,' Maryan prophesied. 'One day – when our ship comes in.'

Amy hadn't the least idea what her mother meant by their ship coming in. But she looked into her eyes and knew that whatever it meant it would certainly happen. Mum was determined that it should. Later she had asked Grandma, who had explained that it meant that something lucky would happen. And now it had begun. Marcus Leigh had taken them out for the day. He was rich. He must be to have such a posh car. They had seen the palace and the coronation. She, Amy Jessop, had seen the new King and Queen. And afterwards they had been for a drive to the country. *Anything* could happen now. Her remark about Mr Leigh marrying her mother had been made on impulse, to shut up that rotten Lily

Smith, but the more she thought about it, the more it seemed possible. They liked each other, didn't they? Maybe that was what Mum had meant when she said they'd go and live in a nice house and have smart clothes to wear. Wouldn't it be lovely to be able to ride in that car every day, whenever you liked? Yes – all she had to do was wait. Wait for the ship to come in.

At playtime Lily Smith was back with her taunts and jibes. She cornered Amy in the playground.

'Go on then – when's the weddin'? You gonna be bridesmaid, are yer? In a big frilly frock.'

'I'm not tellin' *you*, Lily Smith.'

'No – 'cause it ain't true,' Lily sneered.

'*'Tis* true then. Jus' you wait 'n see.'

'I s'pose you know there's rumours going round about you?' Sarah asked Maryan one evening a week later, after Amy had gone to bed.

Maryan looked up from the pile of darning she was helping her mother with. Sarah had started to take in mending lately. Turning shirt collars and cuffs was easy enough for her on her old sewing machine, but the darning tried her failing eyesight so much that Maryan had taken to helping her with it in the evenings.

'No. What rumours?' she asked.

'It's going round that you're engaged to Mr Marcus, that's what,' said a scandalised Sarah. 'I always said nothing good'd come of him taking you up west on coronation day.'

Maryan let the sock she was darning drop into her lap as she stared at her mother. '*Engaged* – to Marcus? Where did you hear that?'

'That Elsie Smith at number twenty-eight. She said her Lily come 'ome from school with the tale.' Her mouth tightened. 'Seems Amy's been puttin' it about. You want to speak to that young madam.'

'Little devil. I'll have a word with her in the morning.'

Sarah looked at her daughter thoughtfully. 'There ain't

no truth in it, is there? Ain't nothin' going on between you an' 'im, I 'ope.'

'Good heavens, Mum, 'course there isn't. You know how shook up he was over his wife dying. He'll never look at another woman – least of all me.'

But Sarah was shaking her head. 'You be careful, my gel. A man's a man. He might not think of marryin' again, but he'll be needin' a woman for you-know-what. They all do. They're not like us, you know, content to keep ourselves to ourselves.'

'*Mum*!' Maryan flushed. 'I'm sure I don't know what you mean.'

'Oh yes you do.' Sarah bent her head over the sewing machine again. 'I'm on'y thinkin' of you. I don't want you losin' your 'ead, gel. Don't want to see you get used – and hurt.'

'You're being unfair,' Maryan said sharply. 'He was kind enough to take us out, Amy and me. That's all. He's a perfect gentleman.'

'They're all perfect gentlemen till they think they c'n get what they wants.'

'I *told* you, Mum. There's no need for you to worry.'

'All right, if you say so.' Sarah's mouth tightened. 'Just s'long as you both remembers it. Meantime, you better scotch them rumours 'fore they gets back to Miss Rachel and Mr Sam. I wouldn't 'ave them upset for the world.'

Maryan bit back her resentment. Apparently even her own mother felt the Leighs would be appalled at the idea of their son contemplating marriage with the likes of her. Nevertheless, she went hot and cold at the thought of the groundless rumour spreading further. If it reached Marcus's ears she'd die of shame. The following morning before school she spoke to Amy about it.

'Have you been saying anything to that Lily Smith about me and Mr Marcus?'

Amy's cheeks turned very pink. 'On'y that he took us to see the King and Queen getting crowned.'

'Nothing else?'

Amy shuffled her feet. 'No – not much.'

'Because Grandma heard a silly tale about him and me getting married. It's supposed to be you that said it. I'm sure that can't be true.'

'No, Mum.'

'So if you hear anyone spreading stories like that, I want you to tell them it isn't true. Do you understand?'

Amy nodded, swallowing hard. 'Yes, Mum.'

All the way to school she puzzled over how she would wriggle out of her boast without losing face. But by the time she came face to face with Lily Smith her face was beaming. She had thought of the perfect compromise.

'My mum's not going to marry Mr Leigh now,' she said, her tip-tilted nose in the air. 'Instead me 'n Mum are goin' to go and live with 'im in a lovely big 'ouse in the country.'

Marcus came back safely from his visit to the Paris summer collections. Nothing was said, but once, when he came into the sitting room while Maryan was cleaning, she asked him if his trip had been successful. He winked conspiratorially and held up his thumb.

'Everything went according to plan,' he whispered. 'Not a word, eh?'

Since then he had been abroad twice more. Maryan had no way of knowing if he'd embarked on any more risky exploits, but she strongly suspected that he had.

Christmas loomed closer and, true to her word, Maryan took Amy to the market after work. Amy loved the market best in winter time when the evenings were dark and the hissing naphta flares lit the faces of the traders and threw exciting shadows. She loved to be out when it was dark and frosty; to hear the stallholders' cheerful shouts as they advertised their wares; smell the mingled scents of oranges and evergreens and chrysanthemums, and hear the happy heart-lifting music of the barrel organ. Sometimes Mum would give her a penny to buy chestnuts from the man with the glowing brazier. The hot nuts would warm her chilled fingers and the smell and taste of the roasted nuts would set her mouth watering in anticipation. Of course it wasn't the same without Dad, but the constant pain of missing him had left her now. Sometimes recently she'd had to remind herself of what it was like when he was here, and the thought made her sad. She couldn't be forgetting him, could she? She'd never do that, because nothing would ever be quite as much fun without him. But Mum did her best. And they were friends again now.

In the year that followed Maryan saw Marcus rarely. When he wasn't working away in his studio or out on business, he was abroad on one of his mysterious trips. If she'd harboured any hopes about their friendship blossoming again they were to be dashed. Her mother certainly needn't have worried.

She searched the papers avidly and worried about what she read. Franco was winning the war in Spain. Had Tom's sacrifice been for nothing? She refused to let herself think about that. Some schools were carrying out experimental gas drills and there were pictures of small children wearing the hideous gas masks. It made her shudder. She read about German children being taught to ignore Jewish children. In the schools they were not allowed to speak to, or play with them. It all seemed so senseless and cruel, teaching innocent children to hate. And even Mussolini was following Hitler's lead, expelling Jews from Italy. It all began to look as though Marcus had been right. Someone should teach Hitler a lesson. If only it could be someone else and not poor old England, she mused wistfully.

In August came the terrifying Czechoslovakian crisis. Maryan was sure, like many others, that war would erupt at any moment. But the Prime Minister saved the day, flying home from Munich with the new peace accord he had struck with Herr Hitler and Mussolini. Desperately wanting to believe the best, the British public let out its collective breath again.

It was early one afternoon in mid-November that Marcus arrived home unexpectedly. Both Leighs were at the factory and Maryan met him in the hall. She was shocked by his appearance. He looked pale and haggard and almost dropping with exhaustion.

'There's a fire in the sitting room,' she told him. 'If you go in there I'll bring you some tea. You look chilled through.'

When she took him the tea and some hot buttered toast she had made for him he turned to her with a smile.

'Thank you, Maryan. You're very good to me.'

'Are you all right?' She poured him a cup of tea. 'You look so tired.'

He sighed and leaned forward in his chair, holding his hands out to the blaze. The firelight on his face highlighted the new sharpness and deepened the hollows beneath his cheekbones. As she turned to go he looked up.

'Don't go, Maryan,' he said softly. 'Stay with me. Bring another cup and share the tea. I need someone to talk to.'

Slowly she lowered herself into a chair. 'What's wrong?' she whispered. 'Tell me.'

He was silent for a moment, then he stood up and began to pace the room restlessly. 'I've been in hell, Maryan. I was in Berlin the night before last. I saw things that will haunt me for the rest of my life.' He went on to tell her of the horrors he had seen – of the marauding storm troopers; of well-dressed women, screaming for blood; of a thousand shattered shop windows and broken bodies. 'It's the end of civilisation,' he said, turning gaunt eyes on her. 'And here people believe that blind fool when he comes home waving his piece of paper and talking of peace.'

'Please. You mustn't go again.' She got to her feet. 'It's too dangerous. Anything might have happened to you. You might have been killed too. Please – you must stop now, Marcus. Say you will.'

He stopped to look at her in surprise. 'Don't you see, Maryan – we can't turn our backs on those people. What will the Nazis do next? Someone must *do* something.'

101

'Of course, but you can't. What good is one man against that?'

He threw up his hands in frustration. 'That's what everyone is saying. In the meantime the madness grows and gathers momentum.'

She looked at his haggard face and love and pity for him overwhelmed her. Throwing caution to the winds she followed her instincts and went to him, putting her arms around him. 'Marcus – please, don't. You're making yourself ill. You helped your brother-in-law get his relatives out. You made sure their money was here for them. You've risked so much, done so much already. Please stop now.'

He leaned against her heavily, seeming to relax for the first time. 'Maryan. What would I do without you? Thank God I have you to talk to.' His arms closed round her and they stood together for a moment.

'You're so tired,' she said at last. 'Finish your tea and toast. I'll go and put a hot water bottle in your bed. What you need is a good long sleep.' She smiled at him. 'Things'll look better then.'

He smiled down at her sadly. 'They'll never look better, Maryan. I've got a terrible feeling deep inside that they're going to get a whole lot worse.' He gave her a little hug. 'But I'll do as you say. You're right. I do need some sleep.' As she made to move away from him he caught her to him and kissed her gently. 'My sweet little Maryan,' he said. 'You re so good to me. Bless you.'

As she prepared his bed for him his words warmed her through and through. He might never love her as she loved him, but she was his confidante. He trusted and depended on her. He told her things he wouldn't even tell his mother. That was worth so much to her.

Summer in Crimea Terrace was never pleasant. The heat seemed to bring out all its worst aspects. The antique drains gave off their noxious odours, dust and flies abounded and the heat in the narrow little streets and alleyways was oppressive and exhausting. Close all the doors and windows and the heat became unbearable; open them and you were obliged to put up with the smells, the dust and flies. The options brought little comfort. And in the summer of 1939 it was worse than ever. The powers that be had decided that precautions must be taken against the possibility of war and air attacks. The sand-bag blast walls that had been built outside the street doors seemed to seal in the heat and keep out the air. It had been suggested that strips of sticky paper be pasted criss-cross on windows, which was supposed to prevent flying glass, and buckets of sand and water were to be kept replenished at back doors in case of incendiary bombs. To most people the precautions were just an irritating nuisance. It was only when gas masks were issued and talk of evacuating the children began to circulate that the prospect of war began to look less like a bad joke and more like a serious possibility.

The previous winter the Leighs had made the decision to take a summer holiday abroad. Rachel had always wanted to go to Norway and, to surprise her, Sam had booked a cruise. Maryan envied them. She had seen the pictures of Norway in the brochures Mr Sam brought home: tall snow-capped mountains, vast blue fjords, cool and serene, reflecting blue skies; forests of beautiful tall trees – a far cry from London's East End, especially in summer. But as the months advanced, the Civil Defence precautions were stepped up and the news grew daily more grave, Sam began to have serious doubts about the wisdom of the holiday he had planned. It seemed mad to risk going abroad unless one had to. Suppose war were to break out while they were away? They might find it difficult to get back into the country. Rachel insisted that he was being pessimistic, but Sam could not agree. War now seemed inevitable. He worried constantly about Marcus. The boy seemed to spend so much of his time in France, almost making it his second home. It was true that Hitler seemed more interested in the countries on Germany's eastern flank, but who knew where he might strike? And if, as was feared, he had his eye on Great

Britain, France would be standing in his way. Sam cancelled the holiday and booked one in Scotland instead. He wrote to Marcus asking him to come home and take over the factory for him as a special favour. In fact he wanted his son back in England and in comparative safety, but he knew better than to say so. To Sam's disappointment and frustration, Marcus replied that he had urgent business to attend to and could not return at the moment. So, for the very first time, Sam was obliged to leave the factory in someone else's hands. Harry Weiss, his partner's son, would be taking charge with the able assistance of Jim Harris, his head cutter. It would be the first holiday Sam had ever had. He and Rachel left for Inverness on 26 August.

On 1 September Hitler invaded Poland.

'You're not tellin' me you're lettin' 'er *go*?' Sarah stared at her daughter, aghast. 'You must be mad. 'Eaven knows where them poor little mites'll end up. You might never see 'er again. Besides, it's Poland that 'itler's invaded, not England.'

'Oh, Mum, do leave *off*.' Maryan was at the end of her tether. Whilst they were away Rachel had left her in charge at 124 Hackney Road and she felt the responsibility keenly. For the past month she had lain awake every night, worrying about Marcus. He had left for France almost a month ago, saying that he would be home in a week. Since his departure there had been rumours by the dozen about what was happening on the other side of the Channel. And where was he? It was quite likely that he wasn't in France at all, but back in Germany again. Surely there was nothing more he could do to help Jewish families. She had read in the papers as long ago as last December that Hitler had seized all Jewish property and possessions. Whatever good Marcus had managed to do had been done in the nick of time. There would be little or nothing he could do from now on. And being Jewish himself he was in constant danger, even with his British passport. If only he would come home. And now she was faced with her mother's opposition to the evacuation scheme. Did she let the child go somewhere where she would be safe, or remain here to face God only knew what? The dilemma was almost more than she could cope with.

'You've already lost a father and an 'usband to war. Ain't that enough for you? Do you want to lose your child as well?'

'I won't be losing her, Mum. They'll be taking her where she'll be safe. Why can't you understand that?'

Sarah shook her head obstinately. 'It's splittin' families. It can't be right,' she argued. 'What'll become of 'er if something 'appens to us – tell me that? She'll be left an orphan. I say we should all stick together.'

Maryan turned on her mother. 'Do you think I haven't thought about all that? I've been half out of my mind with worrying about it, day and night. I've had no sleep since I don't know when. All I do know is that I want her to be safe. So I'm letting her go, Mum, and that's that.'

Maryan had tried to explain to Amy as best she could why she was sending her away.

'It'll be a kind of adventure,' she said. 'Something to look forward to. And when you're settled I'll come and see you as often as I can.'

'Will we live in a big house?' Amy asked, round-eyed. 'Is it because the ship's coming in?'

Maryan smiled to hide the hurt inside her. 'Maybe,' she said, wishing she didn't have to lie to the child. 'Who knows what might happen if you're good?'

Amy hugged the exciting idea to herself. Maybe they *would* end up living in a big house with Mr Marcus just like she'd told Lily Smith. Maybe it would come true. Maybe – as Mum said – if she was very good.

The evacuation was well organised and orderly. The children gathered in the school playground with their little cases and paper bags, name labels carefully tied to their coats. Maryan went along with the other mothers to see them off at Euston station. In spite of her initial eagerness, Amy was tense and silent when the train pulled alongside the platform, clinging to her mother's hand until the very last minute, so that Maryan almost snatched her back and held onto her tightly. It was Miss Vickers who gently prised them apart and said with a gentle smile, 'As soon as she gets there she'll write you a postcard so that you can come and visit. Don't worry, Mrs Jessop, we'll take very good care of them.'

As the train began to move dozens of scared little faces pressed against its windows. Small hands waved frantically and Maryan swallowed a feeling of near panic. Oh God, how could she have let her child go, just like that, to an unknown destination? If Mum was right and they never saw her again it would be all her fault. 'What will become of us all?' she muttered as, blinded by tears, she hurried out into the street again. Would anything or anyone ever be the same again?

To Maryan's relief the Leighs arrived home on Saturday the second, a week earlier than planned, and there was plenty to take her mind off her parting with Amy. Immediately she got to work helping Rachel to make blackout linings for all the curtains and trying to make sure that they'd followed the Civil Defence instructions to the letter. Meantime, Sam was doing the same at the factory. When on Sunday morning war was officially declared and Marcus still had not arrived home, Rachel was distraught. Almost hysterical with worry, she implored Sam to do something. He did his best to calm her, telling her that the boy would not be stupid enough to take any risks. He would surely be on his way home and would arrive any day now. There would be a telephone call – a letter from him by the next post. But no letter came.

Maryan saw and heard their anxiety with an increasing feeling of guilt. When each successive post brought no word from Marcus she became convinced that she should speak. Although Marcus had sworn her to secrecy, the circumstances had changed. He would surely not want his parents to worry so. At last she decided to have a quiet word with Sam when he was alone.

She saw her opportunity on Monday morning, stopping Sam in the hall as he was on his way out of the house to the factory.

'Mr Leigh. There's something I need to talk to you about,' she said. 'Can I speak to you now?'

He pulled out his pocket watch and glanced at it briefly. 'Of course, my dear. I expect you're going to ask my advice about joining little Amy in the country. Why don't you speak to Mrs Leigh about it?'

'No. It's not that. I must speak to you alone. It's about Mr Marcus.'

His expression changed. Taking her arm he drew her into the small room at the front of the house which he used as a study. 'Come in here for a moment,' he said. 'We shan't be disturbed. Rachel is still dressing.'

He walked to the fireplace, then turned to face her. 'You know something?' he said. 'Something he hasn't told his mother and me?'

She nodded. 'He's been making trips into Germany for some time. The first time he went with Mr Weiss – Mr Harry Weiss. They went to try to help get some relatives out of the country. He was very upset by what he saw there and he's been back many times more – times when he was supposed to be in Paris. He was there on the terrible night they called Crystal Night. He's been trying to do what he could to help.' She took a deep breath and clasped her hands nervously before going on: 'I – I've been worrying in case he might have been caught there when war broke out.'

Sam closed his eyes and drew a long breath. Passing a hand over his brow he pulled out a chair and sank into it. 'I had an idea there was something like this going on,' he said. 'But I can't believe that he would be such a fool as to remain in Germany for longer than necessary, not at such a time as this.'

'I'm sorry, Mr Leigh,' Maryan said. 'I've been feeling so guilty knowing about this when you didn't. I couldn't keep it to myself any longer, even though I promised not to say anything.'

He rose and came to her, patting her arm. 'Don't worry, my dear. You kept quiet out of loyalty to Marcus. I understand that. And there was little we could have done anyway.' He sighed. 'I shall say nothing of this to his mother for the moment. All we can do is hope and pray that he's safe.' He looked at her stricken face. 'Marcus must hold you in very high regard to confide in you.'

She bit her lip. 'I – I'm sure he would have told you. It was just that he didn't want to worry you. I think he told me because he needed someone to talk to.'

Sam nodded. 'And he knew of course that we would have done all in our power to stop him if we'd known what he was doing.' He smiled his gentle smile. 'I'm just glad he had someone sympathetic who he felt he could trust.' He took both her hands in his and pressed them reassuringly. 'You did right to tell me, my dear. And I appreciate it. But it shall be our secret for the time being.'

It was just two weeks later that the letter came. It bore a London postmark. Maryan recognised the handwriting as soon as she picked up the post that morning and put the letter in her apron pocket until Sam was alone in his study. He glanced at it and then at her.

'Stay with me while I read it.' She stood by the door and waited while he slit open the envelope and read the single sheet of paper inside. After a moment he gave a sigh and passed it to her. 'Read it for yourself,' he said. 'There is a message for you at the end.'

With trembling fingers she took the letter from him, noticing as she did so that it was dated almost three weeks before. It read:

My dearest Mother and Father,
I don't know when you will get this letter. I'm giving it to a friend who is leaving France today. He will post it for me when he arrives in London, but I'm sure that by the time you read it England will be at war with Germany.
I may not be seeing you for some time. I have made

some good friends here in France and have decided to remain with them and help for as long as they need me. There is much I can do to help our people, work that I am sure you would want me to do. Please forgive me for not getting in touch before, and please try not to worry.
Your loving son, Marcus.

P.S. Please give my regards and my sincere thanks to Maryan for all she has done.

She looked up at Sam. 'What does it mean?'

He was shaking his head. 'I suspect that he's joined some kind of resistance movement.'

'But surely – if he wanted to fight he could have come home and joined up.'

Sam smiled at her ruefully. 'It's my guess that Marcus is fighting a much more personal war,' he said with a sigh. 'The thing is, how am I to tell his mother?'

Rachel took the news badly. She railed so bitterly over what Marcus had done that she made herself ill and had to take to her bed with a severe migraine. Lying in a darkened room, she refused to eat and wept incessantly until finally, two days later, Sam sent for the doctor, who gave her a sedative and prescribed some calming medicine.

Downstairs in the kitchen Maryan remembered Marcus's last words to her. *I've got a terrible feeling deep inside that things will get a lot worse.* Bleakly she wondered just how much worse.

Part Two

Chapter Six

1943

Amy stood on the platform of Rhensham Halt waiting for her mother's train.

It was over six months since they had seen each other and she was looking forward with mixed feelings to the coming Easter. Maryan had written to say that she had arranged to take a week off to be with Amy for the Easter holiday. Since her evacuation to Rhensham, her mother's visits – even at Christmas – had been brief, snatched affairs. This was the first time Maryan had been able to get away for more than a day to stay with her daughter in the Suffolk village.

Amy had been with the Taylors at Mitcham Lodge ever since that afternoon in September '39 when, along with a couple of dozen other tired and bewildered children from her school, she had arrived at the village hall in Rhensham. Almost immediately the tall, dark-haired lady with the gentle smile, whom she later learned to call Auntie Marjorie, had picked out Amy and two other little girls to stay with her at her home.

'I can easily take three,' she generously told the billeting officer. 'There's just my son and me in that great house, and with my husband away in the army there's nothing much else I can do to help the war effort.'

But Amy's two companions had stayed only a few

weeks. When the devastating bombardment of all major cities that everyone had feared failed to materialise, their mothers had thankfully whisked them home again. At the time Amy had expected her mother to come and take her home too, but Maryan had written to say that she was busy helping the Leighs to prepare their new house in Hazelfield for occupation. She had assured Amy that it would be best for her to stay where she was for a little longer. The 'little longer' had stretched to ten months, after which Maryan decided that Amy might as well stay in Suffolk for the summer holidays and get the benefit of the country air. The Leighs were spending every weekend at Hazelfield and needed her to go with them. And as Amy had settled so well in Rhensham, surely she would be happier there, in the company of her new friends. There would be nothing for her to do in London anyway. Maryan concluded the disappointing letter with a half promise: *Perhaps if things are still quiet and you're still homesick you could come home for good when the new school term begins.*

But in September 1940 the blitz had taken them all unawares, coming as it did with the ferocity and unpredictability of a summer storm. When the London raids became a regular nightly occurrence it clearly became unthinkable for Amy to return home. The Leighs moved out of London altogether and took up residence at Whitegates. Maryan and her mother went with them and were installed in the little flat.

Although Amy was homesick for the first few months she had taken to Rhensham, and especially to Mitcham Lodge the moment she had seen it. Her first sight of the house had been late that September afternoon. The setting sun bathed the white walls with a soft, warm glow that made them look as though they were made of gold. To Amy's eyes it had looked just like the gingerbread house in the fairy story and she could hardly believe that she was actually going to live in it. When her two companions had gone home she had felt abandoned, but kind, motherly Mrs Taylor had soon made her feel wanted.

Her son Michael, however, had been quite another matter. An only child, he had deeply resented Amy at first and made no secret of the fact that he would have preferred her to have gone back to London with the others. Three years older than Amy, he lorded it over her, boasting about his army officer father and laughing at her accent and her manners. Her fear of farm animals, and her ineptitude with a football drew the most scathing remarks of all from him.

'Why couldn't they have sent us a *boy*, for heaven's sake?' he was always asking exasperatedly, grey eyes raised to the ceiling. 'Girls are useless. They're no good at *anything*.'

Amy had burned with humiliation. She wasn't useless and she was determined to show him that she was good at things. It was just a question of finding out what.

On the brief occasions when Michael's father, Captain Philip Taylor, came home on leave Amy had felt shy and left out. He was a tall, handsome man and although he was kind to Amy she was slightly in awe of him. It was so long since she had known what it was to share a house with a grown-up male. Having him around made her remember Tom and she began to miss him anew, especially when Michael and his father went off together, unthinkingly excluding her from their expeditions. But on these occasions Marjorie would involve her in helping with the horses or in the kitchen, something they both enjoyed.

The year after war had started Michael passed his scholarship examination and moved on to the Grammar School in Ipswich. For the first few weeks he was quite unbearably conceited and there were times when Amy would have positively disliked him – if she hadn't already become his devoted (but secret) admirer. But as the term progressed and the work became harder his air of brash confidence gradually diminished. For hours on end each evening he struggled manfully with his homework, flatly refusing to let his mother help him. He would not admit that he was finding the work harder than he had envisaged, and his attitude towards Amy grew more amenable as a result.

In September '42 Amy too passed her scholarship and moved to the Girls' High School. She travelled in with Michael on the train each morning and home again at night. Now she had her own homework and, after tea and 'Children's Hour' on the wireless, she and Michael would work companionably together till bedtime. Gradually their relationship mellowed from squabbling rivalry into one of tolerant comradeship.

But Amy knew that the question of where she and her mother would live after the war was over must inevitably arise sooner or later. There was constant talk of a 'second front' which, so everyone said, would turn the tide. The prospect of leaving Rhensham and the Taylors; her new school and the lifestyle she had grown so accustomed to, filled her with foreboding.

The sound of a distant whistle made Amy look up hopefully. A plume of smoke appeared at the bend in the line and a moment later the locomotive chugged into view. In spite of her apprehension, Amy could not help the tingle of excitement in the pit of her stomach. It was so long since she had spent any time with her mother. It was almost as if they were strangers. She stepped back as, with a screech of brakes and a hiss of steam, the train came to a stop alongside the platform. Doors began to swing open and crowds of people streamed out: shoppers laden with parcels; Easter weekend visitors with suitcases; servicemen coming home on leave, heaving bulging kit bags onto their shoulders. She stood on tiptoe, her eyes raking the sea of faces. Then at last there was Maryan, looking so smart in a new black costume with a crisp white blouse, a perky little hat with a spotted half-veil perched on her blonde shoulder-length hair. She spotted Amy and her face lit up in the familiar smile. She put down her suitcase to hold out her arms.

'Amy, love. Heavens, how you've grown. You're quite the young lady.' She hugged her daughter, who was now almost as tall as her. Amy seemed to have grown at least six inches since she saw her last.

'I like your new costume,' Amy said admiringly. 'How's Grandma?'

Maryan laughed. 'Gone back to Hackney. She never did take to it at Hazelfield and everyone reckons the bombing's stopped for good now.'

'But Crimea Terrace was bombed,' Amy said.

Maryan nodded. 'Not directly, though. Our old house is still standing – just about. It can't be very comfortable, but it's where she wanted to be, Amy. There was nothing I could say to change her mind. Mr Leigh says they'll pull the rest of the terrace down when the war's finished. What she'll have to say about that, I don't know.'

Amy took her mother's hand and pulled her towards the barrier. 'Come on, Auntie Marjorie's got a special tea waiting for you.'

When they were seated on top of the bus Amy asked about the Leighs. 'Has Mr Marcus been home on leave?'

Maryan sighed. 'No. It's over three years now since he went away. Sometimes they get word from him to say he's safe, mostly through other people who've seen him.'

'Is he still in France?'

'We think so, but we don't really know, not for sure.' Maryan was silent, thinking about Rachel and the anguish she had suffered since Marcus had left. It was fairly certain from what information they had managed to piece together that he was fighting with the Resistance in occupied France and everyone knew how dangerous that was. It was heartbreaking to see her health deteriorate as she anxiously waited for every post, refusing to believe Sam when he kept telling her that no letter would get through. Daily she prayed to have him home again. But still no word came.

'People are saying that the war won't last much longer,' Amy was saying. 'What will we do then, Mum?'

'Mrs Leigh seems to want to stay on at Whitegates,' Maryan said. 'And my job is with them, so I suppose I'll stay too.'

Amy frowned. 'I'd hate to leave my new school.'

'We'll find you another school, just as nice as this one. You'll see.' She tucked her arm through Amy's. 'We'll make a new life together. We've got so much to catch up with.'

'What about Grandma? Couldn't we go back to London too?'

'The papers say that the Government are to build a lot of nice new houses for people who've been bombed out,' Maryan said. 'Maybe she'll get one of those, or perhaps a little flat. She'll be all right. Anyway, you like the country, don't you?'

Amy's heart sank. She felt confused. It was true that she loved Rhensham, but if she had to leave here she'd rather go back to London than move to Hazelfield. But she could see that nothing would ever be the same as it was before the war.

On her one disastrous visit to Whitegates she had been dismayed and disappointed by the size of the flat, after the build-up Maryan had given it. It felt so small and cramped after the spaciousness of Mitcham Lodge. And the house seemed to be full of sick old people who must not be disturbed. Mrs Leigh had a permanent headache and Grandma had one of her 'chests'. She was told to play quietly and there were parts of the garden where she wasn't allowed. She hated the thought of living there permanently after the freedom she enjoyed at Rhensham.

'I wish you could come and live here, Mum,' she said wistfully.

Maryan took her daughter's hand and drew it through her arm. 'My job is with the Leighs, love. You'll like it all right when you get used to it. Just as you got used to it here.'

As they walked down the drive at Mitcham Lodge, Maryan looked at the house and understood her daughter's reluctance to leave it. The L-shaped house with its white painted walls stood in four acres of land. There was a walled kitchen garden and a paddock with two horses, which Marjorie Taylor stabled for a friend who owned the local riding school.

Marjorie worked hard, tending the garden and growing vegetables; caring for the horses. As they neared the house she came to meet them, a tall, slim figure, her dark hair pulled back into a chignon. She wore jodhpurs and a yellow polo-necked sweater.

'Hello. How nice to see you.' She rubbed one hand on the seat of her jodhpurs and held it out to Maryan. 'Heavens, you look so smart, you quite put me to shame. I can't remember when I last dressed up in town clothes. There's never time any more. And there's so much to do out here at this time of year.'

Maryan shook the slim hand and was surprised to find it work-roughened. 'I hope you get Amy to help you,' she said.

'Oh, I do. She and Michael do their share,' Marjorie said. 'Amy's a little marvel with the horses. She tells me she used to like to visit the ones that were stabled behind your house in London.'

'That's right. Always a great one for the horses, she was. Even as a little kiddie.' Maryan looked at the tall eleven-year-old beside her and felt a pang of regret for the years she had missed. It seemed no time at all since Tom had taken her to the mews to feed the big, gentle drayhorses with carrots. She had a sudden nostalgic vision of Amy, wrapped up warmly against the cold, big blue eyes shining and her little nose like a frozen cherry, holding Tom's hand as she trotted up the street beside him. But Tom was gone. And Amy was a child no longer. Suddenly Maryan realised how little she knew her. Not only was Amy more grown-up than when she last saw her, she was different in a dozen new subtle little ways. Since she had lived with the Taylors she had all but lost her London accent. Now she spoke like they did – not *posh* exactly, but in a more defined, precise way, carefully sounding her G's and aitches and effortlessly getting all the grammar right. It made Maryan proud, yet slightly uncomfortable, though she couldn't have explained why.

'I've got the kettle on. I'm sure you're dying for a cup of tea,' Marjorie was saying, leading the way indoors. 'Amy, why don't you show your mother her room, then you can go and help Michael finish off the horses while we have a cosy chat.'

In the long sitting room with its low beamed ceiling and stone fireplace Marjorie had tea laid out on a trolley drawn up in front of a crackling log fire. The room was pleasantly furnished with a comfortable settee and chairs covered in faded chintz; the parquet floor was strewn with Indian rugs patterned in pastel colours; and there were pictures on the ivory-coloured walls – pretty watercolours of local landscapes, which, Maryan learned later, had been painted by Marjorie's husband, Philip. The room had a lived-in, welcoming look that made visitors feel instantly at home and relaxed.

Maryan looked at the spread on the trolley: homemade bread and scones and two kinds of cake. Her eyes widened. 'Did you make all this?'

Marjorie laughed. 'I like baking – all cooking, in fact. It's no chore to me. And here in the country food is a little easier. But then you live in the country too. I keep forgetting. You must have found that too.'

Maryan nodded, wondering if the remark held a hint of reproach that she hadn't taken Amy back to live with her. 'Food is certainly easier than in London. A lot of people have taken to keeping chickens and pigs, which helps out the rations a treat.' She accepted a cup of tea and a scone. 'I'd like to thank you – for all you've done for Amy. She's been so lucky.'

Marjorie looked surprised. 'Nonsense. I've loved having her. She's a delightful child.'

Maryan sipped her tea. 'You must have wondered why I didn't have her with me when I moved to a safe zone with my employers when the blitz began.'

'Not at all. Amy told me how little room there was there, with your mother being with you.' She smiled. 'To tell you the truth, I was quite relieved. Michael and I would have missed her terribly if she'd left.'

'She's growing up so fast,' Maryan said. 'Quite the young woman. I couldn't get over how tall she'd grown when she met me at the station.' She cleared her throat. 'I suppose I should really have a little talk with her while I'm here this weekend.'

'If you mean a talk about the so-called facts of life, we've already had one,' Marjorie said. 'I hope you don't mind, but she had her first period a couple of months ago, so I really had no choice.'

'Oh? No, of course not. I'm sure it was very good of you.' Maryan swallowed the small stab of resentment she felt. So she wouldn't even be allowed to share this precious-intimate milestone with her daughter. She said quickly: 'This is a lovely place. When you hear of the places some children were sent to . . .'

'I know.' Marjorie nodded. 'And we've been so safe. One would hardly know there was a war on. It makes me feel quite guilty sometimes.' She smiled. 'I'm lucky to have Mitcham Lodge. My parents left it to me, you know. My father bought the house and land quite cheaply in the early twenties. It was badly run down and he restored it. He planned to make it a hobby for his retirement.' She refilled Maryan's cup. 'Being able to grow our own vegetables and stable the horses has helped enormously.' She smiled. 'It's nice to have time to talk, isn't it? We've never had a chance to get to know each other properly before. I don't know Hazelfield, but Amy tells me it's very pleasant.'

Maryan was silent for a moment, remembering the one disastrous visit Amy had made to Whitegates. Mrs Leigh had been ill with a severe migraine that weekend and Sarah, who had left blitz-torn London with great reluctance, had grumbled throughout the entire weekend too, insisting that in spite of the modern conveniences at the flat, she still preferred having her own back yard and taking her bath in front of the range of a Friday night. When Maryan had seen Amy onto the train on Sunday evening she'd felt depressed and exhausted; torn three ways between loyalty to her mother, her daughter and her employers. She was all too aware of how short-tempered she'd been all weekend. It was hardly surprising that the child was eager to leave.

'I hear that your employers moved their business out of London,' Marjorie was saying.

Maryan looked up. 'Yes. The factory was bombed. The building was damaged beyond repair. Mr Leigh and his partner salvaged what they could of the equipment and machinery and found suitable premises in Essex. They've been working on a Government contract – making uniforms. They did it in the first war too.'

'I see. How interesting.' Marjorie pushed the trolley nearer Maryan. 'Do help yourself to more cake. We don't stand on ceremony here. You didn't consider taking up war work then?'

Maryan took a slice of cake and broke a piece off thoughtfully. 'I was tempted. Munition work is very well paid. But Mrs Leigh, my employer, hasn't been at all well since the war began. As she gave me a job when I badly needed one, I felt I couldn't desert her when she needed me. Domestic staff are very hard to replace once you lose someone.'

Marjorie smiled. 'Don't I know it. Before the war we used to employ a full-time gardener and a daily woman here. Now I've had to learn to do everything myself. But you know, I've found to my surprise that I absolutely love it.' She looked at Maryan. 'It's very loyal of you to stay on, though. A good many women would have seized the opportunity to earn more.' She sipped her tea, continuing to look thoughtfully at Maryan over the rim of the cup. 'Amy tells me that her father was killed in Spain – the civil war?'

'That's right.'

'You must miss him dreadfully.' Marjorie shook her head. 'My own husband is in Burma just now. I try to keep myself as busy as possible so as not to worry, but it's always there, at the back of your mind, isn't it?'

'Yes.'

Marjorie looked up with a smile. 'But you're sure to marry again. You're still young.'

Maryan shook her head.

Marjorie nodded. 'Well, I know how you feel. I don't think I could marry again either if Philip – if the worst happened. We keep hearing rumours about this so-called second front they're supposed to be planning. If only it could be soon.' She pushed the tea trolley aside and stood up. 'Well, I must go and have a bath and make myself presentable. Why don't you find Amy and get her to take you for a walk before dinner? The village is looking lovely just now.'

Maryan found Amy at the back of the house in the stable yard, where she was helping a tall, good-looking boy whom she barely recognised as Michael Taylor to muck out. He too had grown since she saw him last. Standing there, watching them, Maryan was struck again by the change in her daughter. She looked so *at home* here; as though she'd been born to this kind of life. As she watched, the boy turned and caught sight of her.

'Oh, hello, Mrs Jessop,' he said politely in his new deep voice. He smiled at her. 'It's nice to see you. I hope you had a pleasant journey.'

'Thank you, Michael. Your mother has suggested Amy might take me for a walk round the village. I hope you can spare her.'

Michael glanced at Amy. ''Course. Glad to get her out of the way for five minutes.' He waved a dismissive hand. 'Off you go, kid.'

Amy pulled a face at him and, leaning her pitchfork against the wall, she crossed the yard to join her mother. 'Right, where would you like to go first?' She'd changed out of the cotton dress she had worn, into jodhpurs and boots, and tied back her dark curls with a length of black ribbon.

'Where did you get those breeches?' Maryan asked as they walked down the drive.

Amy looked down. 'These? Oh they're some that Mike had grown out of.' As they walked down the road and past the church she voiced the thought that was uppermost in her mind. 'Mum – now that Grandma has gone

120

back to London are you here to persuade me to come back to Hazelfield with you?'

By her tone it was clearly the thing she most dreaded and Maryan felt a sharp pang of hurt.

'Not if you don't want to,' she said. 'But you are only an evacuee here, love. When the war is over you'll have to leave. We'll have to start trying to get back to normal sometime,' She glanced at Amy's glum expression. 'Is coming back to live with your mum such a horrible thought?'

Sensing her mother's hurt, Amy slipped a hand through her arm. 'Of course it isn't. I'd just rather not live at Hazelfield though. Do you think the Leighs will go back to London when the war ends?'

Maryan shrugged. 'Who knows, love? Mrs Leigh is getting on in years now. And she hasn't been very well either. It's all the worry over Marcus. I think she'll probably prefer to stay in the quiet of the country.'

'But *you* don't have to stay there too, do you, Mum? Couldn't you get another job?'

Maryan sighed. 'We'll see. The war is far from over yet. And anyway, there's no way of telling what'll happen afterwards. Better wait and see.'

'But until it does – I can stay here?'

Maryan looked at the eager blue eyes, looking so hopefully into hers, and gave in. 'All right. I expect it would be better for you to stay on at this school for the moment. If Mrs Taylor doesn't mind, that is. But it would be nice if you were to come and stay with me for a few days. I think you'd find it better now that Grandma has gone back home. I admit it was a bit crowded before.' She looked at Amy. 'Why not come in the summer holidays? I could get some time off and we could go for days out. We could go up to Town and spend a day with Grandma. She'd love to see you. And we could even slip over and see Auntie Maggie and Granny Jessop too.'

Her mother was clearly trying so hard to make it all sound attractive that Amy felt obliged to agree. 'Okay then,' she said. It was odd, sometimes she felt as though her mother was the child and she the parent.

Later, lying awake in the pretty blue and white bedroom, Maryan thought back over the evening. The dinner Marjorie had prepared had been laid on specially: roast chicken with home-grown vegetables, and sherry trifle to follow, with cream bartered from one of the local dairy farmers in exchange for some of her home-grown broccoli. The table had been exquisitely laid with fine china and a lace cloth. There'd even been candles and serviettes too. Marjorie had changed into a soft wool dress of dark blue, which, although starkly plain, looked sophisticated and expensive, worn with a string of pearls and matching earrings. Maryan, in a frilly white blouse and red skirt, felt common and over-dressed by contrast.

This house, the whole set-up had the ambience of a comfortable middle-class lifestyle that Maryan knew she could never aspire to. To the Taylors, being 'poor' meant having to do without a car, a gardener and a daily cleaning woman. It had nothing at all to do with going hungry or not being able to pay the rent. Maryan could not imagine how Amy would settle down to their old life again. The answer was that she shouldn't have to. Hadn't she always promised something better for them? Of course they had the flat at Whitegates, which was far more comfortable and convenient than anything they had known before the war, but if Maryan had taken the opportunity to go into munitions she could have put enough money aside for something better; perhaps a place of their own. Even Sarah had taken her to task over it during one of the frequent arguments they'd had when they were sharing the flat at Hazelfield.

'I thought you were all for betterin' yourself,' she'd said accusingly.

'I happen to think that this is an improvement on Crimea Terrace,' Maryan said.

Sarah sniffed. 'I seem to remember you tellin' me I was nothing but a servant, yet *you* don't seem to mind bein' one nowadays. This flat might have all mod cons but it ain't yours, is it? If the Leighs chucked you out tomorrer you'd be 'omeless.'

'Well, they're not *going* to chuck me out, are they, Mum? Not today or tomorrow or ever, as far as I can see,' Maryan told her firmly. 'Mrs Leigh needs me. Surely you wouldn't want me to desert her? You've always been the one to point out that she was your *friend*, after all.'

Sarah shrugged non-committally. 'That's as may be. It's true that Miss Rachel an' me was always good friends. But she never took advantage of me like what she's doing to you. She's got you at her beck and call twenty-four hours a day, what with 'er 'eadaches and everything.'

'She can't help it. It's because of Marcus, Mum,' Maryan said. 'Surely you can understand that. He's her only child and the poor woman is worried half out of her mind about him.'

'So's a good many others,' Sarah said. 'After all, from what I c'n make out he didn't *'ave* to go an' put 'is life at risk. He wouldn't never 'ave been called up like all the rest. He'd've been in a reserved occupation, makin' uniforms an' that. There's women losin' their menfolk all up 'n down the country – strugglin' on with kids to bring up and work to do; 'omes to keep together on next to nothin'.' She gave another of her explosive, disapproving sniffs. 'Seems to me Miss Rachel don't know she's born. Wouldn't 'urt 'er to get out and do somethin' to 'elp, 'stead of moping her life away down 'ere in this 'ole at the back of beyond.'

Maryan had been surprised at her mother's vehemence against the employer she had always defended so strongly. It was almost as though their roles were reversed. She put it down to her mother's dislike of the country. The place had seemed to sour her whole outlook. Ever since she'd first arrived she'd done nothing but grumble and find fault. She refused to see that Maryan's relationship with Mrs Leigh had developed beyond that of servant and mistress. Sometimes even felt that what they had was more like a daughter and mother situation. Mrs Leigh depended on her support, as a friend and helper – as a nurse too at times. And, mainly because of Marcus, Maryan was happy to remain at Whitegates and do all she could to support Rachel through this stressful time in her life. Always – right at the back of her mind and barely acknowledged – was the hope that one day, when the war was over, Marcus would come back and he would finally turn to her again. She dismissed her mother's criticism as jealousy, and when Sarah had announced her intention to return to Hackney she'd felt guilty. But on the whole she considered it to be for the best. Sarah was a Cockney, born and bred. She'd never settle in the country.

Before Maryan's weekend was up it had been arranged thay Amy should visit Hazelfield the last week in August. Amy and Michael were involved in a carnival the combined villages were organising. It was to take place in July for the 'Holidays at Home' project. All the schools and organisations were taking part. There was to be a pageant, a picnic, a garden fête with sideshows and competitions, and a flower and produce show, in which Marjorie hoped to exhibit. Everyone was looking forward to it enormously.

But a month before it was due to begin, the excitement was eclipsed by the news of the allied invasion of Normandy. The great push forward that everyone had been longing for had finally come at last. Surely now it could only be a matter of time before the war was won. Michael pinned a map up on the kitchen wall and he and Amy made little flags which they moved every day to check the progress of the invasion: red ones for the British; blue for the Allies.

Then in the midst of all the euphoria came the shocking news of the first of the V-1 bombs falling on London. Hitler was making a last desperate attempt at destruction with this new and deadly weapon. Terrifying robot planes that fell indiscriminately at any hour of the day or night had engulfed a war-weary London in a new blitz. A new flood of evacuees descended on all the 'safe' areas and Marjorie took in the young wife of a naval officer and her twin babies, converting her two spare rooms into a flat for them.

It was while they were having breakfast one morning in July that the telephone rang. Marjorie went to answer it and came back with a worried look on her face.

'That was your mother, Amy,' she said. 'She'd like you to go over to Hazelfield today.'

Amy looked up in dismay. 'But why? I'm going in a few weeks' time anyway.'

'She's worried about your grandmother staying in London now that these V-1s have started. She feels that you should both go up and persuade her to come back.'

'Can't she go?'

'She seems to think your grandma would listen to you.'

Amy was silent. It was because Grandma and Mum fell out badly when they were living at the flat together that Mum wanted her to go too. Grandma could be really stubborn when she dug her heels in. She looked at Marjorie. 'Did you say I could go?'

Marjorie smiled wryly. 'It isn't for me to say, Amy. If your mother needs you, I think you must go.' She began to clear the breakfast table. 'I've looked up the trains and there's one in an hour. I told her I'd put you on it, so you'd better hurry upstairs and pack a few things.'

'You can't go. You'll miss the carnival,' Michael said bluntly.

Amy looked at him. 'I know. Maybe Grandma will agree quickly. Maybe I'll be back by tomorrow.'

Michael opened his mouth to protest further, but a look from his mother stopped him. He stared down at his plate moodily It would all be spoilt if Amy wasn't here to share the fun. He really didn't see why she had to go. He told her so later as she packed her small case for the journey.

'I don't see why your mother can't cope with it,' he said, staring gloomily out of the window.

125

'Because they haven't been getting on too well,' Amy told him. 'When Grandma went to live at Hazelfield before, they were always quarrelling.'

'So – what does she think you can do about it?'

'I don't know, but I have to try and do something. I love Grandma. I don't want anything to happen to her.'

'They'll want you to stay for the rest of the hols,' he said.

Amy shrugged. 'No they won't. But I suppose I'd have to if they did.'

Michael watched her in silence for a moment, then: 'I suppose you know that nothing's going to be any fun with you not there.'

Amy looked at him in surprise. '*Me?* But you've lots of friends of your own.'

Michael went pink and kicked at the carpet. 'It's not the same,' he mumbled.

She snapped her case shut, trying to hide the little smile that pulled at the corners of her mouth. 'I'll probably be back in no time.' She looked up at him. 'Coming to the station with me, Mike?'

'No. I hate stations.' He pulled something out of his pocket and tossed it onto the bed. 'Look, you might as well have this,' he said casually.

Amy picked up the bar of chocolate, looking at him in surprise. 'Thanks, Mike – but, your sweet ration . . .?'

He shrugged off her thanks. 'It was all they had at the village shop,' he said. 'And it's the kind I don't like.'

When the train pulled in at Hazelfield Maryan was waiting. 'I thought we'd go up to Town tomorrow and try and get your Grandma to come back with us,' she said. 'She'll probably argue, but we'll have to persuade her somehow. Those buzz bombs are getting more and more frequent – horrible things. I don't like to think of her there in the thick of it.'

'I know, but did you really need me to come too, Mum?' Amy asked. 'We're ever so busy at Rhensham

126

getting the carnival ready. Will I have to stay long, do you think?'

Maryan stared at her daughter. 'Don't you care about your Grandma?' she asked tetchily. 'I don't know about you, Amy, really I don't. Sometimes I think you've got really selfish, living over there in Suffolk, away from it all. People have suffered terribly in this war, you know. You're old enough to realise that there's a bit more at stake than a carnival.'

Amy coloured, slightly ashamed. 'Okay – sorry, Mum.'

They were having lunch together in the kitchen of the flat at Whitegates when Amy looked out of the window and saw Sam Leigh coming up the drive. 'Here's Mr Sam, Mum,' she said. 'Does he usually come home at this time of day?'

Maryan joined her at the window, a puzzled frown on her face. 'No, he doesn't. He must be ill.' She leaned forward to get a better view. 'I think he must be. He looks terrible. I'd better go down.'

But as she turned away Amy said. 'No need. He's coming up here.'

A quick look from Maryan confirmed that Sam had started to climb the staircase that led up to the flat. She turned to Amy. 'I think perhaps you'd better go in the bedroom,' she said. 'He might want to see me privately about something. Better if you're not here.'

Amy went reluctantly. One minute she was wanted, the next she was being pushed out of sight like a bundle of dirty washing.

As the bedroom door closed behind her Maryan took a deep breath and then opened the door to find Sam waiting, white-faced, outside.

'Mr Leigh, whatever is it? You look done in.' She put out her hand to help him inside.

Inside the closed door he stared dazedly at her. 'Oh, Maryan, I've had some terrible news,' he said brokenly. 'I don't know how to tell Rachel – how to face her. Will you come with me – be with me when I tell her?'

'Of course.' She led him gently to a chair, her heart

thumping with apprehension. It was Marcus. It had to be. Nothing else could affect him like this. She forced herself to be calm. 'Sit down,' she said. 'Take your time. Let me get you a nip of brandy. I think you'd better tell me about it first.'

Sam accepted the brandy gratefully and as he sipped it a little of the colour gradually came back into his cheeks. At last he began to speak, slowly and painfully, his voice husky with emotion: 'This morning I had a visitor. An English airman who had been shot down over France. He'd been taken in and hidden by a farmer and his family after his crash and when he was well enough a small group of Resistance workers were going to try to get him and a group of Jews across the border into Switzerland.' His voice faltered and stopped as he stared into his empty glass.

'And – he had news – of Marcus?' Maryan prompted.

'Yes, Marcus was one of them.' Sam looked up at her, his dark eyes huge and full of pain. 'Maryan – Marcus is dead,' he said, his voice almost a whisper. 'This man couldn't tell me everything because he didn't know. Perhaps no one will ever discover the truth of it. But it seems that someone must have betrayed them. They were meant to hand them over to another group close to the border, but when they arrived it was the Germans who were waiting. They scattered, but it was no use. The airman and one other man escaped, but the rest were caught and – and executed on the spot.' The words caught in his throat and he slumped forward, his head in his hands. 'Oh, my God. My boy – my son – Marcus, *Marcus*.'

Tears streaming down her cheeks, Maryan sank to her knees and put her arms round Sam's heaving shoulders. Putting her own desolation aside she asked: 'And this airman – he knew Marcus well?'

Sam shook his head. 'Not well, but it seems that Marcus had asked him to come and see us if he got home to England safely. He was supposed to tell us that Marcus was safe and – and well . . .' Once more his words were lost in grief. Maryan took both his hands in hers.

'Mr Leigh, Marcus was very brave. He went into it with his eyes open. He'd seen the terrible things that were happening on his visits to Germany before the war. He told me about them. They disturbed him deeply. He did what he felt he had to do. I believe that. And we – you should be very proud of him.' She pressed the cold hands, warming them with hers. 'After Jessica and the baby died I don't think he felt that his life mattered any more. This would have been the way he wanted it. He'd want you to see it that way too. I know he would.'

Sam gathered himself together and raised his head to look into her eyes. 'You're right.' His fingers closed around hers, returning the comforting pressure. 'And I am proud of him. Very proud.' He looked into her eyes. 'You knew him well, didn't you, Maryan? You understood him.' He leant forward to kiss her forehead. 'You've been a good girl to Rachel and me all this time. Don't ever think we don't appreciate the sacrifices you've made for us.' He closed his eyes. 'But I wish – oh God, how I *wish* he could have come back safely to us.'

'I know.' She swallowed a sob. 'I wish he could have too.'

'And my Rachel. How shall I face my Rachel?' Sam asked plaintively. 'You'll have to help me tell her, Maryan. I can't do it alone.'

'Of course I'll help. We must try to be strong – for her.'

'Yes, yes.' He heaved himself to his feet. 'We had better go now. Get it over with.'

When Rachel heard Sam's key in the front door she came out into the hall to meet him. Maryan saw at once the wariness in her eyes. It was almost as though she already knew. She even took a step backwards, one hand held up protectively before her, as though to ward off what she read on their faces.

'Samuel? What is it? Are you ill?'

He took a hurried step towards her. 'Rachel, come into the sitting room, dearest. Maryan and I – have something to tell . . .'

129

'It's not Marcus?' Rachel was shaking her head. 'Not my Marcus? You're not – going to tell me ... She saw from the look in Sam's eyes that it was as she feared. She clapped her hands over her ears. 'No. *Don't*. I won't listen. It's not true. No, no, I can't bear it.'

Sam grasped her by the shoulders, steered her into the sitting room and pressed her rigid body into a sofa. 'Rachel. Please don't make this harder for me. You're right. It is Marcus and you must try to be brave. It's bad news, my dear. The worst, I'm afraid. The very worst.'

Rachel looked from her husband to Maryan and then back again, all the while shaking her head slowly from side to side, her eyes wide and disbelieving. 'He's not – not, dead?' she whispered. 'No, he can't be. No – no – *No!*' she last syllable came from her throat in an agonised howl as she threw herself full length on the sofa.

Maryan ran to her side. 'Oh, Mrs Leigh, please don't take on like that. I'm here. Let me get you something.'

But Rachel would not be comforted. Hysterical with grief she sobbed inconsolably, rolling back and forth and plucking heedlessly at the sofa cushions. Sam stood by, looking helplessly at Maryan.

'I think we should call the doctor,' Maryan said. 'Perhaps he could give her something to calm her down.'

She sat with the distraught Rachel while Sam telephoned the doctor. By the time he had arrived Maryan had managed to get her upstairs to her room. She felt icy cold and her teeth were chattering. The doctor gave her an injection and within minutes she was asleep.

Downstairs in the hall Sam explained. 'We heard today that our only son has been killed,' he said.

The elderly doctor nodded sadly. 'Sometimes I think that this war is especially hard on mothers,' he said. 'I'm sure she will be calmer when she wakes, once the shock has diminished. But don't hesitate to call me if she isn't.'

Back in the flat Maryan explained to Amy what had happened. 'I can't leave them in this state,' she said. 'It may be a couple of days before we can go to London now. You don't mind, love, do you?'

Amy shook her head. The news about Marcus had shocked her too. She remembered him very well, even though it was five years since she'd last seen him. She had never forgotten the day he took them to see the coronation and what fun it had been. It was awful to think that he was dead.

'Mrs Leigh might ask to see your grandma,' Maryan was saying, half to herself. 'She was the one person she wanted when her daughter-in-law died. In fact, this might be the one sure way we'll get Grandma to leave London.'

But Rachel made no requests of any kind. She did not leave her bed at all that day. That night Sam gave her the tablet the doctor had left and she slept soundly till morning. But when she wakened to the horror of reality her agony returned. She turned her face to the wall, refusing to get up, to eat or to see anyone, not even the Rabbi, summoned to the house by a distraught Sam, himself almost sick with grief and worry.

'She says that we have nothing left,' he told Maryan. 'First her poor father perished on the *Titanic*, then there was our dear Jessica and the little one; now we've lost Marcus. She seems to think there is some kind of curse on us; that we are doomed to lose everyone we love because of some unspeakable wrong we must have committed. I've tried to reassure her but it's no use. She won't listen.'

Rachel remained in her room, refusing food or comfort of any kind. On the third day, when Maryan was preparing a lunch tray for her in the kitchen, she looked up to see Amy watching her.

'When are we going to London to get Grandma?' Amy asked. 'It's really boring here, Mum. There's nothing to do.'

'I can't go while Mrs Leigh is in this state,' Maryan said.

'You said she might want to see Grandma.'

Maryan sighed. 'I know, but I haven't had the chance to ask her. She doesn't seem to want anyone at the moment.'

131

'Shall *I* ask her?' Maryan looked up in surprise. Amy nodded towards the tray. 'I'll take that up if you like,' she suggested. 'Then I can ask her while I'm there.'

After a moment's hesitation Maryan lifted the tray and held it out to her. 'Well – all right. You might as well have a try at getting her to eat, I suppose. But don't say anything,' she warned. 'Not unless she speaks to you. We don't want her upset again.'

On the landing Amy knocked on the door. There was no reply, so she opened it and went in. Rachel was sitting up in bed, propped against a pile of pillows, as limp as a rag doll. She stared unseeingly out of the window at the blue sky, apparently unaware that anyone had entered the room.

Amy cleared her throat. 'Mrs Leigh, I've brought you some lunch. It's only an omelette, but Mum says it's very light and it'll do you good.'

Rachel turned her head and looked slightly surprised to see the young girl standing at the foot of her bed. 'Who are you, child?'

Amy moved closer and set the tray across Rachel's legs. 'I'm Amy.'

'Maryan's daughter?'

'Yes.'

Rachel looked without interest at the food on the tray. 'Take this away, child. Tell your mother I'm not hungry. I can't eat it.'

'Oh, please try,' Amy said. 'It's nice and hot and there's home-made bread to go with it, look. And the coffee's freshly made. We're not supposed to waste food, are we? Not with the war on. And Mum's gone to a lot of trouble to make it look nice for you.'

Rachel looked again at the tray with its crisp white embroidered cloth and matching napkin. A small glass vase held two pink roses from the garden. The wisp of steam that rose from the spout of the coffee pot was fragrant and appetising. Rachel looked up at the slim, dark-haired schoolgirl standing by her bed. 'How old are you now, Amy?'

'Twelve and three-quarters.'

'Are you really? You're tall for your age, just like Marcus was at thirteen.'

'I'm sorry about Mr Marcus being killed,' Amy said. 'Mum wondered if you'd like to see Grandma. She's known him since he was a little boy, hasn't she?'

Rachel looked at her. The child was the first person to speak of what had happened openly and frankly. It brought her a strange relief. The shadow of a smile lifted the corners of her mouth. 'Sarah?' she said. 'Oh yes. That would be nice.'

'We thought we might go up to London and fetch her.'

'Would you really?'

'Yes. But only if you eat your lunch,' Amy said daringly. She picked up a fork and held it out. 'Go on, why don't you try a little bit? I bet you'll like it. Mum put herbs and things in it.'

Rachel paused, smiling at the child's naivety, then she obliged by forking up a piece of the omelette.

Amy nodded her encouragement, unselfconsciously sitting down on the edge of the bed. 'That's right. Nice, isn't it? Mum makes lovely omelettes. It isn't made of dried egg either. Go on, have a bit more.'

Rachel ate another forkful – and suddenly her stomach, tantalised by its first nourishment in days, reminded her of how hungry she was. She ate on until, to her own surprise, the plate was empty. When she had put down the fork and dabbed her mouth with the napkin, she smiled at Amy. 'You're a good girl, Amy. You can pour me a cup of coffee now. I do believe I could drink one.'

Downstairs in the kitchen Maryan was amazed and delighted by Amy's success, and when later she went up to Rachel's room she found her employer much brighter. She seemed pleased with the idea of a visit from Sarah, and she was obviously taken with Amy and impressed by way she had persuaded her to eat.

Unable to unleash her own private feelings, Maryan had saved her grieving for when she was alone. Night after night she lay awake far into the small hours, her heart aching for the brief, sweet love whose promise would never be fulfilled. She agonised about Marcus's death. Had he suffered at the hands of the Nazis? Had they hurt him? Had he ever, in those dark and terrible days, thought of her? She searched the corners of her mind for every little scrap of detail about him, carefully storing the few precious times they had shared, pressing them into her memory like flowers between the pages of a book. Maybe one day she would tell Amy about him. Surely she too should share the shining joy that had brought about her very being. As she grew up Amy was getting so much like him. She had his dark curly hair and classic features, and as her body grew and developed it was becoming clear that she would have his tall, supple figure. Her clear blue eyes were all she had inherited from Maryan.

It was almost a week after Sam had brought home his dreadful news that Rachel decided to get up and dress for the first time. She sat in the conservatory at the back of the house, looking out over the garden, ablaze with summer colour. Maryan took her coffee and biscuits to her there and asked again if she would like to have Sarah to visit.

'If you would be kind enough to fetch her for me.'

'Amy and I could go up the day after tomorrow if that's all right.'

'Perfectly.' Rachel looked up. 'I wonder – could you spare me your daughter for a little while this morning?' she asked.

'Of course. I'm sure she'd love to come and sit with you.'

Amy took a draught board with her and she and Rachel played draughts all morning, Amy chattering and laughing uninhibitedly, drawing the grief-stricken woman out until she too was smiling in spite of herself.

The idea came to Maryan in the small hours of the following morning. The more she thought about it, the more she felt that it would be the answer to everything. Amy was the Leighs' grandchild after all. Surely they should know it, especially now that Marcus was gone. Rachel seemed so taken with her. It would be something new for her to live for. And Amy's future would be secure, too; secure in a way that Maryan could never hope for. Of course it meant that her mother would have to know as well, but that couldn't be helped. It was a problem Maryan would meet when she came to it.

She chose the following evening, after dinner. It was the first time Rachel had joined Sam downstairs in the dining room for their evening meal. When Maryan took them their coffee she stood by the door.

'May I speak to you?' she asked, her heart drumming.

Sam looked up at her in surprise. 'Of course. Is something wrong, Maryan?'

'No.' She cleared her throat. Her legs were shaking so much that she longed to ask if she might sit down, but she took a deep breath and went on: 'I have something to tell you. It – it's bound to come as a shock. But – but not a nasty one, I hope.'

Rachel turned to look at her, a slight frown on her face. 'I'm not sure that I want any more shocks just at present. Whatever it is I think you had better tell us quickly, Maryan. I do hope you're not thinking of leaving?'

'Oh no. It's – er . . .' The words died in her throat. It was proving much harder than she'd imagined.

Sam smiled at her kindly. 'Come and sit down, Maryan. Would you like a cup of coffee?'

'Thank you.' Maryan sat down at the table, grateful for the small respite and to take the weight off her trembling legs. She accepted the cup of coffee that Sam poured for her, and it was only then that she noticed that there was no jug of hot milk on the tray. 'Oh – I've forgotten the milk . . .' She made to jump up but Sam put out a restraining hand.

'Never mind the milk, it doesn't matter. Stay where you are. Rachel and I prefer our coffee black anyway.

Now, won't you get this thing that's worrying you off your chest?'

'It's not exactly worrying me.' Maryan took a sip of the hot black coffee. 'It's about – about Amy.' She looked up to find the faces of her employers looking expectantly at her.

'You'd like to have her here to live with you permanently?' Sam prompted.

Maryan shook her head. 'Not that, no – although . . .'

'What then?' Rachel asked sharply.

Maryan moistened her dry lips and looked at Rachel. 'Mrs Leigh – this will come as a surprise to you, but Amy – Amy is your granddaughter.' There was a shocked pause as Maryan swallowed and went on: 'Marcus was her father. It – it was long before he met Jessica. And he never knew. I never told him.' She lowered her eyes. 'I – I loved him very much.'

Having actually got the words out filled her with relief, but this was to be short-lived. She looked up at the two faces staring at her on either side. Sam's expression was incredulous and confused. But Rachel's was dark with suppressed anger. Clutching the edge of the table, she rose unsteadily to her feet to glare down at Maryan.

'How – *dare* you?' she hissed. 'How dare you come to us with this outrageous lie? To think that you are asking me to believe that my son would seduce a *servant* girl – would father her child. It's disgusting – *obscene*.'

Horrified at Rachel's reaction, Maryan rose to face her. 'But – it's *true*. And it wasn't sordid. We were very young and – and in love. Marcus did once ask me to marry him. He was going to speak to you – and then . . .'

'*Be quiet*!' Rachel waved her hands at Maryan as though trying to rid herself of some horrific delirium. 'You are a wicked woman to put us through this. My son is dead and you are trying to blacken his character; to spoil our memory of him. Making him out as some kind of promiscuous philanderer. I know for certain that he would never have dreamed of touching a . . . someone not of his faith. I don't know who the unfortunate father of your child was, but I do know that it was *not – my – son.*' She banged her clenched fist on the table to emphasise the words, then, exhausted by her emotional outburst, she collapsed into her chair, gasping and clutching at her chest. Sam sprang up and poured her a glass of water.

'Rachel, Rachel, my love – don't upset yourself like this.' He glanced round at Maryan, his face white and shocked. 'Perhaps it would be best if you were to leave us now,' he said quietly. As Maryan made a move towards the distressed Rachel he held up his hand. 'I'll see to her. Leave her to me.'

Outside the door a white-faced Amy stood clutching the jug of hot milk that her mother had left on the kitchen table. Hoping to be helpful, she had taken it along to the dining room and overheard every word of the exchange that had taken place behind the door, from her mother's halting revelation to Rachel's hysterical reaction. Turning, she made her way back to the kitchen, placed the jug on the table, then let herself quietly out of the side door to make her way across the yard to the flat.

Sitting there in the dusky light of evening she felt cold and numb with shock. So – the man she had called 'Dad'; the sweet, kind man she still missed so much, was not her father after all. How could her mother have deceived all of them for so many years? Why had she not told her? Surely everyone should know who their father was. Tom Jessop must surely have believed he was her father. He had loved her so much, cared for her like the tenderest of fathers right from babyhood. He had spent so much of his time with her. She remembered the overheard rows between her parents – their angry voices. Harsh words like 'boozing' and 'nagging'. A sentence here and there that she had puzzled over. '*We both know why you married me.*' '*You might be working class but how do you know what class she is?*' She'd never forgotten them or the bitterness with which they were voiced. Now it all slipped into place. A hateful suspicion occurred to her: had her mother sent him away on purpose – because she loved Marcus Leigh? Had she perhaps hoped that Marcus would marry her if Tom were out of the way? Was that the basis for all the vague promises about the ship coming in and the lovely life they'd have when it did? Or was it all lies? Either way it seemed that her mother really was a wicked woman just as Mrs Leigh said.

She got up and ran into her room, slamming the door; sobbing as she undressed and climbed into bed. If her mother came to her she would pretend to be asleep. She couldn't see or speak to her, not tonight. Tomorrow she would go back to Rhensham. But much as she needed to talk to someone, she couldn't even tell Auntie Marjorie about this. It was too bad – too shaming.

Lying in the darkness she tried to sort out the confused, tangled thoughts that chased round and round inside her head. It was no use asking her mother for the truth. She had lied to her and to everyone else for almost thirteen years, so how could she believe her now? But there was one thing she had to know: if it were true and Marcus Leigh was her father, *who did that make her*? Was she still Amy Jessop, or should her name be Brown, like Mum's before she was married? Or was her real name Leigh? And if it was, was she half Jewish? If only there were someone who knew for sure; someone she could trust to be honest, to tell her the real truth.

Grandma. Amy opened her eyes. Grandma must surely know. She wouldn't keep the truth from her. Not if she asked. Somehow she would go up to London and ask her. But she would have to go alone. No one else must know this terrible, shameful secret her mother had imposed on her.

Chapter Seven

Sam reached out his hand for his watch, lying on the bedside table. Peering at its face he could just make out the time: 4.30. He sighed and turned towards his wife, who lay with her back towards him, body hunched.

'Rachel. Are you awake, dear?'

After a pause she sighed and turned onto her back. 'Awake? I haven't closed my eyes once all night. I'm sorry if I've been restless and disturbed you.'

'You haven't. I haven't slept much either.' He sat up and looked at her. 'Shall I get up and make you some tea?'

She shook her head. 'No. At least try to get some rest. You'll be so tired at work all day.'

Sam slid down the bed again with a sigh. There was little hope of relaxing in the same bed as Rachel. He could feel her tension, taut as a tightly coiled spring as she lay stiffly beside him. He dreaded bringing up the subject that he knew they must talk about and searched his mind for something placating to say, but Rachel forestalled him.

'She'll have to go, Samuel,' she said quietly.

He winced. Her use of his full name was ominous. 'Oh, surely not. She's been very good to us, you know. And think how hard life would be without her here to run the house for you.'

'How can you even suggest that she should stay?' Her

voice tightened. 'After last night – the vile accusation she made against Marcus.'

'It wasn't an accusation, my love. She was just telling us a fact.'

'A fact?' She turned to stare at him, her dark eyes glittering like jet. 'You're not trying to tell me that you actually *believe* her?' She was sitting up now, staring down at her husband with an expression of horror. 'How *can* you, Samuel? Our son. Our own Marcus . . .' Her shoulders began to shake with emotion and Sam sat up hurriedly and put his arms around her.

'Rachel, dearest, please don't upset yourself again.' He held her until her trembling ceased, then gently pressed her back against her pillow again. 'Listen, dear. Our boy was a wonderful son, that's true, of course, and nothing he could ever do would change that. He was a loving and devoted husband to dear Jessica and I don't doubt that he would have been a fine father too, if God had willed it. But he was once a very young man, and prone to the follies of all young men. I believe that it is quite possible that Maryan was telling us the truth. And doing it with the best of motives, because she thought we would welcome her telling of it.'

'How could she have imagined that we would *welcome* it?' Rachel said bitterly.

'Because – because of our loss. Because we have no one now.' When she was silent he went on: 'Think, Rachel. Have you ever known Maryan to do anything to hurt us?'

'No. But we have been good employers to her. Why should she?'

'And have you ever known her to tell us a lie?'

'No. But then she has had no reason to – till now.'

'And what reason had she to lie to us now? Now of all times? Tell me that.'

'You are so naive at times, Samuel. She saw her chance, that's why. Saw a chance to gain – for herself and for the child.'

Sam shook his head. 'You think she schemed up the

140

story as some kind of – of blackmail – seizing the death of our son as a chance to gain for herself? Rachel, you shock me. You can't believe that Maryan could even think of such a cruel thing. I don't . . .'

'*I want her out.*' The words squeezed themselves past Rachel's rigid lips and, looking into her face, Sam knew that she would not relent. Nevertheless, he tried once more.

'My dear – please.'

'Can't you see what she is doing to us? Putting us against each other. Driving a wedge between us. And you're letting it work – letting it happen.'

'Won't you wait a few days? Let your anger cool and examine your feelings again. I'm sure you will agree that . . .'

'She has to *go*.' She was really angry now. 'I won't be treated like a fool, Samuel. I won't have that woman under my roof an hour longer than I have to. She must leave as soon as possible. And *you* must tell her this morning. I don't want to see or speak to her again.'

Sam groaned inwardly as he climbed out of bed. How was he to dismiss the young woman they had grown so fond of, who had worked for them so devotedly all these years? And if what she said was true and her child really was their granddaughter, were they driving away their own flesh and blood? Rachel seemed to have closed her mind to the possibility. With a heavy heart he made his way to the bathroom. The sooner he got it over with, the better, he supposed.

Maryan got up as soon as it was light. She was glad to leave her bed where she had tossed and turned restlessly all night. She was in the kitchen making herself a pot of tea when a soft tap came on the door. She opened it and found to her dismay that Sam stood outside.

'Mr Leigh. Come in, I'm afraid I'm not dressed yet.' She pulled her dressing gown around her and tied the belt.

'Forgive me for disturbing you so early, my dear.' Sam

stepped inside the door. 'I felt I must come and see you before Rachel gets up.'

'Of course. I'm just making tea. I expect you'd like a cup.' She pushed her uncombed hair back from her forehead. 'I'm afraid I must look terrible. I didn't sleep very well.'

'It's not surprising.' He reached out to touch her arm. 'Neither did we, if it's any consolation. Though Rachel has dropped off now.' He looked at her. 'Maryan – about – last night . . .'

'Please . . .' Maryan turned away. 'I can guess why you're here. Let's forget it. Telling you like that was a terrible mistake. It's better if we don't talk about it any more.' As he opened his mouth to speak, she held up her hand. 'And there's no need for you to dismiss me. I realise that I must leave now. I'll stay on until you find a replacement – if you want me to, that is. But I think we both know that it would be best all round if I went.'

Sam sighed, trying hard not to show his relief. He had dreaded having to give her notice. With a soft groan he sat down at the kitchen table. 'My dear – if only you had waited a little while.'

'Would it really have made any difference?' Mary poured two cups of tea and pushed one towards him. 'I think we both realise now that Mrs Leigh would never accept Amy as her own flesh and blood. She was obviously horrified. Outraged at the very idea.'

'No, no. It was just the shock,' Sam protested. 'Coming so quickly after . . .'

'*More* bad news, you mean?' Maryan shook her head. 'I made a mistake – a bad one. I thought she was fond of Amy. I was stupid enough to think it might be a happy surprise for her. I was wrong.'

'Maybe – maybe in time . . .' Sam said without conviction. 'She's had such a bad time since the war began. He meant everything to her – the world. You know that. I don't think she will ever get over losing him.'

And from now on Amy and I would be an uncomfortable reminder that he was a human being and not a saint.

142

Maryan stopped herself from saying the bitter words that filled her mind. 'One thing's certain. She won't want to have me around from now on,' she said instead.

Sam drew a long brown envelope from his pocket. 'This is a reference, my dear. It's the very least I can do for you.' He looked at her, his kind brown eyes infinitely sad. 'Maryan. If there's anything I can do – anything at all, you will let me know, won't you?'

'Of course. I'll go into Colchester to the Labour Exchange this morning,' she told him. 'I won't leave without making sure you've got a replacement.'

'It's very good of you to take it so well.' Sam shook his head unhappily. 'I hate seeing you go like this. If only it could have been different. My dear – where will you go?'

'Go? Home, of course. Back to London.'

'And – the child – Amy?'

'She'll stay where she is for the moment. It'll be safer in Suffolk.'

'Then you must let me give you some money. Make you an allowance of some sort.'

'No.'

'But – for Amy's needs. After all . . .'

Amy had wakened to the sound of voices. Slipping out of bed, she went to the bedroom door and opened it. Her mother was talking to someone in the kitchen. She recognised the other voice as Mr Leigh's. The kitchen door was ajar and their voices reached her easily across the narrow hallway.

'After all, you'll need money to bring the child up properly and provide . . .'

'No,' Maryan said sharply, cutting him off in midsentence. 'I hope you don't think that I was trying to get money from you when I . . .'

'No, no, my dear, of course I don't. Nevertheless . . .'

'Please. Don't let's talk about it any more. I'll be all right.' Maryan paused. 'I'll get Amy out of the way this morning as soon as I can; put her on the train for Rhensham this morning. Mrs Leigh needn't see her again.

As for me – I'll do my best to keep out of the way as far as possible.'

'Don't say that, Maryan. You've been so good to Rachel. No daughter could have done more.'

'But I'm *not* her daughter, Mr Leigh,' Maryan said. 'I'm her maid. A servant, that's all I've ever been.' *And now I'm leaving as a disgraced one*, she added to herself.

Amy crept back to her room and began to dress. It sickened her to hear her mother demeaning them both like that. *I'll get Amy out of the way as soon as I can. Mrs Leigh needn't see her again.* As though she was unclean, or some kind of freak, not fit to be seen.

But freak or not, they wanted her out of the way. All of them, even her mother. Now that the secret was out she was an embarrassment to everybody; a mistake, something to be ashamed of – pushed hastily out of sight in case she should cause offence.

She dressed hurriedly and packed her things neatly into her suitcase. Thank goodness Auntie Marjorie and Mike didn't know. They at least would be pleased to see her.

In the kitchen Maryan was busy laying the breakfast table. Mr Leigh had gone. Amy sat in her place, saying nothing. Maryan smiled a little too brightly as she passed her the cereal packet and milk jug.

'I've been thinking, Amy. You might as well go back to Rhensham today. It doesn't look as though we'll get up to see Grandma after all. It isn't fair to keep you here any longer. You'll be wanting to help out with that carnival thing, won't you?'

'Yes. Okay.' Amy poured milk onto her cornflakes, watching her mother out of the corner of her eye. She looked haggard and pale, her eyes red and puffy, as though she'd been crying. But try as she would, Amy couldn't feel sorry for her. Her mother didn't know that Amy had overheard last night's revelation and what followed. It was clear that she had no intention of telling her about it either. Or of telling her the truth about who her father really was. So far she hadn't even said anything about going back to London to live. Did she think that she, Amy, was deaf or stupid – or both? Or was she just so unimportant that her feelings didn't matter? Well, she wouldn't say anything either – wouldn't admit that she'd overheard, or force her mother to confess to her, even though a dozen urgent questions burned to be answered.

After breakfast she put on her coat and they walked to the station together in silence. Maryan was so preoccupied that her daughter's unusual silence went unnoticed. When the train pulled in she kissed Amy, saw her safely into the carriage and handed up her suitcase.

'Don't forget to write,' she called as the train drew out. 'And be a good girl for Auntie Marjorie.'

Be a good girl. Just as though nothing had happened. As though she were still a little girl. Maybe yesterday she had been. Today, weighed down by this shameful secret that questioned her identity – her right to exist at all – she knew she had left her childhood behind for ever.

Amy sat in her corner seat all the way to Rhensham, trying to sort out in her mind who she was and where she was going. Grandma had told her once that Mr Leigh had been a foundling, brought up in an orphanage because he had no parents. Well, now she knew what that felt like. She might as well be an orphan herself. At least orphans knew where they stood. They were at least free to start life with a clean slate and make what they might of themselves. Two days ago Mrs Leigh had seemed fond of her. She'd even asked for her company; chatted and laughed with her. Now she hated her so much that she couldn't even bear to have her in the same house. And all because she had been told that Amy was her own flesh and blood. The thought hurt so much that she wanted to curl up into a little ball and hide herself away from the world.

When she arrived at Mitcham Lodge she was relieved to find that Marjorie Taylor was out. Only Michael was at home. He was upstairs in his room, making posters for the carnival. He saw her pass through his open door and called to her.

'Hello. So you're back at last. About time too, there's heaps to do. I was thinking of going over to Snape tomorrow, to put up some of these posters. Want to come?'

She stood in the doorway. 'I can't. I've got to go up to London, Mike; to see my Grandma.'

He looked up with a frown. 'But – I thought you'd been. Thought that was why you went to Hazelfield in the first place?'

'Yes, but we never got there. The Leighs heard that their son had been killed in France. Mrs Leigh was ill and Mum wouldn't leave her.'

'I see. What rotten luck. So you have to go up?' Amy nodded. He paused in his work to look at her. 'On your own? Are you sure that's what your mother wants you to do?'

Amy walked across to the table and sat down opposite him. 'Mum doesn't know I'm going.' She picked up a paintbrush and dipped it abstractedly into a pot of red paint. 'I – I have to see Grandma, you see – about something – something secret.' While she was speaking she made swirling patterns on a piece of plain paper.

'Hey!' Michael reached out and snatched the brush out of her hand. 'Don't do that, stupid,' he snapped. 'There's a shortage of paper. Don't you know there's a war on?' The phrase was borrowed from the village butcher. It was a running joke with the Taylor family; something the three of them had laughed about many times. Michael was shocked to see Amy's eyes suddenly brim with tears. She fled from the room and crossed the landing to her own room, Michael following. He stared bemusedly at the closed bedroom door through which he could hear her muffled sobs.

'Amy – what's up?' he called. 'Don't be daft. I didn't mean anything. You know that.'

He couldn't know that for Amy his thoughtless rebuke had felt like a cruel slap in the face. It had been the last straw. She was an outcast, she told herself miserably; a misfit whom nobody wanted. This wasn't her home.

She had no home. She didn't belong anywhere – or to anyone.

'Amy – Amy, look, can I come in? I didn't mean to shout at you. He opened the door and stood hesitantly in the doorway, his eyes troubled. 'Look, come on, cheer up before Mum comes home and sees you or you'll get me into a row.'

Amy stopped crying and sat up, fumbling in her sleeve for a handkerchief. Michael crossed the room to stand in front of her.

'Come on, what's up? Did you have a rotten time with your mum?'

Amy nodded, swallowing her tears. 'Sorry, Mike. I didn't mean to be feeble. It's just – something that happened yesterday.'

'And is that why you want to go and see your Grandmother?'

She nodded. 'Don't ask me what it is, Mike. I can't tell you. I can't tell anyone, not till I've talked to Grandma about it. It's too – too awful.'

'Oh, come on. It can't be that bad.'

'It is,' she said despairingly. She looked up at him. 'I'll go tomorrow. I think I've got enough money saved up to pay the fare. I can say I'm going to Snape with you.'

Michael looked doubtful. 'I wish you'd ask Mum first. It's dangerous with these buzz bomb things though, isn't it? I can't just let you go like that, on your own. Mum'd kill me if anything happened and she found out I knew.'

But Amy shook her head adamantly. 'I *have* to go, Mike. It's terribly important. You'll just have to pretend you don't know about it. It'll be all right. And if Auntie finds out I shan't tell her you knew.'

'That's not the point, though.' He was silent for a moment, then his face lit up. 'Tell you what,' he said. 'I'll come with you. I've still got some of my birthday money left.'

It was the first time Amy had been back to London since

that day just before the outbreak of war when she had left with all the other children. Euston station looked much as she remembered it. As she and Michael stepped down from the train a small spiral of excitement stirred in the pit of her stomach. It was a bit like an adventure; scary as well as exciting. There was guilt too – that they'd deceived Auntie Marjorie. But that had been necessary. She would never have let them come if she'd known. Michael looked at her enquiringly.

'Right – what do we do now?'

'We get the Underground,' Amy told him decisively.

'Do you know where to go? Which train to get on?' he asked.

Amy took his hand. 'Come on, we'll ask.'

When they emerged from Liverpool Street Underground station Amy looked around her in dismay. Nothing here was as she remembered it at all. They might as well have been on another planet. Where previously buildings had stood there were now open spaces, rubble-strewn battle scars with blades of dusty grass already pushing their way up between broken walls. Some of the older bomb sites had been cleared, whilst on other, more recent ones, precariously leaning walls still stood, with here and there small reminders of human occupancy: a shred of patterned wallpaper, a broken fireplace. Amy looked away, ashamed of staring. It was a bit like reading someone's private letters, or catching them in their underwear. Where were those people? she asked herself. With a shudder, she realised that they had probably been killed by the bomb that wrecked their homes.

'It's awful, isn't it?' Michael was looking at her. 'I've seen the pictures in the newspapers but I never thought it'd be as bad as this. Where do we go now?'

She pulled herself together, looking at the people, bustling about their daily lives as though nothing had changed. 'Over there,' She pointed to a bus stop. 'We get the bus to Hackney.' At least the bus would still know the way, she reflected.

Even when they got off the bus Amy had trouble

finding Crimea Terrace. As at Liverpool Street, nothing looked as she remembered it. In the end she asked a policeman who was passing.

'Crimea Terrace? Yes, love.' He looked at her doubtfully. 'Not that there's much of it left, mind.'

They followed his directions and when they stood at the corner of the street Amy stopped. The warden was right. Most of the street had gone. The space where the Prince of Wales public house had once stood was flattened; and the mews at the back where Amy had spent so much time with the horses was gone too. The maze of streets, lanes and alleys that had been so familiar to her was changed beyond all recognition. Just two houses and the corner shop were left in Crimea Terrace. Some of the windows were boarded up and the end walls were shored up with strong girders, but the shop was open for business, its familiar trays of vegetables stacked outside for customers to inspect. And at the remaining windows of number ten Amy recognised Grandma's curtains. Her heart lifted a little. They were the first reassuring, familiar sight she had had since getting off the train.

'There it is,' she said, pointing excitedly. 'That's our house.'

'What – that?' Michael quickly tried to hide his initial reaction of shock and dismay. 'Look, I'll go for a walk.' He looked at his watch. 'I'll come back for you in about an hour. That long enough?'

'Plenty. Thanks, Mike.' She watched him till he got to the corner, then knocked on the door. Sarah was so long answering that she thought for one crestfallen moment that she'd made the journey in vain, then suddenly there was the scrape of a bolt being drawn on the other side and the door opened a crack. Sarah's astonished face looked out.

'*Amy*? My Gawd, what brings you 'ere?' She pushed her face a little further out to look up and down the street. 'Is your mother with you?'

'No, Grandma. I'm on my own. Can I come in?'

Sarah shook her head. 'Not this way you can't, love.

You'll have to come round the back. Street door won't open properly since the bombing. Something to do with the foundations shiftin', so they say. Come round an I'll let you in the back door.'

The back, where all the yards had once given onto a narrow passage was now an open space. All that was left of the yard was the remains of one wall and the outside lavatory. Sarah already had the back door open and stood, arms held wide to receive her granddaughter. Her hug was warm and welcoming.

'Gawd, gel, you've grown,' she said, holding Amy at arms' length. 'Proper little woman you are an' no mistake. But what brings you up to see your old Grandma? What's that Mrs Taylor thinkin' about, lettin' you come up alone?'

'I'm not alone, Grandma. Michael came with me. He's gone for a walk so that you and me can have a talk.'

'Oh, yes?' Sarah drew her into the kitchen and pulled a chair out from the table. 'What's up? There's somethin'. I c'n see that. Come on gel. Better spit it out and be done with it.'

Amy bit her lip. 'Grandma – I've been staying with Mum at Hazelfield and – er – Mr Marcus has been killed. A man came to tell Mr and Mrs Leigh.'

'Oh my dear Lord.' Sarah grasped the back of a chair and eased herself into it. 'Poor Miss Rachel. She'll've taken it badly if I know anythin'. The apple of her eye, he was.' She shook her head. 'And to think there was no need for 'im to have gone in the first place. What a waste.' She looked at Amy. 'But your Mum will've written to tell me. There's sure to be a letter in the post. No need for you to come all this way to tell me, love.'

'No, Grandma. That's not why I'm here. There's something else; something I have to know – to ask you.'

Sarah looked at her curiously. 'Come on then. What's this all about?' When Amy remained apparently tongue-tied she made an impatient little gesture with her hands. 'Well? You gonna make me sit 'ere an' guess then, are you?'

'No. It's this, Grandma. I heard Mum telling Mr and Mrs Leigh something the night before last. I didn't mean to listen. Mum had forgotten the milk for their coffee, you see, and I . . .'

'Oh do get *on* with it,' Sarah said impatiently. 'You'll 'ave that Michael back again any minute. What *is* this thing you 'eard?'

Amy swallowed hard. 'I heard her – Mum – telling the Leighs that I was their grandchild. That Mr Marcus was my real father.' She studied her grandmother's face carefully, looking for signs of anything – surprise; shock; acknowledgement. She saw none of them. Sarah stared at her blankly for a moment, then she got up and began to fill the kettle at the sink.

'Well?' Amy pressed. 'Is it true, Grandma? That's why I'm here. That's what I've come to find out. I have to know, you see.'

Sarah turned to her. 'What's she want to go tellin' 'em that for?' She peered into Amy's face. 'And anyway, what does a kid your age know about them sort of things?'

'I'm not a kid, Grandma. I'm almost thirteen. And I do know – about babies and all those grown-up things. Auntie Marjorie told me.'

Sarah looked scandalised. 'Then she'd no call to. Things like that's private, between a gel an' 'er mother.'

'But Mum wasn't there and . . .'

'When I was a gel them things was kept from us till we got married,' Sarah said. 'That's time enough to know if you ask me.'

'But is it *true*, Grandma? About Mr Marcus and Mum?'

Sarah wiped her hands on a teatowel and sank into her chair again. So many things were clear to her now. If she were truly honest with herself she'd known all along that those two were more than just sweet on each other. If Maryan had come right out with it like that, then it must be true. She'd never have said so otherwise. But why in

God's name had she chosen a moment like that to tell the Leighs?

'Grandma . . .?'

She pulled herself up straight. 'If it's true then she never told me,' she said truthfully. 'Far as I know, Tom Jessop was your dad. An' a better one you could never 'ave 'ad. An' if I was you, gel, I'd leave it at that an' be grateful.'

'But I have to *know*, Grandma,' Amy persisted. 'If I don't know who my real father was I'm not – not a real person, am I?'

'Not *real*? What kinda talk is that?' Sarah demanded. But her own mind was travelling along a different track entirely. 'What did the Leighs say?' she asked.

Amy shook her head. 'It was awful. Mrs Leigh was angry – really angry. She said Mum was lying – trying to blacken Mr Marcus's name. Mum's leaving. I think she's coming home. I heard her telling Mr Leigh so this morning.'

'Silly cat,' Sarah muttered under her breath. 'After all these years, to go and lose her job just for the sake of . . .' She looked up at Amy. 'Don't you worry about it no more, luvvie. It'll all come right in the end, you'll see.' Seeing the girl's distressed look she reached across the table and took her hands. 'Why didn't you ask your mum about it there an' then? Why come all the way up 'ere to me?'

'She didn't know I'd heard. She still doesn't. I don't want to talk to her about it, Grandma. And I don't want you to tell her I've been here – that I know. Promise you won't tell – please?'

'I won't say nothin', love. Not if you don't want me to.'

Amy sighed. 'If it really is true why didn't she tell *me* first?'

'I don't know that, love. My Maryan's always been a close one when it come to feelin's. P'raps she was ashamed. Mothers always want their kids to look up to 'em, y'know. That's on'y natural. Then there was Tom

152

to think about. She must've had good reason to keep it to 'erself all these years.'

Amy looked at her. 'Grandma – if it's true, am I half Jewish? Am I really a Leigh?'

Sarah sighed, racking her brain for the right answers. 'You can't be *half* Jewish, love,' she said, frowning. 'Either you are or you ain't. And you can't be Jewish if you ain't been brought up Jewish,' she added slowly. 'It's a religion, see. Like the Catholics an' Methodists, on'y different. An' the name on your birth certificate is Jessop. No doubt about that.'

It wasn't exactly what Amy meant. But then she didn't really know what she meant, so the questions were impossible to pursue any further. Anyway it was at that moment that they both heard the knocking on the street door. 'That'll be Michael,' Amy said, jumping up. 'I'll go round and get him, shall I?'

'I'll make you both a cuppa and a sandwich and then you'd better be on your way,' Sarah said. 'Them doodlebugs comes over any time o' the day or night. Sooner you're out of here the happier I'll be.'

It was only when she and Michael were eating their sandwiches that Amy realised how badly damaged the house was. Looking round she saw that large pieces of plaster had fallen off the kitchen walls, leaving the brickwork exposed. In some places the ceiling was showing bare wooden laths and the kitchen range smoked badly through a crack in the chimney. Sarah saw her looking round and said: 'They sent the builders round after the last lot – to make sure it was still safe. No chance of gettin' nothing permanent done till after the war.'

'Do you go to the shelter when there's a raid?' Michael asked.

Sarah shook her head. 'With these doodlebugs you don't always get any warnin', love. Anyway, I'd rather stay 'ere. I get under me old table.' She patted the chenille-covered table affectionately. 'Oak, that is. Strong as a rock; belonged to my old mother-in-law.'

'It can't be very comfortable for you living here like this, Mrs Brown,' Michael remarked.

For a moment Sarah looked as though she was about to make a resentful reply to the boy's remark, then she smiled ruefully. 'Beggars can't be choosers, love. I was lucky to be allowed back at all. They on'y let me come back 'cause the lav was still working.' She laughed. 'Marvellous, ain't it? Still, can't be long now 'fore old 'itler chucks in the towel, can it? These doodlebugs is just is last kick, so they reckon. P'raps when the war's over they'll build me a nice new 'ouse with a bathroom an a real front garden with geraniums an' everythin'. Never knows your luck, eh?'

Amy was quiet as they walked back to the bus stop together. Michael peered into her closed face once or twice, then he ventured: 'Well – get everything sorted out, did you?'

'Not really.'

'Has it been a waste of time then?'

She turned to look at him. 'Of course it wasn't a waste of time. It was lovely seeing Grandma again.' They'd stopped now at the bus stop and she looked him in the eye. 'You didn't think much of our house, Mike, did you?'

He blushed. 'No one can help the bomb damage.'

'Why don't you say what you're thinking? I expect *you'd* call it a slum.'

'Of course I wouldn't. I . . .'

'Grandma always used to have the whitest doorstep in the street,' she interrupted. 'And the shiniest brasses. The curtains were washed and starched regularly and there used to be nice wallpaper and a sofa in the front room.'

'All right, all *right*. I believe you.' Michael kicked at the kerb with the toe of his shoe. 'No need to go on about it. Anyway, I haven't said a word, have I?'

'No, but you've looked and thought a lot,' she said waspishly. 'Grandma doesn't talk like *you*, does she? I expect you think she's common. Well, *I* used to talk like that and maybe I will again when I come back here to live. You won't want to know me then, will you, stuck-up snobby Michael Taylor?'

'*Amy*. What's the matter with you? Why are you being so nasty? As a matter of fact I think your grandma is very brave. She . . .' He stopped speaking to stare up into the sky, his attention taken by the strange droning sound of an aircraft overhead. They'd been so engrossed in their quarrel that he hadn't noticed it before. Looking up he could clearly see it silhouetted against the sky and flying quite low; a strangely shaped craft with a red flame shooting from its tail.

There was a sudden cry of: '*Buzzbomb. Take cover!*' and at the same moment Michael saw the flame vanish and heard the splutter of the engine as it cut out.

Grabbing Amy by the arm he dragged her into a nearby doorway where they crouched together as passers-by scattered, running past them in all directions for the nearest cover. Traffic stopped. Everything came to a halt. The sudden empty silence of a city street brought abruptly to a frozen standstill was eerie and terrifying. There was a tense wait that seemed interminable, then came a deafening explosion that shook the ground beneath them and almost seemed to batter the breath from their bodies. To Michael it seemed almost on top of them, but he learned later that the flying bomb had fallen several streets away. Amy gave a shrill, startled scream as shattered glass and bits of masonry rained into the street. He put his arms protectively round her, pulling her close and shielding her head with his own as he bent over her. For a moment he felt her heart thumping frantically in time with his and in that moment he wondered how city people had stood this – and worse than this – for so long. He had seen the newspaper photographs and newsreel film of the devastation, but they came nowhere near the reality of it. The raids on the east coast had been bad enough; even Ipswich had had its share, but what he had seen today had shocked him to the heart.

'Hello – you kids all right then?' A man wearing a steel

helmet, with a big 'W' painted on it, bent and held out a hand to them.

'Yes, thank you, we're okay.' Michael got unsteadily to his feet, pulling Amy up with him and brushing the dust from his trousers.

Amy's eyes were round with fear. 'Grandma,' she said. 'Do you think Grandma's all right?'

'Where does your gran live, duckie?' the man asked kindly.

'Crimea Terrace. We've just come from there.'

'Oh no, you're all right. This one landed further up, towards Hoxton.' He pointed in the opposite direction.

'Do you want to go back and see?' Michael asked, looking doubtfully at Amy.

'Where do you live?' the warden asked.

'Rhensham – in Suffolk. We've come up for the day.'

'Well, I'd cut off home sharpish on the first train I could get if I were you. Never know when these blighters will turn up. Daresay your mum'll be worryin' about you.'

'Yes, sir. We will.' Michael took Amy's hand. 'Come on. Look, the buses have started again.'

As they sat side by side in the bus on the way to the station Amy's hand reached out for his.

'Thanks, Mike.'

'What for?'

'You saved my life.'

He flushed a dark red. 'Don't be daft, course I didn't. That thing was nowhere near us. We weren't in any danger really.'

'It felt like it to me.' She looked at him sideways. 'If you hadn't pulled me into that doorway – all that glass and stuff – we'd have been hurt . . .' She broke off, biting her lip. 'You didn't have to come with me, Mike. I'm sorry I said those rotten things to you. I sounded just like Lily Smith.'

'Good job I did come,' Michael said gruffly. 'Heaven knows what kind of a mess you'd have got into on your own.'

'I'd've been all right,' she began sharply, then she smiled. 'Still, I'm glad you were there.' She squeezed his hand. 'Were you scared?'

He shrugged. 'Not really. All I was worried about was what on earth I'd say to Mum if anything'd happened to you.'

She smiled, unimpressed by his bravado. 'Well I was,' she whispered. 'I'll be glad when we're home. I'm really looking forward to the carnival next week, aren't you?'

'Yes – yes, I am.' He was sharing Amy's euphoric feeling of thankfulness at being alive and safe. Suddenly he realised that they were still holding hands. It embarrassed him a bit, but he found to his surprise that he didn't want to pull away. Being in danger together had forged a kind of bond between them and whether he admitted it or not, he too was in need of comfort at that moment. He looked at her enquiringly. 'Amy?'

'Yes?'

'Who's Lily Smith?'

'You don't seem very surprised to see me.' Maryan stood surrounded by her luggage in the kitchen at Crimea Terrace.

'When you gets to be my age and you've lived through two wars there's nothin' much surprises you no more,' Sarah said with a sniff. 'This just a visit then?' She asked ironically as she eyed the two suitcases, holdall and various parcels at Maryan's feet.

'No, Mum. I'm home for good.' Maryan began to take off her coat. 'I've given up my job with the Leighs.'

As Sarah had predicted, Maryan had written to her mother to tell her of Marcus's death. It had been a brief letter, giving only the barest details. The rest – her revelation and the Leighs' reaction – had been impossible to put into a letter and she had finally decided that it would be better to break the rest of her news when they were face to face.

'Given up – just when they need you most?' Sarah

157

challenged. 'How could you do that after all the years you've been with them?'

Maryan sighed and sank into her mother's chair by the range. 'Things change, Mum. I felt I needed a break. I'm not getting any younger. I was sick of being buried in the country.'

'I see. Lookin' for a new 'usband, are you?'

'Of course not. A new job. Something different. I'd like to make a new life for Amy and me when the war's over. She hated Hazelfield anyway.'

'Oh, so it's for Amy you're doing this – letting the Leighs down?'

'If you like, yes.'

Sarah stood in front of her daughter, forcing her to look her in the eye. 'There's more to this than meets the eye, my gel. Are you gonna tell me the truth, or aren't you?'

'Mum – I'm a grown woman, not a kid. I've told you all you need to know.'

Sarah turned away, making a great clatter over putting the kettle on and laying the table. 'I don't suppose you're too old to want your tea,' she muttered. 'And if you won't tell me p'raps Miss Rachel will.'

Maryan looked up sharply. 'What do you mean?'

'What I say. I'll write and ask *'er* why you've left if you won't tell me. There's gotta be more reason than what you've given me.'

'You'll do nothing of the sort, Mum. I won't let you.'

'Won't let me, eh?' Sarah stood on the hearthrug, hand on hips. 'I'd like to know how you think you're gonna stop me?'

Maryan sighed. 'It's not a good idea, Mum. Let it rest.'

Sarah made the tea and set the pot on the hob to brew. 'They give you the push, didn't they?'

'No.'

'But they would've done, if you'd given 'em the chance. That's it, ain't it? Come on, what 'appened, Maryan? Out with it, gel. You know I won't rest till you've told me the truth.'

'We – had a disagreement. Maybe I'd been there too long.'

'A disagreement over what?'

Maryan could see that she would have no peace till she'd told her mother everything. And perhaps she owed her the truth anyway. 'I – told them something, Mum. Told them with the best of motives. It misfired. It was a bad mistake. They didn't want to know.'

'Yes – you told 'em – what?'

'That Marcus was Amy's father.' She glanced up at her mother's stony face. 'I thought they'd be happy, Mum. Mrs Leigh seemed fond of Amy. She was the one person who seemed to comfort her after she heard about Marcus being killed. I thought she and Mr Sam'd be glad to think they had a grandchild.'

'Then you hadn't thought about it enough,' Sarah said bluntly. 'Couldn't you see that everything was against it: their class, their – their culture or whatever they calls it? You should've seen all that. How could you expect them to be pleased? Anyway . . .' She eyed her daughter enquiringly. 'Is it true?'

Maryan stared at her. 'Of *course* it's true. I wouldn't lie about a thing like that.'

'Seems to me you lied enough about it in the past.'

'Tom knew,' Maryan said. 'He knew right from the start. I never deceived him, though he never knew who Amy's real father was. I've never told anyone but the Leighs themselves till now. Even Marcus didn't know. And now . . .' Her voice broke. 'Now – he never will.' She began to cry, leaning forward to hide her face in her hands as tears overwhelmed her. 'I loved him, Mum,' she sobbed. 'I loved him so much – all those years. I never stopped loving him, not even when I knew he'd stopped loving me. I never stopped hoping that some day . . . And – and now there can be no more hope – ever.'

Swallowing her compassion and blinking back her own tears, Sarah took the teapot from the hob and poured two strong cups. Adding milk and two spoons of sugar to Maryan's, she passed it to her. 'Here, drink this, gel.'

She watched as a red-eyed Maryan sipped at the tea. 'So – what're you gonna do now? London still ain't much of a place to be makin' a new start in.'

Maryan looked at her mother. Sarah was close to sixty now, but she looked at least ten years older. She glanced round her. Living in this place couldn't be doing her any good. 'I haven't asked you how you are yet, Mum,' she said. 'The house is a mess. Can't they rehouse you?'

'I'm all right where I am,' Sarah said stoically. 'Everything still works – after a fashion, anyway. I got me wireless. I've still got Vera Lynn and 'Music While You Work' to cheer me up. I'm all right.'

'What about when the winter comes, though? This place won't be fit to live in then. The draughts must be terrible.'

'If you've on'y come 'ome to find fault then maybe you should'a stayed where you were.'

Maryan stood up and took her mother's hands. 'I'm going to look after you, Mum,' she said gently. 'Like you looked after me and Amy and Tom all those years. Time you had things a bit easier. You're not going to argue with that, are you?'

Sarah shrugged. 'Well, we'll see,' she said. But she responded to Maryan's embrace warmly enough. It was true she'd been lonely. It had been a struggle what with the buzzbombs and everything. And she had to admit that the prospect of the coming winter with its inevitable crop of chest colds had worried her too. Yes, it was good to have her daughter back again.

Major Armstrong, who owned Rhensham Manor, had given the Holidays At Home committee the use of his twenty-acre meadow for Rhensham's part in the festivities. It was to take place on the bank holiday Monday and Marjorie Taylor was helping her friend Jane Frencham at the riding school with pony rides. Amy and Michael were helping too. They spent the whole of the Sunday helping to set up their pitch, erecting a coloured awning to keep the sun off the ponies and staking out the rides round the meadow's perimeter.

They were looking forward to the festivities. There were to be sideshows and competitions, a baby show and a dog show, bowling for the pig and other entertainments. Amy and Mike had planned to take it in turns to work and play.

Since the onslaught of V-1 bombings, more London evacuees had arrived in Rhensham. The village school was full to overflowing once again just as it had been in '39 and '41. Amy had already seen many new faces in the village, but they didn't affect Mike and her so much now that they had moved on to the grammar schools in Ipswich. As they staked out the rides on Sunday afternoon Michael mentioned their visit to London.

'I don't think I'd like to live there.' He looked at her. 'Will you really go back there to live when the war's over?'

She shrugged. 'I don't suppose I'll have any choice.'

'You could always stay here. You have to admit, it's nicer.'

'London looks awful now, but it won't when they've built it up again,' Amy said loyally.

'But that could take years.' Michael drove in another stake, hitting it with the mallet. 'You and your mother hardly know each other now. You're not homesick any more, are you? I bet she wouldn't mind if you stayed on with us,' he said. 'At least until you've finished at school. Why don't you ask her?'

'Take a lot for granted, don't you, Mike Taylor?' Amy said. 'What makes you think I want to stay on here with you?' Immediately she could see that she'd hurt him. His face turned a dull red and he turned away quickly so that she wouldn't see.

'Okay. I was only trying to help. I'll be glad to see the back of you if you want to know.' He gave the stake an almighty whack with his mallet. 'It'll be nice to have the place to myself again. You're just a boring little nuisance

161

most of the time. Anyway, I'll be going to college once I've got my Matric, so it's no skin off my nose.'

She looked at him in surprise. '*Mike*. I was only joking.'

'Humph. Funny joke,' he retorted. 'Pardon me while I kill myself laughing.'

Amy giggled and gave him a playful push. 'Don't be such a twerp. Come on, bossy-boots.'

Their quarrel was soon forgotten, but later Amy thought about what he had said. She wondered if her mother would let her stay on at Mitcham Lodge till she'd finished school. If she were honest, it had been a shock, seeing what the war had done to the London she knew. But the war apart, the house in Crimea Terrace had made her think. Had she really lived there – called a place like that home? And could she ever really be happy there again? Would Maryan expect to pick up the threads and make a home again in that *hovel*, or some place like it? Everyone said that after the war hundreds of bright new houses would be built to replace the bombed ones. Some were of the opinion that it was the slum clearance London had always wanted. But as Mike had said, it would surely take an awfully long time? She had her education to finish. Surely Mum wouldn't expect her to leave before it was completed?

The day of the Rhensham Carnival dawned fine and bright. From early in the morning it promised to be a hot day. When the Taylors and Amy arrived at Armstrong's Meadow the sky was a hazy azure blue and a fine heat haze hovered on the horizon. They tethered the ponies and set out the saddles on a bench. There were folding chairs to sit on and a camping table for the tickets and money. Mike went off to fill the buckets with water for the ponies, then they sat down to await their first customer.

By ten o'clock the meadow was full of people and Amy and Mike were kept fully occupied. Pony rides were in great demand, especially among the younger evacuees. Amy was halfway round a ride, leading a nervous little girl on Cobby, the smallest Shetland pony, when a shrill voice hailed her.

'Well, if it ain't Miss High and Mighty Jessop. Wotcher, toffee-nose.'

The voice was unmistakable and Amy could hardly believe her ears. Looking up, she saw a group of children standing watching. Most of them were strangers to Amy, but the one who had called out to her was her old adversary, Lily Smith. Even though she had grown taller in the intervening years, her voice and manner hadn't changed. If anything, she was even more shrewish-looking than before, with her long, pink-tipped nose and small close-set eyes. She was dressed as usual in an ill-fitting dress a size too small for her and she was clearly spoiling for a fight. Unwilling to oblige, Amy continued as though she had neither seen nor heard her – a gesture guaranteed to infuriate Lily.

''Ere, who the 'ell do you think you are?' she yelled. 'Look at 'er,' she addressed the group of younger children. 'Never think she come from the worst slum in 'ackney, would yer? All rigged out like Lady bleedin' Muck.'

Michael caught up with them, leading another child on a pony. 'What do you want?' he asked Lily haughtily. 'If you want a pony ride you pay back there. If not, kindly stop shouting.'

Lily laughed raucously. '*Kaindly stop showtin*',' she mimicked. 'Oh, Gawd blimey. Listen to Lord flipping Snooty. 'E your feller then is 'e, Jessop? Goes for the posh ones, do you? Like your mum and that Marcus Leigh.'

Amy felt her cheeks turn hot as she rounded furiously on Lily. 'Go away, Lily Smith. Mind your own business.'

'Mind yer business, is it? All lies, weren't it – when you said they was gettin' married. Lying little cow.'

'If you don't go away I'll get someone to throw you out,' Amy shouted.

Lily's face turned scarlet and her eyes glittered spitefully in the ominous way that Amy remembered all too well. 'Right. I'll get you fer that, Amy-pissed Jessop. You can't play Lady Muck with me. I *knows* you, remember. Always did think you was better than anybody else. We'll see what you looks like when I'm done wi' you, s'there.' She turned on her heel. 'Come on, kids, let's go. It stinks o' snobs 'ere.'

Michael looked at her. 'What an awful girl. Don't tell me that was *the* Lily Smith?'

Amy gave him a wry grin. 'It certainly was.'

'Really? No kidding. Why does she hate you so much?'

'I don't know. Mum used to say she was jealous.'

'What was all that about your mother and Marcus Leigh?'

Amy blushed and turned away. 'I don't know. Rubbish.'

Mike looked to where Lily stood some way off, whispering to the other children and throwing occasional spiteful glances at them over her shoulder. 'She's a nasty piece of work.' He grinned. 'What was that name she called you?'

Amy's colour heightened. 'You heard her. I'm not repeating it.'

'But why did she call you that?'

'At my old school I used to get teased about my real name. It's Amethyst.'

'*Amethyst*? Wow, I never knew that before. Does Mum know?'

''Course. It's on my ration book for the whole world to see.'

Seething with resentment, Amy watched him walk away, chuckling to himself. At that moment something inside her hardened. The encounter with Lily Smith had made her mind up. She wasn't going back to London and her old life any more. She wasn't Amy Jessop anyway, but someone bewilderingly different. She'd stay here somehow and find out who that new person was. But one thing was certain. The new Amy would be someone special; maybe she'd even be famous one day, that'd show them all. She'd be a person to be respected and envied, not teased and jeered at for being raised in an East End back street. Crimea Terrace where she was born had gone for ever. Well, so had the old Amy Jessop.

Chapter Eight

Maryan found settling back into life at home in Hackney much more difficult than she'd envisaged. To begin with, the house in Crimea Terrace felt cramped and inconvenient after Whitegates, and try as she would, she could not get used to the constant threat of the buzzbombs. Sarah seemed to take it all in her stride, diving for cover under the kitchen table whenever there was a warning, thanking God vociferously when a loud explosion and a few more bits of fallen plaster were the only result. But Maryan, used to the peace and quiet of the Essex countryside, found the constant tension made her jumpy and short-tempered.

Finding a job was harder than she'd foreseen, too. It was true there was plenty of domestic work, but she'd made up her mind to make a new start and try for something completely different. She'd done with being at the beck and call of some other woman, she told herself. She'd always thought her mother's job demeaning – always wanted to better herself. And if she'd deceived herself into believing that she was something more to the Leighs than a mere housekeeper, their reaction to her revelation had put her straight on that count. Obviously her years of loyal service meant nothing to them. They despised her for having the effrontery to love their son and bear his child. Mrs Leigh had even called her a liar. Well, now she was free of any obligation she had felt towards them. Marcus was dead. She had come to the end of a chapter. The wasted years of girlish dreaming were buried with him, once and for all; at least, so she told herself. But on 25 August, when she and her mother listened to the news of the liberation of Paris on the wireless, Maryan shed silent tears. If he could only have been spared another few months all might have turned out so very differently.

Yet hard though it was proving to make that new start, Maryan was determined to survive and make a new and better life for herself and eventually for Amy. Even though she had no qualifications and no experience in anything but domestic skills and machine sewing, she felt sure that somehow something would turn up.

Her dole money and Sarah's tiny widow's pension didn't go very far. By the time the rent was paid and food bought there was very little left over. Maryan had managed to put a little money by while she lived rent-free at Whitegates, but it wasn't very much. She'd sent her mother some each week, knowing how tight money was for her. She was hoping not to touch what was left in her Post Office account, saving it for when she had Amy back again and they would start to build a new home together.

Every day she went hopefully along to the Labour Exchange. She was offered jobs, but there was never anything she fancied and she became increasingly aware that she would soon be obliged to accept one of the positions offered her or lose her dole. Eventually she reluctantly went along for an interview with a greengrocer who had a shop in Whitechapel Road. His wife had gone into hospital for an operation and he was looking for a woman to take over his daily stall in the market.

'It's on'y temp'r'y, mind,' he told her when she applied. 'Till about Christmas I should think. Soon's the missis is fit to take over again she will.' The man pushed his cap to the back of his bald head. 'Mind you,' he said, his eyes sweeping lustfully over the slim figure and blonde hair, 'play yer cards rights, gel, an' I might find some other little jobs you c'n do for me, if yer know what I mean.' He winked at her suggestively.

Maryan swallowed her revulsion and took the job. It wasn't what she would have liked but she badly needed the money. Besides, as the man said, it was only temporary, and truth to tell she was glad of the opportunity to get out of the house for a few hours each day. She and her mother were beginning to get under each other's feet in the confined space at Crimea Terrace, where only two of the rooms were strictly habitable. She wouldn't trust her new employer any further than she could throw him, but she told herself that as long as he was in his shop and she was running the market stall she'd be safe enough.

Running the stall was hard work. Summer had given way to autumn now and there was a chill nip in the early morning air. She had to be at the shop at six to help Arthur Pratt, or Artie, as he insisted on being called, to load up the produce. Then he would run her down to the market and help her set out the stall before going back to open up the shop for the day. On the short drive to Hackney in his draughty, overloaded van he always contrived to touch her knee at least twice whilst changing gear, and as they set out the produce together he was always finding excuses to squeeze past her in the confined space behind the stall, usually leering at her and making some suggestive remark as he did so. Maryan loathed it. It made her flesh creep, but she kept reminding herself that he would soon be gone. She didn't have to spend too much time with him and at least she was earning again.

As autumn turned to winter it grew bitterly cold and Maryan was chilled to the bone standing still behind the stall in the open all day long. Sarah knitted her some long woollen stockings and mittens, made from an old sweater of Tom's which she had unravelled, but in spite of the layers of clothing Maryan wore, the cold and damp seemed to penetrate right through to her skin. The Pratts' pitch was close to a pub which served tea and coffee as well as alcoholic drinks. Once she had paid a boy to mind the stall while she slipped inside for a cup of tea, but to the pub regulars an unfamiliar woman alone was an object for speculation. Acutely uncomfortable with the experience, she hadn't tried it again.

For the most part the stallholders were a friendly, good-natured bunch, but Maryan found their earthy language and ribald humour embarrassing and off-putting. She was no prude, but she had a natural reserve. Sarah had brought her up to believe that nice women didn't swear or shriek with laughter at coarse jokes, and she found the way that some of the women talked embarrassing. She took sandwiches along each day for her lunch and managed with a bottle of cold tea for drink until she got home at night.

The customers at the market were shrewd and discerning. They demanded value for money and were always on the watch for any kind of sharp practice. One morning she had just been harangued for putting a split potato onto the scales when a man's voice addressed her.

'I think some of them would like you to weigh the bag first.'

She looked up to see the young man from the junk stall opposite smiling at her. He wore an ex-navy duffle coat and a striped scarf wound round his neck. Whenever she had the time she loved to browse through the fascinating articles on his stall, and they'd often exchanged a friendly greeting as they set up opposite each other.

She smiled back at him. 'You're right there. I think some of them'd bring their own scales if they could.'

He walked across to her. 'Look, someone is coming to stand in for me in a minute while I go for a drink. Will you join me?'

Maryan smiled wistfully. 'I'd love to, but I've no one to mind the stall,' she told him.

'Doesn't your employer send anyone to relieve you?' he asked. 'You're entitled to a break, you know.'

'He hasn't got anyone to send. It's all right. I don't mind really. I bring sandwiches – eat them when I've got a minute.'

He looked doubtfully at her chapped fingers, soiled

from serving potatoes. 'Can't be very satisfactory. Can I bring you a hot drink when I come back?'

She smiled gratefully. 'Oh, I'd love a nice cup of tea – if you could manage it.'

'Of course I will. I'm Colin, by the way.' He held out his hand. 'Colin Freer.'

Maryan shook his hand. 'I'm Maryan Jessop.'

'Right, Maryan. See you later.'

She watched as he went off whistling in the direction of the pub. He looked about twenty-four and she wondered why he wasn't in one of the services and what an obviously well-educated young man like him was doing serving on a junk stall in Hackney Market. His voice and manner suggested that he was used to something better.

He was as good as his word, arriving with the tea in a thick mug about twenty minutes later. He had thoughtfully placed a beer mat over the top to keep it hot and Maryan took it from him gratefully, wrapping her chilled fingers round the mug and drinking it thirstily.

After that day Colin Freer would wander across to talk to her whenever he wasn't too busy. She learned that he'd been invalided out of the Navy eight months ago after his ship had been torpedoed. He'd suffered severe burns and exposure after being in the water for several hours and had spent long painful months in hospital having skin grafts to his legs and back. Now he was waiting for a government grant to come through so that he could take up the place at university he'd won just before war broke out.

Maryan looked wistful. 'I'd have loved the chance of a proper education,' she said. 'It opens up a whole new world to you, doesn't it? My daughter won a scholarship to high school,' she told him proudly. 'It's more than I ever did.'

'You have a daughter at high school?' Colin looked surprised and Maryan laughed delightedly.

'Yes. She's almost thirteen. I was very young when she was born. She's in Suffolk – evacuated there at the beginning of the war.'

'You must miss her.'

'I do. I'm hoping to have her back soon. With a bit of luck I'll have a better job than this by then. This is only temporary.' She laughed. 'Can't say I'll be sorry when it comes to an end either, even if I do need work.'

He looked thoughtful. 'Have you always been in this line – fruit and veg?'

'Heavens, no,' she told him. 'I started as a machinist in a clothing factory, then I took over my mother's job as housekeeper to the factory owner and his wife. I only took this job because I badly needed to earn some money. I'd really like to learn something new and interesting if only I could get the chance.'

He nodded. 'I see. This is temporary for me too. I'm helping my uncle out. He'll be needing someone else when I leave.' He looked at her thoughtfully, but Maryan changed the subject. She didn't really see serving on a junk stall as an improvement to what she was doing now.

It was at the end of that week that Maryan first met Vincent Donlan. She had seen the tall man in the dark overcoat talking to Colin once or twice before, usually late in the afternoon when he came to help Colin pack up. But on this particular day he arrived in the morning. They left a boy in charge of the stall and went off to the pub together at lunch time. When they came back Colin brought the man across to her.

'Maryan, this is my Uncle Vinnie. I've been telling him about you needing a permanent job.'

The man held out his hand to her and when he spoke she detected a slight Irish accent. 'Hello – Maryan, isn't it? I'm Vincent Donlan. Glad to know you.' He looked at the produce on the stall. 'Colin tells me this isn't really your line.'

She smiled. 'That's right. It's only temporary – till I can get something better.'

'I see. What sort of work are you looking for?'

Maryan served a customer and then turned back to him. She was grateful for the diversion. It had given her time to think. Better put the man straight before they

171

began. 'To tell you the truth, Mr Donlan, I'm fed up with standing on the market all day; specially now that the winter's set in. I don't think I'm cut out for it, whatever line it's in.'

He laughed, the relaxed expression lighting up his rather craggy features. 'Well, that's honest at least. As a matter of fact I wasn't planning to keep the stall on after Christmas anyway. I don't know whether Colin has told you, but I have an antique shop. It's in Chelsea. The stuff I sell here is some of the dross I get landed with when I buy job lots at auctions.' He took a card from his wallet and gave it to her. 'Why not come along and see me on your day off?'

Maryan looked at the card. It was embossed in black italic lettering: *'Vincente', 24 Simons Mews, Chelsea.* In one corner: *Antiques and objets d'art bought and sold.* In the other: *Proprietor V. Donlan.* She was impressed. Judging by the things for sale on the stall, she'd imagined Colin's uncle as the kind of dealer who went around clearing homes. 'I don't know the first thing about antiques, Mr Donlan,' she told him doubtfully.

He gave her his warm smile again. 'Ah, you'd soon learn. And in the meantime there are plenty of other things you could do.' Maryan had a brief recollection of Artie Pratt's leering innuendoes and she must have registered suspicion because Vincent added quickly: 'Young Colin there will vouch for my respectability if that's what's worrying you.'

Maryan blushed. 'Oh – it wasn't that. I just . . . The trouble is, Mr Donlan, I don't really get a day off, except Sunday, that is.' She handed the card back to him, but he waved it away.

'Put it in your pocket. Make it next Sunday if you like. I live above the shop. If you decide to come I'll be there anyway. Just ring the bell at the side door. I think you'd be interested to see the shop, even if you decide you don't want to come and work for me.'

Maryan found Simons Mews without too much trouble.

She hadn't told Sarah where she was going. Better not to raise her hopes in case the job didn't materialise. She wasn't even sure that it would suit her. It was more curiosity that had driven her to brave visiting a man alone in his flat. But she reckoned that Colin was her insurance. He was such a thoroughly nice young man, and if he said his uncle was a respectable businessman she felt sure he was right.

The shop itself turned out to be converted from the original stables, the double doors having been replaced by a Georgian-style bow window. It appeared to be disappointingly empty, but Maryan's ring at the side-door bell was quickly answered by Vincent himself. He looked less formal this afternoon without his long dark overcoat, wearing instead a casual cream sweater over an open-necked shirt. She noticed that his dark hair was on the long side and slightly tousled. Today he had a distinctly raffish, arty look.

'Come in, come in,' he said welcomingly, holding the door open wide.

The flat, reached by a narrow flight of stairs, was surprisingly spacious, and in the comfortable living room Maryan saw that a trolley was laid with delicate bone china cups and a plate of scones and chocolate biscuits. She stopped in the doorway.

'Oh – you're expecting company?'

'I am,' Vincent agreed. 'Isn't it yourself?'

Maryan laughed with him. 'You didn't know for sure that I was coming.'

'Ah . . .' He grinned at her. 'Haven't I the sixth sense for these things? I felt it in me bones as my old mother used to say.'

Maryan looked at the chocolate biscuits and her mouth watered. 'You really shouldn't have gone to so much trouble, though. Look at those biscuits. Your precious points coupons. I know how many they take.'

'Ah, to hell with the points coupons, pesky bits of paper, that's all they are. Just sit down and tuck in,' he invited. 'There's only me to eat the bit of food they let us buy so don't you be worrying your head about it. I eat out most of the time, having no one to look after my creature needs as it were.'

Maryan took off her coat and sat down. As she accepted a cup of tea and a scone she looked around her. The flat was exquisitely furnished. There were beautiful pictures on the walls and carpets of soft pastel colours. 'It's a lovely flat,' she said shyly.

'Thank you. When you've had your tea I'll take you downstairs to see the stock. Since the war I've kept everything of value down in the cellar. It's a good thing I have. I've been bombed twice, though not badly enough to have to move out, thanks be to God.'

As they ate he told her that he'd come over to England with his family as a baby at the turn of the century.

'Irish father, Italian mother.' He grinned. 'That's where the 'Vincente' comes in. It's what I was christened, though I knocked off the last 'e' as a kid. It sounded classy when I took over the business, so I put it back on again.' He also explained that he had one sister, Roisan, who was Colin's mother. 'Father sent both of us kids to art school to help us learn the trade, but Roisan met her husband there and married him, so she never actually came into the business at all.'

He told how his father had built up the business by buying and selling, learning as he went, from a second-hand furniture stall in the Portobello Road through a series of small shops to the present thriving antiques shop in a fashionable area. Colin's mother had settled down to bring up her son, so when their parents died it had fallen to Vincent to take over the business.

'It's been a devil of a struggle to keep the business going through the war, I can tell you,' he told her as he refilled her cup. 'There's not been much call for antiques since '39. Who wants to put their money into things that might get blown to bits? I put in a spell in the army till I was discharged, unfit.' He grinned at her ruefully, 'Flat feet, wouldn't you know. Not as romantic as a consumptive chest, but more practical. Ah, but I haven't wasted

174

the time. I've been buying, investing all I could afford in new stock for after the war. I've been making my living restoring paintings for the big galleries, and in my spare time I've been attending every auction sale I could; buying things at knock-down prices from houses that have been bombed, and restoring them down in my workshop.'

'So you'll soon be able to open the shop again?' Maryan asked, stirred by the man's infectious enthusiasm.

'More than just that. I'm planning to go in for interior design and decorating along with my sister Roisan. We reckon there'll be a big demand when folks start rebuilding their battered homes again.' He reached out and took the cup and saucer from her hand. 'Come on. I'll take you downstairs and show you the stock and the workshop.'

Below the spacious, almost empty showroom was a cellar, reached by a wooden stairway. It was like Aladdin's cave. In it was every kind of antique and curio Maryan could imagine, from the tiniest carved ivory and delicate porcelain figurine to the largest, most exquisite pieces of furniture she'd had ever seen.

'I had the whole place reinforced with steel girders when the war started,' Vincent told her. 'Well, I had to protect my investment, didn't I? I even used to sleep down here when the raids were bad.'

Maryan looked at it all, wide-eyed with wonder at so many beautiful things under one roof. She went from one thing to another, eagerly asking questions till suddenly she stopped, looking at him self-consciously. 'Oh dear, I'm sorry. I'm being nosey.'

Vincent smiled. 'Not a bit of it. You're interested and you're obviously eager to learn. You're just the kind of person I'm looking for. Just as I guessed you'd be.'

In the workshop she saw half-finished pieces in various stages of restoration and the tools of Vincent's trade methodically laid out: finely honed chisels and saws; pots of glue and stain; waxes and varnishes; sheets of veneer.

'Roisan does the soft furnishing side, the upholstery

and curtains,' he explained. 'She has a fine hand with the needle and a wonderful eye for colour and fabrics.' He looked around him with satisfaction. 'All we're waiting for is for the hostilities to cease, then there'll be no holding the pair of us.'

Maryan was wondering just where she fitted into his scheme of things, but she didn't like to ask.

'Roisan is a widow,' he told her. 'Her husband died before the war. She and Colin share a nice little house in Notting Hill, but when Colin has gone off to university I'll be moving in with her. She hates the thought of living alone again and I like her cooking, so it suits us both. Besides, if we're going into business together it'll be more convenient – save time on business meetings. We can have those over our meals.' He smiled at her. 'And that's where you come in, as I daresay you've been wondering. Once the shop is up and running again I'll be needing someone to look after it while I'm working. I'm expecting to be out a lot of the time, at sales and touting for business. I'll be needing someone who'll live here too. I'd feel happier knowing that someone was on the premises.'

'Oh, but I told you, I know nothing about antiques,' Maryan reminded him.

'And *I* told *you* that you'd soon learn.' He smiled. 'Until the peace is declared there won't be much to do up there. You'd just be looking after the flat and keeping the place clean and tidy. But in your spare time you could be learning – coming to sales with me; reading the books I'll lend you and generally getting to know the business.' He patted her shoulder. 'Ah, a bright girl like yourself will pick it up in no time at all. Everything in the shop will be priced and I'll be calling in every day to make sure you're all right. So – what have you to say to it?'

Maryan was sorely tempted. It promised to be the most interesting and challenging job she'd ever had. And with a beautiful home thrown in she could hardly believe her luck. She'd be a fool not to snap the chance up. But there was more than just herself to consider.

'Well, it sounds lovely, but there are a couple of snags.

I'm not alone, you see. There's my mother. She hasn't been too well and I wouldn't be happy leaving her alone. Then I have a daughter, Amy. She's thirteen and she's living in Suffolk at the moment, evacuated. But when the war is over . . .'

'You're welcome to bring your family with you,' Vincent said generously. 'Bring them both with you. There's plenty of room, and they'll be keeping the beds aired.'

'Thanks. It's very generous of you, Mr Donlan.' She paused. 'But – there's the question of references.' She took the envelope containing Sam's reference from her handbag and handed it to him. 'This is from my previous employer. I was with him since leaving school.'

He read it carefully, then handed it back with a smile. 'I'd love to have you working for me, Maryan, but I'm looking for someone permanent – someone I can train to my own ways. Come on a couple of months' trial if you like. Then we'll both be sure it's right for you. Now, as to wages . . .'

As Maryan rode back to Hackney on the bus she thought over all she had seen and heard. The wage Mr Donlan had offered her was generous, especially as she'd be living rent free. And to think that they'd be able to move out of Crimea Terrace with all its draughts and inconveniences, into the comparative luxury of the flat – it was like the answer to all her prayers.

Unfortunately Sarah didn't see it that way. 'You go if you must. I ain't moving from here.' She stood in front of the kitchen range, her arms folded and her mouth set in the stubborn line that Maryan knew all too well.

'But Mum, if you only *saw* the place. It's warm and so comfy. There'd be a bedroom each and a nice cosy bathroom and lav. No going outside for anything. You know how bad your chest has been since the winter set in.

'My bronicals ain't gonna change just 'cause I move into some posh flat Up West.'

'But they *will*, Mum. It's the damp that makes you bad. The draughts and the damp and going from one

177

temperature to the other. The doctor said so last time you . . .'

'I ain't going and you can't say nothing as'll make me.'

Frustration made Maryan want to shake her mother. Seeing her standing there stubbornly refusing the chance to spend her life in comfort was maddening. 'You wouldn't have to do anything, Mum. It's the chance of a lifetime.'

'I'd be bored silly in half a day,' Sarah said.

'All right then, you can help keep the place clean while I work down in the shop, and you can do the cooking,' Maryan said. 'We can share the work if that's the way you want it. But do say you'll come.'

'No. I'm sorry, gel. I know you mean well, but this is my 'ome and I'm stayin' 'ere.'

'Mum – they'll pull it down anyway when the war's over.'

'Then they'll re'ouse me. If I move out of me own accord I'll lose me place on the 'ousin' list. Suppose we move into this feller's flat and you don't suit? What then?'

'I *will* suit. He said so,' Maryan insisted, though she had to admit secretly that her mother did have a point. Mr Donlan had mentioned a month's trial. Suppose she didn't suit him? Maybe it would be as well for Sarah to hang onto her own home – just until she was sure the job was right for her.

Seeing her indecision, Sarah jumped in: 'See what I mean? Better safe than sorry. But you go. I mean it. Don't miss the chance just cause o' me,' she said. 'I reckon you ought to get Amy back soon too. Wouldn't be fair to bring 'er back here. She'll like this new place, no doubt about that. But me – I'm too old a dog to learn new tricks.'

'But once I'm settled – you'll come then?'

'I dunno. We'll see.'

Maryan shook her head. 'I hate leaving you, Mum. I promised I'd look after you. How can I do that if I'm in Chelsea and you're here? And paying out good money

178

for this old place when you could live in comfort seems downright stupid.'

But Sarah's independence meant far more to her than the few shillings she paid each week for the rent.

Although everyone knew that it was likely to be the last Christmas of the war, it seemed to Maryan that no one was in the mood for festivities. She had given in her notice to Arthur Pratt with the promise to work on until after the Christmas rush. On the Sunday after she had formally accepted the job at Vincente Antiques and the final arrangements had been made she took the train to Suffolk for the day to see Amy. She found the girl silent and unresponsive. She showed little interest in her mother's new job and clearly lacked enthusiasm for returning to London. Even the prospect of living in a nice flat in Chelsea failed to arouse her interest.

'I thought I could put your name down at one of the local schools. You could start after Christmas,' Maryan said. 'There are bound to be some nice ones round there. Oh, Amy, just wait till you see the flat. It's ever so smart and really comfy. And I've already started studying the books Mr Donlan has lent me. It's so interesting, reading about the different kinds of antiques. There's so much to learn.'

'Can't I stay on a bit longer?' Amy said. 'There's the school play at the end of next term. I'd like to be in it.'

Trying to hide her disappointment, Maryan agreed that Amy could stay for one more term, but she was deflated by the girl's indifferent response to her good fortune. Later, after Amy and Mike had gone off to feed the horses, she spoke to Marjorie about it.

'She's so grown-up. She's changed so much – even since the summer holidays. I feel I hardly know her any more. I never realised what an uphill job it'd be, making a new life together. I was so looking forward to it, too.'

'Give her time,' Marjorie said. 'I've told her she can come back and see us whenever she wants to. Mike will miss her dreadfully and so will I, but I've already started to prepare them both for the inevitable parting.'

Maryan sighed. Marjorie made it sound as though she was splitting up a family instead of trying to reunite her own. What with Mum and now Amy . . . 'What about Christmas?' she asked aloud.

'You must ask her,' Marjorie said. 'She knows she's welcome to stay with us. But I've told Amy that she should really spend it with you and your mother in London. In the end she must make her own choice. She's old enough to know her own mind now, isn't she?'

Sadly, Maryan had to agree. The days when she could expect Amy to do as she was told were clearly long gone. But she couldn't help feeling that Marjorie made it sound as though spending Christmas with her own family was Amy's duty rather than a pleasure. And when the girl begged with a disconcerting fervour to stay at Mitcham Lodge with the Taylors she felt obliged to say yes. After all, she would be working at the market until late on Christmas Eve now that the blackout had been relaxed, and there would be very little to attract a young girl at Crimea Terrace, especially since all her friends were here. Insisting that she came home would only create more resentment in the girl, and that was the last thing she wanted.

Although it was barely three o'clock the light was already failing as Rachel let herself into number 124 Hackney Road. She hadn't told Sam she was coming, but she'd been planning it for weeks, steeling herself for the visit she knew she must make – and make alone.

There was no electricity and the house smelled damp and musty as she removed her key and closed the front door behind her. The windows had been shuttered both inside and out when they had moved to Hazelfield. Everything of value had been packed away or removed from the house and the remaining furniture was shrouded in dust sheets. She could just make out the ghostly shapes in the winter afternoon gloom.

She'd come prepared. Opening her handbag, she took out a candle and matches. Shielding the flame with her hand, she lit it, then, securing it in a candlestick taken from the dining room, she made her way slowly up to the top of the house, the candle flame throwing large leaping shadows before her as she went.

On the top floor Marcus's studio was just as he had left it. Apart from some powdered plaster on the carpet from blast damage, everything was exactly as she remembered it, the desk behind the door; his drawing board set up under the skylight; the bookcase and the old armchair that had been his grandfather's. She could almost have found her way around it without the aid of a light. She set her candlestick down on the desk and looked around her. The room seemed to breathe his very essence. It was uncanny – as though he might walk in at any moment. She stood quite still, her head on one side as though she were listening for his footsteps on the stairs. She imagined him, whistling a tune as he took the steps two at a time – calling out cheerily to ask if dinner was ready and what she had made. Today would have been his birthday. She'd always made a special meal on his birthday, with all his favourite dishes. They had always made a point of eating together, the three of them. But today there was no sound in the empty house except the faint creaking of the floorboards. Nothing lived – nothing moved – there was only the sound of her own heart beating dully.

On the desk was a picture of Jessica taken on the night of their engagement, radiant in the rose-pink dress he had designed specially for her. She picked it up and looked into the lovely face of the happy, carefree girl, unaware of the tragic future that awaited her.

'You're together now,' she whispered. 'Be happy, my children, my darlings.' She slipped the photograph into her bag and began systematically on her sad task, going through the desk drawers, collecting everything that had belonged to him. For weeks now it had bothered her. It wasn't right, leaving his personal effects here for some stranger to find. She couldn't bear the thought that if anything were to happen to her and Sam some uncaring, faceless official would go through them – see his work, read his letters and his diaries. No. She would take everything home.

Without looking at anything, she piled the letters, folders and papers into the holdall she had brought. Later, when she felt strong enough to deal with it, she would go through them all and deal with anything that was necessary and burn the rest.

She cleared the desk drawers and looked around her, then she spotted a portfolio tucked away at the back of his bookcase. Taking it down she opened it and turned the pages. Her eyes widened and she gasped at the beautifully coloured sketches inside. Design after design, all of them dedicated to Jessica. Her name was written on every page in Marcus's flowing – artist's handwriting. There were day dresses and smart town suits, elegant evening dresses, cocktail and ball gowns, winter coats and fresh casual summer clothes. An entire wardrobe, designed with a beautiful woman in mind. He must have intended to have them made up for her as a surprise after the baby was born. After her death he must have hidden them away, unable to bear to look at them again.

Rachel sat down slowly and turned back to the beginning to go through them again. The designs were outstanding, the style and lines wonderfully and impressively different – like nothing the fashion world had ever seen before. They were quite brilliant; inspired, as they obviously had been, by his love for his beautiful young wife. She stared at them until the lines and colours blurred before her eyes, aware that she must certainly be the first person ever to see them. She devoured them with her eyes; her beloved son's last and most inspired work. Just for a brief moment it was almost like having him back. She could almost feel his presence here in the studio with her as she turned the pages.

Then suddenly in a flash it was all crystal clear to her. She jumped to her feet, her heart quickening. Of course. *This* was the reason she'd been unable to rest all these weeks. He *meant* her to come here – to find these designs. Marcus had spoken to her across the invisible barrier that divided them. Now she understood. She knew what it was he wanted her to do. Hurriedly she wrapped the portfolio in a sheet of drawing paper and tucked it under her arm. Taking up the candle, she made her way downstairs again, picking her way with special care. She must look after herself now. She mustn't fall. Until now she hadn't cared what happened to her – hadn't cared whether she lived or died, but now it was different. Now she had work to do – a reason to live, for him, for Marcus. In the hallway she took a last look round.

'Don't worry, I'll see to it, my darling,' she whispered into the flickering darkness. 'You're free now. Goodnight, my dearest son. Sleep well.'

Sam was frantic. He'd arrived home early that afternoon with the idea that he'd take Rachel out to dinner. Today would have been Marcus's birthday and he knew she would be feeling especially sad. At breakfast she'd been even more preoccupied than usual. He'd scarcely been able to get two words out of her. So when he'd returned early and found the house empty apart from the daily woman from the village who had taken Maryan's place, he'd felt the first twinge of unease. Going to the kitchen he'd asked the woman where Rachel was.

She shrugged. 'I don't know, sir. She went out just after twelve – didn't say where she was going.'

Sam turned away. Maryan would have known. She'd have made it her business to know. She would never have let Rachel go off alone in her depressed state on a cheerless winter afternoon. If she'd been unable to stop her she would have telephoned him at the factory. This new woman did her job reasonably well and took her money. But she would never be what Maryan had been to them. He looked at his watch. It was almost five o'clock. If Rachel left home at twelve she'd been gone five hours. The day was gloomy. Already it was quite dark and a thick mist was rising. Maybe he should telephone the Weiss's. She may have gone there.

When his call drew a blank he began to be seriously alarmed. Perhaps he should notify the police. Anything could have happened to Rachel, the way she'd been since Marcus was killed. He lifted the receiver again and had just begun to dial when he heard the scrape of a key in the front door. His heart leapt with relief as he ran to the door and pulled it open. She stood there on the steps, struggling with her handbag, a heavy holdall and a large, flat parcel wrapped in paper.

'*Rachel* – where have you been? I've been worried out of my mind.' He drew her inside and took her hands. 'My darling, you're frozen. Your hands are like ice.' For the first time he looked into her face. She looked strange. Her cheeks were flushed and her eyes were feverishly bright. He'd been right. She *was* ill. It was some kind of breakdown. He'd been half expecting it. Alarmed, he asked: 'What is it, my love? You're ill?'

'No. I've never felt better.' She threw her arms around his neck and hugged him. 'Oh, Sam – wait till you see what I've got.'

He held her at arm's length, shaking his head in puzzlement. 'You've been *shopping*? Why didn't you tell me you wanted to go Christmas shopping? I'd have come with you. Where have you been – Colchester?'

'No, to London. To Hackney Road – our old house.'

He stared at her. 'Oh, Rachel, no. You really shouldn't have gone alone.'

She waved away his protests. 'Never mind all that. Come into the sitting room and see what I found. It's Marcus's birthday today and he sent me there. I'm convinced of it. He meant me to find this and I know – I just *know* what he wants me to do with it.' She held up the portfolio. The paper was already slipping off it. Pulling off her coat as she went, she hurried into the sitting room, dropping her bag and gloves heedlessly in her haste.

Mystified, Sam followed, picking up her belongings as

he went. What in the world could have happened to put her into this strange, excited frame of mind? And what did she mean about Marcus *sending her to Hackney*? He didn't like the sound of it at all.

But when Rachel excitedly opened up the portfolio and showed him the designs he began to understand her excitement. She was right. They certainly were quite special. He studied them all carefully, then looked at her transformed face. She looked twenty years younger.

'They are certainly very good,' he said. 'But what do you plan to do with them?'

'*Do* with them? Why, have them made up, of course,' she told him.

'Listen, Sam, remember all those luxury fabrics we stored away at the beginning of the war when we went over to uniforms? They're just what we'll need – and all without coupons.'

Sam remembered, visualising the stock they had bought in and never used. She was right. There were brocades, silks and chiffons; tweeds and cotton prints.

'We'll have Marcus's designs made up and we'll put on a fashion show,' she hurried on, unfolding the plan she had made coming home on the train. 'It shall be in aid of Jewish refugees, just as he would have wanted. And we'll invite all the buyers from the West End stores. Soon, when the war is over, women will be hungry for glamorous new fashions to wear, just as they were last time, only more so because so many of them have been in uniform for years.' She looked at him, her eyes shining like jet. 'Don't you remember how well it worked last time, darling?'

He kissed her. His heart filled with joy at having the Rachel he remembered back again. 'I remember how proud I was of my talented wife,' he told her.

'Well, this time it will be our talented son we'll be proud of,' she said. 'Oh, Sam, don't you see? This is the one way we can keep his memory fresh – keep him alive.'

Christmas at Mitcham Lodge was a happy one. Amy and

the Taylors were aware that it could well be the last Christmas of the war, and therefore their last together, which gave the season a slightly nostalgic as well as a festive feel.

At the start of the new term the school play went into serious rehearsal. It was to be a combined effort: girls from the High School and boys from the Grammar. They were putting on Shakespeare's *Twelfth Night*. Amy hadn't been particularly keen to take part at first. Although English had always been her favourite subject, she hadn't really taken to Shakespeare, thinking the language difficult and the plays over-long and boring. But at the beginning of the winter term they had read and analysed *Twelfth Night* in class, and with the aid of Miss Frazer, their dedicated English mistress, Amy had slowly begun to appreciate the poetry and lyricism of the words and the wit and humour in the comedy scenes. She had been fascinated by the story of the girl Viola, searching for her lost brother and having to take on the identity of a boy for her own protection; falling in love with the man she served, the Count Orsino, yet being obliged to carry his ardent messages to the woman who scorned his love. She identified strongly with poor Viola on a personal level – having a secret she couldn't tell and getting so confused about her own identity. When it came to casting the play, she read the part with such conviction that she drew a round of applause from the casting committee. Two days later, to her great delight, she learned that she had been cast in the coveted role of Viola.

Amy threw herself wholeheartedly into rehearsing for the play. Mike, who had grown tall and broadened out over the last few months, had been given the part of Orsino, so the two were able to rehearse their scenes together at home. Mitcham Lodge rang to the Bard's renowned speeches till Marjorie told herself wryly that she could have put on a one-woman performance of the play herself.

One evening she asked Amy if she would be inviting her mother to come to the performance.

'She'll be too busy, I daresay,' Amy said dismissively.

'Oh, surely not. It's going to be on a Saturday and she can stay here overnight afterwards. Surely you'd like her to see you after all the hard work you've put in.'

Amy shrugged. 'I don't think Shakespeare's quite Mum's cup of tea.'

'Nevertheless, I think I'll write and invite her.' Marjorie looked at her curiously. 'Amy – there's nothing wrong between your mother and you, is there?'

'No.'

'I only ask because you were rather cool with her when she came last time.'

Amy looked at the floor. 'I was afraid she'd ask me to go and live with her again.'

'But surely you want to, don't you?'

'With the play coming up? I don't want to miss that.'

'Look, Amy, I know it will be an upheaval for you, changing schools, settling down in London again. But it will mean a lot to your mother, having you home again,' Marjorie said gently. 'She's looking forward to it so much. I think she was rather hurt when she felt you didn't want to go.'

Amy was silent. How could she explain why she felt as she did? No one must ever know how Maryan had deceived her – her own daughter. It was too shameful; the kind of thing that didn't happen to people like the Taylors. If they knew about it they certainly wouldn't want anything more to do with her. It looked as though they wanted her to move out anyway. Auntie Marjorie was just trying to soften the blow.

'I suppose that when Mr – er – Captain Taylor comes home for good you'll want to be on your own again,' she said hesitantly.

Marjorie smiled. 'Oh, Amy, it isn't that, darling. Mike and I have loved having you here. You've been like my own daughter, a sister for Mike, and we both love you. But your mother and grandmother love you too. They've missed most of your childhood and that's very sad. You belong with them, dear, and they'd be desperately hurt if they thought you didn't want to go home to them.'

Amy sighed. 'I suppose so.' Deep inside she felt that things would never be the same again, for her or for anyone. The little boy the Captain had left behind had grown up now. Mike was almost a man. The war had stolen a huge chunk out of all their lives. Time had moved on somehow while they weren't looking. She could see that it would be hard enough for the Taylor family to settle down without a stranger sharing their home. The time had come to stop pretending. She must go home. She must try to come to terms with the rift between her mother and herself. But the prospect scared her so much that she still tried to pretend it didn't exist. She engrossed herself in the preparations for the play. Just for a few precious weeks she could conceal herself inside Viola's skin and pretend – like Viola – to be someone else. When it was over – time enough then to face the future.

The spring of 1945 had been one of excitement and turbulence; triumph and despair. First there was the Rhine crossing with its heavy loss of lives, then the storming of Berlin and the fall of the Reich, and finally the capture and execution of Mussolini and the suicide of Hitler himself. Sometimes Maryan felt that compassion was dead. It was as though all the pity, all the tears in the world had been shed. And certainly no one grieved for two such brutal and merciless dictators. When Maryan received Marjorie's letter she went immediately to ask Vincent for the Saturday afternoon off so that she could travel to Rhensham. To think that Amy had the leading part in a Shakespeare play! She couldn't wait to see it. It was so kind of Marjorie to invite her for the weekend. Since moving into the Simons Mews flat and taking up her new job she had been busy and preoccupied. Amy's play would make a happy diversion.

Vincent agreed at once that she should go.

'You've worked so hard. You deserve a break,' he

said. 'I can easily take over the shop for that Saturday afternoon. And will you be bringing the little lady herself back with you when you come?'

Maryan shook her head. 'I think the play marks half-term,' she said. 'I'm not sure whether she'll want to come till the end.'

'Well, bring her if you can,' Vincent said with a smile. 'I know you'll be happier and more settled when you've got her back.'

As Maryan lay in bed on the Friday night, her case packed and ready, she thought about the visit she'd had a few weeks before from Sam Leigh. His arrival at the shop had been a complete surprise to her. Apparently he'd gone first to Crimea Terrace, where Sarah had given him the Chelsea address. Sitting in the living room over coffee he explained the reason for his visit.

'My conscience has been troubling me,' he said. 'I feel I should do something for Amy.' He held up his hand at the protest he saw in her eyes. 'No. Don't say anything, my dear. I felt so bad, letting you go like that. But Rachel was making herself ill. The shock of losing Marcus was still too great. I couldn't risk making her ill.'

'I know. Please don't blame yourself,' Maryan begged him. 'I should never have spoken. It was all my fault.'

Sam smiled gently. 'I felt bad because I never told you that I believed you, Maryan,' he said. 'I should have given you that comfort at least.'

She looked at him. 'You do?'

'My dear, I know you well enough to know that you'd never lie about something so important. I know that you had the best of motives too. But sadly Rachel doesn't see it that way.' He smiled. 'It was good to see Sarah again. We talked, she and I. She told me that she too only recently learned about Marcus and you.'

'I never told anyone,' Maryan said softly. 'Even Marcus never knew that he was Amy's father.'

'And I'm sure that if he had known he would have made some provision for her,' Sam said. 'Which is why I am here. I want to contribute towards her education.

Sarah tells me that she is bright. I would like to have the honour of encouraging that brightness.'

'Mr Leigh – I couldn't . . .'

'For Marcus's sake,' he added. 'Please, my dear, I don't want you to think I'm just trying to salve my conscience. We owe it to his memory – both of us.'

He had even gone to the trouble of applying to several schools in the area and now he opened his briefcase and took out a bundle of prospectuses. He pulled out two and spread them out on the table for her to see.

'I feel these have the most to offer,' he said. 'But the final choice must be yours, of course. Amy could stay on for as long as she needs to. And if she wants to go to university I'll be only too happy . . .'

Maryan waved her hand in protest. 'Please, Mr Leigh. Let's take it a step at a time. I'm sure I could get Amy into a good state school. Now that we have this new education act there are more opportunities and . . .'

'I want her to have the best,' he interrupted firmly. 'This new act – it's still in its infancy. We'll take no chances with Amy's future.' He leaned forward to take Maryan's hands in his, pleading with his gentle brown eyes. 'Give me the pleasure of doing this one small thing for Marcus's daughter, my dear. It saddens me so much that Amy and I can't know one another – can't enjoy the relationship that we should. Please?'

She could do no other than give in gracefully.

It was six a.m. when the telephone wakened her. Hurrying into the living room, she lifted the receiver and muttered drowsily: 'Vincente Antiques, Mrs Jessop speaking.'

'Mrs Jessop, this is Whitechapel Police Station,' said a crisp voice at the other end. 'I'm sorry to tell you that your mother, Mrs Sarah Brown, has been admitted to the London Hospital with severe double pneumonia.'

Maryan was wide awake at one. 'Right. I'll come at once. Thank you for letting me know.' She put down the receiver, her hands trembling. That tumbledown old house. *Why* had she clung to it so stubbornly? Sarah had caught a bad cold just after Christmas. It had gone straight to her chest and refused to clear up. And she hadn't been there to look after her. As she pulled on her clothes, Maryan blamed herself. She should have insisted on her mother moving out, or she should have stayed on at the market, working for Artie Pratt. If she had been stronger this would never have happened. If Sarah died, it would be her fault.

As the curtain came down on the combined schools' production of *Twelfth Night* the applause was tumultuous. The line-up of young actors stepped forward to take their final bow and Mike took Amy by the hand and led her forward to a renewed outburst of clapping. The production had been faultless and Marjorie, sitting in her second-row seat, could have burst with pride. If only Amy's mother could have been here to see it. She had hoped all evening, but the seat beside her, booked for Maryan, had remained empty.

Once again, Marjorie twisted in her seat to look towards the back of the auditorium. If the train had been delayed, if Maryan had arrived late, even after the interval, she would probably have stood at the back, unwilling to disturb people. But there was no one standing there. And now it was too late.

She'd meant to keep Maryan's visit as a surprise for Amy, but unfortunately she'd been too delighted to keep the news to herself. Now she had the unenviable task of breaking the news to the child that her mother had missed her triumph after all.

Chapter Nine

When Maryan arrived at the hospital the night shift was just going off and the morning changeover routine was in full swing. Behind screens in the bed nearest the doors Sarah lay in a deep coma. Propped up on the pillows and minus her dentures, she looked frail and shrivelled, her face grey against the white of the pillows behind her. Her breathing was laboured and stertorous. Racked with guilt and compassion, Maryan stared down at her.

'Will she – is there anything more that can be done?' she asked the ward sister who stood at the end of the bed.

Sister shook her head. 'She hasn't responded to any of the usual medication. Even oxygen isn't helping any more. Her heart is very weak. If only she'd been admitted earlier there might have been a chance.' She looked at Maryan. 'I'm very sorry, my dear. I'm afraid it's only a matter of time.'

Maryan looked helplessly down at her mother. 'Did she send for the doctor herself?'

'No. A neighbour found her. She hadn't been seen for several days. Apparently someone broke in and found her unable to get out of bed.'

'But why didn't she send for me? I didn't even know she was poorly.' Maryan sank onto the chair at the side of the bed and took one of the hot dry hands that lay limp on the counterpane. 'How long?' she asked.

'It's impossible to say. It could be an hour – a day. Even two.'

'I was wondering if there would be time to send for my daughter. She's in Suffolk.'

'How old is she?'

'Thirteen.'

'Don't you think it would be better to let the child remember her grandmother the way she was?'

Maryan sighed. 'I daresay you're right.'

'I'll bring you a cup of tea,' the sister said kindly. 'I don't suppose you had time to get yourself anything.'

Maryan drank her tea gratefully and waited, watching for any change, any movement or sign of life. If only Sarah would regain consciousness. There was so much she wanted to say to her. An hour passed and still her mother remained unconscious. After another hour Maryan suddenly caught sight of the ward clock over the top of the screens. It was almost nine o'clock; time she should be opening the shop. She must let Vincent know where she was. Slipping out into the corridor, she went in search of a telephone.

Vincent was sympathetic. 'Don't worry about a thing, my dear. I'll slip round and open up myself. Is there anything I can do to help you?'

'No, thank you. I don't know how long I'll be. I'll be back as soon as I can.'

'Stay as long as you need. Never mind the shop.'

It was only after she had replaced the receiver that she remembered her visit to Rhensham. She could have asked Vincent to telephone Marjorie Taylor for her. Never mind. She would do it later.

As she returned to the ward to resume her vigil she saw through a gap in the screens that the ward sister and a doctor were already by Sarah's bedside. As she entered the doctor straightened up, taking his stethoscope from his ears. He and the sister looked at her.

'My dear, I'm so sorry,' Sister said. 'She just slipped away quietly while I was checking her just now. I sent for Doctor Morris at once, but there was nothing more we could do.'

The young doctor patted her shoulder and withdrew and Sister looked at her. 'It was quite peaceful. I'll leave you with her. Stay as long as you wish. I'll be in my office when you want me.' She withdrew silently, leaving Maryan alone.

Sinking to her knees beside the bed, her tears flowing, Maryan whispered: 'Oh, Mum, why didn't you do as I wanted? I shouldn't have left you there on your own. I'm sorry – so sorry.' But even in her grief she knew deep inside that Sarah would never have moved. She'd hated it at Whitegates. Her roots were in Hackney and it was where she wanted to be, bombs or no bombs. Crimea Terrace was the only home she'd ever known. But she had never reproached her, never wanted her to turn down a good job either. Her characteristic acceptance of life was an essential part of her. It was all as she had willed it.

It was much later that afternoon when she had gone through the traumatic business of visiting the registrar and making the funeral arrangements that Maryan returned to the flat in Simons Mews. Walking from the bus stop she felt desolate and lonely among the bustling Saturday afternoon crowds. There was a euphoric air about the people in the streets now. It was spring, the sun was shining and everyone knew that the war was all but over. There was so much to look forward to, so many lives to be rebuilt. But today Maryan could not share the optimism. She dreaded the moment when she would shut the door behind her and be completely alone. Now they were all gone: Tom, Marcus, and now Sarah. As soon as she could she must get Amy back so that they could start to map out a new life together. Amy was all she had now. In her the best of the past and future were invested. She must do all she could to make that future as good as she could, for both of them.

But the moment she closed the door and began to mount the stairs she sensed that the flat was not empty. Looking up, she saw Vincent standing at the top of the stairs, waiting for her, his craggy face gentle with compassion.

'So there you are. Forgive me for letting myself in, my dear, but I couldn't let you come home to an empty flat. What's the news?'

'She's gone,' Maryan said wearily. 'Mum died just after I telephoned you.'

'Oh dear. I'm so sorry.'

As she reached the top stair her legs buckled beneath her and he put out his arms to steady her. 'There, hold up now. Come and sit down and I'll get you something. When did you last have anything to eat?'

Maryan shook her head. She hadn't even thought of food over the past hours. 'I'm not hungry,' she said. 'Just tired and so . . .' Her voice faltered and to her embarrassment the tears began to flow. Her hand over her mouth, she tried desperately to stifle them. 'I'm – sorry. I don't usually make an exhibition of myself like this.'

'Just you have a good cry. Never mind me. I daresay you've been holding it back all day.' He drew her head down onto his shoulder and led her towards the settee. 'Look, hungry or not, I think you should eat something. I'm going to make you a sandwich. It's about all my culinary skills will run to. And I'm not going anywhere till I'm quite sure you're feeling better.' He leaned forward to peer into her face. 'All right?'

'All right.' His quiet words had a soothing effect on Maryan. She stopped trying to hold back her tears and unleashed her emotions, sobbing into his shoulder until finally she felt the pattern of her breathing return to normal and all the tension that had been tying her into tight knots relax.

'She was such a good woman,' she said, wiping away the tears with the large clean handkerchief he pressed into her hand. 'So good and strong and – and wise. She didn't even let me know she wasn't well. I didn't get there in time to say goodbye. I just wish I could have done more for her. I'm going to miss her so much.'

'I know. I remember losing my own mum,' Vincent

said. 'No matter how much you've done, you always feel you should have done more.' He smiled. 'You know, there's a little bit of us that dies with our mothers. Call it the final cutting of the cord. Don't they know us the way no one else ever can? We can never be *quite* the same person with anyone else.'

She looked up at him in surprise. He had put into a nutshell just what she had been feeling all day. 'That's it exactly,' she said. 'You've put your finger right on it.'

He smiled. 'Ah, you're looking better now. There's colour in your cheeks again. I'll make us a snack and a hot drink and then I think you should try to get some rest.'

'So – now that your situation has changed, do you think you'll be staying on?' Vincent looked at her across the remains of the snack meal. 'I mean, I think four months is long enough for both of us to see how the arrangement works. I'm more than happy. Are you?'

'Oh yes. I'm learning so much,' Maryan assured him. She found to her surprise that she'd completely forgotten about the two months' trial arrangement. 'I'm really looking forward to the business starting up again. It's the most interesting job I've ever had.'

'I'm relieved that you feel that way, Maryan.' He looked at her thoughtfully. 'As a matter of fact I was going to talk to you about something else I had in mind. But maybe this is hardly the time to be talking business.'

'Oh, please – I've got to think of the future now more than ever. And I'd be grateful for something to take my mind off things.'

'Well – if you're quite sure. I have a little proposition to put to you. I'll not be needing an answer right away, but will you give it some thought?'

'Of course – if I can.'

'What would you say to taking some lessons in typing and book-keeping? I really need someone who'll help me with the administration side of things, you see. Estimates, costing out, accounts, that kind of thing.' He looked at her doubtful expression. 'As soon as the business gets off the ground I'll employ a full-time secretary. There isn't much to do either in the office or the shop as yet, so until I can afford a full staff it's a question of all of us mucking in. I'd pay you a bit extra for the overtime you'd put in, Maryan. I'm not trying to take advantage of your good nature.'

'Oh, it isn't that.' She frowned. 'To be honest, I'm just not sure if I'm capable.'

'Well, I am,' he said positively. 'If I wasn't I wouldn't ask you. You're a lot brighter than you give yourself credit for, Mrs Maryan Jessop.'

Maryan sipped her tea and thought about it. She'd always wanted to be able to type. And she'd always liked arithmetic at school. Figures gave her no problems at all. Maybe he was right. Maybe she *could* do it. 'Where would I learn?' she asked.

'At evening classes. A woman I know runs a little business school. I'm sure you'd pick it up in no time. And you could be working as you learn.' He grinned at her. 'Nothing like jumping in at the deep end. And I can always turn a blind eye to a few typing mistakes.'

'Well, I'll do my best. And I'd better learn quickly. I'm hoping to have Amy back in July.'

He smiled. 'That's great news. It's just what you need.' Suddenly he frowned. 'You were supposed to be visiting her this weekend, weren't you?'

'Yes.' Maryan leapt up. 'I must ring her. I meant to do it as soon as I got in. She doesn't know about her grandma and she'll think I've let her down, missing her school play.' She shook her head. 'They were close. She's going to be so upset.'

He stood up. 'I'll go. You'll want to speak to her in private.'

She reached out and touched his sleeve. 'Thanks, Mr Donlan.'

He turned to look at her. 'Vincent, please. Or, better still, Vinnie. It's what my friends call me.'

'Thanks anyway. I was dreading coming back here alone. You've helped me so much.'

'Ah, it was nothing – nothing at all.' He patted her shoulder, awkward in his embarrassment at her gratitude. 'Just take care of yourself. And I tell you what – I'll come round and pick you up tomorrow. It's time you tasted Roisan's Sunday roast. Her Yorkshire pudding is as light as the mountain mist. Twelve o'clock all right for you?'

'Well – yes, but . . .'

He was already halfway down the stairs. 'High time you and Roisan met. Hasn't she been nagging me for weeks to bring you round?' As he carried on down the stairs he called over his shoulder: 'See you tomorrow Maryan. Have yourself a good lie-in in the morning.'

As the door closed behind him Maryan walked back into the room and lifted the receiver, but her heart plummeted as she listened to the Taylors' telephone ringing out at the other end. They must have left home already. She'd left it too late. Now there was no way she could let them know that she wouldn't be coming.

Marjorie had arranged a party for the cast of *Twelfth Night* back at Mitcham Lodge. Everyone came, teachers and parents too. It would have been a happy occasion, but for Amy it was all spoilt before it began. She'd felt so bitterly let down by her mother's failure to be there to witness her triumph. After about half an hour she slipped away from the happy throng downstairs and shut herself in her room. Everyone else's parents had made the effort to be there, she told herself, slumping despondently on her bed. Surely her mother could at least have taken the trouble to telephone. It was just like it had been at the beginning of the war. She obviously thought more of that new job of hers than she did of coming to see the play. No doubt she thought it all some childish nonsense like the time she was the fairy in the school panto in Hackney.

Downstairs Marjorie was answering the telephone, her

hand pressed tightly against the other ear as she tried to hear what was being said above the din of thirty excited young people enjoying themselves.

'Who is it? Oh, *Maryan*. My dear, we were so worried when you didn't arrive. The play was such a success. Amy was brilliant. But she was desperately disappointed. Is everything all right?' She listened gravely, her brow creasing into a frown as Maryan explained what had happened.

'Oh, my dear, I'm so sorry to hear that.'

'If Amy is there I'd like to speak to her,' Maryan said.

'Unfortunately there's a party going on here at the moment. You can hardly hear yourself think as you can probably hear for yourself,' Marjorie told her. 'Perhaps it would be better if I broke the news to her myself – upstairs, quietly. I'll get her to ring you later when they've all gone.'

Having got Maryan's permission she rang off and looked around. Seeing Mike passing with a tray of sandwiches, she asked him if he knew where Amy was.

He shrugged. 'I saw her going upstairs a while ago,' he said. 'She's been a bit of a misery all evening since she found out that her mum had missed the play.'

'Didn't you go after her?'

'No. I thought I'd better leave her to it.'

Marjorie took his arm and drew him into the kitchen. 'That was her mother on the phone. It seems that Amy's grandmother died this morning. That's why she couldn't come. I couldn't let her break the news over the phone, especially with this noise going on, so I've got to break it to her now.'

Mike bit his lip. 'Oh, no. Poor Amy. She thought a lot of her gran. Do you want me to come with you?'

'No. I'll go. If she wants you I'll come and get you. In the meantime don't say anything to anyone. Just keep the ball rolling down here.'

On the landing Marjorie tapped on Amy's door. 'Amy – can I come in, dear?'

'Okay,' came the muffled reply.

Marjorie pushed open the door. Amy sat on her bed looking sorry for herself. 'Amy, your mother has just telephoned,' she said. 'I'm afraid she had some very bad news.' She went and sat beside Amy on the bed and took her hand. 'I know you were disappointed and felt let down because she didn't come today. But there was a very good reason. Darling, I'm afraid your grandma was taken ill yesterday. The hospital sent for your mother early this morning.'

Amy's eyes widened as she turned to Marjorie. 'Grandma? What happened? Is she all right?'

Marjorie took a deep breath. 'Amy, dear, I'm afraid your grandma died this morning. I'm so sorry.' Amy burst into tears and she held her close. 'She caught a bad cold that went to her chest. It turned to pneumonia. Your mother said she didn't suffer. It was very peaceful. She was with her at the hospital, that's why she couldn't come.' She tipped up Amy's chin to look into her eyes. 'Amy – your mum is going to need you now. Now that there are just the two of you you'll have to look after each other.'

Amy swallowed her tears. She felt such a bewildering mixture of emotions. Common sense told her that it wasn't Mum's fault that Grandma had died, yet something in her wanted – almost *needed* – to blame her. Her mother had robbed her of *two* fathers. Now Grandma had gone too – all because Mum had gone off to this new job and left her. Why should I go and look after her? she asked herself – a mother who'd done nothing but lie to her all her life, who had always put her job and others first. She didn't deserve it. But, knowing that such bitter resentment would be considered unworthy of her, she swallowed and asked: 'Where's Mike?'

'He's downstairs. Would you like me to send him up?'

Amy nodded. 'Yes please.'

Mike found Amy sitting on the bed, her recent tears drying on her cheeks. He stood by the door, looking hesitantly at her. If she cried again he wouldn't know what to do or say. He wasn't at all sure of how to handle the situation anyway.

'Hello,' he said. 'Mum told me about your gran. I'm really sorry. She was a nice old lady.'

'Thanks.'

She didn't look at him – didn't respond. It was a bit like talking to the wall. What should he do now? Should he go, or try to say something else? What? He stepped towards her. 'Mum says you can telephone your mum later, when the party's over.'

'I'm not going to.'

He frowned. 'Why not? I expect she's pretty upset.'

'If she hadn't taken that job and left Grandma alone it wouldn't have happened.'

He stood uncertainly in front of her. This was a reaction he hadn't bargained for. 'But – you'll be going to London for the funeral, won't you? I mean – you'll need to ring her to know where and when – everything.'

'I'm not going.' For the first time she looked up at him. 'It's her fault, so she can go on her own. I can't help Grandma now. She won't know whether I'm there or not. I'm never going home any more. I hate Mum.'

There was a shocked pause as Mike looked at her. He'd expected it to be difficult, but not this difficult. Her eyes were dark with anguish. He could feel the hurt emanating from her like the vapour from dry ice. What he didn't understand was why. Slowly he sat down beside her on the bed.

'Why do you hate your mum, Amy? It can't really be her fault, your gran dying. And I really think you should go to the funeral.' She was silent and he sensed that she was struggling to hold tears at bay once more. Remembering the day they'd been caught in the buzzbomb raid and the comfort holding hands had given him, he reached out to curl his fingers round hers. After all, she was still only a kid really. 'Come on, Amy,' he said. 'Don't be too hard on your mother. Old people do die, you know – all the time. It's no one's fault and it doesn't help, looking for someone to blame.'

She turned to look at him, her effort not to cry twisting her mouth so that her words were distorted. 'Oh, you – you don't understand. How would you know how it feels?'

'I might find out if you were to tell me.'

For a moment she hesitated. The weight of what she had dragged around with her since last July sometimes seemed as though it would crush her. It would be such a relief to unburden herself. 'Look, Mike,' she said haltingly. 'If I tell you something, will you promise not to say a word to anyone – not even Auntie Marjorie?'

'Of course.'

'Say you promise?'

'Oh, come off it.' He frowned. 'Promises are for kids. If I say I won't tell, then I *won't*. A man is as good as his word, Dad always says.'

'All right then.' She paused, biting her lip. 'Remember that time I went to stay at Hazelfield last summer holidays?'

'Yes.'

'Well, I overheard something the night before I came home. It was something really awful. That was why I wanted to go up to London to see Grandma afterwards. I had to ask her if it was true.'

'I knew there was something. You came back in such a mood. What was it, Amy? What did you hear?'

'I heard Mum telling the Leighs that I was their grand-child,' she said. 'Marcus Leigh, their son – the one who was killed in France – was my real father.'

Mike's eyes opened wide. 'You mean that he and your Mum . . .? Crumbs.' For once he was lost for words. 'But – if this Marcus Leigh person and your mum were – well, you know – *in love*, why didn't she marry him?'

Amy sighed. 'Lots of reasons. Because he was rich and Mum was poor. Because he was Jewish and she wasn't. Anyway, they both married someone else. When Mum told the Leighs they were really mad. She felt she had to leave, after working for them ever since she left school too.'

Mike frowned. 'Just because she loved their son – and had you?'

'No – because they didn't believe her,' Amy told him bitterly. 'They didn't want to believe that their son would mix with someone as common as Mum. She had to get me out of the house quickly so that they didn't have to look at me any more. I heard her telling Mr Leigh she would the next morning. It made me feel like – like something the cat had sicked up.'

Mike looked at her for a long moment. 'But you did *have* a good father,' he said. 'You've often told me. I mean the one you *thought* was . . .'

'That's the awful part. I thought he was but he wasn't. He was just Mum's husband.'

'So – it *was* true then? Your Gran explained what happened – that day?'

'No.' Amy sighed. 'She was as shocked as I was. She said that Mum never told her either. She said I was to forget about it. To think of myself as a Jessop, like it says on my birth certificate. And I've tried, Mike. I've tried and *tried*, but it doesn't work.' She turned to look at him. 'All these years; all these years she's been living a lie – *me*. I've been a lie all my life. I'm not who I thought I was. Can you imagine how that feels? How would you feel if you found out that your dad, the man you feel closest to in all the world, was nothing but a stranger – no relation to you at all?'

Mike couldn't meet the harrowing look in her eyes. 'I can't imagine,' he said, staring at the floor. 'But I know it must feel pretty gruesome.'

'So now can you see why I hate her?'

'But you can't go on hating her for ever, can you?'

'I don't think I'll ever stop,' she said passionately.

'Does she know – that *you* know, I mean?'

'No. I made Grandma promise not to tell and – well, she won't be able to now, will she? Now I've lost her too.' She turned away with a shake of her head. 'I'll never tell Mum that I heard what she told the Leighs that night. I couldn't.'

He looked at her. 'You didn't mean it when you said you wouldn't go to your gran's funeral, did you?'

'Yes. I meant it.'

'Amy?' Maryan was so relieved to hear her daughter's voice at the other end of the line. 'I thought you'd like to know that the funeral went off quite well, love. Granny Jessop, Auntie Maggie and Uncle Bill send their love.' Maryan paused, holding the receiver close to her ear. Honestly, these trunk calls weren't worth the money half the time. The line was awful. She could barely hear Amy's voice. When there was no reply she went on, raising her voice a little: 'Uncle Bill was invalided out of the Army last year – chest trouble. But he's getting on nicely. I wish you could have seen your cousin Johnny. He's so tall, going on seventeen now and quite the young man. He's already in the Air Training Corps. Hoping to join the RAF as soon as he's eighteen.' After another pause she said: 'It was just as well you didn't come, love. Since VE Day the trains have been so crowded. Amy – are you still there?'

'Yes.'

'Did you do anything to celebrate the victory, down there?'

'Not much. There was a bonfire in Armstrong's Meadow with a few fireworks. And they burned a guy, got up to look like Hitler, and there was a bit of dancing.'

'That must have been fun. Mrs Taylor told me how good you were in the play. I wish I could have seen you.'

'Do you?'

'And she sent me the cutting out of the local paper too. It said you were "captivating as Viola". Wasn't that smashing?'

'I s'pose so.'

'I'll keep it always. I've put it in the photo album with all your snaps.'

'Oh.'

'Maybe you'll be in another play.'

'Maybe.'

'I expect you and Mike enjoyed it.'

'It was all right.'

'Amy, I'd like you to come up to Town next weekend,' Maryan went on. 'I've got so much to tell you about my new job. The flat's lovely. I've got your room all ready. I can't wait for you to see it. And I've got a surprise, too.'

'Oh. Have you?'

Maryan felt a twinge of anxiety. 'Amy, love – are you all right? Not feeling poorly or anything, are you? Not upset about Grandma?'

'No. I'm all right, Mum.'

'Good. She wouldn't have wanted you to be upset you know. You always meant a lot to her.' Again there was no reply. 'So you will come, will you – next weekend? I've already spoken to Mrs Taylor about it. I'll meet you off the four-thirty at Euston. That all right?'

'I suppose it's got to be if you've all arranged it between you.'

'Yes – well – I'd better ring off now, love. See you next weekend.' Maryan felt upset and a little put-out at Amy's laconic response, but she told herself that her daughter was a teenager now. Moodiness was all part of growing up, as she remembered from her own adolescence. She would have to employ all her tact and understanding if they were to reestablish their relationship successfully.

As Amy replaced the receiver she caught sight of herself in the hall mirror. Would her eye have returned to normal by the weekend? she wondered. She hated the curious glances she had attracted over the past few days. It would be horrible going up to London on the train, and even worse trying to explain to Mum how it had happened.

Leaning forward she peered more closely at the eye. It had turned from dark red to black and blue at first. Now it was a horrible shade of greenish yellow. Very gingerly she touched the discoloured, still puffy skin and winced at the memory of Lily Smith's well-aimed straight left, consoling herself with the satisfaction that this time she had given back as good as she received. Maybe Lily would stop trying to pick fights with her now.

Ever since that day last summer at the carnival Lily had made a point of making Amy's life a misery whenever their paths crossed. And the news that Mrs Smith had moved the rest of her family to Rhensham permanently after they'd been bombed out had filled Amy with dismay. The large, shiftless family now lived on the council estate on the fringe of the village and Lily, who had left school last Christmas soon after her fourteenth birthday, now worked behind the counter of the village Co-op. But although she now considered herself an adult, she never missed a chance to cat–call and draw attention to Amy whenever she saw her, taking great delight in causing her the maximum of embarrassment and humiliation.

Lily's mousy hair was now bleached and permed to within an inch of its life. She wore bright orange lipstick and short skirts and her jaws permanently rotated on a wad of chewing gum. She was often to be found hanging around the bus stop near the church in the hope of attracting the American servicemen from the nearby camp who sometimes stopped off for a pint of the local ale at the village pub.

As ever, she attracted a string of miscellaneous hangers-on, girls less adventurous than herself who admired her strident outspokenness and her capacity for trouble-making. Lily didn't give a damn. When she was around there was always a bit of fun, usually at someone else's expense; because you were either with Lily or against her. There were no half measures.

On the day in question it was half-day closing and Amy spotted Lily hanging around the bus stop with her usual motley crowd as she stood waiting for the bus to stop. She decided to ignore her. Maybe she'd leave her alone today. And even if she didn't, there wasn't much the girl could do if she refused to take any notice of her. Besides, she was probably waiting for the bus. But Lily wasn't waiting for the bus. She wasn't even waiting to wheedle chewing gum or cigarettes from some hapless American soldier. Today she was waiting for Amy.

She stepped forward eagerly the moment she saw her intended victim get off the bus, the gleefully malicious look on her face that Amy had learned to dread. Her followers gathered round, expressions of smug anticipation on their faces as they waited for the entertainment to begin.

'Well, *well*, if it ain't the great actress 'erself,' Lily sneered. 'Seen 'er name in the paper, did yer? *Captivatin*', it said she was.' She gave Amy a vicious push and snatched off her school hat, throwing it over the wall. ''Ow much did yer 'ave to pay to get 'em to write that then?' She advanced on Amy, who stepped backwards until she could feel the cold stone of the wall pressing against her back. 'Go on, Amy–pissed. Give us a free show then. I reckon us poor sods deserve a treat, don't you? Act us the bit where you was makin' out to be a bloke, like wot it said in the paper.' She turned to the others. 'Reckon it must've been a queer old play, don't you?' she jeered. They tittered and nudged each other. Encouraged by their approval, Lily made a grab for Amy's hair, her eyes glinting dangerously. 'Think you're someone, don't you, *Jessop*? Lookin' down yer snotty nose an' queenin' it over the rest of us in yer poxy school uniform.'

'I don't queen it. I don't even want to talk to you,' Amy said, wincing with pain as the other girl wound a lock of her hair tightly round her fingers and pulled mercilessly.

'Oh, don't wanna *talk* to me, don't yer? Well, pardon me for livin', I'm sure. I s'pose you think you're all set now that your mum's got herself a new feller.'

Amy's eyes opened wide. 'I – don't know what you mean.'

'No? Well, I wouldn't boast about it if it was me neither. Don't think 'cause I don't live in London no more I don't get to 'ear what's 'appenin'. Me Gran still lives there, y'know, an' there ain't much as *she* misses.

She says your mum's living with some bloke in his posh gaff Up West,' she announced triumphantly. 'Some Irish geezer she met when she was working down the market.' She pushed her face close to Amy's. 'My mum says she was always a wrong'un. An now that Marcus Leigh's a gonner I s'pose she's latched onto some other poor bleeder.'

Feeling sick with disgust, Amy kicked out at Lily's shin. The other girl shrieked out in anger.

'Oooh, you little bitch. You've laddered me nylons. New on, they was.'

'I don't care about your nylons, Lily Smith.' Amy's temper was fully aroused now. 'Your skinny legs look stupid in them anyway. Don't you dare say things about my mum. I'll . . .'

Lily gave her no time to complete the sentence. She hit Amy hard in the face with the back of her hand, her knuckles catching her in the eye with a blinding pain. Amy heard the others giggling excitedly and egging Lily on, and suddenly it was as though a red mist of fury rose before her, making her forget every lesson in ladylike manners she'd ever been taught. Wrapping the strap of her heavily loaded school satchel round her hand, she swung it hard at Lily, knocking the other girl off balance and causing her to stagger forward, banging her face against the wall. As Amy seized her chance to escape she heard Lily screech and clutch at her nose, from which a trickle of blood had started to emerge. She didn't wait to see what would happen next. As Lily's shocked admirers gathered round her, enjoying the drama, she ran off along the road and didn't stop until she reached the gates of Mitcham Lodge.

Going round to the back she let herself in at the kitchen door, standing a moment to regain her breath. With luck she would get upstairs to her room before anyone saw her. She felt hot and shaky and close to tears. She just wanted to be by herself to calm down and get over the unpleasant encounter. Lily was jealous as usual, this time it was over the play. But what had she meant about her mother living with a man she met at the market? It was a lie. *Or was it*? Just what kind of woman was her mother? She was beginning to feel she had never really known her. And would she really expect her to go there and live with her and this – this *Irish geezer*? Everything – all of what she had suffered since last summer, including Lily's taunting – had been Mum's fault.

She hurried through the kitchen as silently as she could, but in the hall she came face to face with Marjorie, who was on her way downstairs.

Marjorie stopped in her tracks, her eyes wide with shock. 'Amy. Heavens above, child, what on earth has happened to you?'

Seeing Marjorie's alarmed expression Amy stole a sideways glance at herself in the hall mirror. She was shocked by what she saw. No wonder Marjorie looked as she did. The eye Lily Smith had hit was swollen and already the skin around it was darkening. There was even a small cut where Lily's cheap ring had caught her cheekbone. Her hair was standing on end, too, and she suddenly remembered with dismay that she'd left her school hat where Lily had thrown it, over the churchyard wall. A huge lump rose in her throat and she knew that if Marjorie uttered just one sympathetic word she was in danger of bursting into babyish tears.

'Darling, your poor face?' Marjorie's face was full of concern as she reached out to touch Amy's cheek.

It was too much. A strangled sob escaped Amy's throat as she dropped her satchel on the floor and covered her face with her hands.

'It's all right, darling. Don't cry.' Marjorie put an arm around her. 'Who did this to you? You must tell me.'

'It was – a girl I know,' Amy hiccuped, despising herself for her own weakness. 'She was waiting for me at the bus stop. She's always picking on me for something.'

Marjorie was shocked. 'You mean another girl did it? She actually *attacked* you? Who is this girl? We really should report this, you know.'

Amy swallowed hard. 'It's nothing unusual. She's some-one who used to live near us in London and she's always hated me. Trouble is, she lives here now. Her mother moved them all here for good when they were bombed out.'

'Well, first things first. Come upstairs and let me attend to that eye,' Marjorie said.

As she bathed the eye in the bathroom and applied antiseptic to the cut Amy looked at her. 'You won't tell anyone I've been in a fight, will you, Auntie Marjorie?'

Marjorie smiled. 'Of course I won't. Anyway, it was hardly a fight, was it? More of an assault.'

Amy said nothing, but inwardly she felt a small thrill of satisfaction that this time she'd given Lily as good as she'd got. She'd have a fat nose tomorrow. She'd have a job to wheedle any nylons or chewing gum out of her precious 'Yanks' looking like that. Maybe she would think twice before picking on her another time. But although she'd had the satisfaction of getting even with Lily, the remark about her mother still rankled, echoing like a tolling bell at the back of her mind. It was just another of Lily's malicious lies, of course. It had to be; at best an exaggeration. All the same, there was no smoke without fire, so they said. And it wasn't nice to have to listen to people like Lily Smith saying rotten things about your mother, especially when you were in no position to deny them.

Mike went with her to the station on Friday afternoon. They stood together on the platform, Mike making most of the conversation. Amy was in one of her quiet moods again.

'I bet you're looking forward to seeing your new home,' he said brightly.

'Not really.'

'At least your eye is better. It looks normal again now.'

'Yes.' Amy had slipped out of school in the lunch hour the day before and surreptitiously bought a box of face powder at Woolworth's. A dusting of it, applied with cotton wool hid the faint discolouration left by the black eye, much to her relief.

'It'll be nice, though,' Mike was saying. 'Going back to London now all the bombing's finished.'

'It still won't be like it used to be. That'll take years.'

'Maybe just as well, though, eh? I mean all those . . .'

'Slums? Like where we used to live, you mean?'

'I was going to say places that needed pulling down anyway.'

'Same thing.'

He looked at her gloomy face. 'Oh cheer up, misery-guts. The war's over and you're going to see your new home. You might try and look a bit more cheerful about it.'

'It's all right for you. You haven't got to leave all the things and people you like to go and live somewhere you don't want to,' she burst out accusingly. 'Besides – I told you what Lily Smith said about Mum.'

'But you don't believe it – do you?'

Amy shrugged sullenly. 'I don't know what I believe any more.' He was silent and she glanced at him, suddenly feeling insecure and a little afraid. Mike was her best friend and she'd been horrid to him lately. If he lost patience with her who would she turn to? 'What are you going to do this weekend?' she asked in a lighter tone. 'Bet you won't miss me.'

'Don't know what we'll do. It depends what Dad feels like when he . . .'

'Dad?' She interrupted, staring at him. 'Your dad, you mean? You didn't tell me he was coming home.'

'Oh – didn't I?' He shuffled his feet, his ears turning red. *Blast*, he'd promised his mother he wouldn't say anything in case Amy thought they were trying to get rid of her. She'd been so touchy lately.

'You *know* you didn't,' she said. 'Is he coming home for keeps then?'

'No, only for the weekend. This'll probably be his last leave before his demob, though.'

'I see. You definitely won't be missing me then.'

The train signal changed with a clang and Mike looked up with some relief. 'Oh look, your train's coming.' He glanced at her. 'Dad's getting his old job back with the paper. He's going to see them this weekend. Did you know he was a journalist?'

'No.' She shook her head, too preoccupied to notice his clumsy attempt at changing the subject. 'No, I didn't.'

'That's what I want to be too. Have you decided what you want to do when you leave school?'

'No.' Amy picked up her small weekend case as the train squealed to a stop alongside the platform. 'Have a nice time with your dad this weekend, Mike,' she said, moving away. 'The three of you will be by yourselves now. It'll be just like old times. You'll like that.'

She climbed into the train and found a corner seat where she sat looking straight ahead of her. The train had begun to move when there was a frantic tapping on the carriage window. Mike was signalling to her to open it. She stood up and pushed it down. 'What do you want?'

Running alongside the moving train, he pushed a bar of chocolate at her through the window. 'Here – for the journey. See you Sunday evening. Bye, Amy. Have a nice time.'

She took the chocolate, torn between shame at her own churlish behaviour and annoyance with him for making her feel guilty. 'Thanks, Mike,' she called as the train reached the end of the platform and he stood back, waving. She waved till he was out of sight, then closed the window and sat down again, her throat tight with tears. She swallowed angrily. She was always wrestling with tears nowadays. What was the matter with her?

She couldn't bring herself to eat the chocolate, knowing that Mike had sacrificed his precious sweet coupons to give her a consolation prize she didn't deserve. If only she hadn't been so beastly to him. She gave it to two small children who got on at the next station with their mother, enjoying her own martyrdom as she watched them eat it.

Sitting back in her corner seat she agonised over what she saw as the Taylors' deception. Marjorie must have conspired with her mother to get her out of the way so that they could have their family reunion. Hurt inflated itself inside her like a balloon until everything ached with the pressure. Was there anyone left in the world who really wanted her? Would she ever fit in anywhere?

Maryan met Amy at the station and brought her back to Simons Mews in a state of suppressed excitement. They made the journey to Chelsea by bus so that she could show Amy the bomb damage and how much had already been done to clear the sites. 'They tell us they're hoping to have London back to normal in five years,' she said.

Standing in the little cobbled mews outside Vincente Antiques, Maryan proudly pointed to the window display she had created herself: a pretty little French secretaire and a Regency sofa table, behind which was a graceful drape of crimson and gold striped satin.

'Roisan gave me the drape,' she said. 'She's Vincent – Mr Donlan's sister and she will be doing all the soft furnishing for the business. She's ever so nice and really clever.' Maryan got out her key. 'Vincent is standing in for me at the shop this afternoon so that I can meet you. You'll meet him later. This really is the most interesting job, Amy. There's so *much* to learn: furniture, porcelain and pottery, silver and enamels and glass. Mr Donlan has taken me along to a couple of sales, but I can't imagine ever buying at one myself. You daren't blink without they think you're bidding.' She laughed a little too brightly, aware that she was talking too much. Amy's silence was making her nervous. She had looked forward so much to this weekend and she refused to believe that she couldn't make Amy enjoy it.

'I've even started taking evening classes in office work,' she went on. 'You know, I was really lucky, meeting Mr Donlan's nephew like that at the market. Getting a job with a lovely home that went with it was a real piece of good luck for us – for you and me.'

'It's a pity Grandma couldn't have come too,' Amy said.

Maryan's smile dissolved and she gave a sad little sigh. 'I know. If only she'd agreed to come with me. I did try, Amy, but she wouldn't budge from that awful old place. You should have seen the state it was in since the bombing.'

'I know – I mean, it must have been.'

Maryan looked at her enquiringly. 'Well – shall we go in? I can't wait for you to see the flat.'

To Maryan's relief Amy seemed quietly impressed by the flat, especially the pretty bedroom that was to be hers. For the first time her expression relaxed and something that was almost a smile flitted across her face.

'I made the curtains and bedspread myself,' Maryan told her. 'I thought you'd like the flowered pattern – to remind you of the countryside.'

'Yes. It's very nice, Mum.'

Maryan looked at her daughter, now almost as tall as she was. She was blossoming into a very attractive young girl. Her thin child's body was filling out, her dark hair shone and she positively glowed with health and vitality. And from her reports she was doing really well at school. She had every reason to be happy and confident. Why then was she so quiet and withdrawn? However, encouraged by Amy's obvious approval of her bedroom, she said: 'Why don't you make yourself at home – take off your coat and freshen up? You can unpack later.'

Amy looked at her. 'You said you had a surprise,' she said warily.

'That's right. But I was saving that for later. Tell you what, I'll show you while we're having tea. It's all ready.'

After the meal of cold meat and salad Maryan got up and went to the sideboard, where she took out a folder. She opened it, spreading the contents on the table. 'This is the prospectus of your new school. It's only a short bus ride away from here and it's called St Hildred's. It's actually a convent and the teachers are all nuns, but it's very modern and forward-thinking. And look ...'

Maryan turned the page. 'They specialise in the arts: music and drama, dancing and singing. I know you're going to love it.'

Amy stared down at the photographs in the prospectus. 'It looks very posh,' she said.

'It is. The facilities are wonderful. Just fancy getting a sports field that size in the middle of London,' Maryan said. 'The girls wear these really smart uniforms. Brown and yellow with lovely straw boaters in the summer and felt Bretons in winter. I've put your name down for next year. You start in September.'

Amy had turned now to the last page where the school fees were printed. She looked up at her mother. 'But it's a private school,' she said in surprise. 'It costs an awful lot, doesn't it?'

Maryan blushed. She'd meant to take that page out before Amy could see it. 'That's all right. I mean – you passed your scholarship, didn't you?'

'But that was for the High School in Suffolk.'

'It's all right though,' Maryan blundered on. 'It just has to be transferred.'

'Are you sure?' Amy looked at her with clear blue eyes that Maryan couldn't quite meet. She couldn't tell Amy that Sam Leigh was paying her school fees so she was obliged to bend the truth a little.

'Of course I am.'

They were washing up together when Vincent arrived. He came in unannounced, entering by the back stairs entrance which led directly up from the shop. Maryan heard his step on the stairs and hurriedly dried her hands.

'This will be Mr Donlan,' she told Amy, her cheeks pink. He appeared smiling in the doorway and she went straight into the introductions: 'Amy, this is Mr Donlan, my new boss and our landlord.'

Vincent raised an eyebrow. 'That sounds very formal. You'll be frightening the girl into thinking I'm the wicked squire.' He held out his hand. 'Hello, Amy. Take no notice of your mother. I'm really quite human when you

215

get to know me. I've heard so much about you, I feel I already know you. Welcome to Simons Mews. I hope you're going to be happy here.'

'Thank you, Mr Donlan.' Amy shook his hand, and he bent a little to look at her.

'My nephew calls me Uncle Vinnie. Maybe you'd like to call me that too.' She said nothing and he went on: 'Have you seen the new school yet?'

'Yes.'

'Only the prospectus so far,' Maryan put in, 'but the Mother Superior has promised to show her round in the summer holidays. It's no problem with the nuns living on the premises.'

'Your mother has chosen well. I know you're going to love it there,' Vincent said. 'My sister Roisan went there until she moved on to art college. You'll have the whale of a time at St Hildreds.'

'Mmm.' Amy looked from one to the other of them, then she said: 'Well – I think I'll just go and unpack now, Mum.'

'When you've finished perhaps you might like to come down and see the shop,' Vincent called out to her as she went. 'Maybe we can find a little something for you, a keepsake.'

When Amy had gone, closing the door quietly behind her Maryan let out her breath on a sigh. Vincent smiled.

'Is it heavy going?'

'A bit,' Maryan admitted. 'She's so grown-up. And so – I don't know – reserved is the word, I suppose. It's so hard to know what she's thinking.'

'Did she like her room?'

'Yes. I think so. She seemed to, anyway.'

'I should hope so,' Vincent said. 'The time and trouble you put into it.'

'She's rising fourteen,' Maryan said thoughtfully. 'A difficult age, I suppose.'

'As I remember it, I was never *allowed* to be difficult as you call it. At fourteen or any other age.' He looked at her, his head on one side. 'Tell me, what were *you* doing at fourteen?'

Maryan laughed. 'Working – as an apprentice machinist.'

'See what I mean? I don't suppose there was much scope for being difficult there.'

'No, there wasn't.'

'So – will she settle, do you think? God knows you've done your best.'

Maryan sighed. 'I hope so, Vinnie. I do hope so. It isn't going to be easy, for either of us. Sometimes I feel I've lost her. Five years is such a big chunk out of your child's life. When the war began she was a little girl, now she's a teenager – almost an adult – brought up by another woman too.' She sighed. 'I only hope we can bridge the gap. There's so much I want to make up to her.'

He slipped an arm around her shoulders. 'You'll be fine, Maryan. She's lucky to have such a mother as you, and I'm sure she knows it.'

But Maryan wasn't so sure. There was a lot Vincent didn't know about her; a lot Amy didn't know too. She'd made so many mistakes. Her loyalties had been so appallingly misplaced all these years. And she was horribly afraid that it might already be too late to redress the balance.

Chapter Ten

Rachel sat at her desk in the office she had created for herself at Whitegates. Since the daily woman from the village had taken Maryan's place she had turned the housekeeper's flat over the garage into her own workplace. It now consisted of an office, a studio and a large workroom. Ever since she had found Marcus's designs she had been working feverishly on a collection to be launched later that summer. Once peace was established she predicted that there would be a boom in the fashion world just as there had been after the last war. Feldman's, and more specifically The Marcus Leigh Collection, could begin to make its mark once again.

She herself was working on the business side and the preparation of the show that would launch the new designs, whilst in the workroom a team of meticulously hand-picked cutters and seamstresses were working on the garments. The project had given Rachel a new lease of life. She had begun to take an interest in her own clothes and her appearance once again. After Marcus's death she had lost weight and begun to look every day of her fifty–eight years, but now, with her thick hair well cut and groomed, and the black mourning dresses she was reluctant to set aside relieved by touches of colour, she was beginning to look herself again.

Marcus's designs were being made individually to fit the models Rachel had already chosen. 'They were all girls at the outset of their careers; young and eager; as fresh and as pretty as Marcus's designs demanded and deserved. She had appointed a designer too, to complete the details of some of the sketchier designs and to create further styles; because Rachel was convinced that once the glamour–starved women of Britain had seen the innovative lines and styles Marcus had created there would be a demand for clothes with the distinctive blue and silver *Marcus Leigh* label. She was determined that it would be one of the most sought-after names in the fashion world and she worked tirelessly towards that end.

Eager to encourage young talent, she had invited submissions from art colleges and had finally chosen a talented young woman from an Essex college. Gina Stern was newly qualified and highly recommended by her tutors. At twenty she was fiercely ambitious and determined to get on and make her mark. She admired Marcus's designs and her portfolio revealed a flair and style that were almost uncannily similar and compatible with his. Rachel was well pleased with her choice. Everything was going to plan and life held some meaning for her again.

Outside the window every tree and hedge row was heavy with the bounty of spring. Today Rachel felt its restlessness stirring inside her, making concentration difficult. The venue for the show, a smart Kensington hotel, was booked and the guest list was complete. The invitations were at the printer's and the menu for the buffet luncheon to be served before the commencement of the show was already selected and ordered.

In the workroom next door the hum of machines and the quiet conversation of the seamstresses told of their steady industry. Rachel had no wish to disturb them. They knew their jobs and she knew she could trust them. In a couple of weeks' time things would begin to heat up and she would be busy again. For now there was very little for her to do – except . . .

She got up and opened the window – then closed it again. The singing of the birds and the evocative honey-and-spice scents of springtime made her jumpy and nervous. Her eyes were constantly drawn to the drawer at the bottom of the filing cabinet. Since that day when she had visited 124 Hackney Road and cleared out Marcus's studio she had done nothing about the package of personal papers she had collected from his desk, pushing it into that empty drawer and conveniently forgetting it. Her project for the new collection to be launched in his name had taken up all her time and energy. But she had known all along that she must go through the papers at some stage. Sam, aware of her reluctance, kept begging her to let him take on the task himself.

'We really should do something about it,' he urged. 'There could be something important there, even bills to be settled.'

Rachel had shrugged this off. 'You know that Marcus never got into debt,' she chided him. 'And if he owed anyone money they would have surely asked for it before this.'

But although she knew in her heart that she must do this one last thing for him she shied away from it with a sick feeling in the pit of her stomach. They had not been allowed to bury their son or go through the proper grieving ritual. At the back of her mind there was always the vain hope that he might, by some miraculous turn of fate, not have been killed after all. Even though they had now received his personal belongings and a letter of commendation from the French Government, his death still seemed unreal to Rachel. Going through his letters and papers would make it real; would force her to face the fact that he had gone for ever. And for this reason she allowed the weeks to pass, and the package of personal papers to remain in the drawer.

But today, with everything under control and no other job demanding her attention, she knew that she could put off the task no longer. With a sigh she got up and went across to the filing cabinet. Sinking to her knees she pulled out the drawer and took out the packet, tipping the contents onto the floor. As she had assured Sam, there seemed nothing of any urgency among the pile. Spreading the papers out she could see at a glance that they consisted largely of letters from friends, receipts, invoices, hurried sketches on the backs of scraps of paper, theatre and concert programmes. There were some letters from Jessica. Rachel caught her breath as she recognised the small, neat handwriting on the scented blue envelopes. She destroyed them, tearing them into tiny pieces and dropping them into her waste-paper basket. Her darlings deserved to keep their privacy.

The pile was diminishing nicely and Rachel felt a wave of relief. The job was almost over. And it hadn't taken as long, or been nearly as traumatic as she had feared. Then she saw it.

The large sealed envelope had stuck inside the packet, too thick to fall out with the rest of the loose papers. As she drew it out she saw printed in large capitals: TO BE OPENED IN THE EVENT OF MY DEATH. Her blood chilled and for a moment she turned it over in her hands, weighing it speculatively – trying to guess what it might contain, half afraid to open it. At last, with trembling fingers, she tore it open. Inside were three smaller envelopes, one addressed to her and Sam; another with the address of his bank written on it. But she was surprised to see that the third envelope was addressed to Mrs Maryan Jessop.

Tearing open her own envelope she read quickly.

Dearest Mother and Father,

If you are reading this you will already know that my life is over and that, sadly, we shall not meet again. I want you to know how much I love you both and that I have always been so very grateful for the happiness, the care and the love you have given me all my life. If I gave you pain by joining the Resistance, please forgive me and try to understand that I could not have lived with myself had I not done what I knew I must do.

I do not have very much to leave behind in the material sense, but there is something that I wish you to put right for me, if I am to be denied the opportunity of doing it myself.

A long time ago I did something foolish that had serious consequences and I believe I hurt someone who did not deserve to be hurt. I have good reason to believe that I am the father of Maryan Jessop's child. By the time I returned home she had married another man and seemed unwilling to acknowledge this. I therefore felt it wiser to remain silent, especially when I met and fell in love with Jessica. I now feel that it was very selfish and wrong of me not to face up to my responsibility. Therefore I have instructed the bank in the letter enclosed to invest any money I might leave and hold it in trust for Amy until her coming of age. I know that you and Father do not need it and as Amy is my only living issue I feel it only right that I should provide for her in some small way.

Please try to understand and forgive me for falling short of your high standards and your expectations of me.

God bless and keep you both,

Your loving son, Marcus

Rachel knelt on the floor, reading the letter through again and again, her face wet with tears. How could he be so misguided? If the child had been his Maryan would surely have told him. He was wrong – *wrong*.

But even as she tried to convince herself she knew deep in her heart that he was not wrong. If she were truthful with herself she had known it all along. With her own eyes she had seen the strong attraction between the two young people. She had even witnessed their secret meeting that evening in Whitechapel. And there was no denying that the child, Amy, resembled Marcus. After his death she had subconsciously gained comfort from the fact, feeling a need to have the girl close to her when Marcus's loss was causing her so much pain. The passion she had seen flowering between the two young people had been the very reason why she had persuaded Sam to allow Marcus to study in France. And now she was faced with the fact that if he had not gone to France he would probably be with them, alive and well today. Had she herself set in motion the chain of events that had led to his death?

A sob tore at her throat and she covered her mouth with her hands. *No*. It was unthinkable. It wasn't her – it was Maryan. If it had not been for that girl she and Sam would still have their lovely son. They had employed Maryan, treated her more like a daughter than an employee, and all the time she had betrayed them. She should not benefit from her betrayal.

She looked at the other two letters that lay on the floor in front of her, one addressed to Maryan herself. *No*. She should *not* have it. She picked up the envelope and began to tear it. Then she stopped, biting her lip in anguish. She couldn't do it. Couldn't destroy a letter that Marcus had entrusted to her. But what of the letter to the bank? She struggled with her conscience. These were his last wishes. How could she not obey them? And yet . . .

An hour later she was still sitting at her desk, the three envelopes before her, wrestling with her conscience, wondering what to do. Kitty, the little junior from the workroom, came in with a cup of tea.

'Four o'clock, Mrs Leigh,' she said, setting the cup down. 'Miss Gina said to tell you she's finished the sketches for the white ball gown if you'd like to come and have a look.'

The white fairy-tale ball gown with its sequin-encrusted bodice and bouffant skirt was to be the show's *pièce de résistance*, the climax of the collection. Rachel looked up at her. 'What? – Oh, right. Tell her I'll be through when I've had my tea.'

When the girl had gone she made up her mind. She would not go against Marcus's wishes. She would simply do – nothing. She opened a drawer and took out another large envelope. Into it she put her own letter and the two unopened ones. She sealed the envelope and wrote on it in large clear capitals: ONLY TO BE OPENED IN THE EVENT OF MY DEATH and signed it, Rachel Leigh.

Then she stowed it once again at the back of the bottom drawer of the filing cabinet.

Vincent had invited Maryan and Amy to join him and Roisan for Sunday lunch, and the moment they arrived at the little house in Notting Hill Roisan took Amy under her wing. She had always wanted a daughter and was enchanted by Maryan's, whom she thought pretty and intelligent. Amy, for her part, liked Roisan on sight. Plump and homely, she was the epitome of what a real mother should be, bustling round the big untidy kitchen in a flowered pinny with her grey-streaked auburn hair coming down and her face pink and shiny as she put the finishing touches to the meal.

'Come and give me a hand,' she invited the moment the formal introductions were done with. 'There's no better way of getting to know someone than over a kitchen stove. We'll leave these two to sit and drink sherry like the gentry.'

She hustled Amy downstairs into the semi-basement kitchen and invited her to lay the table while she took a large apple pie out of the oven. Showing her where to find cloth and cutlery she smiled encouragingly.

'I'm sure I don't have to tell you how to do it. You look a very domesticated kind of a girl to me.' As she returned to her cooking she said: 'Vinnie tells me you're going to St Hildred's in September. You'll love it there. I always say it's the best school a girl could go to. If I'd had a daughter myself that's where she'd have gone, so it is.'

Amy soon found she was enjoying herself. She loved Roisan's attractive Irish accent, and the wonderful aromas that filled the kitchen made her mouth water. She had felt instantly at home in the cosy, cluttered little house from the moment she entered it. Upstairs it was all well-worn carpets, their colours mellowed to delicate pastels, and squashy, chintz-covered chairs. But the big living-kitchen was a delight; warm and full of evocative smells. There was a big old-fashioned dresser full of willow-pattern dishes and a huge round Victorian table with Windsor chairs. In a tiled recess stood the Aga stove that Roisan declared she couldn't live without and the floor was covered by an assortment of home-made rugs, each with a history of its own. From the window over the sink there was a fascinating view of people's legs as they passed by in the street above. After half an hour there Amy recognised it, as many had before her, as a haven, the perfect place to escape, to.

'So – have you had a nice weekend with your mammy?' Roisan asked as she took the roast out of the oven.

'Oh yes, thank you.'

'Ah, you must have missed each other with you being evacuated all this time.' Roisan shook her head. 'War's a cruel thing, so it is, splitting up families. I know I missed my Colin. But I was lucky enough to get him back whole, thanks be to God.' She looked up with a smile. 'I hear you went to the theatre last night. Did you enjoy it?'

Amy nodded eagerly. 'It was lovely; a play called *Blithe Spirit*. It was all about a ghost.'

Roisan pulled a face. 'Ugh. I don't care for creepy things myself.'

'Oh no, it was funny,' Amy told her. 'This man married again after his wife died, you see. And his first wife came back to haunt them because she was jealous. There was this funny old lady in it who was a medium. She caused it all to happen when they had a seance.'

'Well, it sounds a bit of a pickle to me. But I'm glad you enjoyed it.'

'Oh, I did.' Amy looked up suddenly. 'I want to be an actress myself when I leave school.'

'Is that a fact?' Roisan straightened her shoulders and looked at Amy. 'Well, you've the looks for it, anyway.'

In actual fact Amy had surprised herself by the announcement that she wanted to be an actress. The notion had been there ever since the school play but she hadn't realised quite how strong the feeling was until last night. The moment she had walked into the theatre's

225

foyer with her mother and Vincent Donlan the exotic atmosphere had hit her. The sense of anticipation conjured by the mingled scents of coffee and cigar smoke had made a deep impression on her and when the curtain rose, sending out its exciting aroma of dust and size and revealing the glamorous drawing-room stage set for the play, she had been completely bowled over. The atmosphere in the theatre, steeped in glamour and tradition, had far surpassed that of the hall where they had performed the school play and as the evening progressed Amy had found herself yearning to be part of it. Back at Simons Mews, alone in her room, she had stood for a long time in front of the mirror, re-enacting some of Elvira's best scenes and thinking how much she would love to play the part of the naughty, wayward ghost. She was sure she could do it. She pictured herself floating across the stage in a dress of filmy grey, delicate and ethereal.

'And what makes you fancy a life on the boards?' Roisan was asking as she stirred the gravy.

Amy came out of her daydream and asked herself the same question. What *was* it? She frowned. It was hard to say. It would be lovely to be applauded and complimented; to have people love and admire you, not for who or what you were but for what you could do. Most of all, though, it would be wonderful to pretend to be someone else for a while. To slip out of your skin, and into another's. But not knowing how to put all this into words, all she said was: 'I don't really know.' She looked up at Roisan. 'I played Viola in *Twelfth Night* at school last term. I think I knew then that it was what I wanted to do.'

'Well, St Hildred's put on some grand plays when I was there,' Roisan said. 'I was never in any of them of course.' She chuckled. 'Put me on a stage and suddenly my hands and feet turn into shovels. My voice goes too. I sound like a squeaking mouse. And as for remembering lines . . .' She raised her eyes to the ceiling. 'My mind goes as blank as a stone wall. Ah, but you, now . . .' She smiled. 'That won't happen to you. I can tell already. Don't you look every inch the little actress? You'll be a great success.' She took a tureen of steaming vegetables out of the warming oven and carried it to the table, which she scanned with a practiced eye. 'Right now. I think that's everything. Will you go and get your mammy and that brother of mine to come and eat this food before it's stone cold.'

Later Vincent went with Maryan to see Amy onto the train for Suffolk. As they waved her off Maryan let out a sigh and Vincent looked at her.

'Don't be sad. It won't be long before she's back for good.'

She shook her head. 'It's not that.'

'What then? The weekend was a success, wasn't it? She seemed to enjoy the play last night. And she and Roisan got along like a house on fire.'

'Yes, so I noticed,' Maryan said ruefully. 'She opened up to your sister far more than to me.'

Vincent slipped an arm around her shoulders. 'You're worrying for nothing. I'm sure you are. It's bound to take time for you both to adjust. You said so yourself. Once you're together, sharing your life again, it'll all come right. I know it will.' He smiled at her. 'Tell you what, let's go and have a cup of tea somewhere. It'll help you relax.'

'No. I've got a better idea. Come back to the flat and let me make you one,' she said. 'It's the least I can do after the way you've helped me entertain Amy this weekend. If I'd been left on my own with her I'd have been at a loss. And that's partly what worries me. We don't seem to have a lot in common any more.'

At the flat Maryan put the kettle on and arranged cups on a tray. Vincent stood in the doorway watching her thoughtfully.

'You've never said much about your husband, Maryan. It must be difficult for Amy, losing her grandmother when her father died at such an early age.'

'Tom was killed in the Spanish Civil War.' Maryan said. 'Amy was only little. They were very close.'

'That's sad. Children can't unburden themselves like us and I think they often bottle things like that up for years.' He paused momentarily. 'Did I ever tell you that I had a wife once?'

She turned to look at him. It was odd but it had never occurred to her that he might have been married. 'What happened?' she asked. 'An accident? Did you lose her?'

'I lost her all right, but it wasn't an accident that took her,' he said. 'Fay left me after just two years. We met and married very quickly. It was just before I was called up in 1940. We hadn't much money but we didn't care. At least I didn't. I thought we'd work together after the war to build up the business and make a home. Fay obviously hadn't seen it that way. I'd no inkling of how dissatisfied she was until I came home on leave. For a while she put up a front of being glad to see me, but then it all came out: she'd met someone better looking and better off than me, and our marriage had been a ghastly mistake. And with that, off she went.'

'Oh, Vinnie, I'm so sorry. So you're divorced?'

He shook his head. 'Roisan and I were brought up strict Catholics.' He shrugged. 'Oh, we're not as devout as we were when our parents were alive, but there are certain rules ingrained into you that you just can't bring yourselves to break. Our church doesn't recognise divorce. Marriage is for life.'

'So you're still married to her?'

'Yes.' He took the tray from her and carried it through to the living room. When they were seated he went on: 'Not that my refusal to give her a divorce stopped Fay from going off to live with her wealthy businessman.'

'I see. Do you ever see or hear from her?'

'Only indirectly. He's in some kind of wholesale racket. I hear he's made a fortune out of the war. Black market – everything from cooking fat to petrol. He wangled his way out of being called up – don't ask me how – they've

228

lived their war in luxury on the fat of the land in some baronial hall in Virginia Water.'

'If you loved her I understand how bitter you must feel.' Maryan poured the tea and passed him a cup. 'But if you're still married and she ever wanted to come back to you . . .?' She was stopped by the look on his face.

'I wouldn't have her back if she came crawling to me on her bended knees,' he said vehemently.

Privately Maryan wondered what the point was of staying married if he felt so strongly, but she kept her opinion to herself. It seemed that this was turning out to be an evening for confessions, and maybe it was time she told Vinnie something more of her own past. 'There's something I'd like to tell you too, Vinnie.' She glanced up at him. 'And maybe when I do you'll see me in a different light.'

He smiled gently. 'Away with you. What could you possibly have done that would make me feel like that? You're not going to tell me you've a criminal record, are you?'

'No. I had Amy out of wedlock,' she said. 'At least, I was married, but not to her father. Tom knew when he married me that I was expecting another man's child. We'd known each other all our lives and he wanted to look after me. He was a good man. He and Amy were devoted to each other.'

Vincent reached out and took her hand. 'And – the other man? Amy's father?'

'He died in the war, fighting with the French Resistance. He was Jewish – Marcus Leigh, the son of my employers. There was never any way we could have been married. But I loved him very much, Vinnie. I always will.'

'Oh, my dear.' His face was gentle with compassion as he looked at her. 'And Amy?' he asked. 'Does she know about this?'

Maryan shook her head. 'Oh, no. She adored Tom. He was the only father she ever knew. There is no way I would ever spoil her memory of him. Even my mother never knew.'

He frowned. 'I'm not sure that's right, Maryan. Amy's not a little girl any longer. Don't you feel she has a right to know who she really is?'

'Tom was a good man. Any girl would have been lucky to have had him for a father,' Maryan said loyally. 'No. I'd rather leave things as they are.'

'And no one knows about this? I'm the only person you've told?'

She hesitated. 'I – did tell someone else. It was a terrible mistake. I told Mr and Mrs Leigh. It was after Marcus was killed. I thought they'd be happy to know that Amy was his – that part of him still lived on in her.'

He squeezed her hand. 'And – they weren't?'

'No. Mrs Leigh was horrified. In fact she refused to believe me – couldn't wait to get me out of the house. Mr Leigh was kinder. He found out where I was and came here later, offering to pay Amy's school fees. I think it was to salve his conscience.'

'Well, at least that's something. I hope you accepted.'

'I did. I couldn't have afforded St Hildred's fees otherwise. I thought about it and I felt Amy deserved a good education at least. But I can't tell her Mr Leigh is paying without explaining everything else to her.'

'So you've already had to lie to her?' Vincent sighed. 'Maryan – you're digging a hole for yourself. A hole that's going to get deeper. Don't you feel it would be better to make a complete clean breast of it? You want to make a new start with her after all, don't you?'

'Yes, but she'd never forgive me if I told her about Marcus. She'd despise me. I know she would.'

'Well, it's none of my business, really. It's up to you.' He lifted her hand to his lips and kissed her fingers lightly. 'All I know is that I was lucky to find you. You've fitted into the job and with Roisan and me so well that I feel you've always been with us, and I'd hate anything to happen to spoil that. Between the three of us I know we're going to make a great success of the business.' He raised her chin with one finger to look into her eyes. 'So, if there's ever anything worrying you that I can help with, I want you to promise you'll come to me.'

She smiled. 'I will, I promise, Vinnie.'

On 15 July the lights in the West End were ceremonially switched on again. Vincent, Roisan and Maryan went up to Piccadilly to witness the occasion. But they were celebrating more than the official end to the blackout. Just that day Vincent had had the firm's first whole house refurbishment confirmed. He'd come leaping up the stairs of the flat above the shop that morning while Maryan was making herself some breakfast, waving the letter excitedly.

'I never thought we'd get it,' he said, his eyes alight with success. 'They're a business couple. Their house overlooking Regent's Park was badly bomb-damaged and it's been closed up since 1943. Roisan and I went round it with them over six weeks ago and I'd just about given up on it. Their letter came by the first post.' He spread the letter out before her on the kitchen table. 'Look, they like the ideas and colour schemes we submitted and they want us to start as soon as possible. The builders have already started on the structural repairs.'

Catching some of his excitement, Maryan flushed with pleasure as she scanned the letter. 'Oh, Vinnie, I'm so pleased for you both.'

'For *us*, Maryan – all three of us. This will concern you too. When I get started on this job you will be in complete charge here, you know. My right-hand woman, in fact. In charge of the shop and the office. I'll be relying on you more than ever. In fact, if we do well we might soon have to take on an assistant for you.'

'I hope I can live up to your expectations. I'd hate to let you down,' Maryan said diffidently.

'Let me down? Never.' He laughed. 'Don't sell yourself short, Mrs Jessop. I've never known anyone pick up the business as quickly as you. You'll be just fine. Oh, I almost forgot.' He pulled another piece of paper out of his pocket. 'Roisan has a job to do next week. It's some kind of mannequin parade at the Royal Hamilton in Kensington. They want to hire a few pieces of antique furniture, just to set the atmosphere, and they've asked Roisan to dress the stage. I'll be sending a couple of men round with a van. They're to take that ormolu and marble console, the royal-blue velvet chaiselongue and the big Chinese vase.' He smiled. 'As a matter of fact Roisan wondered if you'd like to go along after the shop closes and give her a hand.'

'Of course I'll go,' Maryan said eagerly. 'I'd love to.'

Maryan was waiting outside the Royal Hamilton Hotel when Roisan arrived in a taxi, laden with bolts of material and various boxes and bags containing other things necessary for her work. She paid the driver and turned to Maryan, her face pink with exertion.

'I keep telling Vinnie, we'll have to get a van of our own now that the bookings are beginning to come in.' She handed a large cardboard box to Maryan. 'Carry that for me, will you, dear? I'll get a porter to fetch the rest of the stuff. It's so good of you to come.'

The hotel's Duchesse Ballroom had been hired for the occasion. It was an elegant room, decorated in white and silver. Maryan watched, fascinated, as Roisan unpacked the material she had brought and, with the help of two men lent by the hotel, arranged it in graceful drapes and loops to frame the platform at one end. Looking closely Maryan could see that it was only butter muslin, dotted with sequins, but, when it was lit it looked marvelously glamorous.

'You're a genius,' she told Roisan.

Vincent's sister shrugged off the compliment modestly. 'I've got a good supply of fabrics that are obtainable without coupons. And I know a theatrical costumier in Wardour Street that lets me have odds and ends cheap. It's surprising what you can do with a few bits and pieces. Heaven only knows I've had enough practice.'

She sighed. 'Roll on de-rationing. What I couldn't do if I had access to limitless fabrics.'

But Maryan was stunned with admiration. 'I can't believe you could do better than this,' she said, standing back to look at the results.

The furniture had already been delivered and between them they had arranged the console at the back of the stage with the Chinese vase on top, filled with an assortment of tall gilded grasses that Roisan had brought with her. The chaiselongue stood to one side of the stage with one of the gauzy drapes as a background. A catwalk had been erected and Roisan decorated its sides with more swags of her spangled muslin, caught up with blue satin.'

'These are their colours,' she told Maryan. 'Blue and silver. I understand it's a new designer they're launching – some wonderfully elegant gowns by all accounts. Just what most women are longing for after all the austerity.' She pulled a face. 'All those skimpy skirts and horrid military styles. Ugh.'

'I'd love to see it,' Maryan said. 'I used to work for a clothing firm – Feldman Fashions. And I agree with you about the styles. A bit of glamour would be nice for a change.'

Roisan laughed and tugged at her baggy slacks and well-washed jumper. 'Not really my thing, fashion. As if you hadn't guessed. But if you'd really like to come I've got a couple of complimentary tickets. If you can get Vinnie to stand in for you for an hour why don't you slip down and have a gander?' She opened her bulging handbag and rummaged about in it. 'Now where are they? I know I had them this morning. I must have – no, here they are.' Triumphantly, she produced the two blue and silver deckle-edged cards and handed them to Maryan. 'Here you are. Bring a friend if you want to. I understand all the buyers from the big shops will be here; a few film stars and actresses too, I shouldn't wonder. It might be fun just seeing who you can spot.'

But Maryan regretfully passed back the tickets. 'It's very good of you, Roisan, but I really can't take any time

233

off. Vinnie is going to a sale tomorrow. There are some pieces he badly wants for the Grahams' house. I'll be on my own at the shop all day.'

'Oh, what a pity. Oh well, never mind. Can't be helped. Perhaps I'll find someone else to give them to. Seems a shame to waste them.' Roisan pushed the tickets back into her bag and stood back to look at her finished work, her head on one side. 'The florists are coming first thing in the morning,' she said. 'Flowers will make all the difference. Still, I think it could do with something else – a finishing touch.' She chewed her lip thoughtfully. 'I know. There's a little Victorian wine table at the shop; a walnut one – remember?' Maryan nodded. 'It could stand at the end of the chaise with a posy bowl on it. Just the right touch, don't you think? Give the whole thing a lift.'

'Yes. I think you could be right.'

Roisan looked at her. 'Do you think you could bring it round in a taxi first thing in the morning, Maryan?' she asked, smiling sweetly. 'Charge Vinnie up for overtime. Tell him I said so.'

Maryan was up early next morning. She went down to the shop and brought out the wine table, then rang for a taxi. While she was waiting she snatched a quick breakfast and was waiting by the door, the delicate little table shrouded in a soft baize cloth, when the cab turned into the mews. At the Royal Hamilton the driver looked at her enquiringly.

'Don't you want me to wait, miss?' She shook her head.

'I want to see the table safely in place. I've plenty of time. I can get a bus back.'

In the ballroom the florists were already at work. Small gilt chairs had been laid out around the catwalk and the buffet table at the back was already spread with a snowy cloth ready to take the delicacies the caterers would bring later. Maryan unwrapped the little walnut table and put it in place at the side of the stage, then went to tell one of the florists what Roisan wanted, warning them that the table was valuable and to be extra careful not to spill any water on the surface. Finally, looking at her watch and seeing that it was a quarter to nine, she hurried out into the foyer.

A uniformed commissionaire was setting up a board in the entrance lobby, close to the revolving door. As Maryan stepped in and began to push the door she caught sight of the blue and silver poster advertising the fashion show and the breath caught in her throat. The name that had caught her eye. She must have been mistaken. It couldn't possibly have said what she thought it did. Instead of stepping out into the street she followed the door round and stepped out once more into the entrance lobby to stare at the words on the board.

THE MARCUS LEIGH COLLECTION
12.30 in The Grand Duchess Ballroom
Launching an exciting collection of haute couture
by a brilliant new designer
Proceeds to go to Jewish orphans and victims of war

The name seemed to spring out at her. She had *not* been mistaken after all. For a moment the words on the board swam together and she put out a hand to steady herself against the wall. The doorman took her arm.

'Are you all right, madam? Can I get you anything?'

She looked at the man and shook her head. 'No – no thank you. I felt a little dizzy but I'm all right now.'

'Can I call you a cab?'

'No – well, yes. Perhaps I will. Just this once.'

As she sped back to Simons Mews in the back of the taxi Maryan's mind began to stop reeling with the shock of what she had seen and the one vitally important fact emerged. Marcus. Marcus was *alive*. The man who had brought news of his death must have been mistaken. It must have been someone else who had been caught and executed. She had heard of other cases of mistaken identity. It happened often in wartime. Her heart was overwhelmed with joy and relief. To think that this very afternoon Marcus would be no more than a short

235

bus-ride away from her. She must see him. Somehow she must find the time to go back to the hotel. Vinnie would understand. Oh, to think that in a few hours she would see him again. Marcus – the only man she had ever loved. Alive and free. Perhaps their time had come. At last fate was going to allow them to be together.

At the end of the mews she paid the driver and hurried along the cobbled road to the shop. Vincent was just arriving; letting himself in with his key. He looked at her and saw at once that something had happened.

'Maryan?' His eyes looked into hers enquiringly. 'My dear girl, what is it?'

'Can we go inside?' she asked breathlessly. 'I've got something to tell you – and to ask. A very big favour.'

'Well, of course.'

Inside the shop Vincent put away his keys and looked at her. 'Will this do, or would you like to go into the office?'

'Oh, Vinnie. I've just had such a shock,' she burst out. 'I don't know how to begin. It's – it's a *miracle*.'

He smiled wryly and locked the shop door again. 'In that case I think it'd better be the office,' he said. 'And I've a feeling we're both going to have need of my medicinal brandy.'

He closed the office door and took the bottle of brandy and two glasses out of the filing cabinet. Right,' he said, pouring two measures. 'Fire away.'

Maryan eased herself into a chair. 'The fashion show I helped Roisan prepare for . . .'

'Yes?' He pushed the glass towards her across the desk.

'This morning I took that walnut wine table along. Roisan said it would look nice with . . .'

'Never mind the wine table. What happened?'

She swallowed hard and caught her lower lip between her teeth as she looked at him, her eyes wide and luminous with wonder. 'My *God*, Vinnie. I still can't believe it. When I was coming out of the hotel I saw the poster, advertising the show in the foyer. The new designer they're launching is – is *Marcus*. Marcus Leigh.'

He stopped, his glass halfway to his lips. 'Isn't that the man who . . .?'

'Yes – *yes*, Vinnie. The man I loved – love. Amy's father. I thought he was dead. Do you see what it means?'

'I do indeed. So why are you here, girl? What are you doing, sitting here telling me about it?'

'I don't know.' She shook her head and laughed shakily. 'What shall I do, Vinnie?'

'Get yourself back there, girl. Go and grab him. And this time don't let anything happen to get in your way – no matter what.' He got up from behind the desk. 'I'll hold the fort here. Go and make yourself look marvellous. Not that you need it.' He smiled at her. 'I only wish I could put a look like that in some girl's eyes. But put on your glad rags anyway and get yourself over there.'

At the door she paused. 'The sale. What about the sale you wanted to go to?'

He waved an impatient hand at her. 'I'll go to the sale, don't you worry about it. Roisan will come and look after the shop for a few hours. Leave all that to me.'

When Maryan came down from the flat Vincent already had a taxi waiting at the door. As he handed her into the back and gave the driver the name of the hotel he put his head in at the open window.

'Good luck,' he said softly. 'I'll be thinking about you.'

'Goodbye, Vinnie. And thanks,' she said.

In the foyer of the Royal Hamilton Hotel Maryan sat reading a magazine and looking up every time anyone passed through. By the time midday came guests were beginning to assemble and at twenty past they began to make their way through to the Duchesse Ballroom. Maryan got up and followed them, wishing she had taken Roisan up on her offer of tickets. At the door the liveried attendant looked at her enquiringly and with an assurance she hadn't known she possessed, she said: 'I'm with the staff.'

The man smiled and waved her through.

Now that the room was finished it looked magnificent. There were floral decorations everywhere, echoing the theme of blue and silver: tall delphiniums and love-in-a-mist, white roses and lilac, set off by silver-grey and dark green foliage. The food on the buffet table looked delicious and waiters in immaculate white jackets stood waiting with trays of champagne. It was all very grand. Maryan stood at the back and tried to make herself as inconspicuous as possible. There was no sign of Marcus, or of any other member of the Leigh family. But then they had probably come into the hotel by a rear entrance and were busy attending to the last-minute details, she told herself.

She waited while the guests mingled, ate and chattered. As Roisan had suggested she might, she glimpsed one or two well–known faces. A waiter approached her with a tray of canapés and she took one, more to occupy her hands than to eat.

At last the guests were invited to take their seats. The stage at the far end of the ballroom was subtly lit, making Roisan's spangled drapes glitter like star-sprinkled cobwebs. Soft romantic music began to play. Then onto the stage stepped a woman. She wore a long gown of blue velvet trimmed with silver sequins. Maryan took a step forward, peering at her. It was Rachel. But a very different Rachel from the one she had last seen at Hazelfield last year. This Rachel looked slimmer and carried herself proudly. The dark hair, always previously worn in a heavy plaited coil on the nape of her neck, was cut in a short, fashionable style, the white streak at the front caught back with a diamanté clip. She wore discreet and becoming make-up: her cheeks delicately rouged and her lips enhanced by a rosy lipstick. Maryan realised with surprise that if she had passed her in the street she would not have known her.

Rachel began to speak: 'Ladies and gentlemen, I can't tell you what enormous pleasure it gives me to be here this afternoon, and to introduce with great pride the Marcus Leigh Collection which I sincerely hope you will

238

all like. As some of you will know, Marcus was my son – my only son – who died bravely fighting with the French Resistance movement shortly before the war ended. What you are about to see was his inspired vision for the post–war fashion world, which I am proud to have been able to complete and present to you today. The proceeds of this show are to go to the cause that was so very close to his heart: Jewish children, orphaned by the war. The clothes you are about to see were designed exclusively by him and dedicated to his beloved late wife, Jessica. And so, I will now hand you over to your commère, a lovely lady who needs no introduction from me; actress and singer, Madeleine Clare.'

Rachel stepped aside as a curtain swung back to reveal the glamorously dressed actress. 'Ladies and gentlemen. I give you – the Marcus Leigh Collection.'

Madeleine Clare introduced the first model who paused, turned and then began to parade forward down the catwalk. She wore a stunning suit in garnet-red velvet, which was unlike anything the audience had seen before. The skirt swirled around the models's shapely calves and the jacket was nipped in to the tiny waist with a flared peplum. With it she wore a wide-brimmed hat, tipped saucily over one eye and decorated with a huge black silk rose. Gasps of approval were followed by a flutter of applause and journalists at the back of the hall began to scribble furiously in their notebooks.

But Maryan hardly saw any of it. Crushing disappointment and despair floored her like a blow from a pole-axe. How could she have persuaded herself that Marcus was alive? She should have known that Rachel might do something of this sort in her son's memory. To think that she had prepared so excitedly to come here, expecting to see him – all the time savouring the notion that he was no more than a couple of miles away.

Her heart thudding in her chest, blinded by tears, she stumbled out of the ballroom and through the hotel foyer, oblivious to the curious looks that followed her. Out in the street she stood for a moment, taking deep draughts of the fresh air until her heartbeat steadied and the feeling of suffocation that had threatened to overwhelm her gradually began to ease. Then she began to walk slowly back in the direction of Chelsea. At Simons Mews she let herself into the flat quietly by the side door and climbed the stairs with feet that felt like lead. Without taking off her outdoor things she sat in the living room staring at the wall. When Marcus died she had been unable to show her grief. Then, after a while it was as though a skin had formed over an unhealed wound. Today at the hotel that skin had been ripped away, leaving the raw wound to bleed and agonise afresh. The tears she had suppressed all those months before began to flow like a river. It was like being torn apart by a pain so terrible she thought – *wished* she might die of it. Unheeded, the afternoon and evening wore on and the light began to fade. Maryan, her tears drying on her swollen face, sat staring unseeingly at the patterns on the carpet. Overcome by an apathy that drained every ounce of strength from her, she sat on, too weary to get up and change – too stiff with misery and weak with grief to move.

When the door slammed and Vincent called from the bottom of the stairs she didn't even hear him. It was as though she was no longer part of her surroundings – strangely detached – oblivious. When he burst into the room and shouted her name she gave a shuddering start, her eyes opening wide as she looked up into his startled face through the gathering gloom.

'*Maryan*. Good God, girl, what's wrong?' He was at her side. 'Roisan came home and said you hadn't come back. I had a feeling. I was worried so I thought . . .' He had touched one of her hands and found it icy cold. 'Christ almighty, girl, you're like an iceberg.' He began to chafe her hands between his own. 'What in the world is the matter with you?'

Her dry lips began to move stiffly and she heard her voice as though from a long way off. She found it impossible to keep her teeth from chattering so that speech was difficult and disjointed. 'I – was wrong. He's not ... Marcus was dead all the time. It – his mother's show. He ... should have known he wasn't ...' She looked at him and he winced at the pain he saw in her eyes. 'I've been such a fool. I thought – I really *believed* that Marcus was alive – thought I was going to see him. I – I ...' Her voice broke and helpless tears began to slip down her cheeks again.

Swallowing hard at the lump in his own throat, Vincent caught her to him and held her close.

'Oh, my dear. My dear girl. How long have you been sitting here like this, all alone, going through this agony?' He held her away from him and looked into her tear-stained face. 'All afternoon, by the look of you. Why didn't you go down and talk to Roisan?'

She shook her head. 'I couldn't – couldn't tell anyone. Didn't want to see anyone.'

'Never mind. I'm here now. Will you come back to Roisan's with me? Let us take care of you?'

'No. Leave me. I'll be all right.'

'Then I'll stay here. You're in no state to be by yourself. Now ...' He pulled her to her feet and began to pull her towards the door. 'I'll get you something to eat while you get out of those clothes and have a warm bath. You're frozen stiff. It's the shock, I daresay.'

He ran the bath for her and put a hot water bottle in her bed, chivvying her like a mother hen. Her white face and hollow-eyed appearance had frightened him. When she was in bed and he'd managed to get her to drink some hot tea and eat a piece of buttered toast he was relieved to see that she began to look a little better. He took the cup and saucer from her. 'Have you got any sleeping tablets?' She shook her head and he looked down at her apprehensively. 'Maybe I should call a doctor. You need a sedative of some sort.'

'I told you, Vinnie. I'll be all right.'

'Do you think you can sleep?'

'I feel I'll never sleep again. And yet I feel so weary.' She looked up at him. 'It's as though I'm losing them all over again – Tom, Mum, Marcus. As though I'm being punished. I'm so afraid of the future. What if Amy . . .'

He sat down on the bed and took her in his arms. 'You still have Amy,' he said. 'You and she will be all right. You'll see. And for what it's worth, Maryan, you still have me. Maybe you haven't realised it yet, and maybe this isn't exactly the right time to be telling you, but you mean a great deal to me, my dear. A very great deal.' He looked into her face with a mixture of love and apprehension and to his relief he saw that she was smiling.

'Oh, Vinnie, you're so good to me. Without you I might have . . .'

'No.' He shook his head at her. 'No. You're far too strong and far too sensible for that. I'm grateful that I found you, Maryan. And that I was able to be here when you needed me. But you're a born survivor.'

She reached up her arms and put them round his neck, and when he kissed her she felt a sense of peace. The deep ache of her hurt seemed to soften and begin to melt as she returned his kiss. 'Stay with me,' she whispered, her cheek against his. 'I don't want to be alone. Stay with me, Vinnie. Just hold me. Don't let me think.'

'You're sure? Really sure?'

'I'm sure.'

Without a word he undressed and slipped into bed beside her, holding her warm and close in his arms, stroking her soft hair and caressing her trembling body. When she pressed closer to him and he felt desire harden him he drew away and looked apologetically into her eyes.

'Maryan – I'd better not stay. If I do . . .'

'I know,' she whispered. 'And it's all right – really.'

He made love to her slowly and gently, as though she were made of something infinitely fragile. He felt a mixture of guilt and wistfulness. Earlier today he'd thought he'd lost her – that he would never have the chance or the right to tell her how he felt. And to his everlasting shame his heart had actually lifted when he had first learned that she'd been mistaken about Marcus Leigh.

And now – was he taking advantage of her vulnerability, or helping her to shut out what was too painful to think about? Either way he wished it could have been different. In his secret dreams he had imagined how it would be, making love to her for the first time. It had not been like this. In his dream she had been all his – wanting and needing no one but him. It had been *his* name she had called out at the height of their lovemaking instead of the name of another. In his dream love for him had made her eyes sparkle and glow like fire. But when his passion was spent and he looked lovingly into them now he saw only the brightness of bitter unshed tears.

Chapter Eleven

Amy had been packing to leave Rhensham when the news broke that atom bombs had been dropped on Nagasaki and Hiroshima. Almost immediately the Japanese had surrendered and everyone breathed a sigh of relief. At last the war was well and truly over. The enormity of the devastation caused by the bombs or the implications for future peace escaped most of the war-weary public, to whom the end of the war meant only one thing. Life could return to normal – but not so for Amy. To her, normality was about to be shattered. She must leave behind her beloved Rhensham, her school and all her friends to return to live in London for good. In spite of the euphoria all around her, her spirits failed to rise to the occasion.

Four months later, with her first term at St Hildred's coming to a close, she still hadn't become used to the changes in her life. School was perhaps the most acceptable part. At first she'd found it strange. The whole atmosphere was so very different from her previous school. To begin with she'd felt slightly in awe of the nuns, walking on silent feet with heads bowed like medieval saints. Their soft-voiced sternness had unnerved her to begin with. But she soon found that they were kind and fair, and exerted their very positive authority only where it was needed. She found them gifted and interesting teachers, too, and enjoyed her lessons very much.

It was making friends that she found difficult. Whether it was intentional or not she had no way of knowing, but the other girls seemed to her to shut her out. They had their own little cliques, none of which she was invited to join, and because of this she'd been desperately lonely until half term when a new girl arrived at St Hildred's and changed everything.

The new arrival, who was placed in Amy's form, was called Celia Frazer and Amy took to her on sight. She had long blonde plaits, mischievous blue eyes and a wide, expressive mouth. Finding themselves seated at the same desk and each being in need of an ally, the two girls struck up an instant friendship.

Over lunch on their first day together Celia told Amy that her parents had recently parted and were planning to be divorced. She explained that she and her mother had come to London, leaving her father in the Midlands where he worked as stage manager at a repertory theatre.

'When Dad came out of the army he and Mum used to row all the time,' Celia said dispassionately. 'It was horrible. They just couldn't seem to hit it off at all. Mum and I had such a nice time on our own while the war was on. Once Dad came home for good it was awful, rows all the time. He was a staff sergeant and Mum used to say he thought he was still in the army and he could boss us about like he did the soldiers.'

'Did you mind them breaking up?' Amy asked.

Celia sighed. 'I miss him – actually. It used to be such fun when he came home on leave. I always thought it would be lovely, having him home again for good. It's nice to have some peace again, though. I hated it when they kept shouting at each other.'

'You weren't evacuated while the war was on then?'

'Oh no.' Celia took a bite of her sandwich. 'We were able to stay in Northmere. Hardly any bombing there. Quite boring really. But Mum comes from London, so when she and Dad parted she wanted to come back.'

'I was evacuated to Suffolk,' Amy told her. 'So I hardly saw anything of my mother.'

'It must be nice to be together again.'

'Not really. We didn't see each other very often during the war and it's hard getting to know each other again.'

'Is it?' Celia looked at her. 'What about your dad then? He in the army too, was he?'

'He was killed before it started,' Amy said, fighting down the urge to say that he was killed fighting with the French Resistance. 'Mum works for a man who has an antique shop in Chelsea. She practically runs it for him. I don't really see much of her even now, even though we live in the flat above it.'

Celia nodded. 'My mum's got a job too. She's a secretary. She works in Southampton Street for a magazine called *London's Pride*. Perhaps you've heard of it.'

Amy had. She told Celia that Decor Vincente had recently placed an advertisement in it. It seemed to give the two girls yet another thing in common.

'Your mum got a boyfriend?' Celia asked conversationally. 'Mine has this old chap who's always coming round. His name is Reg Thornton. Mum doesn't really like him much. We often have a laugh about him. But he owns one of those toffee-nosed grocery shops and he brings us lovely things to eat, chocolate biscuits and ham and jars of crystallised ginger, stuff like that – off points, of course.' She grinned. 'So we put up with him.'

'How old is he?' Amy asked.

'Oooh . . .' Celia considered, pulling her mouth into a speculative pout. '*Ever* so old – at least forty. He's even got a bald patch.' She giggled. 'He was a lieutenant in the army – catering corps, and his father kept the shop going till he came out. It's in Fulham.'

Encouraged by her new friend's easy openness, Amy said: 'My mum is quite friendly with her boss.'

Celia took a bite out of her apple and looked up. 'Is that this whatshisname, Vincente bloke?'

'Yes. His name is Vincent Donlan, but Mum calls him Vinnie.'

'Is he nice – handsome and all that?'

Amy shrugged. 'Not what *I'd* call handsome. Quite old

too, like yours. He tried to get me to call him Uncle Vinnie, but I won't.' She gave an effective shudder. 'Sometimes I wonder if they might get married.'

'Really?' Celia paused and looked at her enquiringly. 'How would you feel about that?'

Amy pulled a face. She didn't know Celia quite well enough yet to confide her very real misgivings on the subject. 'Don't know really,' she said.

In truth Amy was quite disturbed by the idea. Since she had been at Simons Mews she and her mother had grown even more like strangers than before, seeing little of each other as they went their separate ways each day to school and work. They ate together in the evenings and then separated once again, Amy to her homework, Maryan to her book-keeping or some household job.

It was partly Amy's fault, she acknowledged unrepentantly and with a certain amount of satisfaction. Maryan was always trying to draw her out, but she stubbornly refused to respond, blocking Maryan's every attempt to find a point of contact. Deep inside she was still paying her back for not telling her that Marcus Leigh was her father.

Sometimes she was tempted to give in, to unfreeze a little and be more friendly, knowing that life would be infinitely more comfortable if she did. But somehow, having started her campaign of unyielding silence, her pride wouldn't let her stop.

When she first rejoined her mother she had considered the options. Either she confessed that she had overheard her mother's dramatic revelation to the Leighs, or she kept quiet in the hope that Maryan would one day volunteer the information herself. In fact neither had happened. The secret stood between them like a barrier, unspoken and unresolved, driving an ever deepening wedge between them with each day that passed.

Amy was still bitterly resentful. There was so much she wanted to know about her father. She felt cheated. Having been unaware that he was her father until after his death, she felt that the least her mother could have done was to talk to her about him. But Maryan remained silent on the subject. It seemed she had once again made herself a new and absorbing life here at Simons Mews. She ran the antique shop and the office, doing things Amy had no idea she was capable of. And when Vincent came around they would be closeted together for hours on end, obviously close, sharing jokes that Amy couldn't join in and talking about things of which she knew nothing. Sometimes Vincent took them out, to a film or the theatre. But lately Amy had refused to go, convinced that they would rather be alone anyway. She had a *feeling* about them. It was as though they shared something of which she had no part. She felt in the way.

Some evenings Maryan brought the books and the typewriter upstairs to the flat and worked through the evening in a vain attempt at companionship. Tapping away or totting up figures, she was totally unaware of how excluded Amy felt, sitting at her corner of the table with her homework. Separated by only a couple of feet of carpet, they were as far apart as it was possible to be.

Often in the early weeks there were times when Amy felt achingly homesick for Rhensham and the easy, relaxed relationship she had shared with the Taylors, especially Mike. But she knew that those days were gone and would never come again. On the day she had left, Marjorie had assured her that she would always be welcome at Mitcham Lodge. But Mike would be going away to college next year, where he would no doubt make new friends. Captain Taylor was home now and they were doing their best to pick up the pieces of family life as near as possible to where they had left off. Wallowing in self-pity, Amy felt that, like the war, she was a closed chapter. The one thing that everyone wanted to forget. She belonged to a segment of their lives that they were all trying to put behind them.

Mike wrote to her every week to begin with, but as the months went by his letters grew shorter and the time between them lengthened. She felt like an outsider, abandoned and unwanted. At least, she had until she met Celia.

From that first day their friendship grew. As Christmas drew near excitement mounted at St Hildred's. There was to be a play and a concert, but much to their disgust neither of them was invited to take part in either. Only the fifth and sixth forms were allowed to be in the Christmas entertainment. But they were both selected to sing in the junior choir for the carol service. It was to take place on the last day of term in the school chapel and the parents were invited. Amy and Celia commiserated with each other when they both learned that their respective mothers would be working and unable to attend. To make up for it they threw themselves wholeheartedly into the rehearsals, gaining praise and appreciation from Sister Josephine, the music mistress.

Then, one morning just a week before the end of term, Celia arrived at school with a long face.

'You'll never guess what,' she said gloomily. 'My mum wants me to go and stay with Dad for Christmas.'

'Whatever for?' Amy asked.

'Dad's met this new woman and he's planning to marry her when the divorce comes through. Her name's *Candice*,' she said scathingly. 'Did you ever *hear* anything so pathetic? Mum says he wants me to go and meet her. But I happen to know that's not the real reason,' she added darkly.

'So – what is?'

'It's 'cause rotten old Reggie-boy has asked Mum to go to Scotland with him, *that's* why. I heard her talking to him about it on the phone last night. They've got it all planned. They're going to stay in an hotel.'

'It sounds lovely. Couldn't you go too?'

'Haven't been asked, have I?' Celia said. 'They want to get rid of me so that they can be by themselves. I expect they want to sleep together.'

'Oh, surely not. They're not married,' Amy said naively.

Celia gave her a pitying look. 'Oh, *be* your age, Amy.

What about your mum and this Vinnie bloke? I bet they do.'

Amy coloured. 'Of course they don't. I'd know, wouldn't I? I live there.'

'Not all the time, you don't. It doesn't have to be at night, you know. They can do it any time. Sometimes I think grown-ups are *vile*.' She kicked savagely at the cloakroom skirting board. 'Mum and I were happy till he came poking his nose in,' she said, her lower lip thrust out to prevent it from trembling. 'I don't know how she can – imagine doing it with someone with a *bald* patch. If you ask me, lousy rotten *men* ruin everything.'

Amy looked thoughtful. 'You've probably got it all wrong. Look, if you don't want to go to your dad's I daresay you could come to us. It'll probably be boring, but at least we could make our own fun.'

Celia looked brighter for a moment, then her jaw dropped again. 'Dad did write to invite me, so I suppose I've got to go. Anyway, I would *quite* like to see him. And if I don't he'll blame Mum.' For a moment the two girls looked glumly at each other, then Celia said: 'Hey, *I* know – shall I ask if you can come too?'

Amy looked doubtful. 'Oh, but wouldn't that be a bit of a cheek?'

'I don't see why,' Celia said defiantly. 'After all, Dad will have this ghastly *Candice* person, so why shouldn't I have someone too?'

'Well – I won't ask Mum till you've asked yours,' Amy said cautiously. 'Just in case.'

But the following morning Celia arrived at school wreathed in smiles. 'It's okay,' she announced. 'Mum thought it was a marvellous idea. She phoned Dad and asked him and he's happy too. He'll be busy at the theatre with the Christmas show, so he'll be pleased for me to have a friend for company.'

Amy felt a little thrill of excitement. 'I'll ask Mum tonight.'

'No need.' Celia grinned. 'My mum is ringing her this morning. She can be very persuasive, can Mum. It'll be all right, you just see.' She grasped Amy's arm. 'We're to go up to Northmere by train on the twenty-second. That's on Saturday – so you'd better start packing tonight.'

But Maryan had reservations about letting her daughter go to Northmere for Christmas. When Amy arrived home from school, bubbling with excitement and wanting to know if Mrs Frazer had telephoned, she found her mother looking anxious and doubtful.

'I know you want to be with your new friend,' Maryan said. 'But we don't really know these people at all, do we?'

Amy scowled with resentment. 'We didn't know the Taylors when I went to Rhensham, did we?'

'That was different, Amy. The war was on. We didn't have any choice.'

'Yes, it *was* different,' Amy pointed out. 'I was there with them for over five years and I'm only going to Celia's dad's for a week.'

'It's quite a long way too,' Maryan persisted, ignoring the argument.

'Only an hour and a half on the train – about the same as Suffolk.'

Maryan sighed. 'It's the first Christmas we've been together for such a long time, Amy,' she said. 'I thought you would be looking forward to it as much as I am. We've been invited to go to Roisan's.'

Amy felt slightly relieved. 'Oh, well – there you are then. You won't be on your own, will you?'

'Would it have worried you if I had been? Anyway, that's not really the point.' Maryan looked directly at her and Amy coloured and turned away. 'Amy – what's wrong?' Maryan reached out to touch the girl's shoulder. 'It's nearly five months now since you came home and we haven't really settled down together at all, have we?'

'Haven't we?' Amy shrugged.

'You know we haven't. We don't even talk to each other properly, do we?'

'What would we talk about?' Amy asked sullenly,

shrugging off her mother's hand. 'There's nothing to say, is there?'

'Of course there is,' Maryan protested. 'I'm interested in what you're doing at school. I thought you might be interested in what I'm doing too. You seemed to be interested in the shop when Vinnie showed you round that time.'

'It's all right,' Amy said laconically. She turned and looked at her mother. 'Are you saying I can't go to Celia's dad's then, or what?'

Maryan sighed. 'All I'm saying is . . .'

'He's a stage manager at the Theatre Royal in Northmere,' Amy interrupted. 'Celia says he'll take us behind the scenes and everything. And we'll have free seats for the Christmas show. They're doing *The Sleeping Beauty*. Oh, *please* let me go, Mum.'

Maryan looked at Amy's shining eyes and pleading expression. If she were to say yes, would it improve the sadly impaired relationship between them? She sometimes felt she'd do anything to get closer to this strangely aloof young person who was her daughter. She had hoped that Christmas might bring them closer. The special present she'd chosen with such care; a visit to a West End pantomime; Christmas Day at Roisan's. Amy had taken to Vinnie's sister. She was always at her best when they went there. She'd planned it all so carefully. But it seemed that all Amy wanted was to spend the holiday in some sooty little industrial town in the Midlands with people she hardly knew. Well – if it meant so much to her . . .

'All right then,' she said. 'But if you . . .' Amy didn't wait to hear the rest of the sentence. With a yelp of delight she was already on her way to her bedroom to begin packing.

The Frazers' home was a rambling Regency villa in the centre of the town. It was one of three such villas which stood at the end of the town's best shopping street. It wasn't at all what Amy had imagined and she wondered why they had lived in such a large house.

'It was my gran's house,' Celia explained as the girls unpacked. 'When she got too old to manage it and moved to a smaller house Mum and Dad moved in here. Gran used to take in lodgers; mostly actors from the theatre, and Mum did that too when we lived here.

Celia's father, a stout, rather harassed looking man with a thatch of sandy hair and the same blue eyes as Celia, had met them at the station, brought them home to Arncliffe House and left again in a hurry, explaining that he was due at the theatre for a matinée. Celia took Amy upstairs to her old room, which they were to share. It was a large room on the second floor. From the dormer window there was a wonderful view over the roof-tops to the park and the river beyond. There were two single beds, pushed under the sloping ceiling; between them were shelves on which sat several rather battered dolls and teddies as well as a dozen or more books. Kneeling on the floor, Amy looked at the titles – *Winnie The Pooh*; *Just William*; *Alice in Wonderland* – all of them well remembered favourites.

'Didn't you want to take any of these with you?' she asked. Celia shrugged. 'Mum said there wasn't room. Anyway, they're a bit babyish, aren't they? I'm reading *Forever Amber* at the moment. I'll lend it to you when I've finished it if you like.' She finished her unpacking and held out her hand. 'Come on, I'll show you the rest of the house.'

Amy was impressed. She liked the wide staircase with its elegant curved balustrade, the long windows and the high moulded ceilings. The place had a romantic air of faded grandeur that appealed to her imagination.

There were six bedrooms, most of them now shrouded in dust sheets. Downstairs, on either side of the spacious hallway, there were a dining room and an enormous drawing room that ran the whole length of the house, with a large window at each end and a massive marble fireplace.

'We used to have parties in here,' Celia told her. 'At weekends. While the war was on Mum used to have a lot

of American friends. It was good fun. But when Dad
came home all that changed. He doesn't like parties
much and I think he was a bit jealous. Once he accused
Mum of – you know – *carrying on.*'

'And – did she?' Amy asked.

Celia looked thoughtful. 'I don't think so. I never saw
anything. Mind you, one of them used to bring her an
awful lot of presents, and when men give women presents
it usually only means one thing.'

'What's that?' Amy asked.

Celia gave her a pitying look. 'Oh, *be* your age, Amy.
Services rendered and all that. Like old baldy Reg.
Anyway, Mum used to say how was she to know that
Dad hadn't been carrying on while he was away?'

She led the way back out into the hall and closed the
door. 'It looks as though Dad only uses the kitchen now
he's on his own. I don't blame him. It's the warmest
place in the house. It's hard to keep a place this size
warm in the winter. I expect you've noticed. He'll probably sell up when the divorce comes through. That's what
Mum says anyway. Then perhaps we'll have some money
again.'

Later Celia's father came home again, bringing with
him his new girlfriend, Candice, who, it turned out, was
the new wardrobe mistress at the theatre. She was a little
mouse of a woman with blonde hair and pinched features.
Her nose was pink as though she suffered from a permanent cold. She wore a mouse-coloured fur coat and a
chiffon scarf over her hair. And she carried a bulging
shopping bag, which she began to unpack onto the
kitchen table.

Celia nudged Amy. 'She looks like Mrs Tiggywinkle,'
she whispered.

Celia's father, less harassed now that the matinee was
over, turned out to be quite jovial, and Amy noticed for
the first time that he spoke with a slight Scottish accent.
He insisted that she must call him Jock, which she found
acutely embarrassing until later, when she discovered
that theatre people hardly ever used surnames at all.

Candice took off her coat to reveal an unfashionable mustard-coloured wool dress. The scarf had flattened the limp blonde hair so that it clung to her head like damp cotton wool. From the shopping bag she unpacked the ingredients for a surprisingly good meal, which she cooked and served to the four of them in the barn-like kitchen where a huge black range threw out a welcome heat. Jock Frazer kept up a flow of cheerful chatter all through the meal, questioning Celia about her new school and commenting on how much she'd grown, trying unsuccessfully to drag the obviously shy Candice into the conversation. As soon as the meal was over he and Candice left for the theatre once again, leaving the girls to clear away.

Celia looked ruefully at Amy as they shared the washing-up. 'A good thing you came with me,' she said. 'Wouldn't have been a barrel of fun on my own by the looks of it.'

That night, enjoying the novelty of sharing a room, the girls lay talking long after the light was out.

'Have you got a boyfriend?' Celia asked.

'No. Well, not unless you count Mike,' Amy said.

'Mike? Who's he? You've never mentioned him before,' Celia said eagerly.

'Michael Taylor. He's seventeen and he's going to college in the new year. He wants to be a journalist like his father. He's the son of the lady I was evacuated with in Suffolk.'

'Wow, *seventeen*,' Celia said, impressed. 'Is he handsome? Has he kissed you?'

'I suppose he is *quite* handsome,' Amy said thoughtfully. 'No, he's never kissed me. I've known him since I was seven. He's more like a brother than a boyfriend.'

'Got any photos?

'Yes, I've got some snaps at home.'

'You *must* show me when we go back. There used to be a boy here that I liked,' Celia said wistfuly. 'I thought I might see him this Christmas. He's probably found someone else by now, though.' She raised herself to lean on one elbow, peering at Amy through the darkness. 'What did you think of Candice Tiggywinkle then?'

'She's all right. She's a good cook.'

'Well, she must have *something*, I suppose,' Celia said scathingly. 'Dad seems besotted. Did you notice, his eyes went all gooey when he looked at her. God knows why. I think she's really wet. Can't see what he sees in her. Mum is much prettier – *and* smarter. That awful dress. I wonder if they'll really get married,' she mused. 'Hey – Amy, I've just had a gruesome thought – do you think she and Dad are too old to have more babies?' But Amy wasn't thinking at all. She'd fallen asleep.

What had started out as a slight disappointment for Amy turned into a week of sheer delight. The Christmas show at the Theatre Royal was to open on Boxing Day and Jock took both girls along to the dress rehearsal on the afternoon of Christmas Eve. Going in through the stage door, Amy found herself in a strange new world. Above her head, surrounded by a wooden gallery, was the scenic studio, from which the smell of varnish, paint and size floated down. Down a flight of stairs she found herself in a corridor with numbered doors – dressing rooms, she was told. The corridor gave onto the huge, cluttered prop room, which was like an Aladdin's cave, containing everything you could possibly imagine from table lamps to fire irons. In one corner she saw a rocking horse and an elephant's foot umbrella holder. In another hung a human skeleton, draped in an old net curtain. This was Jock Frazer's domain. He introduced Amy to his band of stage hands; a cheerful group of men in shirtsleeves who showed Amy their own designated corner with a card table and gas ring where they brewed up tea and played cards between acts.

From the prop room they stepped out into the area that was the stage. Amy looked up to a forest of ropes and pulleys and batons of different coloured lights.

'Those are the flies,' Jock told her. 'All the drops – curtains and backcloths – are worked from there. And that . . .' He pointed to an opening high up. 'That is called the perch. It's where the lighting technician sits. From up there he can turn day into night and sunlight into storm clouds, all with his magic switchboard. He works most of the special effects from there too.'

Taking Amy by the hand, Jock led her through the wings and out onto the centre of the stage itself. The fire curtain was raised and she found herself looking out onto the orchestra pit and, beyond it, row upon row of empty red plush seats.

'Why does the stage slope?' she asked him, looking down at her feet.

'It's called the rake,' Jock explained. 'It was designed so that the audience could see the performers better, but you only find it in old theatres. Newer ones have better seating arrangements so it isn't necessary. And those are the footlights.' He pointed to the row of lights at the edge of the stage. 'If those were lit you wouldn't be able to see anything beyond them at all.'

'It's lovely,' Amy breathed.

Jock looked down at her. 'Ever been on a stage before?'

'I was in a play when I was at my old school,' she told him. '*Twelfth Night*. I played Viola.'

Jock looked impressed. 'Quite a part for someone as young as you. Did you enjoy it?'

'Oh, yes. But I'd like to be in a play in a real theatre like this,' she told him.

She was enthralled by everything she saw and when she and Celia took their places in the front row of the stalls to watch the dress rehearsal she completely lost herself in the sheer delight of it all. It was so much better than just seeing the finished show. The ordinary looking people she had seen arriving by the stage door, wrapped against the cold in scarves and mackintoshes, were transformed into ethereal fairy-tale characters in glittering costumes and fantastic make-up.

Watching as the rehearsal progressed she was fascinated to see how all the imperfections were ironed out and put right by the director. She was so impressed by the professionalism of real live actors. The technical side of it absorbed her too; the lighting effects that could turn dull sacking into cloth of gold and a curtain of coarse grubby gauze into a mystical starlit mist. Then there was the music; the songs, worked at painstakingly over and over again, until the musical director was satisfied that they were as good as he and the actors could make them.

And the treat did not end with the end of the rehearsal. When the final scene was finished the girls went backstage again to have tea with the cast, some of them still in their costumes and make-up. Amy thought it was the most exciting day of her entire life. And if she had ever felt any doubt about what the future held for her it was completely erased during that magical afternoon.

'I'm going to be an actress when I leave school,' she whispered to Celia that night when they were in bed.

Celia laughed. 'You must be joking,' she said. 'There isn't any money in it. Ask any of them. If you ask them they all say they don't know why they do it.'

Amy said nothing. She knew why they did it. Because there was nothing else on earth that was so exciting and glamorous; because no one in their right mind could possibly want to do anything else, that was why. As she fell asleep she suddenly realised that she had completely forgotten that it was Christmas tomorrow. Nothing could possibly compare to the excitement of today. Surely when you were an actress every day must feel like Christmas. And she couldn't *wait* to leave school and begin.

Vincent ran down the basement stairs to where Roisan was making coffee in the kitchen.

'Don't bother with coffee for us. I've just rung for a taxi. I'm taking Maryan home. Oh, and don't wait up. I might be late.'

'All right Vinnie,' she said quietly. 'I suppose what you're really saying is that you might not come home at all.'

He stopped in his tracks and turned to face her. 'Don't

look like that, Roisan. Surely you can see how I feel about Maryan. You like her too, don't you?'

She looked at him. 'Yes I do. I like her very much. But you're not being fair to her, Vinnie.'

'She knows the situation. We're neither of us children, Roisan. You surely don't grudge me a little happiness, do you?'

'I don't grudge either of you anything. I just think you're running your head – *and* hers – into disaster. If you thought as much of her as you say you do, you wouldn't be letting it go on. Do you want to see her hurt?' She stood facing him, her blue eyes looking into his in that disconcerting way she had. 'And what about that child of hers? Have you stopped to consider her at all?'

He sighed. 'She's away with her friend. You know that. You surely don't think either Maryan or I would risk her knowing . . .'

'*Knowing* – knowing what? That you're sleeping with her mother? You – a married man?'

He winced. 'You have a positive genius for making things seem sordid.'

'So what else would you call it?'

He sank wearily onto a chair at the kitchen table. 'Don't spoil it, Roisan. Maryan has made such a difference to me. She's given me back my life. It's been a hell of a long time since I've felt this happy. Is that such a crime?'

Relenting, she sat down opposite him and reached out to touch his hand. 'Ah, Vinnie – I know how unhappy you've been in the past, but you've got such a gem in Maryan. She's taken to the business like a duck to water. You don't want to ruin everything and lose her, just when the interior decorating side of the business is taking off so well and you need her at the shop, do you?'

'I shan't lose her. I'll make sure I don't. She's more to me than just an employee, Roisan. Don't you understand, I love her – really love her.'

'Well, if you really feel that serious, and if she feels the same, maybe you should get in touch with Fay and ask her for a divorce.'

He looked up at her with startled eyes. 'I never thought I'd hear you say a thing like that.'

She lifted her shoulders. 'We live in a changing world, Vinnie. The war has broken so many marriages. Maybe it's time for a change. Fay left you. It was she who did wrong and not you. It isn't fair that you should be forced to sin when you could marry the woman you love.'

'*Sin*?' he got to his feet. 'I don't see loving Maryan as a sin.'

'You know as well as I do that it is – while you're still married to Fay. There's no getting away from it.' She looked at him. 'Do you still go to confession? Have you talked to a priest about how you feel and what you're doing?' When he avoided her eyes she rose and went back to the Aga. Taking the percolater off the hotplate she said: 'It seems to me that you've given up your faith anyway, so why cling to the old rules? Ah well, I've said what I think, and probably too much at that. Now it's up to you. I think I can hear your taxi outside. You'd better go.'

He stood where he was, reluctant to leave in disagreement. 'Come up and say goodnight to us properly, Roisan. Maryan wants to thank you for the lovely Christmas you've given us. She'll think it odd if you don't come.'

Roisan turned to look at him and saw the silent plea in his eyes. It said: *Please don't send me away like this*. Ever since he was a small boy she could never resist that look. She sighed. 'Of course I'll come and say goodnight,' she said. 'But I'll not change my opinion, Vinnie, so don't you be thinking I will.'

Upstairs in the hall Maryan was buttoning her coat. She held out her arms to Roisan. 'Thank you for such a wonderful day,' she said. 'Dinner was delicious. I'm sure I won't be able to eat another thing till New Year.' The two women hugged each other warmly and Roisan stood on tiptoe to kiss her brother's cheek. As she patted his arm she whispered: 'Remember what I said.'

She stood at the front door and waved to them as they got into the taxi and drove away, her heart full of doubt and foreboding. In her experience, taking what you wanted when you had no right to it only led to one thing. You usually found yourself paying a far higher price than you could afford. But she'd had her say. There was nothing more she could do.

At Simons Mews Vincent paid the driver and went inside with Maryan. Upstairs, the flat was cold after being empty all day, but Maryan switched on the electric fire and drew the curtains.

'I'll make some coffee,' she said. 'Or would you prefer tea?'

Vincent came to her and slipped his arms around her waist. 'Neither,' he whispered huskily against her neck. 'All I want is you. His kiss betrayed the hunger he felt for her and she put her arms around him, grateful for his warm masculine strength – for his love and his wanting her.

'Oh, darling, it seems so long,' he said, his lips against her throat. 'I want you – need you so much. I wish we could be together always.'

In the bedroom they undressed silently and climbed into bed, shivering a little under the cool touch of one another's hands. Holding him close, Maryan felt a pang of guilt at being glad they had the flat to themselves. She had longed so much to have Amy back with her, but she was finding it hard going, re-establishing her role as Amy's mother. That and the strain of hiding her deepening relationship with Vinnie was beginning to take its toll of her nerves.

Tonight the world was theirs, though. In their first eager need of each other the act of love was swift and quickly over. But as they lay in each other's arms, growing warm and relaxed under the covers, kissing and caressing in the luxury of solitude, they soon became aroused again. And this time their lovemaking was unhurried and wonderful. It seemed to Maryan that each time they made love it was even more perfect than the last. She had known only two men in her life: Marcus, with whom love had been consummated only once and so briefly that she had scarcely had time to realise what was happening, and Tom. Poor, dear Tom, to whom she had never truly given herself. In Vinnie she could lose herself completely. With him she could let the heartache of the past go. He made her feel alive and free in a way she had never known before.

After the launch of the Marcus Leigh Collection every newspaper she picked up had been full of his name. There were countless stories of Marcus's tragic marriage and his bravery – his wife's untimely death and later, his own. Vincent had taken the sting out of it all for her, made her forget with his patient, loving tenderness until the hurt lessened and the gaping wounds healed over. She had been grateful to him for that alone, but soon her gratitude had blossomed into love. The sweetest, most fulfilling love she had ever known.

What had been leisurely lovemaking developed into a hungry passion as it approached climax. Maryan felt the familiar pulsating surge of sensation and arched upwards towards him, wanting to give all of herself, offering him her heart and soul as well as her body. Together they reached a stunning crescendo that left them both gasping and clinging to each other, and Maryan felt tears of joy well up inside her.

'Oh, Vinnie, Vinnie, I love you,' she said softly, her lips against his cheek.

He raised his head to look down at her. 'You've never said it before,' he said. 'If you only knew how much I've wished you would. I love you too, my darling. But I'm sure you know that by now.'

For a long time they lay quietly together, languorous with assuaged love, weightless with relaxation. Then with a resigned sigh Vincent roused himself and began to get up.

'I suppose I'd better go.'

Maryan reached out to pull him down again. 'Oh, please, not yet. Stay a little longer. There's nothing to prevent you staying till morning – is there?'

He lay back against the pillows with a sigh. 'Roisan knows about us. Oh, I didn't say a word. She guessed – in the way that sisters have of guessing what their younger brothers are getting up to.'

'She disapproves?' He nodded and Maryan looked up at him. 'Of me?'

'No, not of you.' He smiled, stroking her hair back from her face. 'Don't look like that my love. It isn't you she's angry with. It's me.'

'Because of . . .?'

'Yes. She actually suggested tonight that I should get a divorce. I never thought I'd hear her say a thing like that.'

Maryan held her breath. 'And – what did you say?'

He sighed. 'In divorcing Fay I'd automatically renounce my faith.'

'How can anyone *automatically* renounce their faith?' she asked. 'Surely whatever you do it can make no difference to the way you feel – what you believe in.'

He shook his head. 'I'm afraid the church doesn't see it quite that simply. And in spite of what Roisan thinks, it does still matter to me. But if Fay were to admit misconduct and desertion . . .'

There was a pause before Maryan said tentatively: 'Do you think she would?'

He shrugged. 'Who knows?'

She paused, searching his face with her eyes. 'But – maybe that isn't what you want, Vinnie.'

He reached out to pull her almost fiercely into his arms. 'Anything that would mean you and I could be married; could be together properly for always, is what I want. Surely you know that.'

'So – what happens next? Will you ask her?'

The question hung in the air between them. Vincent said: 'I could try. Knowing Fay, though, she'll probably refuse, especially if she gets an inkling of what it means to me. I refused to give her a divorce when she left, you see. On religious grounds, of course. She'll certainly throw that in my face.'

'Oh, Vinnie, what are we going to do?' Maryan felt a sudden despair. Why were there always such insurmountable barriers to happiness for her? Why did she always fall in love with men she couldn't have? Must she always have to steal love shamefully and secretly, like a thief? She had more than just herself to consider too. There was Amy.

'Why is life so difficult?' she asked him. 'I have to think of Amy. How will she react to it all? Since we've been together again she's been so difficult. It's been five months now and I seem to be getting nowhere with her. I never expected it to be easy, but I've tried so hard, Vinnie. Sometimes I think she hates me.'

He pulled her close. 'Don't be silly. Why should she hate you?'

'I don't know. I think she feels I've let her down in some way.
Maybe I should have found a way for us to be together during the war. I did try once, but she didn't want to leave the Taylors.'

'Maybe you've been too soft with her, Maryan. I'll admit that there've been times when I've had to bite my tongue not to say something to her. The way she speaks to you sometimes makes me see red.'

Maryan shook her head. 'I try to make allowances. I'm afraid she isn't happy. But why? I'm her mother. I should be able to make her happy, shouldn't I?'

'She doesn't seem to feel any obligation to try to please you,' he said. 'It seems to me that all the trying is on your side. Maybe if you started thinking of yourself more . . .'

She shook her head. 'Perhaps you're right. I don't know.'

'Roisan is afraid I'll hurt you,' he said softly. 'I don't want to make any more problems for you, Maryan. Maybe she's right. Maybe I'm not being fair to you.'

264

'Shhh.' She put her fingers over his lips, then replaced them with her lips. 'At the moment you are the only brightness in my life,' she told him, her mouth moving against his. 'You've given me so much; a home, a wonderfully interesting job. And best of all, your trust and your love. Let's not think too much about the future. Let's just be grateful for what we have.'

They lay for a while at peace in each other's arms, then Vincent said: 'Talking of work, I've got something for you to do the day after tomorrow.'

'You have? What is it?'

'There's a big country house sale down in Sussex. From what I've seen of the catalogue there are some nice pieces to be had. The preview is in the morning, auction in the afternoon. I thought we'd go. Take a packed lunch perhaps. No one will expect the shop to open till Friday anyway.'

'That sounds like fun.'

'Yes, but this time there's going to be a difference.'

She raised herself on one elbow to look at him. 'What kind of difference?'

'This time it's going to be all up to you. You choose the pieces we go for, and you do the bidding.'

She stared at him, wide-eyed with apprehension. 'Oh, Vinnie, I *daren't*. I'm not ready.'

'Yes you are. You've been to plenty of sales with me. You know how it works and I believe you've learned enough about the business now to know what to look for.' She looked doubtful and he added: 'You have to take the plunge sometime, my love. Especially as I'm planning to put you in charge of buying eventually.'

'But – suppose I make a mistake – an expensive one?'

He laughed. 'Easy, I'll fire you.'

'Then I'd better look out, hadn't I?'

He reached out to squeeze her hand reassuringly. 'We'll go through the list of requirements for the jobs on hand tomorrow, so that you can see what we're looking for. Any *mistakes* as you call them can always go into the shop.' He reached across to kiss her. 'But you won't make any mistakes. I'm sure of that. I've got faith in you.' He reached out his hand to switch off the bedside light. 'And now, in case you don't know it, it's two a.m. We'd better get some sleep. Goodnight, my love.'

With a happy sigh, Maryan snuggled close to him in the warm darkness and closed her eyes. 'Goodnight, darling.'

Sam was happy. Mainly because Rachel was happy. He hadn't seen her looking so well or so radiantly fulfilled since before the war. The Marcus Leigh Collection had exceeded even her hopes for it.

The launch last September had been an enormous success. The press had been especially generous to them, taken as much with the story behind the collection as with the designs themselves. The romance of Marcus's wartime heroism, and the designs, created in secret for the beautiful young wife he had lost so tragically in childbirth, had made a wonderful story. Sometimes Sam worried a little that they might be exploiting their tragic loss, but Rachel clearly didn't see it that way.

The whole venture had been her salvation, and for that reason alone Sam was deeply grateful. He reasoned that Marcus would have wished for this outcome. He would surely have been pleased to see his designs becoming so successful. And he would certainly have chosen this way in which to be remembered.

Sam often thought about Maryan and Amy. He would have liked to see them both, but he curbed the desire. If Rachel found out she would be upset. He had paid Amy's new term's fees in advance and in return had received a letter from Maryan, thanking him and saying that Amy liked her new school and was doing well. Perhaps some day he would find the opportunity to see his granddaughter. But not if it meant disturbing Rachel. She had made it clear that she would never believe that the child had been fathered by Marcus and he knew that nothing he could say would ever persuade her otherwise. Best to let sleeping dogs lie.

Their son's prolonged absence during the war and, later, his terrible death had almost destroyed them both, but Rachel had suffered most; her grief aggravated by Maryan's revelation. There had been a time when Sam had feared for her sanity. It was nothing short of a miracle, the way she had discovered the designs and decided to promote and follow them through. It was almost as though some divine hand had been at work, giving Rachel help and strength at the very time when she needed it so desperately.

After the launch, most of the original designs had been ordered by exclusive little boutiques in and around London, but some of the large West End stores had bought a selection too. Now Gina Stern was working hard on a new summer collection, to be shown in early spring. Next year people would be thinking of holidays again. Summer outfits would need to be frivolous and gay, frothy and carefree. And the drawings Gina was creating were certainly all of those things. She had chosen light, colourful fabrics, designed romantic swirling skirts and flattering feminine tops with pretty sleeves. Rachel was delighted with the young designer's work. And it gave Sam a secret glow of pride that at last the garments that were receiving such acclaim bore the name of Leigh instead of Feldman.

After V-J Day Sam had suggested that they might move back to Hackney. He had re-established the Feldman Fashions' factory as soon as the bombing ceased so that he could re-employ some of his old workers who had remained in London and been thrown out of work by the bombing. But Rachel seemed reluctant to go back. He understood that the house held many sad memories for her. It was the same for him of course. But it had been the first home of their own they had shared. He had bought it for Rachel when, together, they had made Feldman's successful. And she had put so much of herself into making it theirs. It seemed so sad to let it go. On the other hand, there was a good train service from Hazelfield. It was pleasant in the country and they had both become accustomed to the peace and fresh air. If it made Rachel happy to stay there, then so be it.

On one of his thrice weekly visits to London he decided to do something positive about the neglected house and he went along to an agent and put 124 Hackney Road on the market. He also arranged for a firm of house clearers to empty it. When they moved to Hazelfield at the beginning of the war they had taken everything they valued with them. And Sam knew that Marcus's belongings had been cleared by Rachel herself. The rest could go. Let the past be buried, he told himself. So many people had suffered loss through the war. At least he and Rachel still had each other. And if she could make a new start, then he would too.

It was on the train journey home that Amy made a startling discovery. As the train chugged through the frosty countryside Celia happened to mention that her grandmother was contributing towards her school fees. Amy looked surprised.

'I passed my scholarship exam,' she said proudly.

'So did I,' Celia retorted. 'But St Hil's is a private school. Mum didn't like any of the London schools I could have transferred to, so Gran said she'd help her pay for me to go to St Hil's.'

Amy was silent. So Mum had lied to her about that too. Someone must be paying her fees and if not Mum, then who? And why was Mum keeping it from her?

'Didn't you know it was private?' Celia asked.

Amy shook her shoulders. ''Course I did. I just forgot,' she said dismissively.

As it was Saturday afternoon and as Maryan was working, Anne Frazer had offered to meet both girls off the train. The taxi dropped Amy off at the end of Simons Mews and she waved goodbye to her friend, then made her way gloomily towards the shop. Maryan had already closed for the night and the place was in darkness except for the one streetlamp near the side entrance. Finding the door on the latch, Amy made her way up the stairs. She felt dreary and flat. Her brief, thrilling sojourn in the world of the theatre was over and so, almost, were the Christmas holidays. School started again in a few days' time. Although she quite liked school the thought of the new term made her heart sink. It was all so dull and routine.

At the top of the stairs she paused in the narrow hallway. She could hear voices, her mother's and Vincent's. In contrast to her own mood they sounded in high spirits.

'I'm so proud of you,' Vincent said. 'You did wonderfully well. Getting that Regency table for the price you did was a real coup. I can soon fix that little bit of damage. I think we'll have to arrange some driving lessons for you next. Then you can take the van along to sales and save us the delivery costs. I'll have to make arrangements at the bank too, so that you can sign cheques.'

Amy had been about to step into the room, but something made her stop. There was an abrupt silence and even out in the hall she could feel the highly charged atmosphere. Instinctively she knew that they were embracing. Shrinking back, she stood for a moment in the shadows. After a moment she heard Maryan say breathlessly: 'Oh, Vinnie, you're so good to me.'

'*I* am. What about you?' came the reply, so soft that Amy barely heard it. 'I can't tell you how wonderful these last few nights alone together have been. It's going to be torture, having to leave you and go home to a lonely bed tonight.'

Amy slipped back down the stairs, her heart beating dully and a huge lump in her throat. So that was it. It must be Vincent who was paying her school fees. Paying them in return for – what was the phrase Celia had used? *For services rendered.* She shuddered. At the bottom of the stairs she opened the street door again and banged it hard. Then she began to ascend the stairs again, making as much noise as she could.

Maryan appeared at the stairhead, her face flushed

and her eyes unusually bright. 'Amy. You're home then? Did you have a lovely time?'

Amy nodded, pushing past her mother unsmilingly. 'Smashing, thanks. Did you?'

Amy lay awake for a long time that night, thinking over her latest discoveries and wondering what to do. Once again there were two alternatives. She could demand to be told the truth about her school fees and make a fuss about her mother's relationship with Vincent, or she could keep quiet. If she made a fuss it might mean that Mum would be forced to give up her job. And that would mean the flat too. They would lose their pleasant, comfortable home. Amy thought of the horrid little house in Crimea Terrace and shuddered at the thought of returning to somewhere like that. Then again, if she made a stand about Vincent paying the school fees she might have to leave St Hildred's; change schools and go to one of the ones Celia had told her about; a school where there might be no drama or music lessons – and certainly no Celia. It would probably even be full of Lily Smiths. Was it worth it? No, she told herself decisively. She had to think of herself from now on. Herself, and her plan for the future.

She rolled restlessly onto her other side and listened to the wind as it rattled the window and tossed the dry leaves about in the mews outside. For a moment she felt like those little heaps of dry, used-up leaves. Useless and forgotten, unwanted, just cluttering the place up. She chewed a corner of the pillowcase thoughtfully. For the moment she had little choice other than to go along with her mother's bewildering behaviour – fall in with the promiscuity, lies and deceit if she wanted the best from life. But one day, she promised herself; one day she *would* have a choice. One day she would be someone special instead of just a child who was in the way. When she was a famous actress people would admire and look up to her. They'd be standing in a line to know her then. It wasn't just a dream either. She would *make* it happen – somehow.

Chapter Twelve

Mike's letter came a week before St Hildred's broke up for the summer holidays. Amy hadn't had a letter from him for some time and as soon as she recognised the distinctive chunky handwriting she tore it open eagerly. His news was mainly about his first year of college, which he seemed to be enjoying, but he went on to say that his mother was giving him a party for his eighteenth birthday on 4 August. He hoped that Amy would be able to come, and perhaps stay on with them for a few days.

Excited at the prospect of a visit to Rhensham, Amy passed the letter to her mother at once, watching her face anxiously for the necessary permission. Maryan read it through to the end and then looked up.

'I don't need to ask you if you want to go, do I?' she said with a rueful smile.

'Oh, *can* I? It'd be lovely to see Mike and Auntie Marjorie again,' Amy said. 'I've been wondering what on earth I was going to do once school broke up.'

Actually the invitation was a blessing as far as Maryan was concerned. She'd been telling herself that she really should try to take Amy away for a holiday of some kind, but she hadn't an idea how to fit it in. Vincent would gladly give her the time off, she knew that, but doing so would be bound to make things difficult for him. Besides, there was so much she wanted to do. Ever since spring she'd been taking driving lessons and she was due to take her test in August. After that she'd be able drive herself to and from sales independently in the van Vincent had bought for the business.

Then there was the shop, now fully stocked and doing a steady trade. Once the antique-loving public had rediscovered Vincente's they had had a flow of regular customers and Maryan was kept busy cataloguing and pricing the stock and keeping the books straight, as well as attending to customers and dealers.

Last spring Vincent and Roisan had divided the business into two separate parts. Vincente Antiques still operated from Simons Mews and was run by Maryan, helped by Paul, the personable young apprentice Vincent had recently engaged, who looked after the shop when Maryan was occupied elsewhere. Decor Vincente was run from Roisan's home, where a secretary had been employed to deal with bookings and enquiries. Roisan had converted one of her ground-floor rooms into an office which the middle-aged, austere Miss Stokes, late of the NAAFI, ran like a well-oiled machine, leaving Roisan free to work away upstairs on her soft-furnishing and colour-scheme planning.

The interior restoration business had gone from strength to strength since that first refurbishment of the Grahams' house. They had a wide circle of friends who, having seen the transformation wrought by Decor Vincente, had positively clamoured to have their own war-tattered homes professionally made over. Vincent was busy from early morning till well into the evening, liaising with clients and supervising his team of painters and decorators. Some weeks Maryan hardly saw him at all, and he had very little time nowadays to spend down in his workshop on the antique restoration work he loved. She didn't even know whether he had managed to get in touch with Fay, regarding their divorce. He hadn't brought the subject up again since Christmas. And Maryan had not liked to broach it herself. She felt that the little time they managed to snatch together was too precious to spend discussing anything so delicate and tenuous.

She began to clear the breakfast table, and for once Amy helped, carrying her own plate, cup and saucer into the kitchen.

'I wonder if they'll think I've grown up at all,' she said, glancing at herself sideways in the mirror as she passed.

'Oh, they're sure to,' Maryan said with a smile. Even living with Amy, seeing her every day, Maryan could see that her daughter had developed dramatically over the past six months. She'd grown so tall, taller now than Maryan herself. And she'd grown her dark hair longer. She wore it curling softly on her shoulders or tied up in a bouncing pony tail. Luckily for Amy, she suffered from none of the usual adolescent problems. Her sapphire-blue eyes and her complexion glowed with health and she had a poise and grace that made her appear older than her fifteen years.

Maryan was very proud of her pretty daughter but she held back from telling her so. There was still a barrier between them that, try as she would, she could not break through. Occasionally they would find something to laugh at together, or a strong view that they shared. There would be moments when they were almost close, when Maryan would feel she had almost beaten down the inexplicable reserve that held them apart. There would be a moment of heartening warmth between them, then Amy's eyes would cloud over and the shutters would go up again. At least this morning she had been able to please Amy; do something to make her smile. If only it could have been she who had been the cause of her happiness and not the Taylors.

At school that morning Amy showed Mike's letter to Celia. 'I'll have a week to get ready and then I'll be going,' she said, her eyes dancing with excitement. 'I can't wait to see them all again.'

'What do you mean, see them *all*?' Celia said, rolling her eyes. 'It's *him* you really want to see, isn't it – Mike? And I can't say I blame you from the look of those snaps you showed me. He's a smasher.'

'Mmm, I wonder if he's changed?' Amy said, looking

thoughtfully into the cloakroom mirror and twisting a curl of dark hair round her fingers. 'Mum says I have. What about my hair? Do you think I should have it done in that new bubble cut?'

Celia had had her waist-length plaits shorn earlier that year. It had been her mother's idea, but when she had gone to visit her father at half term and he'd first set eyes on the jaw-length bob his daughter sported he'd been really angry.

'Men seem to like long hair,' Celia said. 'Remember the fuss Dad made when I had mine cut? No, keep it long. It's so pretty. Not poker-straight like mine.' She grinned. 'Mum says she'll treat me to a perm in the hols. It's a sort of consolation prize, because we can't afford to go on holiday.'

Amy looked at her friend wistfully. 'I wish I could take you along to Rhensham, Cee,' she said. 'Like you took me to your dad's last Christmas. I would if it were up to me, but I'm not related to the Taylors so I can't very well.'

'Course you can't. I know that. Don't be silly.' Celia slipped her arm good-naturedly through Amy's. 'I had hoped to go to Dad's when the theatre closes for a week in August, but he and Candice are off for a holiday in France, rotten pigs.'

'Maybe Reg will take you both somewhere,' Amy suggested.

Celia pulled a face. 'Reg hasn't been round for a couple of weeks. Mum says it's over. I miss the chocolate bickies, but I can't say I miss him.' She giggled. 'Never mind, when you get back we'll think of all sorts of mischief to get up to. We'll have to make the best of it. It'll be heads down and full steam ahead for School Cert. in the autumn, so we'd better have a smashing time while we've got the chance.' She grinned. 'If you and this Mike of yours haven't eloped to Gretna Green, that is.'

Amy coloured. 'Oh, *Cee* – how many times do I have to tell you? Mike and I aren't a bit like that. He's just like a brother.'

Celia winked and nudged her in the ribs. 'Go on, pull the other one. You can't fool me.'

Maryan went with Amy to Liverpool Street and saw her onto the train. All the way to Rhensham she sat looking out of the window in a state of high excitement. This felt more like going home than coming back to London had last year. As they crossed the boundary into Suffolk she watched the familiar landmarks slip past. It seemed to take an eternity. But at last here they were, sliding into Rhensham Station. And there was Mike standing on the platform, scanning the carriage windows as they passed him.

Amy could hardly believe how tall he'd grown, or how handsome he looked in his dark grey flannels and tweed jacket. As she stepped down from the train and saw him take the first hesitant step towards her she felt suddenly shy and tongue-tied. By the slightly puzzled expression on his face, he was having some difficulty recognising her. They met and looked at each other. Amy saw with surprise the pale beginnings of a moustache on his upper lip. He wasn't a boy any longer. He was a young man. Then Mike grinned and to her relief she saw that inside it all he was the same old Mike she had always known after all.

'Hello, Amy.'

'Hello, Mike.'

'It's good to see you.' He held out his hand, 'Here, better give me your case. Come on. The car's in the station yard.'

'Oh. Is Auntie Marjorie with you then?'

He smiled condescendingly. 'Heavens, no. I drove here myself. Passed my test in the spring.'

Captain Taylor's 1938 Hillman Minx had been laid up all through the war, but when he came home for good he'd had it overhauled and resprayed. It stood in the station yard looking like new, its dark blue paintwork gleaming in the sunlight. Mike proudly opened the front passenger door for Amy.

'Hop in. I'll just put your case in the boot.'

It felt so strange, being driven to Mitcham Lodge by Mike in the smart blue car. He drove carefully, keeping his eyes on the road all the time and sitting up very straight. Amy could tell he was trying to impress her, showing off a little in the way he always had. She smiled to herself. Nothing much had changed really after all.

At Mitcham Lodge Marjorie came out on the steps to meet them. She hugged Amy warmly, exclaiming at how much she'd grown.

'You're quite the young lady,' she said. 'And so smart in your London clothes. We can't buy anything as fashionable out here in darkest Suffolk and the coupons are always such a problem. We keep waiting for rationing to end but no sign of it yet.' She drew Amy inside the house. 'Now – I'm dying to hear all your news. I've put you in your old room so you're sure to feel at home. Tea's all ready. I can't wait to hear all about your new school and this exciting job of your mother's, so don't be too long, will you?'

Mike carried her case up the stairs and Amy followed him happily. It was almost as though she'd never gone away.

She unpacked her case and carefully hung up the summer dresses she'd brought. At the bottom of the case lay the new party dress. Maryan had insisted on going with her to Regent Street to Dickens and Jones to buy Michael a birthday present. Amy had chosen a smart pen and pencil set and a card to go with it. Afterwards her mother had steered her towards the 'Junior Miss' department, announcing that they must choose something special for her to wear for the party.

Amy took it out of the tissue paper it was packed in and put it on a hanger, shaking out the folds in the long skirt. Then she hung it on the wardrobe door and stood looking at it critically. It was a proper evening dress, the first she'd ever had. Made of crisp white watered silk, it had a heart-shaped neckline, puffed sleeves and a wide sash that tied in a big bow at the back. To go with it

Maryan had bought her a pair of silver sandals and a silver ribbon hairband.

Amy stepped back and stared at the dress. She had mixed feelings about it. To begin with, she hadn't wanted her mother to spend so much on her and she knew that Maryan had been saving her clothing coupons for a smart new autumn suit she had her eye on. Deep down, she suspected that Maryan was trying to get round her and she hated the feeling of being indebted to her. To make matters worse, the dress was Maryan's choice too, and secretly Amy thought it was a bit childish. She would have preferred a slinky black velvet number she'd seen in the adult department. She'd even persuaded her mother to let her try it on and been cross and humiliated when Maryan had laughed and announced that it made her look like a little girl dressed up in her granny's cast-offs. She felt quite sure that none of the other girls Mike had invited to the party would be wearing anything as babyish as this. She was going to look like the fairy off the Christmas tree.

Jumping up from the bed suddenly, she pushed the white moire evening frock into the wardrobe and shut the door on it. She wasn't going to let anything spoil her stay at Mitcham Lodge. She'd worry about the dress when the time came.

Downstairs, Marjorie had tea ready with all Amy's favourites. She wanted to know about the new school and Amy assured her that she liked it as much as her old school in Ipswich.

'I believe it's a convent,' Marjorie said.

'How does it feel, having nuns as teachers?' Mike asked, looking slightly superior.

'It felt strange at first,' Amy told him. 'I thought they'd be long-faced and serious all the time, but they're not at all. Some of them are really funny and make us laugh. They do all the things other teachers do too. When Sister Sebastian, the sports mistress, tucks up her habit and plays hockey or tennis she can outrun the best of us. And our dancing mistress, Sister Veronica, can dance like Ginger Rogers.'

Mike and Marjorie laughed at the images created by Amy's descriptions, then Marjorie said: 'I've been reading a lot about this new designer, Marcus Leigh, in the fashion magazines and papers. Are those the same Leighs your mother used to work for?'

Amy felt herself blushing. 'Yes. Mr Marcus was their son. He was killed in the war.'

'I know. I read all about him, poor young man. Such a sad, romantic story,' Marjorie said. 'But the designs he left behind seem to be making a terrific impact on the fashion world. So stunningly smart, and delightfully different from what we've been used to.'

'Yes.' Amy hid her face in her cup.

Over dinner Amy was a little shy with Philip Taylor. He was almost a stranger to her and he looked so completely different in his civilian clothes. But he did his best to be friendly and welcoming. When the meal was over Mike invited her upstairs to what had been the old playroom.

'Mum's turned it into a study for me now,' he told her. 'And I've got a portable radio. Radio Luxembourg is on in the evenings. They play all the latest hits.'

Amy was impressed by the room. The old toys were gone and the bookshelves were full of grown-up books instead of the familiar children's favourites. A carpet had replaced the old linoleum and rugs, there was a new desk over by the window and two armchairs drawn up on either side of the fireplace. Mike looked at her enquiringly.

'Like it?'

'Yes. It's smashing. I miss the old table where we used to paint and do our homework, though.' She walked round the room, touching the new books on the shelves. 'And I miss the old teddies and the rocking horse – and your Meccano set.' She grinned at him. 'Not that you ever let me play with it.'

'They haven't gone,' Mike told her. 'They're all up in

the attic. Mum says she's saving them for when I have kids of my own.'

Amy sat down in one of the armchairs. 'Do you like being at college in Ipswich – coming home each evening, or would you rather have gone right away?'

He shrugged. 'I don't mind really.' To Amy's amazement he opened the desk drawer and took out a briar pipe, which he began to fill with tobacco. He cocked a nonchalant eyebrow at her. 'Do you mind if I smoke?'

'Er – no,' she said. 'Does Auntie Marjorie mind?'

He coloured. 'This is my room. I do as I like in here.'

'Oh, I see. Sorry.' She watched, fascinated, as he lit a match and held it to the bowl, puffing furiously, his cheeks growing pink when it became obvious that he was having trouble getting it to light. And when he put it aside and said gruffly, 'Think I'll leave it for now. You probably wouldn't have liked the smell anyway,' she had to bite her lip hard to keep from laughing. Mike sat in the other armchair, one leg draped over the arm.

'So – you've settled down in London after all?'

She shrugged. 'Yes. It's not so bad, I suppose.'

'School Cert. soon, isn't it?'

She pulled a face. 'Next spring. Waste of time really. I've already decided what I'm going to do.'

'What's that?'

'I'm going to be an actress.'

He showed no surprise. 'Well, everyone said you were good as Viola. Matter of fact I've got a job lined up myself.'

'You have?' Amy leaned forward with interest.

'Yes. When I've done my National Service I'm going to the local rag as a trainee reporter.'

'Mike, that's smashing. So you'll still be able to live at home then?'

'Mmmm . . .' He stroked his chin. 'I daresay I'll have to find some digs in Ipswich, I'll have to be on the spot when I'm working. Reporters work all hours, you know. Have to be ready to cover a story at the drop of a hat.'

'Gosh. It sounds exciting.'

He grinned sheepishly. 'Not really. Dad says I'll probably be a dogsbody-cum-tea-boy to begin with – covering the hatch, match and dispatch.'

She frowned. 'The what?'

'Births, marriages and deaths to you.'

She laughed. 'Oh, Mike, it *is* good to be back,' she said. He grinned the old grin.

'Good to have you back.' He looked at her thoughtfully. 'Amy – did you ever get that business sorted out? You know, about this Leigh fellow being your father?'

Amy blushed. 'No. Look, Mike, I've never told anyone but you about that – except Grandma, of course, and you can't count her. I've never mentioned it to Mum and I don't see how I ever can now. You haven't told anyone, have you?'

He shook his head, frowning a little. 'Crumbs no, of course I haven't. I did give you my word, didn't I?'

'I know. Thanks. I just thought . . .'

'His name seems quite big in the fashion world from what I can make out,' Mike went on. 'It seems funny, doesn't it, a chap becoming famous after he dies.'

'Not really,' Amy said. 'A lot of artists and composers get famous long after they're dead, don't they?'

'Doesn't it make you feel odd, though – knowing he was your father, I mean?'

'I haven't thought about it much,' she said. 'There's no point, as no one is ever going to know I'm his daughter. I suppose the best thing I can do is forget all about it, like Grandma said.'

'Yes, but *can* you? I mean, if his name is always going to be cropping up in the papers and so on it won't be easy. And you'll always know, inside yourself, won't you?'

'Yes. I'll always know – inside.' She lowered her eyes for a moment and when she raised them again she was smiling. 'Have you still got the horses, Mike? Can I help you muck out in the morning?'

'*Can* you? We've been saving it up for you. Haven't mucked out for a week specially.'

It was wonderful to be teased again. Her heart full of joy, she threw her cushion at him and he laughed, catching it and throwing it back. 'Hey, we're missing Luxembourg.' He got up and switched on the radio and was rewarded by the strains of 'A Gal in Calico'. He began to snap his fingers in time to the music. 'I like this one. Do you know the words?'

They were still singing along to the record when Marjorie tapped on the door and came in with two steaming cups of cocoa and a plate of biscuits on a tray.

She smiled indulgently. 'Come on, you two. Party tomorrow and a late night. Better not stay up too long.'

Amy sipped the hot, sweet brew contentedly. It was wonderful to be home.

Maryan opened her eyes. It was just getting light, but already the sounds of traffic on the King's Road reached her ears through the open window. She turned her head to look at the alarm clock. Five o'clock. Ages before it would be time to get up.

She turned her head to look at Vincent, still soundly sleeping beside her. Last night she had prepared a special dinner for the two of them, by way of a celebration. They hadn't had a chance to be together, undisturbed in the flat since last Christmas. She smiled, remembering how much Vinnie had enjoyed his meal. She hadn't seen him so relaxed for weeks. He really was working much too hard. But, as he told her, there was nothing else for it if they wanted eventually to expand the business. When they could take on more staff, things would get easier.

It had been a warm night and they had sat at the open window, finishing the last of the wine he had brought with him, then they had come to bed. Their lovemaking had been leisurely and ecstatic. It had been almost 3 a.m. when they fell asleep at last. Now Maryan lay relaxed and warm beside him, looking forward to the weekend they would spend together; a weekend Vincent had promised her, free from work or talk of work. A special time just for them.

He stirred a little and she thought he was about to wake, but he settled back into sleep again. She watched his face. He looked younger in repose, his face smoother and less craggy. Although the dark hair had streaks of grey, it was still thick and wavy. But his eyes were his best feature, dark as treacle; brown and melting. When they looked at her in the special way he had, her knees turned to jelly and she could have died for him. She was so lucky. Since Marcus she had been convinced that she would never love another man. Not that this was the carefree love she would have liked it to be. At the back of her mind the worry that never quite left her began to niggle afresh. Had he contacted Fay? Had he actually done anything about a divorce? Would they ever be in a position to marry?

While she was still looking at him, Vincent sighed and suddenly opened his eyes, looking at her for a second uncomprehendingly. Then he reached out and pulled her close.

'Maryan,' he said sleepily. 'I thought I was still dreaming for a moment.' He sighed contentedly. 'So – what are we going to do today?'

'I don't mind – don't care, just as long as we can be together.'

'In that case, let's just stay right here in bed.' He laughed. 'I can see that I'm shocking you. No, I'm only teasing – I think.' He laughed light-heartedly. 'It looks like a grand morning. We could do anything you like.' He sat up and stretched luxuriously. 'I know. Why don't we take the van and have a run down to the coast – Southend?'

Maryan's heart gave a jerk. She hadn't been to Southend since before the war, not since that memorable Bank Holiday with Marcus. '*No*,' she said sharply. 'I mean – I don't fancy the seaside. It'll be so terribly crowded at this time of year. Let's go somewhere quieter.'

'Ever been to Hampton Court?' he asked. She shook her head. 'Right, then that's where we'll go. Get dressed in your Sunday best and we'll be away.'

'I'll pack some sandwiches.'

'You will not. We'll find a quiet little hotel and have lunch. This is our special day, remember?' He bent to kiss her. 'I love you, Maryan.'

'I love you too,' she whispered.

Hampton Court was a revelation to Maryan as they wandered hand in hand through the magnificent state rooms. She gazed in awe at the brocade hangings, the pictures and tapestries, the beautiful, centuries-old furniture. Just fancy a man giving a palace like this to the woman he loved. Not that any of his loves lasted long. Poor Henry. From what Maryan could make out, Henry VIII had the worst kind of luck, always falling in love with the wrong woman. Vincent laughed when she said so.

'He just wanted an heir to the throne,' he said. 'It wasn't anything to do with love.'

'But surely he must have loved some of them?' Maryan argued. 'Anne Boleyn and Catherine Howard, for instance. I read about them in one of the books you lent me.'

'Books – even history books – don't always reflect real life,' Vincent said. 'If he really loved them how could he bear to order their execution, whatever they'd done? Personally I've always thought Henry a manipulative, self-indulgent lout; bringing people's lives and everything they'd lived for crashing down, simply for his own ends. Think of the good people he murdered merely for their beliefs; the monasteries he overthrew.'

'I suppose so.' Maryan shuddered. 'I'm glad I didn't live then.' She was reminded suddenly that Vinnie was a Catholic. Little wonder he felt no great sympathy for Henry VIII.

Having explored the palace, they came out into the sunlight and went into the maze, losing themselves and laughing helplessly as they tried this way and that. They wandered round the grounds for a while, appreciating their much cherished leisure and each other's company. But by the time they got back into the van for the drive home Maryan could contain her curiosity no longer. All the talk of divorce and the Catholic church had brought the subject that was never out of her mind to the surface. Knowing that she had to know, one way or the other, she turned to him.

'Vinnie, I've been meaning to ask you. Did you ever manage to get in touch with your wife – with Fay?'

He had already started the engine, but now he switched it off again and turned to look at her. 'I've been wondering when you'd ask.' He reached out a hand to cradle her cheek. 'You're patience itself, my Maryan. I should have kept you in the picture more. You deserve better than me, God knows you do.'

'Does – does that mean that you have?'

He sighed. 'Well, I wrote to her. I told her I thought it time we made the break final. It's been so long now. I think we could get an annulment quite easily if she was willing.'

'Yes . . .' She looked into his eyes, trying to read what she saw there. 'Vinnie, don't keep me in suspense. What did she say?'

'Nothing. She hasn't replied. I've written to her three times now. I wondered if she might have moved, or be out of the country or something, so I finally telephoned. His name – her lover's – is still in the book at the same address. I tried several times, but there was no reply.' He shook his head. 'Anyway, talking to her on the phone isn't likely to get me anywhere. She could always deny anything she'd said later, and, knowing her, she would. I need to get something in writing from her.'

'What will you ask her to do?'

'To divorce me on grounds of desertion.'

She frowned. 'But *she* deserted *you*.'

'I know, but it can be made to work both ways.' He looked away. 'She'll be required to say that I made life intolerable for her.'

She stared at him in horror. 'But that's so unfair, Vinnie.'

'Nevertheless, it's the only way I can get my freedom.' He sighed. 'If I knew she was still there I could go and see her, I suppose,' he said slowly. 'Or I could get a solicitor to write, telling her that I plan to apply for an annulment and need her cooperation. First I need to know for sure where she is.'

'What will you do next?'

He squeezed her hand. 'I still haven't decided. To tell the truth I've been putting it off. I've been too busy to think it out properly lately. It needs careful planning. It's not the kind of thing to rush into.'

'Vinnie . . .' She looked at him hesitantly. 'I've been wondering. If your church doesn't recognise your divorce will you really be free to marry again?'

He took both her hands in his. 'Not in the church, my love.'

'And – would you be happy with any other kind of ceremony?'

'I just want us to be together.' He squeezed her hands. 'And for your sake, I want it to be legally binding. Please, Maryan, let's not spoil the day talking about all the difficulties now.' He leaned forward and kissed her firmly. 'Now – shall we go back to the flat or will you let me take you out to dinner somewhere?'

Amy spent Saturday afternoon helping Marjorie with the party food. It was nice, being together companionably in the kitchen and catching up on all the village news. Marjorie told her that the Smith family had definitely made their presence felt. Apparently hardly a week went by that one of them wasn't the subject of local gossip for some misdemeanour or other. Lily's older brother, Norman, had been caught stealing bicycles and had been sent to Borstal for a year. Mrs Smith herself had made front-page news in the local paper, which reported a spectacular brawl she'd had with a neighbour. And Maisie, one of Lily's older sisters, had given birth to a baby boy, fathered, it was rumoured, by an American soldier.

'I miss living here,' Amy said wistfully. 'In London people don't seem to care about each other so much.'

Marjorie laughed. 'They mind their own business, you mean? But you and your mother have settled down together, I hope?'

Amy shrugged. 'Mum's always too busy to chat like we're doing now. I suppose we both are.'

For a minute Marjorie was silent, then she said: 'When Mike goes away to do his National Service I shall miss him terribly. I wouldn't tell him so, of course, because I want him to look forward to his first venture into the adult world and not feel bad about leaving home. And I've been so much luckier than so many other mothers, having him with me all through the war, and even after he went to college. You and your mother have a lot of time to make up. Make the most of it, Amy. All too soon you'll be gone and she'll be alone again. Whatever you might think, she does need you.'

Amy didn't agree. Maryan was clearly too wrapped up in her job and in Vincent to care about her much. But she remained silent on the subject. The Jessops and the Taylors were totally different kinds of people, with two entirely different situations. It wasn't possible to compare them; never had been and never would.

The party was to take place in the large sun-lounge at the back of the house. The parquet floor had been cleared and chalked for dancing and the doors were open onto the garden, which Philip and Mike had decorated with coloured lights. As the day was hot and sunny they expected to be able to overflow onto the lawn until late into the evening. Amy thought the whole affair very sophisticated. She looked forward to the evening with a mixture of excitement and apprehension. Mike had obviously been to a good many such affairs, but it was her very first grown-up party and as the time drew near she was aware of a tingling sensation in the pit of her stomach.

When the time came for them all to get ready she closed her bedroom door and took out The Dress.

Hanging it on the wardrobe door again she sat on the bed to stare at it in near panic. There were *so* many things wrong with it. Maybe she should have gone for a short dress. Suppose no one else wore long? She'd feel such a fool she'd just want to *die*. Then there was the neckline. If only it were lower and showed more of her chest. Not that she had all that much chest to show off. She briefly toyed with the idea of padding her bra with cotton wool. No, best not, she decided. If the padding fell out when she was dancing she'd die of shame. She took off the cotton skirt and blouse she had worn all day and went off to have her bath. Back in the bedroom she brushed her hair and secured the silver hairband in place, then she put on a little of the pink lipstick Maryan had allowed her to buy and dusted her nose with powder to take off the shine. Finally it was time to slip into the dress. She managed to do up the zip, but couldn't tie the sash to her satisfaction. Slipping out of her room she tiptoed along the landing and tapped on Marjorie's door.

'Auntie Marjorie, I wonder if you could tie my sash . . .' She stopped. Marjorie was staring at her. 'Oh – is something wrong?'

'Wrong? Good heavens, child, no. You look so lovely. Quite charming.' Marjorie drew her into the room and closed the door. 'I can hardly believe this is the little girl who came to me as an evacuee.' Philip came out of the dressing room fastening his cufflinks and she said: 'Look at Amy, Philip. Isn't she beautiful? I can't wait for Mike to see her. Here, let me tie that sash for you, then we'll make a grand entrance.'

Much to Amy's embarrassment, Philip insisted on taking her downstairs on his arm. The other guests were arriving and she was relieved to see that most of the other girls wore long dresses too. In the sun-lounge Mike stood talking to an older man who turned out to be one of his tutors. Feeling a little shy, Amy stood back, thinking how handsome he looked in his immaculate evening dress suit. He turned and saw her and his mouth dropped open in amazement.

His father laughed. 'All right, you can close your mouth now, Michael. May I introduce your guest of honour, Miss Amy Jessop.' He bowed low and handed Amy's hand to Mike. 'I suggest that you lead her into the dancing. I'll put on a record.'

The evening passed like a dream to Amy. She couldn't remember ever enjoying herself so much. She was glad that her school taught modern ballroom dancing as she was in great demand. Mike's friends were almost queuing up to dance with her. It felt so strange, dancing with boys. So far her only dancing partner had been Celia. It wasn't until after supper that Mike himself managed another dance with her.

'You've made a hit,' he told her. 'Everyone keeps asking me who you are. It's like Cinderella all over again.'

She looked up at him. 'Are you saying that I usually look ragged and dirty?'

'Well, you don't exactly dress like this to muck out the horses, do you?' He laughed and tightened his hold on her waist as he felt her trying to free one hand. 'Behave yourself. You can't thump me dressed up like that. It wouldn't look right.' He grinned down at her. 'You know, it's a relief to know you're still the tough little Amy I know. Seeing you tonight, I was beginning to wonder if you'd turned into someone quite different. I'm not sure I'd like that.' He slipped a finger inside his collar. 'It's getting so hot in here. Shall we go into the garden?'

They walked across the lawn to the little seat by the lily pond that was screened by a willow tree. Mike took out his handkerchief and dusted it carefully for her.

'Can't have that wonderful dress messed up, can we?'

'I wish you'd stop teasing me about it,' she said, sitting down. 'I know I look like a dog's dinner, but Mum would insist on buying it.'

'The last thing you look like is a dog's dinner,' he told her. 'I'm sure you know that you look absolutely marvellous.' He waved a hand towards the house. 'Ask anyone in there if you don't believe me.'

They sat for a moment in silence, then Amy said: 'Thanks for inviting me to your party, Mike. I've had a smashing time.'

'And thank you for my present. It'll come in really useful.' He laughed. 'Do you remember the birthday parties we used to have when you lived here? Jelly and blancmange and trifle, and cakes with candles for us to blow out? I didn't realise it then, but Mum used to stand in endless queues and hoard all her rations up for months to be able to do it.'

'I know.' Amy sighed wistfully. 'Auntie Marjorie did all the things for me that my own mum never did.'

'Only because she was here and your mother wasn't,' Mike said fairly.

'I still miss you all, Mike.' Amy turned huge blue eyes towards him. The coloured lights reflected in the water made them look luminous and Mike felt the breath catch sharply in his throat.

'We miss you too, Amy. And I'll tell you something else – I'm going to miss you even more when you go back this time.' He bent towards her and brushed his lips across hers. It was like the touch of a butterfly's wing, yet it made them both shiver. Amy lifted her arms and let them rest on his shoulders and he kissed her again, his lips firmer and more confident this time, his arms sliding round her waist to draw her closer.

'I thought you were still a kid last night,' he said when they drew apart. 'You looked grown up at the station, but then later you were the same Amy as always. Tonight though – tonight . . . Oh, Amy, I can't make up my mind which one I want you to be.' He kissed her again until they were both breathless and trembling. The moment hung suspended; bright and shining and magical as the coloured lights in the trees, then suddenly they were aware of voices calling from the house.

'I think they're looking for you,' Amy whispered. 'I expect people are leaving and want to say goodnight.' She stood up and held out her hand. 'Come on, we'd better go in.'

'Amy – wait. Look – when you go back. Will you go out with anyone else?'

She laughed. 'I shouldn't think so with School Cert. coming up. Why?'

'Because . . .' He stood up, laughing. 'Oh, I don't know. Because if you do I'll come up to London and punch his head. That's why.'

She laughed delightedly, catching at his hand. 'Oh, Mike, you are silly. Come on, we'd better go before they come looking for us.'

'Just a minute,' he pulled her down on the seat beside him again. 'Look, when I go into the Army, will you write to me as – you know, my girl?'

Happiness welled up inside her like a bubble. 'Oh, Mike, of course I will.'

Together, hand in hand, they ran through the trees and across the lawn. Two young people with childhood behind them. At that moment each of them felt the future beckoning, just waiting to be plucked like a ripe golden fruit from the tree of life; theirs for the taking.

Maryan was just closing the shop. It was only a quarter past five but business had been slack that afternoon. She'd let Paul, her young assistant, go home early and when no more customers had appeared by a quarter past she decided to call it a day. She was to take her driving test the following morning and she intended to have an early night so as to be fresh and alert.

She was just turning the sign on the door to 'closed' when a woman appeared in the mews outside. Maryan watched as she peered hesitantly through the shop window as though looking for something. It was so typical. No customers all afternoon, yet the minute she decided to close, they seemed to pop up from the cracks in the pavement. With a sigh, Maryan turned the door sign over again and went back to her desk at the back of the shop. Customers didn't like to be pounced on the moment they entered the shop. They liked to browse. She hoped this one wouldn't browse for too long, only to waste her time and walk out again empty-handed.

Her head down, Maryan heard the doorbell tinkle as the woman came in. She glanced up. The customer looked about forty, perhaps a little older. Her clothes were obviously expensive and yet she looked oddly ill at ease in them. She was a little overweight, her thickened waistline straining the buttons of the pink linen suit she wore. And her bleached hair was noticeably dark at the roots as though it was some time since it had seen a hairdresser. Even from the back of the shop Maryan could see that the too bright lipstick that clashed with the suit was badly applied as though she'd put it on in a hurry.

She made no attempt to browse, but hovered just inside the doorway, looking expectantly towards Maryan. Clearly she was looking for something very specific. Maryan rose and went towards her with a smile.

'Can I help you? Were you looking for something special?'

'Not some*thing* – some*one*.' The woman cleared her throat. 'Does Mr Donlan live here? Mr Vincent Donlan?'

'No. I'm sorry, he doesn't. He lives in Notting Hill with his sister. I can give you the address if you like.'

Maryan turned back towards the desk, reaching for a pencil and slip of paper, but the woman said hurriedly: 'Oh, no. It doesn't really matter. It's just that I was passing and I thought . . .'

'He's out of town today,' Maryan said, writing down Roisan's address, 'or I could have called him for you. This is where he lives. If I see him first can I give him a message?'

The woman glanced at the slip of paper Maryan handed her, then slipped it into her handbag. 'Thank you.' She looked up enquiringly. 'Er – you would be . . . ?'

'Me? Oh, I just manage the shop,' Maryan told her. 'And I live upstairs in the flat.'

'I see.'

Suddenly Maryan began to feel uneasy. Who *was* this woman? And what did she want with Vincent?

'Who shall I say called? Are you an old friend of Mr Donlan's?' she asked.

The woman nodded. 'The name's Briggs – Mrs Briggs. Well, I suppose I'd better go, Miss – er . . .'

'Jessop. *Mrs* Jessop,' Maryan supplied.

'Mrs Jessop. I'll call back sometime.' She hesitated, half turning. 'On the other hand – maybe you could . . . Oh dear.' The woman closed her eyes and swayed precariously, clutching at the back of a Victorian spoon-back chair. Alarmed, Maryan stepped towards her and put out a helping hand.

'Are you all right?'

'I – yes. I think so. I just feel a little dizzy, that's all. I'd better go. I've got quite a long journey home to face and the trains will be busy.'

'I don't think you should go anywhere at the moment. Not if you're feeling ill,' Maryan said. 'If you like you can come upstairs and sit down for a little while – wait till the rush hour is over. I was just going to close the shop anyway. I could make you a cup of tea.'

The woman smiled and looked relieved. 'Oh that *would* be kind. I'm diabetic, you see, and I have to be careful. I haven't eaten much today. I expect that's the trouble. Silly of me really.'

Upstairs in the flat Maryan opened the windows to let in some air. The afternoon had been hot and the living room was stuffy. She invited the woman to sit in an armchair near the window and went to the kitchen to put the kettle on.

The tea seemed to revive Mrs Briggs, who in spite of her indisposition seemed remarkably interested in her surroundings. Maryan noticed that while she talked her small pale eyes darted everywhere, taking in every detail of the room.

'So you live here, dear. Nice place, isn't it? Go with the job, does it?' Maryan nodded and the woman looked around her appreciatively. 'This your furniture?'

'No. It's Mr Donlan's.'

'I see. Quite fell on your feet here, dear, didn't you? I

expect it's a well-paid job. I've seen the adverts in the magazines for Decor Vincente. Sounds very posh. And there's always been a lot of profit in . . .'

Prickling with resentment, Maryan said quickly: 'It's such a pity that Mr Donlan wasn't here. Shall I tell him you'll call again, or can I give him a number where he can telephone you?'

'No. I need to see him, dear – talk to him face to face, so to speak . . . It's really *very* important. I – oh dear, I'm so s-sorry.' She began to sniff and her eyes brimmed with tears. She fumbled in her handbag for a handkerchief and Maryan refilled her cup, watching anxiously as the woman struggled to compose herself.

'Look, is there anything I can do? Shall I ring his sister for you?'

'No. It's him I have to see. No one else will do.' She paused. 'I wonder. You look so kind and you've been so nice to me.' The woman gulped hard and lifted her teacup, peering at Maryan over the rim. 'I suppose it's all right to tell you as you're obviously a trusted employee. You'll have to know eventually anyway.'

'Know? Know what?'

The woman smiled coyly. 'I'm Vinnie's wife, dear. I'm not really Mrs Briggs. That's just what I call myself.' The pale eyes were sad and watery under puffy eyelids. 'Vinnie and I were married soon after the war broke out, in the spring of 1940. I let him down, I'm afraid. I met someone else while he was in the army. Eddie Briggs – that's where the name comes from. He was a businessman; clever, good-looking and well off – had this lovely house down in Virginia Water. Central heating and all mod cons. Quite swept me off my feet, he did. I'd never known such luxury. But it was a terrible mistake. Oh, Vinnie knew at the time. Refused point-blank to divorce me, he did. Said I'd find out and be sorry.' She smiled. 'He said I'd come back some day with my tail between my legs. Of course I thought he was just being spiteful at the time. Such a vulgar expression, I always think, don't you? But many's the time I've remembered his words and wished I hadn't been so hasty. Still, all's well that ends well, as they say. Just as well we never got divorced, eh?'

'How do you mean, just as well?' Maryan asked, her heart growing ice-cold with dread.

'Well, because I've come to tell him he was right.' Fay dabbed at her cheeks with the damp handkerchief. 'To throw myself on his mercy as it were and – and to ask him – oh, *ever* so humbly, to take me back.' She smiled. Watching Maryan with a sly shrewdness from under the puffy eyelids, she took in the sudden pallor and the clouded eyes. 'And I know he won't turn me away, bless him,' she went on. 'A good Catholic, my Vinnie is. Believes in the sanctity of marriage and all that.'

Amy travelled home in a state of euphoria. Her week with the Taylors had been the happiest she'd spent for ages. Mike had seen her off on the train and promised faithfully to write every week from now on. Amy had invited him to come and stay for a few days before the start of the new term. Sitting in her corner seat she planned happily how they would spend the days. They'd go to the theatre and the cinema. She'd be able to show him the London she knew; the parts she'd come to know since she'd been back. Kew Gardens and the Zoo. The West End shops.

Amy was certain in her heart of hearts that she loved Mike. Perhaps she'd always known it. It seemed so obvious and natural now, since the night of the party when he'd kissed her. Being in love was the most marvellous feeling she had ever experienced. She felt as though she could fly – as though she walked without her feet touching the ground, light as air. Everything she looked at seemed beautiful, the greyest skies brilliant, the dullest landscape inspiring. Even the rain was like silver spangles falling from heaven. Sitting in the train and thinking of Mike she thought she could understand her mother a little more. Was this how she had felt about Marcus? Her face suddenly grave, she imagined how she must have felt when he married someone else. And when he was killed –

294

how it must have hurt. She resolved to be nicer, and less selfish when she got home. She would try harder to be what a daughter should be, close and companionable – the way she was with Auntie Marjorie. As the train drew into Liverpool Street Station and she stood up to reach down her case from the rack, she found that she quite looked forward to it.

Maryan was waiting to meet the train. Amy spotted her as she walked down the platform. She handed in her ticket and turned to her mother with a smile.

'Hello, Mum.'

'Hello, love. Have a good time?'

'Oh *yes*. It was wonderful. Mike's party was terrific and everyone said how nice the dress was.'

'I told you,' Maryan said abstractedly. 'A good thing you didn't have that awful black thing.'

'Mum, I've asked Mike up for a few days. Is that all right?'

Maryan was busy heading for the Underground and seemed not to have heard. Amy repeated her question.

'Mum – can Mike come and stay with us for a few days?'

'Oh, Amy, I'm not sure I want visitors at the moment. We'll have to wait and see. Things have been happening . . .'

'But *Mum* – he'll be going into the Army soon and I've already asked him.' Amy looked at her mother in horror. It would be too humiliating, not to say disappointing, to have to write and tell Mike he couldn't come after all.

'Well, you shouldn't have asked him till you'd checked with me,' Maryan snapped. 'I run a business as well as a home, you know.' They went down to the platform and waited in silence. A train drew in and the doors opened. Maryan took Amy's arm. 'Come on, Amy, don't sulk. And don't hang about. I can't leave Paul in the shop alone all afternoon.'

'Oh, the shop. It's always the *shop*,' Amy burst out. 'Why does it always have to come first? Why can't you ever think of *me* for a change?'

The train was crowded and they had to stand. Oblivious of the other passengers jostling and swaying against them in the packed aisle, Amy said, 'All through the war it was the Leighs. Now it's the shop and Vinnie, your – your *fancy man*. Everyone else in the *world* is more important to you than I am.'

Maryan rounded on her. 'Stop that at once,' she hissed. 'I won't have you speaking to me like that. We'll talk about this when we get home, young lady.'

Amy stood hanging onto the strap, her cheeks pink and her face sullen as she tried not to notice the amused glances of the other passengers. She hated them all. And she hated her mother more than all of them put together. Her week's holiday – the loveliest week she'd ever spent in her entire life – was utterly ruined. And it was all her mother's fault. She'd never, *ever* forgive her.

Maryan turned away from her daughter's dark expression. Amy's selfishness was the least of her worries. She detached herself from her surroundings as the train continued on its way, automatically counting the stations off one by one as they stopped, wanting nothing more than to be home again.

The past few days had been a nightmare. After Fay's visit she had waited with mounting tension to hear from Vincent. When two days had passed and he still hadn't come to the flat or telephoned, she rang Roisan and left a message that she needed to see him urgently. Roisan sounded strained and awkward on the telephone; something which Maryan viewed with foreboding.

He came that evening. Using his own key he let himself into the flat, arriving as she was cooking herself a meal. The moment she saw his face she knew that he'd already seen Fay.

'You've seen her then – your wife?'

He sat down on one of the kitchen chairs and passed his hand over his brow. 'Yes. I've seen her.'

'She came here first.'

'I know. She told me.'

Maryan turned off the gas under the saucepan she was

stirring and turned to him. 'She told me who she was. And that she wanted you to take her back.'

He sighed. 'She never got the letters I wrote her. She hasn't been living at that address for some time. It seems that the man she's been living with, Briggs, has found himself another woman – a younger one.' He lifted his shoulders. 'Some chorus girl or other. He threw Fay out so that he could bring this woman to the house. She's been living in some scruffy little bedsitting room for the past three months.' He looked up at Maryan. 'She hasn't said it in so many words, but she obviously blames me. She seems to think that if she'd been free to marry him four years ago it would never have happened.'

'She told me it was just as well that you'd refused her a divorce,' Maryan said. 'So – what did you say?'

He paused, shaking his head. 'He treated her appallingly, Maryan. Even knocked her about. Life hasn't been easy for her. She's certainly learned her lesson.'

She looked at him. 'The thing is, Vinnie – have you learned yours?'

He slumped on his chair, elbows on knees and head in his hands as he avoided her eyes. At that moment he looked ten years older and when he looked up at her she saw that he had already given in to Fay's demands. It was all over between them.

'You're taking her back,' she said quietly.

'Maryan, when she left, she was pregnant with my child. She didn't find out till later.'

Her heart froze. '*Vinnie*, that's the oldest trick in the book. How can you believe her? How can she possibly prove it was yours?'

'Because he – this Briggs – wasn't able to father a child. He was sterile and he already knew it. His wife had left him for that very reason. When she told him she was expecting a baby he knew it had to be mine and he gave her an ultimatum: get rid of it or leave. She had no option, Maryan. She had nowhere to go. She was ill and afraid. So she did it. She killed our child – *my* child,

Maryan. Can you imagine how that makes me feel? The only child I'll ever have and it died – thrown away like a piece of rubbish.' He shook his head. 'Apparently she nearly died after the abortion. When she's been through so much, how can I turn my back on her?'

'She deceived you before, Vinnie. How do you know this isn't just a pack of lies to get you back?'

He shook his head. 'She was never that good at lying. If you'd seen her face, Maryan, heard her heartbroken sobbing. No, it's true. She's – she's still my wife when all's said and done.'

Her heart as heavy as a stone, Maryan straightened her back and faced him. 'I see. So when would you like me to leave, Vinnie?'

He looked up at her in alarm. 'I don't want you to *leave*, Maryan. You've become a tower of strength to Roisan and me. We couldn't manage without you.'

'But – the flat. You'll want to live here – with Fay.'

'No, we can stay with Roisan for the time being, just till I find somewhere else.' He stood up and came towards her, his hands outstretched and his eyes filled with pain. 'Maryan – I can't tell you what this is doing to me. It's tearing me in two. It's not what I want. You must know that.'

She turned away from him, her eyes stinging with tears. 'Then why do you have to do it?'

'I told you – because whatever's happened, she's still my wife.'

'She said you'd do what she wanted,' Maryan said bitterly. 'She said you were a great believer in the sanctity of marriage. It seems she was right.'

He took her shoulders and turned her to face him. 'Listen, Maryan. *I love you*. This makes no difference to the way I feel. It never will. But I made vows all those years ago – sacred vows, before a priest.'

'She made vows too.' She looked at him, the tears slipping down her cheeks. 'She broke them. Not you. You made a promise to *me*, Vinnie. Doesn't that count for anything?'

He dropped his hands to his sides, his shoulders slumping helplessly. 'I'll never make you understand, will I?'

'Does it matter whether I understand or not? I'm just an employee, after all.'

The bitter irony of her words went over his head and he looked at her eagerly. 'Does that mean that you'll stay on? Live here at the flat and keep working for me?'

The look of gratitude in his eyes pierced her heart like an arrow and she tried unsuccessfully to swallow the lump in her throat. Her pride wanted to refuse – to pack and leave that very evening and never see him again. But she had more than just herself to think of. There was Amy. This was her home. She'd already had problems settling down after the wartime parting they'd endured. Lately their relationship had seemed to be improving. Reluctantly she looked up at him and nodded. 'Yes, all right. I'll stay. But it isn't going to be easy.'

'Believe me, Maryan, it isn't going to be easy for me either. I love you. I'll always love you. He reached out to take her in his arms but she stepped back, holding him off.

'I don't want you to think because I've agreed to stay that I'm going to be here for you whenever you want me, Vinnie,' she told him. 'If you take Fay back then it's over between us. Over for ever.'

He swallowed hard. 'Of course – if you say so.'

'I do. I've never in my life meant anything more.'

When he'd gone she stood in the empty flat staring out of the window, her heart too heavy with misery to cry any more tears. She stood watching from the window as he came out of the side door and walked to the end of the mews. Before he turned into the street he turned back to look up at the window, but she drew back so that he wouldn't see her standing there. Why was it that happiness always eluded her? Why were the people she loved always beyond her reach? What terrible sin had she committed that fate should punish her so cruelly?

The train rattled to a halt at Holborn Station and Amy

nudged her mother in the ribs. 'Well – are we getting off here then?' she demanded rudely. 'Or do you want to go on to Ealing?'

They changed platforms and this time when the train arrived there were seats, two separate ones, one at either end of the carriage. Maryan was relieved to be apart from her angry daughter for a while. She closed her eyes, swaying in her seat with the motion of the train, thinking of yesterday when Roisan had called to see her. Vincent's sister's placid face had been pink with rage, her mouth folded into an angry button when she arrived at Simons Mews. Maryan took one look at her expression and invited her into the office at the back of the shop.

'I had to come and see you, Maryan. I want you to know that I think he's taken leave of his senses,' she said the moment the door between them and the shop was closed. 'The woman's a devious bitch and always has been. I warned Vincent about her before they married. I always knew she'd let him down. And I knew she'd be back as soon as she thought there was any money to be had. She's seen the advertisements we placed in magazines and decided there were pickings to be had. That's why she's here. I don't for one moment believe that she never received Vinnie's letters asking for a divorce. And as for the story about the child . . .' She threw up her hands. 'Blatant, outrageous lies, all of it.'

Maryan sighed wearily. 'He's taken her back, Roisan. She's his wife and he has every right to do as he wants. There's nothing either of us can do about it. We don't have the right to interfere.'

Roisan sat down heavily. 'Let's face it, Maryan. I know what you and Vinnie feel about each other. This is no time for pretence. How can you just accept it? Fight for him, girl. You don't for a moment believe he really *wants* her back, do you? I know I don't. She's got him over a barrel. She knows he's a soft touch. We've got to stop her somehow.'

'We can't, Roisan. It wouldn't be right to try and come between them,' Maryan said. 'Vinnie's not soft. He has strong principles. He needs to do what he feels is right. He couldn't find happiness any other way. If I tried to push him into sending her away he'd resent me later.'

'Well, one thing's for certain. He won't find happiness with her,' Roisan said. 'She'll make his life a living hell if I know anything about her. She's already started nagging him to find a flat. That's an expense he can't afford at the moment. We need every penny to invest in the business as you know. And she won't be satisfied with anything but the best either. Mark my words, Maryan, he's heading for disaster. She'll ruin us all before she's done. And just when we were all getting along so well.' She looked at Maryan's determined expression and gave an explosive sigh. 'Oh well, if you won't, you won't. At least you're still working for us. That's something, I suppose.'

Maryan walked with her through the shop and saw her out, trying to reassure her that everything would work out for the best; a reassurance she didn't for one moment believe in. And as she closed the door behind her she was overwhelmed by the feeling that nothing could ever be the same again. The excitement of helping Vincent and Roisan to build their business; the way she had believed her luck was changing; her beautiful golden dream of a future with Vincent, all lay in ruins at her feet.

Someone was tugging impatiently at her arm and she opened her eyes with a start. She must have nodded off for a moment. Amy was standing over her, her face pink with irritation.

'Mum, come *on*, wake up. This is our station.'

Getting to her feet, Maryan followed her daughter out onto the platform, wondering how she would explain to her what had happened during her absence; asking herself how she would heal this new rift that had come between them, wishing there were someone she could turn to for comfort. As she came out of the Underground station into the afternoon sunlight and headed for Simons Mews she had never felt more alone in her life.

Part Three

Chapter Thirteen

'Now, put out all the candles with one blow and you'll be sure to get your wish.'

Roisan put the birthday cake with its lighted candles down on the table in front of Amy and stood back. 'Well, what are you waiting for?' She peered, frowning, at the cake. 'I did put on the right number, didn't I? I'm sure I counted out seventeen.'

Amy laughed, her eyes bright. 'Yes, they're all there. It's just that I wasn't expecting a cake too. Oh, Roisan, you are kind.' She jumped up and hugged Roisan till, laughing and misty-eyed, she extricated herself and put the cake knife into Amy's hand.

'Go on with you. It's nothing. Just a morsel of sponge cake and a bit of icing sugar. Can't let your seventeenth birthday pass without a cake, now can we? And your mother so busy. Come on now – blow, wish and then cut before we all die of starvation.'

Amy filled her lungs, then, watched by Roisan and Celia, she closed her eyes and blew hard. When all the candles went out Roisan and Celia clapped.

'Well done,' Celia said. 'You'll get your wish for sure now. And we've no need to ask what it was, have we?'

Amy cut the first slice and Roisan passed the plates round the table.

'Come on now. Tuck in. I don't want any leftovers.'

As Amy ate her cake she thought of all the other

birthdays she'd had. Before the war it had been Grandma and Tom who had made them special. At Mitcham Lodge Auntie Marjorie had always given her a party with all her schoolfriends. This was the fourth birthday she'd had since she had been back in London. On the first two Mum had taken her to the pictures and out for tea afterwards. Last year she'd been too busy even to do that. And when Roisan had invited her round to tea for this one she'd shaken her head, telling her that she was really too old for birthday tea parties now.

Roisan had thrown up her hands in horror. 'Sure you're *never* too old for a little treat on your birthday,' she said. 'And aren't you the only person I've got left to spoil? Now that my Colin has left home for good and Vinnie's gone too I've no one to make a fuss of.'

Roisan's son Colin had got married just over a year ago to a girl he'd met at college and they had set up home in Manchester, where Colin worked as a lecturer at the technical college and his wife taught at a primary school. Since Vincent's wife Fay had returned and they'd moved to a flat of their own, Roisan had been living alone in the little house in Notting Hill. When Amy's birthday loomed she had been only too glad of the excuse to spend some time in the kitchen, making all the things she never bothered with for herself. She'd telephoned Amy the week before.

'A little bird reminded me that a certain young lady has a birthday next week,' she said. 'Now – your mother tells me she has a sale to go to and she's likely to be gone all day, so as it's half term why don't you come and spend the day with me? You can help me in the workroom if you like – or give Miss Stokes a hand.' She laughed. 'If she doesn't scare the pants off you, that is. I know she does me.'

Amy was delighted. 'Oh, Roisan, that would be lovely. Thank you.' She loved Roisan's house with its homely, untidy rooms spilling over with interesting things. 'Can I ask Celia to come to tea as well?' she asked. Celia had taken shorthand and typing in her last year and had left school the previous July. She now worked as an office junior for the same magazine company as her mother in Southampton Street.

'Of *course* you can. Ask whoever you like,' Roisan said generously.

So here they were, sitting round the big table in Roisan's kitchen, stuffing themselves with all the good things that Roisan had made, ending with the sumptuous illuminated birthday cake.

The girls smiled at each other across the table. Apart from growing taller, Amy hadn't changed much in the past two years. Now in her final year at St Hildred's, she was restless. She had longed to leave last year with Celia but Maryan was adamant. As long as her daughter had the chance of a proper education she was going to have it. She'd passed her School Certificate with Matriculation and Maryan had been assured by her teachers that there was every chance the girl would get a good Higher Certificate too.

Celia on the other hand had changed out of all recognition. Gone were the long fair bob and chubby freckled face. Now her hair was cut and permed in the short, fashionable 'bubble cut' and her puppy fat had been whittled away by the diet her mother had put her on. Her newly revealed facial bones gave her a attractive gamin look. She wore make-up every day now, foundation, powder and lipstick; she even got away with a little mascara to darken her pale lashes. Amy on the other hand was only allowed a dash of lipstick at weekends. Celia had smart fashionable clothes too, nylons and high-heeled shoes, which she bought with the money she earned. Amy envied her friend all this sophistication, though she'd never have let her see it. Celia was still her best friend and she never flaunted her new adult status or made Amy feel childish.

Later, as they were travelling back to Simons Mews together, Celia enquired whether Amy had heard from Mike.

'Not since he finished his National Service. He's really

304

busy with his job now,' Amy told her. 'Journalists work long hours, and Mike is hoping to be offered the job of junior reporter on the *Clarion* soon.'

Celia looked suitably impressed. 'He must be coming up for twenty-one,' she said. 'I expect you'll get an invite to his party.'

Amy shrugged. 'Maybe – if he has one. Anyway, it's not for ages yet. Anything could have happened by then.'

Celia looked at her with interest. 'Oh? Like what?'

Amy shrugged. 'I don't know – anything.'

The 'anything' she referred to was her own gloomy theory that the way things were going it looked as if Mike might well be getting engaged on his birthday. His last three letters had been full of a girl he had met. She worked as a secretary on the *Clarion* and her name was Julia Honeywell and she was the same age as him. Deeply wounded by the news, Amy hadn't mentioned her to anyone, not even Celia. The thought of Mike falling in love with someone else hurt too much. At night she lay in bed thinking of Mike's eighteenth birthday party; the night when they had sat by the pond together and he had kissed her. Doris Day had recorded a song last year. It was called 'It's Magic' and the words described exactly how she felt. She'd bought the record and played it over and over when she was alone. Now she tortured herself imagining what this Julia Honeywell would be like. Mike had described her as a redhead. She'd be glamorous, of course. A bit like Rita Hayworth; a great cloud of wavy hair, endless, shapely legs and pouting red lips. And of course she'd wear fabulous, sexy clothes. Amy felt her angry teenage frustration burning her up. It was as if she was a woman trapped eternally in childhood. It wasn't *fair*. Other girls of her age were out earning their own living; allowed to look and behave like adults, whilst she still had to sit in a classroom all day, listening to the nuns droning on and on. She hated the school uniform she was still obliged to wear; the sensible shoes and thick stockings and the dreaded hat. She was quite tall now, almost five foot seven, and she felt ridiculous in her pleated skirt, blazer and Breton hat with its school badge. On the Underground each morning she was sure that people were staring at her – laughing behind their hands at this great tall girl dressed up like a *kid*.

Of course it was all her mother's fault. Amy was convinced that Maryan was determined to keep her dependent on her for as long as possible – just to humiliate her, or perhaps it was just to make herself appear younger. It certainly wasn't because she enjoyed having her around. Most of the time Maryan was preoccupied with her work. She lived and breathed it, having less time for Amy or any kind of home life than ever before. Then there was this mysterious business about Vincent's wife coming back. Instead of leaving when it happened, as Amy thought she would have done, Mum had been throwing herself into her job harder than ever, working long hours and sometimes weekends too. And of course Vincent never came round to see them any more except to talk business. Their love affair, if that was what it was, was definitely finished, and yet the school fees obviously still got paid. Maybe *that* was why Mum had stayed on. In which case Amy fervently wished she hadn't. Still, there was one consolation: at least she wouldn't be getting *Uncle Vinnie* as a step-father.

'Tell me what I've just said?' Celia had stepped in front of her and was staring challengingly into her face. Amy stopped walking and blinked guiltily at her friend.

'I – er . . . Oh, I'm sorry, Cee. What did you say?'

'I *said* I'd read in the paper that clothes are coming off coupons soon. Isn't that terrific?'

'Yes. Sorry. I was miles away.'

Celia gave an explosive snort. 'Huh! You don't have to *tell* me. You're only on this *planet* about half the time lately. What's up, Amy – something on your mind?'

Amy shook her head impatiently. 'It's just that I'm so fed up with school,' she confessed. 'I mean, for instance, it won't make much difference to me, clothes coming off ration, will it? I've got no money to buy any. Anyway, all I ever wear is my rotten school uniform. I feel so – so left

306

behind, Cee. It's so irritating, being made to stay on when I know that all I want is to be an actress. You don't need Highers for acting, do you?'

Celia pulled a face. 'Don't know really. I suppose it's bound to help whatever you do. Anyway, cheer up, droopy-drawers. It's not for much longer, is it? And you've still got your gorgeous Mike.'

But Amy knew she hadn't got Mike. Not any longer. At least, not in the way she would have liked. Although they'd exchanged letters after he began his National Service, they'd met only infrequently. At first Mike had been stationed up north. Later he'd moved down to a camp nearer to London and had come up two or three times to stay with relatives. They'd spent a couple of hours together, usually in the company of others. On the last occasion he'd written to ask if she'd like to see the new musical, *Oklahoma*, and Amy had looked forward to it eagerly for weeks. It made her feel so grown-up to be seen with a young man in uniform. But to her disappointment Mike had brought three other friends along with him and although they sat together in the theatre he hadn't even held her hand – not even during the singing of the romantic hit song, 'People Will Say We're in Love'. She'd hoped to recapture the magic of that summer night in the garden at Mitcham Lodge, but when Mike had dropped her off at Simons Mews after the show he had left her with the briefest of brotherly pecks, his friends looking on from the taxi. As she waved them off she reflected that sometimes it was almost as though she had dreamed it all.

The letters Mike had written since his demob were friendly and filled with news. The Army seemed to have matured him out of all recognition. Now he was eager and full of enthusiasm to get his career off to a good start like Celia and so many of her other contemporaries. They were all moving on while she was still marking time. How could she expect him to be interested in hearing about St Hildred's school concert, or a visit to the Science Museum? He'd probably even be ashamed to admit to his friends that he was writing to a girl who was still at school.

For this reason it had been she who'd let the intervals between letters grow longer. And now Mike had found this girl – this super, sophisticated Julia Honeywell. Her life was over before it had begun, she told herself despondently. Not that anyone cared. Least of all her mother.

'I don't think I can bear school for much longer,' she told Celia. 'It's making my life a misery.'

Celia squeezed her arm affectionately. 'Poor old sausage. You are down in the dumps, and on your birthday too. Come on, I'll treat you to the pictures. I've been dying to see Bob Hope in *Paleface*, haven't you? Everyone says it's an absolute scream, and they sing that song, 'Button and Bows'. I love that, don't you?' She quickened her pace, pulling Amy along behind her, humming a snatch of the song. 'Come on, we'll just catch the last house if we hurry. It's just what you need to cheer you up.'

It was dark by the time Maryan drove the van into the mews. It had been a good sale and though she was tired she had the feeling of satisfaction that a successful sale always gave her. With the help of Geoff Masters, Vincente Antiques' newest employee, she had bought three good pieces that she felt sure were just what Vincent was looking for.

Geoff Masters had been working for Vincente Antiques for a year and a half now. Vincent had discovered him working as a porter for one of the auction rooms. Geoff had been disabled by a war wound and the heavy work was clearly causing him problems. Talking to him, Vincent had discovered that he was an expert restorer and had worked for a well-known cabinet maker before the war. He had offered him a job on the spot. Now Geoff worked in Vincent's workshop in the basement at Simons Mews, restoring damaged and neglected pieces of antique furniture to their former beauty with loving precision. He always accompanied Maryan to sales, examining pieces and assessing their potential. But it was Maryan who had become the expert bidder, often getting valuable pieces that appeared worthless for knock-down prices.

She put the van away in the garage and locked it securely. She had dropped Geoff off at his home in Fulham on the way home. They would unload their purchases in the morning. Fishing in her bag for her key under the streetlamp, she let herself in at the side door and went up to the flat. The place was in darkness, but on the kitchen table was a note from Amy.

Gone to the pictures with Celia. Back at ten-thirty –
Amy.

Maryan took off her coat and filled the kettle. She was hungry. They hadn't eaten much all day. It would have been nice to have had the kind of daughter who would have had a meal waiting. Then she remembered that it was Amy's birthday and felt guilty. Of course she should go out and enjoy herself with her friend, she told herself. After all, I couldn't offer to take her. I'm just being selfish.

But as she set about cutting bread to make herself a sandwich she felt depressed about the relationship that she and Amy shared. Even if she had offered to take Amy somewhere on her birthday she wouldn't have wanted to go – not with her. They were like two ships that passed in the night; communicating mostly like this, by leaving notes for each other. As she prepared her solitary meal she wondered what would happen once Amy left school and began to earn her own living. She guessed that she would want her freedom and independence. The closeness she had looked forward to all through the long war years had never materialised.

She felt guilty in some ways, but in others she blamed the war. If only there had been more time for them to spend together – time to try to understand one another. There was always so much to do, but it was chiefly for Amy that she had built her new career. And she reasoned that if it hadn't been for the war she would never have had this chance to prove what she could do. Life was strangely perverse sometimes.

Then there was that business with the Taylor boy. Amy had seemed so keen on him, wanting him to come and stay. Maryan had seen all the signs and been afraid. It was herself and Marcus all over again. However friendly, the Taylors weren't their class and never would be. Amy would be hurt just as she had. Now she saw that by trying to nip Amy's teenage passion in the bud she had only strengthened it, and made an ogre of herself into the bargain. The girl never confided in her; never wanted to talk about her feelings or ask for advice. Maybe it was all her fault. Perhaps she had never been cut out for motherhood.

Looking back, she felt that she should have left when Vincent's wife came back and their affair came to an end. With hindsight she felt that Amy would not have cared, one way or the other. This flat had never been a real home to the girl anyway. And a clean break would certainly have been much less emotionally difficult.

But in spite of all that had happened Maryan still loved her job. Each day brought with it a fresh challenge. And with the knowledge of the antiques business and the management skills she had acquired, she knew that she had become a valuable asset to the firm. Now that Paul and Geoff had joined the staff at Simons Mews her working life was more organised.

Hoping to prove what he thought of her, Vincent had given her a substantial rise in salary recently. Along with the cheque there had been a short letter, saying that the rise was in appreciation of all her hard work. The note had wounded her to the heart for reasons she was reluctant to probe.

They saw very little of each other these days; communicating mainly on the telephone or through Roisan. She had stuck firmly to her decision to end their love affair when Fay had come back. Not that it had been easy, especially at the beginning. Seeing him; speaking to him on a purely business level; trying to pretend that they had never been more than employer and employee had been torture. She suspected it was for him too. And for that reason she was grateful that he kept his visits down to the minimum.

Fay, on the other hand, was a regular visitor. She arrived at the shop at least once a week, usually at the most inconvenient time. Obviously determined to flaunt her position as the boss's wife, she would wander round the shop pretending to knowledge she didn't possess about antiques, checking for dust and looking for something to criticise. Her interference upset and offended Paul, who loathed her, and Maryan usually took her into the office for coffee just to get her out of his way.

'I can't think why you keep that young man,' she'd said to Maryan the previous week. 'He's got a shifty look about him if you ask me. You want to watch he hasn't got his fingers in the till, especially with you being away from the place so much.'

'Paul is very loyal and he's a hard worker,' Maryan told her stiffly. 'I'd be lost without him. He's always glad to stay on after closing time or help me in any way he can.'

Fay sniffed, arranging the folds of her new fur coat. 'Mmm, I wonder why? In my experience nobody works for nothing. Like I said, you don't want to be too trusting, dear. You want to take my advice and watch him. After all, *you're* the one who'll carry the can back if anything goes wrong, aren't you? Vinnie puts a lot of trust in you, but as I always say, people are only human.'

Maryan boiled with resentment but she held her tongue. She suspected that Fay would do her best to make trouble for any of the staff she happened to take a dislike to – herself included.

Vincent and Fay had moved to a flat in Kensington soon after Fay's reappearance. Roisan worried about him constantly. In the early days she'd made frequent visits to the shop, telling Maryan that he wasn't happy – complaining that she had never known him so withdrawn and worried, until at last Maryan was forced to ask her

311

to stop. As she explained to Roisan, there was nothing either of them could do about it. Whatever Fay was like, it had been Vincent's decision to take his wife back. They must let him live his life as he had chosen.

When the kettle boiled Maryan made the tea. Taking her tray into the living room she went to draw the curtains, but a movement in the mews below caught her eye. Someone was standing at the side door. She waited for a ring at the bell, but the next moment she heard the street door downstairs open and close. Her heart quickened. It was much too early for Amy and only one other person had a key. As she reached the top of the stairs Vincent was already halfway up. When he saw her he paused.

'Maryan. I'm sorry if I startled you.'

'I – wondered who it could be,' Maryan said breathlessly. 'There's nothing wrong, I hope?'

'No.' He followed her into the room. Catching sight of the tray he said: 'Oh, you were about to eat. I'm sorry.'

'It's all right. Perhaps you'd like some tea? It's freshly made.'

'No.' He waved his hand. 'Do have yours, though. I can say what I've come to say while you're eating.'

'The sale was good,' Maryan told him. 'Geoff and I haven't been back long. We did quite well – got a Regency drum table and a lovely Chinese lacquered cabinet. Both badly distressed, but Geoff seems confident that he can restore them. There's a little Jacobean court cupboard too. When I tell you what I got them for you'll . . .'

'Maryan. I've come to ask you something,' he interrupted. 'Roisan and I are going to register Vincente's and Decor as a company. She and I will be joint managing directors, of course, but we'd like you to be on the board of directors with us. What do you say?'

She stared at him, stunned. A director of a company – *her* – Maryan Jessop? The offer was so totally unexpected that she was temporarily speechless. 'I – I don't know what to say – except . . . I mean, don't directors . . . ? Wouldn't I be required to put some money in? I'm afraid

I haven't got very much. I've got some savings put by, but not enough to . . .'

'No, *no*.' He was shaking his head. That's not why I'm asking you, Maryan. Your contribution will be the hard work you've put in and the skills you've learned. You've been with us from the beginning of our venture. Four years of studying and learning; working hard right from scratch. You are our most valued asset now. We simply couldn't have done it without you. So we'd like you to be a real part of the company now that we're becoming established.'

Maryan felt herself blushing. 'But – I'm just – just an ordinary person.'

He laughed. 'And what do you think I am?'

Confused, she shook her head. 'I'm afraid I don't know much about company practice. What would I have to do as a – a director?'

'What it means is that you'd have a say in any future plans we might make; to share your ideas with us as well as reaping whatever benefits there might be. And of course you'd have a vote on any major decisions we might think of making, including the hiring of new staff – dismissals too, of course.'

Maryan was momentarily speechless. It was so unexpected, and so flattering. 'I can't think why you should make me this offer,' she said firmly. 'I've no qualifications for it. I just do my job as best I can. I'm nothing special, just someone who needed a job when you needed someone.'

'Don't sell yourself short, Maryan,' he said. 'The work you've put in these past four years is worth far more than I've ever paid you for. Well . . . ?' He looked at her expectantly. 'Will you accept?' He was leaning forward in his chair. 'Please say yes, Maryan. Roisan and I have talked this over and it's what we both want.'

'Well, I don't know.' She bit her lip uncertainly. 'What about your wife, Vinnie? What about Fay? I take it she'll be a director too?'

'No.' He frowned. 'Why do you ask? What has Fay to do with this?'

'It's obvious, isn't it? Won't she expect to share in any company her husband is forming?'

At the mention of Fay's name Vincent's eyes clouded as he leaned back in his chair. 'Fay hasn't the slightest interest in the firm. Except to spend the money it makes. She's made it clear that she thinks it all a crashing bore and you can rest assured that she wouldn't be interested in getting involved.'

Maryan was silent, remembering the way Fay behaved when she came to the shop. She certainly seemed to enjoy exploiting her position as Vincent's wife on those occasions. 'Well – as long as you're sure.'

'I am. I promise you. Both Roisan and I are firm on that.'

She smiled. 'Well then. Thank you. I'd be honoured to accept.'

'Marvellous.' He beamed delightedly. 'I'll put your name down on the list of directors. You're one of us now, Maryan.'

For a moment they sat looking at each other and suddenly the atmosphere became charged. Anxious to break the increasing tension that was building between them, Maryan stood up.

'Well – thank you for coming – for asking me.'

'Not at all. I'd better go – let you get on with your meal. Your tea will be cold.'

'That's all right. I'll see you out.' They reached the door at the same time and as their hands reached simultaneously for the door handle their fingers touched. Maryan snatched her hand back as though she'd received an electric shock and he turned to look into her eyes.

'It's wonderful to see you, Maryan,' he said quietly. 'To have the chance to talk like this. When you're on the board with us we'll have more chances to meet.'

'Yes – perhaps,' she said, her eyes downcast.

He touched her shoulder. 'Maryan – I can't tell you

how glad I am that you stayed on after – what happened. Are – are you happy?'

Stung by the question she looked up at him. '*Are you?*' In his dark expressive eyes she saw her own pain reflected and the breath caught in her throat. 'You'd better go now, Vinnie,' she said. But he stood where he was, his hand on her shoulder, looking into her eyes.

'I wonder if you've been through the hell I've been through,' he said huskily. 'I know I hurt you, but believe me, Maryan, I hurt myself even more. It's only the business that makes life worth living most of the time. That and knowing that you're still here. Believe me, Maryan, I've had ample time to ask myself whether it was all worth it. Fay and I . . .'

'*Please*, Vinnie. I don't want to hear this. I can cope if I don't have to be close to you too often. If I . . .' She stopped speaking to look at him, her eyes wide as she asked: 'You haven't offered me this directorship because . . . ?'

'*No*. My dear girl, I don't want you to think that; not for one minute. Everything I said is true. Roisan and I have talked it over and we want you with us. It was purely a business offer, because we – we *both* value your dedication.' His fingers tightened on her shoulder. 'I'm sorry, my dear. It's just coming here tonight and finding you alone – seeing you like this. Remembering the times when we . . .'

'*Don't*.' She tried to twist out of his grasp but he caught her other shoulder and drew her to him.

'Perhaps I'm being selfish, but I want you to know that I still love you, Maryan,' he whispered, his voice muffled against her hair. 'I always will, no matter what. I can't help myself.' His lips found hers and for a moment she remained stiff in his arms, then, unable to resist the passionate insistence of his kiss, she melted against him, responding with all the pent-up longing she had denied for so long, her knees weak and her heart pounding. When they drew apart he looked down at her, his eyes full of regret. 'It won't go away, will it, Maryan? It's as agonising for you as it is for me.' She nodded wordlessly and he went on with a sigh: 'But it's something I'm afraid we're both going to have to live with.'

Stung to anger, she pushed him away. 'Not *me*, Vinnie,' she said, almost choking with bitterness. '*I* don't have to live with it. I'm doing my best to forget what happened between us, and I'll succeed if only you'll let me. I'm trying to pick up the pieces and make a life for myself and Amy. I'm going to have to ask you not to come here again, like this – alone. If you can't guarantee that our future association will be on a strictly business footing, I'll have to reconsider the offer you've just made me. I'll have to leave.'

He dropped his hands to his sides and nodded, smiling ruefully. 'I deserved that. Of course I understand. What I've just said and done was very wrong. But please don't leave, Maryan. Without you . . .'

'*Goodnight*, Vinnie.'

He took one last look at her pale face, then turned and walked down the stairs, letting himself out without looking back. Maryan watched, holding her breath until the street door had closed behind him and the sound of his footsteps grew fainter. Then she gave a long, shuddering sigh and sank down onto the top step, one hand over her mouth, unleashing the torrent of harsh, choking sobs that threatened to tear her heart to pieces.

It was two weeks later that Sam arrived at Simons Mews. Over the past four years he had visited Maryan several times. Whenever he had occasion to come up to the West End on business he would look in on her to satisfy himself that she was still all right and that she and Amy had everything they needed. He always came when he knew that Amy would be at school, though. The thought of seeing the girl he could not acknowledge as his granddaughter was too much for him to contemplate.

Paul came into the office halfway through the morning to tell Maryan that Mr Leigh was waiting to see her. Smiling in anticipation, she came out immediately and saw him standing in the middle of the shop; a stocky, dark-coated figure, his black homburg hat in his hand. For the first time she noticed with a twinge of nostalgia that he was growing old. His hair was greyer and thinner than it had been, and he seemed to have shrunk since she last saw him. She felt a surge of affection towards the man who had been like a father to her for so many years. In spite of his unswerving loyalty to his wife, Sam had never let her down. She went to greet him, her hands outstretched.

'Mr Sam. How nice to see you. Come up to the flat and I'll make you some coffee.'

When they were seated in the living room she asked him how he was.

'Fine, my dear,' he nodded. 'Fine, thank you.'

'Business going well?' Again he nodded. 'And Mrs Leigh?'

'Aaah.' Sam sighed and spread his hands expressively. 'My Rachel works too hard. She worries me. But what does she care for my opinion?'

Maryan nodded. 'I knew there was something worrying you. Do you want to tell me about it?'

'It's the new line.'

Maryan smiled to herself. She could imagine how irritated Rachel must be when Sam insisted on referring to the Marcus Leigh Collection as, 'The New Line' – as though it consisted of mass-produced floral print dresses for sale on the street markets.

'Marcus's couture designs, you mean?' she asked.

He nodded. 'She works all hours. Up till the small hours of the morning – making contacts abroad, arranging shows, planning publicity. She won't rest until his name is a household word throughout the world. She's *killing* herself, Maryan.' He shook his head. 'I've told her – Marcus wouldn't have wanted her to ruin her health for him. He never wanted fame and riches. His life was spent in helping people.'

'I know,' Maryan said quietly.

'The thing is . . .' Sam crumbled the biscuit on his

plate. 'The thing is that the designs we're selling now aren't Marcus's any more. They're the work of Gina Stern. She's talented, young and ambitious. I feel it's only a matter of time before she'll want to spread her own wings. What will Rachel do then?'

'Maybe by then Marcus's name will have achieved the fame she wants,' Maryan suggested.

Sam sighed. 'I can't see that ever happening. Rachel drives herself relentlessly. She is never satisfied. I don't think she ever will be. Gina has already suggested leaving once. Seems she had an offer from a rival firm. Rachel was devastated – didn't sleep for nights on end. She almost made herself sick with worry. In the end she offered the girl an enormous salary increase. I tell you, I was shocked. It was out of all proportion – just to keep her designing under the name of Marcus Leigh.' He shook his head. 'Well, then I knew for sure. My Rachel has always been such a sound businesswoman. This thing had stopped being an ambition and become an obsession with her.' He looked up at Maryan, his brown eyes sad and anxious. 'But will she listen to me?' He shook his head sadly. 'There's the money too.'

Maryan shook her head. 'The money?'

'The designs have made a fortune, both here and on the Continent. Now the Marcus Leigh look is sweeping America. But Rachel won't touch the money. She insists that all the running costs are met out of Feldman Fashions. She says she's putting it all in a high-interest, long-term investment.' He lifted his shoulders. 'But what *for*? I've asked her again and again, but she just shakes her head and says it's what *he* would have wanted. I don't know what to do about it, Maryan. It's almost as though she's still expecting him to come back. Sometimes I fear for her sanity.'

Maryan reached out and touched his hand. 'Try not to worry. I'm sure her own good sense will come to her rescue before long. Perhaps you could persuade her to go for a nice long holiday somewhere abroad where she could relax.'

'Maybe. I'll try. I hope you're right, my dear. I do hope you're right.' He drained his cup and passed it to Maryan to refill. 'But – tell me about yourself. And Amy. How is Amy doing?'

'Oh, we're both well,' Maryan passed him his cup. 'Something quite exciting has happened for me. This firm – Vincente's – has been registered as a company. And I've been offered a directorship.'

Sam's sad eyes brightened with delight. 'But that's wonderful. Congratulations. I'm sure you deserve it. You've worked so hard.' He reached out to pat her hand. 'Sometimes, my dear, I believe that leaving us was the best thing you could have done. You were always wasted in domestic work.' When Maryan failed to agree he asked: 'And little Amy? Still enjoying the school?'

'She got her Matriculation as you know,' Maryan told him. 'Later this year she takes her Higher Certificate. The Mother Superior tells me she has every chance of doing well.'

Sam nodded with satisfaction. 'Wonderful, wonderful. I'm proud of you both.'

'She couldn't have done it without your help,' Maryan said. 'She doesn't know you pay her fees, of course. But one day I'll tell her how much you've helped her – helped us both.'

He shook his head. 'No, no. It's enough for me to know she's taken care of and getting the education that Marcus's daughter deserves.'

'I wish you and she could get to know one another better,' Maryan said wistfully.

'So do I, believe me, my dear. But it's better this way.' Sam got to his feet and began to button his coat. 'I wish so much that Rachel could have accepted things as they are. I'd rather she had put her energy and love into the child than into this – this treadmill to madness she's obsessed herself with.'

Maryan walked with him to the end of the mews and saw him into a taxi. As she stood on the kerb, waving to him, a feeling of depression engulfed her. If only her

319

mother could have talked to Rachel Leigh she might have made her see sense as she always had in days gone by. For all the differences in religion, race and class, Sarah and her beloved 'Miss Rachel' had shared the common ground of motherhood and loss that makes all women equal. Theirs had been a very special relationship. If only Sarah could have lived a little longer, things might have been so very different for them all. Maryan turned and walked slowly back to the shop with a heavy heart.

Amy was bored. The Easter holidays stretched ahead and with Celia working there was absolutely nothing for her to do. Maryan suggested that she might like to help in the office or the shop, but she wasn't really interested in antiques and just felt in the way there. She made herself useful around the flat and amused herself trying her hand at cookery, but before long the outdoors beckoned. With spring in the air she longed for Rhensham but had to make do with London streets instead, where the dusty sparrows twittered and quarrelled over discarded crusts under the stunted trees trying to burst into leaf at the pavement's edge. She spent a lot of time looking around the shops, gazing longingly at the colourful new spring clothes that now could be bought without clothing coupons, and wishing she could afford to buy herself something new that was her choice and not her mother's.

It was on the Wednesday of the second week when Celia rang. Amy was alone in the flat and answered the telephone herself.

'Hello, Amy, it's me. How about going out for the day?'

'Aren't you at work?'

'No. I had a bit of a tummy upset last night and Mum thought I'd better have the day off,' Celia explained. 'But I feel fine again now. Seems a pity to waste a day off, so I thought if you felt like it . . .'

'But – suppose someone sees you?'

'Hard cheese. I'll say I was on my way to the doctor's.'

Amy giggled. 'Well, if you like. Did you have anything in mind?'

'Not really. We could have a look round the shops, then a snack and go to the pictures – or even a theatre. In the gods, of course. We'd get a front seat if we started queuing early.'

'Well, all right.'

'Meet me at Alaniano's in half an hour. We can have a coffee first.' Celia dropped the receiver quickly before her friend could change her mind.

Alaniano's was a milk bar the girls often frequented in the King's Road. It had a bar with high stools, freshly made doughnuts and a coffee machine that hissed and spluttered. It also had a coin-operated jukebox which attracted all the local teenagers. The owner's name was Alan Springer, but with his dark, swarthy looks he passed for Italian, in spite of his strong cockney accent, hence the name, *Alaniano's* emblazoned above the bar itself and inside, scrawled artistically across the mirror behind the counter in red and blue paint.

When Amy arrived Celia was already there, dressed to kill in her latest full-skirted dress in a brightly coloured plaid taffeta and a cut away jacket of black wool. She was flirting with Alan as he made up sandwiches behind the bar, and she'd already made her choice of record. Perched on her stool at the counter, she shook her shoulders provocatively, singing along to the record.

'All I need is loving you and music, music, music.' She caught sight of Amy and waved. 'Hi. Come on in. I've already got you a coffee.'

Amy was acutely aware of how dowdy she looked in comparison to her friend. She was wearing her 'best' dress, a button-through design in red wool jersey. She'd had it for over a year and in spite of the fact that she'd changed the buttons and stitched on a new white collar it still looked hopelessly unfashionable to her. She slid onto the stool next to Celia and caught sight of her friend eyeing the dress.

'Okay – go on, say it,' she said, blushing with discomfort.

'Say what?' Celia passed her the sugar in its giant shaker.

'My dress. It's awful, isn't it? You always make me feel like a real frump with your fashionable clothes.'

Celia put down her cup and leaned towards Amy. 'Listen, stupid. You haven't the slightest idea of how attractive you are, have you? You don't even *know* that whatever you wear the boys all stare at you. You're too busy feeling sorry for yourself.'

Blushing, Amy hid her face in her cup. 'It's not true. You know it isn't. I can't flirt like you do.'

Celia sighed with exaggerated patience. 'Of course you can't. And that's *exactly* what fascinates them,' she said. 'You're – oh, I don't know – all coolness and mystery and what-d'you-call-it, *enigma* – like Ingrid Bergman.'

Pleased, Amy laughed and gave her friend a push. 'Oh go on. You're full of rubbish this morning. Drink up your coffee and let's go.'

The girls caught the bus up to Oxford Circus and gazed at the shop windows. They were full of Dior's New Look: long, swirling skirts and figure-hugging jackets a bit like the one that Celia was wearing. But the Marcus Leigh look still seemed to be popular. It had changed subtly since the first designs had been launched, with the introduction of floating panels and looser, more flowing lines, reminiscent of the twenties. Recently Marcus Leigh hats and shoes had been launched too, to complete the Leigh ensemble. Celia stopped as they walked down Argyle Street, riveted by a particularly striking Leigh outfit in the window of an exclusive boutique. Its citrus yellow and gold made a splash of colour in the centre of the small window.

'Now *that* would suit you,' she said, her head on one side. 'It's so fresh and spring-like and the contrasting colours are like sunshine and shadow.'

'It's all right, I suppose,' Amy said, hurrying on. If only she could tell Celia that the famous Marcus Leigh

322

was her father. But she had no right. She had no right to claim anything, it seemed. She was nobody – daughter of no one. Depression descended on her again. She grabbed Celia's arm. 'Come on. Let's get a bus and go down to Leicester Square. We can get something to eat at Lyons Corner House.'

After beans on toast and an ice-cream apiece Amy and Celia made their way to Shaftesbury Avenue to look at the theatres.

'There's *The Lady's Not For Burning* at The Globe or *The Little Hut* at The Lyric,' Celia said, looking up at the rival theatres. 'Which one do you fancy?'

'Don't know that I'm in the mood for either,' Amy said. 'It seems a shame to go inside when the sun's shining.' In actual fact she didn't think she could face seeing people doing the one thing she herself wanted so badly to do. Sometimes it seemed that she would never realise her ambition; never really amount to anything. Celia shrugged good-naturedly.

'P'raps you're right. Maybe a walk and then a news theatre later on. We can drool over the latest film of Princess Elizabeth's baby and have a good laugh at some cartoons, eh?'

They wandered until they lost themselves among the maze of back streets behind Shaftesbury Avenue and were just about to turn back when they noticed a queue of people standing outside what looked like a disused cinema. With her usual open curiosity Celia went up to the last person in the queue and asked what they were waiting for.

'They're auditioning at three,' the girl said.

'Who's "they"?' Celia asked. 'And what are they auditioning for?'

'It's Alex Keynan, the director. He's forming a new repertory company – to tour up north.'

'I see.' The girls walked slowly on in silence, each of them busy with her own thoughts, then Celia turned to Amy. 'Go on, I dare you,' she said.

Amy stared at her. 'Dare me to what?'

'You know damn well. Get in the queue. Audition for a job. You know you want to.'

Amy's cheeks burned crimson. It was as though Celia had read her thoughts. 'I couldn't,' she said. 'What – what about school and – and Mum?'

'Time to worry about that if they offer you a job,' Celia said. 'It'd be a lark just to have a go, wouldn't it? Good experience for you too.' She glanced scathingly at the queue. 'Anyway, I bet you can do as well as that lot. They look like a bunch of drips to me.'

'But they'll all have prepared something,' Amy argued, terrified and excited all at the same time. 'They'll have rehearsed and everything. I haven't got anything ready.'

'Oh, rubbish. What about all that poetry we did at school? And that Shakespeare play you were in – *Twelfth Night*? I bet you can remember some of that.'

In her mind Amy was already going over Viola's lines. *Make me a willow cabin at your gate*, her inner voice recited. She did remember it. *Could* she really do it? Dare she?

There was a sudden buzz of interest as the doors up ahead opened and the line of people began to move forward. Celia elbowed Amy into the queue and began to propel her forward towards the open door.

'Go on, kid,' she hissed in her ear. 'You're as good as them, I bet. *Better*. Tell you what, half a crown says you can do it.'

'All right. You're on.'

As they reached the door a young man with a clipboard took their names and gave each of them a slip of paper with a number on it, then they were ushered through into the empty auditorium which had been stripped of everything except a few rows of chairs in front of a hastily improvised platform. In the centre of the front row sat three people: a man with grey hair and a beard, a woman with glasses, and another man who stood up when they were all assembled, introducing himself as Alex Keynan.

Sitting in the back row, Celia nudged Amy. 'Ever heard of him?'

324

Amy shook her head. 'Don't think so.'

'Quite good-looking, isn't he?' Celia remarked. 'For his age, I mean. Thirty-five if he's a day.'

Amy looked at the slip of paper in her hand. 'Look, I'm number twenty-four. We'll be here for hours. Are you sure you want to stay?'

Celia grabbed her wrist and held her tightly. 'You just stay where you are, my child,' she instructed. 'I grew up in this game, remember. It won't take nearly as long as you think.'

Celia was right. The first few candidates were stopped midway through their audition piece and told to give their addresses to the man on the door. 'Thank you. We'll be in touch in due course,' Alex Keynan told them.

Celia pulled a face. '*Don't call us, we'll call you,*' she muttered under her breath. 'That's the kiss of death. Told you they were a bunch of deadbeats. You'll knock spots off 'em, kid.'

Amy's turn came round sooner than she'd thought. There had been several young actors and actresses who sounded really good to her. They'd been allowed to finish their pieces and, in addition, some had been asked to read from a script the assistant producer handed them. Now it was her turn and she seriously doubted whether her wobbling knees would carry her as far as the platform. To her surprise they did. For a moment she stood there, deeply conscious of the three pairs of expectant eyes that were concentrated on her.

'Right, begin whenever you're ready,' Alex Keynan prompted, looking up at her over the frames of his horn-rimmed reading glasses.

Amy took a deep breath to calm her hammering heartbeat, then began, playing both parts in her favourite scene between Olivia and Viola from *Twelfth Night*. As soon as the first lines had squeezed past her constricted throat she relaxed and forgot where she was. Her nerves calmed as she sank herself into the characters, speaking the lines of both with conviction. At last she came to the end of the scene with Viola's exit line: *Farewell, fair cruelty*. There was a short silence as she came down to earth again. She looked out at the three people lined up before her. Then Alex Keynan looked up, cleared his throat and said:

'Thank you, Miss – er . . .' He peered at the clipboard on his lap. 'Miss Jessop. If you'd like to leave your address with Peter over there we'll be in touch.'

Amy's cheeks were pink with embarrassment as she rejoined Celia at the back of the hall. 'I told you,' she whispered. 'I feel a fool now. Let's go.' But Celia shook her head. 'Don't be daft. You did all right. They let you finish, didn't they? Let's stay and hear the last few. We might as well.' As Amy sat down reluctantly beside her she squeezed her hand and whispered: 'You were better than any of them – honest.'

'No I *wasn't*,' Amy hissed back. 'I got the *don't call us* treatment. You said it was the kiss of death.'

They sat on, Amy with undisguised impatience and Celia placidly enjoying the entertainment. At last everyone had been seen and Alex rose to his feet and thanked them all for coming. They were filing out when the young man who had checked them in came up and touched Amy's arm.

'Miss Jessop. Mr Keynan would like to speak to you. Will you come this way please?'

Amy stared at him, and then at Celia who nudged her.

'Go on then. I'll wait,' she said.

Amy followed the young man back into the hall to where Alex Keynan was standing with his two colleagues, apparently absorbed in earnest discussion. She stood hesitantly on the fringe of the group until the young man touched Alex on the shoulder and drew his attention to her.

'Ah – Miss Jessop.' He turned away from the others to regard her, his arms folded. He was a tall man in his late thirties with thick dark hair brushed back from his forehead and worn fairly long. He had a typical actor's face: long, mobile mouth and strong nose, high cheekbones and bright, sharp eyes that seemed to Amy to look right through her. Then he smiled and his expression changed instantly, exuding a charm that quite took her breath away.

'I wanted a word with you before you left. Are you a drama student?'

'No.'

'How old are you?'

'Eighteen,' she lied. 'Well – almost.'

'And you want to make the theatre your career, I suppose?'

'Oh, yes. It's all I've *ever* wanted.'

He lifted one eyebrow with a hint of cynicism. 'Such enthusiasm. What it is to be young. Well, I should say right away that I've got all the actors I need for the present, but I was quite impressed by your audition. I do still have a vacancy for a student ASM.' Seeing her mystified expression he explained: 'Student-cum-assistant stage manager. What it boils down to is that you'd lend a hand wherever it's needed backstage: running errands, making coffee, sitting in the prompt corner with the script, that kind of thing, in return for learning the craft of acting. There would be the occasional walk-on part to help you get some experience and you might sometimes be required to understudy too.' Seeing excitement beginning to dance in Amy's eyes he added quickly, 'I warn you, we'd work your backside off and the money's abysmal. Just about enough to pay your digs, if you're lucky.' He peered at her quizzically. 'Well, I'm prepared to take a chance if you are. Do you want to go home and talk to your mother and father about it?'

Amy drew a deep breath. 'I haven't got a father and my mother lets me make my own decisions,' she said. 'I'd like to accept your offer, Mr Keynan.'

'Right.' He was already turning away. 'Just give your particulars to Peter over there and he'll give you all the details. The tour begins a month from Monday, but we'll be travelling up to Lancashire to begin rehearsals on Sunday. Peter will let you know the travelling arrangements.'

'Yes, I see. Thank you, Mr Keynan.'

'So – what do you think your mum will say?' Celia asked as they sat over frothy coffee in a nearby café. She was looking at Amy with open admiration, awed by the magnitude of the decision she'd just made. When she'd dared her to audition she hadn't dreamed that she'd actually be offered a job – still less that she'd have the nerve to take it.

'I doubt if she'll be interested,' Amy said, displaying a bravado she didn't feel. Only now was it beginning to sink in. The euphoria of getting her first job in the theatre was rapidly becoming overshadowed by the prospect of the reception her news would receive – both at home and at school. 'Ever since Vincent made her a director Mum's had even less time for me,' she added with a shrug. 'I should think she'll probably be glad to get rid of me.'

Celia pulled down the corners of her mouth. 'Well – I wouldn't bet on it. You do realise that she can stop you, don't you? You're still under age.'

Amy tossed her head. 'She'd better not try.' But as the girls made their way down to Piccadilly to the Underground Amy's stomach was quaking. She wanted to go to Lancashire with Alex Keynan's theatre company more than anything in the world. But she was already wishing with all her heart that the next few hours were behind her.

Maryan had been glad when Amy announced that she was going out for the day with Celia. She'd been mooning around the place, bored and taciturn, ever since St Hildred's had broken up for the Easter holidays. Sometimes Maryan despaired of the relationship between them ever improving. She'd tried to interest her in the shop and its contents, even given her some filing to do in the office and encouraged her to serve in the shop when Paul was at lunch. But the girl had shown no enthusiasm for any of it. She didn't even seem interested in doing the necessary revision for her coming exams. Getting her out of the flat for the day was frankly a relief and Maryan was glad to be able to apply herself more fully to her work.

She was deep in her monthly book-keeping when Paul tapped on the office door and announced that Mrs Donlan was here and would like to see her.

'I did tell her you were busy,' he added in a whisper.

Maryan laid down her pen with a sigh. Just when she had promised herself an uninterrupted afternoon on the books. But before she had time to speak, Fay, resplendent in fur coat and matching hat, pushed rudely past Paul and into the office.

'I think you and I have got to have a little talk, Mrs Jessop,' she said stridently, her eyes flashing.

A feeling of apprehension stirred uneasily in Maryan's breast. It was clear from the expression on Fay's face that the 'little talk' was going to be anything but pleasant. She had a fair idea of what it was about, too. Rising from the desk she nodded to Paul who was still hovering uncertainly in the doorway. 'Thank you, Paul.' To Fay she said: 'Perhaps you'd like to come upstairs to the flat?'

Fay followed her upstairs in bristling silence. When they reached the living room and Maryan asked if she could take her coat, Fay declined, pulling it round her protectively.

'No thank you. It isn't very warm in here. What I have to say won't take long anyway.'

'Well, have a chair at least,' Maryan said. 'Perhaps you'd like a cup of tea?'

'This isn't a social call,' Fay said with a sniff. 'And you might as well know that I don't take kindly to being told by that – that *upstart* downstairs that one of my husband's *employees* is too busy to see me.'

'That was my fault, not Paul's,' Maryan said calmly. 'I told him I wasn't to be disturbed as I was having an afternoon on the books. Now, is there something I can do for you, Mrs Donlan?'

'Yes, there certainly is.' Fay fixed her with an icy look.

'And I might as well come straight to the point. I want to know what the relationship is between you and my husband?'

Maryan felt as though all the blood in her veins had turned to ice. 'I – don't understand,' she said. 'I work for him. I run the shop and do some of the buying.'

'I know all *that*,' Fay snapped. 'It's what you've been getting up to out of business hours that concerns me.'

'There is nothing between Vincent and me,' Maryan said quietly. 'Ever since you came back to him . . .'

'Ah – so I *was* right then.' Fay was on her feet, her eyes glittering. 'There is something. I knew there had to be a reason for him making you a director.'

'Mrs Donlan, please. Making me a director in the firm was purely a business gesture. I was about to say that since you came back Vincent and I have hardly met at all. Most of our communication is done by telephone.'

'Huh. You expect me to believe that? Why did he give you a seat on the board then, while I – his own wife – am left out of it? I'm completely left in the dark about how the business is doing. All I hear are constant complaints about the money *I* spend.' She paused briefly for breath, looking round her. 'And another thing, this flat; if he's so anxious to save money why should you live here, rent-free in comfort in *our* flat, while Vinnie and I have to pay rent for another place?' She drew herself up to her full height. 'I've decided to give you a month's notice, Mrs Jessop. Now that you're going up in the world I'm sure you'll want to buy a place of your own.' Her eyes glinted triumphantly. 'You'll kindly be out of this flat – shall we say by the first of May? That be convenient to you, will it?'

'I'll take notice from my employer and no one else,' Maryan said, her heart pounding. 'I don't think you really have the right to evict me.'

Fay fumed, her face turning bright scarlet. 'No *right*? Well, we'll see about that. If I say you're to get out, then out you go – understand? I'm still not convinced that you and Vinnie aren't carrying on behind my back. Why

330

would he pick up an uneducated, penniless *nobody* like you, send you off on God knows how many courses and then make you a director? It stands to reason there's something fishy going on. I'm not stupid, you know. I'll prove to him that I can be careful with his money. I'll save him the rent on our flat for a start. We can move in here.'

It was during this tirade Maryan heard footsteps on the stairs and realised with dismay that Amy had come home and was on her way up. She mustn't hear this woman's wild accusations, whatever happened. She held up her hand. 'Please – you'll have to excuse me. My daughter is home and . . .' She edged towards the door and Fay gave a triumphant little laugh.

'Oh, *no*, you wouldn't want her to know what a devious mother she's got, would you?' To Maryan's horror she sat down on the settee. 'I'll wait,' she announced stubbornly. 'There are one or two more things I'd like to say to you while I'm here.'

Maryan came out onto the landing and closed the living room door just as Amy reached the top of the stairs. 'I've got a visitor,' she said quietly. 'Will you . . .'

But before she got any further Amy burst out: 'Mum – I've got a job. I'm leaving school.'

Maryan stared at her daughter. 'You've *what*?'

'A job – in the theatre – a touring company. Student ASM, it's called. I went for this audition. I didn't mean to but it was on when we were passing and Celia dared me. It was just for fun really but then they offered me a job and – and I said yes.'

Maryan frowned. 'That was a very irresponsible thing to do, Amy. You're still at school. You know you can't take it.'

Amy's mouth set into the stubborn line that Maryan knew all too well. 'I'm going to take it, Mum. There's nothing you can do to stop me.'

'Oh yes there is. You're under age. I do still have some say in what you do.'

'I don't care what you say, I'm going. I'll only run away if you try and stop me.'

'Don't be so silly, Amy.' Maryan stepped across the landing and opened the bedroom door. 'Just wait in your room for a few minutes. We'll talk about this after . . .'

'*No*. I won't be sent to my room like a naughty child.' Amy stamped her foot. 'This is the chance of a lifetime and you're not going to stop me. You've done enough already to ruin my life.'

'Do as you're told at once,' Maryan hissed, desperate to bring the altercation to a halt. 'I've told you, I've got a visitor.'

'It's always someone else who gets priority with you, isn't it?' Amy snapped. 'I almost have to make an *appointment* to speak to you. Well, it isn't going to make any difference. I'm taking this job no matter what you do.'

Maryan felt her nerves stretched almost beyond endurance. She was dangerously close to losing her temper when she reached out and made a grab at Amy's shoulder. 'For heaven's sake be *quiet*,' she hissed. 'I've told you, I can't talk now.'

Her eyes full of angry tears, Amy shook off her mother's hand. 'Why pretend? You'll be glad you're getting rid of me,' she shouted. 'You left poor Grandma on her own just so that you could come here. Left her in that awful bombed-out house in Hackney to die of the damp and cold.'

Maryan gasped. 'Amy. That's not true. It was for you. I took this job and the flat for *you*.'

'Don't tell *lies*, Mum,' Amy lashed out. 'Nothing has ever been for me. I was a mistake right from the first, wasn't I? Nothing but a great big *mistake*. Why did you never tell me who my real father was? Why did you let me go on all those years, believing I was a Jessop when I was another man's child? Oh yes, I know all about it. I've known for ages. Well, now I'm going for good so you won't have to hush me up any more. And you can tell your boyfriend – *Uncle Vinnie* – that he needn't pay my school fees any more either. So you see, I'm doing everyone a favour, aren't I?'

Maryan winced as the door slammed in her face. She felt stunned. Amy *knew* about Marcus. But how? Who could have told her? Apart from the Leighs, only two people knew – Vinnie and her mother, and neither of them would have . . . And the remark about *Vincent* paying the school fees. Where on earth had she got that idea? She was still trying to make sense of it all when a voice behind her startled her.

'Well, *well*. Quite a revealing little outburst, wasn't it?' Fay stood in the living-room doorway, a smile of spiteful triumph on her face. 'Now I'm really glad I stayed.' She stepped up to Maryan, so close that her over-applied perfume was almost suffocating. 'You and he have known each other longer than you let on, haven't you? *A lot longer*. You and your spoilt, nasty-tempered brat are just a couple of little skeletons, rattling away here in your rent-free cupboard. And to think he accused *me* of promiscuity. When I think of the way I've had to grovel and ask his forgiveness when all the time . . .' She poked Maryan in the chest with a sharp forefinger. 'Tell me – did you *blackmail* him into giving you this job and flat? Is that the price poor Vinnie had to pay you to keep your mouth shut about his bastard?'

Maryan's heart throbbed in her throat and her mouth was dry, but she kept her head. 'You're jumping to all the wrong conclusions, just as Amy did,' she said, outwardly cool. 'Blackmail is a very serious accusation. I think you should be careful.'

There was a momentary flicker of doubt in Fay's eyes. 'Never mind,' she said. 'Now that I know what a hypocrite my dear husband is I'll make sure he pays. By the time I'm done with the pair of you you'll wish you'd never set eyes on each other.'

Chapter Fourteen

As the train rattled through the unfamiliar landscape Amy sat quietly in her corner looking out. It was like nothing she had ever seen before. She had always equated the countryside with leafy rural Suffolk. This raw, wild moorland scenery clothed in granite and olive green seemed bleak and unfriendly; almost awe-inspiring by comparison. Staring out at the massive craggy sweep of it she relived the two traumatic days prior to her leaving Simons Mews.

She had burned her boats; she knew it now. And although she recognised that taking this job was the most adventurous thing she had ever done there were still twinges of doubt and guilt about the way she and her mother had parted. She knew that she had behaved deplorably, making things difficult for her mother by blurting out suspicions that later turned out to be partly untrue. But instead of displaying the anger Amy had expected, Maryan had been strangely silent. Her silence unnerved Amy. It was almost as though her mother had finally given up on her. She had won her fight for independence. But it was a hollow victory.

When she had slammed the door in her mother's face on the afternoon of the audition she had thrown herself onto the bed in a torrent of emotional tears. But once the tears were shed she felt relief that at last the secret between them was out in the open. Maybe she should have told her mother long ago that she had overheard her confession to the Leighs all those years ago. She decided to apologise; to make it up with Maryan. Maybe she would even give up the job if her mother seriously wanted her to.

But when she went downstairs to the office she found Maryan white-faced and ominously silent.

'Mum – I'm sorry . . .' She began.

Maryan laid down her pen and met her daughter's eyes levelly. 'I hope you realise just how much damage you did this afternoon, Amy,' she said. 'It was Mrs Donlan who was waiting in the living room. She heard your disgraceful outburst and she's gone away with all the wrong ideas.'

'Oh.' Amy bit her lip. 'What wrong ideas?'

'If you can remember what you said, you can use your own imagination. You've put me in an impossible position.' She looked up at her daughter. 'And, for your information, Amy, Vincent does *not* pay your school fees.'

Amy gasped. 'I'm sorry. I didn't know. Mum – do you think – could we talk about my real father some time?'

'I don't think there's anything to be gained by that. I don't think there would be much point. But I would like to know who told you.'

'You did. I mean – I heard you telling Mr and Mrs Leigh that night at Whitegates – just after Mr Marcus – my father, was killed.'

'Oh. I see.' Maryan sighed, relieved that at least no third person was guilty of betraying her secret.

Amy stood biting her lip, bewildered at her mother's lack of response. She had said she was sorry, but it seemed that Mum was determined to make her grovel. 'Look – if you like I'll go and ring Mrs Donlan,' she offered. 'I'll tell her it isn't how she thinks. I'll even turn the job down – if you want me to.'

'The damage is done now.' With a resigned sigh Maryan picked up her pen again. 'Talking to Mrs Donlan will only make things worse. And you might as well take the job if it really means so much to you,' she added wearily. 'I've been given notice to leave the flat. From the first of May we won't have anywhere to live.'

Amy's heart sank. Could her outburst really have caused such disaster? 'Is – is that my fault too?' she asked.

Maryan shook her head. 'No, not entirely. What you said didn't help, though. I'm afraid neither of us is popular here any more. Perhaps it's time I looked for another job and you and I went our own ways. Perhaps I've looked on you as a child for too long. You're a woman now, after all.'

Since that afternoon Maryan had been unnaturally quiet. Amy had hardly seen her except at mealtimes, and even then they exchanged scarcely a word. The one thing Maryan had insisted on was that Amy herself went along to St Hildred's to tell the Mother Superior that she was leaving. This she had done yesterday morning and she still cringed inwardly when she remembered the witheringly stern looks and words she had received.

'You are throwing away a golden future, Amethyst.' (The nuns always used the girls' proper names.) 'The sisters have worked hard with you because they felt that you were a highly promising pupil and worthy of all their skills and expertise. Now, on the kind of reckless whim I would have expected of some ignorant guttersnipe, you are tossing all that dedication back in their faces.' She leaned forward, the palms of her hands on the desk and her spectacles glinting ominously. 'You are jeopardising your whole future life, child. You will bitterly regret this decision. And the tragic part is that when you do it will be too late.'

Unable to think of a suitable reply, Amy had sat mesmerised by the formidable dark-veiled figure on the other side of the massive mahogany desk. For one electrified moment their eyes had locked in a wordless, uncompromising duel. Mother Superior was first to avert her gaze. She waved a dismissive hand. 'Very well, that is all, child. If your mind is made up you had better go.'

The train for Lancashire was due to leave Euston at seven forty-five on Sunday morning. Amy had set her alarm clock for six o'clock, risen quietly and made herself a hurried breakfast. Nothing had been said the night before. There had been no last-minute reprieve, no forgiveness or loving reconciliation. It seemed that Maryan had meant it when she said it was time for them to go their own ways.

Amy was careful not to wake her mother. She fought shy of the parting. It would be awkward. She wouldn't know what to say. Instead she scribbled a note and left it on the kitchen table along with her key to the flat, then she picked up her suitcase, crept quietly down the stairs and let herself out into the mews. Closing the street door behind her she suddenly felt very small and alone. Recognising that she was taking her first independent step into the adult world, she shivered a little, half excited, half afraid. If only she could have taken it with everyone's blessing. But she was learning fast that being a rebel didn't come cheaply.

As she came out of the Underground at Euston Station the first person she saw was Celia. Her eyes lit up in surprise.

'Cee – what are you doing here?'

'What do you think, dope? I've come to see you off.' Celia hugged her hard. 'I hope you appreciate the fact that I've sacrificed my Sunday morning lie-in for you.'

They looked at each other, both girls' eyes bright. 'You *do* want to go, don't you?' Celia asked anxiously. 'I mean – don't feel you have to see it through just for the sake of pride. No one's going to think any the less . . .'

'I *do* want to go. Honestly.' Amy hugged her friend. 'But I do appreciate you coming to see me off.' She picked up her case and together they walked to the barrier.

'Was it awful?' Celia asked. 'Your mum and everything?'

'Pretty awful. But she accepted it in the end. Mother Superior was something else though.'

'Oh, hell, poor you. I can imagine.' Celia pulled a face. 'Hey, that looks like your lot over there. There's that Peter whatshisname running around like a headless chicken trying to organise everyone.' She hugged Amy so hard that all the breath was knocked out of her. 'Look, goodbye, kid. I'm off now. I hate standing waving at the back end of a train. Anyway, I might make a fool of myself and blub. You will write and tell all, won't you?'

''Course – you bet. Cee . . .'

'What?'

'I'm going to miss you.'

'Me too. Bye then – have a good time. Make it to Hollywood, or break a leg, or whatever it is they say.' Then, with a final wave, she was gone, to be quickly swallowed up in the mass of people congregating on the platform. And Amy was really alone, facing the future and the results – whatever they might be – of her first major decision. And feeling very far from confident.

Vincent arrived soon after ten, while Maryan was still eating her breakfast. He let himself in and walked up the stairs, pausing to tap on the kitchen door before entering. Maryan knew who it was the moment she heard the street door opening. No one else had a key except Amy, and she had left hers on the table, along with the note she had written. At his knock she called out to him to come in.

He stood in the doorway, taking in her pale face, devoid of make-up. There were traces of tears still on her eyelashes.

'Maryan,' he said quietly. 'My dear, I had to come.'

'Does Fay know you're here?' She got up and turned to the sink to refill the kettle. 'I'll make some fresh tea.'

He sat down at the table. 'I've just come from Mass. And I did tell Fay that I intended to look in on you.'

'Did you manage to calm her?'

He lifted his shoulders expressively. 'Not really.'

'I'm sorry about Amy's outburst. I've no idea what gave her the notion you were paying for her education. It gave entirely the wrong impression. If it caused you any embarrassment . . .'

'Embarrassment's hardly the word for it, but believe me, Maryan, it couldn't have made things any worse than they were already. Every day there's some new outrageous complaint or accusation. I'm getting used to it. I'm just sorry that she came here, interrogating and upsetting you.'

Maryan sighed. 'I should have been straight with Amy as soon as she was old enough to understand. You always said I should, didn't you?' She looked at him. 'I've lost her, you know – Amy. She's gone, taken this theatrical job. She left early this morning.' She pulled Amy's crumpled letter out of her pocket. 'She left this. It's all I have to prove that I once had a daughter.'

Vincent took the note and read.

Dear Mum,

I'm really sorry for any trouble I've caused. I didn't mean to. I didn't wake you because I hate goodbyes and I think we've said all there is to say. You were right when you said it was time we went our own separate ways. Maybe this way I can find out what kind of person I really am. I hope you find somewhere nice to live soon and another job.

Good luck, Amy.

He looked up at Maryan in alarm. 'What does she mean about another place to live – and another job?'

'I thought you knew. Fay gave me notice – of the flat, that is. It's my decision to give you my resignation.'

He stared at her, appalled. '*No*, Maryan. I refuse to accept it. And Fay had no right . . .'

'I think she did,' she interrupted. 'She wants to make this flat your home. She expected to have a directorship in Vincente's. She resented you offering me one. And perhaps she's right, Vinnie. She is your wife, after all.' She glanced up at him. 'And we can't deny that her suspicions about us were partly justified, can we? It's better that I leave – make a complete break. Perhaps it will make things easier for you too.'

He got up from the table and began to walk up and down. 'I won't accept this, Maryan. You are part of this firm. An important part. I can't – I *won't* let you go.'

'But you have to. There's no choice, for either of us.' She reached out to catch at his wrist as he passed. 'If you care anything for me at all, Vinnie, you'll accept my resignation and let me go. There's no future for me – for us. And staying on here isn't going to make things easier.' She looked up at him pleadingly. 'Please – I mean it.'

His face stricken, he pulled out a chair and sat facing her, grasping both her hands. 'But where will you go? How will I know you're all right?'

'I'll be fine. You don't have to worry.' She gave him a wry smile. 'I could always go back and work in the market again if the worst comes to the worst. Summer's on its way and it isn't so bad when the weather's fine.'

'Please – don't joke.'

'I'll keep in touch with Roisan.'

'Will you? Promise me you'll do that?' he asked earnestly. 'I know she'll want you to.'

'All right. I promise. I'll go and see her soon; let her know what I've decided.'

He stood up, drawing her to her feet. Searching her eyes he said: 'Oh, Maryan, what have I done to you, my love? I feel like a man being torn in half.' He looked at her. 'Fay thinks Amy is mine, you know – that we were having an affair long before she left me. Nothing will convince her it isn't true. She's even managed to persuade herself that she knew it was going on at the time and that was her reason for leaving me.'

'I'm sorry. That makes it all the more necessary for me to leave.'

'Sometimes I feel I should have listened to Roisan when she urged me to get a divorce,' he said vehemently. 'Fay is so neurotic – either over-excited or deeply depressed. Perhaps it's something to do with her diabetes.'

His eyes clouded. 'I believe that losing the child must have affected her deeply. God, Maryan, what a mess I've made of everything.' He drew her close and held her for a long moment, till she gently pushed him away.

'Go now, Vinnie,' she said. 'I'll leave at the end of the month. If you want me to help choose someone else to run the shop, I will, but I think Paul is quite capable of managing now. And Geoff could easily take over the buying. Perhaps you could manage with someone to come in and do the book-keeping.'

'Just you look after yourself,' he said. 'You'll get the best reference I can write. The rest is my problem.' He tilted her chin with one finger to look deeply into her eyes and his voice was husky as he said: 'I'll always – *always* love you, Maryan.'

She smiled gently. 'Life will be easier without me, though. Admit it.'

'It will be bleaker, I know that,' he said with a shake of his head. 'You brought the sun back into my life again. Without you . . .' He lifted his shoulders. 'God only knows.'

The three-week rehearsal period was a revelation to Amy. A revelation and, if she were truthful, a slight disillusionment too. Alex Keynan had warned her that the life of a student ASM was hard work, but it sometimes seemed to her that the job was nothing more than that of an errand girl. At the beck and call of every member of the company, she was run off her feet all day long. It sometimes seemed that the principal actors regarded her as some kind of personal maid, and as well as slipping out to buy cigarettes, newspapers and aspirins from the local shops, she was expected to climb ladders and hold tools for the carpenter and electrician, help paint scenery and go round the local shops begging various articles and items of furniture for props on the promise of a free advertisement in the programme. If she'd expected to be able to learn anything about acting she was to be disappointed in those early weeks. She wrote to her mother to let her know that she was safe and well and to send a temporary address, but Maryan did not reply. It looked as though the break between them was permanent, and gradually, as the days passed, she hardened her heart, telling herself she'd been right all along. Maryan had never really wanted her. It would be best if they didn't communicate at all.

The company was to tour several northern towns with a repertoire of plays, working for three weeks in each venue. The plays were varied: Coward's *Tonight at Eight-Thirty*; Shaw's *Pygmalion* and Emily Brontë's *Wuthering Heights*. Once the first three weeks of hectic, intensive rehearsal was over and they had settled into a routine of nightly performances and the occasional morning run-through, things became quieter and Amy was at last able to find more time to observe and glean what she could from Alex Keynan's direction and the professionalism of the cast. The first thing she learned was that it was all very different from school plays.

To begin with she had been quite shocked by Alex's method of direction. It seemed to her that he was rude and insulting to his actors. He frequently shouted and swore at them and often made them go over a scene again and again. She had seen the leading actress in tears more than once. But when she asked Peter King, the stage manager, why they never threw down their scripts and walked out, or swore back at him, he just smiled and said: 'They know he's a good director, the best, and that they're damned lucky to be working with him. They've got the sense to know that he can really bring out the best in them and that doing as he says will further their career. He's tipped for the top, you know.'

'If he's that good why is he taking out a small-town tour like this?'

Peter looked at her in surprise. 'Didn't you realise that this is an Arts Council sponsored tour? The other two bods at the auditions were from there. Alex was just beginning to make a name for himself before the war. He was one of the youngest directors Stratford had ever had, and he was directing in the West End when he was still only twenty-five. He hasn't done much since he came out of the RAF. I think this tour is his way of getting his hand in again.'

Amy was impressed. 'The RAF? Why wasn't he with ENSA?'

'Seems he wanted to have a bash at the Luftwaffe. He was a pilot. He flew Mosquitos. They were death-traps, you know. Not much of a chance of getting out if you were hit. He volunteered for them when his wife was killed in an air raid in '41. They'd only been married a couple of weeks.'

'Oh, I see. How awful.'

After that Amy looked on Alex Keynan with a slightly different attitude. She watched him working whenever she could and soon she began to see that Peter had been right. Alex knew how to coax and cajole as well as bully the very best out of his actors. It all depended on who he was handling as well as the role they were playing. And he certainly got results. They played to packed houses and the local press was generous in praise of the company.

As the weeks went by and Amy performed her endless thankless tasks, running errands, making coffee, fetching and carrying, she longed for a chance to experience for herself the direction of the Keynan Players' brilliant, charismatic director. She already knew most of the lines of each of the leading female roles. She fantasised about one of the leading actresses being stricken by some virus or knocked down – very gently, of course – by a bus, so that she could step into the vacant role just once and prove her worth. But, much to her disappointment, all the members of the cast, both male and female, seemed to have cast-iron constitutions and never succumbed to as much as a headache

Their first date was in Minsdale, a small market town on the Lancashire-Cumbrian border. It was early summer now and on the first Sunday Peter took her walking up onto the fells on the outskirts of the town. The air was sparklingly fresh and larks sang high above the hills, joyful specks hovering in a clear blue sky. A gentle breeze stirred the grass and wild flowers sprang from cracks in the rocky outcrops that scattered the climb to the ridge of the fell. They'd taken a packed lunch and at midday they sat down among the wiry grass to eat. Amy shaded her eyes and pointed to where a sheet of water gleamed in the distance like beaten silver.

'What's that water?'

'Lake Windermere. It's very beautiful – popular too. It'll be getting full of summer visitors soon. We're playing there later in the season. I'm afraid that might mean the digs'll be expensive.'

Amy sighed. 'That's all I need. I hardly have anything left over at the end of the week as it is.'

'I know. The pay is a bit stingy, isn't it?' He took the sandwich she handed him. 'Thanks. Apart from the money, how are you liking it, Amy – now that we're really into the tour, I mean?'

'It's okay.' Amy munched her sandwich thoughtfully. 'I'd like it better if I got a chance to act, though. Alex said there might be the odd walk-on part, but all the parts are taken so I can't see how I'm to get a look-in at all.'

'I expect what he meant was when someone dropped out or wanted time off,' Peter said. He glanced at her thoughtfully out of the corner of his eye. 'Look, if I tell you something will you promise to keep it to yourself?'

Catching the scent of conspiracy she turned to him, her eyes beginning to shine. 'Of course, anything you say. What is it?'

'Well, one of the girls is going to give in her notice shortly. She's had the offer of a part in a film. Only a tiny part, but it's a start and . . .'

'Yes, yes – *who*?' Amy knew that if it was one of the leading actresses someone else would have to be engaged. If it was someone who played smaller parts she might just be in with a chance. 'Come on – who is it, Peter?'

He chewed his lip before replying. 'You do promise

not to let it out, don't you? She only told me because I was there when she got the telegram.' At her emphatic nod he said, 'Okay. It's Natalie Bentham.'

Amy's heart sank. She was an established actress; a woman in her early thirties. She played the leading parts in two of the plays and substantial roles in the others. There was no chance that Alex would risk a raw beginner in parts like that.

But the following day Alex asked her to stay on after the morning run-through. She found him in his cubbyhole of an office, close to the side of the stage in the small theatre they were playing. She tapped nervously on the half-open door and he called out to her to come in.

'Ah, there you are, Amy. You may have heard that we are to lose a member of our company.' Amy shrugged noncommittally and he went on: 'Natalie is leaving us and Rosalind Decker will be taking over her parts. It's going to mean some shuffling around; and it's going to leave some of the minor parts vacant. I intend to start rehearsing again tomorrow with everyone in their new parts.' He took a sheaf of scripts from the table in front of him and handed them to her. 'Perhaps you'd like to begin studying the parts I've marked. There are two: the maid in *Pygmalion* and the little kitchen skivvy in *Wuthering Heights*. I think you'll find the costumes will fit you.'

Amy took the scripts, her heart thudding with excitement. 'Thank you, Alex. I promise you *faithfully* I'll do my very best.'

He raised an eyebrow at her. 'I don't need your undying gratitude, darling. Just say the lines and try not to bump into the scenery, that's all I ask. After all, that's what you're here for – to fill in where necessary. If you turn out to be a bloody disaster I'll have to send for someone else, but we'll see.' He grinned at her. 'Don't look so crestfallen. I said I'd give you a try-out and this is it.'

Slightly deflated, she retreated, clutching her scripts, to spend all afternoon in her tiny bedsitter, learning the lines. By the time rehearsal was called at ten next morning she knew her few lines and moves perfectly. Nevertheless her stomach churned with apprehension as she stood in the wings waiting for her cue. Alex's casual words about sending for someone else if she proved 'a bloody disaster' had made her determined to prove beyond a doubt that she was a born actress.

Halfway through rehearsing the first act of *Wuthering Heights* Alex called out for them to stop.

'*Amy* – what the hell do you think you're doing?' he thundered from his seat in the front stalls.

She looked up, broom in hand, her face pink as all eyes were turned on her. 'Me? Er – sweeping.'

'Ever heard of the expression *upstaging*?' he demanded.

Amy looked nonplussed as a muted titter went round the other members of the cast. 'Yes. But I . . .'

Alex gave an exaggerated sigh and raked a hand through his hair. 'I know you're supposed to be a kitchen maid and realism is very commendable, but you don't *sweep* when the other characters are speaking their lines – *right*?'

Amy blushed crimson. 'Oh, no. I mean, yes. Sorry.'

When the rehearsal was over Peter found her in a corner of the prop room, frantically tidying the shelves, her face flushed.

'Oh, there you are. I've been looking all over for you. We're going to the pub for a sandwich and a beer. Are you coming?'

She shook her head without turning round. 'No. You go. I'm not hungry.'

He paused, then came over to her. 'Amy. You're not upset, are you? I've just heard Alex saying how good you were. How clearly you spoke the lines.'

She turned to look at him. 'You're just saying that. I was awful. Anyway. I've only got three lines *to* speak.'

'Yes, but you got the accent right – spot on.'

'I just copied my landlady. It's supposed to be Yorkshire, but suppose it's Lancashire really.'

He slipped an arm around her shoulders. 'Never mind, Alex thought it was okay anyway.'

She brightened. 'So you don't think he'll send for another actress then?'

He laughed. 'When he can get you to do it for next to nothing? You must be joking.'

It was a backhanded compliment, but it was all Amy needed to cheer her up.

Later that evening Alex came to find her and obliquely confirmed that she was to keep the part.

'Amy, I'm getting next week's programme roughed out for the printer. Do you want your own name on the cast list?'

Her heart gave a little leap. Seeing her name on the programme as a member of the cast for the first time would be quite a thrill. 'Oh – yes please.' At his slightly doubtful expression she asked: 'Why? Is something wrong?'

'No – but . . .' He stroked his chin. 'Amy Jessop's a bit on the mundane side, isn't it? I wondered if you'd thought about adopting a stage name.'

A *stage* name. The idea stirred her imagination; it would be a bit like casting a skin – taking on a new identity. 'My first name is really Amethyst,' she told him. Then she had a sudden flash of inspiration. 'I think I'd like to be called Amethyst Leigh,' she said.

Alex smiled. 'Oh, *very* exotic. It has a gypsyish ring to it. I like it. Amethyst Leigh it shall be. And we'll keep you in as Amy Jessop, Assistant Stage Manager.'

And the fact that when the programmes were printed it came out as Amethyst *Lee* made no difference to Amy. She had a whole new persona. She was Amethyst Lee, the actress. A real person in her own right at last.

By the time Amy had been gone a week Maryan was already packed and ready to leave the flat in Simons Mews. On the Saturday morning after Amy's departure she had left the shop in Paul's capable hands and gone to visit Roisan. The older woman greeted her warmly.

'Come in, my dear. Vinnie said you'd be coming to see me. I can't tell you how upset I was to hear what had happened.' She took Maryan downstairs to the kitchen where she was busy cooking lunch. 'You will stay and eat with me, won't you?' she asked. 'There's plenty for two and it's always more enjoyable than eating alone.'

Maryan sat down at the table. 'I came to tell you what happened,' she said. 'But I don't know where to start.'

Roisan tested the potatoes bubbling away on top of the Aga, then replaced the lid. 'You don't have to. Vinnie has already told me everything; the whole unfortunate business. He's devastated at the thought of losing you.' She joined Maryan at the table. 'In more ways than one, as I'm sure I don't need to tell you.'

'I can't bear the thought of Fay thinking Vinnie is Amy's father,' Maryan said. 'I feel so responsible and I keep thinking that there must be something I can do to put it right.'

Roisan shook her head. 'Take my advice and don't even try. Fay will believe what she wants to believe and if you thwart her she's likely to make matters worse. Taking that woman back was the worst day's work Vinnie ever did. I'm sorry to say it, and God knows I've been a devout Catholic all my life, but if ever there was a good case for changing the divorce rule, Fay is it. I sometimes wonder if she's actually sane.'

'I'm packed and ready to leave the flat,' Maryan said. 'I just want it all to be over now.'

'Have you found another job?' Roisan asked. 'And somewhere to live?'

Maryan lifted her shoulders. 'Not yet. Flats are hard to find in London, as you know. And the rents are so expensive when you do find one. I've been thinking of moving out of town altogether.'

'Well, you're more than welcome to stay here till you get sorted,' Roisan said. 'I've plenty of room and I'd enjoy your company.' She rose to dish up the meal, but as she brought the plates to the table her face was thoughtful. 'I've just had a thought,' she said. 'A young woman I know is about to set up in business on her own and she's needing a secretary – no, a bit more than that;

someone to organise things for her. It might be just your kind of thing.'

Maryan looked up. 'What line is she in, antiques?'

'No, fashion. I met her doing the decor for a show and I've run into her a few times since when I've been buying fabrics. You've worked in the rag trade too, haven't you? Would you like me to put in a word for you?'

'Well, yes. Yes please, Roisan.'

'Better than that, I'll ring her and then you can get in touch yourself. I've got a card somewhere. I'll find it for you before you leave.'

Maryan felt better for Roisan's good beef casserole and apple sponge pudding. Alone in the flat since Amy's departure, she'd hardly eaten at all. Now, with the offer of temporary accommodation and the prospect of a job in view she felt much more optimistic.

'Have you heard from Amy?' Roisan asked as they ate.

Maryan shook her head. 'Not so far. I wonder if I shall.'

'Oh, surely she'll write and let you know she's safe and well,' Roisan said. 'I've always found her a considerate girl.'

'Maybe she has been – with you,' Maryan said. 'The truth is, she and I have never really got on. She was closer to my mother than to me, but I think she still looks on Marjorie Taylor, the woman she lived with all through the war, as more of a mother than me.'

'That can't be true,' Roisan said. 'Blood is thicker than water after all. And you've done your best for her. It must have taken a big slice of your salary to send her to St Hildred's.'

Maryan was thoughtful. Amy knew it had not been she who paid the school fees. How she knew that was still a mystery. She'd been tempted to tell her that Sam Leigh had paid for her education, but she had held back in deference to Sam's wishes. There was always the possibility that Amy might try to get in touch with him and cause trouble between him and Rachel. 'I didn't pay,' she said in answer to Roisan's question. 'Amy's grandfather did. But he wanted it kept secret. Believe me, Roisan,

'I've always tried to do what was best, but somehow everything I touch seems to go wrong. I daresay I'm to blame. But it's too late now to ask where I went wrong.'

'You mustn't be so hard on yourself,' Roisan said. 'Circumstances have been against you. You've had bad luck.'

'I wish now that I'd tried harder to put things right between us.' Maryan sighed. 'But maybe it's better this way. After all, Amy's a young woman now. Time for her to find her own place in the world.'

'And what about you?' Roisan asked quietly. 'Where do you go from here, Maryan? You deserve a decent life too. I know this is a dreadful setback for you after all the hard work you've put in, but don't give up. Go out and get the best for yourself. You deserve it. And I'll be here to help in any way I can.'

'Thank you, Roisan.' Maryan's eyes filled with tears. She wished she didn't have so many secrets. If only she could lay her head on Roisan's shoulder and tell her everything. It would have been such a relief.

'Don't thank me, girl. I only wish there was more I could do.' Roisan got up to make coffee. Her back to Maryan she said: 'For a short while you made Vinnie happier than I've ever seen him. It was you who helped him get this business on its feet. It's us should be thanking you. It's a crying shame we have to lose you.'

It wasn't until Maryan was leaving later that afternoon that Roisan remembered something. She rushed off to find her large, battered handbag and rummaged in its capacious interior. 'I know I put it in here somewhere,' she muttered as she heaped the bag's miscellaneous contents onto the table.

'Don't worry about it,' Maryan said pulling on her gloves. 'Any time will do.'

'No, it won't. You want to apply for the job as soon as you can. I don't want her to go and get . . . *Ah*, here it is,' she said, triumphantly holding up the small rectangle of cardboard. 'Now, I'll telephone her myself tonight and when you have a minute why not ring her yourself? She's a charming person. I'm sure the two of you will get along like a house on fire.'

Maryan tucked the card into her bag, hugged Roisan and made her way to the bus stop. It wasn't until she opened her bag to pay her bus fare that she took out the card and looked at it properly. When she did her heart missed a beat. Inscribed on it in clear black letters was a name she had heard before: Gina Stern. Haute Couture Designer.

When Fay had received no reply to her ring at the bell, she let herself in through the side door at Simons Mews with the key she'd recently had cut from Vincent's. She needed to measure for new carpets and curtains. There was no way she was going to put up with things that woman had half worn out. As she pushed the door open it caught against a bundle of mail, delivered after Maryan had left. Fay picked up the handful of letters and was about to put them to one side when her eye was caught by the rounded, childish writing on the top one. She turned the envelope over. On the back was a name and address: *Miss A. Jessop. Theatre Royal, Minsdale, Lancashire.* It was from the girl.

For a moment Fay stood tapping the letter thoughtfully with her fingers. There might be more information in this letter – things she'd find useful. The girl might make some further reference to the row she and her mother had had. She might even mention her father by name. Proof positive that Vincent was lying. Without further hesitation she slid a finger under the flap of the envelope. Inside was a single sheet of paper which she scanned eagerly. To her frustration it contained nothing of importance. It was just a brief note to say she was all right and enjoying her new job. *Damn.* Fay crumpled the letter angrily and thrust it into her pocket. The stupid girl needn't have wasted her time writing such trivia. And the Jessop woman certainly wouldn't be missing anything by not receiving it.

*

Amy's first week as an actress was one she would always remember. Getting dressed in the costume; waiting in the wings to go on; speaking her few lines and then, at the final curtain, taking her place in the line-up with the rest of the cast and listening to the applause – it was a heady experience and all she'd ever dreamed of. She loved every minute. And when a member of the cast fell victim to a migraine the following week and a chance came for her to play a bigger part in one of the Coward one-act plays she was delighted. The play was *Fumed Oak*, which told the story of a henpecked husband who kicked over the traces. Amy played the whining schoolgirl daughter and enjoyed it very much. She could identify and sympathise with the male character who, having been undervalued and misunderstood by the other members of his family, finally walked out. She'd done the right thing in leaving home, she told herself. Maryan had cheated her of a proper family life. She'd lied to her from childhood and never put her first as a mother should.

On the Saturday night after the performance she stayed on at the theatre. She'd been sharing a dressing room with two other members of the company and her digs were noisy too. She wanted an hour to herself to study the part of Cathy in *Wuthering Heights*. It was the part she coveted most of all and she was sure that one day she'd get the chance to play it. When that opportunity came she would be sure of the lines and ready to step into the role confidently. The theatre was quiet and after a while she made her way up onto the stage where she began to act out one of Cathy's scenes. The fire curtain was raised and the stage was lit only by the small pilot light in the prompt corner. Imagining the rows of seats in the empty auditorium filled with people, she completely lost herself in the part. She spoke her own lines out loud and Heathcliff's under her breath. So she was startled when a deep male voice began to speak them for her. She froze, recalling the tales of a theatre ghost, told by the elderly stage-doorkeeper. Then to her shocked surprise she saw a shadowy figure making its way towards her across the darkened stage.

'Cathy – Cathy, my love, my life.' The voice was heavy with emotion and the figure held out its arms as it advanced towards her. Amy's heart almost stopped in terror, then the figure stepped into the thin beam of light and she saw his face.

'*Alex*! You frightened the life out of me.'

He laughed. 'I'm sorry. I couldn't resist it. Besides, you gave me a bit of a start too. I thought I was alone and when I heard someone ranting away on stage I wondered what the hell was going on. Why aren't you at home in bed? Don't you know it's after midnight?'

'I didn't know you were still here,' she said, acutely embarrassed at being caught out.

'It's a dammed good job I was. Think yourself lucky you didn't get locked in for the night.'

'Sorry. I never thought.'

He chuckled. 'Don't be sorry. I'm quite impressed. Tell me – do you know *all* the lines?' He was looking at her with an expression of amused tolerance.

'Yes. Look, I'll be going now.'

'Hang on. Wait a minute.' He caught her arm as she passed him. 'You're really keen, aren't you, Amy? That's good, of course. But you haven't really got a clue when it comes to a character like Catherine Earnshaw.'

She felt her face stiffen. 'I'm awful, you mean?'

'No. I wouldn't say you were awful. You put up quite a presentable little try just now. But to play a part like that you need to be able to feel as deeply as the character feels. Do you have any idea how Cathy feels when she says those things to Heathcliff? Do you know what it is to be – not just in love, but *obsessed* by a man – even *po*ssessed?' He took her by the shoulders and looked down at her. In the dim light she could see the gleam of his eyes. 'No, of course you don't. You're much too young. And until you know, Amy, my sweet, you're never going to be able to get under Cathy's skin.'

'But – but it's *acting*, isn't it?' she said breathlessly. 'It's imagining. A good actress should be able to imagine how she felt.'

'You think that's possible?'

'Yes, why not?'

'Have you read *Wuthering Heights* – the book, I mean?'

'Yes. At school.'

'What school?'

'St Hildred's. It's a convent.'

He gave a brief bark of laughter. '*Nuns*? That explains a lot.' For a long moment he stood there, looking down at her, then he took her hand and began to stride off the stage. 'Come with me. It's late, I know, but I'm going to give you an acting lesson.'

He closed the door. The tiny office was lit by a single light from the Anglepoise lamp on the desk. Also on it was an open bottle of Scotch and a glass. He indicated a chair and took another glass from a drawer.

'Drink?' He picked up the bottle and looked at her enquiringly. She'd never tasted whisky before but she nodded.

'Oh, yes please,' she said casually, trying to sound as though she drank it every day.

He poured her a generous measure and sat down in the chair opposite. Taking a deep draught from his own glass he said: 'Catherine Earnshaw was the only daughter of a widowed Yorkshire farmer who had high hopes of marrying her into the local gentry. He wanted his daughter to become a lady, and Cathy quite liked the idea too – some of the time. But Cathy was basically a child of nature. She loved the moors. They'd been a part of her ever since she could remember. She was as much a moorland creature as the animals that lived there, as untamed and untamable as the wind and the storm clouds. Heathcliff with his mysterious background and passionate, unpredictable nature was her soulmate. He understood her as no one else ever could. He was all she had ever wanted. Her alter ego. She couldn't live without him. But she

354

couldn't live *with* him either. She both loved and hated him. She resented him for the mirror image of herself that he held up to her and for the irresistible hold he had on her. She tried to be rid of him by marrying another man, but she couldn't.' He leaned across the desk to look into her eyes. 'Can you imagine the intensity of a relationship like that, Amy – *can you*?'

She lifted her glass and took a drink of the whisky. The bitter, fiery liquid almost stopped her breath and it was all she could do not to gasp. 'I suppose not, but I – I could try,' she said, her cheeks pink.

'You could try, could you?' He laughed. 'Have you ever been in love, Amy?'

She took another sip and managed this time to swallow it without wincing. 'Yes,' she said boldly. 'Yes, of course I have.'

He refilled his glass and leaned back in his chair, putting both feet on the desk in front of him. 'Okay – tell me about it.'

'Well – his name was – *is* Mike. We grew up together and I always looked on him as a brother. Then I went to his eighteenth birthday party and I knew – knew that I – I loved him.'

'So he's the same age as you?'

'Oh no. That was ages ago. He's done his National Service since then. He's a journalist now.'

'I see. And did you go to bed with him?'

She blushed crimson. '*No*. Of course not.'

'No?' He looked at her thoughtfully over the rim of his glass. 'No, you'd be pretty young at the time. Have you ever made love with a man, Amy?'

She got to her feet, her heart beating fast. 'I – I think I'll go home now.'

He was on his feet instantly. Coming round the desk he stood between her and the door. Reaching out, he took her hands. 'Amy, I'm sorry. I've shocked you. I've had too much of that damned stuff.' He indicated the whisky bottle. 'I didn't mean to pry into your personal life. I just wanted to assess you as a person – an actress;

to find out what you might be capable of, because you do show promise, you know.' He held her hands warmly in his and smiled gently at her as he went on: 'Do you know that when George Bernard Shaw first wrote *St Joan* and a certain celebrated actress asked him to let her play the part, he told her to go away and have a child first? He meant that she should experience emotion at its very deepest before attempting anything as intense. Do you begin to see what I'm trying to tell you?'

She nodded, though she didn't really know what he was getting at at all. She was feeling slightly dizzy and she couldn't decide whether it was because of the whisky or the compelling eyes that held hers so hypnotically. All she was really aware of was that she wanted him to kiss her. It was giving her the most peculiar sensation in the pit of her stomach. 'I – I think so,' she whispered.

'So you see, my sweet little Amy, I hardly think that a few chaste kisses with your childhood sweetheart behind the bike sheds qualifies you to play a part like passionate, tortured Cathy.' For a long moment he looked down at her. He found the upturned face with those huge, appealing eyes and the soft, slightly parted lips sorely tempting. Didn't the girl know what power she wielded? Was it possible she could really be this naive, or was the wide-eyed innocence merely an act? The next moment she gave him the tacit answer to his unasked question by reaching up and slipping her arms boldly around his neck.

He did what any man would have done. He kissed her; experimentally at first, then, finding her lips warm and yielding, he kissed her again, drawing her close so that her supple body was moulded against his.

Amy was shaken. Never in her wildest dreams had she imagined that a kiss could be like this. When Alex kissed her for the second time he took her completely by surprise. As he pulled her close she was aware of the uncompromising hardness of his body, of his lips moving sensuously on hers. When his tongue parted her lips to explore her mouth she held back for a moment, unsure. She and Celia had talked about this kind of kiss, both of them

356

vowing that they would never allow it; denouncing it in their girlish way as 'disgusting and horrid'. But now that it was actually happening to her she found that it stirred and excited her in a way she could never have imagined possible. She let her lips part, and found that surrendering to this demanding assault on her mouth was deeply erotic. It quickened her heartbeat and sent the blood roaring dizzyingly through her veins. It aroused all kinds of feelings she had never experienced before. She closed her eyes, wanting it to go on for ever. When he released her she felt almost too weak to stand and clung to him for support. He looked down at her, his eyes dancing with a mixture of amusement and surprise.

'Well, *well*. For one so innocent you're a passionate little thing, aren't you?'

She looked up at him. 'Am I?'

'Are you telling me that you've never kissed anyone like that before?' He took her arms from around his neck and held them against his chest. 'I confess you have me puzzled, Amy. You look like a little angel, yet I have the feeling there's a firebrand in there, just waiting for someone to light the touch-paper.' He chuckled softly. 'Come on. It's late. I'll take you home.'

As they walked the deserted streets together Amy had a feeling of anti-climax. She wasn't quite sure what she had expected – or wanted – to happen, but Alex's abrupt decision to take her home was a distinct let-down. The summer night seemed to her to be made for falling in love. It was warm and mellow and although it was still barely two o'clock the sky was already luminous with the promise of dawn. In the shadows near the doorway of her digs she turned to him.

'Thank you – for the acting lesson.'

He laughed softly. 'Don't mention it.' He reached out and pulled her to him. Pinioned to the wall, she could feel his body pressed hard against hers from shoulder to thigh. She caught her breath as, slipping his hand inside her coat, he cupped one breast and stroked it firmly. 'There are lots of things you're going to have to learn, my sweet,' he whispered against her ear. 'And not all of them have to do with acting.' Then his mouth found hers again and this time it opened for him eagerly and without hesitation. At last he stood back, away from her, his arms dropping to his sides. 'I think you'd better go inside now,' he said with a sigh. 'One thing I'm sure I don't really have to tell you is that there's only so much a man can take . . .' He leaned forward to kiss the tip of her nose. 'Without making a beast of himself, that is.'

Amy looked up at him, her eyes tantalising. 'How do you know that's not what I want?' she said daringly.

His eyes opened wide, feigning shock. 'It's a good job it's me you're talking to,' he said sternly. 'And not some unscrupulous cad.' He laughed. 'Go in, girl, before I forget myself and ravish you right here on the pavement.'

On that light-hearted note they parted and Alex went on his way, lightened and cheered by the little encounter. When he'd decided after the show to stay on at the theatre it had been out of a feeling of bleak depression. He'd opened the bottle of Scotch, intending to drink himself into a stupor out of sight of everyone. It was a remedy he resorted to when the memories became nightmares and the heart-wrenching longing grew to unbearable proportions. Amy had unwittingly rescued him from that. He found that innocent eagerness of hers, that adolescent trembling on the brink of sensuous womanhood, quite irresistible. She was like summer morning, warm and untouched, just waiting to be enjoyed. She made him feel young again, as though the war with all its sorrows, its waste and destruction had never been. And he went on his way with a lighter step; refreshed.

But for Amy it was more than a few carefree kisses. She climbed the stairs with stars in her eyes. Alex Keynan had noticed her – not only as an actress but as a person – no, better still, a *woman*. Now anything could happen. Lying in her narrow bed she realised that a metamorphosis had taken place in her tonight. She was suddenly acutely aware of herself; her body and its sexuality – her unexplored potential. Was this what Alex had meant by experiencing deep emotion? Was she falling in love – *really* in love? And if she was, would it make a real actress of her? It was all so exciting – like opening a magic box full of wonderful gifts of which she had so far only unwrapped the first. What other delights lay inside, just waiting for her to explore and experience? She tingled with anticipation. Alex had unlocked the box for her and given her the key. Now she could open it again whenever she wished. And she would. Oh yes – she would.

She fell asleep as dawn was breaking, his name on her lips.

The house was in Gower Street. Maryan found it easily and mounted the steps to ring the bell by the newly painted front door. It was opened by Gina Stern herself. She was a small woman with large, expressive brown eyes and glossy dark hair, cut in a short, fashionable style. She was wearing – surprisingly – a pair of decorator's overalls at least two sizes too large for her, but she smiled unselfconsciously as she invited Maryan in.

'I hope you'll excuse me for a moment while I change into something more suitable,' she said, unbuttoning the overalls as she spoke. 'I couldn't wait any longer for a decorator. They take an age to come these days. I decided I might as well have a go at it myself.'

She led Maryan through a hall shrouded in dust sheets and into a small room at the back of the house, inviting her to make herself at home while she waited.

'Just give me a moment,' she said on her way out. 'I'll be with you in a jiffy.'

The room was furnished as an office and Maryan looked around her with interest. As well as the desk there were two comfortable chairs and a table heaped with fashion magazines. On the other side of the room, close to the window, which looked out onto a small walled garden, a drawing board was set up. On it lay a sketch of a winter suit with a stylish half-cape. It was coloured in crimson and black. She was still looking at it when Gina returned, wearing grey trousers and a crisp white blouse.

'I'm sorry to have kept you, Mrs Jessop. Until I get the place shipshape I'm having to use this room as a combined office and studio. Now . . .' She took a seat behind the desk and looked at Maryan's application which lay on the desk. 'I see that you began your working life as a machinist, went into domestic service and then later worked at Vincente's for the Donlans.' She looked up with a smile. 'You've had a very varied career.'

'Yes. Mainly because of the war,' Maryan said. 'I've been running the shop at Simons Mews since the end of the war, when I came back to London. I've learned a lot about organisation there. I took a business course when I began; shorthand and typing, book-keeping – that sort of thing. I learned the antique trade as I went along, studying from books and going to sales with Mr Donlan – working in the shop.' She opened her bag and took out Vincent's reference, handing it across the desk to Gina, who read it carefully. Coming to the end, she looked up.

'Well, Mr Donlan obviously thinks a great deal of your ability and efficiency, and I'm sure you know that Roisan has given you a glowing report too. But may I ask why you decided to leave? Weren't you happy there?'

Maryan drew a deep breath. This was the tricky question; the one she'd been expecting and dreading. She wasn't quite sure how much Roisan might have told Gina. 'I loved my job,' she said slowly. 'And I got along very well with Mr Donlan and Roisan. It was for purely personal reasons that I decided to make the break.' She looked at Gina, who appeared to be waiting for more. Looking down at her hands, she went on: 'It was Mrs Donlan who . . . I believe she felt the need to make – certain changes.'

Gina held up her hand. 'No need to go on. I think I get the general idea. Sometimes personalities clash, don't they? For no special reason. Call it chemistry. It wouldn't do for us all to be the same. But I feel it's essential to like the people I work closely with. I would never engage someone I didn't feel I could look upon as a friend as well as an employee. I daresay you feel the same.' She smiled. 'I'm pretty sure from what I've seen and heard that you and I would work well together. What do you say we give it a month's trial – on both sides, of course?'

Maryan had warmed to the young woman facing her across the desk. There was nothing she would have liked more than to agree. But first there was another hurdle to get over.

'I'd like that very much, Miss Stern – but there is something I feel you should know before we go any further.'

Gina, who had half risen from the desk, sat down again. 'Oh dear, that sounds ominous. Please tell me.'

'I know that you used to work as a designer for the Leighs of Feldman Fashions. I worked for them too. From leaving school till the end of the war.' She opened her bag and took out the reference that Sam had written for her.

Gina looked slightly puzzled. 'Well, that's a coincidence, of course, but they obviously valued you, so I don't see why it should be a problem.'

Maryan bit her lip. 'I've kept in touch with Mr Sam Leigh, and because of that I know the circumstances of your employment with them. I realise that Mrs Leigh won't be altogether happy about your leaving and setting up on your own.'

Gina shrugged. 'That's true. But why should any of that affect your coming to work with me?'

Maryan shook her head, at a loss to put into words what she feared. 'I just wanted you to – to be aware of the connection between us,' she said. 'I didn't want you to find out later and think I was spying for them.'

Gina laughed. 'Thank you for being so honest with me, but I'm sure you'd never do anything so underhand. If it doesn't worry you it certainly won't worry me. Now – shall I try and tell you a little of what I have in mind?'

Gina was easy to talk to, and so enthusiastic that it was impossible not to catch some of her bubbling enthusiasm and be carried along by it. She told Maryan that she had been saving hard towards starting her own business whilst working for the Leighs and then she'd had a windfall in the shape of a sizable legacy from her grandmother, including the house in Gower Street.

'The house hadn't been lived in for a number of years,' she said. 'Nanna spent the war years in Devonshire. There was some slight bomb damage and it was terribly neglected, of course. But I'm getting it all into shape gradually. I intend to live and work here.' She looked at Maryan. 'By the way, I see that your present address is Simons Mews.'

'Yes. I live in the flat above the shop.'

'Obviously you'll have to move out. Have you found somewhere else to live?'

'I'm living at Roisan Freer's at the moment,' Maryan told her. 'But it's only temporary. I've tried to find a flat, but they're so few and far between – and so expensive too.'

Gina nodded. 'I know. That's why I decided to live here. I hope you find something soon.'

She went on to explain her plan to Maryan. She'd been working on some designs for the middle-of-the-range market, for chain and department stores; a line which she hoped would keep her going until she was ready to launch her innovative top-of-the-range collection, possibly early the following year.

'So you see it's essential for me to find someone I can trust to deal with selling and organisation – oversee the production too,' she said earnestly. 'Take all those things off my shoulders while I get on with my designing. If I'm to have my designer collection ready for next spring I need all the time and space I can get.'

'Are you engaging your own workers?' Maryan asked. Gina shook her head.

'I hope to later, of course, but for now I'm leasing the work out to a really good firm in Islington. I've already negotiated terms with them. It's not ideal, of course, but I know the firm well and I'm sure I can trust them to turn out the standard of work I require.' She leaned back in her chair and looked at Maryan enquiringly. 'Well,

Maryan – I hope I can call you that. I think I know all I need to know about you. Do you have any questions you'd like to ask me?'

Maryan shook her head. 'No. It sounds very interesting.'

'I do have one or two others to interview,' Gina said. 'But I can tell you here and now that I believe you would be perfect for the job – if you want it. I'll telephone you at Roisan's, shall I? Shall we say the day after tomorrow?'

Maryan was glad of the small respite. There was something else she had to do before deciding finally. Instead of going straight back to Notting Hill that afternoon she took the Underground out to Hackney and paid a visit to Feldman Fashions. She was in luck. It was one of Sam's working days and he was in his office. His face lit up with pleasure when he saw who his visitor was.

'Maryan. How nice to see you. What brings you all the way out here?' He stood up and pulled out a chair for her. 'Would you like some tea? I can get you some . . .'

Maryan shook her head. 'It's business really. I'm leaving my present job. There are personal reasons – a disagreement that can't be resolved. I've applied for another job. It would suit me very well and I'd like to take it.' She glanced at him apprehensively. 'But I wanted to talk to you about it first.'

Sam gave her a puzzled smile. 'Well, I'm flattered you should ask my advice, my dear, but it's your life and I'm sure you know best . . .'

'The job is with Gina Stern, you see.'

The smile left Sam's face and he sighed heavily. 'Ah – Gina.' For a moment he was silent, then he looked up at Maryan again. 'Gina is a brilliantly talented designer and a very nice young woman. She deserves to get on. It's high time she spread her wings and I wish her nothing but good luck. As for you working for her, why should I mind? You're free to work for whoever you wish.'

'Thank you, Mr Sam. I just didn't want you to think I was being disloyal to you.'

He smiled gently. 'I hardly feel you owe us any loyalty, my dear. Not after what happened. But I appreciate your candour. Take the job by all means – with my good wishes.'

'Thank you.' She looked at his face. It seemed to her that he looked a little older every time she saw him. 'Are you well – both of you?'

'Well? I'm fine, but Rachel . . .' He spread his hands expressively. 'Ever since Gina left she has been in a state of emotional turmoil. I tell her it is high time she retired. If she would only agree I would retire too. We could go for a long holiday, a world cruise maybe. We both deserve some time together, to relax and enjoy life again. We could even go and live abroad. Somewhere in the sunshine. But Rachel . . .' He sighed and lifted his shoulders. 'She cannot forget this obsession of hers; cannot let Marcus rest in peace. It's ruining her life. And mine too.'

'I'm so sorry. Have you asked her to see a doctor?'

'I have tried everything. I am so afraid she will make herself really ill.' With an effort he shook off his worried expression to smile at Maryan. 'But why should any of this worry you? Go and work with Gina, my dear. Go with my blessing. It is for people like Gina to carry the flame now. I tell Rachel this. Soon we will have completed the first half of this century. So much anguish and suffering we have seen these past fifty years. Surely now the world has learned its lesson and things will improve.' He smiled. 'It is up to the young to build a better world for the next generation. There is so much work to be done to put the world to rights, but Rachel and I are too old to take any part in that. I tell my Rachel that the world belongs to the young – to the *living*. There are so many others who have lost loved ones. We must let go as they have done.'

'Thank you,' Maryan said. 'I couldn't have accepted the job happily without telling you first.'

As she made to get up Sam said, 'Maryan, I've been

meaning to get in touch with you. I was surprised to have my cheque returned from St Hildred's the other day. There was a letter with it to say that Amy was no longer a pupil at the school. Is that right?'

With a sigh, Maryan sat down again. 'I'm sorry. I should have let you know. Amy has left home. She got herself a job with a theatre company in Lancashire. There was nothing I could do to stop her.'

Sam looked concerned. 'Oh, my dear. Is she all right? Have you heard from her?'

Maryan shook her head, her throat tightening. 'No. I'm afraid I've lost her. Since the war we just don't seem to have settled down together. I blame myself. I feel I must have failed her.' She looked at his drawn face. 'I won't worry you with the details. She's grown up now. She wants to go her own way and there's nothing I can do about it.'

Sam touched her hand. 'I'm so sorry. I'm sure she'll come back when she needs you. Children always need their mothers.'

'I'd like to think so,' she said, without conviction.

Maryan made her way back to Notting Hill that afternoon with a heavy heart. If Rachel Leigh had only accepted Amy as Marcus's child so much suffering would have been avoided: for Rachel and Sam; for herself and Amy. If it hadn't been for Rachel's abhorrence she and Vinnie would never have met, loved and parted again. That in itself would have saved so much heartache. Sometimes, fate had a strange way of working.

Chapter Fifteen

To Amy's disappointment Alex ignored her when they met at rehearsal on the Monday following that Saturday evening. Days passed, and then weeks, during which Alex continued to treat her as a very junior member of his company and nothing more. It was as though the encounter between them that night in the empty theatre had been a dream. Amy tried hard to forget, but Alex's arbitrary treatment and the lack of opportunity to play more important roles gradually turned her disappointment into discontent. One morning as she and Peter prepared the stage set for the evening performance he remarked on it.

'Anything wrong, Amy? You haven't seemed yourself lately.'

She shrugged the enquiry off. 'It's nothing. I haven't been sleeping very well lately.'

'I see.' He gave her a curious look. 'Any particular reason?'

'No,' she said. 'Except . . .'

'Yes? Except what?'

'It's just that I'd like a chance to show what I can do. A real part, I mean, instead of all these walk-ons.'

He chuckled. 'You have to learn to walk before you can run. Anyway, why not concentrate on stage management? You could do a lot worse. There are always good openings for stage managers, you know. I've got my eye on working for television. It's the coming thing. More and more people are getting sets. They're saying it'll soon put the theatre out of business.'

'God forbid.' She turned away to put the kettle on for coffee. Peter went on talking about television but his remarks went over her head as she remembered Alex's remarks that Saturday evening, all of which were indelibly printed on her memory. Her lips still tingled every time she remembered his fiery, exciting kisses. He had seemed so sincere. It had all seemed so real to her, yet he behaved as though he'd forgotten the episode. Some days he looked at her as though he could hardly remember who she was.

When Peter left for lunch, Amy stayed on, finding some small jobs with which to keep herself occupied. She liked working alone in the theatre. It was quiet – a friendly silence that gave her space in which to think. She felt as though she had come to a watershed. Maybe she should give up all thoughts of being an actress and go back to London – try for something else. Recently she'd had a letter from Celia. Her mother had remarried and moved out to Richmond. Celia herself had moved to a job as junior secretary for a firm of family solicitors in York. She seemed really happy; earning a good salary and enjoying an independent life in the bachelor-girl flatlet she could now afford. She had even started going out with the boss's son, newly out of uniform after National Service and studying law at university. Celia wrote enthusiastically about their relationship and of how Brian was working hard towards becoming a partner when his father retired. Amy envied her as she sat reading the letter. Celia, always the scatty one, seemed to have her life under control and her future all sewn up, while she still floundered between an insecure past and an unsure future, the one as ephemeral and unsatisfactory as the other.

The lack of a reply to her letter home seemed to confirm that Maryan meant to be done with that part of her life once and for all. There was nothing for it but for Amy to go along with the decision and do the same.

'Good God, you scared the daylights out of me. I didn't know there was anyone here.'

Startled, Amy looked up from the prop bench to see Alex standing in the doorway. Her heart jumped painfully. He wore black corduroy trousers and an open-necked shirt and she noticed that he didn't appear to have shaved this morning. Turning away so that he wouldn't see her blush, she said, 'I thought I'd stay on and finish laying out the props bench ready for this evening.'

'Ah – that's what I like to see,' he said. 'Very commendable.'

He was laughing at her and she felt an impotent fury rising in her breast. 'Time I was going,' she muttered. 'I've got some shopping to do.' But as she made to pass him he stood in her way, his face serious.

'What's wrong, Amy?'

'Nothing. Nothing at all. May I pass, please?'

'You may when you've told me why you're so angry.'

'I'm not angry.'

'You're lying.' Seeing the hot blush that coloured her cheeks he reached out to rest his hands lightly on her shoulders. 'Amy. I think you and I should have a talk. Shall we find a quiet place to have lunch?'

'There's no need – really.'

Disregarding her protest, he rubbed a hand along his jaw. 'When I've been back to my place and shaved, that is.' He grinned at her. 'I overslept this morning. Can't take a nicely brought up young lady out to lunch looking like this, can I?'

'I told you. There's . . .' He took her arm and steered her firmly towards the stage door.

'You can come back to the digs and wait for me. It won't take long.'

He was staying at the Olive Tree, one of the town's best pubs. His room was at the front, overlooking the busy market place. Amy sat in the room's one armchair while Alex took his things into the bathroom and shaved. He reappeared looking clean and spruce in a fresh shirt. Reaching out, he drew her to her feet.

'Now – are you going to tell me why you've been going round for the past few weeks with a face like thunder?'

'I didn't know I had.'

'Oh, I think you did.' He bent to look into her eyes. 'Is it something I did – said?'

Acutely embarrassed, she shook her head, but he persisted.

'You're unhappy about something. Tell me.'

'No. There's nothing. I wish you wouldn't . . .' Her voice trembled perilously and she tried to pull away.

He sighed. 'Oh dear. It's worse than I thought.' He drew her towards the bed and made her sit down beside him. 'Amy – come and sit down. Tell me about yourself.'

'There isn't much to tell,' she said awkwardly. 'I was born in the East End of London, but I was evacuated to Suffolk when the war started. I lived with a family called Taylor.'

He nodded. 'Ah yes, I remember. The famous Mike.'

'Then, when it was over I went back to London and lived with my mother in a flat over the antique shop she runs.'

'And that's all? No dramas, no joy, no pain?'

'Well, my grandmother died, then there was school . . .'

'And – your father?'

She looked at him sharply. 'He – died in the war. My real father, that is. Tom Jessop – the man my mother married – died when I was little.'

He nodded slowly. 'I see. So you never knew him – your real father?'

'I *knew* him. But not that he was my father. I only found that out by accident.' She looked away. 'It was a shock. He was dead by then, you see. It was too late – too late to . . .'

'Get to know him – as a father?'

She nodded. 'There's so much I'd like to know about him. I don't even know if he knew I was his.'

'Have you talked to your mother about it?'

'No.' She shook her head vehemently. 'She let me down; cheated and lied to me all those years. She and I don't talk. I don't suppose she ever wanted me really. She's never really understood me and I certainly don't understand her.'

'What don't you understand?'

'She puts her work before everything.'

He smiled wryly. 'From what you tell me she's probably had to.' He laughed gently. 'You're thinking, what the hell does *he* know about it?' he said, slipping an arm around her shoulders. 'But life is never one-sided, Amy. Maybe if you just let her tell you her side . . .'

'If she'd wanted me to know, why didn't she tell me before? Anyway, she needn't bother because I'm not interested any more,' she said abruptly. 'I'm thinking of *my* work now. And I'm not going home again until I've made a success of it. Probably not even then.'

'Oh dear.' He rolled his eyes ceilingwards. 'Heaven preserve me from avenging angels.'

She sprang to her feet, blushing hotly. 'If you're just going to sit there and make fun of me – treat me like a child . . .'

'I'm not. I'm sorry, Amy.' He caught at her hand. 'It's just that you're so earnest that I can't resist teasing you a little. I do want to understand, believe me.' He looked into her eyes. 'But we still haven't got down to the reason you're so quiet and preoccupied, have we?'

'Do we have to? I mean, why should you be interested – in me?'

He drew back his head and looked at her thoughtfully. 'Ah – so *that's* it. It was our little encounter the other Saturday night?'

She coloured. '*No*. Not really.'

'It was. I can tell.' He gave her shoulders a squeeze. 'You must learn not to take things so seriously, Amy.'

'I don't – *didn't*. If – if you want to know, I'm fed up because I never get the chance to play a real part,' she told him in a rush. 'You promised me when you gave me the job that I'd get the chance. But I – haven't.'

'Oh, but I think you have,' he corrected.

'Bit parts. Walk-ons. I want to do something *real* – something that counts.'

'Like Cathy?' His eyes twinkled.

She bit her lip hard. 'All right, *yes*. Like Cathy.' She looked up at his slightly amused, quizzical expression and something seemed to erupt inside her. 'Oh, it's all very well, you telling me not to take things seriously,' she told him stridently. 'But how am I to get that emotional experience you speak of if I'm not supposed to *feel* anything?' To her horror tears filled her eyes. She blinked them back, swallowing hard, but it was no use. They brimmed over to slip down her cheeks. She got up, making for the door in a panic. But he was there before her, barring the way.

'Amy. Please don't be upset. I didn't mean to hurt your feelings. I thought it was a very pleasant little interlude. I thought you did too. I don't see why you're so upset.'

'I don't go about kissing people I don't care about,' she said angrily. 'When it – happened – I thought it was because – because you – you liked me. And then afterwards when – when you ignored me . . .'

'I'm sure I never ignored you,' he broke in.

'You *did*. You hardly knew I was there. It's *you* who can't feel things. You're the one who's emotionally immature.' She knew she was being silly and childish. To her own dismay she heard the break in her voice, its tearful shrillness. With one determined effort she tried to push him out of the way before he could witness her complete humiliation, but he grasped her arms and held her fast.

'*Amy*. Amy, listen. If you knew the truth about me you wouldn't say a thing like that. We all have to protect ourselves. We all start off soft and vulnerable, but we get hurt so we build a protective shell around ourselves. You'll have to learn to do the same, otherwise life will batter you to death.'

She stared at the floor. 'I know. I'm – sorry.'

'Poor baby. You're very young, aren't you?' He drew her close and kissed her very gently. At once all the passionate feeling she held for him flared up and she clung to him helplessly, her heart beating fast against her ribs. 'If I hurt you I'm sorry, darling,' he said. 'Come and sit down. I want to tell you something.'

Once again they sat together on the edge of the bed. Her hands firmly held in his, he looked into her eyes. 'I was married once,' he said. 'Just once in my life, very briefly I knew what it was to be blissfully happy. Chloe and I met, fell in love and married all within a few weeks in the summer of 1941. I was in the RAF, she was a WAAF working at the War Office. I came home on leave. My first since the wedding. We'd looked forward to it so much. Her parents lived in a village in Essex, but they had a tiny flat in Earls Court that they used when they came up to Town for shopping or the theatre. We'd planned to spend my leave there. Chloe met me at the station that afternoon. We were going out to dinner to celebrate. I left her at the flat, changing, while I went down the road to buy cigarettes. I was gone just a few minutes, but when I came back there was nothing left. The street had received a direct hit. At three o'clock that afternoon my life came to a halt. I was reduced to a kind of mindless machine, going through the motions of life.' He paused and Amy squeezed his hands.

'She was – killed?'

He nodded. 'The emergency services were there. They tried to make me go away but I wouldn't. I helped them dig – tearing at the rubble with my bare hands – hoping against hope. Everyone had miraculous stories of people buried in the rubble who were found alive. But when we found her . . .'

He broke off with a shudder and she saw suddenly that he was no longer with her. He was reliving that part of his past that haunted the darkest recesses of his mind. His eyes were bleak and filled with such raw, naked pain that she couldn't bear to look at him. After a moment he went on: 'We should have gone together, Amy. I'll always be convinced of that. Being left alone like that seemed to me the most cruel thing imaginable. I volunteered for the

372

most dangerous job I could think of, all the time hoping that the danger would take the pain away – even that I'd be killed. But I wasn't. I came through the whole bloody nightmare without so much as a scratch, while friends – good men with wives and families and everything to live for – died. That was my worst punishment. I felt as though God was mocking me. Playing cat and mouse. Can you believe that?'

Amy couldn't answer him, her throat was too tight for words. Instead she put her arms around him and drew his head down to hers, pressing her lips against the corner of his mouth. To think she had accused him of being emotionally immature. She felt ashamed – longed to take his pain away, to be someone special who could make him forget. He sighed and squeezed her shoulders.

'You should thank God you were still a child. Sorry to put you through all that, Amy.'

She shook her head. 'I'm glad you felt you could,' she said. 'I'm flattered that you can trust me enough to confide in me.'

'I just wanted you to understand. You see sometimes, when the memories are too much, I drink. Not because I enjoy it, but to blunt the pain. When I've had too much, I'm not a very nice person. I do things I shouldn't.'

'Are you trying to tell me you were drunk that Saturday?'

He smiled wryly. 'No. That would be rather insulting, wouldn't it? I'd had too much, but I knew what I was doing and saying. I admit that I enjoyed it too. But whisky releases all the inhibitions, makes one forget one's responsibilities. I suppose I was a little ashamed afterwards because I knew I'd no business to let it happen.' He looked into her eyes. 'And you've confirmed that for me, haven't you?'

'Because I behaved like a silly schoolgirl and took it all too seriously? I won't do that again.' Without waiting for his reply she went on: 'Alex – you can't go on for ever living with only memories. She'd want you to be happy again, wouldn't she – Chloe?'

373

'Not at someone else's expense.'

'But why should it be that?'

'Because I don't – I couldn't . . .' He shook his head. 'We're getting much too serious again. Come on, let's go and have that lunch.'

She laid her hand on his arm. 'Alex. Now that you've told me; now that I know, I won't mind if you can't feel as I do. I just want . . .' He stopped her with a finger across her lips.

'Shhh. Don't, Amy. I know what you *think* you want, but you don't. Not really. You're young and sweet. You deserve a nice young man who'll appreciate you. I'd only make you miserable, you know. Write to that nice Mike of yours. Get him to come and see you play Cathy. I guarantee that if he isn't already in love with you he'll fall on the spot.'

She stared at him. 'Play Cathy?'

'Yes.' He held both her hands tightly in his. 'Look, I wasn't going to tell you this and you must promise to keep it to yourself for the moment, but I think you need some good news right now. Remember Minsdale?' She nodded. 'Well, the group of businessmen who own the Theatre Royal have written to ask me to form a resident repertory company there. I've accepted the offer, but as a good many of the present company have commitments to follow this tour, I'll be looking for some replacements. There's a vacancy for a juvenile lead.' He smiled into her eyes. 'So, I'm offering it to you, Amethyst Lee. If you want it, that is.'

When Maryan was officially offered the job with Gina Stern she was delighted and relieved. She had already been staying at Roisan's for six weeks and she felt she couldn't impose on her hospitality much longer. The moment she had read the letter she telephoned Gina.

'I can start next week if you want me,' she said. 'I just have to find somewhere to live that isn't too far from Gower Street.'

'Fine . . .' Gina hesitated. 'As a matter of fact I've got

374

two rooms to let at the top of the house,' she said. 'I've been thinking of converting them into a flat. I think I might be able to get a government grant for that. I would have offered you accommodation before, but I thought you might be put off by the thought of living in.'

Maryan laughed, delightedly. 'You needn't have worried about that, the room will be a godsend.'

'Right, as long as you know you'll be free to move out any time you find somewhere better, that's settled then. Move your things in whenever you like.'

Roisan gave a little supper party for Maryan on her last night. She invited Paul and Geoff. Together the three of them had clubbed together to buy her a parting gift. It was something from the shop that she'd admired for a long time: an exquisite Baccarat glass paperweight. When she unwrapped it her eyes filled with tears.

'Oh, how lovely. Thank you. I'll always treasure this,' she said. 'I've loved working with you all and I'm going to miss you so much. I hope we won't lose touch.'

Paul grinned sheepishly and Geoff cleared his throat. ''Course we won't,' he said gruffly. 'Don't think you can get rid of us that easily.'

Roisan was downstairs making coffee when Vincent walked in. His arrival brought an air of tension down on the little gathering. Paul and Geoff didn't know the true reason for Maryan's leaving and they still blamed Vincent for it. After an awkward half hour when no one quite knew what to say, Paul looked at his watch and got to his feet.

'Time I went,' he said. 'Don't want to miss my bus.'

Geoff seized the opportunity to join him. 'Me too,' he said. 'The missis'll think I've run off and left her if I don't put in an appearance soon.'

When they had gone Maryan and Vincent looked at each other. 'They're smashing chaps, both of them,' Maryan said. 'You were lucky to find them.'

'They think I've sacked you, don't they? They hate my guts at the moment. It sticks out a mile.'

'They know I'm leaving from choice,' she told him. 'I told them I'd found a better job.'

He looked at her. 'And have you?'

'I've found a job, it's true. It's a good one and I'm lucky to get it.'

'They're lucky to get you.' He raised an eyebrow at her. 'Do I know them? Is it one of my rivals?'

Clearly Roisan hadn't told him about Gina. She was grateful to her for that. 'No,' she said. 'It's going to be a case of starting from scratch again – learning a new business – well, not quite new. I've worked in the rag trade before. I'll be glad to keep busy, what with – with one thing and another.'

'Have you heard from Amy?'

She shook her head. 'She hasn't written. I tried to get in touch with her friend, Celia Frazer, but she and her mother seem to have moved. I rang Marjorie Taylor in the end.' She looked up at him with a sigh. 'That took some doing, I can tell you; having to admit that I didn't know where my own daughter was. And when I heard that she'd written to Marjorie it hurt.'

'It must have. Did she give you Amy's address?'

'All she had was the address on Amy's letter. They're on tour, you see; moving around. But she said Amy sounded well and happy. That's all I really wanted to know. Maybe one of these days she'll contact me again.'

'There are ways of tracing people, if you're worried,' he said, his face concerned. 'I hear that the Salvation Army . . .'

'No.' She shook her head. 'As long as I know she's all right. She knows that if she needs me she has only to contact Roisan.'

'I suppose so.' He reached out to touch her hand. 'Maryan, I . . .' but at that moment Roisan pushed the door open and came in with the tray of coffee.

'Pity the fellers had to go,' she said, looking pointedly at her brother. 'I was hoping they'd stay on and talk for a while. This is the last chance Maryan will have to be with them.'

'Maybe I shouldn't have come,' Vincent said, quick to pick up her annoyance.

'Maybe you shouldn't,' Roisan said bluntly. 'I'd have thought you'd have more . . .'

'How is Fay?' Maryan broke in. 'I daresay you must be looking forward to moving into the flat. It'll be so much more convenient for you.'

Vincent avoided his sister's accusing eyes as he said, 'Fay's fine – as long as she keeps taking the insulin injections.'

'That's good.' Maryan got to her feet. 'Well – I think I'd better go to bed now. I've got an early start in the morning.'

Vincent stood up. 'Please don't go – not yet. I want . . .' He shot his sister a pleading look. 'Roisan . . . ?'

Reluctantly she got up and moved towards the door. 'I seem to have forgotten the biscuits.' At the door she paused and looked at Vincent. 'I'll only be a few minutes, so you'd better say whatever it is you have to say briefly and be done with it.'

When she'd gone, leaving the air heavy with her disapproval, Vincent looked at Maryan. 'There's no need to look so apprehensive. I just wanted to wish you well.'

'There's no need.' He looked so drawn and unhappy and she longed to be able to help him. 'It's going to be interesting and exciting, joining a brand-new venture,' she said brightly. 'And in the fashion business too. Back where I started, you could say.'

'Maryan – can I see you sometimes?' His hand covered hers and her eyes came up to meet his.

'I – don't think that would be a very good idea,' she said shakily.

'And *I* don't think I can exist without the prospect of seeing you occasionally. I don't mean to make any demands on you.'

'Then don't.' Unable to bear the tension a moment longer, she got up and walked to the door. 'Tell Roisan I've gone up, will you? Goodnight, Vinnie.'

'Maryan – please . . .' He was on his feet, reaching out for her, but already she had the door open.

'Don't make it harder, Vinnie. It's over. It has to be. There's no other way. Please be kind and let me go.'

Sitting on the bed in her room she heard Roisan's angry recriminations as she admonished her brother downstairs. A little later she heard the front door slam and after a moment Roisan tapped gently on her door.

'Maryan, love. Are you all right?'

'I'm fine, thank you, Roisan. Just fine.'

'Can I get you anything?'

'No. No, thank you.'

She heard Roisan's footsteps going back down the stairs as she sat there on the edge of the bed, her eyes dry and her heart cold and spent. Then, every muscle in her body aching with tension, she got up and began, very slowly, to get ready for bed.

The Keynan Players moved to Minsdale to take up residence at the Theatre Royal at the end of October. Alex immediately put them into rehearsal. Three members of the company had been replaced. Amy had taken the juvenile lead and another student ASM had been engaged; this time a young man called David Handley. The playbills and programmes had already been printed and they were to open 'by popular demand' with *Wuthering Heights*; Amethyst Lee playing the leading role.

In rehearsal Alex was tireless and demanding. At times Amy wondered if she would ever be good enough for him. He bullied and coaxed her by turn, often driving her to distraction as they repeated scenes over and over. But in a strange way his relentlessness exhilarated her. Although she alternated between tears and fury, she knew inside herself that the roughness of his language and his harsh criticism were drawing out the best in her; stirring her emotions and igniting a deep-seated passion within her of which she had so far only touched the edge.

On the opening night she felt as though she would die of nerves. Her stomach churned and her heart pounded every time she thought of stepping onto the stage. Twice she was physically sick, throwing up wretchedly in the backstage lavatory. An hour before curtain-up, convinced that she was too ill to appear, she went in search of Alex to tell him. To her surprise he wasn't angry. He behaved almost as though he'd been expecting it. Taking her hands he drew her calmly into the office and made her sit down.

'Now listen to me. You are Amethyst Lee, the star of this show. You are about to give a stunning performance. I'm your director and I know what I'm talking about. You know your lines. You love the part. You *are* Cathy. Understand?'

'Y-yes, Alex.'

'Right.' Dragging her abruptly to her feet, he pushed her towards the door. 'So go and get your bloody make-up on and try and behave like a pro instead of an hysterical fifth former.' At the door he cupped her chin with one hand and kissed her hard. 'That's for luck. You won't let me down, Amy. I know you won't.'

She didn't. By the time the curtain came down on the last act she was physically exhausted, but her spirits were soaring higher than the moon. It had gone perfectly. The audience had been with her all the way and so had the other members of the cast. Terrence Troy, the actor who had played Heathcliff, led her forward as the cast took their final call and the audience roared and clapped their approval. For Amy, it was a moment to cherish, a dream come true.

Later, as she was taking off her make-up, Alex came to her dressing room. 'What did I tell you?' he said with a smile. 'You were terrific, just as I knew you'd be.'

She jumped to her feet to throw her arms around his neck. 'Oh, Alex, wasn't it *wonderful*? I enjoyed it so much once I'd made my first entrance. I can't *wait* for tomorrow night.'

'Good.' He laughed. 'But you'd better get your beauty sleep first. You look completely frazzled.'

'Oh, Alex, I can't,' she said. 'I can't just go tamely

back to the digs and go to bed. Not after tonight. This has been the most exciting night of my entire life.'

He sighed. 'Oh God, Amy, you make me feel so old. I wish I could get that excited about something again.' He took her face between his hands. 'Make the most of it, darling. Enjoy it while you can. It doesn't last very long.'

The smile faded from her face. 'Alex, don't. I hate it when you say things like that. I want you to be happy too. I want you to share it with me.'

He kissed her briefly. 'Come on, I suppose you do need to wind down a little. I'll take you out for a drink, to celebrate.'

'Can I come home with you afterwards?' she asked, her eyes large and pleading. 'Just for a little while – please?'

For a moment he looked into the blue eyes wistfully. 'If I didn't know how innocent you are, Amethyst Lee, I'd suspect you of trying to seduce me.'

Several other members of the cast were in the Swan, the pub opposite the stage door. Everyone was in high spirits. The Keynan Players' first night in their new resident venue had been an outstanding success and Amy was the toast of the evening. She felt intoxicated by the sheer headiness of it; it was a feeling no mere alcohol could produce, as she told Alex on the way home. He had taken a flat; the ground floor of a Victorian house in a quiet tree-lined street on the town's outskirts. As they walked among the fallen leaves Alex remarked that winter would soon be on them.

'I expect it's colder here than in London,' he said. 'But young blood like yours doesn't feel the cold like my old bones, I daresay.'

'Why do you always make yourself sound so old?' she asked as he unlocked the door. 'You can't be more than – what, thirty-four?'

He grinned at her. 'Don't fish. I'm far too old for you, Miss Lee.'

'Who says so?' She reached up and pulled his head down to hers. He resisted her for a moment, then drew her into his arms and kissed her soundly. 'I'm very nearly old enough to be your father,' he whispered as they drew apart.

'I don't care.' She pressed close to him. 'What does it matter? What does *anything* matter tonight?'

'Mmm. I'll make you a coffee and then I think I'd better take you home,' he said.

'No, Alex. You're not going to get rid of me as easily as that,' she told him.

'Why – what did you have in mind?'

'I'm going to stay here with you. I want to spend the night with you.'

'Oh, no . . .' He removed her arms from around his neck.

'Alex, I'm serious. I don't want to be a virgin any more. I want to be an experienced, mature woman. And I want you to be my first lover.' Her eyes twinkled up at him. 'Just think how good it will be for my art. It's your duty really when you think about it, isn't it?'

He laughed. 'You wouldn't be using me for research purposes by any chance, would you?'

She looked up at him, her eyes clear and candid. 'No, Alex. I promise you it's not that.'

The laughter left his eyes. 'Amy, listen. Don't throw yourself away. I'm no good for you – for anybody, for that matter. You're on a high tonight and you don't know what you're saying. I don't want you to do something you'll regret.'

'You don't get it, do you? I love you, Alex. I *want* you. It's all very simple.' Her arms snaked seductively around his neck again.

'I don't believe I'm letting you do this,' he groaned. 'You're going to hate yourself – *and* me, in the morning.'

'I'll never hate you.' She nuzzled her face into his neck. 'The morning's a thousand light years away,' she whispered. 'Tonight is now, and it's magic. It belongs to us.'

It was just getting light when she woke, but in spite of her unfamiliar surroundings she knew at once where she was. Her whole body still tingled from Alex's lovemaking.

381

She would never have believed anything could be so wonderful. Now she knew beyond the slightest doubt that she loved him. He'd made love to her so passionately that she couldn't believe that he didn't love her in return. He was just being cautious when he said he wasn't good for her. Surely he must know that they were made for each other. And as for the age difference, it was trivial – a mere detail, an accident of birth. She trailed a finger down his cheek and he wakened instantly, looking up at her with eyes slightly unfocused. Then, seeing her face above him – remembering, he groaned.

'Oh, Amy, what the hell have we done?'

She laughed. 'Don't you remember? Would you like me to remind you?' Under the covers she began to caress him. 'We've got hours before we need get up. Plenty of time to . . .' His lips were on hers and he had rolled over onto her so swiftly that it took her breath away.

'You goddamned little temptress, you're enough to drive a man mad. You deserve a damned good hiding, do you know that?' His body was heavy and she could feel his arousal throbbing against her thigh as he lay on top of her. His face was raw with desire as he looked down at her. 'What the hell are we letting ourselves in for, Amy? It's madness and you bloody well know it – don't you?'

She reached up and pulled him down to her. 'Just love me,' she whispered as she arched her body invitingly towards him. 'Just love me and leave the worrying to me.'

The first weeks at Gower Street were hectic. There was so much to do – not only arranging Gina's busy work schedule, but helping her to finish decorating the house and, in particular, Maryan's own flat, so that she had somewhere to lay her head. Gina had promised to have a small bathroom and kitchen installed as soon as she could find a willing plumber who wasn't inundated with work. She had lent Maryan a few essential pieces of furniture until she could buy some of her own and Roisan had offered to make curtains.

Gina worked late into each evening on the designs for her collection, but during the day Maryan and she worked together, making business calls and organising a working plan in the office in the mornings. In the afternoons they worked on the house, donning overalls and turning their hands to whatever was necessary, from scrubbing and cleaning to painting and distempering.

During this time, working side by side, they grew to know one another well. Gina learned of Maryan's family problems and her estrangement with Amy, while in her turn Maryan learned that not all of the funds to set up the business came from Gina's grandmother. The house had been hers and there had been a small legacy to go with it, but Gina confessed that she'd obtained a sizable loan from a businessman friend too.

'Was that wise?' Maryan asked. 'I mean - did you have a legal agreement drawn up so that he can't demand his money back if the whim takes him?' Seeing Gina's expression she blushed. 'Oh - I'm sorry. It's really none of my business, is it?'

Gina smiled. 'I understand what you're saying, but it's really more of a friendly agreement.' She hesitated. 'I might as well tell you. You'll be seeing him around quite often anyway. Robert is a boyfriend.'

'Oh, I see. That's all right then. Are you - I mean will you be getting married?'

Gina shook her head. 'That's the snag. He's already married to someone else.'

'Oh, *no*.' Maryan's face dropped in dismay and at once she bit her lip. 'Forgive me, Gina. I've no business to make remarks. It's just that I've suffered from the same situation myself. I wouldn't like you to be hurt as I've been.'

'I won't.' Gina laid down her paintbrush and sat on the stairs. 'Robert hasn't been happy for years,' she said. 'I didn't break up his marriage. He has two sons and he's waiting till they've finished their education. Then he'll ask his wife for a divorce.'

'I see.' Maryan hoped it was as Gina said and that this

383

Robert, whoever he was, wasn't just playing her along. But she kept silent. She was desperately trying to think of a new subject when Gina did it for her.

'Maryan. I think we know each other well enough now for me to say this to you. You have a nice figure and you're really a very attractive woman.'

'Oh.' Maryan blushed. 'Thank you.'

'But – if you don't mind me saying so, you don't really make the best of yourself,' Gina went on. 'Would you be offended if I gave you some advice about clothes?'

'No, of course not. You're the expert.'

'Then there's your hair and make-up.' Gina smiled apologetically. 'Oh dear, I'm making you sound like a complete frump and you're not. It's just that I know that with a little help you could be quite stunning.' She smiled. 'When we've got some time at the weekend, shall we do a little make-over?'

'That might be fun.' Maryan looked at her enquiringly. 'But what about your friend – Robert?'

Gina sighed. 'That's one of the disadvantages of being the mistress of a married man. He always spends the weekends with his family.'

On Saturday they went shopping. Bearing in mind what Maryan had to spend, Gina picked out the nucleus of a wardrobe for her: a classic suit and blouse, a plain black dress that could be dressed up or down, a smart winter coat and a couple of hats. Then they went on to Gina's favourite beauty parlour for a complete make-up, hair restyling and manicure. Gina insisted that it was to be at her expense; a special thank you to Maryan for helping with the decorating.

When the expert staff at Maxine's had finished with her Maryan stared disbelievingly at herself in the mirror. She hadn't changed her hairstyle since the war ended and now, with the shoulder-length tresses cut into a fashionable short bob with a little half fringe, and the new make-up with its soft colouring and subtle eye-shadow – something Maryan had never worn before – she looked quite a different person. She realised for the first time how dowdy she had grown. Throwing all her concentration into Vincente's, she had quite forgotten to attend to her own appearance. Now she saw that if she was to spend part of her time representing a fashion designer she must be suitably groomed for the job and this was Gina's subtle way of telling her so. Outside in the street she couldn't resist stealing glances at herself in the shop windows they passed. Gina caught her doing it and laughed.

'You should have done this long ago, Maryan,' she said. 'That hairstyle does wonders for you.'

Briefly and wistfully, Maryan wished that Vinnie could see her, then she pulled herself up sharply. This was a new beginning. However much she might regret it, Vinnie was part of the past. She owed it to herself to make a new life. From now on she must look forward and not back.

In the weeks that followed the two women visited the buyers of dress shops and department stores together, showing Gina's portfolio of off-the-peg designs and taking along samples to show the workmanship. Her innovative flair was well known to many of the buyers who remembered her as the designer responsible for the Marcus Leigh label, and most were delighted that she had branched out on her own. Her up-to-the-minute styles interested them and so did her competitive prices. The order book rapidly filled up and after a while Gina was able to leave the selling trips to Maryan, remaining in her studio to work hard on the new season's designs.

One day each week Maryan visited the clothing factory at Islington to supervise the making up of garments. Ken James, the manager, and his head cutter, Ethel, were pleasant and obliging. It was a small, friendly factory and the sound of whirring machines and female voices uplifted in song as they joined in with 'Music While You Work' on the radio brought back memories to Maryan. Those far-off days before the war, when she'd worked at Feldman's, seemed like another world to her now. Watching the girls bent over their work, she was reminded poignantly of the day when Marcus first joined his father's firm and she had shown him how to thread a machine. Poor Marcus. She had loved him right from that very first day: so handsome and gifted with his dark, laughing eyes and curly hair. He had so much charm and talent. He should have had a golden future; a life filled with love and success. Yet the whole of his brief life had been dogged by tragedy and sadness. At times like this she could understand Rachel's endless grieving and Sam's despair.

A date had been set for Gina's show. It was to be at the end of January. Her haute couture collection was of spring and summer clothes to celebrate 1950. The venue was to be the ballroom of a Mayfair hotel, hired at what seemed to Maryan enormous expense. She guessed – correctly – that Robert Kemp was paying for it. Gina had already made out a guest list and given Maryan the task of sending out the invitations. As she worked through it, addressing envelopes, she was a little surprised to see that Sam and Rachel Leigh were included. As she sealed their envelope she wondered if they would accept.

Gina worked through most of Christmas, hunched over her drawing board and breaking only to share the meal that Maryan cooked for them both. Maryan spent most of the holiday decorating her own flat and trying not to think about Amy. There had been no word, not even a Christmas card. Things could have been so very different between them. She was sure that Amy would have got along well with Gina and enjoyed living here. She hoped that, wherever she was, she was happy. She found her thoughts drifting wistfully towards Vincent too. She pictured him with Fay in the flat at Simons Mews and wondered what kind of Christmas they were sharing.

She now had her own bathroom and a tiny kitchen, hastily installed by a plumber whose services had been arranged for Gina by Robert Kemp. Robert seemed to be the kind of man who could pull strings and make things happen. Gina had only to say that she was having difficulty in obtaining something or getting some job done, for it to be attended to next day. Maryan had met him a few times, passing him on his way in or out. He was a tall, well-built man of about forty-five, handsome in an almost saturnine way with his deep-set grey eyes and lantern jaw. She sometimes wondered what vivacious Gina could see in him, but if her employer seemed happy with the far from ideal situation who was she to question it? And she could not deny that he was a great help in getting things done.

As the weeks rushed busily by and the day of the show drew closer, life grew hectic. There was no time to brood over the past or to speculate about the future and Maryan was glad of it. She was busy and fulfilled. She enjoyed her work and at the end of the day she was too tired to think very much. It was enough.

At Minsdale Christmas and New Year were busy and exciting. The Keynan Players put on a production of *Cinderella*; performed more as a musical play than the traditional pantomime, with a male actor in the role of Prince Charming. Amy played Cinderella and had her first experience of playing a musical role. Alex had persuaded a choreographer he knew to come up to Lancashire and teach the dance steps while Harry Palmer, the theatre's musical director, coached them in the singing. It worked well and Amy loved it. She thought about the first time she had stood on a stage, at Northmere Rep with Celia's father. This was her dream come true. Life was good. She had achieved her ambition to be an actress and found the only man she would ever love. She was so lucky. The only problem was that for the moment Alex didn't see things in quite the same way. She was confident that she could make him change his mind, but when she had begged him to let her move into his flat he had been adamant.

'I don't want the other members of the cast to get the wrong idea,' he told her.

She laughed. 'What wrong idea?'

'The moment we let ourselves be seen as a couple they'll start getting suspicious. They'll see every part you get as preferential treatment. Let's just leave things as they are, Amy. Being together at the weekends will give us something to look forward to, eh?'

She said nothing, biding her time and waiting for the right moment, when she would prove to him just how committed she was. She was confident that he would come round to her way of thinking then. And she couldn't help but agree about the other members of the company. Her relationship with Alex had caused a few pointed remarks, especially when she was cast in a coveted leading part. Alex insisted that she was only cast in roles that suited her, and she was sure this was true. He wasn't the type to jeopardise his productions just to please her. But some of the older women in the company would have questioned this. Catty remarks were made and Alex had to be scrupulously fair in order to retain his credibility. He warned Amy not to flaunt their relationship too openly.

'That kind of thing can break a company up,' he told her. 'I've seen it happen. And we've got a very nice rep here. I know you won't want to spoil it, especially when so many provincial theatres are closing down.'

It was true. Peter's prediction about the popularity of television was clearly being fulfilled. As more families bought sets and stayed at home to watch them, one theatre after another closed through lack of business. Experienced actors were thrown out of work and valuable training ground was lost to newcomers. The profession was in the doldrums.

They played *Cinderella* for two weeks instead of the usual one, and on the last night Alex gave them a party. The stage was cleared and everyone invited friends. They ate, drank and danced until the small hours of the morning. After the party Amy walked happily home with Alex, light-hearted and high on wine and success and looking forward to the ecstatic weekend they were about to share.

The night was cold and frosty and the sky was bright with a full moon and stars. She hugged his arm and looked up at him. 'Are you happy, Alex?'

He laughed. 'What kind of damn-fool question is that?'

'A simple one,' she said, slightly put out. '*I'm* happier than I've ever been in my life. Are you?'

He looked down at her. 'It's a long time since I asked myself whether I was happy or not. I've got out of the habit.'

'Couldn't you try and get back into it?' she asked. 'Go on – ask yourself now. Just try.'

He stopped to take out his key, disengaging his arm from hers. 'Isn't it enough for you that you're happy?'

As they stepped into the dark hallway she reached up to wind her arms around his neck. 'No. I want you to be happy too. I want you to be happier than you've ever been before – just as I am. When you love someone it isn't enough to be happy on your own.'

He sighed. 'Let's go to bed. I'm tired.'

She laughed softly. 'What kind of reason is that?'

'It's a bloody good one when you get to my age,' he told her. 'You'll find out.'

'I don't believe you.' She pulled him towards her and began to undo the buttons of his shirt. 'Now, let's see just how tired you are.' Confident that her hands on his bare flesh would make him forget his tiredness, she continued to unfasten his shirt, then slipped her hands inside to caress him. For a moment he stood passively and let her, then, with a roar of angry submission, he swept her up in his arms and carried her to the bedroom.

Their lovemaking was as passionate as ever. Over the months Amy had learned the things that pleased him. She knew how to touch him in ways he found irresistible; how to kiss and caress; when to urge him on, and when to hold back. For her, loving Alex had become almost as much of an art as her acting. When at last they were both spent she lay drowsily in his arms thinking about the request she had wanted to make for some time.

'Alex . . .' She twisted her head to look up at him as she lay with her head on his chest. His eyes were closed and he looked perfectly relaxed. This seemed to her like the perfect moment. 'Alex – will you marry me?'

His eyes flew open. '*What* did you say?'

She laughed. 'I asked you to marry me. Well, if I wait for you to ask *me* we could both be old and grey.' She sat up and looked down at him. 'Well – will you?'

He sat up abruptly, swinging his legs over the side of the bed and reaching for his cigarettes and lighter. She watched as he lit one, inhaled deeply and blew out a cloud of smoke.

'Alex – please say something,' she said quietly.

He drew hard on the cigarette again. 'You're a child, Amy. I've told you so many times before. I'm all wrong for you.'

'You're not. I . . .'

He turned and silenced her with a look. 'I *am*. I'm too old and too – I don't know – world-weary – call it what you like. I don't want to get married. Not now. Not ever.'

Swallowing her disappointment, she reached out to touch him. Angry tears and recriminations would do nothing to help her cause. She knew him well enough to realise that. 'Alex. I'm not a child. You know that. You need someone. You need me. You've been alone too long. I love you. Please don't close your mind to the idea of us being together.'

'We are together. It's enough for me the way we are. Why can't it be enough for you?'

Her hand tightened on his shoulder and she pulled him towards her but he shook her off angrily and stood up, pulling on his dressing gown. 'You don't know what you're saying, Amy – don't know what you're asking. I believe losing your father has a lot to do with this. I think you see me as some kind of father figure.'

She laughed aloud. 'Oh, what *rubbish*. Can you really say that I've treated you like a father?'

He shrugged impatiently. 'It's just a theory, but whatever the reason, I mean it, Amy. Marriage is out.'

She looked at him. He did mean it, she could see that by the determined set of his mouth. The time had come to play her trump card. She had kept it as a kind of treat; the icing on the cake. But now suddenly she saw that it was nothing of the kind. A chill went through her and the thought of what she was about to reveal filled her with dread. Nevertheless, she had to say it. She took a deep breath.

'I'm pregnant, Alex. I'm going to have our child.'

He closed his eyes, rocking back on his heels for a moment. When he opened them again she shrank from the look in them. Glaring furiously down at her he thundered: 'What the *hell* do you think you're playing at, Amy? You said you were taking care of that.'

'No.' She shook her head bemusedly. 'No, I didn't.'

'*Leave the worrying to me*, you said. I thought . . .' He broke off. Stubbing out his cigarette savagely he turned his back to her. 'Christ, what a bloody mess.' He paced the room for a moment then turned to face her. 'Look, there are doctors in London who can fix it. I know where I can get the name of one. A good one. You'll be safe. I'll give you the money and you can . . .'

'*No*. I won't do that.'

He rounded on her. 'You'll do as I bloody well say.'

'No, I *won't*. Not that. You can't make me.'

He raked his fingers through his hair. 'You'll *have* to, Amy. Can't you see? It's not my fault if you've been stupid enough to get yourself into this. Don't you care anything for your career? Or mine? How do you think this is going to look to the rest of the company?'

She was crying now, tears slipping unchecked down her cheeks as she looked up at him. She'd thought she knew him – she'd been so sure that he loved her. 'I don't care about the rest of the company,' she said in a choked voice. 'I only care about you – and me and – and our baby. No one will think anything about it if we get married. Why should they?'

With a despairing sigh he sat down and drew her into his arms. 'Amy – *Amy*. A baby will wreck your career as an actress and I'd make you miserable. Within a year we'd be at each other's throats. You'd wish you'd never met me.'

'I won't. I *won't*. Please, Alex – *please*.'

He grasped her by the shoulders, holding her away from him, his eyes burning into hers. 'Amy, listen to me. I'm trying hard not to be unkind, but you're forcing me. The simple fact is, *I don't love you*. I don't love you and I never will. I can't love anyone – ever. And I can't marry anyone either, because I'll only ever have one wife – Chloe. And I'll never be able to stop loving her.'

She began to sob like a child. 'I don't believe you. It isn't true. You can't love a dead person. You *do* love me. I'll prove it to you, Alex. I'll make you. I'll *make* you.'

With a sigh he held her in his arms and let her cry. It was his fault. He should have seen from the beginning how immature she was. For all her passion and her beautiful woman's body, she was still a child – vulnerable and trusting and naive. He should never have let the relationship develop. God only knew there were plenty of women willing for a quick fling with no strings attached, so why had he chosen Amy? He knew the reasons why. He'd been touched by her innocence; flattered by her admiration; and all his predatory instincts had been aroused by her vulnerability. Christ, how arrogant he'd been. Deep inside he'd known it was folly, seen all the danger signals, so why had he ignored them? Now it was too late. His heart sank despairingly. What in God's name was he to do?

They were married three weeks later, two days after Amy's eighteenth birthday, at the register office in Minsdale. One or two members of the company were present at the ceremony and they all went for lunch at the Swan afterwards. Feeling she wanted someone of her own there, Amy had written to Celia, and to her great delight, she came over from York for the day. After the ceremony they found a few moments to be alone together in the cloakroom at the Swan. Celia hugged her friend warmly.

392

'Well, you made it before me in the end,' she said. 'Are you happy, kid?'

Amy nodded. 'Do you like him, Cee?'

Celia hesitated just a fraction of a second too long. 'Of course. He's terribly handsome and romantic-looking. But . . .'

'Go on, but what?'

'He's quite a bit older than you, isn't he?'

'Not all that much. He's thirty-six.'

'That's twice your age.'

'What does it matter anyway when we love each other?' Amy said, instantly defensive.

'Nothing. Of course it doesn't matter. Where will you live?' Celia asked. 'Have you got lots of exciting plans about working together? I expect you're planning a great theatrical partnership like Kay Hammond and John Clements.'

Amy looked down at the shiny new gold band on her finger. 'I'm going to have a baby, Cee. So my career plans will have to be shelved – for a while at least.'

Celia looked into her friend's face and her heart sank. In the blue eyes she thought she could already see the seeds of unhappiness. Swallowing her dismay, she hugged Amy hard.

'Hey, that's terrific. Congratulations. Promise you'll let me know when it's born, won't you? Maybe I could be a Godmother.'

'Alex has a house in Mill Hill,' Amy went on. 'It belonged to his parents and they left it to him. I'm going to live there when I have to give up my job with the company here.'

'I see. And what about Alex?'

'He's going to try for some film or television work in London when his contract is finished here. But in the meantime he'll travel down to Mill Hill to be with me at weekends.'

Celia was silent. She hoped Amy wasn't about to be dumped and forgotten, like some unwanted animal. She didn't quite know why she should feel this. After all, she had only just met Alex Keynan. It was just an uncomfortable feeling she had. Forcing herself to smile, she said: 'Sounds exciting.' She hesitated, then asked, 'Amy – does your mum know – about you getting married, I mean, and – the baby?'

Amy shook her head. 'I did write when I first came up here but she never answered. I doubt whether she'd be interested.'

'Oh. Well, maybe you're right.' Privately Celia wished that she didn't live so far away. She wished Amy hadn't fallen out with her mother too. She had a horrible feeling that she was going to need someone close to her before too long.

Chapter Sixteen

Gina's first collection was a bigger success than she had dared to hope. The venue she had chosen for the show was a wise choice. Almost everyone who had received an invitation turned up on the day of the show, including – much to Maryan's surprise – the Leighs.

She caught sight of them when she was ushering people to their seats just before the start of the show. For a moment she stood where she was, on the far side of the room, watching as they settled into their seats. They both looked so old and tired that she felt a stab of pity and regret as she watched Sam attentively making sure that his wife was comfortable. Should she go across to them? She stood hesitating. Rachel might be upset – might snub her. Did she even know that she was working for her ex-designer? But at that moment Sam caught sight of her and his face broke into a smile. He waved, beckoning her over. Taking a deep breath, she walked across.

'Hello. How nice to see you both.'

Sam took her hand warmly in both of his. 'Maryan, my dear. Rachel and I were so pleased to be invited. This is a very special day for Gina. We're proud of her, aren't we, Rachel? And we feel so honoured to be asked to share this day with her. I know she must be busy, but if you see her before the show begins, wish her the best of luck from us, will you?'

'Of course I will.' Maryan glanced at Rachel. 'And how are you, Mrs Leigh?'

Rachel turned to give her a brief nod. 'I am very well, thank you.' It was clearly an effort for her. Maryan saw her throat constrict as she swallowed. 'It's – been a long time, Maryan. It – it's good to see you again.'

Maryan reached across Sam to take Rachel's hand. 'It's good to see you, too – very good.' She looked up as the small orchestra they had hired began to play. 'It looks as though we're about to start, so I'm afraid I'll have to go now. But I'll come and see you again in the interval.'

Behind the scenes all was chaos as the models prepared for their appearance. Hairdressers were busy combing and pinning, while the make-up girls worked briskly with their brushes and pots of colour. Gina herself seemed to be everywhere at once, checking hemlines, pinning a seam here and tweaking a sleeve there. As she passed her Maryan managed to say: 'Gina – the Leighs are here. Both of them. They asked me to say good luck.'

Gina looked up with a smile. 'Oh, that's wonderful. Thanks, Maryan.'

In the interval Maryan made a point of joining Sam and Rachel, taking them a tray of tea and picking out a plate of the choicest cakes for them. She found them looking more relaxed, though Rachel seemed a little flushed.

'How are you enjoying it so far?' she ventured.

Sam nodded eagerly. 'Gina has done wonders. Her designs are delightful. We both think so, don't we, Rachel?'

Rachel looked up. 'They are certainly different.' She smiled diffidently. 'I mean that in a complimentary way. I'm so relieved, you see. I dreaded that they might be too like – too close to . . .'

'Too close to Marcus's styles,' Sam said in a hushed whisper. He turned to his wife. 'But I told you, darling. Those styles are out of fashion now anyway. Gina has such flair. She is a trend *setter*, not a follower.' He leaned across to Maryan with a conspiratorial smile. 'Rachel and I are going on holiday next month. I've persuaded her at last. We're going on a cruise to the Greek islands.'

'Oh, how lovely. You'll enjoy it so much.'

Rachel nodded. 'I can't remember when we last had a proper holiday. There was the war and everything.' She smiled reminiscently. 'Though I always felt that working to promote Marcus's name was a holiday for me. I loved it all so much.'

'But it will be so nice to be together,' Maryan said. 'To have no one else to think of but each other.'

Sam smiled and squeezed his wife's hand. 'A second honeymoon, I tell her.' He chuckled. 'Though she tells me not to be a sentimental old fool.' He looked at Maryan. 'We are thinking of winding up Feldman's – maybe even selling up,' he said quietly.

Maryan glanced at Rachel, wondering how she felt about this. The firm had been started by her father and left to her. It had always been meant as a family business, to be handed on. But now there was no one to hand it to. She must feel that. 'I see,' she said. 'Well, whatever you decide, I'm sure it will be the right decision.'

Gina joined them and Maryan left her to speak to the Leighs alone. She felt happy to have seen them and spoken to Rachel. Although no one had mentioned Amy or the circumstances in which they had parted, she felt instinctively that she had been forgiven. And she was glad that they bore Gina no ill will.

The fashion magazines and trade papers were full of praise for Gina Stern's spring and summer collection and she was soon receiving invitations to exhibit her work at larger shows both in England and on the Continent. By summer she was inundated with orders, both for her range of off-the-peg fashions and for her more exclusive designs, so much so that the factory in Islington could no longer cope with her orders as well as their other commitments. After a meeting with her bank manager to find out just how much she could afford to spend, Gina decided that there was nothing for it but to hire a whole factory instead of just a few machines. She discussed it with Maryan over supper one evening.

'It's going to be so expensive,' she complained. 'And where will I find a place like that anyway? In the end the only answer is to buy, and that would mean taking on a big mortgage. I'd rather wait till I'm more established before taking a step like that.'

'Would Mr Kemp – Robert help you?' Maryan ventured.

Gina stirred her coffee pensively. 'I'd rather not ask,' she said. 'I want to stand on my own feet. I already owe him a lot. Too much, in fact.'

Maryan was surprised at Gina's tone. 'I'm sure, from what you tell me, that he doesn't look on it like that.'

Gina looked up at her. 'You might have noticed that Robert hasn't been around much lately,' she said. 'I'm afraid it's on the cards that our relationship is coming to an end.'

'I see. His wife . . . ?'

Gina shook her head. 'No. That I could come to terms with. Robert is going in for politics. He's standing for Parliament in next year's General Election. He's been selected for a constituency in Essex. It's something he's always wanted, so I'm sure I don't have to tell you that he won't allow a scandal to ruin his chances.'

'I see.' Maryan looked thoughtful. 'It's bound to be expensive, organising an election campaign. Is he asking for his money back?'

'No. But he's going to get it,' Gina said determinedly. 'Every last penny, which is why buying a factory could be something of a problem just now.'

'Yes, of course.' A gloomy silence descended between them. Then Maryan had an idea. 'Why not ask Sam Leigh if you can rent Feldman's premises? He's talking of winding the business up – even selling it off. He might be willing to let you rent the workshop for a while with the option to buy later, when you're ready.'

Gina stared at her. 'My God, Maryan, that's brilliant.

Do you really think he would? It seems an awful cheek to ask after I left them.'

'They don't hold that against you,' Maryan said. 'Anyway, there's only one way to find out. Ask him.'

Gina's eyes lit up with excitement. 'I will. I'll ring him tomorrow. No – better than that, I'll go and see him.'

Number twenty-two Willow Drive hadn't been lived in since 1947, when Alex's widowed father had died. One of a row of neat semi-detached residences built between the wars, it had once been the ideal suburban home. Now it was sadly neglected and run down. The garden was a wilderness of weeds and long wiry grass and the house itself, closed up for the past three years, smelt musty with damp and was badly in need of decoration.

When Amy saw the place for the first time she was deeply disappointed, and the thought of living there alone depressed her beyond measure. The removal of dust sheets revealed ugly, old-fashioned furniture; dark in colour and heavy in design. The curtains were dusty and in need of washing, the carpets were worn almost thread-bare and cobwebs festooned every corner.

'I think Dad became a bit of a recluse after Mother died,' Alex told her. 'He wouldn't have a cleaning woman in or help of any kind.'

'I can see that,' Amy said dryly. She had wandered into the kitchen, where the first thing to catch her eye was an ancient black gas cooker which squatted in one corner on four bandy legs. It was encrusted with grease, welded in position by layers of dust. Its rusting plate rack held two cracked dinner plates and a filthy tea towel. The half-tiled walls, once white, wore a film of grime and the linoleum on the floor was cracked and torn, showing the floorboards in places.

Seeing her look of dismay, Alex said cheerfully, 'It just needs a bit of a clean. You'll soon get the place shipshape. It'll be something to occupy the time, won't it?'

Despair gripping her chest like an iron band, she wrapped her arms around his waist and laid her head on his chest. 'Oh, Alex, do I really have to stay here on my own? Why can't we be together? I know I can't act at the moment, but I wouldn't be a nuisance. I'd help backstage if you like. Anything so's we could be together.'

He put her from him impatiently. 'Amy, look, we talked all this through and we decided. It's better for you to be here in a stable home, at least until after the baby's born. Later – well, we'll see.'

'But we could make a stable home in Minsdale. I don't know anyone here.'

'You'll soon make friends. I daresay you'll be going to some sort of clinic where there'll be other young mothers-to-be. You'll be fine.' He kissed her. 'Look, I know this place looks pretty awful now, but at least it's ours and it's paid for. When my contract runs out at Minsdale I'll be getting work in London. This will make a good central base for me.'

'But it's so – so shabby and creepy,' Amy said, looking round at the dark green paintwork and peeling ceilings. 'Couldn't we sell it and find something nicer?'

'That's easier said than done,' Alex told her. 'Houses like this are at a premium. You have to go through heaven knows how much red tape, not to mention building permits, to build a new place and even then it wouldn't be as sound as this.' He ruffled her hair. 'Cheer up. You won't know the place once we get a bit of paint slapped on and some new furniture.'

'I don't really know how to paint. You will help me, won't you?'

'Of course.'

'When, Alex?' she asked him eagerly. But he shook his head.

'Might have to wait a bit,' he hedged. 'I'm tied up in Minsdale for the next twelve months. After that – well, we'll just have to wait and see.'

In the early weeks she occupied herself by cleaning the house. At first she found that she couldn't even light the boiler for hot water. Whenever she tried clouds of smoke filled the kitchen, almost choking her, until she realised what the trouble was. Once she had found a local sweep and had all the chimneys swept it was easier. Then, armed with buckets of hot water, soap and soda, she scrubbed the house from top to bottom until her hands were red and raw. She washed the curtains, hanging them out to dry in the spring breezes. She'd already discovered that the beds were not too bad. The double one in the front bedroom had an interior spring mattress, and after a good airing it was warm and comfortable. The airing cupboard was full of good quality linen, too, yellow with age and disuse, but whole and some of it exquisitely embroidered; a relic of better days when Alex's mother was alive, she guessed. To add to this there was good cutlery and china in the sideboard downstairs. It seemed that Alex's father had put it all away, using only the two cracked plates in the kitchen and a pathetic chipped cup with a saucer that didn't match.

All through the hard-working weekdays Amy looked forward to the weekends when Alex would come. But to her disappointment he didn't always get away. She knew of course that it was difficult for him, making the long drive down from Minsdale after two shows on Saturdays, then driving back on Monday to arrive in time for the evening performance. Because they had no telephone she often waited in vain, sitting up until the small hours of Sunday morning, hoping against hope that he would come. The usual reason he gave for not coming was that the second-hand car he had bought soon after they married had let him down.

She wrote long letters to Celia, making her marriage and pregnancy and settling into the house sound like an exciting adventure. Celia wrote back with news of her busy and interesting life. She was training to be a legal executive, now; studying in her spare time. She invited Amy to go up to York and stay with her at the flat for a weekend. Amy declined, saying that Alex always drove down to spend the weekends with her. Of course this wasn't strictly true and she suspected that he would be only too happy for her to have an alternative to occupy her weekend. The real reason was that she was short of money. Alex's weekly cheque often failed to arrive and she had to eke out the previous week's money as best she could. Dearly as she would have loved to see her friend, the train fare to York would have been beyond her means. She often toyed with the idea of writing to her mother. She had sent her a note, telling her that she was to be married, addressing it to Simons Mews, confident that one of the Donlans would forward it to wherever Maryan had gone. But, as before, she had received no reply.

She did write to Marjorie Taylor, however. As with Celia's letters, she made everything sound much happier and grander than it really was. As well as passing the time, writing letters boosted her confidence and made her feel that things were going to be all right. Marjorie replied, telling her that Mike was working for the BBC and hoping eventually to become a foreign correspondent. She promised to pass on Amy's good wishes.

Month by month the baby grew inside her. She was remarkably well. She had registered with a local doctor and had her monthly checks without fail. She had been booked in at a local hospital for the birth and everything seemed to be going according to plan. As Alex had predicted, she did meet other young mothers-to-be, but no one with whom she felt she had anything in common. When she told them she was an actress they looked at her with open suspicion and disbelief, preferring to talk amongst themselves about babies and shopping and what they were going to give their husbands for tea.

Alex declared that pregnancy suited her. In the early days when he came home he loved to lie in bed and watch her undress. Seeing the nymph-like figure growing increasingly ripe and voluptuous excited him. It was like making love to someone new. He was delighted too at the way pregnancy seemed to increase Amy's appetite for love. But as the months passed and the pleasantly rounded figure grew larger, his interest waned. Privately he thought she looked bloated and grotesque. Making love to her became little more than a duty. The list of stock excuses for staying away lengthened and the week-end visits grew even more infrequent.

His obvious lack of interest was a cause of anxiety and distress to Amy. She lay awake at night, worrying about it. He had made no attempt to hide the fact that he no longer found her desirable and it hurt unbearably. Surely once the baby was born and she regained her figure he would find her attractive again? In the meantime she was lonely, lonelier than she could ever have imagined. She often thought nostalgically about the happy times at Rhensham, and of the Taylors; of her schooldays and Celia. And she thought of her mother too. It would have been nice to have had a proper mother at this time in her life – someone she could talk to about the pregnancy, sharing her fears and apprehension about the coming birth with someone close who loved her. Her feelings towards Maryan swung between anger and wistfulness, resentment and regret. But however much she might want it, her pride would not allow her to beg for her mother's attention. Maryan had always been too busy for her in the past. Clearly nothing had altered.

As spring evolved gently into summer her thoughts turned to the garden. Looking out of the windows at the tangle, she realised that something would have to be done with it. With the warmth and the gentle spring rain the weeds and grass were shooting up. Day by day it grew increasingly out of control. She was struggling to cut the front lawn one afternoon in late May when she made her first friend.

'You'll never make no headway like that, missie.'

The voice made her look up. A little man with a brown face and bright blue eyes stood looking over the front gate. She straightened her back and he noticed for the first time that she was pregnant.

'Oh,' he said, taking off his cap and scratching his head. 'Sorry, I didn't notice you was a missis. Like me to give you a hand with that, would you?'

Amy smiled and wiped the sweat from her forehead

with the back of her hand. 'I'm afraid I couldn't afford to pay you, but if you could just show me how to get it started . . . I don't know anything about gardening, you see.'

'I can see that all right.' A smile lit up the blue eyes as he eagerly opened the gate and came in. 'Bless your heart, I don't want no paying. Glad of something to do. Since my retirement I've been getting under my missis's feet something chronic.' He held out his hand. 'Jack Shaw from number twenty-nine.'

Amy smiled and shook the large knobbly hand. 'How do you do, Mr Shaw. I'm Amy Keynan.'

Jack slapped his cap back onto his head and looked pointedly at her thickened waistline. 'Apart from anything else, m'dear, you got no business doing heavy work like this in your condition, if you don't mind me saying so. Hubby work away, does he?'

'Yes.'

'Right. Better let me get on with it for you then, eh?'

Amy handed over the mower gratefully. 'Well, if you're sure. I'll make a cup of tea. I expect you'd like one.'

'Well now. That'd be very nice.'

Jack did wonders with the garden. Having convinced him that the exercise was good for her, Amy helped, and once they had cleared the tangle of weeds they found a pleasant lay-out underneath, with borders and a shrubbery. Jack brought bedding plants from his own greenhouse to plant in them. It wasn't long before he brought his wife across to view his handiwork and to meet Amy.

Addie Shaw was plump and motherly with tightly permed hair. The sharp blue eyes that twinkled behind her spectacles missed nothing that went on in Willow Drive. Right from the first she showed a friendly curiosity towards her new young neighbour. She admired the work that Amy had put in on the house and then, as they sat down to a cup of tea together, showed a lively interest in her private life.

'Hubby work away from home then, does he, luvvie?' she observed, her little finger crooked as she drank tea from one of Alex's mother's bone china cups that Amy had brought out of retirement.

Amy explained that the house had belonged to Alex's parents and that he was up north for the time being.

'He's running a repertory theatre in Lancashire at the moment, but when his contract is up he'll be looking for film work,' she said. Addie was impressed.

'There now. Just fancy. A film producer. We never saw much of old Mr Keynan, of course. Kept himself very much *to* himself, if you know what I mean. There's plenty would have been willing to help him after his poor wife passed on, but he wouldn't have it. Oh no, very independent.' She looked up over the rim of her cup. 'Tell you the truth, dear, we never even knew he had a son. Your hubby didn't visit much – hardly ever that I can remember.' She looked around her. 'Always wondered what sort of a state this place was in. A man on his own usually lets a house go to pot, don't he? But it's all good stuff, you can see that. And you've made it quite nice, dear – considering.' She nodded in the direction of Amy's stomach. 'When's baby due then?'

'The end of August.'

'Oh. Not long to wait now then, eh? Exciting, isn't it – the first baby.'

But in spite of the improvement to the house and garden, Alex bristled with annoyance when he knew that the Shaws were partly responsible.

'Interfering old fools. Who asked them to poke their noses in? I hope you haven't been telling them too much. People like that have nothing better to do but ferret out other people's business and gossip about it all over the neighbourhood.'

'That's a horrible thing to say,' Amy retorted. 'They've been so kind. I don't know what I'd have done without them. It hasn't been easy, getting this place shipshape as you call it. I haven't noticed you doing much – when you ever bother to turn up, that is. It seems you never came to see your parents, though, so it's nothing unusual, I suppose.'

'There, you see? They've already started making trouble.' He rounded on her angrily. 'Thanks a *lot*, Amy. That's what I call *real* gratitude. I work bloody hard all week, then wear myself out, driving all the way down here as often as I can, to make sure you're all right. And you reproach me because I don't spend all day Sunday digging the damned garden or sloshing a paintbrush about.'

'You hardly ever come any more,' Amy said reproachfully. 'I don't think you really give a tuppenny damn whether I'm all right or not.'

'Oh. I see.' His face darkened. 'Well, if that's what you think I might as well go now. There are plenty of other things I could be doing that are a bloody sight more rewarding than this.' He strode into the hall and began to put on his coat. 'Maybe it'd be better if I didn't bother coming home any more,' he said, shrugging his arms into the sleeves. 'Maybe you prefer the Shaws' company to mine.'

Heaving herself out of her chair, she hurried after him. 'Oh, Alex, don't. You know I didn't mean it. I get so lonely, that's all. I miss you. And I can't do everything on my own, specially now.' She put her arms around his neck, attempting to pull off his coat as she did so. 'Don't go, darling. Come up to bed.'

'It's the middle of the afternoon.'

She smiled up at him. 'So – when did that ever bother you?'

He frowned, pushing her away. 'No, Amy. I can't. It isn't – isn't good for you.'

She let her arms fall to her sides and stood looking at him. 'You could give me a cuddle,' she said, her lip trembling. 'You never cuddle me any more.'

He turned away, his expression a mixture of guilt and distaste. 'Oh, Amy – don't be so childish.'

She managed to persuade him to stay, but for the rest of the day he was morose and silent. In bed, when she reached for him he kissed her briefly and turned his back. Long after his breathing had deepened she was still

406

awake, staring at the ceiling, the tears drying on her face. Perhaps she should have done as he wanted in the first place and gone to London for an abortion, she thought despairingly. As though responding to the thought, the child inside her stirred and she clasped her stomach with protective hands.

'I didn't mean it,' she whispered. 'I didn't really mean it, baby. I'll never let anyone hurt you.' She promised herself that whatever happened, whatever came out of this, she would have her baby to love; someone who truly belonged to her. And she vowed that she would always be honest and truthful with her son or daughter. There would be no secrets between them. No shocking surprises. No lies or deception. Never.

Alone in the house she often thought about the couple who had lived there before her; Alex's parents. She was always coming across things – little things, clues to the life they had led here, which she gradually fitted together like the pieces of a puzzle. A photograph album she found at the bottom of a drawer held all the Keynan family memories. A wedding photograph bearing the inscription, *Henry and Florence July 9th 1910*, showed Alex's parents as a young couple on the day they'd wed: a shy young man with a waxed moustache, wearing a high, stiff collar and Windsor knotted tie; and his bride, her face almost hidden under the enormous cartwheel hat loaded with flowers. Further on there were pictures of Henry as a young soldier in the Great War and Alex as a chubby infant on his mother's knee. He was their only child. They must have been so proud of him. She often wondered why he had neglected them and tried to imagine their puzzled sadness and, later, the loneliness of poor widowed Henry, left in this house with his memories and his solitary grief. Sometimes in the night when she couldn't sleep she held imaginary conversations with them in her head, and wondered if she was about to be abandoned too in this house of disillusionment and loneliness.

It was six weeks before Alex came again, arriving

unannounced one Friday evening. The baby's birth was less than a month away now and Amy, lonely and tired of the endless waiting, forgot all her fears in her delight at seeing him. Everything was ready now. She had made most of the baby's clothes herself, finding Alex's mother's old sewing machine carefully put away in the boxroom. The needlework lessons she had complained of so bitterly at St Hildred's had finally come into their own. She proudly showed Alex the little flannel nightgowns and the vests and jackets she had knitted. Addie Shaw had found her a second-hand pram in good condition. She'd made some baby clothes for her too, but Amy kept those at the back of the drawer, in case Alex might be annoyed again.

But he showed scant interest in the baby clothes. He'd driven down earlier that afternoon to attend an interview for a job he'd applied for with Gainsborough Films, but by the end of the afternoon he knew that the job he wanted so badly had gone to someone else. He had repaired to the nearest pub in an attempt to dull the pain of disappointment. But drinking only made him feel worse, and by the time he arrived at Willow Drive the mixture of alcohol and disillusionment had plunged him into the blackest of moods.

'What's the matter?' Amy asked. 'Aren't you interested?'

He waved a hand at her impatiently. 'I've got more on my mind at the moment than bloody knitting and baby clothes.'

Stung, she rounded on him angrily. 'Well, isn't that nice for you? I wish *I* had other things on my mind. All I've got to look forward to is the baby, Alex. You might try to take an interest in it, if only for my sake.'

'If it's all you've got, then you've only yourself to blame,' he said, erupting hotly into anger. 'Do I have to remind you that you forced me into this marriage? That it was *you* who threw yourself at me and *you* who was careless enough to get yourself pregnant? Well, now you've got it all your own way and I'm stuck with a wife and child I don't want. So if I were you I'd just keep my mouth shut.'

She turned away, tears springing to her eyes. 'If you're trying to punish me, Alex, you're succeeding. I wonder if you know how cruel you are.'

He got up and flung out of the room. She followed him. 'You're bored with me, aren't you? God knows you've made that clear enough these past months. Do you want a divorce? Is that it?' she demanded. 'If it is, just say so. You obviously don't love me any more.'

He spun round, his face a mask of fury. 'I've *never* loved you, Amy. I thought I'd made that clear to you right at the beginning. What we had was meant to be just a fling – a bit of fun. I thought you knew that. I thought you were keen on a career and that you'd take proper care.'

'So – it's over then?' She stood staring at him, her eyes wide and her lip trembling.

'*Over*? How can it be over now that you've landed us with *that*?' He threw a look of disgust at her swollen belly. 'We're trapped, Amy. You and I are well and truly up the creek in the same bloody boat, and I just hope you like it.'

Her hand to her mouth, she went into the kitchen and shut the door. How could she have come to this? she asked herself. She wasn't even twenty yet and her life was over. She'd had such plans. She'd been so determined to make a success of her life. And she *would* have, too. She was a good actress, everyone said she had promise. Everything had been going so well. And in spite of that she hadn't been unhappy when she found out about the baby because she loved Alex. But if he resented her so much; and meant to go on blaming her, then there could be no future for them.

She felt bleak and alone. Standing at the kitchen window, she gripped the edge of the sink and tried hard not to cry. Tears cured nothing. She'd already proved that. She must let Alex go. Somehow or other she must manage on her own. How could she stay with a man who clearly despised her? She couldn't take it any more.

When the first pain gripped her it came as a shock. She'd always thought labour began slowly and gently, besides there were still three weeks to go yet. It caught her low down in her back and abdomen, like a giant hand gripping and squeezing her. The intensity of it took her breath away and left her gasping. She gave an involuntary cry and bent almost double, clutching at the kitchen table for support. Slowly the contraction relaxed its iron grip and she was able to breathe again. She was crossing the kitchen when another pain seized her, sharper and even more intense this time. Her scream brought Alex, running down the stairs and bursting into the kitchen.

'What's the matter? Have you hurt yourself?'

'I think – think it's the baby,' she said between clenched teeth. 'I've got to go – to the hospital.'

'I'll take you.' His face was white with shock. 'I'll get the car started.'

Minutes later they were on their way. Amy sat hunched in the passenger seat, her teeth clamped over her lower lip to stop her from crying out. There was scarcely a break now between the pains. They were fierce and relentless. It was as though something else, some demon, had taken her body over. She was no longer in control, however hard she fought. With every contraction she wondered just how much longer she would be able to bear it. Already her breath was coming in hiccuping gasps. Would they get there before the baby thrust its way into the world?

When they reached the hospital the staff took over. She was lifted onto a trolley and whisked away, leaving Alex to wait in the corridor.

Amy's son was born less than an hour after her arrival at the hospital. Although he was three weeks premature he weighed almost eight pounds and cried lustily at birth.

'Here he is. Little master impatience.' The nurse smiled as she put the baby into Amy's arms. 'He had no intention of waiting around for anyone, did he? A real go-getter he's going to be.'

Amy looked down in wonder at the enormous blue

eyes that stared up at her. His dark lair lay against his little round head in flat, damp curls. She adored him instantly, and from that very first moment she knew exactly what his name was going to be.

'Mark. I want to call him Mark, after my father,' she told Alex when at last he was allowed in to see her.

He looked down at his son. 'Yes. It suits him.' He bent over Amy. 'Darling, I'm sorry – about earlier. I didn't mean what I said. It's all the rushing up and down from Minsdale and the partings. We haven't had a chance to settle down to marriage really, have we?'

She smiled, pushing aside the memory that living apart had been his idea. The baby's birth seemed to have made everything else insignificant somehow. 'Never mind. Everything will be all right now, won't it?'

'Of course it will.' He took her hand. 'Poor love. I felt so useless out there, waiting.' He lifted the hand he held and kissed the fingers one by one. 'Was it ghastly?'

'It was, a bit.' She smiled sleepily. 'But at least it was quick.'

'I didn't tell you. I had an interview this afternoon for a job with Gainsborough. I didn't get it. It hit me hard. That's why I was so bloody to you.'

Her eyes clouded as she looked up at him. 'Why didn't you tell me, Alex? We should share the disappointments as well as the happiness. I'm your wife.' She held his hand against her cheek and closed her eyes. Suddenly she was terribly tired. She wanted to talk to him. There was so much she wanted to tell him, so many promises and plans for their future, theirs and Mark's. But her eyelids felt as though they were weighted with lead and try as she would she could not make them stay open.

Alex stood looking down at them both. His wife and child, both sleeping peacefully. It was hard to take in. Through all the past months, haunted by doubt, he'd kept telling himself that once it happened – once the child was born – he would be able to come to terms with the fact that he was a married man again. But as he looked down at the girl sleeping so serenely in the bed

411

the image of Chloe's face seemed to superimpose itself on Amy's. Not Chloe's face as he wanted to remember her, but the image that haunted his worst dreams of that horrific day when he had helped to dig her out from under the debris of the bombed building.

He closed his eyes in an attempt to shut out the dreaded pictures but it was no use. Even behind his closed eyelids he could still see the fair hair caked with dirt and the lovely face bruised and blackened, streaked with blood. The grotesquely twisted limbs. His stomach heaved and bile rose in his mouth. It was a sight he would never get out of his mind if he lived to be a hundred. One regret would torture him for ever. He should not have left her that afternoon. They should have gone together.

Fighting his nausea and blinded by tears, he stumbled out of the room and along the corridor. The birth of his son should have marked a new beginning; this should be the day when the past could finally be laid to rest and he could start again. But even today the past would not free him from its grip. Maybe it never would.

Sam Leigh agreed happily to let Gina rent the old Feldman premises. Refreshed after his holiday, he was feeling buoyant and optimistic. She was to have first refusal to buy whenever she felt ready.

'You gave up so much for us, my dear,' he said. 'You gave us the benefit of your talent for far longer than we deserved. The least we can do is to help you get established in your own career.'

He and Rachel were to live in peaceful retirement at Hazelfield, he told her. But by letting Gina rent the factory they would be able to remain in touch with the trade and take an interest in the progress of her career. It seemed that Rachel had at last given up trying to keep Marcus alive. She was content now to live with her memories and let him rest.

But in spite of having the problem of factory premises solved, Gina still seemed restless and uneasy. When

Maryan asked her why, she admitted that she was still going to be short of money once she had repaid her debt.

'I'll have machinists to engage, twelve at least; a good cutter and someone to supervise.'

'Do you really have to pay back the money you owe Robert right away?' Maryan asked. 'I'm sure he wouldn't mind waiting a little longer.' But Gina's mouth set in a firm line.

'*He* wouldn't, but I would. I want it over and done with,' she said. 'While he still has a financial interest in the business I'll have to go on seeing him from time to time. I want to make the break complete.'

Maryan looked at her employer. The end of the affair had obviously hit her hard and she wanted no loose ends to prolong the agony. She understood that well enough. But tying them up could prove costly. 'I suppose there's nothing you could sell, is there?' she suggested.

Gina shrugged. 'All I have is the business and the house – apart from a few old sticks of Nanna's furniture down in the cellar.'

Maryan's heart jumped. 'What kind of furniture?' she asked. 'Can I have a look?'

'If you like, but there isn't much. She took anything of value down to Devonshire with her when the war started. Other things she gave away to friends and relatives. The house was virtually empty when I inherited it. There are just a few items of furniture that have always been down in the cellar as long as I can remember.'

'Never mind. They might be worth a look,' Maryan said. 'Shall we go down?'

At first glance it seemed that Gina had been right. The few effects that Gina's grandmother had left behind were stacked at one end of the cellar and covered in dust sheets. On removal, Maryan saw that there was a hide-covered Victorian chaise longue; some balloon-back chairs and an enormous and quite hideous Edwardian sideboard. Gina stood back and folded her arms.

'You see, I told you.'

'Mmm, none of it is really old enough to be called

413

antique.' Maryan opened one of the sideboard cupboards. 'Did you know it was full of china?' Taking out a plate she turned it over. 'Limoges. An early design. I wonder how much of it there is? If it's a complete set it might be worth quite a bit.'

Excited, Gina bent to help Maryan take out the pieces, counting them one by one as they stacked them carefully on the floor. 'I remember this dinner service,' she said as she brought out an ornate tureen. 'Nanna always used it when the family came for Christmas when I was little. There should be two dozen of everything if I remember rightly. Four kinds of plates, soup cups, four tureens, two sauce boats, four meat plates . . .' She was kneeling now, surrounded by the dinner service, and she looked up at Maryan with shining eyes. 'I do believe it's all here. It's a miracle. What do you think it'll fetch?'

Maryan shook her head. 'I can't say offhand, but you should get a good price at auction.' She looked at Gina, whose smile faded.

'But not enough to repay my loan, eh?'

'Well – not really, I suppose. Is there anything else?'

'There's a picture over there against the wall, but I don't think it can be worth anything,' Gina said doubtfully. 'Nanna surely wouldn't have let it moulder away down here if it'd been anything valuable.'

'You can never tell. Often it's just a matter of taste,' Maryan said. 'Let's see.'

The picture was covered and leant against the wall. She pulled off the sacking that covered it. It was a mediocre still life, Victorian and probably a copy. Gina was looking at her hopefully.

'Any good?'

'Sorry, I'm afraid not. And this is all?'

Gina was pulling out the sideboard drawers. 'I think so, except – there's a box in here.' She drew it out and took off the lid. 'Oh, look, aren't they pretty?'

Inside was a collection of miniatures. It was a subject that Maryan had found fascinating when she was studying the books Vincent had lent her, and as she looked at the tiny, detailed portraits she felt excitement stirring inside her. There were eight in all, exquisitely painted and carefully wrapped in tissue paper and laid on a bed of cotton wool in the box. The fact that every one of them was gold mounted and painted on ivory told her that they were important, but when she peered closely and saw that some of them were signed too her heart began to drum with excitement.

'Are they any good?' Gina asked.

Maryan looked up. 'I think we've got a real find here,' she said. 'I don't want to get your hopes up too high in case I'm wrong, but I believe that at least two of these are by Fragonard and this one . . .' – she held up a miniature portrait of an eighteenth century-beauty – '. . . is by Richard Cosway. See – it's signed.'

'Oh. Does that make them valuable?' Gina asked, holding her breath.

'It certainly does. And if we could find out who the sitters are as well it would make them worth even more.' Maryan sat back on her heels, wishing she had Vinnie's book with her. 'You really should get an expert opinion,' she said. 'Perhaps you could get someone from Sotherby's to look at them.'

'I'll get onto it at once,' Gina promised. 'Thanks, Maryan. I'd never have thought of looking down here for the answer to my problems.'

It was later the following day that Gina told Maryan what she'd arranged. 'Last night I rang Roisan,' she said. 'I can't think why we didn't think of it before. She's promised to get her brother, Vincent, to come and look at the miniatures.'

Maryan's heart lurched and she felt the colour drain from her face. 'Oh,' she said faintly. 'Well, he'll certainly be able to help value them.'

She looked forward to Vinnie's visit to Gower Street with a mixture of excitement and dread. Working hard over the past months, she had been able to put aside her own heartache. But the thought of seeing him again, of being close to him, filled her with apprehension.

Determined to be strong, she steeled herself as the day drew nearer. She would not let him see that she had suffered. She'd hold up her head and greet him as a colleague and friend.

Gina had arranged for him to call at about eight-thirty, when the day's work would be over and they would have plenty of time to examine and discuss the miniatures. After she had eaten, Maryan waited in her flat for Gina to call her. As the time drew near she found her nervousness increasing and when at last she heard the doorbell ring downstairs and Gina's voice calling up the stairwell to summon her, the breath caught in her throat. Admonishing herself for being a fool, she took a deep breath and went downstairs to meet them.

He looked tired and drawn, but when he saw Maryan his eyes lit up and he held out both hands.

'Maryan. How nice to see you. It's been so long.'

She put her hands into his and smiled, wishing that her heartbeat would steady. Surely by now she should be able to greet him calmly? It was ridiculous.

'It's nice to see you too, Vinnie,' she said. 'Are you well – and Fay – how is she?'

He smiled and nodded. 'We're both well, thank you.'

'I can't wait for you to see what we've found,' she went on. 'There is definitely a Cosway and I think there are two Fragonards. I hope I'm right about them.'

Gina had the box of miniatures all ready and she took off the lid with a flourish, holding her breath with suspense as Vincent took out the loupe he always carried in his pocket and examined them minutely one by one. He took a lot of time over his examination, putting four of the eight miniatures on one side. When he had finished he looked at Maryan.

'You were right about the Cosway and these two are certainly Fragonards,' he said. 'I think I know who the sitters are, too, but it shouldn't be difficult to verify. The Cosway is of Mrs Fitzherbert.' He picked up the fourth one. 'This is by John Smart; late eighteenth century.'

'And the other four?' Maryan asked him.

'Military souvenirs. A lot were done of young soldiers at the time of the Napoleonic Wars. They're all good, but they need a little more research.' He looked at Gina. 'Would you mind if I came back again and made a closer study? I'll do some more research in the meantime. I believe you have a very important find there. I'd insure them well if I were you. I'll let you have a firm valuation figure when I've done some more research.'

'They're for sale,' Gina told him.

He stared at her for a moment. 'Are you serious?'

She sighed. 'I know they're beautiful and I'd love to keep them, but I need the money. They could save my business. At the moment that is the most important thing in my life.'

He nodded. 'I understand. Well, if you're quite sure that's what you want, I can arrange it for you so that you get the best deal. I'll look into it and tell you what reserve to put on them. I'd advise auctioning them and I think they should be sold individually and not as a collection. I believe you'd do better that way.'

Gina looked mystified. 'Reserve? I don't understand.'

Vincent smiled and looked at Maryan. 'Maryan will explain it all to you. In the meantime put them away somewhere safe.'

Gina's face was flushed with excitement as she stowed the miniatures carefully back in their box.

Vincent smiled. 'Well, it's nice to be the bearer of good news for once. Now I'd better be on my way.'

Gina looked up. 'Oh, how rude of me. Can I get you a drink, or a coffee or something?'

He shook his head. 'No thank you. I'll be on my way. I'll be in touch in a day or two if that's all right.'

Seeing that Gina was engrossed in the task of putting away her treasures, Maryan went with him to the door. In the hall he looked at her.

'You look wonderful, Maryan,' he said softly. 'You've done something different with your hair. It really suits you.'

'Thank you.'

'It's obvious that you're happy in your job with Miss Stern. I'm glad.'

'Yes. It's very interesting.'

'We still miss you at Vincente's.'

'I'm sure that can't be true.'

'It is. If you only knew . . .' He broke off to sigh. 'Paul has left us, you know.'

'No, I didn't. I haven't seen Roisan for some time.'

'Fay and he never got along. And with her working in the shop . . .' He lifted his shoulders. 'But I don't need to burden you with my troubles. Roisan was saying the other day that it would be nice to see you.'

'I know. I feel bad about it, but we've been so busy, what with Gina's show and everything. Tell her I'll come round to see her soon, will you?'

'I will.' They stood by the front door now. Maryan made to reach for the handle but he stood in her way. 'Will you be here when I come again, Maryan? It's so good to see you.'

'I might be,' she said brightly. 'It all depends.'

'On what?'

She shrugged. 'All sorts of things – what time of day it is. How busy I am . . .'

'Of course.' His eyes sought hers. 'If I come in the evening – at the same time as this? Please be here, Maryan.'

'I – I'll try.'

'There can be no harm in our seeing each other now, can there? Not after all this time.'

'No, I suppose not.'

He moved aside to allow her to open the door. 'I'll be in touch again soon,' he said as she let him out. 'Goodnight.'

'Goodnight.' She closed the door firmly behind him and leant against it, her heart hammering. Why had she said she would be here when he came again? Why had she meekly agreed to subject herself to all that agony again? She would not let it happen. When he came again she would be out. She had all but convinced herself that she was over him; that seeing him this evening wouldn't affect her at all, and it *mustn't*. But when she closed her eyes she could still see the sadness in his dark eyes and the fine network of lines that unhappiness had etched on his face.

Inwardly she screamed in protest. 'No. *No*. I won't give in. He made his decision. He made it impossible for us to be together and now he must live with it.'

'Maryan – *why didn't you tell me?*'

Startled at the voice interrupting her inner struggle, Maryan opened her eyes to see Gina looking at her. 'Tell you – what?'

'That you and he were – that close. It's why you left, isn't it? Because he's married.'

'Is it that obvious?'

'Only to someone who's been through the same mill. I saw it the moment you looked at each other. If you'd told me I would have asked someone else to value the miniatures.' She took Maryan's arm. 'Come and sit down. Tell me about it – if it would help.'

The first days of looking after little Mark and settling down to motherhood were serene and happy ones for Amy. It was as though his birth had put all her worries and fears to rest. While she was still in the hospital a trolley came round with things to buy. There were little cards announcing the baby's birth. On impulse Amy bought one and sent it to her mother. On the front was a picture of a stork carrying a baby suspended from a blue ribbon. Inside she wrote, *Announcing the arrival of Mark Alexander Keynan – July 24th 1950. Seven pounds fifteen ounces*. But the weeks went by and, as before, there was no response, and Amy's time was too consumed with the baby to brood over the reason why. Mark thrived and grew bonnier every week and for a little while life was better, and when Alex got a job with the Rank Organisation it looked as though their luck was changing.

He was making travel documentaries and was away from home even more than before, but the money was good and they began to improve the house a little. Alex had a telephone installed, as he said it was essential now that he needed to be available.

Mark's first Christmas came and went. His first tooth appeared and, a week before his first birthday, he took his first steps. Amy was so proud of him. He was a happy baby, placid and contented. Jack and Addie Shaw adored him and sometimes came across to spend the evening at number twenty-two, while Amy went to the first house of the local cinema for a treat.

Now that Mark was no longer a baby, Amy itched to get back to the stage. She reminded Alex that they'd said they'd think about her resuming her career when Mark was old enough. But Alex, fiercely protective of his son, was adamant.

'It's out of the question, Amy. How can you be a mother and have a stage career?' he said. 'No child of mine is going to be brought up by strangers.'

And with that Amy had to be satisfied. She loved little Mark and enjoyed being with him and watching him grow. But privately she promised herself that she would somehow find a way of returning to the stage before too much time had passed.

Alex's new job was taxing. When he was at home he was irritable and terse, snapping at Amy for the smallest thing. It became obvious that he was drinking too much. The smallest thing would trigger off a row and when he found out that she often left Mark in the Shaws' care while she went to the cinema he was furious.

'How could you?' he demanded. 'Suppose something went wrong? What use do you think they'd be if anything happened? Why can't you grow up and think of the child for a change, Amy?'

His harsh criticism stung her. 'That's not fair,' she shouted. 'I hardly ever get out. A couple of times a month – if that. I have to have *some* time to myself. And you're wrong about Jack and Addie. They love Mark. They'd never let anything happen to him.'

'You're right. They won't, because he won't be left

420

with them again, do you hear? You wanted a baby, but now it seems it's too much trouble to stay at home and look after him.'

Amy turned away, swallowing the defensive retort that she longed to make. The more she tried to defend herself, the guiltier she sounded. And she wasn't guilty. Alex was never at home. He had no idea how demanding a small child could be, or how boring and repetitive her days were. His criticism hurt her deeply and he knew it. It seemed to her that all he wanted was to sting her into retaliation and start a row so that he could say the things he knew would hurt her.

In September, just a month after Mark's first birthday, Alex was assigned to a film that was to be made on location in the north of Scotland. It meant several months away from home. And for the first time Amy felt nothing but relief at the prospect of parting.

Chapter Seventeen

Autumn came to Hazelfield early that year. By the beginning of September the nights were too cold for Sam and Rachel to spend idyllic evenings sitting on the terrace at Whitegates. Log fires were lit in the pleasant drawing room and they resigned themselves to the end of summer.

The news of the King's illness and operation in September had shocked everyone. Having a lung removed seemed so frighteningly serious. And when Rachel caught a bad cold which went to her chest she dwelt on the subject more and more.

Sam grew increasingly worried about her. Her cold refused to clear up and her persistent cough became troublesome and exhausting, robbing her of sleep and making her look haggard and drawn. To Sam's concern she seemed to lose interest in her appearance and grew more and more depressed. She began once again to dwell on the past and fret for Marcus. Sam begged her to see a doctor, but every time he suggested it she became so upset and agitated that he was obliged to let the subject drop.

One night he woke to find her standing at the bedroom window in her nightgown, her feet bare. Shocked, he got up at once and went to her.

'Rachel, my love, what are you thinking of? You'll catch your death.' He picked up her dressing gown and wrapped it around her shoulders, feeling the chill on her skin as he did so. 'What is it, darling?' he asked, peering anxiously at her. 'Why won't you talk to me? Are you ill?'

She leant wearily against him. 'Oh, Sam, I think I am – very ill indeed. I – I'm afraid I haven't much longer to live.'

Sam was shocked, but he tried not to show his fear. Putting his arms around her he said: 'Rachel! You mustn't say such things. Whether you want me to or not, I'm sending for the doctor tomorrow. You're feeling low after your cold. You should have had treatment for it long ago. He'll give you something for the cough and a tonic too. Then we'll take a nice long holiday in the sun.' Very gently he led her back to bed and tucked her in. 'I'm going downstairs to make you a hot drink. I won't be long.'

'But she grasped his wrist, refusing to let go. 'Sam, no. Stay here with me. There's something I want to tell you.'

He sat down on the edge of the bed, glad that at last she was ready to talk. 'Well – as long as you don't tire yourself. What is it?'

'I have a confession to make. It's been preying on my mind for so long. I have to tell you now, while I have the courage. While there is still time.'

He pressed her hand. 'Surely it can't be anything so terrible.'

She looked up at him, her brow furrowed with anxiety. 'Oh, but it *is*, Sam. You don't know how terrible. I've deceived you and it was wrong of me.'

He shook his head, clicking his tongue at her. 'Now, now, you really mustn't get things so out of proportion, Rachel. You're depressed.'

'No, Sam, hear me out. When I've told you you'll probably be angry with me but I can't help it. It couldn't be any worse than carrying this burden of guilt around. I can't bear it any longer.' The rush of words made her cough a little and Sam poured her a glass of water frown the carafe beside the bed. When she had finished drinking she lay back against the pillows and looked at him.

423

'You remember the time I went to Hackney Road at the end of the war and brought back Marcus's things?'

'Of course. The day you found his designs. It was the turning point. It seemed to cheer you – give you a new reason for living.'

'Yes. But later, going through his papers, I found a letter he had left for us – in case he was killed.'

His eyes clouded. 'A letter? And you didn't tell me? Never showed it to me?'

'I didn't show it to you because I couldn't.' She pressed his hand even more tightly. 'You see, in the letter he explained about Maryan's daughter. About Amy. He *was* her father, Sam.'

He sighed deeply. 'Oh, Rachel.'

'You always believed her, didn't you?'

'Of course. I know she would never have lied about a thing like that. I think you knew it too, but you wouldn't let yourself believe it.'

She nodded. 'Are you very angry with me, Sam?'

'I can't be angry with you. You know that. I do think it's a pity that we have missed so much, though. Amy was such a lovely child. She would have given us so much pleasure and comfort. We could have done so much for her – Maryan too. She was good to us, Rachel. She didn't deserve what we did to her.'

'I know. I *know*. And I haven't told you everything.' Rachel moistened her dry lips before going on: 'There were two other letters. One to the bank and one to Maryan. I – still have them. I never passed them on.' She looked up at Sam anxiously. 'But I did carry out Marcus's wishes.'

'His wishes?'

'About the money. I didn't go to the bank, as he asked, to have all the money from his estate invested for Amy. But I did put aside all the proceeds from its fashion collections. Apart from the charity donations, I invested it all. It's still there, untouched. And it's for Amy. That's why I had to tell you before anything happened to me. You must see that she gets it. If I died without making sure she got it I'd have betrayed Marcus.'

She burst into tears and, deeply moved, Sam gathered her into his arms and held her. So much was clear to him now. This was the reason that she wouldn't touch any of the money – why she had insisted so adamantly that all expenses must come out of Feldman's. 'Please, my love, don't cry. Everything will be all right, you'll see. Tomorrow we'll get the doctor to take a good look at you. I'm sure he will soon have you fit and well. Then after that we'll go and see Maryan. Or ask her to come here. We'll tell her everything you've just told me.'

Rachel shook her head. 'How will she ever forgive me, Sam – for keeping Marcus's letter from her all this time?'

He smiled. 'She will. I know she will.' He wiped the tears gently from her cheeks. 'And I'll tell you why. I've got a confession to make to you too. Although I knew nothing of all this I kept in touch with Maryan. I paid for Amy's education. Not because I wanted to go against your wishes, but because I wanted what was best for the child I truly believed was our granddaughter.' He looked into her eyes. 'So – do you forgive *me*, my Rachel?'

For the first time she smiled. 'Forgive you? Oh, Sam, you're such a good man. I don't deserve such a husband.'

Next day Sam summoned the doctor, who diagnosed acute bronchitis and prescribed complete bed rest and one of the new antibiotic drugs. Tired and run down, Rachel was content to stay in bed and allow Sam to spoil her, but she responded to the treatment very quickly. Sam secretly felt that unburdening herself of the secret she had kept from him all these years was better medicine for her than anything the doctor could have prescribed.

As soon as he felt Rachel was well enough to receive visitors he telephoned Maryan and invited her over to Hazelfield for the day the following Sunday. She sounded slightly apprehensive, but he was able to reassure her that Rachel was anxious to see her and that they had something of importance to impart.

It was with mixed feelings that Maryan returned to Whitegates. The last time she had seen the place had

425

been on the day she had left after Rachel's hostile reaction to her disclosure and she wondered what her ex-employers could possibly have to say to her. When she got down from the bus by the church gate the village looked much as she remembered it. Leaves were falling from the tall elms in the churchyard. They swirled around her feet as she walked, dry and rustling in the wind. The sky was dark and heavy with threatening storm clouds. Somehow the weather seemed to reflect her mood. Whatever the Leighs had to tell her now, it was too late to heal the breach she had created when she had confessed her secret to them.

Sam opened the door to her himself. He looked pleased with himself. Inviting her in, he took her coat. 'Rachel has been ill,' he said. 'A bad bout of bronchitis. But she's better now, and she wants to see you – to tell you something. Do come into the drawing room, my dear. We'll have lunch in an hour, but first we'll talk.'

Rachel rose to greet her, but in her smiling eyes Maryan saw her own apprehension mirrored.

When Rachel explained the contents of Marcus's letter Maryan was stunned.

'But – I never told him about Amy,' she said. 'When he came back from France I'd married Tom Jessop. Then he met Jessica and everyone seemed so happy. If I'd told him about Amy it would have upset everything – caused so much trouble. I couldn't do it.'

Rachel smiled sadly. 'He must have guessed. Marcus was always a sensitive man. I suppose he must have felt as you did – that to bring it to light would upset too many people. And you never seemed unhappy with the man you had married.'

'No. Tom was a good man and a good father to Amy. That's why I never told her either.'

Rachel reached for the large envelope into which she had put the three letters. Drawing out the opened envelope, she passed it to Maryan. 'Here is the letter Marcus left for us, Maryan. Read it for yourself.' She passed a second, sealed envelope to her. 'And this is the one he meant for you. I hope you can forgive me for keeping it from you all these years.'

Maryan felt her throat tighten as she read Marcus's words to his parents. To think that all the time he had guessed that Amy was his child and never spoken of it to her. But he had tried to make it up to her – done his best to see that she was provided for. She tried to stifle the resentment she felt against Rachel for keeping his letter secret for so long, and for not passing on this other, personal letter intended for her. It seemed that even when Rachel knew the truth her bitterness would not let her accept it. When she came to the end of the letter she passed it back.

'Thank you for letting me see it,' she said. 'If you don't mind I'll keep my own letter for later. I'd like to be alone when I read it.'

Sam and Rachel both nodded their agreement. 'Marcus didn't have a lot to leave, as he says in the letter,' Rachel went on. 'But I invested all the money we made from the Marcus Leigh Collections for Amy. It's all in an account for her. I had to keep faith with his wishes.' She paused, then looked at Maryan. 'It's such a long time since we last saw Amy.' She smiled wistfully. 'I was always very fond of the child. Do you think she would come and see us if I wrote and asked her? I would like to tell her about her inheritance myself. Would you mind?'

Sam looked at his wife in dismay and Maryan said quickly, 'I'm afraid Amy left home two years ago. I haven't heard from her since. I'm sorry to say that I don't even know where she is.'

Rachel's face fell. 'Oh dear. Was there some kind of quarrel between you?'

Maryan cleared her throat, glancing at Sam before she said, 'It seems that on the night I told you about Marcus being Amy's father she overheard the conversation. She said nothing at the time and I never suspected until just before she left home. She was waiting for me to tell her and I let her down. I'm afraid it caused a rift between us. She hasn't forgiven me. She was very young at the time.

427

What she heard must have made her feel rejected. I think she decided to show me she didn't need me; didn't need any of us.'

'And she never even wrote to you?' Rachel looked upset. 'Oh my dear. How hurt you must have been.'

Maryan sighed. 'Perhaps it was no more than I deserved. I should have been honest with her from the first. Now it's too late.'

Rachel was frowning. 'But we must find out where she is. I want to see her – to get to know her before it is too late. And above all, I want her to have the money that is rightly hers.'

Sam laid a hand on his wife's arm. 'The money will be there when she needs it,' he said calmly. 'I'm sure that Amy will come home to Maryan again one day soon. And if she doesn't, then we'll find her somehow. The main thing is that the three of us are reunited.' He reached for Maryan's hand, linking the three of them. 'I'm so happy that now at last I can say that.'

In the train on the way back to London, Maryan opened Marcus's letter. It felt so strange, drawing out the sheet of paper and knowing that the last eyes to look at it had been his. Tears blurred her vision as she read the words he had written.

My dear Maryan,

If you are reading this you will know already that we shall not meet again. I know that you will look after my parents and help to ease their grief. I know that they look upon you almost as the daughter they never had, and I thank you for all you have done for them in the past and no doubt will do in the years to come.

I want you to know, Maryan, that I guessed a long time ago that Amy was mine. She is a daughter to be proud of and I only wish that I could have acknowledged her openly before this. I needn't go into the reasons for not doing so. I think they were shared by us both. We were young and thoughtless, but that makes my omission none the less regrettable. I will never forget the young love we once shared, Maryan. I think of you often and I pray that you won't remember me as a coward who shirked his duty.

Because I want to do what is right I am leaving Amy all my money, such as it is. And – if you feel it is appropriate – I would like you to tell her that I was her father and perhaps speak of me sometimes.

Take care of yourself, Maryan. Take care of Amy too. I hope and trust that you will love her for both of us.

Goodbye, my dear. Ever yours, Marcus.

Blinking back the tears, Maryan slipped the letter back into her handbag. Perhaps one day she would get the chance to show it to Amy. She hoped so. If only Rachel had given it to her all those years ago, their lives might have turned out so very differently.

On fine days Amy always took Mark to the park. He loved to get out of his pushchair and play on the grass. They would take bread to feed the ducks on the pond and sometimes a ball to play with. He enjoyed it so much, and usually came home happily tired and ready for his tea. But when Amy had bathed him and put him to bed the evenings felt endless. When Mark was tiny she had sometimes put him into his carry cot and taken him over to Jack and Addie's. Now he was too big for that and would only fall asleep in his own bed. They had been in the habit of coming across to sit with her some evenings, but they had recently bought themselves a television set and now spent their evenings in their darkened living room, their eyes glued to the small flickering screen, oblivious of everything else.

Alex's absences on location grew more frequent and she had almost come to welcome them. When he was at home he constantly picked quarrels with her, criticising her housekeeping and her cooking and, depending on his mood, accusing her alternatively of spoiling or neglecting Mark, in whom he now took an almost obsessive interest.

Sometimes, she asked herself how she could have fallen in love with him. When he had told her bluntly that he could never love her she should have realised that the marriage wouldn't work. But naively, she had imagined she could change him; that she could make him love her – that the baby would draw them together. How wrong she had been. His irritation and resentment of her were all too obvious. Sometimes, when he looked at her in that withering way of his, she was convinced that he hated her. She hadn't meant to trap him. She'd loved him so much when they'd married. But loneliness was preferable to putting up with his constant carping and the cruel criticism that wounded her so much. Now, as she sat alone night after night in the silent house, it was her turn to feel trapped. Trapped by a man who had neither love nor need for her, and by a child who had. She felt her youth and her talent slipping away like sand in an hour glass. Inside, a voice nagged her constantly to do something about it. But what could she do? She had a child dependent on her, no money and nowhere to go.

It was one wet Monday afternoon in early November when the front doorbell rang. Mark was playing happily in his playpen and she was ironing. Switching off the iron, she went to answer the door and gasped in shock. A man stood there, a smile of anticipation on his face. For a moment Amy stared at him, then her face almost split in half with delight.

'*Mike*. How lovely to see you. But what are you doing here?'

'I had to be in this area and I've got some time to spare, so I thought I'd look you up. Mum gave me your address.'

'Come in.' As she ushered him into the hall she took a quick look at herself in the hall mirror. She was wearing an apron and her hair was tousled and untidy. She'd been playing with Mark and he'd been pulling it. Quickly tucking a loose strand behind her ear she laughed. 'Heaven knows what I must look like. Come and meet my son.'

Mike was enchanted by the chubby toddler standing clutching a toy bear in the playpen. Suddenly shy at the sight of a stranger, he looked up at Mike with huge solemn blue eyes, then, after a moment, offered him his teddy.

Amy laughed. 'You're honoured. Teddy's his favourite.'

Mike accepted the toy graciously. 'Thanks, old chap.' He looked at Amy. 'What a terrific kid. He looks just like you. Same blue eyes and curly hair.'

She laughed. 'Thanks. Look, just let me put this lot away, then we'll have some tea and a good old natter. I want to hear all about this job of yours at the BBC.' She began to bundle the linen basket and iron into the hall cupboard.

'And I want to hear all about this producer blokc you've married,' Mike called to her. 'I hope he knows how lucky he is.'

As she filled the kettle at the sink she smiled wryly to herself. 'Far from it,' she said under her breath.

They talked over the tea. Mike told her all the news from Rhensham. His parents were well and Lily Smith had added twin boys to her family and now worked as a daily cleaning woman for the vicar.

'I think when Lily applied for the job he felt obliged to be charitable,' he said. 'Fallen women are a hobby-horse of his. Mum tells me that Lily's mother looks after the kids. I don't suppose she even notices another two among her own brood.'

Amy was silent, reflecting that even the feckless Lily had a mother who was willing to support her.

Mike told her about his work with the local rag and how he had come to get his present job with the BBC.

'I'm only very junior at the moment, of course,' he said modestly. 'But I'm in the news room and working my way up.'

'You'll get there,' Amy told him with shining eyes. 'I can just see you reading the news on TV in your dinner jacket. Very posh and suave.'

He laughed. 'So, what about you?' he asked. 'As I remember, you had ambitions too.'

She shrugged. 'They went by the board when Mark came along, I'm afraid. But I did do well, Mike. I joined the company as a student but I did get to play leading parts before Alex and I married.' She went on to tell him how she had played Cathy in *Wuthering Heights* and all the other things she'd done with the Keynan Players. When he had first arrived, Mike had been dismayed at her appearance. She'd looked hollow-eyed and weary, but now, as she spoke about her brief career in the theatre, he saw a change in her. She became animated. Her eyes sparkled and the colour came back into her cheeks.

'You must miss it.'

'Oh yes. I do.'

'Obviously you'll be going back as soon as you can.'

The sparkle in her eyes snapped off. 'Not in the foreseeable future,' she said. 'Not now that I've got Mark.'

'Why not?' he asked. 'I mean, there are nannies and nurseries. He's getting older now and . . .'

'Alex doesn't believe in working mothers. In the theatre the hours are so erratic. Besides, people soon forget. If you stay out for more than six months your chances of getting back are poor – even if you've already made a name for yourself. Apart from all that, television is killing off all the provincial reps.'

Mark chose that moment to remind them that he was still with them and, looking at the clock, Amy saw that it was past his bedtime. When she scooped the little boy up in her arms Mike looked at his watch and got hastily to his feet.

'Heavens, I didn't realise it was getting so late. I'd better go and let you get this chap to bed.'

'Oh, don't go, Mike,' Amy begged. 'I mean, not unless you want to, of course. I get fed up spending every evening on my own. You can help me put Mark to bed if you like and then I'll make us a meal.'

He looked pleased. 'Well, if you're sure . . .'

'No, if *you* are. You've probably got some glamorous girl waiting for you somewhere?'

His eyes twinkled with mischief. 'Well, if I do, what the hell? It'll do her good to wait.' He laughed. 'No – there's no one – honest injun.' He gave her the Scout's salute and she laughed aloud. Suddenly she was back at Mitcham Lodge and they were children again.

Upstairs in the bathroom Mark was delighted to have two attentive people to play with him in the bath, and Mike volunteered to sing him to sleep while Amy went down to start the meal. Downstairs in the kitchen she could hear his pleasant baritone rendition of 'Baa Baa Black Sheep' and she reflected sadly that if only Alex was at home more they would be more like a real family. Nowadays he only seemed interested in talking to Mark. He didn't even talk to her about his work any more. She might never have been an actress at all.

She laid the table and made a quick meal of fried eggs and chips. Coming into the kitchen Mike sniffed appreciatively.

'You remembered,' he said. 'Egg and chips was always my favourite meal. Mum wouldn't let me have it when I lived at home – said too much fried food would give me spots. But now on the rare occasion when I get to Rhensham she spoils me rotten.' He sat down at the table. 'That's the best of leaving home, don't you find? It makes going back special.'

Her back towards him as she worked at the stove, Amy shrugged. 'I wouldn't know,' she said. 'I haven't been home for two and a half years. Not since I left to join the Keynan Players in fact.'

'Oh, why's that?'

She sighed. 'A lot of reasons. Mum and I never really hit it off, not since I found out about my real father. She never really seemed to have much time for me. And when I said I was taking the job with the Keynan Players – leaving school before taking my Highers – well, you can imagine.'

'But she knows you're married?'

433

Amy shrugged. 'I wrote when I first left, and again when I got married. Then I sent her a card when Mark was born. I don't know why I bothered. She never replied to any of them. I think I've got to accept the fact that she's written me off.'

Mike frowned. 'That doesn't sound like the Mrs Jessop I remember.'

'No – well, you never really got to know her, did you?' Amy ate in silence, her eyes downcast, and Mike watched her for a moment, his face concerned.

'So – you haven't been home – tried to see her?'

'I don't think there'd be much point. I haven't even been up to Town since I came to live here, even though it's only a short tube ride away.' She smiled wistfully. 'I must be the only person in England who hasn't seen this fantastic South Bank Exhibition. My neighbours went up when it first opened in the summer and they came back full of the Dome of Discovery and the Skylon and Battersea Park Funfair.'

'What a shame. Maybe you'll get up to see it before winter sets in.'

'Oh, I doubt it.'

He looked at her. It was plain that all was not as it should be. 'Tell me about your husband. He must be quite a bit older than you?'

'Yes. Nineteen years to be exact. He was beginning to make a name for himself before the war began. He was in the RAF. A fighter pilot. He was married and his wife was killed in an air raid. After that he didn't care much about anything.' She looked down at her plate. 'Nothing's changed. He still doesn't.'

Her words were almost inaudible and there was a silence between them as Mike began to guess the reason for her obvious unhappiness. 'Does that mean what I think it means?' he asked.

She looked at him, her eyes dull with pain. 'I wanted him, Mike. I thought I could make everything all right for him again. Make up for what he'd lost. I wanted him so *much* and I thought he wanted me.' She looked down at her hands. 'I got wanting and loving all mixed up.'

'And – now?'

'Now it's neither. Sometimes I think we just torment each other. His work takes him away from home a lot, and frankly I think it's a relief for both of us.'

'Oh, Amy.'

She looked up at him quickly. 'It wasn't always like that. When Mark was on the way I used to long for the weekends. I looked forward to seeing him so much. I *did* love him, Mike. It was real. I know it was. But now it's just – gone – dead.'

'I'm so sorry, Amy.'

'It's my fault really. He warned me, you see. He kept saying he was too old for me. He told me quite openly that he'd never love me. He still loves her, you see – his first wife. He was completely frank with me. I should have listened.'

Mike tried to conceal his amazement that Amy had walked into a marriage so obviously doomed. 'What about the baby?' he asked. 'Has his arrival made no difference?'

'Oh, he loves Mark,' she said. 'He's fiercely protective of him. That's why he won't even think of letting me go back to work.'

'I'd no idea about all this, Amy. You sounded so happy in your letters to Mum.'

'Of course. I don't really want people to know. I'm slightly ashamed, I suppose. And I shouldn't really be telling you all this. It's just that there's no one else and sometimes I think . . .' She got up and took her plate to the sink. As she filled the kettle for coffee she said, 'Let's talk about something else. In a minute you'll be so depressed you'll wish you hadn't come.'

By the time coffee was made she had swallowed her depression and put on a show of light-heartedness. She amused Mike with stories about the struggle she'd had with the neglected house, turning her inept attempts at decorating and her worst domestic failures into amusing anecdotes. She left out the times she had sat in the middle of the floor, surrounded by pots of paint and distemper, weeping helpless tears at her own inadequacy. Or the times she'd cried herself to sleep, sick with sheer loneliness and fears about the future.

She describe Jack and Addie Shaw, their well-meaning kindness and their preoccupation with their newly acquired 'telly'. And made him laugh with her description of the chimney sweep and her struggles with the overgrown garden. When Mike finally looked at his watch and announced that it was almost eleven o'clock they were both surprised.

Getting up to leave, he hugged her briefly and said, 'Thanks for a super evening, Amy. I can't tell you how wonderful it's been to see you again.'

'Thanks for coming. I don't get many visitors. Come again if you're at a loose end.'

At the front door he paused. 'Look, I've got two tickets for the new musical at Drury Lane, *South Pacific*. One of the perks of my job. Do you think you could come?'

Her eyes lit up. 'Oh, Mike. I'd *love* to. When are they for?'

'Next Monday. I'll be going straight from the office, but if you could come up on the train I could run you home afterwards.'

She bit her lip. 'Oh, it does sound tempting. I wonder if Addie would have Mark for me. I'll ask her. I'm sure she wouldn't mind, just this once.'

'Fine. Give me a ring if you can make it.' He found a scrap of paper and scribbled his number on it. 'You can get me there in the evenings. I share a little house in Chiswick with two other blokes. They're never off the phone, so if it's engaged do keep trying, won't you?'

'I will. Thanks, Mike.' Standing on tiptoe she kissed his cheek. 'It's lovely to see you again. Give my love to Auntie Marjorie when you see her – your father too, of course. Oh, and Mike . . .'

'Yes?'

'Forget all that gloomy nonsense I bored you with, won't you?'

Mike put his hands on her shoulders. 'Listen, silly. What you told me is strictly between ourselves. We never split on one another, do we?'

She stood on the step and waved as he drove away in his smart little Ford Prefect. It had been wonderful to see Mike and to have someone understanding to talk to; reminiscing over old times and hearing about what was happening out there in the world of work and entertainment. Would she ever be part of that world again, she wondered?

Closing the door and locking up for the night, she climbed the stairs. At least she had something to look forward to for once. She'd read about the exciting new American musical, *South Pacific*. And now – if she was lucky – she was actually going to *see* it. Maybe her luck was changing.

On 26 October Robert Kemp was elected Conservative Member of Parliament for Bradfield with a very healthy majority. By a narrow margin the Tories were in power again, with Winston Churchill once more at the helm. But it wasn't for political reasons that Gina received the news with relief.

'I think Robert's planning to move to his constituency,' she said. 'I've heard on the grapevine that his wife has been looking for a house in Bradfield for some time. All I have to do now is to pay off my debt to him, then I can start to get on with my own life again.'

The date for the antiques auction in which the miniatures were to be sold was set for Monday 10 November. Vincent had advised Gina to use an auctioneer he knew well and who could be trusted to make sure she had the best deal possible. Meanwhile the miniatures were in safe hands at the bank and now all they had to do was to wait.

Then, on 6 November Gina had a telephone call. Maryan put it through to her in the studio and five minutes later the office door flew open and a flushed Gina stood on the threshold, her eyes shining with excitement.

'I've been asked to fly to Paris on Monday,' she said breathlessly. 'To discuss plans for a fashion show being organised at the *Musée des Art Décoratifs* for next spring. Only top designers are being invited to exhibit. Oh, Maryan, imagine – *me*, Gina Stern – showing alongside people like Fath, Dior and Chanel. Thank God I've been working flat out on my new collection.'

'That's wonderful. Congratulations.' Maryan was looking at the calendar. 'When did you say it was?'

'Monday, the tenth.' Gina's face fell and her hand flew to her mouth. 'Oh, *no* – the sale.'

Maryan smiled encouragingly. 'Never mind. You must go to Paris. It isn't essential for you to go to the sale.'

'Oh, but I wanted to be there. Maryan, will you go? It won't matter if we close the office just this once. And you must take the car, of course. Oh dear, I'm so excited I can't think straight. What shall I take to wear? It's *so* important to create the right impression. There's that black suit I wore for the last show. It'll have to do. There isn't time to have anything new made up. You don't think I've put on weight, do you? Suppose I can't get into it? Oh – will you ring and book my flight? They want me there for three o'clock, so it'll have to be an early one. Oh – and a hotel too.'

She was like a whirlwind as she flew around the house, making one decision after another and changing her mind every five minutes. Maryan remained calm and smiling as she busied herself with the telephone, booking the flight and hotel and rearranging appointments that seemed to have gone right out of Gina's head.

Gina left Gower Street in a taxi at six o'clock on Monday morning. Maryan had made sure that she would have plenty of time to check in at her hotel and have lunch and a breathing space before the meeting. It was with some relief that she waved the taxi off. All weekend Gina had been in an agony of indecision. Would she make the right impression – say the right things? Was her schoolgirl French good enough or would she sound provincial and unsophisticated? And what about her portfolio? Would her spring collection be considered avant-garde enough to exhibit in a show of this calibre? She had promised to ring Maryan that evening, when they would exchange news about the day's events, though Maryan suspected that the importance of the sale had temporarily taken secondary importance in Gina's mind.

The sale was to take place in a country house in Surrey. Maryan drove down in Gina's car and arrived in plenty of time to look round before the start of the sale. Queensthorpe Hall was an imposing Georgian manor house standing in grounds which swept down to the river. It had clearly been very elegant indeed once, but during the war it had been requisitioned by the Army and after being abused and neglected for so long it had now acquired an air of crumbling grandeur. But in spite of its ill-kept appearance, it was the perfect venue for the sale with its spacious oak-panelled rooms and carved staircase.

When Maryan arrived there were already a good many people wandering round inspecting the numbered lots, ticking off items on their catalogues and making notes. She recognised one or two dealers from sales at which she had represented Vincent. The miniatures had pride of place, displayed in a room set aside for smaller articles, under glass in a locked cabinet to avoid excessive handling. They looked very special and she saw that they were described in the catalogue as being 'of outstanding quality – a rare find'. She felt a little frisson of excitement as she wondered what they would fetch and if it would be enough to relieve Gina of her debt. Their lot number was sixty-four, so she calculated that they would not come up until the afternoon. She would have a lengthy wait.

The auctioneer arrived, a small, dapper man in a grey pinstripe suit and bow tie. He had a pencil-thin moustache and quick, bright eyes, and the moment he arrived things began to happen. Two porters carried lot number one, an ornate Louis XVI console table, down to the front of the hall and the auctioneer's clerk tapped his gavel and asked everyone to take their seats as the sale was about to begin.

The bidding had been in progress for about half an hour when Maryan saw Vincent arrive. From her seat at the side of the hall she saw him slip quietly in and take a seat at the back. Her heart gave an involuntary lurch and she chided herself sharply. She was reacting like a schoolgirl. All that was over long ago. Surely she was too old for such nonsense? But when, a few minutes later, during a lull in the proceedings he slipped into the empty seat beside her and whispered a greeting, she could scarcely reply for the traitorous drumming in her chest.

'Maryan – hello. Isn't Miss Stern with you?'

'No.' She turned to look into the dark eyes, steeling herself to remain calm and unruffled. 'She was called away to Paris on business. I'm here to represent her.'

'I'm glad – that you're here, that is. I was wondering whether I'd see you today.' He bent towards her. 'Look – the lot I'm interested in won't come up until after lunch and neither will Miss Stern's miniatures. There's a very good pub in the village. Shall we slip out after this next lot for a bite of lunch?'

She intended to refuse – to tell him she'd brought sandwiches – anything. She actually opened her mouth to do so – and, to her astonishment, heard herself saying: 'Yes. I think that would be very nice.'

They left the sale just before twelve and under his direction Maryan drove the mile and a half to the Fox and Grapes in Gina's car.

'They always get really busy by one,' he told her as they parked. 'This is the best pub for miles. They do what they call a ploughman's lunch.'

Maryan laughed. 'What's a ploughman's lunch when it's at home?'

'Cheese, pickle and crusty bread with salad,' Vincent told her. 'Very satisfying.'

The pub was small and cosy with a welcoming fire crackling away in the huge open fireplace of the bar. There was an evocative scent of ale that reminded Maryan

440

nostalgically of the old Prince of Wales in Crimea Terrace where she and Tom had celebrated their wedding twenty years ago. That pub was long since gone, bombed to the ground along with so much of the old East End she remembered. And here the smell of ale was mingled with the country scents of beeswax and burning apple logs. She settled happily in a corner by the fireplace to enjoy the atmosphere while Vincent went to the bar for drinks. When he rejoined her he was smiling.

'This is a real treat. I never thought when I left home this morning that I'd be sitting here having lunch with you.'

'You wouldn't if it hadn't been for Gina's business trip.' She took a sip from her glass of sherry. 'But it's good to see you too, Vinnie,' she added quietly. 'How are things with you? Is the business doing well?'

He sighed. 'Not as well as I'd like.'

'Oh – why is that?'

He looked as though he was about to say something, then changed his mind and shrugged. 'My fault, I daresay. I haven't the same enthusiasm I once had.'

'I'm sorry to hear that. You worked so hard to build the business. It always meant so much to you.'

'*We* built it, Maryan. Roisan and you worked hard too. And it meant everything once. But lately business has dwindled. God knows why. We give the same service we always have, Roisan works as hard as ever and so do I.' He held her eyes with his. 'The truth is that since you left nothing has been the same. Paul left as I told you. Fay does the job you did and runs the shop as well, but sometimes – sometimes I wonder . . .' He trailed off. Covering her hand with his, he said, 'All the zest has gone out of life. I'm sure I don't have to tell you why, do I?'

She tore her eyes away from his. 'But there's nothing to be done about it, is there?'

The landlord's wife brought their food and Maryan applied herself to it, but somehow her appetite had gone.

'Tell me about your work with Miss Stern,' Vincent

said. 'You seem happy with her. It's good that you were able to have a flat in the house.'

She told him a little about Gina's work, trying hard to sound interesting and light-hearted, but all the time she was wishing she was anywhere but sitting here with Vinnie, skirting around the subject uppermost in both their minds.

They finished their meal and Vincent looked at his watch. 'Better be getting back,' he said. 'Don't want to miss seeing the miniatures come under the hammer, do you?'

As they threaded their way among the customers now crowding the bar he remarked that he would have liked to buy the miniatures himself. 'They're not really my line though,' he explained. 'My customers like to choose their own pictures. I always think they're a very personal . . .' He broke off as the door opened and a familiar figure stood facing them on the threshold.

'*Ah. I thought I'd find you here.*' Fay's bleached hair looked unkempt but her eyes were bright with triumph as she confronted them.

Vincent looked shocked. '*Fay.* For heaven's sake. What are you doing here?'

'You might well ask. Thought you were safe out here, didn't you? Thought you could meet your *whore* in secret.'

Her voice was shrill and piercing and the other customers in the bar stopped talking to look curiously at the irate woman in the fur coat. Vincent took her by the arm and tried to guide her outside.

'Please, Fay. Don't make a scene in public.'

She shook his hand off and stared venomously at Maryan. 'I heard him talking to his sister on the telephone,' she hissed. 'He confides a lot in her, you know. They're both in this thing against me. Can't you see that they're just using you to get at me?' She shook her head. 'No. You're only too willing to fall in with their plans, aren't you, you devious *bitch*. Why can't you keep out of our lives? Why don't you leave us alone?'

Maryan stared from one to the other in horror. 'You've got it all wrong,' she said. 'It was sheer chance that we met here today. Gina Stern, my employer, should have been here, not me.'

'*Liar.*' Fay's lip curled into a sneer. 'If only you could see yourself. You're *pathetic* with your innocent blue eyes and your outraged expression. Butter wouldn't melt in your lying mouth, would it? But you don't take me in. Not for one moment. I know your sort.' She laughed, her eyes glittering with rage. 'You think I don't know that you've been meeting secretly for years? To talk about your bastard daughter, no doubt. But I could tell you things about *her* that you don't know yourself.'

The colour drained from Maryan's face and Vincent made another attempt to steer his wife away.

'Fay, for God's sake let's get away from here. You're making an exhibition of yourself.'

'What do I care?' she shouted. 'If they want to listen, let them. Let them all know what I've had to put up with all these years. A cheating husband who fathered another woman's child.'

'It's *not true.* Why won't you believe it?' Vincent made a move towards her but Maryan intervened.

'Wait. I want to hear what she has to say.' She looked at Fay. 'What do you know about my daughter that I don't know?'

Some of the triumph went out of Fay's eyes and they took on a wary look. In the heat of the moment she'd almost given away the fact that she'd opened and kept the letters that arrived at Simons Mews addressed to Maryan. But what did it matter? Who could prove anything? Serve the bitch right anyway.

'I can tell you she's *married* for a start.' Fay spat the word out triumphantly. 'Got herself into trouble, I shouldn't wonder. Like mother, like daughter. Bad blood will out, they always say, don't they?' She watched with satisfaction as Maryan's colour changed. 'Yes, she's got a child.' She looked at Vincent, a spiteful gleam in her eyes. 'She's a grandmother, your bit on the side. You didn't know that, did you?' She laughed bitterly. 'But then I suppose that makes you a grandfather too.'

White-faced, Maryan looked at Vincent. 'Did you know this? Did she write to Roisan?'

His face was as shocked as hers. 'If she did I knew nothing about it. It's probably all lies anyway.'

'It's not *me* who's the liar,' Fay screamed. 'It's *you* two.' She turned to Maryan. 'You'll find out. You'll suffer for what you've done. Even your own daughter walked out when she found out what kind of woman she had for a mother.'

Maryan turned and ran blindly for the car, Fay's hysterical voice following her as she got in and fumbled with the ignition key. Through the windscreen she could see Vincent struggling to calm her. She felt as though she was deserting him but she couldn't help it. She had to get away. She couldn't listen to any more of the woman's ravings. Was it true? Could Amy have married and become a mother without even trying to get in touch with her? Although no letter had come from her she had always believed, as Sam said, that Amy would come home to her eventually; that somehow or other they would be reconciled. Now she knew without a doubt that it would never happen. Now that Amy had her own life – her own family – she knew she had truly lost her, just as she had lost everyone she had ever cared for.

As Mike drove Amy home to Mill Hill she hummed the memorable tunes from the show she had just enjoyed. 'Some Enchanted Evening', It was such a beautiful, romantic song and it summed up what this evening had been for her – enchanted. It was so long since she'd been able to lose herself in an evening of pure pleasure. Mike's seats in the stalls had given them an excellent view of the stage. He'd taken her for dinner first and now she would have the memory to take out and enjoy whenever she felt low.

Mike glanced at her. 'It was a good show, wasn't it?'

She stopped humming to look at him. 'Oh, *yes*. Thank

444

you so much for taking me, Mike. I haven't enjoyed myself so much for ages.'

'Mary Martin was terrific, wasn't she? That bit where she washed her hair.'

Amy laughed and sang a snatch of the song. 'I'm Gonna Wash That Man Right Outa My Hair.' She sighed. 'Oh, Mike, I *wish* I could get another acting job. I miss it so much.'

'I know you do.' For a while they drove in silence, then he said, 'Look, I've just had a thought. I hear they're planning a daily radio serial at the Beeb. The sort of thing the Americans call a "soap opera". They seem to think it could really take off. Why don't you audition for a part?'

Amy shook her head. 'How can I take anything on when I've got a child to look after?'

'It's only a fifteen-minute slot and as far as I can make out they record a number of programmes in one session,' he told her. 'It might mean you'd only need to come up about once a week. Couldn't you get someone to have Mark for you just for one day?'

A tiny twist of excitement made her heartbeat quicken. 'Well – I don't know. Maybe I could.' She turned to look at him. 'Oh, Mike. Do you think I'd stand a chance?'

He laughed. 'I haven't a clue, but I'll make some enquiries for you if you like. It's worth a try.'

'If I could get another job it would help in so many ways,' she said thoughtfully.

'With cash, you mean?'

'Not just that. You know, ever since I found out that Tom Jessop wasn't my father I've felt sort of lost.'

He glanced at her. 'In what way?'

'Oh, I don't know. So many ways. I keep looking for something in myself, yet I don't know what. I never knew my real father properly, so even if I was like him how would I know? I suppose I feel that I don't really know who I am – or what I might be.'

'*I* know who you are,' he said. 'You're Amy Jessop,

445

the girl I grew up with. You'll never be anyone else as far as I'm concerned.'

'It's not as simple as that, though.' She sighed. 'When I was acting up in Minsdale I took the stage name of Amethyst Lee. I was happy with it. I really thought then that I'd found the real me. Now I'm not sure all over again. I'm Amy Keynan, and yet I'm not Alex's wife. She was called Chloe and she died in the blitz ten years ago. But she's the only wife Alex will ever have. She's the real Mrs Keynan.'

'It's more than just a name though, isn't it? You're Mark's mother,' Mike said firmly. 'That's a *real* identity. Never forget that. And never let Mark forget it either.'

'Oh, I *won't*,' she said fervently. 'Whatever happens I'll always be there for him. I'll never lie to him or let him down.'

Mike dropped her off at the end of the road with a promise to ring and let her know about the audition. There was still a light burning at the Shaws' where Mark was staying for the night, so she decided to go across and make sure that he was all right.

Jack opened the door, but before she could speak he said, 'The little lad's gone. Right upset, Addie was. Just come across and insisted on taking him, he did. And the little'un fast asleep in bed too.'

Amy stared at him, her heart thudding with fear. '*Who*? Who took Mark?'

'Mr Keynan, of course. Come home unexpected. In a right temper he was. Said some real nasty things to Addie and me – uncalled for things. Insisted on taking the baby. Poor little mite cried something chronic, being woken up so sudden like.'

Amy apologised, thanked Jack and told him not to worry. Then, her heart in her mouth, she hurried across the road to let herself into number twenty-two.

Alex was in the dining room. He sat at the table, his collar and tie loosened and his hair awry. On the table beside him stood a glass and an almost empty whisky bottle. He looked up at her with bloodshot eyes, his voice slurred.

'Where' er bloody'ell've you been?'

'I've been to Drury Lane to see *South Pacific*,' she told him. 'Mike Taylor came to see me last week. He had two tickets and he asked me . . .'

'You – *what*?' He got to his feet to stand swaying in front of her. 'You left my son with those two old cretins while you went off gadding with one of your ex-lovers?' His face took on a dark red flush. 'I ought to give you a bloody good hiding for that.'

'Mike isn't an ex-lover,' she said. 'I never had a lover before you, Alex. You know that. You had no right to do what you did tonight.'

'No right? No bloody *right*?' The dark red flush turned to purple. 'You go off and leave my son and you say I've no right.' He made a lunge for her but she side-stepped his flailing arms and he staggered against the wall.

'I suppose you think you're the right person to look after a child,' she said contemptuously. 'Look at you. You can hardly stand up. He was fast asleep. You could have dropped him.'

He laughed dryly. 'And you're the devoted, caring mother, I suppose? You're the one who abandoned him.'

'I'm shut up in this house seven days a week, Alex. I never get a break. I hardly see anyone but tradesmen from one week's end to the next. I needed an evening out. I *deserved* it.'

Alex picked up the bottle and poured the last of it into his glass, regarding her with distaste as he did so. 'Fed up, are you? Well, what a *shame*. I might remind you, Amy, that it was you who wanted to be married.'

She swallowed hard at the lump in her throat. 'I wanted to marry *you*, Alex. There is a difference.'

'Oh yes. You wanted me. You even got yourself pregnant just to prove it. Well, now that you've got me the least you can do is take proper care of my child.' He swallowed the contents of the glass and slid it across the table. Steadying himself, he glared blearily at her, his eyes dark and hostile. From above came the sound of Mark's frightened crying, wakened by the commotion. But when Amy made a move towards the door Alex grabbed her by the shoulder and pinned her against the wall, leaning all his weight against her.

'*Leave him*. I'll see to him.' He pushed his face close to hers, breathing the sour odour of whisky into her face. 'You've got a choice, Amy,' he said. 'You can leave me any time you like. I don't give a damn what you do. But don't think you're taking that child with you. Don't you ever try to take my son away from me.' His fingers pressed into her throat until she could hardly breathe. 'If you decide to stay, you'll stay on my terms, understand? You'll behave as a mother should. And that means that you will not leave my son with strangers any more. Step out of line once more and out you go – got it? Out on your arse – and *on your own*. Got that, have you, Amy?'

Chapter Eighteen

Amy sat up, dozing fitfully in the armchair all night. After Alex had stumbled off to collapse on the bed upstairs she had remained where she was, numb; too stunned to think straight. An hour passed and she went upstairs to check Mark. He was sleeping peacefully, but when she went into the room she and Alex shared she found him sprawled across the bed, snoring loudly and still fully dressed. As she stood looking down at him he stirred and mumbled something. She couldn't make out what he was saying except for the name, *Chloe*. Going out quietly, she closed the door and went downstairs again, resigned to spending the rest of the night in the armchair.

Watching the hours pass she tried to make some kind of sense out of the tangle of thoughts milling around in her brain. Her marriage to Alex would never work. She had to face the fact. He had never got over losing Chloe and he never would. Now she recognised that his understanding of the character, Heathcliff, the interpretation that had impressed her so much, was based on his own experience. Alex himself was tortured in much the same way. He too knew the torment and slavery of obsession, and the crushing power of a lost love that refused to die. He was incapable of loving another woman. He'd warned her of that. But he adored Mark; adored him with a fierce, possessive love that frightened her in its intensity.

Surely he must realise, though, that if she were to leave he couldn't possibly care for the child himself? It wasn't possible. She should call his bluff, take Mark and leave. But where could they go, and what would they live on?

It was getting light when she finally slept, only to be wakened an hour later by Mark's hungry cries from above. Rubbing her stiffened neck muscles, she went upstairs to wash and dress him. Her own bedroom door was still firmly shut. Alex was obviously still sleeping off the effects of the whisky.

But Alex wasn't asleep. Mark's cries had wakened him too. At first he couldn't make out where he was and why he was lying across the bed, fully dressed, then the events of the previous night slowly filtered up through the alcoholic fog inside his head. He heard Amy's footsteps as she came upstairs to attend to the child and her voice as she spoke softly to him.

He rolled onto his back and lay staring at the ceiling. The sick pounding in his head reminded him painfully of the previous night's excesses and he felt a stab of fear – a fear that was becoming frighteningly familiar. He knew his drinking was getting out of control but try as he would he didn't seem able to overcome it. It helped him forget; chased away the images that haunted him. He could no longer ignore that fact that his work was suffering. He'd already received a couple of warnings about being late on the set and, more recently, turning up too drunk to do his job. Not that he cared about that. Trivial little travel films were a waste of his talent anyway. He had a better job in the offing if only he could pull it off. If he did he'd stop drinking. He'd have the motivation then, something more interesting to absorb himself in.

The most worrying part was that lately he found he was unable to remember things he had done and said during one of his drinking sessions. All he really remembered about last night was his anger at finding Amy out when he had arrived home; his son farmed out like a dog with neighbours while she went to the theatre with another man. He hadn't been drunk when he arrived home. Last night's drinking bout had been down to her.

Had he been offensive to that old couple over the road? He hadn't meant to be. Well, he was damned if he was going over there to grovel and apologise. It wasn't his fault if he had an ineffectual wife. Let her go and apologise.

What had he said to Amy? Had he threatened – struck her even? He knew he'd been angry enough. He remembered the anger. Whisky always did that to him. Well, whatever he'd done and said it was no more than she deserved, going off like that.

He rolled onto his side, turning his back to the window and closing his eyes against a shaft of sunlight penetrating a chink in the curtains. It gouged through his eyes and into his brain like a red-hot gimlet.

Since Mark had been born he'd felt different. It was as though the boy was an extension of himself; a replacement, waiting in the wings, ready to step into his shoes. An understudy. If he died now he would have done at least one worthwhile thing. He had fathered a son. And Mark was no ordinary son. He was special. Born into a better world – destined for a better life than he had led. Watching the baby grow into a little boy he had seen himself mirrored in the child. And strangely, he could see a likeness to Chloe too. So much so that at times it was almost possible to imagine that Mark was Chloe's child and not Amy's; to persuade himself that through some mystic power beyond his comprehension Amy was the mere vessel for the child he and Chloe were destined to create.

'I'll take good care of him, my love,' he whispered drowsily into the pillow. 'I'll see that she does too. Some day we'll all be together. It might take time, but we will, never you fear.' And, as he drifted between sleeping and waking, he thought that he saw Chloe smile her lovely smile and nod her approval. He thought she looked happy again.

*

451

Mark had been fed and was playing happily in his playpen when Amy heard Alex stirring. Above her, there was the sound of doors opening and shutting – footsteps, the bath running. Her heart quickened. What mood would he be in this morning? Would he still be angry with her for going out? What right did he have to threaten her? She was his wife, a woman with rights of her own, not his prisoner. She stood at the sink, her hands trembling as she busied herself with the baby's washing. She dreaded Alex's appearance and wished that their confrontation could be over. Suddenly, to her horror and dismay, she realised for the first time that she was actually afraid of Alex – afraid of the unpredictable and increasingly violent behaviour that drink induced in him.

When at last he walked into the kitchen he looked grey and haggard. Amy glanced at him.

'Do you want breakfast?'

He groaned. 'God, no. I'd like some coffee though. Black. And a couple of aspirins if you've got any.'

She put the coffee on and fetched the aspirin bottle from the medicine cupboard. As she tipped two into his outstretched palm he looked up at her.

'Was I a bastard last night?'

The tightly wound spring of her emotions was suddenly released and she turned away as her throat constricted. 'You – were drunk,' she said. 'Mark was perfectly safe with the Shaws, you know. I hardly ever go out and leave him.' She spun round to face him. 'I don't care what you say to me – or what you *think* of me. I do the best I can, Alex, and I can't do more. But I won't have you upsetting the Shaws. They've been kindness itself to me. They've been there to help me when you haven't.'

He winced as he washed the bitter tablets down with the strong black brew she poured for him. 'Oh, Christ, don't start giving me a hard time, Amy,' he growled. 'I can't take it this morning. Look, to be honest I really don't remember much about last night. It's all a bit of a blur. I'd been out for a drink with some of the film crew. I've been shortlisted to direct a major film for Ealing. I made the journey all the way home specially to tell you about it. And then, when you weren't here . . .' He shrugged irritably. 'Oh, what the hell? Why am *I* apologising? It was you who let me down. Not the other way around.'

'You told me I could get out any time I liked,' she reminded him. 'But that I couldn't take Mark.'

He laughed uneasily. 'Oh, come *on*, surely not. You must have misunderstood.'

'I didn't misunderstand anything, specially when you started pushing me about,' she told him. 'You said I wasn't to go out again, and that if I did I'd be – I'd be out on my arse.' She was angry now. The previous night's hurt and bewilderment combined with lack of sleep brought her simmering anger to boiling point. '*Out on my arse*,' she repeated. 'That was the delightful phrase you used. I didn't misunderstand you, Alex. *On my own*, you said. Without Mark. Without my baby.'

He frowned. 'A man will say anything when he's had a few drinks, Amy. You should have known there was nothing in it. Just the whisky talking.'

'I don't know how much more of this I can stand, Alex,' she said, ignoring his alleged memory lapse. 'I should have listened when you told me you didn't want a wife. You certainly never wanted *me* – or Mark either – *before* he was born. Now you're using him as a kind of weapon to threaten me with.'

'That's not true, Amy, and you know it. I love the boy. I care more for him than anything else in the world. That's what this is all about.'

'You care for him, but not for *me*, Alex. That's what it's really all about. You live the life of a single man, use this house like a hotel and you treat me like dirt. I don't deserve that.'

'Oh, don't be so bloody melodramatic, Amy.' He got up and refilled his coffee cup from the percolator on the stove.

'If you really want me to go, I will. But let's get one thing clear. I won't leave my baby. You couldn't look

453

after him yourself and you don't want strangers caring for him. If you don't want me any more you'll have to provide somewhere for Mark and me to live – and money for us to live on until he's old enough for me to get a job.'

Seeing the logic of her argument, he put down his cup and looked at her. 'Look, I'm sorry if I upset you last night, but it's nothing to get in such a state about. We're married and we've got Mark. Life might not be ideal for either of us at the moment but there's nothing else for it but to make the best of it.'

Amy bridled. Now that he'd sobered up he wanted to soft pedal the whole thing. Well, she wasn't going to be as easily talked down as that. 'And – if I say I'm sick of making the best of it? That I don't want this kind of life any longer?' she challenged. 'If what *I* want is a divorce?'

He took a deep draught of his coffee. Normally her truculence would have angered him, but all last night's fury had evaporated in the cloud of alcohol that filled his head. Instead a warning bell tinkled softly. Divorce meant she'd get custody of Mark. They'd live apart. He'd hardly see the boy. It was out of the question. He took a deep breath to control the pounding inside his head, and looked up at her.

'But you *don't*, do you? Not really.' He stood up and went to her, lifting her chin with one finger. 'Look, I'd had a few last night. I went over the top a bit. I'm sorry. If you want to go out occasionally, okay, I understand that. But pay someone to come and sit with Mark. The Shaws mean well, but they're past it. You must admit that they are.'

'And what am I supposed to pay a sitter with?' she asked him. 'You keep me so short of money we hardly have enough to eat.'

'Oh, that's a bit of an exaggeration, surely. Anyway, all that will change when I get a better job.' He pulled her to him and nuzzled her neck. 'Come on, love. Come down off that high horse of yours. I've said I'm sorry.' He blew gently into her ear. 'Hey, tell you what – I was a damned fool to get too pissed to make the most of being home last night. We didn't even get to sleep together – did we?'

'Don't you remember that either?'

For a second he looked unsure, then he laughed. 'You're teasing me. That's better. That's more like the Amy I know.' He caught sight of the kitchen clock and gave a gasp. 'Christ, is that really the time? I should have been away from here half an hour ago.'

'When will you be home again?' she called to him as he hurried into the hall and began to pull on his coat.

'God knows,' he called. 'We've got to go over to Ireland the day after tomorrow. Could be gone for anything up to a month, depending on the weather.'

She heard him go into the living room and pick Mark up. Heard the child's gleeful shriek and Alex's laugh as he tossed the child into the air and caught him. It was Mark's favourite game, and when Alex put him abruptly back into his playpen and hurried off the little boy let out a dismayed wail of disappointment. Amy sighed. She'd be half the morning pacifying him now. Alex didn't have a clue what it meant to be with a small child twenty-four hours a day.

Maryan was in the office at Gower Street on the morning after the sale when the door opened and a familiar face looked round it. She looked up from her typewriter in surprise.

'Roisan. How nice to see you.'

'Well, if Mohammed won't come to the mountain . . .' Roisan smiled. 'Actually I've come on a business errand, but I've been meaning to come and see you anyway.'

Maryan got up from the desk and fetched a chair. 'I was just going to make some coffee. Will you have some with me?'

'I certainly will.' After Maryan had plugged in her electric kettle Roisan opened her handbag and handed her an envelope. 'This is the cheque for the miniatures,' she said. 'Less the auctioneer's commission, of course.

Vinnie asked me to bring it. He said to tell you they went well over the reserve price. Gina should be well pleased.'

'Thank you.' Maryan fingered the envelope, longing to look at the cheque – to know what the miniatures had fetched. But it was sealed and addressed to Gina. She must wait patiently till she came home to find out.

'I hope Vinnie has taken his commission too,' she said as she slipped the envelope into a drawer.

Roisan shook her head. 'Not a bit of it. He was only too happy to be of help.' She peered at Maryan, noticing her pale face and red-rimmed eyes. 'My dear, I heard what happened,' she said. 'Vinnie was so upset that you had to be humiliated like that.'

'I had no idea that Vinnie would be at the sale,' Maryan said. 'And certainly no notion that Fay might turn up. But she seemed to think we'd planned to meet.'

'I know. And once she gets an idea into her head . . . He would have come in person to apologise. But he thought you might not want to see him after yesterday. Anyway, he's leaving this afternoon for a sale in North Wales.'

'Fay is still convinced that he is Amy's father,' Maryan said. 'Nothing will persuade her otherwise. She made a terrible scene. I felt bad about leaving him with her like that, but my presence was making things worse.'

Roisan nodded understandingly. 'She's paranoid. I'm very worried – for Vinnie's sake. Living with her is such a strain. And since she's been running the business side of things the orders have fallen off dreadfully. We're not getting half the contracts we were and business at the shop is almost at a standstill. Apparently, when she's in a bad mood she's appallingly rude to the customers. At the rate we're going Vincente's will be bankrupt before the end of next year, and Decor won't be long after it.'

Maryan was appalled, but not surprised. 'It's such a pity Paul left,' she said. 'He was so good with people. He knew the job too.'

'Never mind our business problems.' Roisan touched Maryan's arm. 'You were badly upset by the scene with

Fay yesterday. I can see that. I wouldn't mind betting you didn't sleep last night.'

'I'm all right,' Maryan said. 'I just wish I hadn't gone to the sale. It was just that Gina had to go to Paris and I promised I'd be there.'

'And then you had to leave before the miniatures came up.' Roisan smiled. 'Still, I think Gina will be delighted with the price they fetched.' Her smile faded and she said quietly, 'You're still in love with Vinnie, aren't you? Oh my dear, I'm so sorry. I know it won't help when I tell you that he feels the same. If only he'd applied for an annulment as I wanted him to – before she came back.'

'It's just that I can't bear to see him so unhappy,' Maryan said. 'And the business he's worked so hard for – all going to waste. Isn't there *anything* you can do, Roisan?'

'I only wish to God there were.' Roisan was thoughtful for a while as she sipped her coffee. 'I've got all kinds of suspicions. I know I shouldn't say this, but I can't help thinking that the fall-off in business has something to do with her. I don't know what she's up to and even if I did I couldn't prove it, but if I could only . . .' She sighed. 'Ah, but that's only wishful thinking. She's convinced Vinnie that he owes her his loyalty and protection. God knows what lies she's told. Personally I wouldn't believe that woman if she had a halo and wings.' She looked at Maryan. 'Do you mind being here on your own? I could go and get my things and stay with you till Gina gets back.'

Maryan shook her head. 'No. It's good of you but I'm all right. There's plenty of work to do and Gina should be back in a couple of days' time.'

'Well, you know where I am if you need me.'

Roisan rose to leave but Maryan said quickly, 'Roisan – you haven't had a letter from Amy, have you?'

'No. You know I'd have let you know at once if I had.'

'Of course. It's just something Fay said yesterday. She said she knew things about Amy that I didn't know. She said she was married – that she had a child. I've been wondering if Amy did write to me after all. But surely Vinnie would have seen any letter that went to the flat?'

'Ten to one she made it all up to hurt you,' Roisan said. 'That woman is capable of saying anything that comes into her head. She's either as gloomy as doom or as high as a kite. Vinnie puts her changing moods down to her diabetes, but I'm not so sure. No other diabetic I've ever known has behaved as she does.'

Maryan sighed. 'I suppose you could be right. It's just that I've had this feeling.'

'What kind of feeling?'

'I don't know – a sort of intuitive feeling – that Amy isn't happy; that something is wrong. Oh, Roisan, I wish I hadn't let her go like that. She was so young. Anything could have happened. And if she did write letters . . .'

Roisan put her hand on Maryan's arm. 'You couldn't have stopped her, Maryan. She'd made up her mind. That job was what she'd always wanted. But leave it with me,' she said. 'I'll see what I can find out. If there were any letters I'll get to the bottom of it.'

'But – how?'

Roisan winked and tapped the side of her nose. 'I'll play it by ear as they say. Try not to worry. I'll be in touch.'

Amy was coming in from the garden, a basketful of washing, rescued from a sudden rain storm, on her hip. She heard the telephone ringing as she opened the back door and, dropping the basket on the kitchen floor, she hurried into the hall to lift the receiver.

'Hello,' she said breathlessly. 'Amy Keynan here.'

'Amy, it's me, Mike. Look, I've only got a minute, but I've got those audition details I promised you. I'll give you the address. You have to apply, giving your age, experience and so on. Then, if they think you might be what they're looking for, they'll send you a script and an audition date.'

'Will I stand a chance with the little training and experience I've had?' she asked doubtfully.

'Anyone's guess,' he said briefly. 'Just write in and take it from there. It's got to be worth a try.'

Amy took down the address as he gave it to her. 'When will I see you again, Mike?' she asked.

'Heaven only knows. They're sending me on an assignment to Derbyshire this afternoon. There's been a pit accident up there and I'm to interview some of the victims. It's my first solo assignment, so it'll be quite a challenge.'

'Mike, that's marvellous. Congratulations.'

'Listen out for me on the nine o'clock news tonight,' he said. 'And don't forget, when you come up for the audition ask someone at the reception desk to ring me. We could have a drink – lunch even.'

'Right. I'll do that – if I get an audition. Thanks, Mike.' She hung up with excitement tingling in her veins. Mike's enthusiasm was infectious. Would they really allow someone as inexperienced as her to audition for a BBC serial? Well, as Mike said, it would do no harm to give it a try.

She wrote her application out carefully while Mark had his afternoon nap, signing it with her stage name, Amethyst Lee. Then, when Mark woke up, she walked down to the post box with him in the pushchair. As she dropped the envelope into the box she wondered what she had started. If she did get an audition, and if by some miracle she was actually offered a part, what would she do about Mark? And, even more to the point, what would Alex's reaction be?

She turned the pushchair and set out towards home. I'll meet that when I come to it, she told herself. Might as well worry what I'd do if the moon dropped out of the sky.

The room was small; much smaller than Amy had imagined it would be. The girl who had shown her up had taken her coat and pointed out the microphone.

'Someone will tell you what to do and when to begin,' she said as she left.

What she hadn't prepared her for was that the instructions would come via a loud speaker on the wall, and when the disembodied male voice addressed Amy for the first time she almost jumped out of her skin.

'Good morning, Miss Lee.'

'Oh – er – good morning.'

'I take it you have read the script we sent you.'

'Yes – thank you.'

'Good. I'd like you to read the piece of your own choice first. After that I'd like you to read the part of Estelle in our script. It begins on page three. Have you got that?'

With trembling fingers Amy turned the pages and found the place. 'Yes, I've got it.'

'Someone will read the other character for you. You may begin when you see the red light and there is no need to wait in between. Just carry straight on.'

'Right. Thank you.' She stood poised, staring at the bulb. Her heart was beating so loud that she was sure the microphone must pick up the sound, but she didn't dare move away in case they couldn't hear her. The light flashed on. She took a deep breath and began to read.

She had chosen a piece from *Wuthering Heights*. It was a longish speech, highly charged with emotion, and reading it reminded Amy of Minsdale and the Keynan Players. Life had been so full of hope then. Hope and love, so soon to be shattered.

When she had finished she paused, picked up the other script and began to read as instructed. The character of Estelle could not have been more different from that of Cathy. Having read the script she knew that Estelle was a teenage girl, the flighty daughter of an East End family. It gave her the chance to use the Cockney accent she had grown up with. As she relaxed she found herself slipping easily into the familiar accent; a language that brought its own memories – of her visits to the brewery mews and the big gentle horses; her early schooldays and playing the fairy in the pantomime; of Lily Smith's envious spite. Of the death of Tom Jessop, the man she'd mourned as her beloved 'Daddy'.

After she'd conquered her initial nerves, Amy thoroughly enjoyed the audition. It was wonderful to be doing the work she loved best, even if it was only for a short while. It was with regret that she laid down the script when it was over. She waited. When the voice addressed her again it was cool and impersonal.

'Thank you very much for letting us hear your work, Miss Lee. You may leave the script on the table. Someone will be in touch with you very shortly. Thank you for attending. Good morning.'

'Good morning.' Amy went down in the lift, wondering if the brief dismissal meant the same as 'Don't ring us, we'll ring you.' Thank goodness Mike would be waiting for her in the entrance hall. He was taking her out to lunch. Going straight home would have been such an anti-climax. She couldn't wait to tell him all about her audition.

Gina came home bubbling over with the visit to Paris and the sightseeing she had managed to squeeze into her brief visit to France's romantic capital. But she had serious news to impart. It was too important to blurt out, especially as it concerned Maryan herself. Realising that tact and diplomacy were needed, she invited Maryan to have dinner with her on the evening of her return, booking a table for two at her favourite restaurant.

When they were seated Maryan handed over the envelope containing the cheque for the miniatures. So far Gina hadn't asked about them.

'I've been saving this. It's the money for the miniatures,' she said, waiting in anticipation as Gina tore open the envelope.

'My God, I'd completely forgotten.' When Gina saw the amount written on the cheque she gasped. 'I hadn't expected them to fetch quite this much.'

'It's enough to cover your debt then?'

'Yes. And plenty to spare.' Gina looked up, puzzled. 'But – you were there, weren't you?'

Maryan sighed. 'Well, I was – and I wasn't. I was forced to leave before the miniatures came up.' She went on to tell Gina about Fay's sudden appearance and the scene she had created. When she had finished her employer shook her head.

'She sounds impossible. How on earth does Roisan's brother stand her?'

'I think it's hard for him. But he's a Catholic. Divorce is out of the question.'

Gina looked thoughtful. 'If you and he still love each other . . .'

'There's no chance it can ever come to anything,' Maryan interrupted. 'It's better if we don't see each other under the circumstances.'

'That's what I thought,' Gina said. 'In which case the proposition I have to put to you might be just what you need.'

'Proposition?' Maryan looked up.

'Yes.' Gina took a sip of her wine. 'While I was over in Paris I had an offer. The real reason that I was invited was that my designs had impressed one of the big houses. Word had got out that I was responsible for the Marcus Leigh Collection. Well, to cut a long story short I've been offered a job – by Fath.'

Maryan looked puzzled. 'But – you're a designer in your own right. You're building your own house – your own name.'

'A very small house and a very small name. It'll take me years struggling alone.'

'But it's why you left the Leighs. I thought you'd always wanted to be on your own.'

'Of course. I still do.'

'Then – what about your new designs?'

'They're to be shown at the spring show. Fath will buy them. I'll be working for them by then – if I take up their offer.'

'But – I don't understand. Won't that put you back where you were before?'

'No. Not at all.' Gina leaned eagerly across the table.

462

'With a name like Fath behind me I could come back after two or three years with a real head start. The Marcus Leigh label did well, but only as long as I was there. It was a flash in the pan. How could it be anything else when the original designer was dead? The public is fickle, Maryan. People want a face – a personality to put to a name. When they don't get it they soon forget.'

'Yes, I see.' Maryan felt her heart contract and Gina reached across to touch her hand.

'I'm sorry. Did that sound hard and insensitive?'

'No. I see what you mean. It's a wonderful opportunity for you. Will you take it?'

'Well, I'm seriously considering it,' Gina said. 'There's an awful lot to think about, of course. I'd keep the house on. I might let it on a short lease. I haven't started working it all out yet.'

'Then I'd better start looking round for another job and somewhere to live.'

'Oh *no*. That's what I was coming to. If I go I'd like you to come with me.'

'*Me*?' Maryan stared at her.

Gina laughed. 'Yes, *you*. I'll still need a secretary and the salary they're offering will certainly run to it. I'd have the rent from the house and what's left over from this too.' She waved the cheque. 'We could share a flat. Oh, just think, Maryan. It'd be such *fun*. I know you'd *love* Paris. And we'd both be getting away from the unhappy memories we'd rather forget.'

'I don't know.' Maryan shook her head. 'I've never thought of living anywhere but England.'

'You've nothing to keep you here, have you? Your daughter has her own life now, and you've said that there's no future for you and Vincent Donlan. Anyway, I wouldn't be going until early next spring. You'll have plenty of time to make up your mind.'

Maryan slept little that night. The thought of leaving England and spending two or three years in Paris had taken her completely off guard. It was something she had never even dreamed of. Yet suddenly it was a real possibility. And it was certainly tempting. As Gina had said, there was plenty of time to weigh up the pros and cons, but even so, Maryan had the feeling it wasn't going to be easy to decide. If only she didn't have this uneasy feeling about Amy. If only she knew where she was. And just how much truth there was in Fay's spiteful allegations.

The letter came with a batch of cards just a few days before Christmas. Amy opened the cards first, trying not to look at the other, smaller envelope lying face down on the mat. There weren't many. She'd lost touch with most of the people she used to know, and Alex seemed to have few friends. There was one from Celia, one from Mike and another from Marjorie and Philip Taylor. She bent and picked up the remaining letter. It had BBC printed in one corner, so she knew at once what it contained. She carried it through to the living room, put it on the table and sat down to stare at it. It would be brief and to the point, politely declining her services and thanking her for attending. Oh well, might as well get it over with.

She tore open the envelope and drew out the sheet of paper inside. She read the letter through once. Then, the words dancing before her eyes, she read it again, slowly and carefully, hardly able to believe what she read. *They were offering her a part.* Not the part she'd read for, but another, better part. If their offer was acceptable she was to go in and meet the producer and sign her contract on Friday, 21 December. It was a wonderful Christmas present, the best she'd ever had. She tried not to think about the new set of problems it brought with it. A reliable person would have to be found to take care of Mark while she was working. Preferably someone who didn't charge too much. And then, even more difficult, there was Alex. She must break the news to him. He had telephoned at the end of last week to tell her that he'd got the job he wanted. He was to direct a feature film for Ealing. The crew and cast, which included two big-name stars, would be leaving for location work in Greece right after Christmas. Should she tell him before he went, or wait and see how things worked out? She decided on the latter. If she got everything well organised and Mark wasn't suffering he would have nothing to argue about.

'It went really well, Mike. All the cast were there – and the producer. Even the writers, four of them. We talked about the main storyline and we each got a chance to say how we thought of the characters we will be playing.'

They faced each other over tea in the canteen. Amy's eyes were bright with excitement. She hadn't enjoyed herself so much since her days at Minsdale with the Keynan Players.

Catching some of her enthusiasm, Mike urged her to tell him more. 'Go on, what's the title? Have they got one yet?'

'Yes. It's to be called 'This Year, Next Year',' she told him. 'It's about two families. The middle-class Owens who own a printing business and a group of their workers, most of them from the same East End family.'

He grinned. 'Sounds good. So when do you start work?'

'Right after the Christmas holiday. We'll be working two days a week, one for rehearsal and one for recording a set of five fifteen-minute programmes.'

'Have you got a crèche or a sitter of some kind arranged for Mark?'

'Addie Shaw has put me onto this young mother who takes care of several children while their mothers are at work. She's a qualified children's nurse and very capable. I went to see her yesterday and took Mark. They seemed to take to each other on sight and she's actually got a vacancy coming up after Christmas, so everything looks like working out well.'

'That's good news.' He smiled at her. 'You know, you look like the old Amy today,' he told her. 'Your eyes are shining and you're full of excitement and enthusiasm. It's good to see you looking happy again.'

465

Suddenly embarrassed, she avoided his eyes. 'Thanks, Mike. If it hadn't been for you I'd never have had this opportunity.'

'Rubbish. I only told you about it. You got the job because you're talented.' He raised an enquiring eyebrow. 'Was Alex pleased for you?'

She sighed. 'I haven't told him yet. I wanted to have everything cut and dried first. Besides, he hasn't been home. I could hardly tell him over the phone, could I?'

'I suppose not. How will he take it?'

'He can hardly object to me earning extra money, especially when he can see that Mark is going to be well taken care of, can he?'

Her confident tone belied the uneasiness in her eyes and Mike smiled encouragingly. 'Of course not. What are you doing for Christmas by the way?'

'Alex will be home. He'll want to spend Christmas with Mark before he goes on location to Greece. He's likely to be away for at least six weeks.'

'Oh, that's all right then. I was going to invite you to Rhensham if you were going to be alone.'

'Oh, Mike. Were you really?' Amy sighed wistfully. 'It'd be lovely to spend another Christmas at Mitcham Lodge. I'd love Auntie Marjorie to see Mark. And to show him the village and the horses. Does she still help at the stables?'

He smiled. 'Yes. She's still got a couple at home too. Never mind. Some other time, eh?'

'That would be wonderful.'

'Amy . . .' He looked into her eyes. 'Look, Amy – you do know that if ever you need anything – if ever you need me, I'll be there.'

'I know, Mike. Thanks.' For a moment they looked at each other, then Amy noticed the time and jumped to her feet. 'Heavens, I must fly. Mark is with Addie this afternoon. I must go and collect him or she'll think I'm taking advantage.'

This year Mark was old enough to understand and catch

the excitement of Christmas. He loved the coloured lights in the streets and the shop windows, and his own small Christmas tree, decorated with lights and tinsel and placed out of reach of his grasping little hands, was a source of sheer delight to him.

Alex arrived home on Christmas Eve. He'd had a drink, but to Amy's relief he wasn't drunk. He played with Mark until bedtime then he and Amy ate supper together before creeping upstairs to fill the stocking, hung up at one corner of Mark's cot. For once he was in a good mood and seemed to be looking forward to the challenge of the new job. He even discussed it with her, sounding more animated and enthusiastic than she'd known him for some time. Maybe it would make him less frustrated, she told herself hopefully. Perhaps it would bring about that change in their lives that he had promised.

All through the Christmas holiday she meant to tell him about the BBC job. Once or twice she even began, but each time something happened to stop her and when he left on the day after Boxing Day she still hadn't broken her news. As she stood on the doorstep with Mark in her arms, waving to him as he drove off, she regretted not getting over that one final, very important and difficult hurdle. But things had been so much better between the three of them. She couldn't bring herself to spoil it. It wasn't really that she was too cowardly, she told herself.

When Gina told Maryan that she had definitely decided to accept Fath's offer Maryan realised that the winding down process must be put into operation at once. One of her first tasks was to contact Sam and tell him that they would no longer need to rent the Hackney factory.

As soon as Christmas was over she telephoned, asking him to meet her for lunch. The purpose of her meeting with him was twofold. Besides asking him to release Gina from their arrangement, she was badly in need of advice and could think of no one better than Sam.

He agreed at once to meet her, suggesting lunch at a quiet restaurant in Soho. He was waiting when she arrived and had already ordered her a glass of wine. When they'd studied the menu and ordered their lunch he looked up at her with his kindly smile.

'You sounded a little anxious on the telephone, Maryan. You're looking peaky too. I hope everything is all right.'

'I'm fine. It's just that I've got some news.'

He looked up hopefully. 'About Amy?'

She shook her head. 'No. It's Gina. She was invited over to Paris last month with a view to taking part in a show next spring at the *Musée des Arts Décoratifs*.'

Sam looked impressed. 'That sounds wonderful. Marcus told us so much about the *Musée* when he went to Paris before the war. It's marvellous that it's up and running once again.'

'She took her portfolio with her new collection and had a terrific time. But while she was there she had an exciting offer – of a job with the house of Fath.'

Sam nodded. 'I see. She should take it, of course. I presume she accepted at once.'

'Not right away. She's been thinking it all out carefully. But now she has decided to take up the offer.'

'So she will wish to be released from our agreement about the Hackney premises.' Sam smiled. 'Tell her not to worry. It's not a problem. I can easily re-let the factory.'

'Thank you. I'm sure that will be a relief to her.' She hesitated and Sam peered at her, sensing that there was more on her mind.

'You didn't ask me to meet you just for that, did you, my dear? There's something else.'

'Well – yes. The fact is, she's asked me to go with her and I don't know what to do, Mr Sam.'

The old man reached across the table to squeeze her hand. 'Maryan, I think it's time you dropped the Mister, don't you? After all, we're almost related. So – you're finding it difficult to decide, and you want me to help you make up your mind. Is that it?'

She sighed. 'I can't go without knowing what's become of Amy,' she told him. 'I must find her before I can even begin to think of leaving the country. Do you understand?'

'My dear, of course. Rachel and I would like to know where she is too. Rachel in particular worries about her. She hasn't been well again. The doctor says her heart isn't strong. Worrying is so bad for her.'

'The problem isn't so much finding her,' Maryan said. 'That would be fairly easy, I imagine, if I put my mind to it. The question is, does Amy *want* me to find her?'

'Maybe to begin with we could make some discreet enquiries – just to be sure that she's all right,' Sam said. 'If you knew she was well and happy you could go to Paris with peace of mind, eh?'

She looked uncertain. 'It would help. But what I really want is . . .'

'A reconciliation?'

'To be forgiven, I suppose.' Maryan looked at her old employer. 'I wasn't a very good mother, Sam. Looking back now I can see where I went wrong. I should have made more effort to spend time with her – not kept secrets from her. Everyone deserves to know the basic truth about their parentage. I was so wrong not to tell her.'

'And Rachel and I made so many demands on you. Oh yes, we are to blame too.' He looked at her with his gentle brown eyes. 'Maryan, listen to me – do you really want to go to Paris?'

She sighed. 'I know I'm lucky. It's a wonderful opportunity. One I might never have again . . .'

He waved a hand at her. 'Putting all that aside – do you *want* to go?'

For a long moment she looked into the wise, candid eyes. 'No, Sam. No, I don't.' She sighed, suddenly filled with relief. 'This is the first time I've really admitted it. I feel I ought to want to go. But I don't, not really. I'm a Londoner, you see – born and bred. This is where I belong and I know I'd be homesick. I know now how

Mum felt in the war when we tried to get her to stay with us at Hazelfield. If I went I'd feel I'd abandoned Amy. Even if she doesn't want to see me any more, I'd still feel that.'

'And all this has been keeping you awake at nights, eh?' He patted her hand. 'Making those blue eyes of yours so sad? I do know how you feel, my dear. Perhaps more than you can guess. So – what will you do when Gina goes?'

She shrugged. 'I haven't got as far as thinking about that yet.'

'How would you like to work for Feldman's again?'

She stared at him. 'But – there *is* no Feldman's. You retired.'

His smile was almost impish. 'I want to come out of retirement, Maryan – to start again. Maybe with your help I could do it. You see, I feel like you. Feldman's has been my life since boyhood. It *is* me. Without it I'm nothing. I've been thinking about it so much lately. Now that I have someone to leave the business to I can't let it die. I could do a lot of the work from Whitegates as I did before. I just need a good, reliable manager to run the factory for me – be on the spot. The job is yours if you want it, Maryan. I can think of no one better. It would be like having my own daughter run it for me.'

Maryan's heart lifted. She had started as an apprentice machinist at Feldman's when she left school at fourteen. Now she was going back as factory manager. Back to the East End where her roots were. What would her mother have said, she wondered? She could just imagine her shaking her head and saying that she should have the good sense to know her place. But life had changed since Sarah's day.

'You could have free rein,' Sam was saying. 'Use your own initiative and ideas with the workforce. After all, who better to understand their needs than you? And you're so much more up to date with the world of fashion than I am now. What do you say, my dear?'

She looked up with a smile. 'Oh, Sam – I'd *love* to come back to Feldman's.'

He squeezed her hand tightly. 'And maybe – just maybe we could look for Amy together?'

She smiled. 'Yes. Maybe we could.'

With the New Year came the usual crop of bills. At Decor business was at a virtual standstill and trade at Vincente's was no better. Things were even worse than Vincent had visualised. There seemed to be a slump in the antique and house refurbishment business in London and the Home Counties. If he wanted to continue he was obviously going to have to widen his sights and look further afield for work. He placed advertisements in the county 'glossies', offering to go as far as Scotland, and when he received a telephone call from a man in Caithness who had just bought a castle and wanted to refurbish it he was filled with new hope and excitement. He promised to travel up to Scotland to look at the property and give a brief assessment of its potential, and a date was made. But early on the morning of the day he was to drive north Roisan received an urgent telephone call.

'Roisan . . .' He sounded worried. 'I wondered if you could come over to Simons Mews today?'

'Of course, if you need me. Is something wrong?'

'I can't go into detail.' He lowered his voice so that she had to press the receiver close to her ear to hear what he was saying. 'I can't talk at all really. It's Fay. She isn't well, and there's no one to open the shop. I wouldn't ask you, but I might need to be away for at least three days.'

Roisan sighed and raised her eyes to the ceiling. Fay was up to her old tricks again. 'You must go, Vinnie,' she told him firmly. 'This could be the turning point for Decor. You mustn't let it slip through your fingers. I'll cope at this end. Is Fay in bed?'

'Yes. She couldn't sleep. She was up half the night, walking up and down, shivering – sweating. I tried to help but she didn't want me near her and she refused point-blank to let me send for the doctor. I dropped off myself in the end and when I woke, about four-thirty, she wasn't in the flat. God knows where she went. Maybe she thought some fresh air ... Anyway, she seemed a bit better when she came in.'

'Did she have some insulin?'

'Yes, when she came in. She's asleep now.'

'How long was she away?'

'I don't really know. About an hour – it could have been longer.'

Roisan clicked her tongue in exasperation. 'What was she thinking of, wandering about in the middle of the night? She might have caught pneumonia. All right, Vinnie, I'm on my way. Just you get off, and don't worry. I'll take care of everything.'

On the way over to Simons Mews Roisan worried about Vincent, driving all the way up to Scotland after so little sleep. It was typical of Fay to spoil his chances. Surely if she had felt ill she could have allowed him to help instead of worrying him by taking off into the night like that. It was so typical.

She had her own key to the flat and it was just before nine o'clock as she let herself in at the side door. At the top of the stairs, she paused to listen. There was no sound. She tiptoed into the bedroom. Fay was lying on her back, her mouth open and sleeping like a log. Roisan looked at her in disgust. If she hadn't known better she'd have thought Fay was drunk. She closed the door and went down to open the shop.

At lunchtime she put up the 'closed' sign and went upstairs to the flat to make herself a snack lunch. She put the kettle on, then put her head round the bedroom door. Fay would most likely be awake and hungry by now.

The moment she saw her she knew that something was wrong. She was a bad colour and her breathing was deep – much too deep. Maybe she wasn't asleep at all, but unconscious – in a diabetic coma. Roisan knew enough about the disease to know that if insulin wasn't administered the result·was a coma. Yet Vinnie had said she'd had insulin in the small hours. Something wasn't right. In the living room she dialled for an ambulance. While she waited for it to arrive she collected up the syringes and ampoules from the bathroom cabinet. Then she remembered that diabetics carried a card. They would need to see that at the hospital. She went through Fay's handbag, but to no avail. There was nothing among the contents to certify a medical condition at all. It was as she heard the ambulance turn into the Mews that she found the slit in the lining. Slipping her hand inside she felt an envelope, but already the street doorbell was ringing downstairs. Cramming the envelope into her pocket, she went down to open the door.

The ambulance man agreed immediately that Fay was unconscious. When Roisan mentioned that she was diabetic he looked puzzled.

'This doesn't look like a hypo to me,' he said, bending over Fay's prone body and sniffing. 'But you'd better bring along her insulin and any other medication she's on.'

'It's all right, I've already done that.' Roisan held up the paper bag and saw that the ambulance man was examining the puncture marks on Fay's arm with a thoughtful expression. Straightening up, he looked at his assistant.

'Better get her to hospital right away.'

Fortunately, the journey to the hospital was short and as soon as they arrived in Casualty Fay was whisked away. It was while Roisan was waiting that she remembered the envelope in her pocket. They would need the card. She pulled it out and looked inside. There was no diabetic card, just two crumpled letters and a small card with a picture of a stork on it. She caught her breath. Amy's letters, and a card announcing the birth of a baby boy. So this was where Fay's information came from.

'Are you the lady who brought Mrs Fay Donlan in?'

Roisan looked up to see a tall man in a white coat looking down at her. She rose to her feet, thrusting the envelope back into her pocket. 'That's right. How is she?'

'Are you a relative?'

'I'm her sister-in-law.'

Looking around the crowded waiting area, the man said, 'I'd like a word in private. If you could just come with me.'

Mystified, Roisan followed him to a small office where he closed the door and indicated a chair. 'I am Doctor Leverton, the Casualty Officer,' he said. 'And you are?'

'Mrs Freer.'

The doctor nodded briefly, making a note on a pad. 'Now – the ambulance man who brought your sister-in-law in tells me that you told him she was diabetic.'

Roisan nodded. 'That's right. I brought her insulin and syringes with her, but I couldn't find a card.'

He looked at her thoughtfully. 'Does she live with you?'

'No. She lives with my brother – her husband.'

'Do you happen to know the name of her GP?'

'I'm sorry, no.'

'So you wouldn't know if she'd been ill lately?'

'Not that I know of. At least, not till this morning. My brother telephoned me earlier on and said she wasn't well. He had to go away on urgent business and he asked me to go and stay with her.' Roisan frowned. 'Is she all right? What's happened?'

'How long had she been unconscious before you called the ambulance? Please think carefully, Mrs Freer. It's very important.'

'I don't know. Not long. I arrived at about half-past nine. She was sleeping then, quite peacefully, I thought. My brother has a shop, so I was busy till one. When I went up to the flat I found her collapsed. Apparently she'd injected some insulin early this morning . . .'

'Your sister-in-law is *not* diabetic,' the doctor said abruptly.

Roisan stared at him. 'She's not . . . ? Then what's wrong with her?'

'I have reason to believe that she has administered an overdose of a narcotic. The substance in the ampoules you brought with her is diamorphine, not insulin.'

Shocked, Roisan stared at him. 'But – I thought . . . Diamorphine, you said?'

He nodded gravely. 'Perhaps better known to you as heroin.'

Chapter Nineteen

It was much later that evening when the hospital telephoned to tell Roisan that Fay had regained consciousness and could be visited. She lay in bed in the small side-ward, her face grey against the white of the pillowcase. When Roisan closed the door and sat down by the bed she turned her face away.

'Why did you do it?' she muttered. 'Why did you have to bring me here?' She turned her accusing eyes on her sister-in-law. They burned like hot coals in her white face. 'You've always hated me, haven't you?'

'I thought you were in a diabetic coma. What was I supposed to think? You're addicted to that vile stuff, aren't you? How long has it been going on?'

'I told the doctor the drug was prescribed abroad when I broke my arm and afterwards I couldn't get off it.'

'And is that the truth?'

'What business is it of yours?' Fay glared malevolently at her sister-in-law. 'And what does it matter, as long as they swallowed it? You'd guessed anyway, hadn't you? This is just the chance you've been waiting for. It must have seemed like a godsend, finding me flaked out like that.'

'You're wrong,' Roisan said. 'I didn't guess, not about the drugs. It was a complete shock when the doctor told me. But if I had, Fay, and if you'd been anyone else but Vinnie's wife, I'd have blown the whistle on you right away. Make no mistake about that.' The two women looked at each other for a moment, then Roisan asked: 'So what happens next? Are they giving you any treatment?'

Fay grimaced. 'They've offered me a spell in some drying out place, to get off it. It sounds ghastly. I shan't go.'

'I would if I were you,' Roisan said dryly. 'As it happens I've had my eyes opened in more ways than one since this morning.'

'What do you mean?'

'I've spent the afternoon in the office – going through the books and checking bank statements.'

Fay raised herself on one elbow, her eyes staring. 'You've *what*? You have no right . . .'

'I have *every* right. It's my business you've been cheating too, remember? I've also been in touch with some of our previous clients. I know now why the business has been failing. You've been quoting exorbitant prices and creaming off the profits to supply your habit, haven't you?' When Fay turned her head away Roisan bent her head closer. '*Admit it*' she hissed. 'There's a name for what you've been doing, you know – one the police might well be interested in.'

'They can't charge me with cheating *myself*,' Fay said. 'Vinnie is my husband. Decor is my business as much as his.'

'The Inland Revenue might see things differently,' Roisan put in. 'You see, I found a bank book and statements too, Fay. The account is in the name of Kendal. Your maiden name, I think. The receipts tally with the extra cash you quoted clients. And the statements show some interestingly large cheques paid out regularly to the same person. It doesn't look good, does it?'

Fay swallowed hard. 'How dare you go through my personal papers – snooping and poking your nose into what doesn't concern you?'

'Doesn't concern me?' Roisan's face was flushed with anger. 'You've cheated, lied and stolen from Vinnie and

477

me. Now you've been found out and you're going to pay for it.'

Fay turned her head on the pillow. 'Go away, or I'll ring for a nurse,' she murmured. 'I'm supposed to be resting.'

'I've no wish to spend a second more than I have to in your company, Fay, I promise you that. But I haven't finished with you yet. There are things I must say. You deserted Vinnie – went off with this man who you thought had more to offer. Then you came back and shattered Vinnie's life just when he was finding success and happiness again. Since then you've made his life a living hell. Well, now your little game is over – understand?'

'I'm still his wife,' Fay said with a maddening smile. 'You know Vinnie. As long as he feels he has a duty to me . . .'

'But he *hasn't*,' Roisan interrupted. 'There never was any pregnancy or abortion, was there? You made the whole thing up to use as emotional blackmail.'

'You can't prove that,' Fay snapped.

'I don't have to. I have enough proof of other things to put you behind bars if I choose to. You've almost wrecked the business Vinnie, Maryan and I worked so hard to build. You're going to pay for that.'

'We'll see. When Vinnie gets here . . .'

'He isn't coming,' Roisan interrupted. 'I haven't told him about this little episode.'

Fay's eyes blazed. 'I'll telephone him myself. I'll ask the doctor to.'

'I wouldn't if I were you.' Roisan took a small bundle of crumpled papers out of her handbag. 'While I was looking for your non-existent diabetic card I found these. You kept the letters that Maryan's daughter wrote to her. Vinnie might just be saintly enough to forgive you for stealing his money and wrecking his business. But this – never.'

'So – the girl *is* his child then?'

Roisan smiled wryly. 'You'll never know, will you,

Fay? You'll never be able to prove it either way. On the other hand, all the cards are stacked against you.'

The defiant look faded from Fay's face and for the first time Roisan dared to feel confident that she was winning.

'It wasn't all for me – the money,' Fay said quietly. 'He – the man I was living with – has been blackmailing me. When he got tired of me and threw me out he promised to keep quiet about my habit and to keep supplying me with – what I need, if I made monthly payments.' She looked at Roisan. 'All right. What now?'

Roisan drew a deep breath, trying hard not to let it sound like a sigh of relief. 'I'm prepared to offer you a deal, and if you're wise you'll take it. Make yourself scarce. Get out of Vinnie's life and I won't go to the police. They tell me you'll be discharged from here tomorrow. I'll bring your clothes and the bank book. You can keep the money that's left in it. It'll be worth it to see the back of you. Later, you'll put divorce proceedings into action; set Vinnie free.'

'You don't want much, do you?'

'I want what's due to my brother,' Roisan said. 'He deserves it.'

'What's going to become of me?'

Roisan shrugged. 'That's up to you. You've been offered a cure. Why not take it?'

'And – if I refuse to co-operate?'

'Simple. I go to the police with the evidence I've got first – and tell Vinnie what I've done afterwards.' She raised an eyebrow. 'Well – what do you say?'

Fay made one last effort. 'I say you're bluffing.'

'*Try me*,' Roisan challenged, her mouth set in a determined line. 'The jail sentences for embezzlement are quite stiff, I believe. Illegal possession of narcotics is probably even stiffer, I wouldn't know. And of course your friend and supplier would be involved too. He might not be too happy about that. Think about it, Fay. So far you've been lucky. Damned lucky.'

There was a long pause. Then the door opened and a nurse came in.

'I'm sorry, Mrs Freer. I'm afraid I'll have to ask you to leave now.'

Roisan got to her feet and walked to the door. She paused and looked back. 'Well?'

Fay nodded briefly, her face bleak with defeat. 'All right,' she said quietly. 'I'll do as you say.'

Roisan felt drained as she walked out of the hospital into the March evening. It was raining. Raincoated figures hurried past, the wind tugging at their umbrellas. The traffic swished by on the wet roads, throwing up a fine spray of oily water, and the pavements glistened underfoot. But as she joined the bus queue she saw that the woman in front of her carried a bunch of flowers, and as she breathed in their fragrance her heart suddenly lifted. The air seemed filled with the joyous promise of spring.

Since reopening Feldman's Sam had taken over the flat above the garage at Whitegates, using part of it as his office, as Rachel had done when she launched the Marcus Leigh Collection. He felt happier and fitter than he had for a long time. He was back in harness, running Feldman Fashions once again. And what was more, he had Maryan to help him. Every Friday he went up to Town to spend the day with her at the Hackney factory; going to the bank, paying the wages and helping out in any way he could. He loved to do the rounds, chatting to his workers, enquiring after their families and their health. He prided himself that he could remember all their names and personal details. He knew that it made them feel a valued part of the firm and encouraged them to take a special pride in their work. Maryan seemed happy too. She had found a flat nearby and settled into her job well. And she was certainly efficient. The factory had never run so smoothly or so profitably.

Rachel, on the other hand, was taking life quietly these days. The King's death in February had affected her deeply, but since the Princess Elizabeth had become Queen and the papers had been full of the new young royal family and the exciting arrangements for the coming coronation, she seemed to have cheered up. She had taken up an old hobby, embroidery, and was busy making a set of elaborate cushion covers to commemorate coronation year. While Sam worked she seemed quite content to stitch away, listening contentedly to the wireless as her needle flew in and out.

It was as Sam was working one Wednesday morning that Rachel burst into the office. Her face was flushed with excitement and she was quite breathless from hurrying across the garden and climbing the stairs to the office. He looked up in surprise at her sudden entrance and admonished her sternly.

'Rachel, my love. How many times has the doctor told you you mustn't rush about like that? You know you . . .'

'Samuel – *listen* to me,' she interrupted impatiently. 'Something wonderful has happened.'

Frowning, he got up from his desk and took her arm. 'Sit down and catch your breath. Whatever it is, it can't be so wonderful you would kill yourself for it. Now – take your time.'

But Rachel flapped her hands at him frustratedly. 'Oh, do stop *fussing* and listen to me. I was listening to the wireless just now. A new programme was on. I was interested to hear it because they said it was all about an East End family who run a printing business – it sounded rather like us. Well, as I listened it struck me that one of the characters sounded just like . . .' She looked up at him. 'I know you're going to think I've taken leave of my senses, but she sounded just like – Sarah.'

Sam looked blank. 'Sarah?'

'*Our* Sarah – as she was when we first knew her. Sarah Brown.' She waved her hands again, anticipating his next remark. 'Yes, I *know* you're going to say that Sarah has been dead for years, but hear me out, Sam.'

Nonplussed, Sam sank back into his chair. 'All right – all right, I'm listening.'

'Well – when the programme came to an end I listened for the cast of actors. The name of the one who sounded like Sarah was . . .' She bit her lip with suppressed excitement. 'It was *Amethyst Leigh*.'

Sam shook his head. 'I'm sorry, but I don't . . .'

'Oh, *Sam*, how can you be so slow? It's Amy, don't you see? Amethyst is her full name, don't you remember? We know that she left home to be an actress. And obviously she has taken Leigh as a stage name.' She spread her hands. 'What other name would she choose but her true father's?'

Sam still looked doubtful. 'It's most likely all coincidence,' he said. 'I wish you wouldn't get yourself so worked up about it, my love. It isn't good for you.'

'Good for me? *You're* not good for me.' Rachel was on her feet. 'Can't you see how frustrated you're making me? At least we can find out, Sam. We can write to the BBC and ask for the address of this actress. Better yet, we could telephone them.' She clasped her hands together. 'Oh, Samuel, just think – our granddaughter might be no further away than the end of our telephone.'

'Now, Rachel, you must calm yourself,' Sam said firmly. 'All right. It may be as you say. But first we must go and see Maryan and tell her what you have heard. We can't do this without her permission.'

'Yes, yes – so when can we go?' Her eyes were bright with anticipation as they looked hopefully into his.

'You can come with me when I go up on Friday.'

'*Friday*?' She stared at him. 'How can you expect me to wait until Friday? Oh, Samuel, please – can't we go now – today?'

When she looked at him like that Sam had never been able to refuse his wife anything. He sighed resignedly. 'Oh, very well, if it will satisfy you – anything. But only if you promise me not to build up your hopes too high.'

By the beginning of March the first week of 'This Year, Next Year' had already been broadcast and the reaction had been marvellous, even better than the predictions.

Letters flooded in from listeners to say how much they had enjoyed the heart-warming show with its memorable characters. The producer and cast settled down confidently to a long run.

Amy was radiant. Over the past two months she had learned so much about herself. Not only was she sure now that she could act – and act without Alex to guide her – but she could successfully combine her other roles of housewife and mother with her artistic career. It helped, of course, that she was working away from home on only two days of the week. There was plenty of time for her household jobs and for being with Mark. She usually studied her scripts in bed when the house was quiet. And of course there was the added advantage that radio work did not involve memorising lines.

Since Christmas she had seen a lot of Mike. On her two days in London they usually lunched together and he had been out to Mill Hill to spend the occasional Sunday with her and Mark, who was growing fond of him. Alex wrote from time to time and he had telephoned her twice. But he gave her little indication of how the film was progressing. Greece was fine, he told her. The weather was warm and sultry but they had been held up by a lack of sunshine. He had no idea when they would complete the location filming. On the two occasions he had telephoned he had made it unflatteringly clear that his chief reason for ringing was dire necessity. He needed her to wire him some money. Boredom and inactivity were proving expensive, he said enigmatically. He rang off without saying once that he missed her. But then she didn't expect him to.

On the day that the first programme went out Mike suggested they celebrate. He rang to say he had booked a table at a restaurant by the riverside in Richmond and would pick her up at eight. Amy went across to ask Addie if she would have Mark for the evening. The older woman agreed at once, but Amy noticed that Jack looked less than pleased.

'Mr Keynan isn't likely to come back, is he?' he asked meaningfully.

'Oh no. He's in Greece, filming,' Amy reminded him. 'That other time was a misunderstanding, Jack. It won't happen again.'

Jack looked doubtful. 'Does he know about you and this Mr Taylor?' he asked.

'*Jack.*' Addie looked scandalised. 'Fancy saying a thing like that to Amy. It's none of our business.'

'It will be if he comes back and blames us for colluding,' Jack muttered ominously.

'Mike is a very old friend. We grew up together during the war. He's like a brother,' Amy told him.

'Yes, but he's *not* your brother, is he?'

Amy looked at Addie. 'Maybe I should ask someone else to sit for me,' she said. But Addie would have none of it.

'Take no notice of *him*,' she said, throwing her husband a reproachful look. '*I* know there's nothing going on that shouldn't be. That's good enough for me. You've worked hard and you deserve a little celebration. She smiled. 'Jack and I both listened to "This Year, Next Year" on the wireless and we thought you were ever so good in it.'

The restaurant was cosy and intimate. Checked table-cloths covered the small tables and on each was a small candle lamp. Lights along the river bank made the flowing river look like rippling black satin and Amy sipped her wine with a feeling of happy satisfaction. She smiled at Mike.

'Since I've been working again I feel like a real person,' she told him. 'A whole person. Acting is what I was meant to do. I'm sure of it. And everything seems to be working out really well. Mark is happy. He looks forward to going to Rosemary's two days a week and I'm sure I'm a better mother now that I feel more fulfilled.'

Mike took a thoughtful sip from his glass and looked up at her. 'And Alex?'

Her smile faded. 'Ah – yes, Alex.' She twisted the stem of her glass between her fingers. 'When I didn't manage to break it to him at Christmas I thought I'd write and tell him.' She looked up at him. 'But I couldn't put it in a letter. It wouldn't be right, would it?'

'I don't think you're being quite honest with yourself, Amy.' He looked at her. 'You're afraid he'll make you give it up, aren't you? That's your real reason for not telling him.'

She sighed. 'I suppose so. I couldn't bear it if I had to give the job up now, Mike.'

'Then don't. Telling him doesn't mean you have to give in. You have a right to your own life too. You've made it work, after all.'

'You don't know what he can be like.' She avoided his eyes.

'Amy . . .' He reached across the table, touching her hand – making her look at him. 'Are you afraid of him?'

'It's when he's been drinking. He's so unpredictable. I sometimes feel he isn't quite . . .'

'Isn't quite what?'

'In control of himself.'

'Then tell him when he's sober.'

'Yes. Yes, I will. When he comes back from Greece, I'll tell him. And I'll insist that I'm keeping the job. After all, I do have a contract to honour.'

'Leave him, Amy.'

Her eyes widened, startled by the sudden bold statement.

'I mean it,' he went on. 'You're terribly unhappy and you're afraid of what he might do to you. For God's sake, get out while you still can.'

Amy closed her eyes briefly and swallowed hard. 'Do you think I haven't thought of it?' she said almost inaudibly. 'But it was *my fault*, Mike. I forced him into marriage – into this situation. Anything that's happened to him is my fault. And there's Mark now. Alex loves him. I couldn't take his son away from him.'

'You're overrating your own part in this,' Mike said. 'And Alex could have access to his son. After all, how much time does he spend with him now?'

485

'But – where would I go?'

'You have a job now, Amy. You're independent.' He pressed her fingers lightly. 'And you could always come to me – if you wanted to. And bring Mark of course.'

She looked at him. 'You mean – to the house you share with . . .'

'I mean to a place of our own. Amy, I'm asking you to free yourself and marry me.' For a long moment they looked at each other, then Mike smiled wryly and said, 'Does that sound terrible? I suppose I'm what the Victorians would have called an "unprincipled cad".'

She smiled in spite of herself. 'It's not terrible at all, Mike. You're very sweet. I can never repay you for all you've done for me.'

He winced. 'Oh dear, that sounds ominously like the prelude to goodbye.'

'I didn't mean it to. It's just that I'd hate you to feel you have to be responsible for me.'

'But I want to be.' He looked into her eyes. 'I've always loved you, you know,' he said. 'I can hardly remember a time when I didn't. I think it might have started that day we went to London to see your grandmother, and got caught in the air raid.'

She smiled. 'I remember. Did Auntie Marjorie ever find out about that?'

He shook his head. 'She'd have had forty fits if she had. Do you remember the time you came to Rhensham for my eighteenth birthday party?'

'How could I forget?' she said, her eyes misty. 'It was my first grown-up party and I was so shy. You all seemed so sophisticated. Mum chose my dress and I thought it looked so babyish.'

'It was a beautiful dress. You looked like a princess in it.'

She looked up at him. 'You made the evening for me when you said you liked it. And you kissed me. It was my very first kiss – so romantic. I fell head over heels in love on the spot. But later when you were in the Army and came to London you seemed so loftily grown up.

And then when you started your job as a journalist, I felt sure that you wouldn't want to be bothered with me any more. Especially when your letters were all full of that girl, Julia Honeywell.'

'Julia Honeywell?' He looked astonished. 'Oh, there was nothing going on there. I admit I had a brief crush on her, but we never really had anything in common. It fizzled out.' He laughed. 'So I was loftily grown up, was I?'

I felt you must be ashamed to be seen with a school kid.'

'What a pair of idiots.' He chuckled. 'That *terrible* convent school uniform.'

She winced. 'Please – don't remind me.'

'I suppose you don't want to be reminded of the time Lily Smith blacked your eye, either.'

She grinned wryly. 'It was after the play, remember? *Twelfth Night*. She thought I'd forgotten my origins and needed taking down a peg. Perhaps I did.'

Their mood lightened and they enjoyed their meal, but later, when they were alone together in the car, Mike turned to her.

'I meant what I said earlier. You still haven't answered.'

In the darkness she looked straight ahead, afraid to look into his eyes – afraid that she would see her own longing mirrored there. 'I know you meant it, Mike. And I love you for it.'

'Only for that? Only for meaning it?' He turned her face, making her eyes meet his. 'Just say what you have to say. Just tell me the truth, Amy. Don't worry if the answer is no. I won't get upset and I won't let it spoil our friendship, I promise. I have to know, though.'

With all the courage that was in her she tried to tell him that she didn't love him. But she couldn't. Tonight they had reached a watershed in their relationship. Nothing could ever be the same between them now. She couldn't tell him she would marry him. Yet losing him would be like losing a limb. Not just because he had become a vital lifeline, but because she now knew that the teenage love that had flowered on that lovely August evening had developed into something strong and sweet and infinitely enduring. She drew his face down to hers and kissed him gently.

'Of course it isn't just for that, Mike. I loved you when I was fifteen and I still do – for everything you are. For always. Whatever happens I want you to remember that.'

Flight 218 from Athens circled London airport. Passengers were requested to extinguish their cigarettes and fasten their safety belts in preparation for landing.

Alex swallowed the last of his whisky. He had been drinking ever since take-off. Ever since this morning if the truth were known – and before that. In fact he had hardly stopped for long enough to sober up since arriving in Greece with the cast and crew at the end of December.

Directing the film had not been the happy experience he had expected. Right from the start it had been one long series of catastrophes. To begin with he'd had a severe stomach upset – something to do with the food, or the water, he decided. After that the weather had been against them and there had been endless days of boring inactivity, waiting for the sun to shine. He'd started drinking seriously then – local wine, retsina, ouzo, anything he could get his hands on. There had been a brief and torrid affair with one of the starlets, until he had realised she was just using him to make her cameraman boyfriend jealous. That had led to a sordid brawl in which he had come off worst, collecting a bruised jaw and a warning cable from London. Apparently someone had had the bloody cheek to complain about his behaviour to central office. It was when he found out who that someone was that the real trouble came. After an evening's heavy drinking at the local taverna he'd gone out looking for the offending actor; finally hauling him out of a restaurant where he was dining with friends and challenging him to a fight. But his informant had omitted to point out that the actor in question was the nephew of a major shareholder.

His arbitrary dismissal came by cable. A few words, short and very much to the point. Two days later his replacement arrived and he was on his way home.

An hour after landing he was at the studios, clearing his desk. In the filing cabinet he found a whisky bottle still a quarter full. He took out the hip flask he carried and filled it, tipped the surplus into his mouth, and dropped the empty bottle into the wastepaper basket. His head was pounding with a fury fuelled by alcohol and a sense of injustice that tortured his guts even more painfully than the booze. 'They'll go a long way before they find another director as talented as me,' he muttered as he emptied the desk drawers into his briefcase. All his pre-war experience seemed to count for nothing. 'Inept, short-sighted bloody fools, the lot of them,' he growled. Just because some jumped up little ham took exception to his having a few drinks to break the monotony he was dismissed without warning, like some bloody shop assistant with his fingers in the till. If he'd had any say in the matter that cretinous little stuffed shirt wouldn't have got a job in a bloody sausage factory, never mind a part in a major film. Well, he wouldn't forget. Oh no. 'If ever I get the chance to get even with the little swine I'll do it,' he vowed as he stormed his way out of the building.

He collected his car from the parking lot behind the building and set out on the drive to Mill Hill. It was mid-afternoon and the roads were busy with heavy lorries. His tongue was like thick dry felt in his mouth and his head felt as though it was stuffed with cotton wool. He found it difficult to judge distances and twice other drivers hooted at him for almost hitting them. Finally he decided that what he needed was coffee, strong and black, and he pulled off onto the forecourt of a transport café.

The café was steamy and cheerful. Only a handful of customers sat at the plastic-topped tables. On the counter a radio played some nameless, mind-numbing music. He

489

collected his coffee at the counter and carried it to a table near the window, but his hands were shaking so much that by the time he got there half of it was in the saucer. It was then that his fury suddenly drained away and the reality of his situation hit him. Christ, but he was in a mess. He had no job and no prospect of getting one – all through no fault of his own. He was a brilliant bloody director, damn it. He could knock spots off all the rest of them. Why could no one see it? Why were they all so petty and small-minded? To make matters worse, he had a wife and child at home, dependent on him.

Resting his elbows on the table he dropped his head into his hands. Why in God's name had he taken up with Amy in the first place? Young and naive, her gamin charm had flattered him. At first she had made him feel young and alive again. He'd enjoyed moulding her raw talent and seeing her blossom into a promising actress under his direction. Why on earth couldn't he have left it at that? How could he have been fool enough to fall for such an age-old trick – to let her trap him into a marriage he didn't want? She'd misled and used him all along, just like any little back-street tart on the make.

Mark was the only good thing to come out of it. And now he had let him down. Tears of maudlin self-pity coursed down his cheeks. 'I'm sorry, Chloe,' he muttered. 'I wanted to do well for our boy. And I will. I know you'll help me. Tell me what to do, darling. For Christ's sake, tell me what to do.'

Suddenly he was aware that the radio had stopped playing music and an announcer was introducing the next programme. One of the waitresses called out to another: 'Hey, Doris – it's that new serial. You gonna come and listen, or shall I turn it up?'

Alex looked up to see the two women lean their arms comfortably on the counter and prepare to listen as the introductory music faded and the episode began.

Radio drama. That was an idea. Maybe there might be an opening for him there. It was something he would have to look into. Who did he know at the BBC? Then, while he was still mulling the notion over, his attention was suddenly riveted by the sound of a familiar voice. Good God. He could have sworn . . . The coffee machine hissed and spluttered, drowning the radio. When it stopped someone else was speaking.

He downed his half-cold coffee and went to the counter for a refill. As he did so the serial episode came to an end and the announcer began to read out the cast list. Alex found himself listening intently. One or two of the older actors' names were familiar to him. Then, to his astonishment, the announcer said: '*The part of Freda Owen was played by Amethyst Lee.*'

'That'll be fourpence, please sir.' The waitress held out her hand to the stunned-looking man on the other side of the counter. He stared at her.

'What?'

'Fourpence – for the coffee.'

Pushing his hand into his pocket he threw the coins onto the counter and hurried out, his open mackintosh flapping behind him. The girl stared at his retreating back.

'Sir – don't you want your . . . ?' But he'd gone, leaving the door swinging open behind him. Through the window she saw him get into his car and the way he swung off the forecourt onto the road without even looking left or right made her gasp. It was nothing short of suicidal. She sighed and shook her head. *Honestly* – some people. You got all sorts in here.

'You mean you haven't heard it?'

'I'm sorry, no. I haven't.' Maryan had sent one of the girls to make tea for her unexpected visitors. Rachel was so flushed and animated that she felt slightly alarmed. Clearly Sam was concerned about her too.

'There's a radio in the factory,' she went on. 'The girls like to sing along to "Music While You Work". But I'm afraid I can't concentrate if I don't have quiet. I usually close the door while it's playing.'

'Of course you do,' Sam said. He turned to his wife.

'How do you think Maryan can listen to the wireless and do her work properly?' he admonished.

The girl came in with the tray of tea and Maryan poured Rachel a cup and passed it to her, hoping it would help to calm her down.

'It's a new daily serial, you say?' she said. 'And you think Amy is playing one of the parts in it?'

'I don't think, I know.' Rachel leaned forward. 'I ask you – how many people do you know with the name Amethyst?'

'Well, only the one, I admit.'

'And why would Amy take the name of Leigh?'

Sam broke in. 'I bought a copy of the *Radio Times* on the way here,' he said. 'It's spelt L double-e, not L e i g h.'

Rachel waved her hand at him dismissively. 'It could be a printing error. I just know deep inside that this is our Amy – your Amy, Maryan. Even if those silly people at the BBC wouldn't give us her address.'

Seeing Maryan looking puzzled, Sam explained, 'We asked them – on the telephone this morning. It isn't their policy to give addresses. Well, it's hardly surprising, is it? I told Rachel they'd say that but she wouldn't listen.'

'If you were to write a letter,' Rachel went on. 'Addressed to Amethyst Leigh, care of the BBC.'

Maryan hardly knew whether she was on her head or her heels. Just this morning she'd had a telephone call from Roisan – with news so stunning that Maryan had already had difficulty concentrating on her work. Fay had gone. Gone for good, or so Roisan said. She sounded quite sure about it. Vincent was to get his divorce at last. She said mysteriously that she couldn't go into details over the phone but promised to come and visit as soon as she could, adding that she had other news too, and something to show her. Now here was Rachel, insisting that she had found Amy. It was almost too much for one day. Thank heaven for Sam's steadying influence.

Maryan took several deep breaths, trying hard to calm the churning excitement in her stomach. *Mustn't hope for too much*, she warned herself. And yet she couldn't help feeling that there was a distinct possibility that Rachel was right. Amy might well be the person in this radio serial. It was certainly worth investigating further.

'Look,' she said. 'Tomorrow morning I'll make a point of listening to this programme myself. And if I'm convinced that it is Amy, I'll do as you say and write.'

Recharged by several deep pulls from his hip flask, Alex drove like a maniac. Hardly able to focus on the road ahead, he pressed his foot down hard on the accelerator. He was dimly aware of going through two sets of red traffic lights – of angry motorists hooting at him – a lorry driver lowering his window to yell an obscenity. He ignored it all. All he could think of was that Amy had disobeyed – defied him. She was working again.

At the back of his mind and unacknowledged, he burned with the thought that Amy – an inexperienced girl of twenty on whom he had lavished the benefit of all his experience – could find work when he couldn't. It made her the breadwinner. The thought of living on his young wife's earnings was overwhelmingly humiliating. He wouldn't tolerate it.

He told himself that it meant she must be leaving Mark alone. His son – his son and Chloe's – was at the mercy of some stranger. He'd warned her what would happen if she did that again. Well, now he would teach her that he did not make empty threats. She wasn't up to caring for his son. Chloe would never have left their child alone. Amy must suffer the consequences of what she had done.

Net curtains twitched in Willow Drive as the car drew up with a screech of tyres outside number twenty-two and Alex leapt out of the car. The house looked deserted as he let himself in with his key. He sensed that the house was empty as he stood in the hall, but still he ran upstairs two at a time to look into every room, calling in a loud, angry voice for his absent wife.

By the time he re-emerged neighbours were standing at

their front doors, peering apprehensively at the wild-eyed man with his flying coat; wondering what could have happened to send him into such a frenzy. They watched as he strode across the road to bang loudly on the door of number twenty-nine with his clenched fist, still shouting his wife's name.

Addie was alone. Jack had gone down to the shops on his bike to collect the weekly grocery order from the Co-op. When she opened the door and Alex pushed his way past her she uttered a frightened little squeak and fell back in alarm.

He strode through the house, throwing doors open to look into all the rooms, then he turned to glare at her. 'Where are they?' he demanded. 'Where is my son?'

Clasping her hands together, Addie shook her head. 'She – they aren't here, Mr Keynan.'

'Where are they then – *where*? Tell me, woman.' Eyes blazing, he advanced towards her and she stepped back, wincing in alarm at the expression on his face, convinced that he was about to attack her.

'They – they aren't here – *really*,' she stammered breathlessly. 'On the days Amy's recording Mark goes to Rosemary's.'

'Rosemary? Rosemary who?' His face dark with anger, Alex grabbed Addie's wrist and twisted it painfully. 'What has that bitch done with the child? *Tell* me, woman. It's my son we're talking about, for Christ's sake.'

'She – it's Mrs Carter,' Addie said, her teeth chattering with fear.

'*Where*? Where does she live? Come on – come *on*.'

'N-number eight M-meadow Walk.'

Rubbing her bruised wrist, Addie watched as he ran down the path and jumped into his car. What on earth was the matter with the man? she asked herself. Fighting drunk at four o'clock in the afternoon. He'd absolutely reeked of drink. It was disgusting. Who did he think he was, bursting into people's homes, shouting and manhandling her like that? And what would he do to poor little Amy when he found her? She wondered if she should call

494

the police. But they never interfered in domestic matters, did they? Should she ring Rosemary Carter? Jack would tell her not to get involved, and maybe he was right. She chewed her lip apprehensively. All the same . . .

Amy's heart was light as she sipped her cup of tea. Through the window she could see Mark playing happily in the sandpit with Rosemary's other three charges in the sunny back garden. Spring was well and truly here now. The trees were bursting with new leaf and blossom and the birds were singing. Life was good again. It had a pattern and a purpose.

'I don't know when I've had a happier little boy,' Rosemary was saying. 'He really enjoys being with the other children and he's so good at sharing the toys.' She laughed. 'Except that teddy of his, of course. He never lets that out of his sight. But then they all have a favourite toy, don't they? By the time he goes to school he'll be quite used to mixing with other children.' She smiled at Amy. 'We all listen to you in the mornings, you know. I get the children their elevenses and we all sit down to hear Mark's mummy on the wireless. You should see his little face light up when he hears your voice.'

Amy laughed. 'Thank you. It's nice to know that someone is out there listening.'

'Oh, I'm sure you have a huge audience,' Rosemary assured her. 'Everyone I've spoken to says how much they enjoy "This Year, Next Year".' She looked out of the window. 'But here I am, chattering on when you'll be wanting to take Mark home and give him his tea.'

'I do like to spend some time with him before bed when I've been away all day.'

'Of course you do. I'll get him for you.'

Mark's eyes lit up when he saw his mummy waiting to take him home. He chattered to her as she fastened his coat, telling her in his baby way what he'd been doing all day, and what Teddy had been doing too.

They'd just stepped through the gate when a car

stopped two doors down the road. When it began to reverse at speed, Amy pulled the child out of the way to avoid the back wheels as they mounted the pavement.

From where she stood at the front door, Rosemary watched with horror as a man leapt from the car and snatched Mark from Amy's arms, bundling the terrified child into the back of the car. Then, as Amy made to join him, he grabbed her roughly by the collar of her coat and pushed her into the front passenger seat. A moment later, before a shocked Rosemary could do anything, the car roared off at speed, leaving her watching helplessly from her doorway.

Rigid with terror, Amy hardly dared to look as they careered into the main road without stopping, narrowly missing a passing car and tipping a cyclist onto the pavement.

'Alex, for God's sake, be *careful*! What's the matter with you?' Gritting her teeth, she held tightly to the sides of her seat as the car wove perilously in and out of the traffic. 'Why are you here, Alex? What's wrong?'

'*What's wrong*?' he mimicked. 'You might well ask.'

She glanced at him, alarmed by his strange grey-green pallor. There were beads of sweat on his forehead and his lips were drawn back from his teeth in a menacing travesty of a smile. Alone in the back seat, Mark was being thrown about like a shuttlecock by Alex's erratic driving. He was wailing loudly with fear and calling out for her. Amy turned in her seat and tried in vain to comfort him.

'It's all right, darling. We'll soon be home.' But the baby's wails drowned her soothing. She turned to Alex. 'Please stop,' she pleaded. 'You've been drinking. You don't know what you're doing.'

'I know what I'm doing all right.' He threw her a look of pure hatred, so ferocious that it made her recoil. 'Of course I've been drinking, you bitch – driven to it by you. Why didn't you tell me you'd taken a job? You can have no idea what you sound like in that rubbishy thing. Like some guttersnipe hamming it up in a village hall. How do you think I felt, sitting in some tatty transport café, hearing my wife making a fool of herself? And knowing that half the bloody country knew about it before I did. That must have given you the best laugh of all.'

She bit her lip. So that was it. 'I'm sorry, Alex. I should have told you. And I would have. It was just that . . .'

'That you knew I'd put a stop to it – right?' He turned to glare at her with bloodshot eyes. 'Well, if you want to make a fool of yourself, do it. I don't give a damn any more. You're a selfish little cow and you always were. But I won't have you farming my son out on some idiot stranger. I told you what would happen if you ever did that again, and by God I mean to see that it does.'

'Alex, *don't*. It's not like you think. You can't imagine how lonely I've been – how frustrated, alone in that house with you away all the time. It's wonderful to be working again. It's not doing Mark any harm . . . *Oh* . . .' She gasped as he swung the car across the road directly into the path of an oncoming lorry. The lorry's brakes screeched and the driver leaned out of his cab to hurl abuse at Alex. There was a thud, followed by a scream as Mark fell from the back seat onto the floor.

'*Alex*! For God's sake, stop. You've hurt Mark now.'

The little boy was wailing with pain and bewilderment at what was happening to him. But the child's cries only served to anger Alex even more. As the car lurched forward again he rounded on Amy.

'*I've* hurt him? That's rich. It's you who's hurt him. If he's crying it's because of what *you've* done to him – to Chloe's child. He's all I have left of her, but what do you care? Dumping him like a parcel of rubbish, anywhere that suits you. You've done it on purpose, haven't you? You've done it to get back at me – at *us* – me and Chloe. But you shan't have our child. *We won't let you*. Do you hear?'

Cold with fear, Amy stared at him. What was he talking about? His eyes were wild, the pupils dilated. He was completely out of control – living in some fantasy of his own making. Did he even know what he was saying? Had the drink fuddled him so much that he'd lost his mind? How could she reason with him in this state?

They were speeding through the tree-lined streets of the estate now. Children were playing outside after school. A ball ran into the road and a little girl stepped out from between parked cars to retrieve it. Amy screamed, clenching her fists and closing her eyes, waiting for the inevitable horror. But the child jumped back in time and somehow the accident was miraculously avoided. Next time – oh God, next time they wouldn't be as lucky.

She turned and pleaded with him, her voice thick with tears. 'Please. Oh, *please*, Alex. You must stop and listen to me. We can talk this out quietly at home. I can make you see, if only you'll calm down. Please – *please* stop before you kill someone. If not for me then for Mark. He's hurt. Can't you hear him?'

They had turned into Willow Drive now and suddenly Alex stood on the brakes. The tyres shrieked and the car shuddered to a halt, throwing Amy forward so violently that her forehead met the windscreen with a dizzying thud.

'*Get out*,' he snapped. 'Go on, get out – *now*, before I throw you out.'

Her head still spinning with the pain, she opened the door and got out of the car on trembling legs, almost weeping with relief. Thank God he'd listened to reason at last. She reached for the handle of the rear door to get Mark but before she could open it Alex slammed the car into gear and revved the engine. With a roar the car leapt forward, gathering speed as it roared down the road.

In a blind panic, she ran after it, her arms outstretched, oblivious to the blood trickling down her face from the cut on her forehead. In vain she screamed for him to stop. She could see Mark standing on the back seat, looking out of the rear window as the car sped away. His little face contorted with terror, he held out his arms to her as the distance between them lengthened. As it rounded the corner and disappeared Amy staggered to a stop. Her legs gave way beneath her and she sank to her knees on the road, tears coursing down her cheeks.

'Mark. Oh, Mark – my baby. Oh God – *God*, what shall I do?'

Shocked neighbours, who had watched the incident helplessly from their front windows, ran out to help, but it was Addie who was first at her side. She helped the almost hysterical girl to her feet and wrapped her arms tightly around her.

'There, there, luvvie. It'll be all right, you'll see. You come home with me. Jack's already ringing the police. They'll catch him, never you fear.'

She hugged the sobbing girl close, reproaching herself. She'd always known something like this would happen some day. Why hadn't she tried to help – to warn her? If anything happened to that kiddie now she'd never forgive herself.

Chapter Twenty

'I've put her to bed in the spare room.'

Jack looked up at his wife as she came into the room. 'I doubt if she'll sleep.'

'She will. I made her some Ovaltine and I dissolved one of my sleeping tablets in it.'

Jack shook his head. 'You shouldn't have done that. Suppose the police come and want to speak to her?'

'The girl needs rest more than anything else at the moment. She's worn out.' Addie sank into her armchair with a sigh. 'And let's face it, it isn't likely to be good news, is it? The way that maniac was driving.' Her face crumpled. 'Oh, Jack, I'll never forget seeing her running down the road, screaming for the baby, blood running down her face – I thought my heart would stop. If only I'd had the sense to do something earlier. When he came here throwing his weight about I could see he was drunk. I might have been able to stop him. That poor girl.'

'Come on now, love. Don't take on like that. There's no sense in blaming yourself,' Jack said. 'It's a good thing I never forget car numbers. The police'll soon get onto him with what I was able to tell them, never you fear.'

'But the kiddie – little Mark. Thrown about in the back of that car like a pea on a drum, poor little mite.' She sighed. 'I always knew that marriage was all wrong. Didn't I always say so? May and September. It never works. That girl needs her mother at a time like this.'

Jack nodded. 'D'you know where you can get hold of her?'

'I asked her. She never said so, but I got the feeling she'd like to see her mum. It's only natural. But she said she wasn't sure where she lived any more. Seems they had a falling out some years ago and haven't been in touch since. She did give me the name of a friend who might know, though. A Mrs Freer.'

'Some relation?' Jack asked.

'I don't know. She called her – now what was it?' Addie frowned. 'Ro-sheen, or some such queer name. It's an address in Notting Hill. Do you think I should phone?'

Jack nodded. 'I do, love. Sooner the girl has someone of her own with her, the better.'

Maryan was sitting at the table in her flat, carefully composing a letter to Amy. On the table before her the envelope lay, addressed, as Rachel had suggested, care of the BBC. As she had promised, she'd listened to the radio serial that morning and was convinced beyond a doubt that Rachel had been right; the voice was Amy's. But in spite of her desire to get in touch with her again, the letter was proving hard to write.

There was so much she wanted to say, that was the trouble. How did one put into a letter the regrets of a lifetime, and the reasons for them? Also, she had to keep reminding herself that it wasn't a girl she was writing to. At Amy's age three years made the difference between girlhood and womanhood. And Amy had become a wife and a mother since they last set eyes on each other. She didn't want to make her feel obliged to see her again. Yet at the same time she didn't want to appear diffident. There had been too much of that in the past.

She wanted, more than anything in the world, to see Amy again. She had no illusions. She knew there was no hope of making up all they had lost as mother and daughter. But at least they could try to make a fresh start

– as equals – two grown women with a blood link. She was sure they could make it work, if only Amy was as willing as she was to try.

But how did she put all this down on paper? She read through what she had written, then, with an impatient gesture, she tore the top sheet off the pad and screwed it into a ball, tossing it into the already overflowing basket. The written words sounded so trite – false, almost. Why was it so hard to put on paper things that seemed so simple in your heart?

She was starting again when the telephone rang. With a sigh, she put down the pen and went to answer it.

'Maryan – it's Roisan.'

'Roisan. How are you?'

'Listen, dear, I have news.'

'So do I. I think I know where to find Amy. I was just . . .'

'Mine isn't good news, I'm afraid,' Roisan interrupted. 'And I'm afraid it concerns Amy.'

Maryan's legs trembled beneath her. 'What is it?'

'I would have come over instead of ringing.' Roisan sounded strained. 'I hate having to tell you on the phone like this, but it was the quickest way. I think – I know you'll want to go to her as soon as you can.'

'She's hurt? In hospital?'

'No, *no*. It's nothing like that. Listen, Maryan. It seems that Amy's husband has abducted their child – driven off with him in the car. I don't know the full details, but there appears to have been some kind of disagreement. The worst aspect of the situation is that he was very drunk as well as angry at the time.'

'My God. When was this?'

'This afternoon. About three hours ago. The police are out looking for him now.'

Maryan sank onto a chair, her knuckles white as she gripped the receiver. 'Oh dear God, poor Amy. Just tell me where she is. I'll go at once.'

'It's Mill Hill. She's being comforted by a neighbour – a Mrs Shaw, at twenty-nine Willow Drive . . . Maryan . . .'

'Yes?'

'You remember last time we spoke I told you I had something to tell you? Well, it was this: there were three letters from Amy, addressed to you at Simons Mews. I found them in Fay's handbag when she was taken ill. One was a card to tell you about the baby's birth.'

So she *had* written. Maryan bit her lip hard. Amy had written and Fay had opened the letters and then deliberately kept them back. That was how she knew so much. And when she received no replies – what must Amy have thought?

'Maryan – are you still there?' Roisan sounded anxious.

'Yes. I'm still here.' Maryan took a deep breath to steady her emotions. 'Thank you for letting me know, Roisan. I'll get a taxi and go at once.'

'You'll let me know if there's anything I can do, won't you? And keep me informed about what happens?'

'Of course I will. Thanks again for letting me know. Goodbye, Roisan.'

When Amy opened her eyes and saw her mother sitting beside the bed she thought at first that she was still dreaming. She closed her eyes, then opened them again.

'Mum?' She framed the word tentatively.

'Yes, it's me, love. Your friend Mrs Shaw rang Roisan and she got in touch with me.'

Slowly the reason she was here in Addie Shaw's spare room filtered back into Amy's mind. Filled with sudden alarm she sat up. 'What time is it? What's happened? Have the police found Mark?'

'No, love. Not yet. It's eleven o'clock. Mr and Mrs Shaw have gone to bed.' Maryan put her arms round Amy. It seemed so right and natural to hold her own child. And Amy didn't stiffen in her arms or turn from her. Instead she returned the embrace gratefully, pressing her face into her mother's shoulder.

'Oh, Mum. They *will* find him, won't they? Alex wouldn't hurt him. Not on purpose. I know he wouldn't.'

503

'Of course they'll find him, love. Everything will be all right. You'll see.'

For a long moment the two women held each other, each drawing comfort from the other. Then Amy drew back to look into her mother's face.

'I did write to you, Mum – after I left home and again when I was married – when Mark was born. Didn't you get my letters?'

Maryan shook her head. 'No, love. Fay Donlan didn't send them on. It was only recently that Roisan found them. It's a long story. One that needn't worry you now. I'm here with you. That's all that matters. We must concentrate on getting that baby back, then we'll talk.'

But Amy shook her head. 'No. I want to talk now. I daren't let myself think – about Mark and Alex – about what might happen. Don't let me think about it, Mum.' She looked at her mother. 'You've been on my mind such a lot lately. I wanted you to get in touch again. I thought that if you heard me on the radio you might . . .'

'I *did* hear you. At least, it was Sam and Rachel Leigh who heard you first and told me. They were so excited. They want to find you too, Amy.'

Amy looked puzzled. 'They do? But why?'

'Rachel has accepted that you're Marcus's daughter now.' Maryan sighed. 'I chose the wrong time to tell them. Rachel was still deeply shocked by Marcus's death. Sam always believed you were his granddaughter, though. He never lost touch, you know. He always made sure we were both all right. It was he who paid your school fees.'

'Oh, Mum. If only you'd told me. I imagined – well, you know what I imagined.'

'I know, love. I've made so many mistakes. Too many.' She took Amy's hand. 'I want so much to make it all up to you, if you'll let me.'

'I wish we'd talked more,' Amy said. 'All those years in the war, when I was at Rhensham. We hardly knew each other. Your work seemed to mean more to you than I did. Then when I found out that Marcus Leigh was my father I was so confused. And when you didn't talk to me

504

about it I thought it was because you didn't understand – or even care how I felt.' She shook her head. 'Since I married Alex I've seen things differently. Since Mark was born and I've spent so much time alone, I've understood what a struggle you must have had and what you must have gone through.'

Maryan nodded. 'Yes, it was a struggle in those early days, trying to keep the four of us together – you and Tom, your grandma and me. Tom felt it so badly, me being the breadwinner. He felt so useless and I did nothing to help him feel better. I regret that. He was a good man, taking on another man's child, and he loved you every bit as much as a true father would, Amy. Every bit.'

'I know, Mum. I remember that.'

'My worst mistake was in thinking I could cover up what I did – pretend it hadn't happened. Two wrongs can never *ever* make a right.' Maryan sighed. 'It was just that you and Tom were so close. After he was killed I couldn't bring myself to tell you he wasn't your real father.'

'Did he – Marcus, know about me?' Amy asked.

Maryan smiled gently. 'I never told him – or anyone else till that night at the Leighs'. But I've found since that he'd guessed. Too late for both of us, he guessed.'

Amy was silent for a moment. 'At least you didn't force him to marry you,' she said softly. 'That might have turned out worse. It's what I did to Alex. That was *my* worst mistake. 'It's terrible to be married to the wrong man, especially when you love him. And now I know how it feels to – to lose your child.' Her voice faltered and Maryan drew her close again.

'You mustn't say that. You haven't lost him.' *And, please God, you're not going to*, she added silently. Inwardly she was asking herself impatiently what the police could possibly be doing all this time – and why they hadn't found Alex Keynan's car when Jack Shaw had given them the colour, make and registration number. How much more could they need? Unless – unless . . .

She closed her eyes, shutting out the unthinkable possibility. Somehow they were going to have to get through the night – somehow she must help Amy pass the dark hours still to come in any way she could.

'We've got some catching up to do, you and me,' she said cheerfully. 'Such a lot has happened to me. Some good and some bad. I hardly know where to start. I want to hear about your last three years too. Shall I start, or will you?'

Amy needed little encouragement to talk. She told her mother about her brief stage career and the powerful attraction Alex Keynan had held for her, first as mentor, then as lover; the fiery passion so quickly roused, only to be extinguished by Alex's inability to love her. She told her about his first tragic marriage and how he had never recovered from it; the shattering disillusionment and loneliness marriage had brought them both and, overriding all, the sense of guilt she felt for causing Alex's decline into bitterness and alcoholism.

'He wasn't ready to share his life with anyone else, Mum,' she said. 'And I don't think he ever will be. I was too young and naive to realise it at the time. Even when he told me I wouldn't believe him. I was so sure I could take her place – make it all up to him. But I was wrong – so *wrong*. I think he must be going through some kind of breakdown. I'm afraid it's been coming on for some time. And the awful thing is that I caused it.'

'No, Amy. I'm sure you did your best to bring him happiness,' Maryan said. 'You mustn't blame yourself. Tell me about the happier things – about Mark – your baby.'

Amy went on to talk about Mark and what a joy he was, then about her renewed friendship with Mike and how getting the part in the radio serial had helped to restore her self-confidence. Talking seemed to relieve some of her tension and when she had finished she lay back against the pillow again, looking more relaxed.

'You tell me your news now,' she invited. 'Where did

you go after Mrs Donlan took your job and moved into the flat?'

Maryan started at the beginning, filling in the years they'd been apart. When she'd finished Amy smiled. 'You've done well, Mum, haven't you? You've come such a long way since we lived in Crimea Terrace. I wish . . .'

She trailed off, looking uncertain and Maryan said: 'Yes, what do you wish?'

'I wish you'd tell me about Marcus Leigh. I hardly remember him and I want to know so much – what he was really like; how you fell in love; his bravery in the war and how he died. I've wished so often that I knew more about the man who was my father.'

Maryan was reminded sharply of the words Marcus had written to her in his letter. His last words: *Speak to her of me sometimes*. She began haltingly, but once into her story the words poured forth. She talked until her mouth and throat were dry and her eyes stung with fatigue and the unshed tears of the past years. It was so long since she had talked about Marcus – or even thought about him as anything but a sweet and distant memory. And as she unfolded his story to Amy something seemed to happen. Just for a while it was almost as though he was alive again, sitting there beside her, smiling his approval. It gave her a sense of peace that she hadn't known for a long time.

It was only when the first pale rays of early morning sun began to lighten the room that she realised how long she had been talking. She looked at Amy and saw that she was sleeping. One minute she had been listening intently – the next she was fast asleep; all the anxiety and fear smoothed from her face.

Creeping silently out into the landing Maryan went into the bathroom, splashed her face with cool water and ran a comb through her hair. Then she went downstairs to the kitchen.

Addie was already up. Clad in her dressing gown, her grey hair tightly wound in curlers, she was filling the kettle at the sink. She turned when Maryan came in and raised an enquiring eyebrow.

'How is she?'

'Sleeping. We talked for most of the night. I think it did her good to get things off her chest.'

'Doesn't sound as though you got much rest,' Addie remarked. 'Got to admit I hardly closed an eye myself.' She spooned tea into the pot. 'Still, nice cup of tea, eh? That'll soon put us to rights.'

It was while they were drinking it at the kitchen table that the front doorbell rang. The two women exchanged a startled, apprehensive glance.

'Better go,' Addie said jumping to her feet. 'Don't want the whole house roused, do we?'

A young policeman stood on the doorstep. Behind him hovered a WPC. Both looked uneasy. From where she stood behind Addie in the hall, Maryan saw the young constable remove his helmet and finger his collar nervously.

'Mrs Keynan?' he said, looking from one to the other. 'Mrs Amy Keynan?'

'You've got news?' Addie asked.

Maryan stepped forward. 'I'm her mother,' she said. 'She's sleeping at the moment. If there's any news – bad news, perhaps you'd better tell me first.'

Addie led them both into the living room where the young policeman stood in the middle of the carpet, shifting his weight from one foot to the other.

'You've found them?' Addie prompted. 'The car – Mr Keynan and the baby?'

'We've – found a car.' The policeman cleared his throat. 'We have reason to believe it may be the car in question, but . . .'

'But my hubby gave you the number,' Addie interrupted. 'And the colour and make. You must surely know whether it's his or not.'

'This car was totally burned out when we found it, I'm afraid,' he said. 'Apparently it had hit a tree and burst into flames on impact. It was on a quiet country road about ten miles north of Chelmsford. There were no houses within a couple of miles, so no one had seen or heard anything. A farm worker found it on his way to work. We think it must have happened late last night.'

'And the driver? The – the occupants?' Maryan's mouth was suddenly so dry that she could hardly get the words out. She saw the policeman's Adam's apple bob up and down as he swallowed hard.

'The driver's – er – body was found at the wheel, I'm sorry to say, madam. The doors of the car had burst open and there were some items scattered nearby. One was a briefcase. It was badly charred but some of the contents were readable. Mr Keynan's name was on some of the papers.'

'Oh, my dear Lord.' Addie sat down with a bump and clasped her hand to her mouth.

'And – the baby?' Maryan whispered, her face ashen.

'There was no sign of it – *him*,' the policeman said. 'But with a very small child it's hardly . . .' Unable to finish the sentence he trailed off, looking at his feet. Nudged by his woman colleague, he went on: 'There was another item found near the car, though. Perhaps you might be able to identify it.'

The WPC stepped forward. Unzipping her shoulder bag, she produced a small, half-burned teddy bear. Maryan looked at Addie who nodded, then began to sob noisily.

'*That's Mark's.*' They all turned to see Amy standing in the doorway. White-faced, she stepped into the room and held out her hand. 'That is my son's. He never goes – never went anywhere without it. May I have it, please?'

Dry-eyed, she took the charred toy from the police-woman's hands.

Maryan hurried across the room to her. 'Amy – love . . .' But before her hands reached out to catch her Amy had slipped silently to the floor.

It was late afternoon when the police car turned into

Willow Drive and stopped outside number twenty-two. In the back the elderly couple peered out of the window.

'Yes, this is the house, George,' the woman stated. 'Don't you remember? We came here to visit Alex's parents in '41. I wonder if they're still alive? They were getting on in years then if I remember rightly.'

George Downes nodded. The journey had been long and his arthritis was playing up from sitting all that time. 'Yes, yes, I'm sure you're right,' he said tetchily. 'Shall we go in and get this business over with? I'm sure the inspector and his assistant here are anxious to get back to the station.'

The policeman driving the car winked at his female colleague and turned to them with a smile. 'Thanks for the promotion, but it's sergeant, sir, not inspector. And we're not in any hurry at the moment so you can take your time.'

He got out of the car and helped the couple out, first the man, who leaned heavily on his stick, then the elderly lady, who stood on the pavement looking at him apprehensively.

'What about the – er?'

'WPC Jennings had better wait here, I think, madam. It would be better to explain things first,' the sergeant advised.

It was Maryan who opened the door. She'd persuaded Amy to go up and rest and she found the interruption irritating. 'Yes?' She glanced towards the stairs. 'Do you think you could come into the living room? And could you keep your voices down, please? My daughter's terribly distressed and I've just got her off to sleep.'

The policeman stepped inside and removed his hat respectfully. 'I take it your daughter is Mrs Amy Keynan?'

'That's right.'

'This lady and gentleman are Mr and Mrs Downes,' he said. 'They have something of importance to tell you.'

Maryan closed the door and invited them to sit down. Kate Downes began: 'Our daughter, Chloe, was Alex

Keynan's first wife,' she explained. 'She was killed in the blitz, poor lamb, shortly after they married in 1941. Alex was badly cut up about losing her. He didn't seem to care much about anything or anybody afterwards and we lost touch with him after a while. It must be all of ten years since we saw him last – until he turned up on our doorstep right out of the blue late yesterday evening.'

Maryan's interest was instantly aroused. 'You *saw* him – yesterday?'

'Yes. We still live in the village in Essex where Chloe was born, you see. We don't get many visitors nowadays and it was really extraordinary, his turning up like that. He'd changed quite a lot and just at first I couldn't think who he was.' She shook her head. 'Not that he gave me time. He just rang the bell and when I opened the door he pushed this sleeping child into my arms. "This is Chloe's son," he said. "I want you to take care of him for me." Then he was gone – just like that. Well, it gave me a terrible turn, him saying a thing like that. And of course we knew right away there must be something badly wrong. Alex looked so strange. Tired and sort of wild-eyed. I was about to ask him in, but before I got the chance he'd jumped into his car and driven off as though the hounds of hell were after him.'

George Downes took up the story. 'The child woke up in a distressed state. When my wife undressed him we saw that he had a few bruises too. We didn't know what to do for the best. My wife fed and comforted him as best she could and after she'd put him to bed we talked it over and decided that our best course would be to notify the police and take him to the local hospital.'

'It was then that we heard the dreadful news about poor Alex,' his wife put in. 'The accident must have happened when he was on his way back to London. Thank God he left the child with us.'

Maryan was on her feet. 'Where is the baby? Is he still in hospital?'

'No. He's fine, madam,' the policeman reassured her. 'He's been thoroughly checked over by a doctor and apart from one or two bruises he's none the worse. He's in the car with a WPC at this moment. Mr and Mrs Downes insisted on coming to see him safely home with his mother – them being slightly connected, as it were.'

Maryan shook hands with them both. 'Thank you so much for what you've done,' she said. 'It was very good of you to make the journey. You have no idea what this is going to mean to my daughter. It's like the answer to a prayer.'

Kate Downes smiled. 'I'm so grateful that Alex thought of us,' she said. 'Even if his mind was confused into believing the baby was Chloe's, at least his concern was to make sure the child was safe.' She smiled wistfully at Maryan. 'You're very lucky, my dear. He's a dear little boy. I only wish he was our grandchild.'

Mark seemed none the worse for his ordeal. When the policewoman put him into Maryan's arms he struggled impatiently to the floor, clearly happy to be home again. He made straight for his toy box and was soon playing happily as though nothing had happened.

After saying goodbye to her visitors, Maryan sat down and looked at her grandson for the first time. Thank God he was safe. He was a beautiful child, so much like Amy at the same age that she felt her throat tighten. Her grandson. And Marcus's. How he would have loved him. What did the future hold for him? she asked herself, watching him play. Riches and happiness, success and love? Love above everything, please God, she prayed silently. All the rest is empty without it.

She held out her arms to the little boy. 'Mark – come to Grandma,' she invited, marvelling at how natural the name sounded on her lips.

He stood looking shyly at her for a moment, studying her face solemnly as though weighing her up. Than he dropped the toy he was holding and toddled towards her, a big grin on his baby face. Laughing, Maryan scooped him into her arms and hugged him close, tears of thankfulness slipping down her cheeks.

'Oh, your mummy is going to be *so* pleased to see you,'

she said, nuzzling his soft little neck. 'Shall we go and wake her? Shall we go and give your mummy the biggest, *best* surprise she's ever had?'

He smiled. 'Mummy,' he said eagerly. 'Want to see Mummy.'

At the inquest, held to determine the reason for Alex's tragic end, the verdict was 'accidental death'. Maryan was relieved and grateful. If there had been the slightest suspicion that he had taken his own life Amy would probably have blamed herself for the rest of her life. It would have clouded her future and prevented her from going forward. Now, once over the trauma of it all, she would be free to pick up the pieces and make a new start.

Once the funeral was over Maryan persuaded Amy to close up the house in Mill Hill and return with her to Hackney, but for the first few weeks the girl went about her life as though in a kind of daze. She hardly let Mark out of her sight, panicking if they were parted even for a minute. Maryan would often wake in the night to hear her getting up to go into his room, just to reassure herself that he was still there. In spite of her mother's attempts to get her interested in the world outside she remained indoors, engrossing herself in her small son to the exclusion of all else.

Maryan found Mike Taylor a godsend. He was an almost daily visitor, bringing Amy small gifts of fruit or flowers; sometimes a book he thought she would enjoy. And perhaps best of all, he brought news from outside – from the world she seemed to have turned her back on – snippets of news and gossip about his work and colleagues, many of whom Amy knew; things to surprise her and make her smile and look up with the first sparks of interest. Gradually, as the weeks passed she began to come round to the idea of returning to work. The producers of 'This Year, Next Year' had been kind and considerate. She had been written out of the story temporarily to allow her time to recover from her tragedy, and Maryan was afraid that if she kept them waiting too long she might lose the job she had prized so much. But thanks to Mike's patience and good sense she eventually agreed to return. Once the decision was made her energy and enthusiasm began to return and she immersed herself totally in her part again.

Soon she was studying her scripts as meticulously as ever and making the two trips to the BBC each week to rehearse and record. Everyone remarked on how brave she was to throw herself so wholeheartedly into her work, but Maryan understood that the work Amy loved gave her a sense of normality – reassured her that she was still a person in her own right with a positive pattern to her life.

On the days when Amy went to the West End to work, Maryan brought her own work from Feldman's home, so that she could care for Mark. He was a contented child and truth to tell she enjoyed having the opportunity to care for him. There had been precious little time to enjoy Amy when she was little.

On the days that Sam came up to Hackney he often brought Rachel with him. The elderly couple were totally bewitched by their small great-grandson, and loved to spend as much time with him as they could. Rachel's health even seemed to improve with her new interest. Maryan was astonished at the way the years fell away from her as her relationship with the little boy developed and grew stronger.

Mike was Amy's constant companion and support. He was attentive and infinitely patient; never expecting too much of her; making sure that she ate properly on her working days, and did not tire herself too much. Whenever his own work allowed he would drive her home after work, and gradually, as time went by, he persuaded her to go out with him in the evenings, at first for short drives in the car and perhaps a quiet drink, then to the theatre or cinema. Finally one evening, to Maryan's delight, he managed to coax her into dressing up and going out for dinner.

He took her to the restaurant down by the river in

Richmond where they'd dined to celebrate the first episode of 'This Year, Next Year'. It was a mild evening in early November and the restaurant was quiet and intimate. Maryan had persuaded Amy to buy a new dress for the occasion, and she had chosen a soft wool skirt in garnet red with a white lace blouse. Mike thought she had never looked more beautiful. The past months had brought a new maturity to her. Her face had lost some of its youthful softness. There were shadows under her cheekbones and soft smudges still beneath her eyes. But for Mike they seemed to give her a new beauty, a quiet dignity which, although born of her traumatic ordeal, gave her a new enigmatic quality that he found irresistible.

As they sipped their pre-dinner drinks he reached for her hand. 'Amy – in all this time you haven't talked to me about how you really feel, about – what happened. Maybe you should. If you want to get things off your chest, you know I'm always ready to listen, don't you?'

She smiled at him. 'I know, Mike. You've been wonderful, and so has Mum. I could never have got through it without the two of you. But I've talked as much as I want to. Nothing can ever undo what happened to poor Alex. In a strange way I think it was somehow inevitable. It was what he wanted. He was so unhappy.'

He nodded. 'Just as long as you don't still feel that you were the cause of it all. Or that you have to spend your life in eternal limbo because of it.'

She shook her head. 'I don't feel that any more. I know I have to put it behind me now and make a new life, for Mark's sake as much as mine.'

He looked at her for a long moment. 'That brings me to what I want to say. Amy – I once asked you to leave Alex and marry me. I've felt my own particular guilt over that. But it doesn't make me want you any the less.' He looked into her eyes. 'Maybe it isn't the right moment. Maybe there's no such thing as the right moment, I don't know. But will you at least think about it? I want you to know that however long I have to wait I'll never change my mind. I'll always love you and want you.'

She curled her fingers round his and squeezed them tightly. 'I told you once, Mike, that I'll always love you. Without you this whole nightmare would have been intolerable.' She lowered her eyes. 'But maybe we should both take time to think it through. You'd be taking on a package, you know. Not just a wife but a stepson too.'

'Do you think I haven't thought of that? You know I love Mark. I'll do my best to be a good father to him.'

'But you wouldn't be his *real* father, Mike.' She looked up at him honestly. 'I'd have to make that a condition. I was kept in the dark about my own real father. I remember what I felt when I found out the truth. I've promised myself that I'll never let that happen to Mark. Alex taught me so much. If only what I felt for him hadn't got in the way he would have taught me much more – about my craft. He was a brilliant director, you know. I'll always want Mark to know about that side of him and be proud.' She looked up at him. 'Do you think you could come to terms with that?'

'Of course. I agree, absolutely.' He looked into her eyes. 'So . . . ?'

She shook her head. 'I don't know, Mike. It's still a bit too soon. Is it unfair to ask you to have a little more patience with me? I married too hastily before and it ended in tragedy.' She held up her hand as he made to speak. 'Oh, I know this is different. We've known each other most of our lives, and I do love you – truly. But I need a little more time – just to be certain. For your sake as well as mine.'

Swallowing his disappointment, he smiled, leaning across to kiss her lightly. 'Take as long as you need, darling. When you decide I'll still be here, waiting.' His eyes sparkled with a hint of mischief. 'I'm making one condition of my own, though.'

'Yes?'

'When and if you decide you want to marry me, *you* propose to *me*.'

516

She laughed. 'All right, it's a deal.' She held both of his hands. 'I'll make you a solemn promise, Mike. There'll only ever be one man I can marry and that's you. There will never be anyone else I could love or trust more.' Her eyes glowed softly as they looked into his. 'You are my first love, my last love and my very best friend.' She raised her glass. 'So – just for now, shall we drink to that, Mike? To us – first, last and always.'

Mike smiled and whispered, 'To us – first, last and always.' And as they sipped their wine they each made a silent pledge of their own.

On Amy's twenty-first birthday the following February, Sam and Rachel gave her a dinner party at Whitegates. At the end of the meal Sam proposed a toast to her, wishing her long life and happiness, and when Amy got to her feet everyone looked at her, faces upturned, as they waited expectantly for her response.

'First, I'd like to thank you all for being here this evening,' she began. 'And especially my grandparents for giving me this lovely dinner party. I owe very special thanks to Mum for her help and support over the past months – and to Mike too . . .' She looked across the table at him, fingering her glass nervously. 'Mike for whom I now have a very special question.'

The guests were silent as they waited for what was to come, but already Mike's eyes were beginning to sparkle in anticipation. Amy went on: 'A few weeks ago Mike did me the honour of asking me to marry him. I told him I needed time to think. I promised him I'd tell him when I'd come to a decision. Well, now I have and I want you all to be witnesses to what I'm about to say to him.' Looking directly at Mike, she said, 'Michael Taylor, will you marry me, please?'

Instantly he was on his feet, his arms around her, to the delight of the onlookers who laughed and clapped. Maryan surreptitiously brushed a tear from her cheek. It was what she had prayed for. The perfect happy ending.

*

The wedding took place in April at a small ceremony in the village church at Rhensham. It was what Amy wanted and Maryan had been eager to fall in with her wishes. Rhensham was the place where she had known the most happiness. It was where she had grown up; where she and Mike had met as children. And now neither of them blamed that on anything but the war.

The church looked beautiful, decorated with spring flowers, and Amy looked radiantly happy in a cream dress and picture hat. Marjorie Taylor had offered Mitcham Lodge for the reception and she and Maryan shared the preparations equally.

Although it was a quiet wedding no one had been left out. The entire cast of 'This Year, Next Year' was there, plus Mike's colleagues from the newsroom. Celia came down from York to be Amy's only bridesmaid, bringing her fiancé with her. Sam and Rachel; Vincent and Roisan, and the Shaws came. Even Gina flew over from Paris to join Maryan in celebrating her daughter's wedding.

After the telegrams had been read, the toasts proposed and the cake cut, Maryan slipped out into the garden to be by herself for a while. Finding the little seat under the willow tree, she sat down to assess the past year and the future. On Amy's twenty-first birthday Sam and Rachel had presented her with a cheque for the money Rachel had invested for her from Marcus's estate. And Sam had announced that they had willed Feldman Fashions to their great-grandson, Mark.

Over the past few months, due to her success in the daily serial, Amy had been offered other parts in radio drama and Mike's career looked set to flourish too. He was getting regular news assignments and there was talk of promoting him to television, where his good looks and pleasing personality would be ideally suited. It seemed that the future was rosy for her little family. She was reminded sharply of her marriage to Tom Jessop back in the early thirties. The world had changed so much in the past two decades. Pray God there would be no poverty to sour love for Amy and Mike as it had soured theirs;

that there would be no wars to tear them apart and rip away their roots. They deserved an assured future, after they had all fought for it so long and hard and bitterly.

But what of her own future? Where did she go from here?

Maryan looked into the water of the little pool pensively. Vinnie and she had seen each other from time to time over the past months. His divorce had come through recently and he had driven out to Hackney to ask her to marry him. Her refusal had shaken him badly.

'I won't pretend I haven't thought about it, Vinnie,' she told him. 'But I've made up my mind that marriage isn't for me. Sam is going to need help with Feldman's. A lot of help. He isn't as young as he was and Rachel's health is poor. She needs him with her. Now that I know that Feldman's will pass to Mark some day, I want to make sure that when he's ready to take over it's still flourishing.'

He looked at her and the hurt disappointment in his dark eyes tore at her heart. 'Of course, I understand that,' he said. 'I'm not asking you to come back and work with Roisan and me, much as I would like that. I just want us to be together, Maryan; to be married. I've always wanted that – more than anything in the world. You know I have.'

'*Have* you?' Maryan looked into his eyes. She couldn't find it in her heart to tell him that she no longer felt able to trust his love and his promises; that she thought him weak for taking back a wife who used and almost ruined him. She loved him still, it was true; loved him too much to risk the heartbreak of being let down again.

'Why won't you marry me, Maryan?' he asked. '*Why*, now that I'm free and we've waited so long?'

'I'm trying to fulfil the family obligations that I should have fulfilled long ago,' she told him truthfully. 'I have so much to make up to Amy. I may not be able to give as much of myself to the marriage as I'd want to.'

He took her hand. 'I'll take whatever there is,' he said. 'I'd rather that than lose you.'

'You won't lose me,' she told him with a smile. 'I'll always be there. We've been friends for too long not to go on seeing each other.'

But somehow it hadn't worked out like that. Since her refusal there had been a barrier between them. She hadn't meant to make him feel rejected, but he was clearly hurt and upset. She hated the feeling of estrangement, but she wasn't sure what she could do about it.

'So this is where you are.' She looked up to see Sam looking down at her. He lowered himself onto the seat beside her. 'I saw you creep away from the festivities and I wondered if you were all right.'

She smiled and tucked her hand into his arm. 'Bless you, Sam. I'm fine. I just wanted some fresh air and time to think.'

'About – what?' He cocked an enquiring eyebrow at her. 'Maryan, is there something you want to talk about? You know I'm always ready to listen.'

'I know you are, Sam. No. It's nothing you can help with.'

'I thought you might have something to tell me,' he prompted.

She looked at him in surprise. 'Tell you?'

He gave her hand a little squeeze. 'My dear, I know something has been troubling you lately and I think I might have guessed what it is. Do you want to go back to work for Vincent Donlan?'

Her eyebrows rose. 'No. Whatever makes you think that?'

He lifted his shoulders expressively. 'I'm not blind, my dear. Vincent is free to marry now. You'll be making plans. And a man's wife should work at his side if she works at all.'

'I'm not going to marry Vinnie,' she said quietly. 'So it doesn't arise.'

'He hasn't asked you?'

'Oh, he's asked me. It's just that I've decided not to.'

'I see.' For a moment he was silent. Then . . . 'You can tell a nosey old man to mind his own business if you like, but – do you want to tell me the reason?'

Maryan sighed. 'It's complicated. There are so many, Sam. We fell in love while he was still married but separated. That was wrong, I know. But although his wife had let him down, left him for another man, he took her back without question, without thinking of what it did to me. Oh, yes, I know that he's Catholic, and divorce is against his religion. But he had lapsed, Sam. He didn't even go to church regularly any more.'

'And you feel that made him – what, weak – unreliable?' He looked at her. 'You're afraid he might let you down – hurt you again?' He took her hand and held it tightly in his. 'My dear, I believe we've known one another long enough for me to give you the benefit of my years – yes?' He looked into her face and she nodded. 'Our religion frowns on divorce too. This is a matter of culture rather than actual religion. It's ingrained – in the roots. Marriage is for ever, a commitment. To hold to that isn't weakness. Being loyal to a wife who is bad takes strength, sacrifice and a great deal of fortitude. Vincent must have suffered so much, losing you. Must you punish him still?'

'There's Amy and Mark to think of too,' she said. 'I want to be a proper mother to Amy. I want to protect Mark's inheritance and make sure that Feldman's is a flourishing business for him when he's ready to take over.'

'And for this you would sacrifice the rest of your life?' Sam shook his head. 'My dear, you're still young. Young enough even to have another child, if that is what you wish. Don't live your life for those who are to come. Live it for yourself. For *now*. Amy is married to a good man who loves her. She'll be fine. And for all we know Mark might want to do something entirely different when he's a man. And if he does, then we must let him. We must do what we can – be there to support and to love. We can give them the benefit of our experience, but we can't live their lives for them. I learned that lesson long ago.'

For a moment they were silent, both of them thinking

of Marcus. Then she looked at him tentatively. 'So – you think I should marry Vinnie?'

He smiled gently. 'I think that this time you should do what your heart tells you,' he said. 'You've been through so much, Maryan. You've loved and lost, kept your true feelings hidden from everyone and put yourself last. You've tried so hard to please and serve everyone else all your life, and you haven't always been rewarded as you should. Now it's time to please yourself.' He bent to plant a kiss on her cheek. 'Follow your heart, my dear. Take the happiness you deserve – with my blessing.'

When they went back into the house everyone had gathered in the hall, waiting for the newlyweds, who were about to leave for their honeymoon.

When they appeared at the top of the stairs Amy's eyes shone with happiness and Maryan felt her heart swell as she looked at her daughter, lovely in her lemon suit and the little straw boater trimmed with daisies. Mike looked so proud and happy at her side too. Catching her mother's eye, Amy tossed her posy to the waiting guests and Maryan caught it, blushing at the laughter of the other guests around her.

As they were about to get into their car out on the drive, Amy put her arms around Maryan and hugged her.

'Thanks for everything, Mum. I don't know what I'd have done without you this past year. And you and Auntie Marjorie have given us a wedding we'll always remember. I'm so happy.' Pressing her lips close to her mother's ear she whispered, '*I love you.*'

As the car drove away and the others turned back into the house, laughing and chatting, Maryan stood alone at the gate, watching the car until it was out of sight. Amy had said, *I love you.* Could she possibly know how much that meant to her? It was the first time she'd ever heard her say it. And she knew it came from her heart.

She felt an arm encircle her shoulders and turned to see Vinnie smiling down at her.

'Sam Leigh has just given me a mysterious message,' he said. 'He said you wanted to see me. When I asked him why, he said he had an idea that you'd come to an important decision.'

She smiled. 'Dear Sam. I believe he can see inside my mind sometimes.'

'So it's true?' He looked into her eyes hopefully. 'You do have something to tell me?'

'Yes.' She smiled up at him. 'I think I might just have made the most important decision of my life.' Reaching up, she drew his head down to hers, and as their lips met and his arms closed around her she knew that she had no need to tell him what it was.